V. T. Bovalino

The Second Death of Locke

orbit

orbit-books.co.uk

ORBIT

First published in Great Britain in 2025 by Orbit

1 3 5 7 9 10 8 6 4 2

Copyright © 2025 by Tori Bovalino

Map by Rebecka Champion (Lampblack Art)

The moral right of the author has been asserted.

A CIP catalogue record for this book
is available from the British Library.

HB ISBN 978-0-356-52488-7
C format 978-0-356-52489-4

Typeset in Garamond by M Rules
Printed and bound in Great Britain by
Clays Ltd, Elcograf S.p.A.

Papers used by Orbit are from well-managed forests
and other responsible sources.

Orbit	The authorised representative
An imprint of	in the EEA is
Little, Brown Book Group	Hachette Ireland
Carmelite House	8 Castlecourt Centre
50 Victoria Embankment	Dublin 15, D15 XTP3, Ireland
London EC4Y 0DZ	(email: info@hbgi.ie)

An Hachette UK Company
www.hachette.co.uk

orbit-books.co.uk

For Matt

Part One

The hand and the heart

A well without a mage is nothing. What is the point of power with no way to use it? Alone, a well is no better than a common soldier; untrained in fighting and healing, they are even less useful than a typic.

If one cannot protect their master, their mage, they do not deserve to hold power.

Wielding Power, Volume 1: Third Edition, revised Post-Destruction (PD)

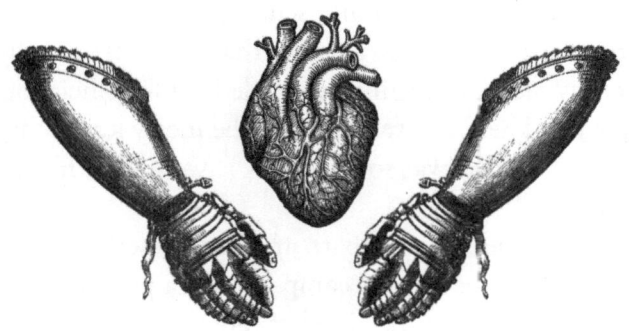

one

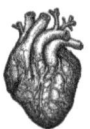

IT WAS RAINING AGAIN in Mecketer as Grey stalked across the encampment toward the command tent. She had nearly finished washing, was almost properly clean for the first time in days, when Kier had thrown her a tether and sent a pulse through it. They had so little time apart from one another that he didn't usually disrupt hers, so it only meant one thing: he needed her for official business. It was too cold and her hair was still wet, the messy knot of it dripping on her cloak, but if he was somewhere . . . well. That meant she was needed, too.

They were not meant to be apart, and they took that duty seriously.

Each step across the sodden camp felt like a perpetual battle with some unseen enemy, as if the blood of those they'd fought and those they'd lost was determined to claim her boots for the bones buried below. Equally uncomfortable was the fluttering of her heart in her chest, the lump in her throat – she wasn't *anxious*, really, but the station she and Kier shared required a sort of unhealthy co-dependency that Grey only allowed herself to think on very late at night when she was certain that Kier was asleep.

She didn't know if the captain fostered the same reactions in her absence. She'd never asked.

Grey slipped through the flap of fabric into command – which wasn't one tent at all, but rather a shoddy collection linked together with other-worldly tunnels of fabric. She thought it had once been the color of natural canvas, but it was now a dingy gray with smoke from the campfires outside and speckled brown with mud. She hated the tents. They smelled like damp and mold, the inescapable result of rain seeping into every crevice, and it always made her skin itch. In other assignments, they were sometimes in one of Scaela's many old fortresses, surrounded by candlelight and thick stone walls and real floors, but this was not the case with Mecketer. It wasn't even near a city – the encampment was its own entity, and though it had persisted for most of the years of the war on the border between Luthar and Scaela, it had been burned down or shifted too many times for anything permanent to remain. It existed now, as it always had, to defend the supply road from the sea that ran between Scaela and one of Luthar's old ports, constantly changing hands between the two nations.

What she wouldn't give to be back in one of those fortresses, with a roof over her head and stone underfoot. What she wouldn't give for dry boots and a warmer cloak.

The clerk looked up as soon as she entered, exhaustion plain on their face – they weren't really a clerk at all, but either a typic being punished with secretarial work or a young person-at-arms too injured for patrolling. They stood, inclined their head to Grey, and said, 'Can I help you, Hand Captain?' in the flat tone of someone who'd stopped caring a dozen deaths ago.

'I'm here to join Captain Seward,' Grey said. She had not been summoned by Attis or Concord, but she didn't have to be. If Kier was here, she was meant to be, too.

The clerk sighed, but led the way out of the administrative tent, through three drenched, gauzy passages, stopping at a tent flap marked with the High Lord of Scaela's seal: an open hand, palm out, making the sign of justice over a light blue field. There, they paused and squared their shoulders – Grey tried not to read too much into this – then called, 'Master Attis, Hand Captain Flynn is here.'

No sound on the other side. Master Attis was powerful with

standard magics and the well she drew from was strong enough to make a difference, so she was able to hold a sound shield long enough to keep most of her business private. She was thorough. Grey appreciated that, even if the woman herself vaguely terrified her for reasons she hadn't yet gotten to the bottom of.

Finally, a voice called, 'Enter.'

Grey muttered a quick thanks to the clerk. She noted their limp, the way they favored their left side – she thought about directing them to visit Leonie, but the healers were already overworked.

She shook it off and slipped past Scaelas's seal, inclining her head to Master Attis and her Hand before moving in further. Her ears popped slightly as she passed through Attis's shield, and it took a lot of effort not to wrinkle her nose or rub her ear.

Like most other tents at Mecketer, there was barely any furniture within, and certainly nothing that could count as permanent or well constructed. An open brazier blazed on one side, filled to the brim with light purple magic-fed flame, and Grey relaxed slightly in the warmth. It was a small tent, containing only a table laden with maps, a desk and two chairs. Attis sat ramrod straight on one side of the desk, her salt-and-pepper hair pulled back into a tight bun that rendered her features even more severe, her Hand lurking against the back of it like a badly angled shadow. Kier had the other chair, somehow giving the impression of rumpled insouciance even sitting straight and prim as Attis herself. It was something about the untidy curve of his mouth, the lock of his hair that never quite managed to stay where he put it.

'Apologies for proceeding without you, Hand,' Attis said, not sounding apologetic at all. She barely even looked at Grey as she straightened the papers on her desk.

Who am I to delay you? Grey wanted to say, but she'd already gotten in trouble for her tongue more than once here. The mud made her irritable, and the constant salt scent of the sea a few miles off made her antsy, but Attis was no treat either. It was one of the many reasons this assignment grated on her: that she had to keep her true feelings quiet unless it was only Kier within hearing range. Usually, with only the fate of either a violent death or a lifetime of battle looming ahead, their masters had a better sense of humor.

Grey nodded once, turning her attention to Kier. Grey scanned over him quickly, as she always did when they were reunited, even after the shortest period. It was another one of those anxiety-induced habits. The shape of Kier was committed to her memory, as familiar to her as her own reflection: the uneven hazel of his eyes; the deep, rich brown of his hair, curlier than usual, like it was when they were children, with the salt in the air; the variations of his skin, leaning darker olive whenever they had more than an hour of true sunlight in the day (but not now, because at Mecketer, there was rarely any sunlight, and Kier, who loved the sun as much as it loved him, was uncharacteristically pallid). The fullness of his lips and the crooked line of his nose, the shadow of his eyelashes over his cheekbones.

Nothing new broken. No wounds besides the scrape along his jaw from a skirmish the week before.

She slipped into place behind him. For his part, Kier's shoulders relaxed when Grey was there, if only a fraction.

In the practiced pose of mages and their Hands, their wells, their power, Grey rested her own hand on Kier's left shoulder, fingers curving so the tips just barely grazed the line of his collarbone, her thumb the merest inch from his skin over the collar of his cloak. Submission and protection. Fealty and power, all in one.

'As I was saying, this is not going to be easy,' Attis said.

'It rarely is,' Kier allowed in his calm, lovely voice, so far removed from the terror of what he could do. The small part of Grey that still tittered with anxiety quieted immediately. 'But please, continue.'

Grey glanced over the papers on Attis's desk. Most were maps: annotated with arrows and wins and losses, showing how the Scaelan army was spread across the borders. The main one showed all the nation states that made up the island of Idistra. Grey's gaze traced over the corners: knots of fighting between their own nation of Scaela and the northern nation of Cleoc Strata, then to the east with Eprain, the south with Luthar. The western border with Nestria was quiet, thankfully – their new High Sovereign had no taste for blood – but who knew how long *that* would last.

It took her a half-second to realize that the paper on the desk between Kier and Attis was yet another map, badly marked up in an untidy hand, much smaller than the others that blanketed Attis's large table. She didn't lean close to scrutinize it – that was not her job. Thinking was not her job. Strategy was not her job.

Grey was a well, and beyond that, she was Kier's official Hand, the well dedicated for his use. As such, she had two roles: the first, to feed her mage the power he needed to perform magic. The second, no matter what, to keep him alive. In the past, being a Hand was a lifelong position, requiring a ceremony of binding, but that practice had long since fallen out of favor, and recently had been forbidden.

'This is their path,' Attis was saying, tracing her finger along a marked ridge, clearly in the middle of a conversation Grey had missed. 'And this is where the resource is. They are traveling with a retinue of eighteen mages' – which meant eighteen wells, too, because within the system of Idistran magic, one could not operate without the other, but Attis didn't mention the Hands, and Grey couldn't keep her gaze from flicking to Attis's own Hand – 'and seem to be operating in shifts for constant movement. Four identical carriages, equally guarded. A complete decimation is the desired outcome, as ordered by the High Lord.'

Kier didn't even flinch. After years and years of this, of course he didn't. Grey had lost count of the lives on their hands, the blood staining every single skirmish they only just scraped out of.

'Decimation might be tricky,' Kier said. 'How many am I taking with me?'

'Your full company, Captain.'

He made a small noise. 'Everyone?'

'The High Lord's orders.'

Grey didn't realize how much her fingers were digging into his shoulder until he subtly dipped it, their signal to let her know she had tensed.

There had always been significantly more wells than mages in Idistra, but with the constant wars and waning power, that was no longer something to count on – even in Scaela, the nation that held the most power when everything changed.

'Based on the last census of wells, it doesn't seem like good strategy—' Grey started.

'It may be more sensible to leave some of our wells behind,' Kier agreed, taking the fall for her boldness, smoothly covering her misstep. She felt a tug on the tether between them, a pulse of caution, and pressed her lips together. Though she and Kier were as balanced as a pairing could be and treated one another as such, not every mage saw the relationship with their power source as one of equals.

And, of course, she knew what else Kier would say to her if they were alone: *If you keep calling authority into question, you* will *draw attention*, to which she usually replied, *We always draw attention. It's your fault, for being so alarmingly grotesque*, to which he would almost certainly respond, *Alarmingly striking, you mean.*

Attis shook her head, aiming a warning glance at Grey before she turned back to Kier. 'Not every specialty is as developed as yours. Every mage in your company must be accompanied by their Hand, with enough typics to match and cover, and all will move with you. I am not taking any risks.'

Kier had no protest to that, but Grey knew what he was thinking. In the time when magic was strong across Idistra's nations, mages were only limited by the power of their wells. But now, everything had changed – everything had weakened. Though mages had always had affinities for flesh and blood, or materials, or natural forces, they were now restricted in what they could do with that magic. The mages with affinities for flesh and bone all had a specialty, a body part they had an ability to affect within their opponents; materialists could only home in on one type of metal or wood or object. In her time working as a healer in Scaelas's army, Grey had seen the whole bloody assortment of it: those with the ability to cut off air to the lungs, leaving the dead blue-lipped and haunted; flesh affinites who could stitch giant ropes of skin over the mouth that Grey had to cut through with narrow blades, covered in sluices of blood; bone mages who could lock jaws and break bones with barely a look. Though internal affinities were rare, when they occurred, what they were capable of was utterly ghastly.

Perhaps Kier's affinity with the heart was better. Clean. They had limits, of course – a full aortal separation took so much of her well of power that they could only do ten an hour, maybe a dozen at a push, but there were other ways to harm the heart. Other ways to ensure the enemy did not fight back. And though Kier's affinity lay with the muscle itself, he had every other benefit of basic magic.

'They're taking the trade route here. If they take the resource across the river into Luthar, we have no way to recover it. Do you understand, Captain Seward?'

'Perfectly,' Kier said, frowning at the map. Which was fortunate, because Grey understood very little. She sent a pulse down the tether – they could not fully form sentences between them, but they had been paired as mage and Hand for long enough that Kier could read her intentions by how she shaped her feelings as she pushed them through the tether of her power, and he could reciprocate in kind. He caught her curiosity and understood easily.

'And what exactly is the resource?'

'Not for you to know, Captain Seward.'

There was a short pause. Grey wished she could see his face instead of trying to imagine his expression based on the back of his head. Very carefully, Kier said, 'Master Attis, surely ... you must understand that I cannot retrieve the resource if I do not know what it *is*.'

Another pause. Grey kept her eyes straight ahead, face blank, trying once again to fit into the picture of a perfect Hand, more befitting of Kier's station. Across from her, Attis's Hand was doing the exact same thing. Her name was Mare Concord, and she was thirty-eight years old. She'd been Attis's Hand for eighteen years, long enough that even her thoughts had become someone else's. Grey had learned these facts when Attis had borrowed her two years ago, on another assignment, when Mare was injured in the field and required medical attention.

'You'll know it when you see it,' Attis said, clipped. 'That's all you need to know. You set out before first light. Is that understood?'

A pause, and Grey knew Kier wanted to press. He knew better. That was the difference between them – Kier knew when to stop.

'Yes, Master,' he said.

'Good,' Attis said, already accepting the next paper from her Hand, already turning to the next task. 'Dismissed.'

For just the barest of seconds, the Hand Master's eyes locked on

Grey's. Grey remembered the skin of Mare's face, gray with blood loss, her lips cracked and chapped as she'd drunk from the cup in Grey's hand. Mare was unconscious while Grey sutured the wound in her liver, but by the time she moved to the external wound, the anesthetic draught had worn off and Mare's gaze was empty, feeble as Grey stitched up the jagged gash over her ribs. She remembered what Mare had told her when it was done, the other woman's bloody hand clenched around her wrist: *Get out. Now. As soon as you can. They never need you as much as you need them.*

She'd told Mare then that Kier was different and was rewarded with a pitying gaze so motherly that it made Grey's heart ache. *None of them are different.*

Mare made a full recovery without infection, thanks to Grey's careful action. That night, alone in their quarters, Grey lay awake long after Kier's breathing evened, studying his face.

We're going to die in this armor, Mare had told her, gripping her hand, slippery with blood. *We're going to die under Scaelas's banner, and for what?*

For what they did to Locke, Grey did not answer then, even though the truth of it echoed all the way to her bones.

Dismissed, Kier was already moving, and Grey fought her way out of her memories and hurried to follow. He set off across the room, then through the tunnels and out of the tent. Grey kept as close behind him as she could – they didn't match mages and wells based on stride length, but perhaps it should've been taken into consideration – as they stepped out into the clamor of the camp.

'Kier—' she started.

'Hold on,' he said, not turning. He didn't need to. She was so closely attuned to his voice, so firmly aware of him, that she was able to hear it even as a whisper in the middle of battle.

They stopped at one of the fires for hot tea and food, then headed to their tent with wrapped bread and cheese and jerky in their pockets and tea clasped between their hands. As they passed the infirmary, Grey couldn't tune out the cries of pain from the injured. She itched to help, but she did not. Her duty did not lie in that tent or any like it, hadn't since she was pulled from her post as a healer six years before and assigned as Kier's Hand. She still helped in her free time, but they were both already low on sleep, and judging by what she'd heard of the conversation, they would not have much more of it tonight. Onward she pressed.

They cut through the camp, the sea of faces all different but ground down into familiarity through exhaustion and the long-lasting post-battle weariness. As was the case in the rest of Idistra, Scaela had no uniformity of appearance – a thousand years ago, the whole Isle was uninhabited, until the first ships came, and the magic came with it. Before its wars, the nation states were known for their fishing, textiles and northern trade; nearly everyone here had heritage linking some-where else, and the appearance to match the mix of it. Grey herself was a mosaic: if anything, she could trace her lineage to Lindan, maybe a bit of Ruskaya; more relevantly, to the older families that had reached the Isle and learned its magic. The cool steel of her eyes, paleness of her skin and dark brown of her hair blended in here, among the mix of soldiers from all over Scaela, as it never had when she was growing up on the coast, where more were descended from Isbetan and Maroushan traders, who shared Kier's coloring.

Back in their tent, it was easy. It always was when it was just them, when the trappings fell away and she didn't have to *think*.

Calm as always, Kier undid the pin at her throat and helped her out of her cloak, then hung his on top of hers. He dragged the small brazier over to the space between their bed pallets and grabbed her hand as he lit it. She felt the siphoning, a pinch and then a trickle of warmth down her spine. He didn't have to touch her to use her power, but it was always easier when there was some sort of contact between them: he used less of both of their energy, and when they were alone, there was no point in siphoning without contact. Who would care?

She took off her boots and tucked them next to her pallet. He shifted over to make room for her on his, moving the blankets of his bedroll to make a cocoon for her. Grey crawled up and sat cross-legged, knees warmed by the fire, Kier's left side pressed to her right. He'd dragged the small table over for their cups of tea and food.

'So?' she asked.

He made a low noise in his throat, eyes miles away. She nudged him with her shoulder, and he handed her a piece of cheese and a hunk of bread as if to say, *Eat, I'll get to it.*

'I don't like the sound of this one,' he said finally. 'Feels off.'

'What about it?' Grey asked.

'The High Lord, for one thing. It can't mean anything good if he's involved.'

Grey chewed her lip. He had a point – Grey and Kier were fighting in the southern border, against Luthar; the High Lord, known only as Scaelas, in the fashion of all Idistra's sovereigns, was in the northeast. For him to be involved, their mission had to be *big*.

That wasn't the only thing that bothered her about the High Lord's involvement, and possibly bothered Kier, too. Grey and Kier and his brother, Lot, had grown up in a village on Scaela's northeast coast, close to the capital and the High Lord's seat. It had been years since Grey had worried about the presence of Scaelas in her life.

'It means you're trusted,' she said.

Kier shot her a look. 'It means we've been *noticed*.'

'It could be a good thing,' she said decidedly.

'Do *you* trust me?' Kier asked, which was absolutely the most pointless question he'd ever posed to her.

'Eternally,' she said. She watched his fingers as he dissected his bread. They were long and scarred, and he wore a single silver ring on the middle finger of his right hand even though he really wasn't supposed to, given the constant, looming risk of degloving in battle. It had once belonged to Lot, before he died in a skirmish against Eprain.

Kier sighed, setting the gutted rind of his bread aside, tossing a few crumbs into the fire. 'I'm afraid of this one. I have a feeling that … I don't know, Grey. I don't like it.'

It was the use of her name that gave her pause. He did it so rarely that her knee-jerk reaction was to say, 'I didn't know you gained the gift of prophecy while I was bathing.'

That was enough to get a half-smile out of him. Grey studied his face, the lines at his eyes that had only appeared recently. He'd started going gray at the temples last year, a fact that she teased him about relentlessly even as it made her stomach ache. At twenty-six, he was one of the youngest captains in Scaela, and she hated how every day of his duties made that fact less and less clear.

Kier frowned. 'I didn't like the look on Attis's face ... and there was something else on her desk. I know I shouldn't have read it, but I did.'

Grey shouldered into him. 'Kier Seward, you charlatan. Reading the master's secret correspondence? That's not like you.'

He smiled, but it didn't reach his eyes. 'It looks like Luthar found something that they *think* can make more wells. Fight the waning. If they believe they've found something that could generate wells, restore power ... well, I can see why the High Lord is involved.'

Grey stiffened for half a second – Kier was watching her intently, taking in the planes of her face, and he would catch her the second unease flickered across. So she didn't let it. 'The only way they can restore power,' she said, 'is if they found the heir to the Isle.'

'I know,' Kier said.

Grey fidgeted with the edge of her blanket. She did not want to think of what it would be like if they found the heir to the Isle of Locke, a feat that had long since become improbable, since someone had attacked the Isle, the source of the five other nations' power, and reduced it to nothing.

Detonated or submerged, when the Isle of Locke had descended into the sea sixteen years before, any fragile peace that existed between the remaining nation states dissolved completely – and the hunt began in earnest when Scaelas received a letter from Severin of Locke, signed with his true name, proving that the heir apparent had survived the decimation.

Grey remembered the patrols through the villages, Scaelan soldiers interrogating every boy between twelve and twenty, just in case. She remembered one of the half-dozen times when they came for Lot, and his blank look when he returned from his questioning late that night. She remembered listening at the door, stacked with Kier, as Kier's ma quietly answered Lot's questions about the war: *Why did they question me? Because you're a boy of about the right age. What are they looking for? The only person who can end this war – but even he is just a child. What would they have done to me? What will they do to him? I don't know, love. I don't know.*

It was an unfortunate truth, and one that had led to the war between the remaining nation states that made up Idistra. The Isle of Locke had always been the root of power for Idistra's other nations: Scaela, Cleoc Strata, Nestria, Eprain and Luthar. As the foundation and source, it supplied wells from those nations with the power needed for mages to draw from.

No one knew exactly why or how Locke had been destroyed, nor which nation was guilty of the destruction, but one thing was clear: without it physically existing, without the heir being able to tether to the source, there had not been a single well born in Idistra in sixteen years.

Kier persisted. 'Unless they found some other way. Maybe an ancestor? With shared blood? A forgotten cousin?'

'I don't think that's how the power works,' Grey hedged. 'That sort of connection, a lost cousin of the Isle, would not be strong enough to restore all the power that was lost.'

'Someone more direct, then? A bastard?'

'Everyone with the Isle's blood was killed,' Grey said sharply.

Each nation had individual alliances with Locke, but Scaela was bound to the Isle by blood and vows. Scaelas, the High Lord who bore the nation's title, was the first to go to war in an effort to uncover the fate of Locke's lost son – first with Epras for going after any cousin with the Isle's blood within reach, and then with Nestrias for killing the High Lady of Locke's sister after the destruction of the Isle – and then it was only a matter of time before Cleoc Strata and Luthar followed.

Kier was quiet for a long moment. 'I don't like to think about that part.'

It was impossible to forget, when it was the very reason they were at war. But: 'I know,' Grey said.

'So they think they found the heir, then,' Kier said, twisting his ring. 'That's the only explanation.'

'I suppose it is.'

He shrugged. 'Not my job to worry about it. Not yours, either.

We'll retrieve whatever it is they want and go from there. It's a fool's errand, but if Attis thinks we're able to do something big, then it at least reflects well on your power. Maybe they'll move us somewhere kinder.'

She raised her hand to his temple, skimming over the silver shooting through his thick, dark hair. He was due for a haircut – they'd been on the defensive non-stop for weeks as Luthar pressed for possession of the supply road that went from the bridge across the river and wound down on their side all the way to the port. Kier was in charge of sixty others (though he always said, 'You're just as much in charge as I am,' and she always laughed at that), so it made sense that a haircut was the last of his priorities. If she was a better Hand, a more militant Hand, she'd handle it now. She had the kit in her bag. But for all her dedication to their duty, she so loved the feeling of his too-long hair curling against her fingertips.

'Attis gave us the assignment because we're capable,' she said.

He sighed. 'She gave us the assignment because you're the best well we've got, and she's finally figured that out, though it pisses her off to admit that you're stronger than Concord.'

Grey shrugged. There was no true response to that. 'Rest easy, Captain,' she said. Then, because there were duties she *did* have to carry out for his health, she nudged his hand toward his bread scraps. 'And eat.'

Kier grimaced, but he obeyed.

They'd been at war for nearly two decades now, the unrest ruling their memories for most of the time either of them had been alive. Before, back when Locke was there as neutral territory, the six nation states that made up Idistra were as peaceful as the continent. Grey couldn't remember what that felt like.

Grey's parents and brother were casualties of the war. Following the tradition of Scaela, the orphan girl who washed up on the shore on that gloomy day, found half starved and feral in the woods, was given to a widow of the war. It was hoped that it would ease suffering – and it solved the issue of what to do with orphaned children, giving them a home despite the distinct lack of caretakers. It was certainly less helpful that Grey's new guardian was newly eighteen, only just married and widowed just as quickly, and barely able to look after herself, let alone a grief-stricken child.

So it was a stroke of luck that the kind couple next door to Imarta had two boys just a bit older than Grey and the capacity to love two more unmoored stragglers. Grey barely remembered her first days in Imarta's house besides a few snippets: Kier's ma stirring a great pot on the stove as his mum tied the laces of Grey's boots, checking them for a sturdy fit; how the older boy misheard her name the first time she said it and then exclusively called her Grape; sleeping tucked against Imarta, barely able to get through the night without screaming terrors; rifling through a pile of hand-me-down shirts as the younger of the boys peered at her from across the table.

She was glad she remembered meeting him. She was glad she had half a memory of life without Kier, if only because it reinforced the understanding that she felt unmoored without him. They'd known each other so long, grown into each other like roots of neighboring trees rather than neighboring children until Kier was so intrinsically tied with her understanding of magic that she sometimes had trouble separating the two.

Maybe that was fate. Self-fulfilling prophecy. Now, Kier was as close as she would ever come to true magic herself.

It was late evening when they were finally alone again, after a strategy discussion with their officers for the ambush and a round of sparring.

Sore and tired, Grey lay on her back on the scratchy rug that protected their tent floor from the mud. She'd shucked her cloak and most of her layers, leaving her in fitted sparring trousers and a compression vest. She stared straight up, watching the movement of the tent fabric in the wind.

Kier finished sharpening his blade and sat down next to her. When his hands found her calves, massaging out the knots, the sound she made was borderline indecent. His low chuckle answered. She clapped a hand over her mouth before anything else could escape and she'd have to shamefully and dishonorably remove herself from the situation, her position and perhaps all of Scaela.

'Turn over,' Kier murmured.

Grey pressed her lips together, but did as she was told. She slipped her straps over her shoulders and Kier helped her pull her vest down to her hips, exposing her back. Grey shivered, folding her arms to pillow her head. Kier moved over her, his hands shifting to her back. The problem with being trained to protect him and his person at all times, at all costs, was that it was actually quite hard on her body. At least, unlike most mages, Kier did his best to show her he appreciated it.

'I keep trying to work it out,' he said, his knuckles digging into the knots in her lower back. 'You're *certain* there's nothing that can just make a well, right?'

'You know as much as I do,' Grey said.

'Lies, blasphemy, slander.'

She sighed. 'No. There's nothing that can *make* a well.' She chewed her lip, distracted by the gentleness of his touch as his fingers traced up her spine, digging in again when he reached the too-tight muscles of her shoulders.

He thought for a moment. 'Then maybe it's something from another system.' Though Idistran magic relied on both a well and a mage, other systems of magic in other places didn't. 'Maybe a rock?'

'A *rock*?' Grey asked, turning her head to look at him over her shoulder.

He smirked at her, and *oh*. She could often pretend that she and Kier were nothing more than the most devoted of friends, but sometimes the ache in her chest was difficult to ignore.

'Or an elixir,' he said.

'Kiernan Seward, if we are risking our lives for a rock or an elixir, I am leaving you and this entire blasted camp and deserting.'

He laughed, his hands moving down to clasp her waist, thumbs pressing on either side of her spine. She bit her lip to stop any inappropriate noises from escaping. 'You wouldn't leave me,' he said.

She closed her eyes, hiding her face behind her arm. No, she would not leave him. But perhaps, someday, it would be far easier for her heart if she did.

'It's probably a mistake,' Kier said. For a half-second, she thought he was talking about what they were doing, and her heart dropped – though it was not uncommon for him to be so affectionate, or so kind to her body. 'A fluke.'

'Perhaps,' Grey said.

He went back to his ministrations, the quiet swelling between them. Grey shifted, aiming for subtlety, because though this seemingly didn't impact him, it did affect her in ways she would be mortified for him to discover.

Unless it was requited. In which case, this was quite a good moment for him to make that discovery, or a move, or cross a line that she herself wouldn't without certainty – but the position they were in and the fact that he *didn't* cross that line was answer enough for her.

'You had a nightmare last night,' Kier said, unprompted.

She rolled under him, narrow-eyed, moving her arm to cover her breasts as she did. Kier shifted up to give her space to move. If he was affected by the sight of her, shirtless beneath him, he did not let it show.

He leaned to adjust her hair so it wasn't caught under her, then picked up the arm she wasn't using to cover herself, massaging her right forearm. Annoyingly, after years and years of this, he always knew exactly where she was the sorest.

'I'm sorry I disturbed you,' she said.

'It's fine,' Kier said, brushing it off like he brushed off any inconvenience she offered. 'What was it about?'

Grey tipped her head back, staring at the canvas again. 'I don't remember.'

He poked her hard in the stomach.

'What? I don't.'

'*Flynn,*' he sighed, brushing the hair out of her face.

She pushed his hand away and pulled her vest up. Now he did look down, for only a second, before he glanced away, swallowing.

'You remember everything,' he said softly.

I don't want to remember this, she wanted to say, but it wasn't worth it. She stayed quiet until he moved, stretching out on his back next to her. He hated doing it, she knew, because he always expected the damp to seep up through the rug (it never did) and he insisted that the pallets were more comfortable than the ground (they were not; she would sleep right here, on the floor, if he did not kick up such a fuss about it). His arm pressed into hers; she laced their fingers together and felt the lazy attachment of the tether between them, her power flowing easily into him and falling dormant. The room glowed warmer, the fire going a tinge brighter purple, as she pushed the power at him.

Kier, she wanted to say, *why are we doing this? Why are we fighting?*

But he would only say that they were fighting for Scaela because it was their home, and because everyone was fighting. Scaela against Luthar for the ports and Cleoc Strata for the fertile land and Eprain for access to the eastern sea. It was Scaela against the others, and the other nation states against one another, all the way down – the only place to get any peace on this doomed island was possibly in Nestria, because they fought only Cleoc Strata and were mostly free.

Scaela against them all because decades before, someone had killed Locke in a failed attempt to seize control of Idistra's power, and their own High Lord Scaelas would never forget it.

Because there would soon be no power left at all, not unless the Isle's heir returned to resurrect it, and someone had killed the rest of the family and no one knew who or how or if it was possible to bring the power back.

Grey felt all of it pressing on her chest, the hopelessness and her nightmare adding equal weight.

'Captain,' she said, voice catching in her throat.

'Hand,' he said, easing into their roles, waiting for her confession. He imparted so much tenderness into that one word that she had to swallow hard twice before she could even consider speaking.

She closed her eyes, focusing only on his hand in hers, the ebb and flow of power between them.

'Fire,' she said. 'I dreamed of fire.'

'Past or present?'

'Past,' she said. 'All over – I felt my hair singeing. I felt my clothes burning away.'

'And then?'

She shrugged, words failing to encompass it. There was no 'and then'. She was on fire. She was awake, sitting up on her pallet with her fingers knotted in her blankets, soaked in sweat, panting into nothing. Barely a second passed between the two.

And they were screaming. That was the one thing she wouldn't tell Kier: around her, they were all screaming.

'That's all,' she said, punctuating with another squeeze to his hand.

He didn't push. He knew better by now.

They lay like that for a while, listening to the sounds of the camp outside: boots in the mud and half-heard conversations and the wind through the tents.

Finally, Kier sighed. 'We should sleep.' His fingers left hers as he eased himself up. She watched him, his shirt untucked from his trousers, revealing a dimpled sliver of skin on his back.

'We should,' she agreed.

Kier gripped her hand and tugged her up from the floor with him, pulling just enough power to adjust the fire to a comfortable temperature for sleeping. She went to her trunk to rifle for clean sleep clothes. Kier pulled off his boots and shucked his clothing, folding it on his own trunk. He'd always been comfortable with his body in a way she was not with hers: even now, she turned to the wall to undress.

It didn't matter. Whether she cared or not (and truthfully, *cared* was not the correct word), they'd seen every inch of one another. She knew every scar on his body as well as her own, every expression his face could create. There was no real modesty between them, nor could there be. Even when they pretended.

It made everything more difficult, the knowing. Most notably for her traitorous heart.

'Flynn?'

'Hmm?'

She turned to see him sliding into his bedroll, rolling onto his side to face her. After she shrugged into her sleep shirt, she slid into her own blankets and mirrored the posture. In training, their bedrolls had been so close that she could see every detail of his face when they lay like this.

'Last night,' he said uncertainly. 'Your nightmare.'

'*Kiernan.*'

'You shouted your brother's name.'

Grey sucked a breath through her teeth. 'What of it? You shout your brother's name, too, when you're sleeping.'

His face did not change. With two dead brothers between them, what else was there to say?

'You just ... haven't had a terror like that in a while. If something is happening ... if something is *changing* ... '

She rolled on her back angrily before he could see her face or say anything further. 'Sleep,' she said. 'You use so much of me when you're tired.'

He was quiet after that, and she felt the sting of her words hanging in the air between them. He never used too much of her, no matter what she said, and that was the truth – however much he needed was just as much as she was willing to give.

The knights of the Idistran order enter the High Sovereign's service as men-at-arms. The order of ranks is as follows: soldier-at-arms, officer, lieutenant, captain, master and then commander. Mages and typics are promoted on their own merit. Wells, assigned as Hands, follow the ranking of their assigned mage and share the rank – but deference is, in all cases barring death, given to the mage who has earned the rank.

The Idistran Military Order by Master Aluna Hutchins

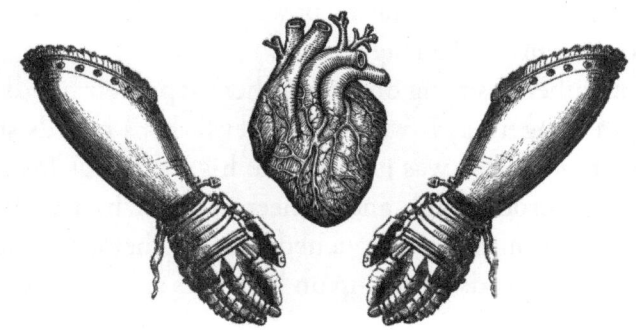

t w o

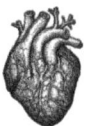

GREY WAS FOUR WHEN she learned what it meant to be a well. There was no magic without wells: mages had to draw power from them, tether into a well and siphon to perform any action. It was like a water wheel, generating power. As a well, she was the river, the source that made the magic move.

She remembered sitting on her mother's lap, their hands linked, heads bowed together. It was one of her father's guards she tethered to first, when she was just a child: his name was Iowain, and he had a boisterous laugh and a sheet of silver hair and a beard down to his stomach. He crouched next to them, his face open and earnest, his hands palms-up on his knees as if to prove himself harmless.

'It'll hurt, at first,' Alma, her mother, murmured into her hair, 'but only because it feels like a loss – your body doesn't know yet what it's doing.'

'Push away as much as you need, child,' Iowain said.

Grey sucked in a breath. She felt the reach of the tether and she wanted to recoil, but more than that, she wanted to make her mother proud. So she felt the thread of magic within her, warm and endless and unfurling, and something inside of her felt like it was cracked right open. She felt the moment the tether took, the stomach-ache pain of it, then felt it dissolve.

'See?' Alma said, stroking Grey's hair back from her face. Grey felt the presence of her brother behind her, waiting in case she needed more support, his hand pressed to her back. 'Nothing to be afraid of.'

Iowain put his hands together, and Grey sensed that tugging. Alma nodded to her, and Grey let the tiniest thread of power slip into the tether. When Iowain opened his hands, smile growing, he held a luminous opal in his palm. Iowain was a materialist, and after that day he was constantly making her opals and pearls, sapphires and rubies, presenting them to her like a magician from a children's play. She still thought of him every time she caught the glimmer of a fine jewel on some nobleperson's skin.

Only a few years after that, the rest of them were dead, and Grey was not. She sat on a hillside with a boy she'd only met days before; she hadn't spoken in nearly as long. But he was kind, and he didn't ask her any questions, and he was just as comfortable in silence as she was.

They sat on the hill and looked out at the sea, the flatness of it stretching still unfamiliar to her. When she reached out her hand, he took it without hesitation. When she offered a tether, he took that too. She already knew he was a mage. It was obvious: the energy of unfulfilled magic fizzled around him.

It only took a moment for the boy's brows to draw together. Another moment, and he drew a tiny flame between them, the earliest kind of standard magic they taught mages. He pulled back and said, '*Oh.*' Kier looked at her hand, then at her. 'What *are* you?'

Grey only looked at him. It was the first question he'd asked her, and she felt compelled to answer. She could not remember why she'd opened up her power. She only knew she trusted him, the kind dimples that carved into his cheeks, knees and elbows always scraped from playing too hard with his brother and now her, his eyes green on the outside and brown on the inside. Hazel, but only just.

'You don't have to answer that,' Kier stammered. 'I'm sorry I asked.' He was always like that, back then – full of doubt, uncertain of himself. It was an imperfection that years of fighting and leading had long since taken from him.

Sometimes, now, she still looked at him and *missed* his imperfections. She even missed his doubt, because that meant room for mistakes without the consequence of death.

'It's okay,' she said, and she meant it. She looked out to the open sea where the Isle once was. 'It's only, I don't know.'

The mud was thick and cold, soaking the crest of Scaela she wore on her chest. Grey barely felt it, armored as she was for battle. She'd shifted her baldric and most of her blades to her back when they'd gotten down, to avoid the mud. It was still utter misery, lying between Kier and Eron Fastria, one of their typic officers, eyes trained on the road at the bottom of the hill. Further down the road, the Iolis was swollen with the rainfall, nearly spilling over its banks.

Their company was divided into four groups of fifteen, half scattered over this ridge and half on the other side of the road, hidden among the scrabbling weeds and underbrush, blending with the barren trees of the woods. Intelligence delivered to Attis and then to Kier estimated the convoy of carriages would be rolling through two hours after sunrise. They'd been here waiting for three already, just to be safe, in position for an ambush.

She was comforted by the familiar weight of steel on her back – it was gauche to be armed to the teeth walking around camp, but she liked the presence of her weapons, and she was always most comfortable when she had her sword at easy reach. It reminded her of her father, who had taught her to wield a sword as soon as she was steady enough to stand on two feet and strong enough to lift a wooden practice blade.

She liked knowing she could protect herself. And Kier, if needed. In return, he did everything in his power to keep her safe.

She risked a glance down the line. The sun shimmered, murky through the clouds, as the rain picked up from a drizzle to a patter. She was already soaked to the bone, rain seeping through the gaps in her leather armor, through her padded shirt and plain cloth undershirt. Next to her, Eron offered her a tight smile. He was not usually a smiler, so he must've felt the tension rolling off her. Grey only grimaced back. Fastria sighed, his dark eyes losing some of their glimmer.

It was hard for Grey not to lose focus when they were like this. She tried to keep herself present by running through muscle groups, then organs, then bones. When she was younger, fresh out of her extra training as a healer, out of those years spent up to her elbows in blood, she used to imagine viscera in diagrams and memories of injuries she'd treated. Now, years separated, she imagined all manner of it on Kier. Open his chest, split the pectoralis major down the middle. Count the ribs. She imagined the pinkish white of his manubrium, the ridges of his xiphoid process. It was impossible not to imagine all bodies as Kier's, all parts as Kier's. She'd seen too much of him, opened him up too many times and sealed him shut, felt the nodules of his bones and the slick heat of his bare muscles.

That was what it meant to be a Hand. To be just as comfortable, just as *capable* with the inside of him as she was with the outside.

Before she finished her recall of bones, a small noise like birdsong sounded from the field down the road to their right, just loud enough to be heard over the river. Grey drew her sword in the quiet before the storm. On her left, Kier stiffened.

'Captain?' a muffled voice asked in the near silence.

'Prepare for attack,' Kier said, his own voice barely above a whisper. It didn't matter – Grey heard the gentle shift of the soldiers-at-arms tensing, taking position. The signal meant that dust from the road had been spotted in the distance, that the convoy was in sight. In her veins, she felt the pre-battle tension.

She tightened her fingers around the sword, flexing her hands in her leather gauntlets. Her hands were bare, ungloved, in case Kier needed direct contact with her skin in the heat of battle. She focused on the shuffle of boots on the packed road. Soon enough, she too could see the dust cloud in the distance, the four carriages surrounded by tidy lines of soldiers. On her right, Fastria drew a quick breath and murmured a prayer in Arkunish, probably to one of their gods.

'Approaching the first marker, Captain,' he muttered in the moment after he finished his prayer.

'Keep holding,' Kier said. 'I'll give the signal when the time comes.'

The convoy came closer, and every muscle in Grey's body was

wire-tense. They were entering the danger zone – if any of the mages in that convoy had an affinity like Kier's and a strong enough well, they'd be able to sense other life forces, other *magic* waiting up ahead. If that happened, if their cover was blown – well, they wouldn't be totally ruined, but it would be a fairer fight than she wanted.

The first of the carriages passed the next marker. Grey didn't usually second-guess Kier, but she did give him a look, judging his face. His jaw was tight, anxious.

'Approaching the third marker, Captain,' Fastria said.

'Kier?' Grey murmured.

He whistled twice, sharp, through his teeth. That was all it took – Grey spotted movement in the group closest to the convoy as they sprang to action, then the second team raced down the hill. Kier shifted a hand to her shoulder, gripping the edge of her pauldron, as Fastria and the others surrounding them leaped into a run.

Their job was not with the first wave. Though Kier was unnervingly eager to throw himself into battle, he and Grey had a more specialized task for this particular skirmish.

Grey watched the first wave of soldiers crash into the unsuspecting convoy. She gritted her teeth through the flashing of steel as meat met meat. A spray of blood flew up from one of the smaller skirmishes closer to them, speckling the side of the first carriage with crimson. She watched the typics with their steel, the mages and their Hands, all entangling with the thirty-six mages and Hands opposite. She had to watch, because if she did not, she would panic – and she could not panic.

'Now, Grey,' Kier said, just for her.

She kept a steady pace behind him down the bank. One dark shape rose to her left, a mage-less Hand, but she cut him down with one swift move of her sword and only vaguely winced at the spray of hot blood that splashed on her face. She felt Kier's magic tugging at her middle, power unfurling from her chest. He wasn't severing any aortas with that trickle of power, but Grey heard a shout to one side and glanced that way just long enough to see a mage fall to his knees with no apparent injury, blood trickling from his gaping mouth. Kier finished the job with his own sword.

She did not stop. She pushed more power at Kier and kept moving.

It was her job to keep him safe, keep him alive. As a well, Grey herself was impervious to harm by magical means, but the other mages and typics in their company weren't. She kept close to Kier, kept power flowing to him as he strategically targeted their rivals. With her sword, she fought off anyone else who could do him harm.

She cut through another mage – their swords clanging overhead, her dagger to his side, recovery with her sword, finding a seam in his armor, stabbing through his belly – and pushed forward to the line of carriages. All around her was the ebb and flow of magic, so thick she could taste it, as a dozen skirmishes were lost and won and recoupled. It was a sick feeling, how the magic in the air refilled her own personal store even faster.

Kier kicked the door of the first carriage open and Grey stabbed the guard who slid out to protect whatever was inside – which turned out to be a whole lot of nothing. She felt Kier pull from her and turned just in time to see him wince as he blocked some magework.

'You okay?' she asked.

'Fine,' he insisted.

There was no time to waste. They pushed back into the battle, Grey gasping halfway through slitting a man's throat as Kier pulled the magic from her in heady ropes. There was nothing to be found in the next carriage either, and she felt the uncomfortable desperation in her stomach – even though she was good at it, she hated active fighting, hated the vulnerability for both of them. She caught movement out of the corner of her eye and turned just in time to see the edge of a blade catch Kier's cheekbone, a hilt smash his nose crooked and bloody – then his slick hand grasped her left hand, skin-to-skin contact drenched in blood. A great tear opened up inside her middle, power torn away in a torrent. On Kier's other side, the offending soldier fell, with another three going beyond him.

'Easy, Captain,' Grey managed through gritted teeth. She caught sight of a well taking a knee, trying to revive their fallen mage, to no avail. Kier's aim was always true.

She stayed with Kier as they pushed back through the mess of blood and mud, trying to avoid the worst of the fighting.

'Third's a charm?' he muttered, pushing a body from the end of Grey's sword. He turned to slash at another attacker, favoring his blade now rather than his magic as Grey focused on rebuilding her well of power. Alongside the convoy on both sides, the battle was quieting; she watched with detached, familiar horror as one of her men delivered a blow that nearly decapitated an enemy soldier, but she kept moving. That was the awfulness of warfare, the fact that kept her up at night staring at the ceiling of every room they'd ever slept in, from the rain-soaked canvas tents to the thick stone fortresses: she had to see it all, watch it all and keep going. This war wasn't about winning or losing. It was about enduring. Watching flesh tear, tasting the blood of strangers in her mouth, taking lives in her hands and pushing forward into a stretching maw of time in which she hoped the killing would end.

Kier kicked down the door of the third carriage. Grey slipped in first, grabbing the hair of the Hand who lurched forward and slitting his throat in one easy, neat movement before he could raise his blade against her. This time there was a mage waiting for them too, but Kier dismantled him with some trick that left Grey gasping, feeling like something had been chewed from the middle of her.

There, in the center of the hollowed-out carriage, unmistakable – there was the resource.

It took them both a second to process, blinking down at it, because it wasn't a rock, or a forgotten aunt, or an elixir. It was a girl. A scrappy thing, thin to the point of boniness, with pitch-black hair cut jaggedly to her chin, and eyes the blue of ice chips. Grey couldn't place her age, but didn't think she could have been older than eighteen or twenty. She scowled up at them – it was impossible to do anything else with her wrists and ankles bound, her mouth gagged.

'Captain . . . ?' Grey found herself saying.

But Kier was already moving. 'We're not going to hurt you,' he said to the girl, perfunctory, as he dragged her over his shoulder. 'Go,' he urged Grey when the girl was in place, and Grey slipped from the carriage back into the mess of the fight – but at least that had calmed down. Lieutenant Chappelle had rounded up the wounded from their company behind the convoy. Anyone still well enough to stand was on clean-up, making sure there were no survivors remaining.

Attis had asked for decimation, and she would have it. Grey swallowed hard, turning her face away. She'd been on clean-up one time too many, and she couldn't bear to watch it now.

'Resource acquired,' she called to Chappelle, keeping close to Kier's back. 'Grab who you can and we'll go.'

She kept her sword drawn as the company regrouped, carrying the wounded and dead they were able to. She scanned over them, chewing her lip. 'Five dead,' she reported to Kier, unease heavy in her stomach.

But Kier wasn't next to her. She turned to see that he'd carried the girl over to the bank, separated from the blood and battle, and set her down facing away from the worst of it. He'd already removed his helm and unbuckled his pauldrons, his fingers quick as he took off his armored leather breastplate. Grey stalked toward him – over or not, they were still in obvious danger, and it was too risky to be apart.

He was speaking in a low voice that Grey wasn't close enough to hear. Her stomach tightened as he pulled the breastplate over the girl's head, tightening it to her body, offering her protection. She felt frozen, watching him like that, as he ceded his armor to the girl they had been sent to rescue. Fool that he was, he cut away the restraints on her hands and was rubbing the blood back into her wrists, the exact same way he'd rub feeling back into Grey's limbs after a long day.

He was always too prone to tenderness.

She looked away, just for a moment. Down by the carriages, the company was very nearly ready to go.

'On your signal, Captain,' she called to Kier. 'Let's get back.'

Something within her prickled – it wasn't power, thick in her middle. There'd been an odd kindness in his face, and she … she didn't know. It reminded her too much of when she was just a girl, rescued by some soldier far away from here. She didn't want to see it when she was still covered in blood, still aching with the power he'd drained from her. She didn't want to accept that she'd become the very type of person she'd had so many nightmares about.

There was no sound behind her, no acknowledgement from Kier. Lieutenant Chappelle turned to say something from the front of the column – she saw the shape of the word on his lips – and then behind her, very clearly, Kier said, '*Hand.*'

Grey turned. He had the girl by the wrists, holding her awkwardly as he pushed her down the ridge. She was sobbing, great breaths shaking her thin shoulders. In Kier's armor, she looked like a child play-acting at knighthood. Kier's face was twisted oddly, looking almost like shock. He tethered to Grey, and she felt something strange coming through: pain, guilt, apology, surprise.

Something was very wrong.

'Kearns, Pacet,' she called, and two of the typics from the back of the column detached at her command. 'Take the resource.'

It took a moment for them to clear the girl, lead her away, another moment for Kier to take a step, stumble. He gripped Grey's arm for stability, clutching the edge of her pauldron. Grey's hands went to his upper arms, holding him upright without thought, fingers digging into the bulk of his padded shirt.

'What? What is it?' she asked, searching his face. It was difficult – he was a mess of blood anyway, all drama with very little true injury besides a cut cheek and perhaps a broken nose, but none of that was enough to explain the glassy look in his eyes.

'She stabbed me,' he said. He moved closer to Grey, shielding his body from their company. Very carefully, he pulled up the bottom of his padded shirt, revealing the blooming stain on his undershirt. It was very quickly going red and wet.

'How badly?' Grey asked.

Kier winced.

'I'll kill her,' Grey gritted, pressing her fingers to Kier's side. 'I'll fucking kill her.'

'No . . . ' Kier was saying, his hand tightening on her arm.

She couldn't kill the resource. She couldn't kill the resource, because that order hadn't been given, and yet, and *yet* – when she looked back, the girl's hands were red with Kier's blood. Kier leaned in, his breathing ragged on Grey's muddy cheek. All she could think of was the overwhelming crush of her own failure; all she could hear was the pounding of her heartbeat in her ears.

'You *gave her your armor,*' she seethed.

'She's just a girl,' Kier said, unsteady. 'She was – is – terrified.'

Grey herself had been 'just a girl' once, and look at her now. She wondered if Kier would've underestimated her, too, when she was a girl – or if she would've made the same decision their prisoner had. To cut. To wound. To run.

'How did you not check if she was armed?'

'Grey,' he said. 'It was my own dagger. It . . . it probably did a lot of damage coming out, and I won't let you put yourself at risk for me.'

She knew the dagger. Dark metal, barbed on the lower edge. She'd given it to him herself – had presented it to him on his twenty-fifth birthday with a note that read, *So you can be deadly all on your own,* partially as a joke. He must've recovered it before handing over the resource – good move; it wasn't a solid plan to leave her armed – because he shakily offered it to Grey. If only the girl had left it buried in his lower intestines, she wouldn't be quite so panicked now. Removing it had only done more damage.

'Listen to me,' she said, holstering the dagger then moving one hand to grip his chin, forcing him to look at her. It was shock, probably – he was fine. He'd had worse. He'd be *fine.*

'Grey—'

'*Don't,*' she chastised. He'd been stabbed before, worse than this. They'd *both* suffered worse than this. She pressed a hand against his wound and sent a push of power at him. Kier let out an awful noise, staggering against her, his eyes going very dark.

'I just need to get you to camp,' she said. 'Once we get back, I will fix it. Okay?'

'Grey,' he said, scrabbling for her hand. She let him take it, his slick and wet with his own blood.

'No,' she said, feeling him resist the tether. 'Take it. Siphon from me. Take it all – don't you *fucking look at me like that.*'

There was blood between his teeth. It took her a minute to recover the gauze from her pocket kit, another to wrap his torso as tightly as she could under his shirt. Once that was done, she kept his hand in hers, forced him to move forward, draped his arm around her shoulder. He was so heavy, too heavy – she staggered, nearly dropping him. One of the other Hands was there before she was even off the bank, taking his other side, giving Grey the freedom to press her hand firmly against his wound. She could not do that much now, not without stopping to clean and inspect the wound, but he wouldn't get any worse with a constant thread of power running into him.

Mages could not heal themselves, even with a steady flow of magic. It was like trying to tickle oneself – an impossibility. Just as it was impossible to harm a well with magic; the power didn't allow for that kind of direction. But Grey's hands paired with Grey's power . . . Though she had no affluence to perform her own magic, her medical training and undiluted power worked in tandem to put Kier back together. And until she could get her hands on him, could actually *help*, she could keep him indefinitely stable with power alone.

If she could sustain it.

'Let's move!' she shouted, hating the shrill note in her voice. But she was his Hand, his voice – she was in command when he could not be.

The Hand on Kier's other side said very softly, 'You must move your feet, Captain Seward.' Grey looked over just long enough to register that it was Ola Et-Kiltar, a sharp-tongued well who had caught her eye often enough that she and Kier were planning to put her mage, Brit, up for promotion. Grey couldn't see Brit now – usually their pale hair was easy to spot in the heaving mass of soldiers – but she forced herself to stay calm, because if Ola wasn't panicking, Brit probably wasn't dead.

But Kier was still resisting her, and losing valuable time because of it. '*Take it*,' Grey seethed into his shoulder. He hissed a breath through his teeth, coughed, and spat out a mouthful of blood. She pressed her hand firm against the gauze, feeling the muscles of his stomach and another sluice of hot, sticky blood.

But this time, he listened. She felt the thread of her power moving into him, unraveling like a loose bit of yarn on a knit sweater. He took another unsteady breath.

They supported him, shuffling along as Grey's head pounded with the agony he was unable to keep from slipping down the tether. She felt the thread unspooling further and further, the tugging against her. She had quite a lot to give before she ran out, but she had to keep just enough to heal him when they got back to camp, and avoid suspicion on top of that.

Halfway back, Ola switched with her mage, Brit – this was a relief to Grey, because it confirmed that Brit was not dead – but that left a new problem. Kier stumbled, once, and Brit sucked a breath through their teeth as they caught him, looking over at Grey.

'Is he siphoning from you?' they asked. 'Has he been siphoning from you all this time?'

'That's none of your concern,' Grey snapped. But Kier was grappling against the tether like a dying man – he wasn't doing it intentionally, but he was drawing a *lot*. For a normal well, it would be too much.

Ola, within earshot, hurried to Grey's other side. 'Surely it's too much – Hand Captain Flynn, you can't let him drain you.'

Grey shot Ola a fierce look. 'I know what I'm doing.'

'Hand,' Kier said, very quietly. He'd always been better at propriety. A terrible irony, that was.

She didn't know the edges of her power, the barriers – it'd been a long time since she'd gone looking. She had felt the fatigue of true emptiness only once, after a particularly awful battle years ago, when Kier had overdone it. Then, she'd slept for three days straight and woken to his guilt.

They'd taken measures since then, legal and otherwise. And he'd always been so careful. She didn't think she was going to run out of power, but they were so far from home.

She couldn't think of it. Not now.

'Hand Captain,' Ola said again, more urgent.

Her vision was graying out a little bit at the edges, going grainy from the force of her focus. Her jaw was clenched hard enough that it felt like her teeth would shatter. The spool was ever spinning, but Kier's feet were moving, and his heart was pumping, and if he stopped siphoning . . .

'He's going to kill you,' Ola said urgently. She exchanged a look with her mage and held out her hand. 'Let me. Please.'

The idea of giving Kier over to someone else was so sweet – and utterly impossible. Grey looked at him, his eyes half shut. There was a scar through his eyebrow from falling out of an apple tree when he was nine. The scratch on his cheek was now clotted, crusted nearly black.

'I'm fine,' she insisted. She adjusted his arm across her shoulders, gripping the hand that hung limply on her chest. It was so, so cold.

'Hand Captain,' Brit said, very carefully, 'if you do not disengage, we will be dragging back both of your bodies. Let Ola take him.'

All she wanted was to give him up. Push him out. Let him go. But she could keep holding him; the well of power inside of her was not empty.

If she kept holding him, they would know. They would know she was not normal, that there was something wrong.

If she let him go, Ola would try to tether to Kier, and she would find that she could not.

'Drop it,' he said to one or both of them. His voice was utterly unlike himself – it was like listening to a version of Kier already years in the grave. His head lolled to one side, his forehead pressing to Grey's temple. 'Let go,' he muttered.

'I'm *not* going to,' she said. She was going to throw up. There was so much of her going, so much of her gone, it felt like she was pulling her intestines out through her navel. 'You can't ask that of me.'

He sucked a breath. She stumbled, pressing her hand tighter. She felt his lips on her temple, chapped, uncoordinated with pain. 'Hand Captain,' he said, the lips brushing her skin so very cold. 'I order it.'

'You don't outrank me.' If she let go, there was no guarantee he'd get back alive. No guarantee he'd get back at all.

'Like hell I don't.' If she didn't let go, there would be even more eyes on them. Suspicion.

A pause. A breath. How nice it would be, Grey thought, to lie next to him and die. For all of this to be over.

'I have enough,' Kier said.

She snapped the tether.

The relief was so dizzying that she very nearly lost consciousness, and in a moment of panic, she realized that she *had* given a lot, and she was not as powerful as she thought. Her neck was clammy with sweat under Kier's arm, her stomach awful with bile, her head pounding. There was a great, caving emptiness within her, the well of magic nearly dry, and then she heard Kier suck in a breath. She couldn't even imagine – without the power of a tether, any pain he'd kept at bay rushed in, doubling, trebling.

'If you die on me,' Grey hissed into Kier's shoulder, 'I'm going to come right down with you and haunt your bones, Kiernan Seward, you absolute fucking bastard.'

His laugh was weak, breathy and full of blood. 'I'll hold you to that.'

The relationship between a mage and well can be complicated enough, based on the delicate balance of power, without emotional entanglements entering the equation. For the best working relationship, it is recommended that the pairing remains as close as is necessary for trust, but otherwise avoid any feeling more powerful than friendly respect.

Mage's Codex, Fifth Edition, published 4 years PD

My love is yours, as that which beats within my heart is yours, and that which powers the fabric of the world is yours through mine own hand. Take from me, that I may be thine.

Binding ritual recovered from Locke, author unknown, date unknown

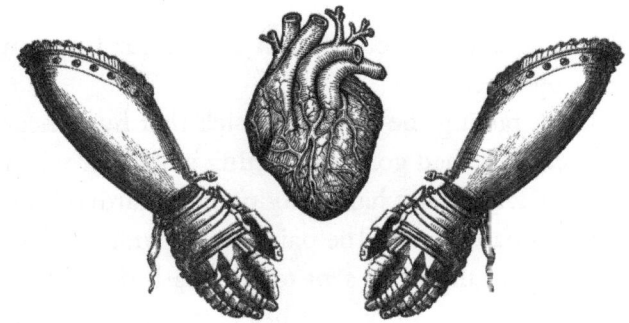

three

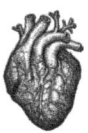

IT HAD NEVER BEEN a sure thing, her becoming his Hand. Two weeks after her eighteenth birthday, in a time that felt like a different life entirely, Grey was wrist-deep inside a chest wound when the door to the infirmary opened and an officer stepped inside.

'Flynn?' they called, searching the ward.

Grey looked up, registered the caller. 'I'm currently unable to curtsy,' she said apologetically. Beneath her careful work, the mage on the table made a strangled noise. Grey nodded to the trainee healer beside her, who leaned close to the mage's nose with a cloth soaked in an herbal anesthetic.

The officer grimaced. 'You've been requested. Captain Pickett requires your presence.'

Grey inhaled, tasting the blood and sick that hung heavy in the air around them. She had gone to training with Kier when she was nearly sixteen, Kier's steady hand forging her guardian's permission on the necessary parchment. The pair were separated when she had been deemed too young to be sent to her death right after training and instead was sent to work as a healer, while Kier went with a company of mages to fight.

Until a couple of weeks ago, she figured everyone had forgotten that there was an able-bodied well working in the infirmary – after all, wells made the best healers, though they usually weren't held back from battle until they'd lost at least one limb. And she wasn't shy about her talent – she was a *good* healer. Good enough to be requested by captains and masters; good enough to find little bottles of liquor or extra parchment for her letters tucked into her apron pockets by those who'd survived under her hands.

It will be boring, she had written to Kier in her latest letter, *but I might not die before my twentieth birthday if they keep me here. Maybe.*

He had not written back. In fact, she had not heard from him in months, which filled her with more anxiety with each day that passed. All she could do was pray to her gods that he wasn't dead, and send increasingly panicked letters to her adopted mother, Imarta, to ask if Kier's mothers had heard anything.

Each letter from Imarta came with *Laurella and Pia have not heard from him, but he is not dead.* It was okay, she thought. No news was good news. After all, when Lot was killed, they knew immediately.

Besides, Kier could not be dead, she figured, because if he *was*, she was certain she would know. She would feel some sort of reset in her bones, some eternal agony, no matter how much distance separated them.

She finished her work, frowning despite herself. She couldn't even remember *wanting* to be anything other than a healer. But when she finished working on the mage, washed the blood away and made her way to the old farmhouse where the officers worked, all the things she'd once wanted fell away.

She was led into the office of Captain Pickett. The cranky, peevish man in charge of the healers at the camp sat behind his desk looking mercurial as always, and . . .

Another man stood in front of the window, half illuminated by the afternoon sun – it made his hair shine dark and glimmering, made the polished pin at his throat gleam. He wore the red-trimmed blue cloak of a mage, both hands folded in front of him.

Grey froze in the doorway, barely able to breathe. Half of her life she'd revolved around him, one tiny planet around that great sun. Two years of her life she'd read every letter a dozen times until the paper wore thin, tucking each into the inner pocket of her cloak for safe keeping. For nearly three months he had occupied hours of worry as she waited for any word of him.

Now here he was again, and she couldn't move – she didn't know if she knew him at all anymore.

'Healer Flynn,' Pickett was saying, perfunctory, ready to get this over with. 'You've been reassigned. A lieutenant has requested you as his Hand.'

Grey curtsied before she could be written up for disrespect yet again – she wasn't being unintentionally disrespectful, just forgetful, her brain always skipping from one injury to the next, one patient to the next, without taking stock of who in the room mattered more than her – and skittered three more steps into the room so she could shut the door behind her.

'Kier?' she said, the word escaping her lips before she could stop it. She hadn't seen him since the day he was sent to the Nestrian border. Then, two years before, he wasn't this broad-shouldered, he wasn't this stern, and he certainly didn't have that scar tugging on the corner of his lip, or the other snaking across his left hand into the cuff of his sleeve.

'That's Lieutenant Seward,' Pickett said. 'You won't be warned again, Healer.'

'I'm sorry. I . . .' She shook herself out, forced herself to focus, squared her shoulders. She'd known about his promotions. Of course she had. He had written to her about them himself. Any semblance of coherence fled. 'Lieutenant. I . . . Sorry. Your Hand? Me?'

'If you wish,' Kier said, steady as ever. His face, inexplicably different, even as her memory shifted the new angles of him into recognition. His voice, utterly unchanged.

'She does not get the choice, Seward,' Pickett said. Kier winced.

'Of course,' Grey said, swallowing hard. 'Of course.'

'Then it's done,' the captain said, going back to his stack of missives. 'You'll leave right away. Gather your things, Flynn. The carriage is waiting to take you both back to Lieutenant Seward's post.'

Her head felt full of air as she curtsied again, following Kier in an orderly line down the stairs. It took her far too long to realize that he'd diverted from the path and drawn her into a broom cupboard, and then before she could even process anything other than the smell of bleach, he was pulling her into his arms.

She was stiff, still against him for two more seconds – and then she was wrapping her arms around him, digging her fingers into his shorn hair, hiding her face in his chest.

'You're alive,' she said into his chest, breathing too hard, as if she needed to reassure herself. He smelled like he always did, sunlight and clean linen and his mothers' lavender soap. He smelled like *home*. 'You're alive.'

'I'm alive,' he said, just as desperate, as if he too needed convincing. 'A near thing, but I'm here. I'm alive.'

'You didn't write back.'

His expression flickered. 'It's been difficult,' he said. 'I'm sorry. I'm so, so sorry. I just haven't been able to think, let alone write.'

'And you want *me*?'

'I didn't mean to pull you from safety,' he said, 'but when I saw you listed as a well, for reassignment— Oh, Grey, I shouldn't have, and you must think me selfish.'

She gripped his shoulders, pushed him away just enough so she could see the gleam of his eyes in the dim. He looked— She couldn't think, couldn't focus. He looked like every dream she'd had of him, stretched over two years and too many heartbeats fearing she'd never see him again. He looked like an absolute stranger.

She moved her hands up, cupping his face. 'I'm so sorry,' she said, the words coming unbidden – and she had to say them in person, write them into the space between them like she'd never been able to write them in letters. 'I'm so sorry about Lot.'

He closed his eyes. Turned his head to press his lips to her palm. He was always so affectionate, even when they were children, always one to kiss her temple or link his arm through hers or lay a hand over her shoulder. She used to read something into it before she considered that it might be the only way he knew to prove she could trust him.

'Don't,' he murmured against her skin.

His shoulders shook, and he was just a boy again. She pulled him down – when he'd gotten so much taller than her, she didn't know;

unless he'd always been so tall and she'd forgotten, which was un-
thinkable – and buried his head in her neck. Neither acknowledged
his tears.

Soon after, once she had collected the single bag of her belongings
and her ill-fitting new cloak trimmed in Hand's black, he said,
'Pickett is wrong. You didn't have to agree.'

'You said they were assigning me anyway. Best it's with you.'

'Yes, but . . . where we're going. It's not anyone's first choice.'

'Why?'

'It's . . . it's bad. It's bloody. It's awful. And I . . . I shouldn't bring
you into it.' He looked at her, then, in the darkness of the carriage.
She longed to run the tip of her thumb over that new scar, feel the
swell of his lip under her skin.

'Then why did you?'

He didn't speak for a long time, just watching her. 'We're not
bound,' he started.

Grey laughed. Binding significantly increased the power that a
mage and well shared. It allowed the mage to draw from only one
power source, allowed the well to only respond to that mage. And in
return, the connection was so much more sensitive: Grey could give
Kier much more of herself, and Kier could take even the smallest
power and run with it.

It was also illegal, forbidden and punishable by death.

She elbowed him in the ribs, hard, and laughed harder at his pout.
'We're not allowed to be.'

Kier shrugged, allowing it. *Nobody* was allowed to be bound. Not
for a decade; not since the High Sovereigns realized that the magic
was waning in earnest. To cut off the abilities for mages and wells
to be interchangeable was to cut down their usefulness dramatically,
and Grey was not harboring any illusions. She was only valuable to
the army for her usefulness.

'I don't want anyone else to hurt you,' Kier said, 'and I know you
like I know myself.'

He turned to her then, urgent like he usually wasn't. This wasn't
the Kier she remembered, but the Kier she knew, the boy she'd grown

up with, had never nearly died. That Kier's brother was still alive, not buried next to the tree they used to play on as children. He reached for her hand, and she let him take it – she felt the draw immediately, the pull, the unfurling of power in the middle of her chest. An unreadable look flickered across Kier's face.

'How easily,' he murmured, 'you give up your magic to me.'

She blushed despite herself, pulling away from him with something like embarrassment. 'It's not magic when I have it. It takes you to make it into something.'

'We're not bound,' Kier said again, his hands knotted in his lap as if he couldn't bear to say what he needed to. 'But the way you know me – it's close to it, isn't it? Binding makes the tether stronger. If you were matched to someone else – there would be too much to know, Grey, and I couldn't stand it, imagining you in that kind of danger.'

She chewed on her lip. In truth, she was grateful, and he was right. If she'd become Hand to anyone else, there would be a lot of hiding, or else a lot of explaining.

'Will you be my Hand?' Kier asked. 'My companion?'

How could she say no? How was she ever meant to say anything other than yes?

She narrowed her eyes. 'What's in it for me?'

That drew a laugh out of him, and she was grateful – she didn't know what to do with this new, serious version of the boy she'd always known. 'Better quarters? My cheese portions?'

'You've got to try harder than that.'

'Unlimited access to my shirts?'

Grey shrugged. 'I could be convinced,' she said finally. The answering smile on his face was utterly dazzling.

I have received further reports that the Isle is gone entirely. There are no survivors. I have seen the empty bay with my own eyes, and though it has been days, no bodies have washed ashore. It is reported that the High Lady, the Lord Consort and both children are dead, along with their court.

More personally: I am so sorry, your majesty. I know what they meant to you.

Letter from Commander Finnegan to Scaelas, 2 days PD

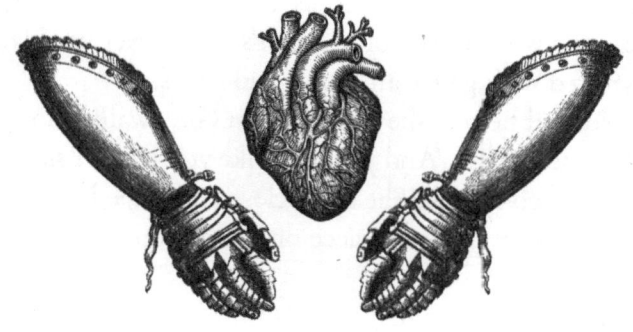

four

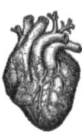

Kier didn't die on the walk back to camp, which was a small miracle in itself. Ola and Brit half-dragged him, mostly unconscious by this point, into the medical tent. In a side area, Leonie, the lead healer at this camp, waited for Grey. Leonie's dark curly hair was piled on top of her head, stuck through with a pencil to hold it in place. She wore a deep blue healer's apron over her black dress, pockets stuffed with gauze and tools and herbs.

'You've looked better,' she sighed when Grey walked in.

Grey frowned at her. 'And you look like you haven't slept in days.'

'Only two,' Leonie said. She came close and helped Grey unbuckle her armor, laying it piece by piece on a cloth-covered table. 'You're filthy.'

'Thanks, love,' Grey said.

Leonie's fingers lingered for a second too long on Grey's waist, working at the leather buckle that clasped her breastplate on. Grey took a shuddering breath, finding an odd comfort in the steadiness of Leonie's hands, the coolness of her brown eyes as she scanned Grey over quickly. 'None of this blood is yours?'

'The captain's,' Grey said crisply, stepping away. She recounted Kier's idiocy as she wiped down her sword.

'Should I begin without you?' Leonie asked, gathering instruments on a tray after Grey finished reporting the extent of Kier's injuries in a measured, emotionless voice. 'Or delay? Surely an hour won't make a difference. You look—'

'No.' Grey took the three packets of prepared nutrient-dense sludge that Leonie held out, cursing the mages who formulated this shit years ago, cursing herself for needing it, then cursing herself again for not washing off first – the mud added flavor of the worst variety.

But she had to replenish her power in whatever way she could, as quickly as possible.

When the sludge was gone, swallowed in uncomfortable gasps, she fought her way out of her padded shirt, then pulled her soaked under-shirt and vest off too for good measure. Naked to the waist, she did her best to ignore the chill of the air as she washed the dirt and blood away from her skin. Every muscle *ached*: from battle, from carrying Kier back, from her depleted stores of power. She sluiced mud away until the water rolled clean down her chest and arms, then washed once more for good measure. Finished, she pulled on the clean shirt Leonie offered. The pair walked through the flap of fabric that led to the back of the infirmary.

An assistant had already stripped Kier, washed his wounds and rendered him unconscious with a cloth soaked in an anesthetic herb blend placed over his mouth and nose. They sat by his head now, carefully monitoring his breathing. She noted the dark streaks pooling under his eyes, the remaining crust of blood on his cheek, the crookedness of his nose under the damp white cloth – but she'd worry about setting that for him later.

'The captain has left his last words,' the assistant said quietly when Grey entered the room, and Grey very nearly threw her out in a fit of rage even though it wasn't the assistant's fault that Kier was such an absolute disaster.

But it was good to feel *something*. Strong feelings, anger and rage and desperation, made her power replenish faster. She felt the swell of it crawling from somewhere in her lower belly.

Good. She needed it.

'He can tell me himself,' she muttered, glaring at the folded piece of paper, 'when he's awake.'

There was no further argument to that. Leonie set the instruments out for Grey as she slipped into a set of sterile gloves and surveyed his injuries. She had six years of putting him back together under her belt. It was her duty to do it yet again.

She took him in, the slope of his pectoral muscles, the shadowy peaks and valleys of his ribs, the scar from yet another near miss over his heart.

She turned her attention to her own well-being. Her power was moderately replenished – she cursed the sludgy porridge, but it *was* effective – but this could be a long one. Her inspection of his wound revealed that the blade had gone in through his lower intestine, so she had to deal with any contamination to ensure the wound didn't go septic.

She laid her palm flat on his chest and focused. The power came slowly at first, an exhausted trickle. But that was all she needed. She felt the strands of him in her fingers, the tether between them tightening.

She took a thin blade and opened him up.

She had fixed him up after battle more than once, but Kier was usually better behaved than this. She'd only really been wrist-deep in him thrice before: once after a mage from Cleoc Strata with intriguing internal capabilities tried to turn his spleen inside out, another time when he'd been stabbed in the stomach by a soldier from Eprain, then the final chest wound from a Hand after he'd killed their mage. All of these had left her utterly terrified, anxious with every move that she'd fuck up something inside of him permanently.

She'd had so much experience with internal surgeries, but when it was Kier she was working on, Kier under her hands . . . it was like all her training turned to sludge in her brain, overpowered by the realization that despite the fact he was beloved, he too was just meat.

This time, she was too tired for fear. She focused on that tiny thread of power, easing it out as she worked. Leonie helped her, handing her instruments when she asked for them, holding together tissue, wiping away blood. She didn't offer to tether her own power to Kier, to give Grey a break – she'd worked with Grey long enough to know better.

To her credit, the assistant at Kier's head didn't ask questions or black out, even when the effect of Grey's power and direction had his flesh pre-emptively knitting back together and they had to cut him open again.

Grey lost track of time, focusing only on the slippery feeling of his insides and breathing evenly. Finally, she surveyed her work, probing for anything out of place, and sighed with relief. 'Let's close him up,' she said, glancing at Leonie – but it wasn't Leonie at all.

Hand Master Mare Concord stood on the other side of Kier's body, waiting for instructions. Grey didn't even know how long she'd been there. She had only seconds to recover before Mare was handing her a needle and suture.

Grey was too tired for this. She focused on maintaining that last little thread as she stitched the layers of Kier back together. Mare was a great help, at least: she was ready with the tools Grey needed before she even asked.

Of course she was. She had probably done very similar surgeries on her own mage.

Grey cleaned the stitched wound one final time and affixed gauze. Once that was done, she washed her hands three more times until every trace of Kier's viscera was gone from her skin, if not her shirt.

'Good work, Hand,' Mare said. 'Neat stitches.' At some point while Mare was watching, the assistant had left too – it was just the two of them, three if Kier counted.

'I'm very good at mending socks, too,' Grey said, sorting the equipment into the appropriate wash buckets. She did an internal check for her well. It was waning again, but not empty. Worse than it had been in years, but she could deal with that. She focused very hard on finishing the conversation – the sooner she could curl up in her bedroll, the better. She'd settle for the break room in the back of the infirmary at this point.

'It's a dangerous game you two are playing. Your mage should know better than to use that much of you. If you need to file a complaint with a request for retraining, Hand Captain—'

'He doesn't take any more than I'm willing to give,' Grey snapped. She was so, so tired of these conversations.

'You have . . . quite the capacity,' Mare said carefully. 'We're meant to report high-capacity wells, you know. In case a higher-ranking officer is in need.'

Grey stiffened. Mare was the type of weathered that wells usually didn't live long enough to become. Grey forced herself to focus, to watch her face for any sign of – well, anything. 'I'm already serving a captain, Hand Master.'

Mare shrugged, allowing this. 'Unless there's another reason for the capacity you're able to offer Captain Seward.'

Grey did not let any emotion show on her face. 'What are you trying to say?'

'I'm just saying,' Mare said firmly, steely, 'it's notably unusual, and there are very few reasons for unusual power.'

That was enough, the last of it her brain could handle. 'I don't know what you're talking about, Hand Master, but I've used quite a lot of myself today and I cannot keep going.'

'Hand Captain Flynn . . . ' Mare reached out, gripped Grey's shoulder, but Grey shrugged her off. She always made her worst decisions when Kier was indisposed.

It was insubordination to leave this room, risk on top of risk, but she did it anyway. Grey dragged herself out of there, freezing, and across the encampment, barely upright when she slipped into the safety of her own tent. As soon as the flap closed behind her, her knees hit the floor and then she was slumped, the air running from her lungs. She forced herself up, clawed her way onto her pallet. She was still sticky with Kier's blood.

She'd be punished for that, she knew. For leaving without being dismissed. For not answering Mare's questions. But to stay, to try to cobble together something coherent – that was an even greater danger.

She gave up and let herself slip into emptiness.

Fire. When she dreamed, she always dreamed of fire.

This time, the fire was in the shape of a boy in front of her. He sat cross-legged, and she was no longer a soldier, no longer a woman, no longer a well. She was a girl, a child. She might've been fire, too.

The fire-boy said, 'Stay quiet.'

She stayed quiet. They were sitting on hard-packed ground in a stone room. A basement. It smelled like salt and ash. When she snuffled, raised her fist to wipe her nose, the boy caught her hand. It did not burn, but it should've.

There was pounding overhead. She was covered in blood, drenched in it. She remembered whose it was, but she did not let herself think of it.

'Do you promise,' the fire-boy whispered, 'to let us go?'

'No,' she whimpered. She wanted to hug him, but she was afraid; she was so afraid that her heart pounded rabbity in her chest and her hands were sweaty and her teeth ached from clenching her jaw. Just an hour ago, she and the boy were at the big table, squabbling over dessert. She could still taste the sour tang of sugar between her teeth.

He gripped both of her hands so hard, and this time, it hurt.

'You have to,' he said, leaning his fire-head close to hers. She remembered the color of his eyes under all that licking flame: they were silt-brown, shell-brown, sargassum-brown. 'I can't hold it much longer, but I will until you promise.'

She sobbed, and he let her, even though it made so much noise. There was a shout overhead, then the pounding of feet down the stairs and someone at the door.

'I promise,' she said. The fire-boy kissed her, once, on the forehead, and held her hands so very tight.

The world around her exploded.

Grey woke to an empty room and a dry mouth. Across from her, Kier's bed was terribly devoid of Kier, and for one half-second of unremembering, her heart flew to her throat.

Then she realized her shirt was still stained with his blood, and now her blankets were too, and that was enough to remind her. She sat up, folding her legs under her, and stared out at nothing.

The fire wasn't burning. The cold was good; it made the anxiety in her chest dull to a low-level thrum. She hurriedly changed into a clean shirt from Kier's trunk and her own trousers – she'd need to wash properly soon, but it could wait – and laced her still-damp boots over a pilfered pair of Kier's socks. She swung her cloak over her shoulders and set out into the frigid morning. There was no note pinned to her tent, no letter of dismissal waiting for her, so her interaction with Concord was apparently not enough for *immediate* action.

When she reached the infirmary, Leonie was at the herbalist's desk near the door, filling a tray with measured-out herbal tablets and salves. She took in the half-scrubbed traces of blood on Grey's hands, the shadows under her eyes, and sighed, the breath blowing her curling fringe up over her face. Unlike Grey, Leonie looked a bit better rested today, her deep brown skin shining with a healthy glow, the shadows under her eyes less pronounced.

'Is it too much,' she asked mildly, 'to ask you to take care of yourself?'

'Yes,' Grey said, pulling the little booklet of overnight notes from Leonie's apron pocket and searching for Kier's name. The only reason she was able to do it without a disapproving look was because Leonie already knew that if Kier was in the infirmary for a few days, she'd at least have Grey's help to lessen the load. 'How is he?'

'Alive. How are *you*?'

'Alive,' Grey muttered, reading over the notes from the overnight healer. It was helpful, at least, to know she'd only been out for approximately twelve hours.

'Have you eaten, Hand Captain?'

Grey didn't hazard that with a response. It wasn't anything personal – she *liked* Leonie. In fact, she'd more than liked Leonie on one frantic fever-dream of a night three months ago when Kier was in the infirmary, recovering from a broken rib.

As if to bring that memory into stronger relief, Leonie laid a hand on Grey's arm. She had short fingers, but they were nimble and strong, trim and clean, capable to a fault.

'You smell like old blood and you're still wearing the battlefield,' she said. 'Eat. Clean yourself up. He will be here when you're back.'

She met Grey's gaze, held it for an immeasurable moment and muttered something uncomplimentary about the obsessive nature of

Hands under her breath when Grey swept past her into the depths of the infirmary.

She stopped on the way to his bed, briefly, to check on the three others from their company who were still here with injuries from the day before. If Kier was awake, he would check if she'd done it first.

Satisfied once she'd completed her due diligence, she made her way to his bedside.

His skin, usually a medium olive tone, was nearly as pale as the sheets. He was shirtless, the sheets pulled up over his chest. She pulled off her cloak and considered throwing it on the empty cot to Kier's side for a moment, but that would just make more work for Leonie, so she folded it over his feet instead.

She took the time to check his heartbeat and the frequency of his breathing, only pausing for a moment of relief when he flinched at her frigid hands on his skin. He was dry, not clammy with fever. When she pulled the blanket down and lifted the gauze, the area was not inflamed. She found her well of power restored, so she let herself unspool, a tether attached to him, nudging the power to the wound. She kept her eyes open in case Mare Concord happened by – in case she actually was being watched.

In these moments, when he was incapacitated, she allowed herself to be tender. It always came easy to Kier to brush her hair behind her ear or grab her hand, possibly because even the slightest touch came with a rush of power, but she didn't have the same freedom. It never seemed to mean anything to him when he took her hand, when skin met skin. Not like it did for her.

She glanced around – Leonie was near the front of the ward, treating an injured person with a salve, and everyone else around was sleeping. No sign of Mare.

She skimmed her fingers over his cheekbone. Under her touch, the scratch across his cheek healed. She took another quick glance around, tracking Leonie's progress, and let her hand snake under the covers, palm pressed to the uneven stitching of his wound.

'Hand.'

She glanced down at him. Her other hand was still pressed to his cheek, thumb skimming over his eyebrow without her telling it to.

She withdrew both hands. He winced at the loss of contact, so she pushed a bit more power in his direction.

'You're doing the thing again,' he murmured, eyes sliding shut.

'Keep that to yourself,' she chided – but she put her hand back over the wound, watching as he instantly relaxed.

'You look like shit,' Kier said.

'You've got your eyes closed.'

'So I don't have to see you looking like shit.'

'Unfair. I'm the reason you're alive.'

'Doesn't change anything.'

Grey sighed, pulling her hand away. She had to stop – any further healing and people would start asking questions. Kier's eyes rolled back open. 'Thank you,' he said.

'A draught to ease the pain, Captain,' Leonie said. Grey's gaze snapped up to her, her apron, her tray, her neutral expression. She was favoring her right leg again – always did, in the rain, and there was near-constant rain here – but it would do no good for Grey to ask how she was feeling. Leonie's left leg had been amputated from the knee down years before, replaced with a wooden materialist-crafted prosthetic, and she'd confessed to Grey once that the rain made her badly healed hip throb.

'Thank you,' Kier said, taking the draught like a good patient. Grey and Leonie exchanged a glance. Both of them would've refused. Neither of them were good patients.

'And as soon as you're able to get up, Attis has requested you.'

'He is unable to get up,' Grey said quickly, which didn't stop Kier from trying. A firm push to his shoulder was effective enough.

'Noted,' Leonie said. 'It can wait.'

'Did she say why?' Grey asked.

Leonie shook her head. 'Something to do with the prisoner you recovered, I think.'

It wasn't a guarantee, but perhaps Grey wasn't completely fucked for her behavior the other day. Maybe Concord still owed her for saving her life. Maybe – though Grey very much doubted it – she would get off easy this time.

Leonie took note of her fidgeting. 'Hand Captain, if you're going to

be loitering here, I'd appreciate your help if you have time to spare —
but I will require you to clean up and eat first.'

'And that's an order,' Kier said.

'You still don't outrank me,' Grey said, but she conceded anyway.

Torrin –

It is over. It is done. Let me live in peace, I beg of you. It is barely a life at all, and has not been since they died by my side. The last thing I ask of you is to let all of it die, as I should have.

I know, in your stubbornness, you may never stop looking for me, but I ask as the last of my name that you do.

Letter from Severin of Locke to Scaelas, 3 months PD

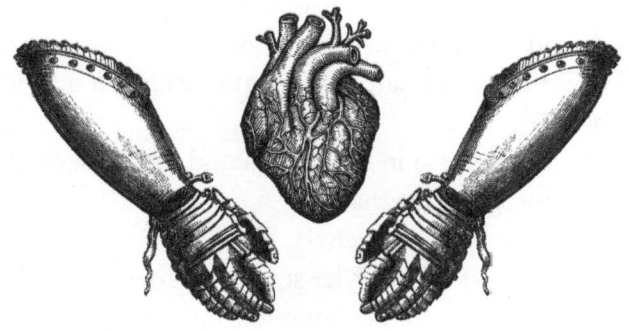

Five

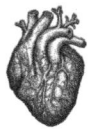

'Give me one reason, Captain Seward,' Attis said, fingers steepled in front of her on the desk. Her clear, stern eyes were focused on Kier as if Grey wasn't even in the room, and Grey chewed on the inside of her cheek at the weight of that stare, glad it wasn't anywhere near her. 'One reason why I shouldn't demote you, separate you and your Hand, send her on the first convoy out to an infirmary as far away as I can manage and keep you on the front as a typic. One.'

Because Kier was a pain in the ass first and a mage second, he said, 'Because we're too good for that.'

Grey very nearly kicked his chair.

They were in Attis's office, Kier seated in front of her desk, Grey positioned behind him with her hand resting on his shoulder. He was fully dressed, which was an improvement, and only winced occasionally when he moved – partially for the drama. She'd possibly gone too far in healing him, into a territory that was nigh unattainable for a regular well, but having him whole and hale was more important than anything else.

She'd warned him about what Concord had said, but shockingly, Grey was not the one being reprimanded, and no one had asked about her capacity. Hopefully Kier was playing it up enough that Attis wouldn't want to see his wound, wouldn't want to look any closer.

'You nearly killed your Hand.'

'Hand Captain Flynn knows her limits.' A dangerous line of conversation, if they went probing into Grey's limits.

'But do *you*?'

Grey's fingers dug into Kier's shoulder: a warning. 'I trust her,' he said, very carefully. 'She untethered from me, Master Attis, when it became too much, as she was trained to do.'

Behind Attis, Mare's face twitched – the only indication that she was paying any attention at all. Grey wanted to jump over the desk and shake her: *What did you say?*

'You let your guard down,' Attis snapped, and that was the one thing Grey couldn't argue with. With Kier in the infirmary, she hadn't had a moment to speak to him alone. Why had he given the girl his armor? Why had he untied her restraints? What had the girl said to him? These were the questions she'd wrestled with the night before, alone and insomniac in their tent.

'She was just a scared girl,' Kier said. 'I was doing my duty. Trying to help.'

'She's a *prisoner*, Captain.'

Silence hung between them, and Grey swallowed any protestations she had. She felt herself softening, her own angry questions withering away.

This was the line, the thing that she and Kier could never quite get over: the people they fought, the people they *killed* . . . It didn't matter what Attis or the others high up in command said. They were just people. These wars, these endless battles over land and territory, they all amounted to nothing. She'd been disillusioned with war since the first soldier died under her hands at sixteen, but it wasn't like there was anything better. The battles never ceased. The armies were never sated. No one was actually going to avenge the death of Locke, and until that happened, Scaelas and the other high rulers would not be satisfied. She, Kier and Lot, had realized when they were children that they could either wait for some attacking army to stomp through and burn their village or they could enlist and fight back. There were no other options. Never had been.

The soldiers they fought had the same choice. The prisoner was just another person with no other decisions to make.

Attis sighed. 'I need to know you can follow orders, Captain Seward.'

'I don't believe I've ever put that in doubt. Though you might dislike my methods, I did deliver you the asset.'

'Nearly at the cost of your Hand,' Attis snapped. 'Captain Seward, I know your history. I know you and Hand Captain Flynn have been paired for a while. I know you two are *very good* at what you do.'

Grey tensed, her gaze flicking to Mare. But the Hand's face was unchanged. If she'd told Attis something, there was no way to know now.

'Your power is like that of a bound pair,' Attis said. 'Which you could be investigated for if an accusation is made.'

It took a lot of Grey's concentration not to let anything show on her face. Binding was foolish and forbidden, and the military didn't care about the value of sacred acts or devotion.

It was a shame they'd been forbidden from doing it. It was an even bigger shame that they'd disobeyed that order years before.

But it was the only guarantee of Grey's safety. She did not regret it.

Kier did not give in. 'This isn't about my command, or the fact that you can't accept my Hand is powerful. This is about the prisoner. And you sent us in without any indication of the stakes or the cost. It's no wonder my Hand was forced to use so much of herself and I was nearly killed – we did not know what they were fighting for, and we still don't.'

It was justified, but perhaps not the best way to go about it. Grey wanted to point out that they had bigger problems – if Attis could prove her suspicion that she and Kier were bound, they could be punished, or discharged, or even sent to the High Court if she was angry enough. It *wasn't* a small infraction.

Attis's lips twitched. 'Then let's talk about the prisoner.'

Grey's chin inched up. She hadn't had time between keeping Kier alive, putting herself back together and helping Leonie with the wounded to get more information on the girl – or to find her and give her a solid kick in the stomach to repay her for what she did to Kier.

'Very well,' Kier said.

Attis was silent for a moment, gathering her thoughts. Grey watched Mare's hand on Attis's shoulder – she'd flinched, calling attention to it, and now Grey saw how tightly the Hand gripped her mage.

'Hand Master Concord and I have our suspicions, but in this case we are willing to set them aside. There are bigger issues afoot, and it has become clear that you and your Hand are a strong pairing, for whatever reason.'

'Master Attis, I can assure you—'

'Keep your lip service for someone else, Seward. We have an assignment, and it looks like you and Flynn might be the only two here equipped to carry it out.'

That was . . . a far cry from being reprimanded, and Grey couldn't fight the feeling that they were being tricked. She wished she could tell Kier to be careful in how he proceeded. She didn't like the narrow line of Attis's mouth, the way she kept her gaze on her own hands, the tight grip Mare had on the master's shoulder.

'Are we being reassigned?' Kier asked, and Grey knew him well enough to detect the palpable relief in his voice. After all, they'd been here, on the front against Luthar, for six months, and right on the border of Cleoc Strata for nearly a year before that. They were due an easy assignment.

'Not exactly,' Attis said. It took Grey a second to identify the emotion on the master's face, but when she did, her chest felt very, very cold. Master Klara Attis, the most put-together of any commanding officers they'd yet faced, was *terrified*.

'Master,' Kier said, finally betraying the depths of his exhaustion. 'I don't mean to push, but in the last forty-eight hours, I have been stabbed and nearly died at least twice. I am tired. My Hand is tired. I have followed each instruction you have given me to the letter.

The least I can ask of you is that you are forthcoming with our assignment.'

'I need your discretion. This assignment – the future of Scaela, the hopes of our military, the promise of a day without battle, they all rest on this. Do you understand the weight of what I am telling you, Captain?'

Kier made a small noise, a half-sigh. Grey interpreted it as one of his favorite lines, reserved for when he was ill and she asked him to do the bare minimum, like eat: *I suffer and I suffer, and yet. And yet, you ask me to suffer still?* She felt his pulse jump, ever so slightly, and she frowned at the master in front of them.

'Yes,' Kier said, resigned, because he could not accuse the master to her face of adding to his suffering. After all, what could they possibly do to protect the future of Scaela?

Do you promise to let us go?

Grey wrestled with the memory like it was a physical attacker, pushing it away before it could take root. She set her jaw, clenched her teeth. She'd need to ask Leonie for a sleeping draught tonight. She couldn't keep dreaming like this.

'What do you know of the Isle of Locke?'

A pause. Grey's back went ramrod straight, and she had no doubt her fingers were clenched on Kier's shoulder tight enough to bruise. When Kier spoke next, his tone was even, cautious. 'I was a child when the Isle was destroyed, Master. But my Hand and I are from a village on the eastern coast – we know enough of it.'

'You remember its destruction, then.'

Grey bit the inside of her cheek. Kier said, 'The air tasted like smoke for days, when it vanished.'

'I imagine it did,' Attis said, sweeping right past the trauma of the event. 'Captain Seward, every nation has been searching for years for the lost heir to Locke, to no avail. Could you imagine the sheer power in Scaela if our own High Lord found Severin of Locke, if he restored it?'

Grey *could* imagine the sheer power. She worried that she was breaking Kier's skin under his jacket. As if he could hear the thudding of her heart, he reached back with one hand, covertly hidden by the desk, and wrapped it around her thigh.

Perhaps it was the combination of Locke prickling in her ears, Kier's near-death, and the warmth of his hand on her, but it only took that much for Grey to forget herself.

'No one could have survived that,' she said before she could think better of it.

A silence. Mare and Attis both regarded her like she was something left to rot on the battlefield for a good long while. 'You mustn't, Hand,' Attis said, raising one dark eyebrow. 'I would expect more . . . discretion from one of your rank.'

Grey bit her tongue before she could lash out. Again. She stepped back half a pace, shaking off Kier's hand.

'One does not get to our position,' Kier said, always diplomatic, even in the face of her sharp tongue, 'by ignoring obvious truths, no matter how inconvenient.'

Master Attis did not look impressed. 'Then you must know the truth of your mission. Captain Seward, Hand Captain Flynn, I'm trusting you with a lot. I know that you two may have committed an egregious error, and I will not investigate whether you are bound, because I *need* the kind of power you have for this mission. But if you refuse this quest, then I cannot guarantee that your precarious position will *not* be investigated.'

They were caught, and there was nothing they could do about it. Kier rubbed his face, long-suffering as always. 'I understand. And who is the asset?'

'The girl,' Attis said, 'is Maryse of Locke, daughter of the last High Lady of the Isle.'

A sharp indrawn breath – Grey didn't know if it was her or Kier, or both of them, because they knew the truth and neither of them could say it. Under her hand, Kier was very, very still. His own hand snaked back again, gripping her thigh with a new ferocity.

'But Maryse of Locke is dead,' he said. 'If anyone survived the death of the Isle, it is Severin. The boy. It *must* be the heir. He wrote to Scaelas after—'

'Maybe the letter was forged. After all, Severin Locke was never found,' Attis said.

Kier did not look at Grey, but he stiffened beneath her hand. 'He didn't *want* to be found. When excerpts were released, that much was clear. It can only be speculation.'

Attis waved a hand in dismissal. 'It's *all* speculation,' she said. 'Yes, the High Lord did receive a letter, supposedly from the elder child – but what if it was the girl who survived? What if the letter was a fake? What if, all this time, we have been looking for the wrong one?'

'And what are we meant to do?' Kier asked, and Grey was so very grateful in that moment that he was the one responsible for responding.

'I expect you and your Hand to deliver Lady Maryse to the High Lord Scaelas, who will be waiting for you on the eastern coast. There he will reunite with his god-daughter and work with her to restore the Isle. You are to protect the girl on your journey and be at Scaelas's disposal when you get there,' Attis said. 'Unless that is too difficult a journey in your current state.'

The High Lord. They were to deliver the girl to the coast, the coast that haunted Grey always as her childhood home – and something more. The High Lord, Scaelas, probably now graying with age and changed by loss, but when she'd seen him last, he was—

No. She refused to think of it, as if Mare and Attis could see right through her, could read her expression even as she fought to keep it placid.

If Kier let go of her now, she would come unmoored. 'It's not too much,' he said, like an absolute fool.

He insisted on coming back to their tent instead of the infirmary, and Grey was not in a position to protest. When they returned, there was a tray on her bed with a note from Leonie warning her what would happen if she didn't take the time to eat. She sat, half catatonic, and unwrapped the bread, eating with mechanical precision. It took her almost a full minute to realize Kier had pulled his bag from the trunk at the foot of his cot and was unceremoniously shoving clothes into it.

'Hey, hey,' she said, abandoning the bread for a moment, grabbing his hand. 'Attis didn't say we were leaving *now*.'

He looked at her, confused. Nothing remained of the cut on his cheek, not even a scar, and she was proud of her work – though his nose was still a bit crooked.

'Grey,' he said, perplexed as ever. 'We're not going.'

She glanced at his bag, half-full, then back at him, wondering if she had finally, utterly lost it. It was bound to happen sometime – no surprise it had happened now.

'We're *leaving*,' he said, looking back down at his pack, shoving in his shaving kit.

His words hit Grey like a punch in the stomach – like the punch she still owed the damn prisoner, whenever she found her. 'Leaving?' she repeated, considering the idea that she had also lost understanding of common speech.

Kier straightened, huffing a breath, and it was something when he looked at her straight on like that. When she was a girl, she'd convinced herself that she valued him more than he valued her, and sometimes she still deferred to that line of thought – but then he looked at her in that way, the measure of devotion clear on his face, matched to her own, and it was all moot anyway.

'Don't make me say it.'

'Kier . . . are you *deserting*?'

He laughed, short and harsh, and the sound went right to her chest. Reality zoomed in around her again, pounding like a migraine against the back of her eyes. 'What other choice do we have?'

She blinked at him, waiting for an explanation. For the rest of the sentence. He stared back at her, just as shocked, and she realized that for possibly the first time, they very much weren't on the same page.

'Where would you even go?'

'To the continent. Lindan, or Nisielle, or Arxun,' Kier said, completely serious. 'Two travelers, unobtrusive . . . We can make our way to the south coast and hire a boat to the continent, like we should've done years ago.'

Her brain quite possibly stopped keeping up. Though Scaela was doomed to lose its power forever, though all the nations that made up Idistra were doomed, they were home. They were *hers*. She and Kier and Lot might've spoken about running when they were children, or in the early days of recovery after battle, but she couldn't bear the thought of it now. And they didn't have the resources to escape.

'You can't leave this behind,' she said mildly, keeping level to staunch her own panic, smoothing imaginary wrinkles from his shoulders. 'We don't have the money for that. Not by far.'

He caught her hand. She didn't look at him, because if she did, that would be the final crack in her composure, and it would be over. She had the sudden, awful memory of digging around in his insides less than two days before – it was a miracle he stood in front of her now. It was a miracle of her own making.

'I promised you,' Kier said.

'Promises don't—'

'I swore on my brother's grave that you'd never have to go back there, Grey,' he said.

'I would never ask you to give up everything.'

'You wouldn't *have* to,' he said, his voice taking on a new urgency. 'If we go at nightfall, then we have time . . .'

She wanted to throw something. She was obtusely, immediately angry, the flames of it crawling from her stomach up her throat and into her mouth, and she wanted to pull down this tent and this entire camp and cast it into the sea. At the end of the day, all Grey was was an endless well of anger with nowhere to put it all.

'We're not leaving,' she snapped, turning away. She shrugged out of her cloak in protest, as if that would keep him here, draping it over her trunk, relishing the prickle of cold on her bare arms.

'Then what? We're going on this fool's errand? What happens when we get there?'

'I don't *know*,' Grey said, desperate.

'When Locke fell,' Kier said, 'they found the sister of the High Lady in Nestria and drowned her and her three boys in the bay in an attempt to restore the Isle. They dismembered the bodies to see if their blood or flesh would resurrect it. Killed the servants, slaughtered the entire household.'

'Kier—'

'In Eprain, a cousin. Burned as an offering to the old gods. In

Luthar, they got a child from one of the uncles of the dead High Lady to bring the power back. They killed the man, and then the child, when they proved useless. Across Idistra, hundreds of boys fitting the vaguest description of Severin of Locke were kidnapped in attempts to resurrect the Isle and control the power it once held. Do you need me to catalogue them all? Every single remaining bit of Locke's blood was hunted, tortured, *trialed* to find out how to bring the Isle back.'

How much of that was my fault? Yours? Let's? She pushed the thought away, her anger mounting. 'Scaelas never killed one of them, Kiernan,' she said. 'He *would* never.'

'But he cannot protect them. How many times have you told me that? There is no way to know, no way to trust anyone else, because that could be our very undoing. If we take this girl to Scaelas, she will be identified, and what? They'll try to use her to resurrect the Isle and find that they cannot? Or worse, someone else will kidnap her and kill her trying to bring Locke back?'

'That is not my responsibility,' Grey said tightly. 'When she's out of our hands—'

'When she's out of our hands,' Kier said, 'they will know she is not truly the blood of Locke.'

Grey knew what he was doing: after all, every barb he threw at her now, she had supplied him with herself.

'Grey,' he said. 'The only reason you are safe now is because everyone is certain you are dead. I'm just trying to—'

'Trying to save me?' she snapped, turning back to face him. His cheeks blazed with color, his eyes alight with anger. They fought so rarely that the effect was something to be savored. She wondered with a fierce swell of desperation if this was what he looked like in other fits of passion, then pushed it away immediately – that was a thread she couldn't bear to untangle.

He reached out, tugging her against him. It was awkward with the pallet between them, banging against her shins. She caught herself with both hands against his chest. His hand cupped the back of her skull, nearly big enough to cradle her from ear to ear. He lowered his mouth so his lips were against the shell of her ear when he spoke the name she'd only said to him a handful of times, always under the cover of darkness.

'What will we do,' Kier said, 'if they discover that *you* are Maryse of Locke?'

She has my eyes and her mother's power, and she will not stop screaming, no matter what any of us do. We are all, predictably, besotted.

Letter from Isaak Masidic Locke to Genevieve Masidic, his mother, 8 years Ante-Destruction (AD)

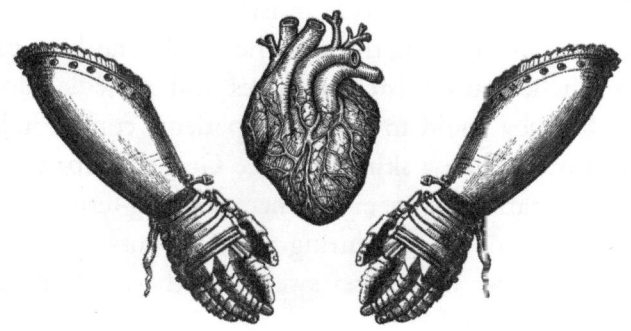

SIX

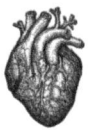

WHEN GREY REACHED THE infirmary, she found Leonie and a few assistants moving through the wards, checking bandages, removing stitches, administering salves and remedies and doing whatever else they could to make the patients comfortable. There hadn't been more than a skirmish since Grey's company returned, so most of the patients were either there for long-term treatment or had sustained minor injuries during practice bouts.

Leonie glanced up when Grey swept into the ward. 'Back for another round?' she asked.

Grey snorted as she moved past Leonie, past the beds, into a small room at the back of the ward full of changes of clothes and cots for healers taking breaks. She shrugged off her cloak and pulled on one of the navy-blue aprons the healers wore to protect their clothes from bodily fluids.

'When was your last break?' she asked, returning to the line of beds and taking the tray of labeled poultices and salves from Leonie's hands.

'Yesterday,' Leonie said. She was many things, but she was not a liar – there was no reason to hide her exhaustion from Grey.

'Go. I'll take care of things. I have a few hours.'

Leonie looked at her, lips pursed. 'Are you okay?' she asked. 'You look—'

'Go.'

Leonie sighed, but she didn't argue. 'We'll talk when I'm back,' she said. She hesitated, just a second, laying her hand on Grey's arm. 'Thank you.'

Grey only nodded. Leonie didn't need to know that she wasn't just here to help. She was hiding.

When Leonie was gone, Grey settled into the familiar pattern of the infirmary with the easy relief of an old routine. It wasn't required of her to do anything when Kier was injured – as his Hand, as a Hand captain herself, her duties extended only as far as his. But she had never been particularly good at staying still, and she'd worked in Scaela's infirmaries long enough to know the need for extra hands, particularly capable ones. So she'd made a habit of filling in when she could. When they had a few days between skirmishes, or in instances when Kier needed time to recover, she found herself drawn here. Unlike her previous tenure as a healer, as Kier's Hand she was not required nor requested (nor able) to use her power for speeding up the healing process for mages who were not her own. All she needed was her own natural skill. That suited her just fine.

She didn't allow herself to think of their usual routine: often the captain accompanied her, providing company for the injured while she worked, or doing some of his endless paperwork at one of the empty tables used for writing notes. Too many times she looked up to see him staring into space, chewing on the end of a pen, or tracking her around the infirmary with his ringed hazel eyes.

Perhaps it was a relief to be alone for once. To have the time and space to think. So she distributed remedies, and when that was done, she started on the cleaning. They were always creeping toward filth, the infirmaries, and with all the mud, this one was no exception – despite Leonie's careful cleaning schedule, it was impossible to keep everything sterile and tidy.

As she cleaned, her thoughts turned to their argument: Kier's grip on her, the words he'd whispered in her ear: *Maryse*, always Maryse;

but Maryse was not her true name. Kier knew that, too, but he wasn't fool enough to say it out loud.

When she was little, she'd hated it: Gremaryse, named after the old god of the sea, one of the mythical protectors of the Isle. But that was her true name, at least the first of it; and in the short span of time she spent having one, her mother always said, *Keep it close to your chest, Maryse. True names are for Hands and husbands.*

If her brother, Severin, was around to hear it, he always laughed and responded, *More like mages and mistresses,* which never failed to earn him both a loving thwack to the ear and a small smile.

So her true name stayed close to her chest, and it was shortened for public knowledge, and she was Maryse of Locke until the Locke name and nation died underneath her feet.

Days after the destruction, she was found by a Scaelan regiment. She'd wandered perilously close to the burning remains of a town Eprain had reduced to rubble, so she was left with the rest of the rescued orphans. At first, when they asked her name, she'd said nothing. It was only later, when she was handed over to Imarta, that the problem presented itself.

Hands and husbands. Mages and mistresses. Locke is gone, and I am gone with it.

Grey, she decided, was a better shortening anyway. She couldn't bear to be Maryse anymore, nor could she risk it. Close enough to cling to something of her old self in desperation, close enough that she couldn't fully forget.

Grey of Locke, she whispered to herself sometimes, alone in the small hours of the morning. It was the name of a girl who had never existed.

If she had grown up, grown into herself, she wouldn't be Grey *or* Maryse anymore, anyway – when a ruler came of age in Idistra, they took the diminutive of their nation. Their true name, then, was known only by the closest family members. Scaela had Scaelas; Cleoc Strata had Cleoc; Eprain belonged to Epras and Luthar to Luthos; and Nestria was ruled by Nestrias. It was only the High Sovereign of Locke, the oldest and most traditional of Idistra's nations, who took the name of the Isle, unchanged.

Grey's mother had herself been Locke, both the heart of the nation and its High Lady. It was only fitting, Grey thought exhaustedly, that the name died with her.

She did not whisper any of her lost names now, as she cleaned – she was not a fool. No one spoke the name of Locke lightly anymore.

Grey found solace in her work. By the time everything was finally still and quiet, night was falling outside. Leonie returned to find her sitting at one of the tables at the back of the infirmary, redacting a letter to Imarta.

'I know you're avoiding *something* when you take the time to write to your mother,' Leonie said. 'Anything catch on fire while I was gone?'

'Nothing to report,' Grey said, folding her letter and slipping it into her pocket.

'Good. I brought you food.'

Grey sighed as if this was an inconvenience, but in truth, she *was* hungry. She'd been so focused during the afternoon that she hadn't even thought about eating.

'Come to the back,' Leonie said. 'Things will be fine out here for a bit.'

Grey went to the back room while Leonie stopped to speak to one of the attendants. Alone, she pulled off the apron and put it in the wash bin with the rest, then eyed her cloak. It was a good idea to get into it, but she relished the cold for just a second. The frigid air, the icy sea – they were among the few things she still kept of Locke, that she was able to find in Scaela. She always felt more like herself with goosebumps prickling on her arms and a chill in her chest.

'How was your meeting with the master?' Leonie asked, bustling into the room and drawing the curtain. Her deep black curls were up again, gathered now in a tight bun on the back of her neck, but when her hair was released, it floated around her shoulders and face in a cloud of jet and onyx. Grey remembered the feeling of it between her fingers, Leonie's mouth on her skin. She frowned, pushing those thoughts away.

'As well as could be expected,' she said. She had the urge, again, to throw something.

'Do you want to talk about it?' Leonie asked, hopping up onto one of the extra beds by Grey's makeshift table. Grey forced herself to sit down, forced herself to put bread in her mouth and chew it and swallow instead of picking a fight with the wall.

'Talk about what?'

'Captain Seward.'

'Why would I want to do that?'

'*Flynn.*' The name was weary, a sigh caught on an ocean of exhaustion.

'We don't have to talk about him,' Grey said, looking up from her tray of bread and porridge and dried fruit, gazing at Leonie through her lashes. 'We could talk . . . about you? About *us*?'

'Grey Flynn, you absolute rake,' Leonie said with a laugh. 'There is no *us*. There was one time—'

'Two,' Grey corrected primly.

'Doesn't count if it's the same evening. One time, and we both knew what it meant before, during and after. I'm hurt, Hand – I thought you considered me a friend.'

Leonie was right, and they worked better as close confidantes. Moving between places the way they did, Grey found friendship hard to find and harder to stomach, but there was just something about Leonie that she trusted.

Leonie's expression wasn't hurt at all. That mischievous smile curved on her face and she looked at Grey with eyes like dark polished river stones. 'I knew from the start you were not open territory.'

Grey pushed the uneaten half of her food away. 'I don't know what you're talking about.'

'You're hiding in the infirmary. There are very few people here you would hide from other than Captain Seward. And don't look at me like that – finish eating, or else I'm making you take a whole host of vitamin draughts.'

'Who said I was hiding?' Grey muttered.

Leonie shook a packet of herbs in her direction, somehow managing to make the action look threatening.

Grey groaned, but she turned back to her food. 'He's stubborn,' she said, conceding on the more obvious point. 'Too stubborn sometimes.'

Leonie got up to prep the night-time medications, dividing herbs into tiny capsules for easier consumption, cross-checking her notes. 'Yes, I imagine so. But so are you.'

Grey shrugged, allowing it. 'And we know each other too well, I think.'

'It's the nature of wells and mages – you're required to have some level of . . . intimacy.'

Grey wrinkled her nose. 'That's not how Kier is.' She didn't know, exactly, what she was protesting.

'You practically live on top of each other.'

'We all do.'

The healer pressed on, ignoring her. 'You nearly let him drain you, Grey. And the worst thing is, it's clear you're not just obsessed with him. He's as devoted to you.'

Grey chewed the inside of her cheek. 'He would die for me,' she said. He would desert for her, at least, which was a death sentence in itself.

'Undoubtedly,' Leonie said in a voice that made it very clear she didn't see that as a positive trait. 'But . . . Grey, you know the way of wells.'

She did. It was a dizzying sort of thing, to have this much power – enchanting, even. And that was the worry with Kier: she did not know if he adored her or the power she provided.

'I still have years on my contract until retirement,' she said, as if that was anywhere close to the true problem. 'I can't . . . go anywhere. This is my life, whether I like it or not.'

'Maybe,' Leonie said, finishing her sorting and putting the tray on one of the carts. 'But you *are* a good healer. You could write to one of the continental cities to find work there, or seek respite at a university further afield. You don't have to stay if they buy your contract.'

Grey sighed. She'd thought of it before, desperately, on nights when Kier was injured. Thought about leaving, working until she was wealthy enough to buy out his contract, too.

'They'd never let a well leave,' she said, and it was the simple truth. With magic waning, conscripted wells were not a resource Scaelas could squander.

'They might,' Leonie said.

Grey shook her head. Not after the stunt she'd pulled – not after Attis and Concord realized that she had real worth. 'I appreciate your worry,' she said. 'But this is what I've chosen.'

'It seems,' Leonie said carefully, 'to be what the captain chose.'

Grey closed her eyes. It was impossible to explain without revealing too much. But the truth was, Kier never would've chosen this without her. It wasn't about him chasing titles or needing her as his Hand. Above all, as long as they were enlisted, as long as they were two faces in a sea of nondescript armor, even if he gained rank – as long as they were unextraordinary – she would never be discovered. She would never have to go back. Even with Kier's promotions, she was the girl in the shadows, standing behind him. It was a delicate dance, trying to rise high enough to make it safely out of the worst battles but to hold back so that no one would question her power. So that no one would suspect that the captain's Hand was the long-lost daughter of Locke.

But he'd promised her they'd never go back.

Grey got up and grabbed Leonie's sleeve before she could return to the infirmary, to work. Leonie's face was a mask of surprise when Grey cupped her cheek and pressed her mouth tenderly to hers.

'Thank you,' she murmured, 'for caring.'

When she pulled back, Leonie was holding back a smile, her lip between her teeth. 'Get out of my infirmary and fix your own problems,' she said, but she also swatted Grey's ass on the way out, so all was forgiven.

Kier was a different matter.

Grey found him working in the office tent they shared with two other typic captains, bare except for three rickety tables and four chairs, dully lit with the fire in the brazier. She tethered to him of her own accord and felt the threads of his answering magic. There was a buried line of pain in him, echoed in her own body – for the moment, she couldn't tell if it was physical, emotional or both.

She could read so much of him through the tether of her power – and it still left so much unsaid between them.

He looked up when she hesitated in the doorway, clearing her throat. He pressed his lips together. She saw a hint of apology in his eyes and nodded her head behind her, back toward their tent. They couldn't talk openly here. Kier rose, saying a quiet word of farewell to the others, swinging on his cloak.

Back in their tent, he shrugged off his cloak and lit the fire without touching her. 'I thought you'd stay with Leonie tonight,' he said.

'Why's that?'

He gave her a long, level look.

'How do you even *know* about that?'

'Gossip spreads,' he said mildly, shucking his shirt. She didn't look at the newly healing scar on his stomach or the fine dark trail of hair traveling down from his navel, though all of these things were burned into her memory whether she wanted them to be or not.

'I'm not sweet on Leonie,' she sighed, pulling off her boots and dropping to her bedroll fully clothed. She fought out of her cloak and spread her arms wide, letting the warmth of the fire creep through her.

He perched on the bottom of her pallet, taking her ankles and dragging her feet onto his lap. 'It wouldn't matter to me,' he said, 'if you were.'

She threw an arm over her face to hide her wince. It was, quite possibly, the worst thing he could've said. She wanted him to care. She could've fallen on her knees right then and there and *begged* him to care.

Kier had explained his version of attraction to her when they were teenagers: how it was less about the gender and more about the person themselves; that his taste did not lie one way or another but with whoever enchanted him at the time. Grey didn't have a preference for one gender over any others, either – but she wished, above all, that there was something about her that ensnared *him*. It was a desire that was left unrequited.

'I'm sorry,' Kier said. 'About earlier.'

Grey sighed. She felt the apology coming, maybe even guilt through the tether.

'Flynn.'

'What.'

'We should talk about what happened. During the battle.'

'I should've let you die,' Grey lamented.

'You probably should've,' Kier agreed, but he grabbed her hand and hoisted her up into a sitting position, then arranged her bodily to sit with her legs crossed, knee to knee. 'You used too much of yourself on me. You should've snapped the tether earlier. Far earlier.'

'When you have power,' Grey said, 'you can tell me how to do it.'

'Grey,' he said, so soft on her name that it broke her heart. He picked up one of her hands, brushed his lips against her knuckles. 'You cannot put yourself at risk for my sake. I cannot live without you. Okay?'

'And I won't live without you,' she said, like it was simple. 'But I will try to be safer, for both of our sakes.'

His eyes were very serious, dark shadows never fully gone from underneath. She remembered again how it had felt to see him for the first time in that sunny office, superimposing the remembered boy over the man he'd become. Sometimes she looked at him and it was like nothing would ever change about him; not his scars, not even the silver of his hair.

'Concord pulled me aside today,' Kier said. 'Threatened in earnest to send me to retraining.'

Grey snorted. She could imagine it: Mare, she suspected, was a force to be reckoned with. 'I was not kind to her when she brought the matter up with me.'

One eyebrow arched. 'When?'

Grey waved a hand. 'While I was stitching you up. After I – very kindly, might I add – did not let you die.'

He moved slowly to cup her face in his hands. It was easy to read this as something it wasn't, and she kept her own hands balled into fists in her lap even as she leaned into the warmth of him despite herself – mages usually ran hot, and Kier was no exception. 'You,' he said, 'are a credit to your profession.'

'Fuck off,' she said. But she let him press a kiss to her forehead and did not allow herself to think what would happen if she asked for more of him.

Think of Hands as devoted hounds. The handbook encourages 'healthy respect', yes, but it often appears more as obsession. A good Hand will do everything in their power to protect their mage, murder included. It would be in your best interest to encourage your own Hand to take a path of mercy and sensibility rather than retribution. You do not want to be on the receiving end of their fiery anger, nor should you wield it without careful consideration.

Surviving the Front: An Unofficial Military Companion by Captain Iowain Jessop, published 4 years PD

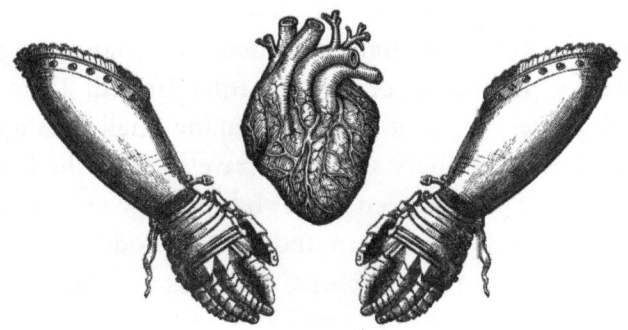

seven

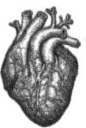

THAT NIGHT, GREY WAITED until Kier's breathing was heavy and even. She sat up, watching his face for any signs of consciousness. He was a light sleeper, but perhaps he was immune to noises as long as they were hers. And he did not wake now – he slept on his side, facing her, one knee tucked to his chest.

She didn't bother with a light. The moon was round and full over-head when she pushed out of the tent, fully dressed. The camp was quiet on this side: their tent was one of many small ones for officers and the masses of auxiliary staff who traveled with the companies, with a line of fire pits between them and the large tents reserved for the rest. Grey picked her way around the fire, nodding to a sentinel who stood guard near the kitchens. She hesitated for the barest of moments outside the infirmary, thinking of Leonie, before she hurried on her way.

They kept prisoners in the middle of camp, in a tent guarded by day and night. The two typics standing guard in front of the door eyed Grey as she approached, moving through the dark camp like a ghost. One bowed his head when she came close and the other, probably barely older than Grey had been when she first joined Kier in battle, hurried to follow.

'Can I help you, Hand Captain Flynn?' the older one asked. Grey didn't recognize him – he wasn't from her company. It was for the best. Kier was well liked among those in his command: it wasn't hard to imagine them exerting unnecessary cruelty on the prisoner.

'I have orders,' she lied, 'to assess the girl's health.'

The man's eyebrows rose. 'In the middle of the night?'

She pulled gauze and a jar of salve out of her pocket, displaying both for the guards. She'd stolen them from the infirmary earlier – they wouldn't be missed, and she'd use them eventually so they weren't wasted. 'If you don't believe me, you can wake the master yourself,' she said. 'And I guarantee she will not be pleased.'

The soldiers exchanged a look, the younger chewing on his lip. Finally, the older sighed. 'You get five minutes,' he said.

'I'll take two minutes and your discretion.' Grey slipped him a small flask of liquor as she passed by. He glanced at her, lips pressed together, but he didn't protest or hand her bribe back.

The tent was lit by a flickering orange magelight, casting long shadows in the dim. The girl sat alone in the center, hands and feet bound, but she was not gagged. She looked up as Grey entered, her eyes scanning over her in a way that made her feel frankly scrutinized. Grey wondered again at her age – she looked younger now than she had in the carriage, in the heat of battle; she was a teenager, but Grey couldn't say how old.

She wasn't even fully certain why she'd come. The idea had popped into her head earlier, intrusive as a migraine, as she'd gone from bed to bed in the infirmary. But part of her wanted – no, *needed* to see her. The girl who claimed to be Grey herself. The girl who'd tried to kill Kier.

Maybe it was a sick sense of curiosity – perhaps if she got close enough, she'd be able to feel the truth of this girl. She could not be Maryse of Locke, so she had to be someone else. All Grey could wonder was *who*.

Silence stretched between them. Grey tried to maintain her cool composure, tried to look like a captain herself instead of an exhausted girl who'd never fully come into her own. The prisoner didn't even look that much younger than her, and Grey felt every one of her twenty-four years as a decade.

The girl's eyes didn't stay on Grey's face – they flicked to the knife at her belt, the hilt of her sword at her hip, the glint of the golden pin over her left breast that signified her rank.

'You're the well,' she said finally. 'I can smell the power on you.'

Grey's lips curled into a grim, vicious smile. Wells could not *smell* the dormant power of others. Even Locke herself could not do that. The girl was trying to intimidate her.

In an instant, her dagger was under the prisoner's throat, her hand in her hair. She would not kill her – even knowing what she knew, she wasn't willing to risk *that* – but she needed her to have a healthy amount of fear.

The girl looked up at her, breathing hard through her teeth, eyes wild with fear. *This is why*, Grey thought, *you don't play games you can't win.*

'Then you know,' she said. 'You know what I'm capable of. What he's capable of through me. And I swear to you – if you try to harm the captain again, if you raise one finger against him, I will kill you. I don't care who you are. To me, you are nothing.'

You're threatening a child, *Hand,* Kier would've scolded. But Kier wasn't here.

The girl whimpered. Grey released her and stepped back, blending once more with the shadows. Before the prisoner could collect herself, she turned on her heel and went out. Her palms were slick with sweat; her teeth chattered with pent-up power. She wished she had Kier to tether to, but it all fizzled out of her, unused and wasted, unsatisfying.

Back in her tent, she stripped down to her shorts and vest and threw her clothes over her bedroll. It would only be a matter of hours before she was in them again. She kneed Kier over and crawled into his bedroll, barely big enough for him, let alone both of them. Kier made a low noise in his throat at her cold hands pressed to his skin, eyes flicking open wearily.

'You can't die on me,' Grey whispered, tucking her face firmly against his neck. His arms encircled her out of muscle memory.

'I'm not going anywhere,' he murmured into her hair, still half-asleep.

She lay awake for a long time like that, his fingertips stroking the long line of her spine, her fingers digging into his shirt. Their legs tangled together until she was no longer certain whose limbs were whose.

'Promise me,' she whispered. 'Make me an oath.'

'I don't think that's the kind of—'

'I promise on your name, Kiernan Trevaine Seward, sworn Locke. As I am your Hand and your power.'

He pulled back just enough to see her face. 'Are you okay?'

'*Swear to me.*'

He grabbed her hand from his chest, knotted their fingers together. 'I promise on your true name and your taken, Gremaryse Pellatisa Carnelion Masidic Locke, sworn Seward, Grey Flynn, that I will not die on you.' He pronounced every syllable carefully, breathed directly into her ear. She shivered – they hadn't sworn an oath since their binding, and it was the first time she'd heard his name in proximity to hers. 'Happy?'

Grey dropped her head to his shoulder, seeking comfort, and nodded. It was easy, in the dark, to let herself be convinced.

I fear writing these words, but it is impossible to ignore: my magic is . . . restricted. Waning, even, if I should be so brave to say so. I keep hearing rumors, and I must be honest with myself, even if I cannot admit it to anyone else: I think our very magic may be dying. Mare has never before felt so weak to me.

Journal of Master Klara Attis, 3 months PD

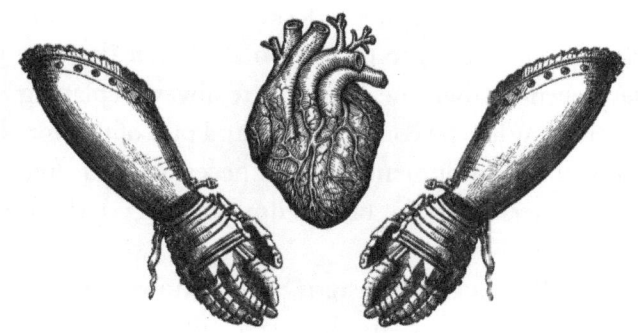

eight

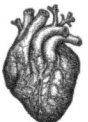

IF GREY EVER HAD to see Attis's office again, it would be too soon. This time, they both sat at the desk, Grey across from Mare, Kier across from the master. The map from the other day was replaced with a new, even smaller one – they were always replacing maps on this assignment. With the constant push and pull of territory between the port and the encampment, it was a necessary evil. According to Kier, cartographers were the best bedmates. Grey had never tested that theory herself.

The map itself focused on eastern Scaela, showing the routes from the southernmost point, where they were, all the way up and across the mountain passes, between Luthar and Cleoc Strata, toward the Bay of Locke. She scanned over the path, trying to recall places they'd been along the way. Moving north, back toward the village where they grew up, the land turned from dense forests to scrubby volcanic cliffs and thin trees, then sparse mountains speckled with gorse. By the sea, it became brown-green cliff grass and pebbled beaches rising up toward slate cliffs that looked out at the bay.

Scaela was a kinder place than Locke, she always thought, though the terrain was not so far removed. Sometimes, when she was at home in Leota, the seaside village where she and Kier had grown up, she looked at the dark cliffs of the shore and imagined them even rockier, sharper, like the place where she was born. They called Locke 'the Obsidian Isle' for the way its sheer black cliffs rose against the sea, and there was nowhere else like it in the world.

'You were previously in Grislar, is that correct?' Attis was saying, running her fingertip along Scaela's indented coastline. Grislar was the base twinned with Scaela's capital city, Easlar, but it was still perilously close to Luthar's border – and also their closest assignment to Leota.

'For nearly a year,' Kier said. He frowned down at the map. 'It's a little late in the season to be crossing the mountains.'

'Sorry, Captain,' Attis said drily. 'Can't control the weather.' She paused, rubbing her eyes, and Grey glanced at her. Attis looked exhausted. Whatever they were doing, she'd been up all night preparing. It was lucky she hadn't caught Grey in the middle of the night, out on her way to threaten the prisoner. 'It'll take you two weeks to get from here to Grislar on foot, three if the weather turns.'

'On foot?' Grey asked. She didn't care about walking one bit – but. She scanned the area on the map. She had been all over the country, had fought by Kier's side on every coast, but she'd never been asked to *walk* across it.

Attis pressed her lips together. 'Carriages are too conspicuous. And it's the last push of the harvest – civilians on horses are bound to look suspicious.' Grey found herself nodding at this; Attis had a point. Horses at this time of year were either doing farm work or requisitioned by the military; any others belonged to nobles, who wouldn't be safe on the roads without a retinue of guards anyway, and would still fall into the realm of 'conspicuous'.

'We can send you with enough funds for travel and to alleviate the journey of the mountain passes, but we need you to be as low-profile as possible. Merchants, or even better, pilgrims traveling to the abbey at Pontille. We don't have time – Luthos already knows the prisoner is missing and that her body was not found among the dead. They could suspect another nation, but the easiest explanation is that we have her.'

Kier looked up. 'Another nation?'

Attis's smile thinned. 'We must operate on the assumption that Cleoc Strata, Eprain and Nestria already have the same information about the girl's existence – with the possibilities of her power, I'm certain they will be looking too. That's why you need to go straight across, through the mountains, and stay as inconspicuous as possible.'

Kier leaned back, pinching the bridge of his nose. He hadn't shaved this morning and his cheek bristled with the first sign of a beard. Grey held her tongue from telling Attis outright that she was sending them to the slaughter.

'And how many of us will go? With the prisoner?'

'We've planned for you and one other.'

'Give me three.'

'Captain.'

Kier gazed at Attis, hazel eyes unyielding, and these were the times Grey knew him best. He was so goddam stubborn and, when it wasn't directed at her, she fucking adored it.

'I'm not doing this without another mage-and-well pairing, and I want a typic too. If this is as precarious as you say it is, I need to be sure we're not going to die exhausted in the mountains. I need to know that we can have consistent sleep patterns. I need to know that my team is being protected just as much as your prisoner, and if you put my Hand at risk—'

'No one is asking you to put your Hand at risk,' Attis snapped. 'Fine. Three. Your choices.'

Grey did not answer Kier's look. Attis would not defer to Mare, like she had any stake in the master's choices; Kier ought to do the same in public, even if he asked her opinion on everything in private.

He sighed, reading her avoidance. 'Okay. But hold on. What happens when we get to Grislar, when we deliver the prisoner? Will we be reassigned?'

Attis held his gaze, unflinching. 'If you and your team do what is required of you,' she said, 'you will get six months of leave. For everyone.'

Grey drew a breath. They hadn't had more than a month of leave in all the time they'd been in Scaelas's army – six months was an impossible amount of time. She couldn't imagine how they could be spared for that long.

Her heart nearly stopped when Kier said, 'I want a break in contract. Honorable retirement. For me *and* Hand Captain Flynn. If we reach Grislar alive and with the prisoner intact, I want to hand her over to Scaelas and receive our commendations within the same hour.'

'Captain?' Grey had never seen Attis so thoroughly caught off guard. The answering silence was opaque, unbreakable, and Grey herself wasn't even sure she was breathing . . .

And he was still, staring right at her with that insouciant curve to his mouth that was more scar than attitude. Her heart leaped to her throat – if they were given honorable retirement, it would come with wages. They wouldn't have to fight anymore. They wouldn't have to go day after day, waking at first light, putting their bodies through torture.

There would be no logical physical reason for them to remain together.

If she was not his Hand, what was she? Had she pushed too far? Hurt him too much? Perhaps this was betrayal disguised as liberation; perhaps Kier would rather never do magic again instead of enduring more time by her side.

She caught herself before she could spiral too far. No matter what he had in mind, she had every belief it somehow included her. If he got his way – and this was the danger of it, her mind racing over the possibilities, skipping toward a joy that set her chest aflame – then she could imagine it. Maybe they'd find a little house on the southwest coast, far from the battlefield, and she'd work as a healer in a village, or they'd run away to the continent. He could bed all the cartographers he wanted – she wouldn't care. It wouldn't *matter*.

They'd never speak the name of Locke again. She'd never again feel the burned-out match of another well dying next to her on the battlefield, her hand and sword dripping with blood, out of her mind with terror.

Maybe, alone, together, he would finally see her as something more than his friend, his Hand, his sword.

'Could I interest you in a promotion instead?' Attis asked, a little desperately.

She felt the doubt in the tether – he was posing her a question. She sent back certainty, and with it, the tiniest thread of joy.

'No.'

'Captain Seward, I . . . You know you are valued. You *know* that you have been recommended for promotions, that you are very nearly a master yourself. If you complete this mission, you will have command of any post you require. You could even request a transfer to Scaelas's personal guard, or serve directly under Commander Reggin, I'm sure.'

'I don't care,' Kier said. 'Based on what you're saying, this mission is a death trap. We have a target on our backs. Luthar, Cleoc Strata, Eprain, all after us? Nestria will be there too, I imagine. They'll all be just as savvy as we think we are. For all I know, there are soldiers waiting for the minute we set out from camp. If I make it – if *we* make it – we're not coming back.'

He was so good at this, but under the table, he gripped Grey's hand. His was clammy with sweat, and she realized that despite his posturing, he was terrified.

Attis stared him down, grim-faced, for another full minute. Finally, she opened one of her desk drawers with an angry clatter. Mare's eyebrows were drawn together, furrowed, her thin-lipped mouth twisted in a pucker of surprise.

Grey watched as Attis conspicuously wrote a note on fresh parchment. She finished, read it over twice, folded it, and sealed it with wax and the stamp of her office.

'If you live through this,' she said, holding it out to Kier, 'you are free to go.'

Kier squeezed Grey's hand hard enough to bruise. With his other hand, easy as anything, he took the missive and handed it to her. She tucked it serenely in the inner pocket of her cloak.

'Pick your team,' Attis said. She was an unusual shade of red – and Grey almost felt bad for her. If she wasn't sending the pair of them on a suicide mission with a girl who'd just stabbed Kier (and who was also pretending to be Grey), she would find some measure of sympathy in herself.

But Kier was right. Attis was only agreeing because the likelihood of them coming out of it alive or fit for service on the other side was . . . slim.

'Hand Ola Et-Kiltar. Brit Wyvern. Officer Eron Fastria.' Grey sent a wave of approval for choosing Brit and Ola – they were a strong pairing, and they'd seen the blood. They knew what the girl was capable of. Grey had figured Kier would want Chappelle over Fastria, but Chappelle would probably take over command in his absence.

Mare noted the names, chewing on her lip. Grey resisted the urge to stick out her tongue and shout, *I told you so. I told you we were different.*

'I will notify them. You leave as soon as preparations are finalized. Report to the infirmary for assessment.'

Kier nodded, thanked the master and finished with a salute. They were halfway out when Attis called, 'Seward.'

He turned, one hand gripping the cloth to hold it aside. Grey lurked in the shadowy path between tents.

'It's not always easier,' she said, 'to be free of duty.'

'Not everything is about duty,' Kier said. Something odd flickered across Mare's face – maybe she disagreed. Grey had one fixed image of them, the two women who'd spent more time together than any Hand and mage she had ever met, who she could never really understand.

'Freedom does not guarantee you the world,' Attis said mildly.

Kier smiled, the move not quite reaching his eyes. 'I would choose freedom over anything, Master.'

Attis inclined her head, both allowing for Kier's words and dismissing them.

Grey waited until they were halfway to the infirmary before she said, 'You didn't have to do this for me.'

Kier didn't look at her, but the corner of his mouth quirked up. 'Who said you had anything to do with it? Each assignment chisels away more of my beauty.'

'You were never beautiful to start with.'

'That is a bold-faced lie, Flynn.'

It was. She didn't care. There was something clawing up inside of her, and it felt an awful lot like happiness. She pushed power toward him, a blaring supernova of it, so much that he stumbled and nearly took a knee in the mud.

'Gods and seas,' he muttered, rubbing idly at his chest. 'I can feel every heartbeat in the camp when you do that.'

She pushed him a bit more, just to be an ass.

'Don't celebrate too soon,' he said. 'We've got to survive this first. And figure out some way to keep our hand firmly concealed.'

'With your unchiseled beauty on the line,' Grey said, 'I'm sure you'll come up with something.'

They entered the infirmary to find three assistants and a healer Grey didn't know manning the ward. 'Where's Leonie?' she asked before she could stop herself, earning a sly grin from Kier, who knew nothing about anything.

The healer stood, curtsied and said, 'Doing paperwork in the back. She asked for a moment undisturbed.'

'But—'

'Send them in,' Leonie said, poking her head out from behind a curtain.

Grey made her way through the beds to the room where Leonie waited, sitting on a little stool, reading a recipe for an herbal concoction. She patted the nearby bed without looking up when they came in. 'Who's first?'

'Don't you need to know what we're doing?' Kier asked, pulling off his cloak and folding it neatly over a chair.

'Chappelle got word he's taking the company. You're moving?'

'Something like that,' Grey said, folding her arms over her chest, leaning against a cabinet of medication. God, how she missed *leaning*. Solid walls. A floor that wasn't constructed from packed dirt, waterproof padding, scratchy rugs and the tears of those who came before.

Leonie poked and prodded at Kier, checking inside his mouth and ears, looking at his eyes, listening to his heartbeat and the sound of his lungs as he breathed, tested his reflexes. She also examined his mostly healed wound, blowing a low whistle. 'That's some Hand of yours,' she said.

'She's too good for me by half,' Kier confirmed.

'At least you know it. You're good to go, Seward. Flynn?'

Grey hated these examinations, even though nothing ever came up. She endured Leonie's prodding. 'When was your last monthly bleed?' Leonie asked while she checked on an old wound on Grey's right arm, a slash from a skirmish weeks before.

'Uh . . .'

Leonie sighed. 'Have you had recent relations of a sexual nature with anyone with the ability to produce semen?'

'That depends on your—' Kier started.

'Gods, no,' Grey said, cutting him off before she could think better of it.

'Interesting,' Leonie said clinically, very careful not to look at Kier. Grey kicked her shin and pretended it was a reflex.

'Can't say the same for the captain,' Grey said, because if he was going to tease her about Leonie, she was more than capable of firing back. Kier only shrugged.

'That is none of my business,' Leonie said. 'Presumably you'll be due for your monthlies during your travels – I'll grab you a pack.'

She disappeared through the thin corridor that went between supply rooms.

'She *is* pretty,' Kier said with a glint in his eye that Grey couldn't quite read.

'And too good for me by half,' Grey said, repeating his earlier words so she didn't say, *So are you – by chance, are you interested in relations of a sexual nature?*

'Doubtful,' Kier said. 'I can leave, if you want to say goodbye to her properly.'

Grey rolled her eyes at his wink. 'What, so you can go say goodbye to the dozen paramours you've acquired at this camp?'

'You wound me, Flynn.'

'I know you, Seward. There's a difference.'

'If only any of them were enough to steal my heart, but I fear I'm too much a fool for that,' he lamented, his gaze lingering on her for a moment too long. The words sent a pang to her stomach, but she had no idea how to respond. Then, quieter, 'I didn't speak for you, back with Attis, did I? Make an assumption? I know I do that sometimes.'

'What do you mean?'

He moved across the room, draping his cloak over her shoulders – he must've seen the goosebumps rising on her arms. 'I'm not forcing you into an early retirement against your will?'

The laugh that bubbled out of her was half hysteria, half exhaustion. 'Me? Stay here? Without you? Not a chance.'

But that uncertainty hadn't gone. He picked up the little hammer Leonie had used to check their reflexes and fiddled with it, his thumb rubbing at a ridge in the metal. 'Six months would've been nice,' he said doubtfully.

She laid a hand over his, releasing another pulse of power that made his eyes flick shut. 'Forever will be nicer.'

His eyes opened, hazy and indistinct. 'Grey, when I said—'

The supply pack hit Grey in the arm. Kier jumped back. Grey grabbed the pack, flipped through it and nodded. 'Thanks,' she said to Leonie, sliding down from the exam table as the other woman came back into the room.

'Can I have a moment with you, Hand?' Leonie asked. 'I have a med kit for your travels, things to run through. Attis sent a brief – you'll be the healer?'

'You know more than me,' Kier said.

'Go on,' Grey said. 'I'll be along.'

He looked at her for a second, and she remembered that he'd been in the middle of saying something – possibly something important. But he didn't protest. He took his cloak back, pushing hers toward her. 'I'll start packing up,' he said.

Leonie didn't move until they were alone. When Kier was gone and enough time had passed that he was safely out of earshot, she leaned her good hip against the exam table.

'It's not a reassignment, is it?' she asked. She set the healer's bag on the table and opened it. Grey took a cursory glance, taking in the sachets of herbs, the tiny jars of salve.

'I can't say.'

Leonie made a small noise in her throat. 'They had me check the prisoner for injuries.'

That caught Grey's attention. 'And? Is she in good health?'

'Yes, mostly. A few cuts and bruises, and her shoulder was dislocated when she arrived – whatever Luthar did to her, they didn't do it kindly. She has had dental work done. Looks like it was performed on the continent.'

'The continent?'

'Mm. They use different materials. It's easy to see, if you know what to look for.'

Grey turned this over. It wouldn't be unexpected for the lost daughter of Locke to seek refuge in the continent – it just wasn't what happened.

'A few other inconsistencies. I left you notes.'

She chewed her lip. 'Why are you telling me this?'

'Because we're friends,' Leonie said, with no hint of irony. She hesitated, looking up at Grey with a solemn expression. 'And I hope, someday, if you have need of me—'

'Leonie . . .'

But Leonie only raised a hand to Grey's cheek. 'You're not a normal well either, Hand Captain.'

Six years of serving Kier across nearly a dozen assignments, and no one had discovered her – yet in this camp, it felt everyone was suspicious. What had changed? What had slipped? Or was it only that she'd let her guard down, that she'd let others get close to her?

Grey smiled sadly, catching Leonie's hand. 'I'm obviously far better-looking.'

Leonie rolled her eyes, the moment broken. 'You spend too much time with the captain. Now, stop your flirting, and come here and say goodbye.'

It was not meet, in the army, to depart with a hug. But Grey so rarely found others on assignments that she cared for, that she *liked*. So when Leonie opened her arms, Grey didn't hesitate to tuck herself against the other woman, to let herself be embraced.

'Write to me, if you can,' Leonie said.

'If I can,' Grey said instead of a smart-ass retort, which she thought was very noble of her.

'And be safe,' Leonie added against her hair. Grey did not bother to respond to that, because on this mission, safety was very much outside of her control.

Part Two

The Blood of the Retinue

Sorry it's taken me so long to write. You know how things are. Kier is fine, and I am fine, and there's nothing to report that I wouldn't have to redact later. You probably know too much already because Kier tells you/Lo/Pia everything anyway. So I guess this is me saying that we are still, unfortunately, alive and at war.

Letter from Hand Captain Grey Flynn to Imarta Flynn, 15 years PD

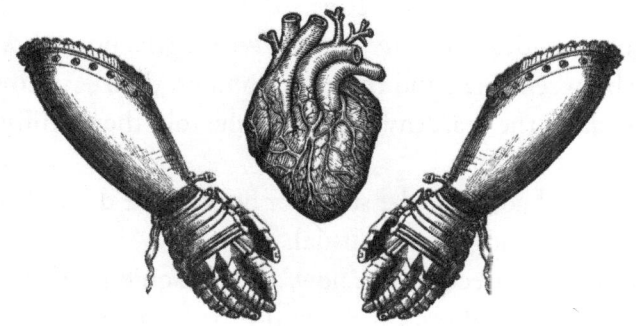

nine

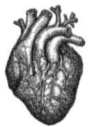

THEY SET OUT AN hour later, moving quietly out of the far side of camp, heading north. It was the only instruction Attis had given them, besides *Stay alive and deliver the girl*: north first, to put distance between them and the encampment; then east, toward the mountains and the sea. Anything else, she told them stiffly, was up to Kier.

Later, as he'd adjusted the straps of her bag, he'd met Grey's eye. Deferring to her judgment, as usual.

'Follow Attis's directions for now,' she said quietly. Kier nodded.

Now, they trudged on, off the main roads, on a small path that farmers from this area once used to bring their wares to the port, when the port belonged to Scaela. It was overgrown, but at least they were not up to their knees in mud.

Grey barely knew herself out of her black-trimmed Hand's cloak or the armor of the Scaelan army. She would not admit it to anyone, but she missed the familiar weight of the leather, the scuffed armor broken in by ages of sweat and battle. Now, she wore a loose-fitting rough-spun shirt and a leather vest buckled over her stomach – the closest thing she could find to armor without actually reaching for her breastplate and helm. The trousers were black, just nearly too thin for the season, but at least she had her well-worn boots, and they were dry for once. She kept her knives on her belt and her sword across her back, like the merchants wore them. It wasn't unusual for travelers in these parts to be armed: with the military's attention diverted elsewhere, there was no one to keep the paths or the main roads clear of bandits.

She and Kier walked in front, followed by Ola and Brit on either side of the girl, then Eron at the back. The prisoner was out of her dirty travel clothes and wearing a new thick gray dress and too-big coat. Glancing at her, Grey was reminded of the uncanny feeling of seeing her on the battlefield, wearing Kier's armor; how much she then looked like a child.

Attis had handed something over to Kier upon their departure with a quiet word, which Kier explained to the others as he opened his hands to reveal cuffs.

'They'll hurt,' he told them and the girl as he strapped them to her wrists with unshaking hands. He didn't seem to care that she had stabbed him only days before. 'A constant flow of magic needs to run through them – Grey and I will take the first shift, then Ola and Brit. But if she strays too far, they'll do some damage.'

Ola had winced. Grey had not.

After the cuffs were secure, Grey had looked the girl straight in the face and said, 'I'll need your name.'

'Maryse,' she said, her voice high and clear. Grey had not quite been able to figure out her accent. It had taken Grey herself months, when she first settled in Scaela, to eradicate any traces of the burr of her own, but the prisoner's accent bore no trace of the Isle.

'Something else,' Grey said, flippant.

Only then did the other girl look at her, ice-chip eyes sad and empty. 'I suppose it doesn't matter.'

Grey gritted her teeth. 'It matters to us,' Ola said. She glanced at Kier, and seeing no sign of protest, she took a step forward. She pulled the girl's coat tighter around her shoulders (did no one re-member that she'd just stabbed Kier? Was Grey the only one who carried that?) and wrapped a scarf about her neck. 'What would you like to be called?'

'Sela,' the girl said finally.

So Sela she was, and now they walked.

'So,' Brit said, not too long after they left Mecketer, loud enough that
they all could hear. Grey startled, already lost in her own thoughts.
'What are our roles, Captain?'

Kier glanced up at Brit, then at Grey, then back at Brit. He seemed
just as lost as Grey felt. 'What?'

'Our roles. Responsibilities. What are we in charge of?'

'The prisoner,' Grey said flatly, ignoring the frightened look Sela
aimed in her direction. 'We're in charge of the prisoner, and making
sure she doesn't die. And that we don't either.'

The group flattened a little, forming more of a line than a pod.
'It's not a true quest if we don't have our own roles.' Brit smirked at
Grey, their bright blue eyes sparkling. Next to them, Ola rolled her
own eyes. Grey had noted Ola's power early on when the pairing
had joined Kier's company, and in turn, Brit's humor. She was never
really certain what to do with people who were funny rather than
just bitter, self-deprecating or sarcastic – they always left her feeling
a little on the back foot, like she wasn't sure if they could genuinely
be trusted.

She wasn't sure if *Brit* could be trusted.

'It's not a quest,' Grey said. 'It's a mission.'

But Kier glanced down the line, then at Grey, then at the girl, and
Grey realized he was actually going along with this. 'Well,' he said,
considering. 'Flynn is our healer, for obvious reasons. That, at least,
was assigned. And I'm in charge. What other roles are there?'

A pause.

Brit elbowed Ola in the ribs. 'I can ... navigate?' Ola offered,
uncertain.

'That would mean handing over the maps,' Kier said.

'If I'm navigating, you don't have to worry about guiding us in the
wrong direction.'

'Kier is already good at directions,' Grey said, hoping to put an end
to this ridiculous discussion. They didn't need *jobs* – they just needed
to survive. 'And everyone else can just be very good at listening.'

'I'll care for the weapons,' Brit said. They opened their coat, revealing belts of blades that shone in the sunlight and dark metal axes and thin bars of raw metal. Grey stopped in the middle of the road, shocked despite herself.

'Where did you even *get* all of that?' Kier asked. 'Attis didn't . . .'

Brit shrugged. 'I made them. I'm a materialist. A metalworker.' Which Grey knew, of course – she knew the affinities of everyone in their company. But she hadn't realized what Brit was capable of.

She and Kier exchanged a long look. *I told you Ola was powerful*, Grey tried to convey. *They could not have done all of that without a strong well, and I knew she was good, and I told you so.*

This mission is fucked, Kier's expression said, his lips pressed tightly together. Finally, he sighed, raising his eyes skyward. 'Okay. Ola, you navigate. Brit, you're in charge of weaponry. Fastria?'

Eron looked up. He was quieter than the others, and always had been – when he was promoted to be one of Kier's officers, Grey had questioned it at first. But whenever he did open his mouth, it was like he always said the right thing, at exactly the right time. She'd wondered sometimes what he would be like if she was actually in his confidence. Perhaps, on this mission, she would find out.

No. She caught herself – they were not here to become friends, or confidantes. She sent a pulse of annoyance down the tether to Kier, hoping he'd wrap up this foolishness soon.

'I'll cook, I guess,' Eron said.

Kier raised an eyebrow. 'Are you good at cooking?'

'Guess we'll find out,' Eron said. 'I've always wanted to try.'

Kiernan, Grey thought at her mage with all possible force.

'And what about me?' Sela asked. Badly timed – Grey turned a glare on her. To her right, Kier sighed.

'Your job is to listen,' Kier said. A beat. 'And not piss Flynn off.'

'Not piss Flynn off any further,' Brit amended. It was the only sensible thing they'd said since the retinue left Mecketer.

'Don't lose focus,' Grey said. She nodded to Kier, and they re-formed their pod around the girl, falling back into silence.

*

The signs of failure should've been obvious, because it was Eron who questioned the mission first, to her surprise – Eron, who was usually much more considered.

He caught up to the pair of them when they were safely in the woods. Eron cleared his throat, looking between the two of them. 'Captains? A word?'

Grey and Kier exchanged a glance. Kier nodded. 'Yes, Fastria?'

'It's confidential,' Eron said, rubbing the palm of one hand with the thumb of the other. A nervous tic if Grey had ever seen one.

Kier pulled a trickle of power from her, then drew a sound shield around the three of them. 'We're protected,' he said, his voice going fuzzy for the barest moment.

'Right.' Eron took a deep breath. 'The prisoner. She's meant to be the heir to Locke. But isn't Maryse ... dead?'

Grey winced. 'She's meant to be,' she said. She did not like her own name in so many mouths after so long, distorted by the Scaelan accent.

'Severin lived,' Eron said, pressing forward. 'He even wrote to Scaelas. Fled to the continent. No one has ever suspected Maryse of surviving, given the proof. So why are we on a mission to the death to protect her?'

'It is believed, due to recent discoveries,' Kier said shortly, 'that the letter from Severin was a forgery.'

He sounded like that, Grey thought grimly, because they *knew* it was.

'We are to protect the girl and deliver her safely. If Scaelas believes she is the heir to Locke, then we are not to question it,' he went on.

A pause. A beat. Eron ran a hand through his close-cropped hair – another fidget. Perhaps he, like Grey, wore his anxiety in his inability to stay still. 'Yes, Captain. Very well.'

'Thank you for your honesty, Eron,' Kier said, the dismissal clear as anything. When Eron fell back, Kier aimed a long, telling look in Grey's direction.

The truth was, there *was* a letter. The first time Scaelas's forces came to Leota, searching all the children for any trace of survivors, Grey was so ill with the pox she was nearly unrecognizable. Imarta had carried her to meet the soldiers, showing her face for only the barest of moments before they demanded she take the contagious girl away. It was a lucky thing she had been far too sick to tether.

The second time the soldiers came, weeks later, she was struck with such unbelievable terror she could hardly move. If they saw her, they would know. If they tethered to her, they would *know*.

She poured these fears into Kier, who summoned Lot down to their protected cove by the sea. Lot paced as Grey spoke, telling him of Severin's death, of her own identity, of the destruction of Locke.

Except buried in all of that, she kept one final lie.

'Severin,' she said, finishing. 'He was the heir to the Isle. He was a well, too. I was just . . . the extra. A backup.' She let Lot comfort her as she cried, ignoring the seed of guilt that grew in her stomach. She watched Kier's face as he heard the lie, believed it, swallowed it down.

Finally, Lot asked, 'Do you want to go to Scaelas?'

'No,' she said, voice cracking. 'I don't know if it's safe.'

He nodded then, a decision made. He was twelve, nearly thirteen, and to Kier and Grey, he was the smartest person they'd ever known.

'Then here's what we'll do,' he said. 'Grape, go and get parchment. *Good* parchment. Kier, bring me Ma's sealing wax. I will write a letter to the High Lord saying I'm your brother, asking him to leave me alone. That way, it looks like Severin survived, and they'll stop looking for you. Maybe they'll take the letter to heart and stop searching entirely.

Grey blinked at him. 'How can we be sure they'll believe it?'

'Do you know your brother's true name?'

True names are for Hands and husbands. But Severin was dead, so what did it even matter?

'Yes,' she said. Then, chewing her lip, 'And diplomatic symbols. I know the one for my mother's line. It will get the letter to Scaelas faster.'

'Then Scaelas will know it, too, and he'll believe it.'

'Yes. I can show you how to make it,' Grey allowed. 'And Sev's signature.'

It was the only good option, and they couldn't think of another. So Grey fetched parchment and writing instruments, and Kier got the sealing wax. Lot wrote the letter, because he was the oldest and his handwriting was the nicest, and Grey taught him Sev's true name and signature, then drew the lines of Locke's symbol under the forgery.

After, Lot decided it would be too close to send the letter from Leota, so the trio packed a single bag and slipped out of the Seward house after dark. They walked inland all night, ducking into ditches and behind bushes when they saw others on the road.

An hour after dawn, they reached a minuscule village. Lot went alone to send the letter. When he returned, he took Grey's hand and they made the long walk back. On their return, they found Pia and Laurella and Imarta angrier than they ever had been before. Imarta left the punishments to Pia and Lo, because she was barely more than a girl herself, and she knew little of raising children.

That night, they went to bed grim-faced and silent, holding their secret, mad at one another and themselves in the way of children caught misbehaving – but it was worth it. The plan worked, in some ways. After that day, no one went looking for Maryse again.

It failed in some ways, too – because they never stopped looking for Severin.

After a few hours, Ola moved up to the front of the group, trading places with Grey, so she and Kier could mutter and argue over the map. They came to a place where the path ran parallel to the wood. Kier turned, finding Grey's eye, and she nodded. Kier led them into the wood. The route through the underbrush was too narrow to walk three abreast, so Brit and Grey let Eron and the prisoner go ahead and followed behind. Grey waited, tense – she was certain Brit would break the silence between them soon enough.

She was unsurprised when they finally cracked. 'What will you do with your six months of leave?' they asked.

So Attis hadn't told the others about Kier's proposition, what he and Grey would get. Grey filed that away for later chewing.

'Sleep,' she said. She was still feeling irritable, but also a bit bad about how sharply she had spoken earlier. A conversation with Brit would not kill her – and perhaps it would help her uncover what lay under their humor.

Brit snorted. 'That would be something. And then a new assignment . . . Can't say I'm sad to go. That place was a shithole.'

Grey wrinkled her nose, stepping delicately over a tree root. The last thing she needed was to sprain her ankle on the first day. 'I'm just glad to be out of the mud,' she admitted.

'Where were you before?'

'Karlot. Then Orakey before that. We were at Grislar on our first assignment.'

'Ah. Familiar territory.'

Grey shrugged. She'd never much liked Grislar – it was too close to Locke. She'd grown up near the coast, always aware that Locke was there, but in Grislar she had to look at the place where it had once been. They were higher on the cliffs, with the camp built backing the sea, so sometimes she'd wake up to the smell of phantom smoke in the air. It was a sensation all of the wells claimed to have, looking uneasily over their shoulders as they discussed it over bowls of mealy porridge at breakfast.

The other wells, she realized soon enough, did not hear the screams that came along with the smoke.

That was the assignment when Kier had promised her, after night after night of nightmares, that they wouldn't go back.

She glanced up, saw the back of his head. She didn't resent him for it, for the fact that he couldn't keep his promises. Perhaps she just had to stop asking him for things he couldn't control.

'It's also a shithole,' she said apologetically. 'Or at least it was when we were there, and I doubt the situation has improved.'

Brit sighed, looking up through the trees. 'My first was Lanavin.'

Grey quirked an eyebrow. 'Oh?' She'd heard of it: no one wanted to go to Lanavin. In fact, it wasn't *un*heard of for soldiers to be sent there strictly for punishment. She herself had been threatened with it more than once. 'How was that?'

Brit simply looked at her. There was no use speaking of the blood when they were out of it.

'Here's hoping Grislar has improved,' they said.

Grey snorted. 'Doubtful.'

In a lower tone – though it didn't matter, Grey thought, because

Ola and Kier had moved from conversing over the map to arguing over the map, and Eron was now arm in arm with their prisoner, quietly asking her questions she didn't answer about her schooling – Brit asked, 'What do you know of Locke?'

She had to stop jumping every time someone mentioned it. She had to get used to it. Not in public, but they'd want to talk about it within their retinue. There was no way Ola and Brit and Eron would not have a single word to say about their mission. Perhaps she didn't trust them, but she had to figure out a way to dance around the topic all the same.

'Not much,' she lied. 'I was a child when it happened.'

'But you and the captain – you're from the seaside, aren't you?'

'We are. Kier remembers better than me.'

'Who do you think did it?'

Grey raised her eyes skyward, looking at the dappled sunlight streaming through the trees. Even after all these years, that was the question. No one knew *how*, exactly, the island had vanished – but the overarching theory was that it hadn't been unprovoked. All that the few witnesses of its destruction reported was this: a ship was spotted by one of Scaela's port guards, gliding across the bay toward Locke from an unknown origin. Then, an hour later, it appeared that most of the Isle was on fire. Just as Scaelas was sending his own ships to its aid, there was an explosion, and when the smoke cleared, the Isle was gone.

Evaporated or submerged, it didn't matter – Locke vanished that day, and no trace of it had been seen since. No bodies. No debris. No survivors. Just a blank span of sea in the Bay of Locke, with nothing remaining of the Obsidian Isle and its thousand-year legacy of power.

Besides her.

'I hope,' she said, 'we never know. It doesn't matter anyways. Locke is gone.'

'*She* might know,' Brit said quietly, their eyes cutting to Sela.

Grey shrugged. 'Maybe.'

Brit must've read her discomfort, even if they did not know the reason. 'The captain,' they said, switching directions. 'You're from the same town?'

This train of conversation was easier to swallow. 'Nearly the same house.'

'What was he like as a boy?'

Grey considered this. She didn't usually talk to mages other than Kier unless she had to, and she certainly hadn't since Kier had been raised into command. It wasn't that she disliked them – but she saw him, how he felt when someone much older than him pushed back, the strain it took for him to claim some semblance of authority. She'd felt it too, but with wells, power was more a sign of authority than age, and she'd always been quietly capable. She was respected because she had power. For all of Kier's miraculous triumphs on the battlefield with that power, he'd had to fight for every bit of respect he'd garnered.

But this was different. For one thing, Brit wasn't digging for ammunition to use against him, which Grey might have otherwise suspected – that they were looking for the subject of a joke, or a way to tease him. They already respected Kier. And they couldn't have been that much older than him either, so it wasn't that.

Let go, Grey chided herself. *Not everyone is trying to hurt you.* But her gaze flicked to the prisoner, the *girl*, Sela, and she bit her tongue.

'The same, in some ways,' she said. Then, before she could stop herself, 'He was always kind. Even to me. Even to his brother. Even when he didn't have to be.'

'Mm.' Brit walked in silence for a few paces, long enough that Grey figured they'd ceased the need to talk and could continue the rest of the day's journey in relative quiet. 'I think I've forgotten how to be kind.'

Grey looked at them as if seeing them for the first time, taking in the shorn shimmer of their pale hair, traced through by and growing oddly around scars that had long since healed. She understood their humor now, despite herself. It was a mask over the anger they all carried, the fear. It was its own kind of armor.

She glanced at the four ahead, at Ola's laughing face – she and Kier had finished their argument with some success – and the prisoner's drawn, angry mouth. She flexed her hand, remembering the feeling of the girl's hair in her grip. 'I don't think I ever knew,' she confessed.

*

It was easy to be lulled into a false sense of security, to forget it wasn't just an adventure, especially now that she had warmed somewhat to Brit's unfailing optimism and noted how it spread so easily to the others.

The Scaelan south was not much to look at, but in comparison to Grey's memories of Locke, it was verdant and green. They would reach the foothills of the Aloducan peaks in a few days' time, according to Kier's calculations, but for now, they were cutting through miles of forests interspersed with rolling hills of green grasses and grazing sheep, past stands of closely crowded trees. They were careful to avoid the villages, choosing farmers' fields and bits of woodland to travel through instead.

The night came too quickly in the wood, and Kier paused in a small clearing, just big enough for the six of them, and declared, 'This will do.'

'No town?' Eron asked. Grey glanced around at the ferns creeping into the clearing, the shady canopy of birch and ash that hung above. It wasn't muddy, which made it immediately better than Mecketer.

'Not tonight,' Kier said. 'I want to stay in the wild a bit longer.'

They unpacked their bedrolls and Eron set to food preparation, using Brit and Ola to heat the pot of thick reconstituted gruel without lighting a fire. He whistled as he stirred, rifling through the supply kit and adding a mysterious combination of things to the pot. Grey watched with resignation as the gruel turned a frightening shade of gray, speckled with unknown herbs.

'Are you sure this was a good idea?' she muttered to Kier. 'Leaving Eron in charge of feeding us?'

'I refuse to be the one to break his heart,' Kier whispered back. But he did go to his own pack and slipped her a bit of dried fruit when no one was looking.

'We'll take the first watch,' he said, louder, so the others could hear. Grey turned away, pretending to search through her pack for another knife as she chewed on the leathery strips of apple and apricot. 'Ola, can you and Brit handle the cuffs for a while?'

'Of course, Captain,' Ola said.

'Kier,' he corrected. They all paused, glancing at him uneasily. Kier shifted his weight. 'We're not in a position for titles. So, Kier. Just Kier, or Seward, if you have to.'

'Right. Sorry.'

Once she had swallowed the last of her haul, Grey checked that the others were thoroughly occupied as she retrieved her healing kit. 'Sela?'

The girl looked up from watching Eron stir. Grey felt Kier's gaze on her, and the question within it.

'Leonie said you have some injuries in need of care,' she said, clipped as ever. She was investigating, and she would do her job to the letter – it didn't mean she had to be nice about it. 'Ola, could you restrain the girl?'

'Is that necessary?' Ola asked.

Grey stood, kit in one hand, eyes hard as flint. 'Need I remind you,' she said, leaning into the authority she so rarely used, 'that she nearly killed Kier?' Was she the *only one* who remembered this?

'*Flynn*,' Kier sighed.

But Grey held firm. Leonie didn't know who this girl was – and until Grey did, she would not let her guard down. There was no reason for someone to just *pretend* to be Locke with no reason for it.

'She has the cuffs,' Eron said.

'Doesn't stop her from attacking me,' Grey pointed out.

'I won't hurt you,' Sela said quietly. Grey didn't bother with a response – she'd like to see the girl try.

But Ola only held Grey's gaze for a moment longer, then went in her bag for a length of rope.

'In front of her, please,' Grey said. Her shoulder was probably still sore, and that was a mercy she could grant her. When Sela was bound, Grey went to her and hauled her up by her good arm. 'I'll take her for some privacy. Kier, a light?'

She felt the thin trickle of power and then the light flared cool and blue in Kier's hands. 'Need backup?' he asked.

She could tell from his look that he was displeased about her tying Sela up, but he wasn't going to say anything about it in front of the others. She didn't want to hear it alone, either.

'No.'

She led the prisoner a little ways away to the edge of the clearing, still within open view of the camp. She nodded to a fallen tree trunk thick with moss. 'There,' she said, 'please.'

The girl lowered herself to the trunk. Kier's magelight was, as always, a neat piece of work: Grey could see, and the girl probably could too, but no one more than a few feet outside of its warm glow would be able to catch it. She felt the threads of magic within it, his work tidy as ever. She set the magelight next to Sela and crouched in front of her.

Leonie had left detailed accounts of her examination. 'I should put you in a sling,' Grey murmured, looking through the notes, then up at the girl. Sela was small in stature, fine-boned – she looked too breakable to be a soldier. Grey suspected that she hadn't been conscripted at all before she was taken captive. 'Let me check for swelling.'

She eased the coat off the girl's shoulders – awkward when Sela's hands were bound, but she wasn't compromising on that point just yet – and probed with her fingertips, pausing only for a moment when she heard Sela's quick indrawn breath.

'It'll still be tender,' Grey said.

'Can you give me anything for the pain?' Sela asked, surprising Grey with her trust. Grey could just as easily slip her poison. 'Polla weed? Something like that?'

Grey blinked, hesitating before she caught herself. 'Yes,' she said after a moment. 'I'll make you a solution when we get back to the fire.'

She let go of Sela's shoulder and pulled the coat back up, then worked through the rest of her injuries carefully, applying antiseptic salve and a new dressing to the wound on her shin, rebandaging the broken skin on the knuckles of one hand. Sela was quiet the whole time, her heart too fast in her chest.

'Done,' Grey said, sitting back on her heels.

Sela's head snapped up. She was on guard, tense, and probably for good reason. Grey had, after all, threatened to kill her.

Something was shifting inside of her, something she didn't like at all and would not acknowledge to Kier or any of the others. Sela's eyes were wide and blue, her chin sharp, her face round and young. The severe cut of her hair did nothing to make her appear any older – if anything, she looked like a girl in need of protection.

Grey sighed. She untied the restraints and moved the girl's arm carefully, refashioning the rope into a sling. She could hold a grudge with the best of them, but cruelty didn't suit her.

'Do not give me any reason to distrust you,' she said, annoyed with herself. 'You'll be tied right back up again before you can blink.'

'Understood,' Sela said, her voice very small.

Grey nodded and hauled the girl back up. At camp, Eron had finished cooking the beige abomination and was spooning it into a line of collapsible bowls. Grey stopped to mix some of Leonie's pain-reducing solution with water and handed it to Sela. After, she took the bowl she was given with a quick nod and thanks, then settled against a tree at the edge of camp with her food, the magelight and the stack of Leonie's notes on all of their previous injuries. If she was to be the team medic, it was good for her to be informed.

It only took her two mouthfuls to decide that making Eron the cook was a terrible idea, but it was too late to change things now. Grey leaned back, setting her bowl aside for now, listening to the night-time sounds of the forest: the rustling of small animals in the ferns and brush, a creek babbling nearby. Against her tree, the air smelled of autumn: leaves decaying into rich soil, and the barest bite of winter on the wind.

The others chatted idly in soft tones while they ate: Eron and Brit compared notes on previous assignments; Ola held a one-sided conversation with the silent girl about a pastry shop in Grislar. Kier was off on the perimeter watch, tethered to Grey but not pulling any magic since they'd switched with Brit and Ola for Sela's cuffs, the connection dormant but still comforting.

She flipped through Leonie's notes. There was nothing dramatic: Eron had suffered a concussion three months before, so he had an alert for further head wounds. Ola's left arm had been nearly cleaved off in a previous assignment and the muscle still ached sometimes; Grey made a note to apply a heat compress when they reached the next town. Brit had also had a concussion five months ago, a broken ankle two assignments ago, and recurring but treatable kidney stones due to a run-in with an internal mage on the frontline near Nestria. Then there was Kier: a patchwork of so many injuries over the years that she'd lost count. There was no point in reading them: she knew them all by memory.

She went back to the girl's papers, searching for Leonie's report about healed injuries. It was short, perfunctory: none. Nothing. No sign of previous injury. Not even an interesting scar. Sela certainly hadn't been fighting before: that empty injury report would be nigh impossible if she had. And Leonie was thorough – she'd even noted Kier's eyebrow scar, even though that had been acquired in childhood.

Grey chewed on her lip, flicking back to another page: Leonie's notes on Sela's general well-being. She ran her finger over the writing, careful not to smudge the ink. She read the line again, *Missing third molar, no sign of surgery*, and her tongue immediately traced the place where her own back molars had come in – and been removed – only a couple of years before. Further down, Leonie noted that she'd employed help from a bone mage to make sure nothing had been broken. There, she'd written, *Humeral head unfused*, and included a diagram.

It stirred a memory within Grey, of one of her worst days as a healer. She had been called out of her bed and taken to a back room in the fortress full of tables laid with bones. There, the lead healer of the camp had asked for her help: they'd found the remains in a village nearby, the flesh picked away by scavengers. It was her job to determine how many of the bones belonged to children, make an assessment of the sex of the assorted bodies and find any other nuances in the remains, in the hopes that relatives could be informed. They had worked for hours trying to line the bodies up, Grey's mind clouded with the progression of bones and how they grew in the body until she could barely think of anything else.

She sat now staring at nothing until her eyes went dry with strain. She stared until someone nudged her on the shoulder and she looked up to find Eron standing over her.

'You should finish eating,' he said kindly. 'Do you want to join the ca— Kier on the first watch?'

She fussed with the papers, putting them in order before she buried them at the bottom of her kit. 'Yeah, I have to be awake if he's on watch – can't siphon without me and all,' she said. Eron probably knew quite a bit about mages and wells, but not being one himself, she wasn't sure how aware he was of the technicalities. It was true that a normal mage couldn't draw on their well if they were sleeping, but with Kier bound to her, that left another loophole. She got up, knees popping, and took the med kit back to her bedroll.

The others had finished their food and were settling in for the night. Grey should've made more of an effort to talk, to get to know them – but this wasn't a mission for friendship.

They'd arranged their bedrolls in a haphazard formation with Sela at the center. The girl was already down, lying on her uninjured shoulder, eyes closed but not asleep. Brit and Ola were on either side of her, angled in, with Eron at her head.

'Everyone feeling okay before I head off on watch?' Grey asked. She kept her head low as she searched her pack, coming up with the stub of a pencil and a ragged notebook she'd purchased in a mountain village three assignments ago.

'Mmph,' Brit muttered, burying their face in the jumble of a coat they were using as a pillow.

'Would love a cup of tea,' Ola said, one arm thrown over her face to block out what little glow emanated from the dimming magelight.

'Fuck off,' Grey said kindly. She pressed her hand on the magelight to take the power back into herself, evaporating the glow, then set off toward the perimeter, where Kier lurked, pausing on the edge of camp to scribble.

She found him perched on a stump, worrying at the hilt of a knife as he stared into the darkness. She slipped him a mug of gruel and the note she'd written. 'I'll take care of the other side,' she said. 'Sharp pull when you need me. Pass and switch whenever.'

Kier winced around his first sip of stodgy porridge. She should've watered it down. 'God. Three weeks of this?'

'Two if we're lucky.'

'We won't be.' They never were.

'It's your fault,' Grey muttered, 'for allowing them to treat it as a quest.'

Kier cast her a wounded look. 'If it gives them the morale to survive? I'm not taking it back.'

She didn't bother responding. She moved quietly through the perimeter of the camp, her eyes soft and searching in the darkness. It had taken her a while to adjust to the forests of Scaela. The Isle of Locke was a scrabbly, mountainous thing, half cliff and sea spray. The trees that grew there were sparse and tall, so she could see her brother even halfway across the old patch of growth they called the Ghostwood, which separated the fortress from the Isle's villages. Severin, seven years older than her and barely more than a boy when he died, used to take her into the largest of the villages when they had time away from tutors and lessons. She remembered holding his hand as they made their way through the scant forest, listening to the scream of the wind (on Locke, the wind was always screaming) as Sev tried his best to convince her they wouldn't be eaten by ghosts. Sometimes they'd go off the trail, into the trees, all the way past the little creek to the circular clearing, climbing over the ruins of the temple that lurked on the cliff's edge. That was where all Lockes were buried, all the way back as far as they went, all the way to the first well.

It hurts my stomach, Grey, then Maryse, always said when they went there. She didn't like to go in, didn't like the feeling of a cavern opening all the way inside of her, like it would turn her inside out and swallow her up.

It's nice, Sev said. He liked to raise flowers there, when they went, and little saplings that bent to him. It was the only place on the Isle that she could remember being rife with color, from Sev's flowers. Everything else was unchanging, steely gray, from the sky to the stone of the cliffs to the angry expanse of the sea.

Far off in the distance, depending on where they were on the Isle, they could see Cleoc Strata or Scaela or Luthar or Eprain. There was only one bit, far up in the highest reaches of the Barrens, the part of the Isle uninhabited and covered by rocky cliffs and thin trees, where they could look out and see nothing but sea.

That's where I want to go, Sev said.

Where?

Anywhere but here.

She hadn't realized, when she was only a girl, how difficult it had been for Severin. In the tradition of the Isle, the heir to the title and its power would not be declared publicly until all children in consideration were fully grown. Until that came to pass, all eligible children were kept on the Isle for their own protection, apart from closely guarded diplomatic journeys. With seven years separating Grey and her brother, he had a long time to wait before he could officially either take up the role of Locke or leave the Isle and its customs behind for her to rule.

They never made it that far. The heir to the Isle was never revealed. On the mainland, it was assumed that Severin was the true heir, that he would inherit; after all, in the rest of Idistra, inheritance followed the right of primogeniture.

In Leota, there hadn't been much more in the way of forests. Cliffs overlooked the stony beach, and the rest was seagrass and scrubby old rock. She remembered the long ride to the training camps, her arm pressed to Kier's in the convoy as they wound toward the mountains, further from Locke than she'd ever been before. They stopped to stretch their legs and they were in the middle of a wood, trees stretching on either side and high above, so thick and dense that she worried they'd all fall in on her.

But now she'd been everywhere, seen every terrain Scaela had to offer. Forests were no longer unfamiliar, and she found she liked them. There was something peaceful here that she'd never found by the sea – she could move through the trees without her heart in her throat.

For years, she looked at every single view, forcing away that awful thought that Severin had never gotten to see any of it. That he died only really knowing the Isle.

Grey eased into the monotony of the watch and the pain of her own unceasing guilt, scanning the forest ahead, moving every so often. Her sword was drawn, but there was no need to use it.

When her joints were just beginning to ache, she heard a stirring in the wood. She searched for the source and saw Kier cutting through the brush before her. He slipped the note back to her, stub of graphite wrapped inside.

'Switch,' he said. Grey nodded and moved away. At her new post, she checked the note and frowned.

The girl's shoulder joint is unfused

MEANING? EXPLAIN LIKE I'M A CHILD

There was no point in saying she'd talked him through this process hundreds of times before purely out of boredom. Kier had not lived her life, her training: he had not been brought the bones of lost villages like she had; he had never been asked if there were children among the dead.

Twice more in the deep hours of night, they switched positions and notes. When Grey's eyes were heavy, she gripped the tether between them and sent two pulses of exhausted power in Kier's direction. She felt an answering two pulses and turned back to camp.

He caught her just outside the clearing and handed her the note. She skimmed over it.

Like a child: shoulder ball fuses to arm bone. Full fusion happens in late teens. The girl has too big a gap. Her bones are too young.

WHEN DID L GO?

16 yrs

IT'S ALMOST YOUR BIRTHDAY

She looked up at him, gaze steely. 'That's not the point.'

Kier shrugged. He took the note back, and with a fine twist of his fingers, the paper burned in a quick, flameless burst and crumbled to ash.

'She was probably a baby when Locke disappeared, if she was alive at all,' Kier said quietly. 'You got all of this from, what? *Bones?*'

'Mm.'

He sighed.

'To be discussed,' she said, turning back toward camp.

'To be shared?'

Grey hesitated. 'Not yet.'

She followed his tracks through the darkness back to camp. He roused Ola and Brit while she stretched out on her bedroll. The rough-spun shirt she wore was uncomfortable, but she'd deal: they each only had space for one other change of clothes in their packs, so she wouldn't switch until they had the time and means to properly wash.

Sela and Eron slept soundly, Eron snoring just slightly. After a moment of consideration, Grey abandoned her own bedroll and slipped into Ola's recently vacated pile of blankets instead, putting herself closer to Sela in case the girl tried to escape in the middle of the night. Years of training had made Grey a light sleeper. Plus, Ola's blankets were already warm.

Kier mirrored her, slipping into Brit's bedroll and turning on his side to look at Grey over Sela's head.

She looked back.

The corner of his mouth quirked up and she tried not to read too much into it, first because it was half scar tissue, after all; and second because they'd gone to sleep like this every night for years, face-to-face and sometimes closer, though never with someone between them like Sela was now. Maybe it was because they were out of camp and only three weeks of gruel and hiking stood between them and the rest of their lives, but she ached for him to reach out and push the hair out of her face like he sometimes did when they were on the edge of sleep, as if he couldn't bear to drift off without seeing her face.

Somehow, in the indeterminate haze of Eron's snoring and Sela's measured breathing and the liquid hazel of Kier's gaze, Grey fell asleep.

The situation in Idistra has become beyond unstable. It's their fault for destroying the very root of their power – I cannot think of a single other nation that would do something so unbelievably foolish. I will be surprised if any magic survives this war as the nation states continue to cannibalize. It's been years, and there's been no sign of that boy – chances are he's either far from here, or dead.

Nowhere in this damned island feels safe. Our own lord is still impulsive with his anger, and still bitter with grief.

Official report from Piotr Ralkonikov, Ruskayan ambassador to Scaela, 3 years PD

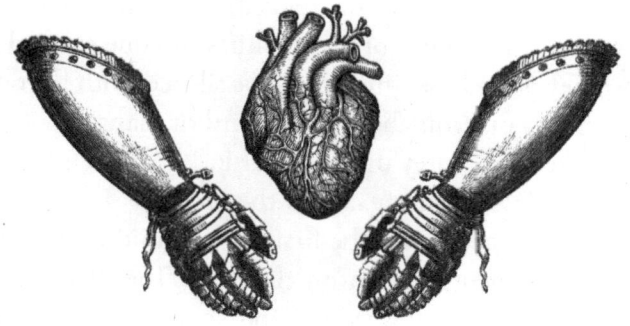

ten

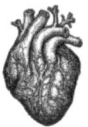

ℱOR THREE DAYS, THEY followed Kier and Ola's bickering ne-
gotiations through the forest. Grey found herself mildly amazed.
She herself had the directional awareness of a blindfolded toddler
dropped map-less into the middle of Nestria at all times, without
exception. She didn't know how either managed (though she couldn't
fully discount some odd magical transference from the number of
cartographers Kier had reportedly fucked). After the first day of mon-
otonous walking and night of watch shifts, no one seemed keen on
talking, so they passed the time in relative silence, with the occasional
remark from Ola or Eron about a nice bird or plant.

If Sela spoke at all, Grey did not hear it.

'Be on guard,' was all Kier said to the group.

When they stopped to eat the first of their mid-morning rations,
he showed Grey their location on the map. The distance between
them and the encampment was miserably short, the distance between
their location and Grislar frustratingly far, and they still had the
mountains to worry about.

'We'll have to pick up the pace,' he murmured to her.

Out of the woods, they kept carefully alert for signs of other travelers. They were on an infrequently used supply road, so it was hours

before they saw anyone else; even then, only a handful of travelers shared the road with them, and all traveled in the opposite direction. Few were going to the mountains at this time of year, when the shepherds were leading their flocks down from the hills, which made them more conspicuous than Kier liked, and on the morning of the fourth day, he directed them back to the wood, parallel to the road, until the trees ran out.

Grey's back ached so much that Kier kept eying her, clearly feeling her discomfort through the tether. When their afternoon rest came, he insisted on shouldering her pack. On the next bladder relief break, Grey was grimly unsurprised to find the onset of her monthly and instantly annoyed she'd given Kier her pack.

'Need something?' Eron asked, catching her grimace. He unshouldered his own pack and dug around in it for his pouch of supplies. 'Take what you need. Mine is finished.'

Grey thanked him with all the gratitude she could manage when caught with her trousers down.

When they rejoined the group, she allowed Kier to re-tether, cursing the sluggishness of her power and her craggy irritability, which possibly had more to do with the fact that she'd spent the better part of the week sleeping on the dirt and hadn't changed her clothes in as many days. Kier took one look at her face and sighed.

'I think,' he said, 'we need a supply run. A night in an inn, if we can. We'll be starting on the hills tomorrow – I want everyone rested.'

No one actively cheered, but the slackened shoulders and tired smiles were just as clear as any sign of relief. After Kier's declaration, he and Ola bent over the map, tracing along the path once more until he said, 'That'll do. There should be somewhere for travelers on the road to Pista.'

Grey had never heard of Pista. It wasn't a surprise – they were in the middle of the country, in the nowhere of farmers' fields, the exhausted recovery zone for those who couldn't be bothered with the fighting or who'd left the army years before but still grew the food and paid the taxes to support them.

They found an inn by late afternoon. It was alone, not even in a village, which was probably why Kier had chosen it.

'Will we be noticed here?' Grey asked.

He sighed. 'Hopefully not. It seems to only be travelers.' He didn't tell her that they were stopping because she was tired, grumpy and in pain and he wanted her to rest – he didn't have to.

She sighed, knocking her shoulder against his arm.

The windows of the tavern glowed with warmth, and the smell of roasting meat and grain was enough to send Grey's stomach grumbling the instant it hit her nose. The other four dragged two tables together while Grey and Kier went to the counter to enquire about rooms. There were a few others in the tavern, and Grey regarded them carefully as they waited: a pair of sunburned farmers with pints of ale in the corner and a woman and a child eating dinner near the door. Grey kept her eyes open, but she did not feel as if they were threatening.

The tavern keeper, when she appeared, was a bracing woman with a crooked nose and three fingers missing on her left hand. Ex-soldier, Grey surmised, based on both the missing fingers and the sword bolted to the wall behind the keeper's head, a twin to the ones Grey and Kier wore across their backs, except hers was mutilated and bent out of shape from some long-over battle.

'My companions and I are passing through. Do you have any rooms?' Kier asked in his soft, pleasant voice, the one Grey internally referred to as his 'charm the pants off your mother' tone. It had worked, unfortunately, on more than one mother and at least one father, though she could not confirm or deny if all had affinities for mapmaking.

The keeper eyed them shrewdly. 'What's the nature of your journey?' she asked in a voice sharp enough to cut glass.

Kier doubled down, leaning his arm against the counter, that smirk working up on his mouth. 'I've just been honorably released,' he said, not clarifying – there was only one profession that someone could be released from in Scaela. And though Kier was too young by far for release unless he'd been seriously injured, not all career-ending ailments were visible. 'My wife' – he put an arm around Grey and dragged her against him, and she ignored both the way her heart tripped at the title and the way he said it – 'and her sisters and their families – we're resettling. Looking for a patch of family land left in the mountains.'

It wasn't an unfamiliar story. Many a family estate had been abandoned when the children were sent to fight. Not all of them lived to return.

The innkeeper regarded them for a long moment. It made Grey uncomfortable, but the woman probably just didn't want to rent rooms to bandits, only for them to steal anything not bolted to the floor. She supposed this place had few other travelers.

She tried to look as innocent as possible, leaning further into Kier. His arm tightened around her.

The innkeeper nodded and opened a drawer full of keys. 'How many rooms?'

'Two will do,' Kier said, probably because he couldn't say *one* without her asking questions about how six adults would fit into a bed. 'We're not rife with resources at the moment.'

Another lie. Grey had seen the bulging mass of coin Attis had given Kier before their journey. They certainly had enough for three rooms – they had enough for each to have their own room, Sela included, but Sela had to be watched at all times, and someone had to stand guard, which would not work if they were split up.

Grey sighed, because Kier was a liar. Two rooms or not, she doubted he was going to let them split up: they were going to squeeze six adults into one bed and she just fucking knew it.

Once they had their keys and the tavern keeper was getting food and drink for everyone, Grey looked up, letting her nose skim the stubble of his jaw – he didn't usually like to go unshaven, and seeing him like this now, five days into an almost beard, was positively novel. 'Thrilling plans for the evening, husband?'

When he laughed, the sound hit her right in the stomach. He adjusted his arm around her waist, slipping it under her coat to pull her fast against him. He pressed a kiss to her temple that was mostly the vibration of his mirth against her skin, and because she had no sense at all, a shiver of excitement fluttered down her spine. 'I suppose you could tempt me.'

She rolled her eyes, pulling away before she could let her bruised, crumpled little heart believe him.

The tavern keeper returned with two pitchers of ale and a stack of glasses, saving Grey. She took the drinks back to the others and distributed them while Kier stayed behind to ask about the best places to get supplies, listening as the woman described the path to the next village over. Grey tried her best not to look at him as she settled into her seat, pretending to be interested in Eron and Ola as they debated the relative merits of knuckle guards over gloves.

She sat back, one hand around her ale, and forced herself back into sense.

Flirting wasn't new. They *always* flirted. And Kier was the kind of person who required affection for everything: when they were alone, he was always catching her hand or pulling her feet into his lap or rubbing her shoulders or sitting at her feet with his head on her thigh, and they barely went to sleep at night without him pressing his lips to her hand or her forehead or her temple. But that's how he was. How he always had been.

Beyond that? Nothing. He had always been her right hand, the other half of her, her best friend, the person she knew better physically and mentally than anyone else, and it was clear in every waking moment that he was just as dedicated to her. This was just ... this was the line they didn't cross.

It wasn't as if they spoke at length about their other dalliances or the nights they spent away from one another. It was just, sometimes he went out after sparring or a late-night patrol and came back in the small hours of the morning, hair wet from washing, and she forced herself not to say anything and was careful not to tether to him then in case any jealous emotions slipped through. She kept it for the light of morning, when it was easier to heckle him without her true feelings escaping.

It was just, she couldn't fault him. It was so good to feel alive, to feel someone *else* alive with them when they were so often staring death in the face. Between his rank and his annoyingly undeniable handsomeness, he was never short on offers. And she'd done the same, though not as often, sneaking off with someone like Leonie or a Hand from another company in the brief spans of time when she was certain Kier wouldn't need her, infrequent as those were. She just couldn't separate her heart from it unless she was desperate, but when she *was* desperate, it was almost easy. There happened to be, to her surprise and horror at sixteen, a *lot* of fucking in the army.

It was just, she wondered. He knew every single thing about her except for that clawing, desperate want. He knew the span of her power, the feeling of her vulnerability, her true name. And she wondered sometimes (more often than she'd ever admit to anyone, let alone herself) what it would be like to be with him.

And Grey was a liar too, because she longed for him. Endlessly, immeasurably, ceaselessly.

She pushed those thoughts away as Kier came closer, but it was like trying to beat back the rising tide. When he sat next to her, his leg casually pressed to hers, she actively considered death as an alternative.

Usually, it was easier to bear. It was the retirement looming, she decided; once they were no longer forced to be together, where would that leave them?

Her thoughts were interrupted by the arrival of food, and silence settled over the group as they ate their first non-beige meal in days. Grey was rather proud of herself for not making any noises of contentment over the thick stew and warm bread, even though the tender meat and potatoes seemed to melt against her tongue. It was far superior to their diet on the road of Eron's gruel and Grey's sneakily ingested dried fruit and strips of salted fish.

'I'm a disaster,' Eron announced, sighing.

Ola said, 'Generally, or . . . ?'

He sat back, groaning, hands on his stomach. Grey had also eaten too much too quickly. She adjusted, but that just pushed her further into Kier's side, so she decided it was easier to settle with the discomfort for now. 'Give me a new task. Reassign me,' Eron was saying. 'I can't cook for you.'

'That's why you're a soldier, not a cook,' Brit said. Grey kicked them under the table – they were not soldiers, not here.

'You didn't give us much of a choice,' Ola muttered.

' . . . Didn't you volunteer for the responsibility?' Kier asked around a sip of ale.

'I like feeling useful,' Eron lamented.

'You do a good job,' Sela said, 'with what you're given.'

That silenced whatever words were forming on Grey's tongue. She looked at the girl – they all were looking at her – as she ate delicately, in a way that made some alarm go off in Grey's brain. But she'd spoken. She'd spoken without prompting, and she'd been *nice* about it.

Sela looked up from her plate, saw their eyes on her and blushed deep red. 'Sorry, Captain,' she murmured, ducking her head.

'No, no, it's a good observation,' Kier said, taking another sip of ale. Grey knew the look in his eyes: he was calculating. She nearly kicked him under the table too.

Though they hadn't been able to speak in private beyond a few passed notes on their watch shifts, Grey knew the curiosity was killing him. They couldn't just announce that they knew Sela wasn't who she said she was, not without revealing that they knew something about Maryse of Locke that they shouldn't.

His eyes flicked to Grey's, brows arched. She sighed, but nodded. For now, for *this moment*, she could play nice.

'Speaking of responsibilities,' she said. 'After we finish here. Who is doing what?'

'Like, for the *quest*?' Brit asked, eyes sparkling.

'Absolutely not,' Grey said, because she still refused to consider this a quest. 'Replenishing our supplies.'

'Can you and Brit stay?' Eron asked. 'I can acquire the food – thank you for the encouragement, Sela – and Ola can get new clothing, if we can find it. Kier, you can be our devilishly handsome patron.'

'Kind way of asking me to throw my money around,' Kier said. 'And accepted.'

Grey swallowed hard. 'Ola should stay,' she said. 'I can go, if you need another set of hands.'

'Grey,' Kier said, 'you need to rest.'

She glanced up at him, betrayed. Even though he knew her exhaustion – she had not been hiding it, through the tether – she could not bear the idea of him going. 'Kier—'

'Please,' he said, a touch quieter.

The others looked at her. Kier's face was carefully blank, but of course he knew what she meant. She *hated* undermining his authority in public, even though he deferred to her in private more often than not. But if something went wrong, he wouldn't be able to pull power from Ola any more than he'd be able to pull it from a rock.

Grey swallowed. 'It's only,' she said, 'we should have enough here to fully guard our ... friend.'

'As always, my Hand is quite right,' Kier said smoothly. 'Ola, you stay. Grey, you're in charge.'

Grey thought about protesting further, but at Kier's look, her words died on her lips. Any more wrangling would cause suspicion.

But she didn't like letting him out of her sight, and though Eron was a good fighter – no, a *great* fighter – she wasn't sure how safe she felt about this.

'Any medical supplies?' Kier asked, sending a warm rush down the tether. *I'll be fine.*

'Bandages, probably,' Grey said, conceding. Because, after all, he was right. She was exhausted, and cramping, and irritable. 'Just in case.'

After they finished eating, they made their way up to the two rooms, and Grey was annoyingly grateful when Kier told them the plan: 'I want two on guard in the room with Sela, one in the bed with her – sorry, Sela, nothing personal ... '

'It absolutely is,' she muttered.

'You *stabbed Kier*,' Grey reminded her, in case anyone had forgotten, which earned her an exasperated look from her mage.

' ... and two off-duty sleeping in the other room. *Sleeping*. This is not the goddam army.'

Ola said, 'It very much is the goddam army.'

'I'm leaving all of you,' Kier announced, separating some of the coin into a smaller pouch, 'and walking directly into the sea.'

'That can be arranged,' Brit said from the corner, where they'd sat against the wall and gotten straight to oiling their sword.

Grey did her best not to smile. After days traveling, it was getting more and more difficult to remain distant from the retinue, as she usually did with other soldiers in her command – it was getting more and more difficult not to *like* them.

Liking them, caring about them – it was a vulnerability she could not afford.

Kier gave one more withering look before he went into the other room to put his pack down and lock up, and Grey was following before she could stop herself. She hesitated in the doorway.

'We'll take first watch again tonight,' he said, 'if that suits.'

'Will you be careful?'

There was something in her voice that made him look up at her, pausing in his search for something in his bag. 'Of course,' he said. 'I'm always careful.'

Another lie, but she swallowed this one.

He came close to her on his way out of the room, touching her hand with the barest brush of his fingertips. 'Two more weeks,' he promised, 'and then we're done. Wherever we want to go. Whatever we want to do.'

She nodded, ignoring all the questions that rose up in her heart at that statement.

He nodded back, the corner of his mouth tugging up, and then he was gone.

There were only so many blades to oil and sharpen, but Grey and Brit did them all, checking the edges on the clothes they planned to burn when they left this place. Ola got the innkeeper's permission to do the washing, and she went back and forth from upstairs to the wash house across the yard, paying for the use of it by doing some of the inn's linens alongside their clothing. Sela sat on a chair in the corner, watching them, then watching Ola through the window, but her gaze always returned to linger on Grey.

'How old are you?' she asked suddenly when they were halfway through.

'Who?' Brit asked.

'Both. Either?'

'Classified,' Grey said.

'Twenty-nine,' Brit said with only a small, withering look at Grey.

'This is the knife you stuck in Kier's intestines,' Grey said cheerfully, holding up one of the short blades, letting it glimmer in the light.

Sela blushed, chewing on her lip. 'I don't think it is,' she said, voice small. 'I seem to recall the handle was black, and that one is navy.'

'My mistake. Perhaps this is the one intended for *your* intestines.'

'Hand . . . Grey,' Brit chided.

Grey set the blade aside, leaning back against the bed. They were all sitting on the far side of the room, away from the door, Sela in the furthest corner. It was hard not to feel restless with Kier gone, but Grey really had been trying even as she counted the minutes in her head: it was meant to be less than an hour to Pista, then an hour for purchases and errands, and the return journey home. Eron and Kier were trained soldiers, deadly, armed and aware.

'I'm going to check on Ola and get a pitcher of water,' she announced. 'Will you be okay in the meantime?'

Brit, another trained, deadly, armed, aware soldier, rolled their eyes. 'Yes,' they snapped.

Grey strapped on her sword out of muscle memory, then locked them in just in case and took the key with her. She felt . . . odd. Uncomfortable. Uncertain why. Sure, she'd been tethered to Kier for the better part of a week, even if he wasn't pulling power from her, and that was longer than they usually went without a break. But she thought the absence of the tether had more to do with it. Their range, though much larger than other pairs, spanned about the size of Mecketer; a half-mile at most. Kier was on his own, and so was she.

She found Ola sweating over the crank-operated washbasin. It was so loud that Grey had to shout to ask the other woman if she wanted help or needed anything, and Ola only waved her away with a half-smirk. Grey made her way back across the yard, now understanding perfectly the distance between the wash house and the tavern.

She went back to the dining area and leaned against the counter. There were two men there, too, leaning further down, squabbling over a little bag. Grey sighed, digging her nails into the wood. She wished there was water out that she could just take, so she could hurry and return upstairs and away from the men and the coins they were laying out on the counter . . .

Accents. The little group arguing next to her spoke common

Idistran, the language shared by all nations on the island, but they spoke it in Luthrite accents.

Grey froze. Inconspicuously, she tried to look harder, cursing herself for not paying closer attention.

The coins on the counter were auros – gold Luthrite coins. Back when the nations were allied, auros would be accepted here just as easily as Scaelan ornen, with a direct one-to-one exchange rate. But since the wars, no one in Scaela would accept Luthrite auros. No one in Scaela would even *carry* auros, let alone take them out in a public place. They must've brought them from Luthar directly.

And by her calculations, by the place Kier had pointed to on the map, they were many days' walk from Luthar. Perhaps they were merchants, but this was a sleepy inn with no village, and there was no reason for them to be here . . . unless.

Unless someone else had evaluated all paths from Mecketer to Grislar and sent packs out to hunt.

Unless they had noticed that Pista was the last large market village before one reached the easiest of the mountain passes, and decided that a retinue moving quickly would aim for it, too.

One of the men was looking at her, taking in the tension of her jaw, the grip of her hands on the counter. She knew what they were seeing immediately: her age, her bearing, her scars. Her hand went to her hip unconsciously – and she realized she wore her sword there, like a soldier, instead of across her back like a merchant or traveler. Muscle memory.

So much for being undercover.

The tavern keeper returned with two glasses of ale and took the men's Scaelan money – Grey didn't miss how one of them shuffled off all the Luthrite, stuffing it in his pockets.

'Your husband left a tab open,' the woman said cheerfully, turning to Grey. 'Can I get you anything?'

One of the men said something to the other. They made their way to a third and fourth, sitting at the back table.

'Just water,' Grey said, her voice small and awkward. 'If you please.'

The innkeeper nodded, turning back to get glasses. 'Busy day we're having,' she said to Grey, maybe to no one. 'Not often so many travelers rolling through at this time of year. Where did your husband say you were going? Coastal, right?'

Grey's fingers dug into the counter. The men were clearly listening. She itched, above all, to run. 'No,' she said, smiling as the woman offered her the pitcher and glasses.

The innkeeper grabbed her wrist. 'Ah, well these folks said they're heading to Grislar. They were asking around if there was anyone here heading to the coast, looking to share resources. Wasn't sure if you were going that way, too.'

There was something in her voice. She'd noticed Grey's sword, and probably Kier's. Perhaps she'd even heard Sela call Kier *Captain*. Whatever she'd observed, she did not trust the men in the corner, and neither did Grey.

Behind her, she felt a shift, a fizzle, a change as one of the mages tethered to their well.

'Thanks,' she said. She turned on her heel and headed back through the doors that led to the rooms. There was no time to warn Ola, let alone retrieve her. As soon as the door swung shut behind her, Grey dashed up the stairs.

Lesson one of protecting your mage: you have no natural advantages. Train to fight as if there is no difference between you and a typic. In a battle situation, even with your mage's abilities, you have only your own blade, your own body's strength, your own combat skills. Do not shirk this training.

Wielding Power, Volume 1: Third Edition, revised PD

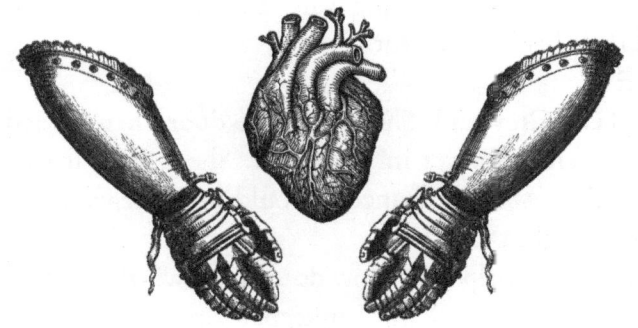

eleven

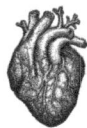

'TUTHRITE TRACKERS DOWNSTAIRS,' SHE said as she burst through the door, spilling water all down her shirt. Brit looked up from their blade, brow furrowed.

'What?'

'Move fast,' Grey said. She locked the door, then started to drag the flimsy wardrobe over in front of it. She wished it was heavier, sturdier – there was no chance it would hold. 'If we can't get out, we'll have to fight them.'

Brit jumped to help her. 'How do you know?' they asked.

'How they spoke. Coin. Innkeeper tipped me off,' she said through gritted teeth. 'Doesn't matter if I'm being paranoid – I'm not taking any fucking chances.' She examined the window, the drop below, but the garden was fenced all along, and there was no sign of a gate. Plus, if they ran, she wasn't sure she'd be able to lead them back to Kier.

It was better to fight. Leave no survivors.

'Are they here for us?' Sela asked. She stood uselessly on the other side of the room, her hands fluttering like she didn't know what to do with them.

She's a kid, Grey chided herself. For all her annoyance, that fact still hung heavy in her stomach. Whoever Sela was, *what*ever Sela was, she was just a kid.

'Don't worry,' she said. 'We'll deal with it. Now get down. Away from the window. In that corner, under the desk.'

Sela nodded, but Grey could see the panic in her face. Grey flipped the desk so the top protected Sela's body, so she could curl up in the middle of it and be safe on all sides. She dumped the weapons they wouldn't use with the girl. Those cool blue eyes peered up at her, devoid of any of the arrogance she'd had in camp. This time, Sela was scared.

It was only because she was listening very carefully that she heard the boots on the stairs.

'Captain?' Brit murmured.

'Tether to Ola,' she instructed.

Brit looked away. 'She's not reaching, and I can't initiate the tether myself at this range. I have to tether to you.'

Grey swore – she *couldn't* tether to Brit. She threw open the window and shouted Ola's name. There was no response. She swore again.

'Swords,' she said. They both drew, and Grey grabbed a dagger for good measure – the room wasn't *that* big, and swords weren't always great in proximity. Brit armed themselves with some assortment of metal; Grey didn't question it.

Someone knocked on the door. 'Ma'am?' a voice said. Not the innkeeper.

Brit and Grey exchanged a long look. Brit, too, drew their knife.

Another knock. Someone tried the doorknob. 'We'd like to compare routes, if you please. We think we're going in the same direction.' Their tone was silk over glass, tension clear in every word as they tried to smooth out their accent, to sound Scaelan.

'No thank you,' Grey called back firmly.

'I'm reaching a tether,' Brit said, and Grey felt a strange sense of prodding, like her stomach was the closed door of the room Brit was knocking at. An odd expression flickered across Brit's face.

Something rammed the door – it held. Muted voices conversed on the other side.

'Hand Captain?' Brit asked.

Grey's terror was cold and even. 'I . . . can't,' she said.

'I won't use—'

'No,' Grey said, facing the truth of it – the truth of what they'd done. 'Brit, Kier and I are bound. I *can't* lend my power to another.'

Brit's eyes were blank for a terrible time. 'Well, *fuck*,' they murmured. 'I had a thought when you wouldn't let Ola . . . *Fuck*.'

Something hit the door again, and Grey heard the cracking of wood. She thought again of calling for Ola and dismissed it. 'Hope you're just as good with your sword,' she muttered, sinking into position. 'We've got to get out of here without your magic.'

'When the captain gets back,' Brit seethed, 'we are going to have a long discussion about trust.'

'If we're still alive, I look forward to it.'

Grey didn't need a tether to know Brit was furious. It wasn't that they couldn't fight – but mages *liked* the edge of magic, and they were taught to fight with it as another limb. It would be awkward and uncomfortable for Brit to go without it.

But there wasn't time. Something else hit the door, cracking it fully. Brit jumped back as a boot kicked down the dresser, and managed to get in the first hit, stabbing out as someone tried to enter. There was a howl of pain in the hall.

'You have two minutes,' a voice called. 'Surrender the girl or die.'

'What girl?' Grey shouted.

There was another murmur from the hall. Grey felt the swell of magic building, and before she could warn Brit, the door and wardrobe exploded in a shatter of wood. Grey threw a hand in front of her face to protect her eyes.

'Fucking *materialists*,' Brit groaned – ironic, because Brit too was a fucking materialist.

Grey only had time to bring her hand down and duck out of the swing of a blade. The air was heavy with the sound of metal on metal and the ashy smell of magic – there were four of them, probably two mages and two wells, and she was so incandescently angry that she hadn't forced Ola to stay inside, that she had been so preoccupied with being separated from Kier that she hadn't kept the other pairing together, that she hadn't *thought*. Just past her own fight, Brit dodged a hit, rolled over the bed and took a lunging swing at one of their opponents that caught them in the shoulder.

Grey gritted her teeth, leaning into the blow she blocked, swinging forward with her off-hand. She caught the man in the ribs, a deep hit that made him suck a breath through his teeth. He withdrew, stumbling back. Grey lunged forward again, driving lower than he expected, getting him in the stomach – he fell to his knees, that flash of disaster clear in his eyes, and she felt the fizzle of a snapped tether.

'Flynn.'

She turned just in time to catch the slash on her arm instead of her back, which hurt like a *bitch* but wouldn't kill her.

'This would be so much fucking easier,' Brit seethed, bleeding from their forehead, 'with *magic*.'

Grey blocked another blow and hazarded a glance at the mage, who'd been forced into a corner.

'Tether!'

The small voice caught them both off guard enough that Grey nearly missed a block and Brit did – but it didn't matter, because Grey felt the new strand of magic as Sela pushed her power forward and Brit latched on.

'Drop!' they shouted, and then the metal shavings they had clenched in one fist went flying through the room at a killing speed. Grey hit the floor, face-down, covering her head with both hands as the metal pattered around her and at least two more bodies thudded to the ground.

Silence rang in the air. She smelled blood, and felt the sweet aftermath of worn-out power even as her own well brimmed overfull with adrenaline.

She opened her eyes. One of the Luthrite soldiers was on the ground next to her, their face half obliterated by metal. For that force of an explosion, that much projection, Sela was probably spent.

Grey sat up, wiping the blood away from her face, taking careful stock. The four soldiers were dead. The desk Sela had hidden behind was a mess of wood splinters, but she could hear the girl crying, so at least she was alive. It was Brit she focused on, slumped over the bed, breathing hard.

'Brit?' She pushed herself up, stepping over a body. She pulled the mage over onto their back – their eyes were wild with pain. Blood dripped down their forehead; another wound soaked their sleeve, and there was one more that Grey couldn't see across their ribs.

'You didn't tell us,' Brit said, staring straight up at the ceiling.

Grey did not cry – she'd lost that instinct to cry in the face of danger years ago – but she did curse fantastically under her breath. She opened Brit's shirt, slicing through buttons with her bloody knife, and took in the injuries. The one across Brit's ribs was deep but she didn't think it had punctured anything important; there was another just to the side of their navel, not deep enough to pierce the gut, but she could not fully tell without inspecting further.

'Sela,' she said very carefully. 'Are you okay?'

'Um.' The girl sniffled, trying to breathe through sobs that racked her body. 'I don't . . . I'm not . . . I'm not bleeding.'

'Good. Sela, dear heart, can you do something for me?' Grey had a choice to make: concentrate on Brit or worry about Sela. If the girl wanted to run – well. She was more trouble than she was worth. And though her own retirement hung in the balance, though Kier might actually kill her if she lost the prisoner, she wasn't going to let Brit die. She pressed a firm hand to the worst of their wounds to staunch the bleeding.

'I think,' Sela said. Grey glanced over at her. She was standing now, breathing heavily, probably in the middle of a panic attack. When her eyes landed on Brit, half unconscious under Grey, then on the body of a soldier close to her on the ground, the blood drained from her face.

Grey held out a key. 'Don't look at them. Sela, next door, my bag is on the bed. I need my kit from it. The one with salves and herbs and antidotes – you'll know it when you see it. It's okay to bring the whole bag. I'll need you to do a few other things and then I'll send you for Ola, okay?'

'Okay,' Sela said. She took the key. Grey wondered, her thoughts fuzzy with adrenaline and the pain of the fight, if she would regret this.

She couldn't think of that now.

With the girl fetching her kit, Grey got to work. She moved around Brit, stripping the bed to the top sheet to give herself a level surface. She dragged the bodies into a pile in the corner, swearing profusely at the waves of blood that drenched her shirt as a result, and draped a sheet over them – the others could deal with them later. Grey hurried downstairs, not caring about the sound of her boots on the ground. The inn was eerily quiet, empty – the door was locked from the inside, covered with a heavy crossbar. She found the innkeeper, collapsed on the other side of the bar. Grey paused for a moment to check her breathing, her heartbeat; she didn't wake when Grey kicked her arm, so she must've been poisoned or ingested a sleeping draught.

There was no time to worry about it. Grey dragged the woman into a back room, then stole the keys from behind the bar and locked the innkeeper in just in case.

Then she steeled herself and returned to the room where Brit lay.

Amazingly, the pitcher hadn't been shattered by Brit's improvised projectiles. Grey pulled off the pillowcases and dipped them in the water, using them to clean the blood from Brit's wounds. They were breathing shallowly now, eyes closed.

Sela returned with the med kit and sat quietly on the night table in the corner, as far away from the bodies as she could get, even though her eyes kept flicking to the pile – the white sheet was starting to stain red in places.

'Sela?' Grey said, washing her hands thoroughly with water and soap powder.

'Yes?'

'I want you to breathe.' Grey said as carefully as she could, trying to keep her own voice from shaking. She found a jar of numbing salve among her medicines. 'Breathe in for five counts, then out for five. Can you do that?'

'Yes,' the girl said. Grey listened, timing her own breathing to Sela's as she numbed the areas around Brit's wounds.

'How are you feeling?' she asked.

'My stomach hurts.'

Grey's hand stilled, halfway through her kit. 'You weren't trained, were you? You're a well, but you don't know how to do it.'

The answering silence was so loud that she had to glance up to make sure the girl hadn't passed out. Finally, 'Yes.'

Grey nodded. She took a second to assess. Brit was still breathing, and there was nothing blocking their airway.

'Okay. I need you to go get Ola. Once she's here, you can sit with us or on the stairs and wait to let the others in. Okay?'

'Yes,' Sela squeaked. She hesitated for only a moment. 'Will they live?' she asked.

Grey glanced up. Sela stood with her hands pressed to her chest, like something had wounded her. She had a scrape across one cheek, Grey noticed, but it had missed the eye.

'If I have anything to say about it, yes.' She forced her tone to soften. 'It will be okay, sweetheart. Go get Ola.'

Sela was out the door in a second, and Grey glanced over her shoulder to make sure the girl ran across the yard into the wash shed. Then she spent an agonizing minute cataloguing everything that could go wrong.

A moment later, Ola appeared, running across the yard. Sela followed, not as fast, still shaky on her feet.

Grey turned back to her work.

The worst of the injuries was the slash across Brit's ribs, then the wound on their stomach. The arm was gruesome to look at, but overall fine, and the head wound looked much worse than it actually was. Grey could worry about a concussion after she was certain none of Brit's insides were about to become their outsides.

'What the *fuck*?'

She lifted her head to see Ola in the doorway, but she needed to focus. Her hands were shaking, half from fading adrenaline. Though she'd helped in the infirmary often, it had been a while since she'd actively operated on anyone who wasn't Kier. She forced herself to remain calm now, to think only of her training and those endless days of surgery after surgery when she was a healer. She didn't have the tools to keep Brit unconscious and cursed herself for it, but she could only work with what she had.

'I need you to tether,' Grey said very carefully.

'*Locke's bones*, Captain—'

'*Tether*,' Grey hissed through her teeth. She noticed Sela edge into the room behind Ola. The girl went very quietly back to the night-stand and sat with her knees pressed to her chest.

Ola narrowed her eyes, but Grey could feel the greenness of new magic as the tether took. 'Yes, Hand Captain.'

Brit sighed in relief, their face relaxing just a fraction. Ola sat at their head, her hand pressed to Brit's uninjured arm.

'Can you remain tethered and secure downstairs?' Grey asked, detached as possible. 'I didn't have the time to do a thorough search.'

A pause. Then, 'Yes, Hand Captain,' Ola said, brimming with anger.

Neither wound had perforated the internal organs, but they were still serious. Grey cleaned them up, nudging the threads of Ola's magic to heal what she could, and carefully stitched Brit's stomach. Ola returned when she was tying off the thread, settling back into the space next to Brit.

'Why didn't you have them tether to Sela immediately?' she asked, her voice strained and bitter. 'Isn't Locke meant to be some great well? Some unbelievable power?'

Grey froze, her breath caught in her throat. She looked up at Sela – but the girl only hid her face.

'I cannot answer that,' Grey said through her teeth. She went back to her work, her own heart pounding with the lies she held.

When she was finished, she moved to the wound over Brit's ribs. She focused on bringing the muscle together, then the flesh; she forced herself to think only of that, and not of Sela sobbing in the corner, or of Ola's hard, unforgiving glare.

If she stopped, she was going to fall apart, or throw up. She'd lost so much fucking blood herself and she couldn't even tell if Brit was dying under her.

'What's going on?'

Grey lifted her head to see Eron in the door, shock clear on his face. She couldn't deal with it right now.

'Where's Kier?' she asked, tying off her knot and examining her work.

'Downstairs.' He grimaced, and Grey thought again of the inn-keeper; she wasn't sure if she was awake, or even still alive.

'Can I just ... What the *fuck*?' Eron repeated, as if they had not heard him the first time, as if Grey had the capacity to answer. She was busy adhering a strip of gauze to Brit's forehead.

'Can you take Sela into the other room?' she asked. 'And – Kier. I need Kier.'

It was only then that her voice broke. As if he sensed it, the tether she'd been reaching out found its mark. Kier caught her, and before she could stop herself, she sent a pulse of agony through. *Help.*

Boots sounded on the stairs, then in the hall. Then, a quiet inhale in the doorway. 'Eron, can you help me with the bodies?'

Kier's voice, calm and sure, always so much better with emergen-cies than she was. Grey finished her work on Brit's forehead and cut away their jacket, revealing the slice to their arm. It was not deep enough for stitches, merely a graze.

A hand landed on her shoulder. 'Are you okay?'

She did not look at him. If she looked at him, it would all be over. 'Yes,' she said. 'The keys are on the nightstand by Sela. I don't know if the innkeeper is dead or just unconscious.'

'I'll handle it.'

He brushed the hair away from her forehead. She swabbed gently at the blood crusting around Brit's wound. Ola had shifted closer to their head, humming softly as she fed a constant thread of power into them.

Grey finished at around the same time Kier and Eron removed the last of the bodies, and Eron took Sela into the other room. She looked up to find Ola's eyes, hard as flint.

'Why didn't you give them power?' Ola asked, clearly seething.

Before Grey could answer, Kier said, 'Now's not the time. Can I trust you to keep watch in here for a moment?'

Ola looked up at him, silhouetted in the doorway. Her mouth thinned into a line. 'Yes, Captain,' she said very quietly.

'Good. Hand, bring your supplies.'

Grey packed the kit with shaking fingers. Kier had already disappeared down the hall, but the door was open to a new room – the six of them were the only ones there, so she figured he'd commandeered an empty room. She walked in to find him sitting on a chair he'd dragged to the bed.

'Are you hurt?' he asked, his eyes catching on her blood-soaked sleeve.

'Not mortally wounded, no.'

'Take off your coat,' he said, all authority. 'And shirt. Please.'

Grey didn't know what to do – what to say. The tether between them was unbroken, but he didn't pull from her, nor did he send anything through. It just sat heavy on her chest, her power unspent.

So she did as he asked. She shrugged off her coat, biting back a sob at the pain in her arm, and unbuttoned and discarded her shirt with one hand. He did not look at her face when she sat in front of him in her vest.

'I . . . You know more than me,' Kier said. 'What do you need? Stitches?'

Grey forced herself to look, breathing in through her mouth and out through her nose. 'It's deep,' she said. 'There's gauze in there – yes, take that, and the soap there.' Her voice felt very far away as Kier shuffled through the kit, picking up the items she indicated. 'Clean your hands, then me. It will hurt.'

'Okay,' he said. He disappeared for the barest moment to retrieve an ewer and basin. She focused on her breathing, watching him as he washed his hands before turning his attention to cleaning her skin. When he rubbed at the wound, she gritted her teeth against any noise that threatened to escape – the world went white in a frizzle of electric pain around her. When she came back to herself, her fingers were gripping Kier's thigh so very tightly. Her mouth tasted of blood – her teeth had pierced her lip.

Despite her reactions, Kier hadn't stopped. His face was close to her wound; it was still leaking blood. He wiped it away in a pink smear of salve and blood.

'Let me see,' she said.

'I don't think,' Kier said very carefully, 'a kiss will heal it.'

Her laugh was cloudy with the lump firmly lodged in her throat. She took in the wound: when it was cleaned, it didn't look so deep. 'I think it's okay if you just wrap it very tightly,' she said.

He looked at her, finally, and she saw the raw guilt on his face. He hadn't been angry at her at all. 'If that wound was on me, would you be satisfied with wrapping it?'

She chewed on the inside of her lip. 'No.'

Kier nodded. He found a fresh needle, thread. He'd patched her up many times, bandaging wounds she couldn't reach herself, rubbing antiseptic salves and ointments into her skin, getting her stable if anything major happened during a battle, which it almost never did. But for anything more serious, she'd always gone to the infirmary – it had nothing to do with Kier's experience or lack thereof; even though he'd watched her do stitches so many times, he probably knew how to as well as she did.

'Anesthetic, please. That greenish-gray salve, in the pot with the blue lid,' Grey said, looking at the wall. He rubbed the salve over the edges of her wound, the catch of his rough fingers making her hiss.

'Sorry,' he murmured. She didn't look as he prepared, but she *felt* it when he started stitching.

It wasn't his fault – actually, it absolutely *was* his fault that it hurt as much as it did. She sucked a breath through her teeth, her nails digging into his thigh, feeling every single puncture of the needle, every tug of the thread.

'You're doing so well,' he murmured, pausing to wipe a tear from her cheek.

'Keep going,' she snarled. 'Get it done. Quickly.'

Halfway through, she dropped her head to his shoulder, numbing to the ceaselessness of the pain. Finally, he tied off the knot and cut the thread and his arms were around her.

'Fuck you,' she said into his neck, wet with her tears.

'I'm sorry. I'm so, so sorry.'

His arms tightened, one wrapped around her bare back, one tangled up in her sweat-and-blood-filthy hair.

'I shouldn't have gone,' he said. 'I shouldn't have left.'

With her good arm, she curled herself around him. He tugged her, pulling her off the bed, onto the chair, onto his lap. He moved one arm down, draping it over her thighs, hand under her knees, holding her against him.

'I nearly killed Brit and Sela,' Grey said against his skin.

'It wasn't your fault,' Kier said.

It didn't matter; it didn't dull the pain. She couldn't remember the last time she'd cried, and she didn't now. She only hid her face in Kier's neck, as if burying herself in him could solve anything at all.

She didn't remember falling asleep. When she woke, she was curled in bed with Sela at her back, in the second room they'd had originally. Grey turned and looked over to find Brit arranged on another mattress on the floor, Ola curled up next to them.

She sat up, the blanket dropping to her waist. She was in a clean shirt that smelled like Kier, her arm aching. The captain himself sat by the window, looking out. Eron perched cross-legged in front of the door.

Kier glanced up at her, the early-morning light illuminating the dark shadows under his eyes.

'How long did I sleep?' she murmured, pitching her voice low so as not to wake the others.

'A while,' Kier said. 'You needed it.'

She slid out of bed. He'd taken off her trousers, too, stained with blood as they were – she wore only the shirt and her own shorts. 'Give me a moment to sort myself out, then I'll take over watch.'

'You should keep resting.'

Grey leveled a look at him. They'd talked about this. 'You need sleep. You too, Eron. I can handle it.'

She didn't wait for protest. She grabbed her supply bag and wash kit and made her way to the small washroom on the second floor. The door to the room where Kier had stitched her up was ajar, and the room where they'd fought had no door at all. Grey hesitated in the empty entry, taking in the bloodstains on the bed where she'd tended to Brit, the dark marks soaked into the wood floor where the bodies had lain. She shuddered, moving on down the hall.

In the washroom, she changed over her padding – honestly, after all the fucking drama the day before, the fact she was still bleeding was a travesty – and took stock of Kier's stitches. They weren't necessarily neat, and she imagined the scar would be ghastly, but they would get the job done. She looked at her face in the glass, taking in the tangle of her hair and the flaking spots of dried blood on her skin.

I am the High Lady of Locke, she thought as she took in her reflection, nearly cracking into a fit of hysteria.

She rinsed her skin with water and tried to brush out the tangles before giving up. She needed to bathe properly, but there would be time for that when everyone was better rested.

Back in the room, Eron lay on the bed next to Sela and Kier was curled up in the corner in a nest of blankets.

'You sure you're okay?' Kier asked her. He handed over a pair of trousers from the pile of clothes near the door. Someone must've gone back for Ola's washing and hung it to dry. They were still a bit damp, and too big. She cinched them around her waist with her sword belt.

'I need time,' she said. It was as honest as she could handle being right now. She locked the door behind her, checked it twice.

She found her sword in a heap of her pack and bloodstained clothing. She sat in the chair Kier had vacated and rested it across her knees.

'Not too long,' Kier said, eyes slipping shut.

'Whatever you say, Captain.'

No well shall complete the unification process, known colloquially as 'binding', with a mage without explicit written consent, approved by the High Lord. If any mage-and-well pairing is found to be unlawfully bound, they shall face a trial of their peers and receive sentencing. Depending on the circumstances, recommended punishment is imprisonment, forced separation, or, in the most extreme of cases, execution.

The Diplomatic Articles of Scaela, Article 3, Addendum 8

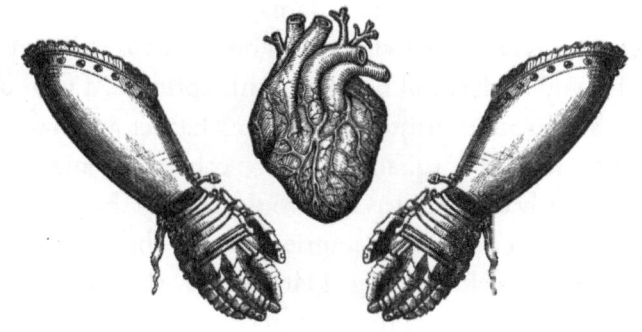

twelve

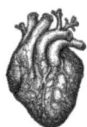

GREY WAS TWENTY THE first and only time Kier used too much of her. They were in the east, fighting both Eprain and Luthar in equal measure. The Eprainish were a particularly nasty lot: they trained mages for as much internal damage as possible, so walking into the battlefield was an open invitation for one's organs to be eviscerated. Kier was heavily in demand because of his aptitude, a feral dog on a leash that their captain insisted on pushing harder and harder.

They commanded a squad of twelve others, six mages and six Hands, constantly changing as they couldn't keep them from getting injured. She'd never seen Kier angrier than in those days, spending long hours on the field holding their ground, then ages in middle-command meetings as captains and masters who hadn't set foot on the battlefield in years yelled about strategy. It was in that time that they stopped caring about tears, and at night she did not comment if his eyes were damp when they sparred after day after day of death surrounding them.

'How many can you take? Quickly?' the captain, a rugged and scarred man with a propensity for drink, asked them at the end of every meeting.

'With magic or force?'

'Magic. Don't fuck with me, Seward.'

'Four,' Kier said, voice sturdy, always. 'Five at a push.'

'Not good enough,' the captain growled, even though the answer never changed. 'If you can't take eight, you shouldn't be a lieutenant.'

They practiced, when they had time: Kier drew from her until the pain of emptiness brought tears to her eyes, until the power could come from her in great ropey lengths. They made it through battles where Kier destroyed six hearts at a time, then seven. She felt each one of them like a quiet supernova within her, wrenching her insides apart.

It happened after he'd used too much of her, after he'd destroyed too many hearts and nearly torn apart her own. They'd been on a bluff, their backs against the wall, too many of the enemy – outnumbered, half their mages dead – and she'd felt the ice in her stomach as cool and depthless as the sea below the cliffs of the Isle.

She turned – trying to cover him, trying to keep him safe, trying to get out alive. But when she turned back, he was not there. If he wasn't still tethered to her, she would've been certain he was dead.

There was another mage, one of the Eprainish, his face half blood. He hadn't even hesitated when he saw the black trim around the Scaelan seal she wore on her chest. He lowered his sword and grabbed her throat, slamming her back into the cliffside. He lifted her, her feet scrabbling for purchase as she dropped her sword, as her hands went to his as if she could peel him off her neck.

'Fucking *bitch*,' he snarled, and that was when she felt it – a tether pushed at her. She tried to bat it away, but she couldn't breathe, and she lost the tether with Kier entirely. When she went to reconnect with him, blind with panic that this was it, he was dead, it was all too slippery and she couldn't focus. She found a tether and grasped it.

The mage's smile grew in front of her. But then something flickered in his eyes: recognition. Understanding. He started to pull from her, power that she didn't want to relinquish, and the pain was so great that she nearly lost consciousness. He slammed her against the cliff again, and Grey felt everything inside of her giving up, shutting down.

Severin, she thought desperately. *Severin, I'm dying.*

Maryse, someone said, very far away.

She fought. She grappled for the knife in her belt and tried to stab at the man's arm, but she was too weak, and everything was going shadowy and uncertain. Then she was covered in blood, warm and metallic, and the mage's face changed. She only just realized that his throat had been cut; she was covered in *his* blood. His hands went slack on her, and she fell, sliding down the wall, crumpled at the bottom. The unwanted tether snapped.

Kier kicked the body aside. He dropped to his knees in front of her, his hand cupping her head. Everything hurt. It hurt so much she couldn't think past it.

'Grey?' he asked, shaky and terrified.

She gripped his surcoat, the blood leaving a mark on the coarse fabric. 'Take it,' she murmured, tethering to him and pushing as much power at him as she could. The surge rushed through her so hard she choked as she gritted through her teeth, 'Take it all. Get us home.'

And he had.

Grey didn't know what happened nor how Kier got her back to camp after, but she slept for three days straight, interrupted often as healers monitored her concussion, and spent two more in the infirmary under careful watch.

He came to her on the evening of the second day, his eyes dark with grief and something else she didn't recognize. It took Grey a moment to realize that he was ashamed. 'I've applied for reassignment,' he said.

'Where are we going?' Grey asked, barely able to speak through the tightness in her throat. She'd glanced in the mirror, once, and nearly wept at the bruising. She hated the way he looked at her, as if he expected her to recoil, to fear him – as if he himself had bruised her.

'We're not,' he said, deflated. 'I've asked for retraining. And for a new Hand.'

Grey sat up so fast her head spun, so fast she knocked her forehead against his chin and hissed at the sudden burst of pain. 'Hand Lieutenant!' one of the healers nearby shouted. 'Watch yourself.'

Grey waved him off. 'What have I done wrong?' she asked Kier, unable to keep the devastation out of her voice. 'Send me for retraining, or ... I don't know, Kier, you have to—'

'It's not you,' he said, taking a quick glance around, his hands fluttering above her shoulders like he wasn't sure how to touch her but couldn't keep himself from trying. 'Dear heart, Hand ...' He winced, as if her station brought back all the things she'd sacrificed for him, and looked away. 'Grey,' he said unsteadily. 'It's not you. I can't keep doing this.'

She shook her head, gripping his hands to stop his fluttering. 'No. Don't. You're not—'

'I've requested medical dismissal on your behalf. Go home, Grey. Don't come back.'

'Kier—'

'I'll send my wages. Stay with our mothers, and when I can leave my contract, I'll come.'

She didn't care who saw. She gripped the back of his head, vise-like, and drew his forehead to hers, nose to nose. Her hair was lank and greasy, falling in her face, but he just pushed it back like always. He was always so careful with her.

'You would be so much safer,' Kier said, 'away from me.'

'Don't ask that of me.'

His hands were at her waist, gripping the coarse fabric of her shirt. 'He stole your power, Grey. I can't even think of that kind of violation without getting ...' She heard the anger rising in his voice. He took a deep breath and continued, 'He knew who you were, *what* you were, when he tethered. I will *not* risk you again. The things I wish I could say to you ...' He caught himself again. 'Losing you, living without you would be a fate worse than death.'

She shook her head. She couldn't think of it, of the invasion of that other tether. It made her sick to remember it. 'I don't ... I can't. It's just, with the tether as it is, it's so slippery sometimes. It's hard to manage. Hard to grasp. Because there's you, and then sometimes the power goes elsewhere in offshoots, and I can't hold it in battle – but Kier, if it was *just you*, if I could guarantee that ...'

He'd gone very, very still under her hands. 'You want to bind to me.'

She chewed on her lip. They'd spoken about it before, on other assignments that hadn't felt so life-or-death – to bind oneself to a single mage, to limit power like that, was so dangerous … but it changed the quality of magic entirely. She could give him so much more, and he'd be able to take with abandon. There were other rumors, about the power of a bond: they'd be able to communicate without words, pushing feelings along the tether. It wouldn't feel like a fraying rope between them, but like a strong tie, a knot.

But.

If they were bound, she wouldn't be able to use her power on another mage – those tethers would be closed to her unless Kier died. And he would never be able to use another well. His tether would only work for her, would only seek her. It didn't matter if *she* died – he would only ever be able to use her. If she died before him, in battle or in age, he would never be able to do magic again.

He leaned back, cupping her face.

'You can't want that.'

'It would be a protection,' Grey said quietly. 'For me.'

Kier studied her face. They both knew what she could not say, not in public: to bind to her was to bind to Locke.

'You'd really do it.'

Her voice was fierce, insistent as she laced her fingers through his. 'There's nothing I want more. Only you, Kier. No reassignments. No retraining. Bind to me, take what I have. Let me be your Hand in earnest.'

'And what about you?' he murmured.

She squeezed his hand. 'Never ask me to leave you,' she said, voice cracking. 'Use my power well. Protect me. It has always been this; it has always been us. Let it be us until the wars end or we find our deaths – whatever comes first.'

When she was out of the infirmary, alone in their little lean-to – it was the first assignment they weren't in one of the long communal tents, and she was absurdly grateful for the privacy – they sat together on the floor, cross-legged, knee to knee. It was a binding of blood and power, true name to true name, and when he took the name of Locke into his heart, she swelled with such great power that the magelight between them glowed pure, warm gold.

They were fools when they were young: so often on the edge of death, so desperate for someone else to fall into the chasm alongside them, as if the reaper's teeth would not gnash them to nothing as long as they remained together.

She kept watch by herself as the sun rose fully over the not-so-distant mountains. No one came down the road by the inn. Eventually, she felt a hand on her ankle, gently rubbing the knob of her bone. She looked down to find Kier's eyes open.

'We have to keep moving,' he said quietly.

Grey glanced around. No one else was awake yet. 'I don't know if we can move Brit. I need to assess.'

Kier sat up, rubbing his face. 'There's a farm close by. I'll see if I can buy a horse. The faster we move on, the better.' He didn't say they'd already been loitering there too long. If one group of spies had already found them, the rest weren't far behind.

He leaned forward, resting his forehead on her thigh. She stroked his hair. 'The innkeeper,' he said quietly. 'What would you do with her?'

Her hand paused, his hair like silk against her fingers. She knew what her mother would have done: the last High Lady of Locke had a reputation for ruthlessness, to match the bloodlust of their ancestors. The best option, the safest option, was to kill her.

But right now, Grey's stomach turned at the thought of more blood. More killing. Another life on their hands, the life of someone who had not done her any harm.

'Drug her again,' she said. 'I can make something – it will make her ill for a few days, but it will leave the memory clouded.'

'If you're sure,' Kier said. He did not say, *If you're sure we can let her live.*

'I'm sure,' Grey said.

He woke Ola, who blearily agreed to keep watch but was awake enough to aim another firm glare at Grey.

'This is not going to be a good morning,' Grey muttered as they left the room, padding down the hall in their socks.

Kier sighed. 'We'll have a tactical meeting. Preferably out of town.'

Grey's stomach growled. 'And over breakfast.'

'As long as Eron isn't cooking,' she said.

She found her kit and sorted through the packets of herbs, labeled in Leonie's hand. She picked out the appropriate ones and ground them together, then added water to make them into a paste. She sniffed it, wincing at the immediate trace of a headache, and handed the concoction to Kier.

'She has to ingest it,' she said.

'I'll find a way.' He pulled a heavy ring of keys out of his pocket and hesitated outside the doorway. 'You are still ... Grey, don't take this the wrong way, but you look like you nearly lost a battle. I think it's best if I go in alone.'

Grey pursed her lips and crossed her arms over her chest. 'Not pretty enough for you, Captain?'

He smirked, but it didn't reach his eyes. 'You are a vision, even with blood clots in your hair. But I don't know if all would share my depraved tastes.'

She sighed, but relented, going into the room with the packs by herself while Kier tried his best to poison the innkeeper.

It didn't take more than a few minutes for Kier to work, but to her, it felt like an eternity. She set her medical kit back to rights and tried not to worry. She heard a door shut downstairs, then footsteps. He came back, leaning on the door frame.

'Did it work?' she asked, closing the kit and replacing it in her pack.

'She's asleep,' Kier said. 'We'll leave her ample pay for damages when we go. Now we need to get moving.'

'After I examine Brit.'

'If Ola lets you close enough. She's ... not happy.'

Grey was not ready to think about that. 'Where are the bodies?'

'Burned. In the woods. Eron and I dealt with it.'

'Mm.'

'There's new clothing for you in there,' Kier said, nodding to a gray-green saddlebag they must've bought in the village. 'And ... not to put too fine a point on it, but it might be a good idea to clean up. I wasn't kidding about the blood in your hair.'

She flipped him a rude gesture as he shut the door, leaving only his laugh behind, ringing in her ears.

She did not have the luxury of time, so she raced through bathing.

She scrubbed the blood out of her hair and off her skin, careful not to pull her stitches. The clothes Kier had gotten her were nondescript but softer than what she'd been wearing: a loose black shirt and black breeches, thick woolen socks, her same buckled leather vest. She liked the vest; it reminded her of a similar one her mother used to wear, and it had the close, heavy feel of armor.

He'd gotten her a new coat, too: heavy dark gray fabric, trimmed in black, with wide lapels and deep pockets. It was too big, but she preferred that. She folded it and left it on the bed, retrieving her kit to go check on Brit.

It was only Ola and Brit in the other room when she went in. Ola had moved the mage to the bed and was halfway through changing the bandage on their arm.

'I'll need to look at those stitches,' Grey said wearily.

'What? Do you care now?'

She was too tired for this. 'Of course I care.' she snapped.

'She did her best,' Brit said, eyes closed. 'With the stitching, at least.'

'Not to remind you of your station,' Grey said, even though that was exactly what she was doing, 'but leave off. And listen. Ola, I need you to tether to Brit—'

'Ah, because you have no power left, do you?'

'Fucking *listen* to me,' she snarled.

Ola did not respond. She only glared at Grey with a ferocity that made her oddly sad – but she listened. Grey sensed the tether as it took, felt the flow of magic from the well into the mage. She could not give Brit her own power, but she was still a Locke, still a daughter of the very place where the power took root.

She sensed the fiber of the tether – like all other times, she found herself wondering idly how other mages and wells could cope with such a slippery, unstable connection; she'd grown so used to the thick knot of her tether to Kier – and nudged it. She directed the wealth of Ola's power to the wound in Brit's stomach, pushing it to bind the meat of them.

Brit clapped a hand over the wound, hissing, *'Brine and bone*, Ol, what in Locke's name—'

'I'm not doing anything!' Ola insisted.

Grey felt the heat of infection starting in Brit – 'Focus, Ola, I need more' – and nudged it to the fore. Pinkish-white pus seeped through Brit's skin and she wiped it away, then layered on more antiseptic salve. She probed around the wound, but it was otherwise clean, and much better than it had been yesterday.

'You can detach,' she said.

Brit pushed themself up on their elbows, grunting at the movement. Ola stared at her, wide-eyed. Kier was used to the itching of her forcing his wounds back together, but Grey didn't usually do something like *that* unless the mage was unconscious and beyond notice – but there was no point in hiding. Ola was right: they had to be honest, and they were relying on one another for survival. What was she meant to do? She would never get over the guilt of nearly letting Brit die because she couldn't tether to them. She'd never forget the agony in Ola's eyes when she returned to find her mage nearly dead.

If it had been Kier . . .

She gathered up her things and packed her kit. Before either of them could stop her, she went downstairs to find Eron and Sela sitting at a table with steaming cups of tea. Cloth-wrapped bundles sat on the table in front of them: breakfast, Grey surmised. It was dark in the tavern, the curtains pulled over the windows.

'Where's Kier?' she asked.

'Seeing a man about a horse,' Eron said. 'Close by – don't get your nerves in a knot, Hand.'

'Impossible not to,' Grey muttered. She glanced at Sela. Though she knew the girl had slept, her face was still pale and drawn. 'Are you okay?' she asked, softer. She realized Sela wasn't wearing her cuffs, but with one mage down and Ola untrusting of Grey's power, she couldn't find herself surprised by it.

'I think so,' Sela said. It was unconvincing.

Kier returned a short while later, smelling of the cold, and soon Ola was helping Brit down the stairs too. They assembled around the table and . . . waited.

'We need to go,' Kier said.

Ola crossed her arms. 'I'm not leaving until I have answers.'

Grey gritted her teeth. 'You're endangering our mission.'

Ola looked at her. *So are you*, she didn't say.

Kier sighed. She felt the tug of him tethering, then her ears popped as he created a sound shield around them. 'You have ten minutes,' he said, his voice sounding like it was underwater for the briefest of moments before it came back into clarity. 'And then we're leaving. We have food for the road.'

'A picnic. Quaint,' Ola said, sitting back, arms crossed – but she'd stopped glaring. 'Now. Sorry, Captain, we need to talk about your Hand. And you.' She turned on Sela. 'You didn't tether to Brit either, until the very last moment. Isn't that something you should, I don't know, *control*?'

Grey drew a breath. Ola stared Kier down across the table. Brit, looking pale and caught in the middle of it, said, 'If there's information the captain deems unfit for us to know . . .'

'That information nearly got you killed,' Ola said. 'I have just as strong a memory as your Hand, Captain. Sela might have harmed you, but your well did not tether to my mage in a time of need, and that is, frankly, despicable.'

Grey flinched, but after all, she agreed.

'What Hand Captain Flynn determines to be necessary action would certainly be my call—'

'And you'd let a mage *die*?' Ola said at the same time Grey said, 'Kier.' He didn't look at her, but his jaw tightened, pulsing with tension. She wasn't sure how much she liked the beard anymore – it made his expressions uncanny, harder to read.

At least they'd given up on pretending they weren't in the army.

Grey folded her hands on top of her reports. 'There are a few things we need to discuss.'

'Either you're a heartless bitch who only thinks of your own mage,' Ola said, leaning back even further, 'or you and the captain are bound.'

'We are.'

Ola blinked owlishly, like she hadn't expected Grey to actually confirm – it was odd how well Brit mirrored that expression, how similar the two of them were, yet Brit had not told Ola that Grey and

Kier were bound. It was information, Grey thought, that she would not keep from Kier. Eron choked on his tea, sputtering, 'Since *when*?'

'A while,' Grey snapped.

'Sorry,' Sela said, very quiet, 'but what does that mean?'

Meanly, Ola said, 'When a mommy well and a daddy mage love each other very much—'

'Oh, fuck *off*, Ol,' Brit said, surprising Grey. She raised a brow before she could stop herself, then quickly schooled her expression into neutrality. 'You're pushing this too far.'

'*I'm* sorry,' Ola exclaimed. 'I thought that would be necessary information! We are on a highly dangerous mission, and the least – the literal *least* – I expected was to know if we had two capable, interchangeable wells and mages in case of injury, and I can't even get that? Not to mention that binding is highly forbidden in the first place. What kind of mission are you running, Captain?'

'I'm bound to Grey,' Kier said. 'It has never been detrimental before. I apologize for not telling you – for not telling any of you – but it was a matter of safety.'

'Not to come back to this,' Sela said, 'but why does it matter?'

'How do you *not* know what a bond is?' Eron asked. 'Isn't that basically mage/well "don't do this if you don't want to fucking die" rule number one?'

'She's not a soldier,' Grey murmured. 'Not everyone is a soldier, Fastria.'

But Ola was frowning too – and Brit.

Kier sighed again, rubbing his eyes. 'Grey, don't.'

Grey did. 'She'd know if she wasn't a fucking kid. What are you, thirteen?'

'I'm fifteen,' Sela said, indignant as only a mislabeled teenager could be.

'Hold on,' Eron began at the same time Brit said, 'Fifteen? Impossible. That's ...'

The blood drained from Sela's face.

'How old was Maryse?' Eron asked.

'It is impossible,' Ola said very carefully, 'because Locke disappeared sixteen years ago. And you didn't tether to Brit earlier because ...'

'Because she couldn't,' Grey said. 'Because she wasn't trained.'

'Congratulations, Ola,' Kier said, ever-suffering, ignoring Grey for now. 'You win the prize.' To Sela, he said, 'You're not Maryse of Locke. So who are you? And *why*?'

'Wait,' Ola said, even more indignant. 'You two *knew*?'

Sela had gone a very interesting shade of greenish-yellow ivory. Grey, who'd spent quite a lot of time with the ill and dying, did not associate that shade of skin with a living body. 'If I tell you,' the girl said, pulling at the fabric of her dress anxiously, 'do you promise not to kill me?'

'No,' Grey said, but there wasn't any heat to it. At the girl's stricken expression, she said, 'Sorry, Sela; we promise. You were . . . very helpful yesterday when I could not be, and I am thankful for that. You're forgiven for stabbing Kier.'

'I don't think you can apologize for *my* stabbing,' Kier said. 'But . . . Sorry. What happened with her yesterday?'

'We'll talk later,' Grey said. She turned back to Sela. 'We won't kill you. But we do have to know – because there are a lot of people after us, and if you're just a peasant girl caught up in a lie, this is going to be very difficult to explain. Sela, who are you?'

For another moment, the girl looked like she was going to vomit all over the table. She put her elbows on the surface and dropped her head to her hands, her dark hair falling in a choppy curtain around her, hiding her face. 'My name is Wilisela Naudé.'

'Naudé?' Eron repeated, chewing it over. 'Why do I know that name?'

But Kier was staring at Grey, sending a heady blend of frustration and exhaustion over the tether. She caught all of it, sending back equal measures of annoyance. He was basically telling her he'd told her so – they should've deserted. They should've left and not even considered this damn mission.

He raised his eyes skyward. 'I suffer and I suffer,' he muttered. 'And yet. And *yet*.'

And to his credit . . . The horror was prickling and insistent. She had a memory tugging from some distant past of running her fingers over the name in cursive, flicking up the accent on the e. She remembered the shape of it in her father's voice, his hand caught on her mother's waist as he said, *There's a letter on the desk for you. Naudé – the new Cleoc – sent a proposal* – and she was again on the island, again watching the wind through Severin's hair; and her mother was leaning over to kiss her forehead before bed, the cold silver of her necklace skimming over Grey's nose; and her father was carrying her up to the tallest tower of the fortress, up and up and up, and she sat on his shoulders as he pointed at the different masses of land and said, *Look. You have to know them all, Maryse. You have to understand them all, and determine who you can trust.*

'Eron,' Kier said, 'you know that name because the Naudés are the High Family of Cleoc Strata. And if my incomplete knowledge of political inheritance is correct – which I *really fucking hope* it isn't – Sela is the First Daughter of Cleoc Strata, heir to our enemies.'

Sorry it's been so long since I last wrote. We're on the northern coast, near Cleoc Strata. Being so close to the sea has me feeling tense. I don't think Kier has noticed, thank the gods. I don't want him to worry about me with everything else going on.

Letter from Hand Captain Grey Flynn to Imarta Flynn, undated

Grey has been having nightmares again. They don't wake her, but her fear keeps me up at night.

Letter from Captain Kiernan Seward to Imarta Flynn, 14 years AD

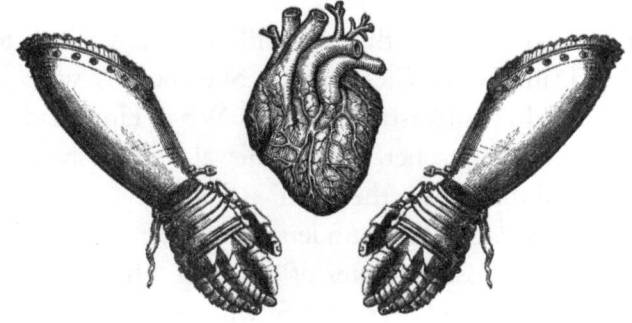

thirteen

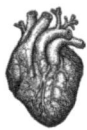

'BRINE AND BONE,' OLA swore, the first to recover. 'You've got to be kidding me.'

But Kier was already moving. 'Look. Let's chat on the road – we've stayed too long. Pack your things. Brit, you and Sela will ride.'

Over the years, Grey had become very good at compartmentalization. That was the only reason she was able to launch herself up, finish tidying the room and pack her bag and Kier's, don her new gray coat and stand ready at the door without utterly falling to pieces.

The First Daughter of Cleoc Strata. She couldn't wrap her head around it, couldn't understand – *how*? Why? How had she even ended up as Luthar's prisoner, and did they also think she was Maryse of Locke, or did they know the truth?

And, uncomfortably, Grey understood better than anyone what it meant to be the lost daughter of a nation. She realized all over again, with a sick sort of desperation, what would happen to her if that secret got out.

She sent a pulse of worry down the tether. Kier answered with his own tentative comfort, but it wasn't strong enough to be believable.

Her mage actively relaxed when they were back on the road, the inn fading into the distance behind them, the mountains looming ahead. Sela and Brit rode the horse Kier had acquired, Brit's arms framing the girl in a way that wasn't fully restraint but wasn't *not* restraint.

'Captain,' Ola started, but Kier said quietly, 'Wait. There will be time. I want to get out of here.'

They continued in silence, Kier shushing them any time one of them got anywhere close to probing the matter. The captain kept his own counsel, chewing on his lip, clearly preoccupied. Grey glanced up more than once to find him looking at her sideways, his expression unreadable.

But he did not confide in her. Grey did not know what to think of that, of all things.

She focused instead on the walk. The scenery changed as they wound up into the foothills, from forest to grassy hills, then rocky paths with cliffs that rose up and up. They kept to the trail now, Ola pausing every so often to peer at the map and the compass, sometimes consulting Kier. It grew colder, too: Grey's breath came in great puffs, and she was grateful again for her new coat. She buried her fingers deep in the pockets, thumbs tracing over the bits of lint and coin left behind by the previous owner. Her sword clinked against one of the straps of her bag, more sensation than sound, and she lost herself in the monotony of it until Kier said, 'Okay. Let's eat and talk.'

She stopped. Brit pulled the horse to a halt, too; it snuffed gray-white clouds of breath and pawed at the rocky trail. Grey didn't know its name. She reached to gently run her hand across the beast's nose, damp with the condensation of cooling breath.

Brit and Sela slid down, and Kier took the reins. He nodded to a rocky formation to the side of the path. They sat in a loose circle, waiting, as he tied the horse to another rock near a patch of grass so it could graze. Eron distributed their afternoon helpings of cheese and dried fish. Finally, Kier seemed to come to some decision – perhaps he'd been wrestling with it all day. Grey felt the tug on the tether as he siphoned, the pop of her ears as he shielded them.

'Sela,' he said. 'I have two questions. Why does anyone think you're Maryse of Locke? And how did you end up Luthar's prisoner?'

The girl kept her head down, chin to chest. Grey remembered the first time she saw her, bundled and tied up in that carriage. She felt an uncomfortable stirring of pity.

'I was staying with nobles in Lindan, getting my education.' Lindan was on the continent, and like all other continental powers, it stayed far out of the warring within Idistra. They did allow children to journey to the continent for safety, though, particularly those from the noble families. One of the Lindle universities had offered Severin a place, back when there was peace, but since Grey was still a child, he could not leave the Isle to accept it.

'Nicer than here,' Brit muttered, nudging a rock with the toe of their boot. Grey took in their pallor, even paler than their usual alabaster. She made a mental note to give them a draught for pain relief before they moved again.

'I don't know why I did it,' Sela conceded. 'Homesickness, maybe? I . . . I feigned illness and slipped out of my lessons, went to the harbor and boarded the first ship I could find that was going to Idistra.'

Despite herself, Grey reached over and took Sela's hand. The girl looked up at her, eyes big and glassy with tears.

'We all made bad decisions at fifteen,' Grey said evenly.

'Speak for yourself, Flynn,' Ola muttered.

But this seemed to strengthen Sela ever so slightly – or perhaps she, like Grey, was just happy that Ola no longer looked murderous every time Grey spoke. 'I wanted to come back. I knew it was foolish. I didn't care.'

'Does anyone know you left?' Kier asked, arms crossed. That scar on his lip was tugged down, making his frown deeper on one side than the other.

'I don't know. And if they do, I don't know if they care. Lindan was never . . . kind to me.'

'Ah.' Kier glanced at Grey, then away. 'So you took a ship back. Then what?'

'I didn't expect . . . ' Sela trailed off. Grey didn't know what it was she didn't expect: that she'd be returning to a nation at war? That someone would care about one girl coming back from abroad? She was anxiously ruining a bit of bread with the hand Grey wasn't holding. 'The ship was trying to land in Scaela, but it was searched

and I was not on the manifests, so they knew I was not meant to be there. They asked for papers, and I didn't have them. So they . . . '
She stopped, thin lips pressed together.

Grey squeezed her hand. Sela looked away.

'They were going to drown me. I knew if I revealed my identity, they'd kill me. So I said I was Locke.'

Grey pretended to be very interested in her fish to hide any reaction to the story, and immediately regretted it. It tasted like post-battle leather armor. 'Why?' she asked finally, saying out loud what everyone else seemed to be thinking.

Sela looked at her, only her; those big eyes were doing their best to appear earnest. But Grey didn't doubt her for a minute. She was a kid. Grey herself had run away when she was sixteen, looking for the first place that made her feel something. It just so happened she actually *was* the long-lost lady of a dead house in hiding, while Sela was not.

'Because I didn't want to die, and I know Locke is important,' Sela said. 'No one has ever found Severin – so what if he wasn't the one who survived after all? What if it was me?'

'Because you're twelve,' Eron said, exasperated.

'Fifteen,' Sela corrected.

Kier had gotten up at some point, and he was now pacing back and forth. 'Eat, Captain,' Grey chided, and he grudgingly bit off half of his dried fish and struggled to chew it, wincing the whole time. 'Okay,' he said once he recovered. 'The problem with taking you to Cleoc Strata, even if you tell the truth, is it'll look like *we* kidnapped you. Plus, it's much farther than Grislar, and we'd probably be killed at the border. Too many complications.'

'Why take her to Cleoc? Why not bring the High Lady to us?' Grey asked. Kier looked at her, withering, but she was his Hand, and often, his reason. She went on. 'If we go to Grislar, like we're supposed to, and send word ahead to get an ensign from Cleoc – we can barter for peace, Kier. If Sela says we rescued her from Luthar when we're actually protected . . . '

'But our leave,' Brit said sadly. 'We're meant to deliver Maryse of Locke.'

'They only said we had to deliver the *prisoner*,' Grey said. 'If we get caught on the way, we're fucked. But if we make it there, if we're able to arrange it? That will mean something, won't it? Perhaps it will even lead to an alliance on one front?'

Kier looked at her for a long time, sending something down the tether that she couldn't quite read. That was the problem with feeling someone else's emotions, even someone as close to her as Kier: there was not always a direct translation from his heart to hers.

'What if that doesn't work?' he asked.

Grey shrugged. 'Then we'll figure it out.'

He looked at her, the expression clear on his face: *What if they find out about you?* She tried to school her own expression into an answering gaze of *We will deal with it if it happens.*

Ola blew out a long breath, tugging on the end of one of her braids. 'It would be nice to have one less border to worry about.'

'I can do it,' Sela said, without anyone asking her. 'I can get the truce – I'll push for it. I'm supposed to inherit in a few years. My mother has to listen to me.' She was still squeezing Grey's hand and ruining the bit of bread, still just a girl who'd run away from safety into something she didn't understand – but Grey understood better than anyone that little girls grew up, and little girls with titles grew into rulers with power.

Grey looked away, far past the mountains, toward the sea. Something like longing stirred within her.

They made camp that night halfway up one of the rises, in a shallow dip protected by crests on either side. The cliffs above had just begun collecting little drifts of snow. 'It will only get colder,' Kier warned as they set out out blankets and bedrolls. 'Keep close together.'

They sat together as Eron cooked up a new variety of beige. Grey changed the bandage over her stitches, then inspected Brit's healing wounds. Kier was a ways away from them against the cliff, reading a book. Sela sat near Grey, stroking the horse's side. It was called Pigeon, she'd learned, which made absolutely no sense. Horse names rarely did.

'Eron,' Ola said. 'I can *hear* your wheels turning. What are you thinking about?'

Eron looked up, nearly knocking the pot over. 'Sorry.' He cleared his throat. 'How do we know for certain that someone survived Locke? What if the whole survivor thing is a lie? Didn't the entire isle ... explode?'

'If everyone had died,' Ola said, 'there would be no magic at all.'

Eron considered this as he poured in the mush to soak. 'But how do we *know*?' he asked finally. 'It could still be possible that the letter from Severin was forged, and no wells have been born since the Isle's destruction. How do we know that that isn't because Locke is well and truly dead?'

'Because Locke is the root and foundation of power,' Sela said quietly. Grey focused on Brit's skin, on the task at hand. 'There is no power at all without Locke.'

'Then how were *you* born a well, if you were born after Locke?'

'Cleoc was pregnant with me when Locke disappeared,' Sela said, like it was a normal thing to know. 'I was born just a couple months after. That's probably why I don't ... have much to draw on. I'm barely a well at all.'

Grey did not want to think about this anymore. Because Sela was right: Locke *was* power; *Grey* was power. If she took her secret to her grave, kept fighting other wars and perished in them, she would take all of Idistra's power with her.

If she did not reclaim Locke before her death, the nation's magic would die. For good.

This was what she lay awake thinking of late at night; the one thing she could not fully discuss with Kier. He would push for her safety at any cost. Even if it meant the death of magic.

And the truth? She was afraid. She knew the death of each remaining member of her family – she remembered when word came of her beloved aunt Wren, who had been slaughtered in Nestria. She understood, then, how her godfather, Scaelas, immediately went to war with Nestria in retaliation – if Grey had been a sovereign and not a girl of eight, she too would've set the very seas on fire to avenge Wren's death.

She knew of her cousins and aunts and uncles, those who had not been heirs to the Isle's power and had instead been sent to marry into other nations to strengthen alliances. All of that fell away when Locke perished. None of them were safe, and Grey least of all.

She was a coward, at the end of it, willing to let the entire system die instead of putting herself at risk of facing the same fate.

She did her best to tune the others out. She finished her ministrations and tapped on Brit's arm, signaling for them to move. They nodded, pulling their shirt down and shrugging back into their coat.

There was no further discussion on the topic. Kier marked his page and set his book aside, face-down, then looked out over nothing. Grey left the fire and went to sit by his side.

She leaned her head against his shoulder. After a moment, he wrapped an arm around her back and tugged her close. 'How are you holding up?' he asked.

'Just dandy.'

'Less than two weeks, Flynn. Then the rest of our lives awaits.'

She sighed.

Lower, he said, just for her, 'Power in bravery.' It was the motto of her family, her house, her isle. It was as if he knew what she'd just been thinking. Sometimes she wondered if he could take one look at her face and see every thought her brain held.

'I don't feel very brave,' she admitted. 'Or powerful.'

'Nor do I.'

She leaned further into him, looping her arm over his knee. The cliff face sheltered them from the swirling snow that had started, but it was cold against them – the wind was so loud here that she couldn't hear the others; it was just as effective as being in a bubble.

'The wind,' she said, 'reminds me of home.'

There was a beat of uncertain silence. 'Does it?'

'Not that one.'

'Ah.' His arm tightened around her. 'You dreamed of them last night.'

'Is that a statement or a question?'

'Statement. Your breathing changes when you do.' He laced his free hand together with the one she had on his knee, and the power flowed through them, a full unbroken circuit. 'Has this been bringing up memories?'

'Here and there,' Grey admitted. 'Nothing I can't handle.'

'Do you want to talk about it?'

'Do you remember when we were her age?' she asked.

He was quiet for a moment. 'I do,' he said finally, his hand tightening over hers.

It had been the last close call they suffered in Leota — and it had *terrified* her. Lot left during the summer before her fifteenth birthday, going to train, leaving them behind in a lopsided arrangement made worse by the fact she could no longer hide from her affection for Kier.

That winter, in a brutally cold storm that whipped the sea into frothy peaks below the cliffs, they had been sitting in Leota's village square with a new letter from Lot and hot tea clasped in their hands. They were there when Mika, the town's bailiff, strolled through with a loose knot of his friends. Grey had always wondered how he managed to hold his post with his proclivity for drink — she preferred to just avoid him and his crew.

She'd been leaning on Kier, her cheek on his shoulder as they read, when she heard the laughter from the group of armored soldiers loitering nearby.

'All's I'm saying is this.' Mika's voice carried across the square, his words slurred with drink. 'That boy can't hide forever. Someday, someone's gonna find him. And if I got my hands on 'im . . .'

At first, she thought he was talking about one of the village boys. She glanced up, frowning, wondering what they'd gotten into now.

'Could ransom him,' one of Mika's friends said. 'Imagine the payout.'

'Scaelas would find out,' another said.

'Nah,' Mika replied. 'Nah nah nah. You're thinking all wrong. You know what I'd do? I'd kill him. Stop this whole bloody business. No more power, no more magic, no more stuck-up mages with their bullshit. Then I'd chop 'im up and sell his parts.'

Grey froze — not even the hot tea in her hands could ease the chill in her bones.

One of his companions snorted. 'Well, that's one way to do it. You really think killing that kid would kill the whole system?'

'I think that if I had the chance, I wouldn't hesitate to find out. Fuck Scaelas, and fuck this war. Let me rule, eh?'

More boisterous laughter filled the square, but Grey barely heard it. Her stomach swam with bile. Kier's arm was tight around her, drawing her close, shielding her – because even at seventeen, he knew.

They had left the square, risking death on the icy cliff path that led to the shore; in their favorite pebbled beach cove, there was no risk they'd be heard. Grey's panic was a tangible thing in her chest, her breathing uneven.

'Do you think,' she had asked, pacing back and forth, 'others would feel the same? That it's easier to kill me than to restore Locke?'

'I don't know,' Kier admitted. He leaned back against the damp, cold rock, watching her. 'But they're not looking for you. They still think it's Severin.'

Grey shook her head. 'We can't bank on that forever. Someday, they'll figure it out.'

'Would that really be enough? If someone killed you, would they kill all power? Couldn't someone else find the source again, or create it?'

'Yes,' Grey said bitterly, rubbing her eyes. 'It would kill the power, to kill the source. The only way to take the control of power away from me is to get an heir, forcing a new line of inheritance, and then control that. I'm old enough to bear a child now, if forced, and I'm sure they would kill me after I gave them a well who could take on the power—'

'Grey, stop,' Kier said, gripping her arm. Her voice had taken on a new, high pitch of fear. He was pale, confronted with the truth of her worst fears. 'That's barbaric.'

She laughed, a short, harsh sound. 'Then you doubt they'd do it?'

He pressed his lips together, a muscle ticking in his jaw. It was not the first time he'd been furious on her behalf, and she had the awful suspicion it wouldn't be the last. 'I won't let that happen to you, okay?'

'You can't control what happens to me.' She let him pull her into his arms, to wrap her up. She tried to time her breathing to his own, pressing her cold nose against his neck. 'If Mika ever finds out—'

'He won't, and I'll kill him if he even gets close. But we can't stay here waiting for someone to find you.' A pause, a beat. 'Do you . . . *want* to be Locke?'

'No,' Grey said immediately, remembering the blood, the smoke the flame. She pulled away, putting space between them – he was just comforting her, as any friend would. 'I would rather die.'

'Then we'll find a way to keep them from finding you. We'll find somewhere to hide.'

'There *is* nowhere to hide,' Grey said, covering her face with her hands, her stomach heavy with the truth. 'No matter where I go, the knights will be looking for me.'

'Unless,' Kier said, looking away from her, 'you *were* one of the knights.'

She looked up at him. He did not seem afraid, nor did he wear that mischievous smile he had when they were doing something deliciously impulsive and ill-advised. He looked completely serious.

'Join them, you mean,' she said. 'Follow Lot to training.'

'We could go together. They would probably let us stay together, even.'

She'd nodded, bitterness blooming. 'When the patrol comes back next summer,' she said, arms crossed over her chest, leaning against the salt-soaked rock, 'we will join up.'

'You're too young to do it next summer. But if we wait a couple of years, train more . . . '

'We'll lie.'

'Grey . . . '

She shook her head, fierce. 'I'm not going to sit here and wait for someone to find me. To kill me. Maybe my father trusted Scaelas, but I—' She broke off, the tears ragged in her throat. 'I don't know if I can. I don't know if I can trust anyone.'

'You can trust me,' Kier said. He reached out, his hand brushing hers. 'Grey, no matter what happens, you can always trust me.'

So he had lied for her, and run away with her, and fought Imarta and both of his mothers on her behalf when they found out. When word got back to him, Lot had only written her a gentle letter about the dangers of battle. He had written Kier a much meaner, strongly worded letter about Grey's safety, but he had ended it by telling his brother he was proud of him. Grey had found that letter again recently, still tucked into Kier's pack.

Now, Kier took a deep breath, and Grey anticipated his next question, because he could always read her, especially when she least desired it – *Do you want to be Locke?* all over again, the same question nearly a decade later – which was why she was surprised when he said, 'Do you want to go to Lindan?'

'What?'

'It might be nice,' he mused, his thumb skimming over the meat between her thumb and forefinger. 'Lindle magic is different. No wells, no mages. Some are just … magicians, like they learned it. Like math.'

Grey knew all this, and Kier knew she knew. Like Idistra, Lindan functioned on an intrinsic system, meaning magical aptitude was a trait the Lindle were born with. Unlike in Idistra, *all* had some access to Lindan's magic, though wielding it well was a matter of practice. 'We probably wouldn't have any magic at all,' Grey said carefully. 'Not that far from Locke.'

'Mm. Maybe not.' He didn't say, *But you* are *Locke.* He didn't have to. 'We could leave all of this behind.'

You can let the magic die, if you want to, he did not say. *You do not have to save us and sacrifice your own freedom.*

'Do you ever think,' Grey said, glancing at the others, but Eron had Sela stirring the pot as he chopped up bits of jerky to flavor the travesty that was dinner, and Brit was carefully braiding Ola's hair next to the warmth of the magelight, which brought out the shimmers of red in her dark curls. 'Do you ever think we'd be better off if we stopped running?'

'Stopped running from what?' Kier asked.

'Locke,' Grey said, the word barely more than an exhalation, and Kier stiffened – it seemed they were both surprising each other tonight.

'I don't think it's a good idea,' he said.

'A terrible one, actually,' she agreed. But she paused, listening to the screaming of the wind – and sometimes they were so heavy on her heart, the family she'd lost, the place she'd never grown to fully know. Sometimes, when she closed her eyes, she was right there in the Ghostwood, and she'd open them and her stomach still hurt, but it ached with emptiness instead of power.

'You know what it would mean,' Kier said. 'What could happen to you.'

And that was the crux of it, wasn't it? Kier knew as well as Grey did why her family had been killed: to control the power. Whoever controlled Locke controlled all of the magic in Idistra. It was a simple miscalculation that had led to their downfall: they did not know that Locke would rather die than be controlled, that they would take everything down with them rather than allow the heir to be taken.

'You think they'd kill me.'

'Or worse,' he said. 'We can't be certain of Scaelas's intentions. It's too much of a risk.'

'We don't need Scaelas,' Grey said. 'We don't need anyone.'

'We need allies,' he said. 'You and I do not an army make.'

'Where's that ego I know and love?'

He smiled, but only just. 'I will go wherever you want to,' he said, 'but we shouldn't rush into a hasty decision, or do something because we're backed into a corner.' He squeezed her hand, two short pulses. 'If you want to go, it should be a genuine choice. Not the result of a forced hand.'

'I know,' Grey said.

'That's a decision that can't be reversed.'

She snorted. 'Like retirement?'

'We could always re-enlist.'

'Gods, no.'

They sat for a moment in silence before Kier said, 'Once you open that box, there's no going back. It would reveal the truth of you.'

Grey nudged his jaw with her head. 'You know the truth of me.' It was easy, like this, to pretend that there was something else between them other than friendship and the tether of power.

He laughed. Kier raised her hand to his lips, and she felt the brush of his new beard. 'I do,' he agreed, 'though sometimes I wonder.'

'Are you two going to eat, or are you just going to keep necking in the corner?' Ola called.

Grey sighed, untangling from Kier's side. 'We're not necking,' she grumbled, even though she blushed as she said it. She half crawled back across the rocks to the circle of warm light. Sela handed her a bowl with a tentative smile.

'Captain Flynn?' she asked, moving closer with her own bowl, and Grey immediately knew from the girl's tone that she was in for something.

'Grey works, kid. What do you need?' she asked, already mentally cataloging the things she had to do before sleep. Kier was across the light with Ola, going over tomorrow's route.

'Can you explain binding to me?'

That again. Grey forced herself to get down three spoonfuls in rapid succession, thinking it over. 'Maybe when you're older,' she said finally. She was rewarded with a pout that made Sela look even younger.

'I don't believe it has anything to do with *that*,' Sela said primly. 'But you and the captain are bound. Why?'

Grey nodded. There was no point in edging around it: the fact was out there. 'Why didn't they train you as a well?' she asked. She knew the girl had power – she also knew how little she was able to use it.

Sela shrugged one shoulder. 'I've tried, a few times, but I'm no good at it. So we decided to focus on my education instead. Diplomacy, magical history, geography. All that.'

Grey took this in. She remembered what Sela had said before, about barely being a well at all. Perhaps she was too weak for training – but she'd tethered to Brit in the battle, so there was *something* there.

Beyond that, she wished someone had been able to make such a decision for her. There were so many gaps in her own knowledge, holes that she didn't think she'd ever be able to fill: history and geography, mathematics, continental languages. Her schooling had been so singularly dedicated to preparing her for a life at war, life as someone else's tool, a life as a well and a healer, that she sometimes didn't know who she would be if she'd genuinely had the choice.

'So why did you come back?'

Sela sighed through her teeth, poking her spoon around in her sludge, which she hadn't finished. For all her sweeping declarations about the passable mediocrity of Eron's cooking, she didn't seem keen to eat it now. 'I don't know if I can explain it,' she said. 'Do you ever miss your home? Familiarity? The place you know better than any others?'

Grey shrugged. She'd been moving around since she was sixteen. And though she'd lived in Leota for years, though that had been her home for most of her childhood, it wasn't Leota she thought of when she smelled the salty brine of the sea.

'I guess that answers your question,' she said slowly, choosing each word with deliberate care. 'About Kier and me. With power – with your mage. It's like that, sometimes. You find someone, and they feel like home, and everything is stronger. I think that's how it's meant to be, for some of us. Not moving from mage to mage with every reassignment. I know Kier just as well as I know myself.'

'Do you love him?' Sela asked with the shamelessness of a teenager.

'Of course I do,' Grey said. There was no point in clarifying the way she loved him, or the ways it was unreciprocated. 'But . . . there's more to love than that.'

'Ola said it's a foolish thing for anyone to do,' Sela admitted. For a second, Grey thought she was talking about love, and that she and Ola had been gossiping, but Sela clarified. 'Binding, I mean. She said that Kier is useless without you, and that if you die, he'll never be able to do magic again.'

'He'd be useless without me anyway,' Grey said, trying to make a joke, and finding it bitter in her mouth. She shrugged. There was no way to break a bond, no way to undo it, and they'd known that four years ago when he whispered her true name and pressed his blood to her mouth. 'But we're capable of a lot, bound as we are. It has its benefits. It makes both of us stronger.'

She looked at Sela's full bowl, her upturned face. She wasn't even pretending to eat anymore. Grey elbowed her gently in the ribs. 'Eat something,' she said. 'We've mountains to cross, kid.'

Sela sighed, but she did as she was told. A few moments later, when she'd finished shoveling the gruel in – speed was the only way to make the meal palatable – she said, 'Can you train me?'

Grey had been expecting this. She watched the steady glow of the magelight, felt the warmth on her fingers. 'I can try,' she said, 'but I probably won't be any good at it.'

'Trying is nice too.'

'And Brit needs to agree to help.'

'They probably will, if I ask nicely.'

Grey did not contest this. She sensed a shadow over her, then Kier came close. 'We should probably get some rest,' he said. He'd clearly already told the others – Brit and Ola were already setting up their bedrolls. 'Eron is taking the first watch.'

'Thanks,' Grey said. She watched him go back, setting out their sleep areas, leaving Sela's closest to the warmth of the magelight. To Sela, she said, 'Then we'll try.'

I expected a lot of things from this marriage, but not love. It's Isaak's fault for loving me first and I am a fool because I have allowed it. The fact that it has found me, *weakened* me, makes me incandescently angry. I think of him, always, and nothing could enrage me more.

Letter from Alma, High Lady of Locke, to Wren Locke Teinek, her sister, 18 years AD

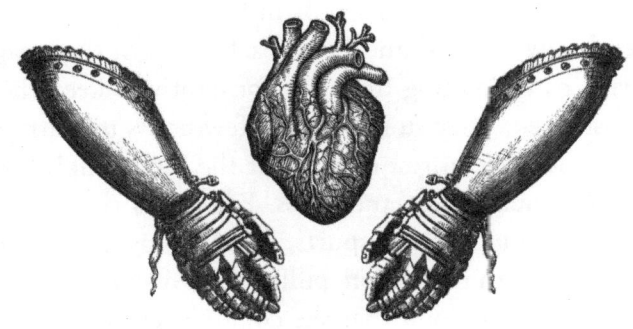

Fourteen

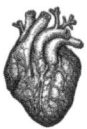

IT WAS NOT AN easy thing, to cross the mountains at the turn of the season. Grey kept her hands in her coat as often as possible until Kier finally relented and made each of them tiny magelights, one for each hand, pulling from her constantly to keep them from getting frostbitten. They stopped every few hours to warm up their feet or eat or let Pigeon rest or graze at the increasingly infrequent patches of mountain grass and moss. Four days they spent in the mountains, sleeping in short spurts, huddled together on a double layer of bedrolls with three more pulled tight over the top. At night, the wind screamed so loud that she couldn't tell the difference between waking and her nightmares. She often woke tangled in Kier's arms, in Kier's coat, her legs entwined with Brit's or Sela's, to find the captain's eyes open and staring into the night.

'Stop worrying,' she murmured to him every time, but he only sighed and stroked her hair until she went back to sleep. Between hours of sleep, they took their watch shifts, pacing and frigid, forcing themselves through exercises to keep their circulation going.

As they walked through the mountains, Grey did her best to teach Sela. 'I want you to imagine it as a ball of yarn,' she said, as her own mother had told her. 'Find a thread and tie it to Brit, and let it unspool little by little. Not like a ball you throw – a thread, Sela. That's all they need.' They practiced until Sela was able to connect to the mage without any directional nudging from Grey. She was a weak well at most, but she was a well. Just being an unbound well made her more useful than Grey herself, a fail-safe if they needed one.

Closer and closer they drew to the other side of the mountains, until Grey realized that they'd spent most of the afternoon going downhill instead of up. As evening fell in earnest, she hurried her footsteps, moving around Eron, then Pigeon, to catch up with Kier. 'Where are we?'

He pulled out the map and said, 'Aloducan peaks, crossing east.'

'Kier,' she said, fully accepting that her tone had slipped into whininess. She didn't think she could identify the unmarked Aloducan peaks on the map if they stabbed her in the chest. He only sighed and pointed at their location with a brief tap. She traced her finger over it, examining the space between there and Grislar, and something like hope swelled in her chest.

'What are you thinking about our next move?'

He cast his eyes skyward. The clouds were steely gray, heavy with the promise of fresh snow. Grey was tired of the stuff, but at least the hard-packed frozen ground was better than mud. 'I'll defer to you on this,' he said. 'I think we need to send letters from the next village we come to. We're about five days out, and I need that time.'

Five days. The thought was nearly incomprehensible.

'Let's camp here,' he said, louder, so they all could hear him. He nodded toward a sheltered patch of grass a few feet off the path.

Grey set herself up on a rock, laying her kit out as Eron began preparing the food. 'Brit,' she called. 'The big day has arrived.'

The mage came over, a smile creeping across their lips. 'Time to take the stitches out?'

Grey nodded. When she had her workstation set up and had cleaned her hands, Brit removed their shirt, shivering in the cold, and stretched out. Kier positioned himself nearby, ready to help if needed.

Grey focused on her work, humming just a little as she did. There was quiet contentment around the camp – it took Grey a second to realize that Eron was telling stories as he worked.

'That's not how I heard it,' Ola protested.

'You're from the southwest. They can't be correct,' Eron retorted.

'And what do farmers know of folk tales, then?'

Grey had no idea what they were talking about. She finished up and applied more salve to Brit's wounds, then bandages. The mage dressed and Grey took off her own coat, then her shirt, wincing at the cold of the wind. Kier moved to sit next to her, taking her arm in his hands. She forced herself to pay attention to Eron for a distraction, if nothing else, as Kier started his work.

'They say that magic is a gift from the gods,' Eron said grandly. 'That all gods came down, and chose a nation, and blessed it as they saw fit. And here in Idistra, we were blessed most of all, by our own gods: for we are never forced to endure alone.'

'Bullshit,' Ola said. She was sitting on a rock, stroking Pigeon's nose. Sela sat at her feet, her head on the well's lap. 'No one says that.'

'Well, then you explain it.'

'In Lindan,' Sela said, 'they think magic is a responsibility, and it must be learned.'

'Good thing we aren't Lindle,' Brit muttered. 'Eron, you'd be fucked.'

'I don't *have* to feed you,' Eron said. 'And besides – I can use Arkunish magic, and my father left me some of his spellstones.'

'Do they work here?' Kier asked, genuinely interested. He had always loved knowing as much as he could about how other systems of magic functioned.

'Not well,' Eron admitted. 'And anyway, not to say too much about my father, but he only left me the shitty ones. They're very specialized. So I suppose I'm really useful, but only if you have a drain blockage, or a thread that keeps snagging.'

'Alas,' Kier said. 'I do not.'

Brushing past this, Sela said, 'And in Ruskaya, did you know that the magicians are demons?'

Kier snorted. Grey looked up at him, at the careful concentration on his face. 'To be fair,' she said quietly, 'some would accuse you of . . . demonic qualities.'

He smirked, finishing the last stitch. Grey directed him to apply a salve and wrap the healing wound as the others bickered over the relative merits of other types of magic.

'Captain,' Eron said when he saw they were getting up. For a second, Grey thought he was talking to Kier, but he was looking at her. 'You grew up on the coast. Tell us, what were the stories there? Where did they say our magic comes from?'

'Oh. Um.' Grey chewed on her nail. She knew the stories she believed, the variations they used to tell around the fire at night on Locke. She glanced at Kier, but he only gave her a smile. Bastard.

She accepted the bowl Eron handed her, pausing to let it warm her hands as she settled in next to Brit. Kier took a spot across the magelight from her, closer to Eron.

'Surely you heard *some* stories growing up,' Eron said, tucking into his food.

Grey pushed her spoon around. 'Well, they say that this land existed before we did, don't they? Hundreds of years ago, when no one lived here – actually no one; it was an island of sheep – there was a ship lost in the sea. It bore explorers from what is now Lindan, where magic is freer. Looser. But when they landed, they found that they were so far from home that the magic did not come as it once had.' She paused, looking up. 'Have you heard this one before?'

Ola wrinkled her nose. 'I think so?'

Brit and Eron shook their heads.

Grey chewed her lip, but she continued. 'Now, after a hard winter, only two explorers remained. But they were out of food, and though they'd retreated to a small isle for protection and made a home for themselves, they could not live another winter there alone. So one suggested she could go searching the mainland, close by, to find provisions. The other woman feared she would never come back for her. So in the night, she stole her heart, and with it, her magic. The intrepid explorer went in search of food, and found it, but she did not feel whole – and she could not perform any magic on her own. When she returned to the isle with her provisions, she was delighted to find that her magic had returned, but only when she remained with her lover and betrayer. And for that reason, we need both: one to love, and one to betray.'

There was quiet for a long moment. She knew Kier was looking at her, but she did not look back until he cleared his throat and said, 'I think I know a different version of that.'

'Gods, I hope so,' Ola muttered. 'That was bleak.'

'In the version I heard, she gave her heart freely, as a promise to return.'

Grey felt her cheeks warm. She looked up, meeting Kier's gaze. 'Who told you that version?'

'Mum,' he said.

'Hopeless romantic.'

He shook his head, but he couldn't hide his smile – the dimples of his cheeks were dark in the dying light of evening. Mum had heard that version from Imarta, Grey knew, who had heard it from Grey herself. And both versions were passed from Grey's own mother, who decided which version she would tell based on how well behaved Grey and her brother had been that day.

There were other stories after that, but Grey didn't participate in the telling. It was too easy to slip, to say something she wasn't supposed to know. That night, when she and Kier went on watch, she looked out into the valley below and thought of the remains of the temple that went down with Locke, dedicated to the goddesses of love and betrayal – or of love and devotion, depending on who was there to make an offering. Retarik, Locke's goddess of forgiveness, was also the goddess of devotion, the first of the named mages.

She hadn't thought about the temple of Retarik, she realized, in many years. It was partially intentional, since the temple had been repurposed into a festival hall – the very same hall where the Isle had met its end.

Even that made her sad: there were so many things on Locke, so many details, and she was the only one to hold them, to go on remembering when everything else was lost.

She hadn't believed in the gods, not really, even though she'd been named for one of them: Gremaryse, the goddess of the sea. Sometimes, she wondered if that was the only reason she survived the sea that night after Locke burned, if it was her namesake pushing her further and further toward Scaela's foreign shores.

She tucked her knees to her chest, thinking of the ruins on the edge of the Ghostwood, looking out at the sea. Alma, her mother, was named after the other character in the origin story: Kitalma, the first well, the patron goddess of Locke. *That*, Grey thought bitterly, hadn't been enough to save her.

In Scaela, there used to be more monasteries and altars devoted to Locke's gods, but half were destroyed by Eprain and Nestria, who held no respect for the Isle's superstitious ways. Grey herself had only been to one altar on the mainland, the one in Grislar, dedicated to Kitalma. She'd gone there to think and stare out at the sea, but most of all, to ask the goddess if the burden of her blood could be taken from her. If Grey, the last of her daughters, would be blessed with the mercy to forget.

They found the abandoned remains of an old shepherd's cottage as the dark bled through the sunset. They were dotted all over the hills in this part of the country, out of season, closed up for the year. Kier inspected it thoroughly by magelight, repeating the process he'd gone through with the one they'd stayed in two nights before, though that one had been far nicer and less shack-like.

Grey stood in the doorway with her hands clasped in front of her, leaning into the power that flowed through the tether. She'd used so little of it lately, Kier only drawing from her when he was making magelights or clearing brush or seeking heartbeats in the path ahead: it left her feeling restless and overfull, to keep her reservoir of power so high.

He moved carefully through the two little rooms and up to the loft. The floor was half rotted, glassless windows looking out over the valleys that spread below. It might've been nice, once, she thought. Scraps of cloth hung from the bars over the windows, and she could just barely see the cheerful blue floral print. There were the ashes of a hearth near one wall, the chimney open to the dark night. It might've been cozy. Quaint.

She leaned against the wall, watching as Kier examined a patch of writing on the arched doorway between rooms. There was just something about looking at him. She'd never get tired of the familiarity of his shoulders, the shifting hazel of his eyes. He had his hand against the wall now, that ring from his brother shining dull silver – how many ghosts they carried, the two of them – and she imagined, aching, what that hand would feel like on her skin.

'What are you thinking, Flynn?' Kier asked, voice soft. She realized he was pulling from her, the tether showing more than she wanted. It happened, sometimes, that her emotions came through without her pushing them.

'Just, somewhere like this would be nice, maybe. In the hills. Away from it all. When we're retired, I mean.'

He looked over, the corner of his mouth tugging up. 'We've been living on top of each other for years. You're not sick of me yet?'

'Never,' Grey said before she could think better of it. 'And I wouldn't even make fun of you if you brought a whole league of cartographers to your bed.'

He snorted, glancing out the window. 'I wouldn't worry about me bringing anyone else to our bed,' he said. He caught her hand, pressing a kiss to the back of her fingers.

Grey rolled her eyes, pulling back before he could feel the way her heart thudded faster. 'Keep dreaming,' she muttered, because it was what he expected of her; because they always flirted, and nothing ever came of it; because he didn't know how much she wished he could be sincere and let her down easy, for once.

His smile widened. 'It's clear,' he called to the others.

They filed through the open doorway. Sela and Brit laid out the bedrolls while Ola launched herself up the ladder to explore the tiny loft. Eron took the water buckets to the stream behind the house, then left one for Pigeon and brought the rest back. Grey turned away from the activity, from the domesticity of it, and leaned against the open window. Only days left, and then she and her mage would be – what? Just two good friends in a cottage somewhere? A cozy bed for her and Kier and all his would-be lovers, with just enough space for her own broken heart?

She chewed on her nail. She'd thought of telling him a thousand times, a million, how she felt. But he was just . . . There were so many opportunities. He had to *know*, somehow, and the simple fact that he had not said anything sincere was confirmation enough for Grey that he did not feel the same.

She loved him in every way it was possible to love a person. And for the most part, she knew he loved her back, in his own way – but as she stared into the emptiness of the mountains, she wondered for the first time if that would be enough.

Most rites of the Isle are unknown to those outside of the High Family and the close company they keep, but no processes are quite so obfuscated as the selection of the heir. It does not pass by age. If there is some divine right, a predetermined selection made by the old gods the Isle still holds dear, it remains unknown to the rest of Idistra.

'Even the seas burned': A Brief History of the Rise and Fall of the Obsidian Isle by Bell Owndig, University of Isidar

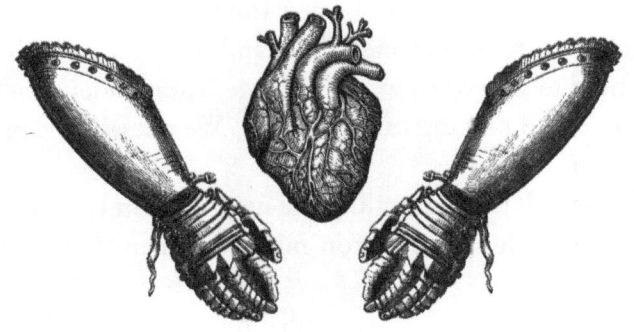

Fifteen

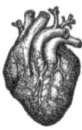

THEIR ROUTINE WAS so well oiled now that Grey barely needed to think. They ate whatever mystery Eron created, then Sela and Brit washed up with buckets of water from the stream while Ola set out bedrolls and Kier examined the map.

'We'll need to stop when we see a village,' Eron said, unpacking the stores of food and making careful tallies. 'We guessed the provisions well, Captain.'

'That's good,' Kier said, rolling the map up. 'Grey, a hand?'

'A hand from the Hand,' Eron muttered, then sighed. 'I need a break.'

'Six months of leave,' Kier reminded him.

Grey lowered herself to the floor next to him. He sat in the corner, one knee tucked up with a stack of papers propped on his thigh, the other leg straight out in front of him. He had a pale blue magelight balanced on his lap, casting ghostly light over the paper, deepening the shadows of his face. He kept rubbing at his straightened knee, pain written in the line of his mouth – he'd ripped a tendon in a skirmish three years ago, and it acted up when it was cold, or when he overdid the walking. Grey laid her hand flat over his knee and pushed a swell of power to him, relishing his sigh of relief.

'Thanks,' he muttered. Brit and Sela came in from the cold, closing the crooked door behind them; Kier barely looked up at the noise. 'Can you read this? I don't know if I'm phrasing any of it right.'

Grey took the paper. Neither of them was uneducated, and part of their training involved a certain measure of diplomacy – and with every promotion, there'd been further training on how to speak to officials. But there was a difference between 'this is how you write a missive to a master' and 'this is how you propose a truce between two nations who have been fighting for nearly two decades'.

She leaned against his shoulder, closer to the magelight, and skimmed the lines, half distracted by Ola and Eron's joking. Her belly was warm with power, overwarm really, and she pushed a great knot of it to Kier.

He made a low noise in his throat, his hand closing over her knee. 'You're making me *very* sensitive, Flynn,' he murmured.

'I think it's a start,' she said carefully. 'But I know so little about diplomacy, so perhaps Sela—'

Kier's hand tightened on her knee, fingers digging in. He wasn't looking at her – he wasn't looking at *anything*. His eyes were focused straight ahead, mouth half forming something he didn't say.

'Quiet a moment,' Grey said to the others, pushing another knot of power at Kier. 'What is it?'

He was on his feet in an instant, drawing his sword, swearing in a lovely mush of anger. 'Heartbeats,' he said, stalking into the back room. There were no windows there, but he launched himself up the ladder to the loft. Grey hurried up after him, the others starting to follow until Grey made a quick sign with her hand. Eron pulled Sela into the corner of the back room, away from the door and windows. Ola and Brit lurked by the door, swords drawn.

Kier hoisted himself up into the loft and threw open a flue he must've found earlier. Grey hesitated, watching him push up through the ceiling, then followed suit, dragging herself to sit on the roof with him.

'We are absolutely going to fall through the ceiling,' she muttered, her heart pounding in her chest. Kier looked . . . She couldn't say it, couldn't come up with the words. She pushed him more power and he winced.

'What do you sense?' she asked, squinting out into the frigid night. The dark was cold and clear, the sky cloudless above, but it was a waxing moon – it was so unbelievably dark, and they were down the mountain enough that they didn't have the lightening effect of the snow.

'I hope I'm wrong,' Kier muttered. He reached out blindly and she pressed her hand to his, squeezing tight. He took a shuddering breath, the tether between them running thick and taut with power. 'There are heartbeats, Grey. Human ones. All around.'

She twisted around, looking behind them, up the ridge; then over. There, in a copse of trees behind Kier's back, she only just made out the barely-there glow of a magelight.

'Kier,' she said, nodding in that direction. He craned around, sucking a breath through his teeth.

'How many do you feel?' she asked.

His eyes flicked shut, and she felt the fizzle of magic. 'Thirty, at least,' he said, defeated. 'Maybe more. We're so close to the border – I wanted to avoid the higher elevation. *Fuck*, Grey.'

'Hey, hey,' she said, squeezing his hand. 'We've gotten through worse.'

'They're surrounding us,' Kier said, his magic mapping a scene that she couldn't see. 'I don't think we can fight them. Not with Brit still injured, not with only five of us and Sela.'

'Don't panic,' she said, but she was also panicking, so it was unhelpful.

Kier was gazing off into the distance, away from the mountain ridge – she did not like the look on his face. 'You could get them out, you know,' he said quietly.

'Kier, I'm not leaving you.'

'You could at least let me try to protect you,' he said, frustrated.

She shook her head. She was not going to be the survivor again, not when it was Kier she risked losing. 'Hold the martyrdom for a second. What if . . . Do you think we could take them? You and me?'

His gaze snapped to hers, brow raised. 'Thirty? Forty? An entire company? Not a chance.'

'We could try.'

He shook his head. 'There are wells too. Even if we take out the mages and typics, we wouldn't have the strength to fight the Hands after.'

She chewed on her lip, assessing the well within her. She had not told him, out of fear, what it really meant to be Locke. What it really meant to be the first and last point of power, to hold the fate of all wells in her hands.

She had not told him, in her sixteen years of loving him, what she had done. What she could do. There was the chance, when he knew, that he would not love her back.

He saw that she was thinking something and grabbed her hand. The power flowed stronger between them. 'We can't take them alone,' he said.

Behind Kier's back, she saw movement as the first line of soldiers crept down the ridge toward the little house – they hadn't been spotted on the roof, she suspected.

'Not alone,' she said quietly. The reality of the situation was dawning on her, watching that line of soldiers move slowly but steadily toward them. She saw Kier's gaze shift and suspected he was watching the same thing over her shoulder.

'Captain?' Eron called from below. 'There's movement ahead.'

'Do you trust me?' Grey asked.

He looked at her, serious as she had ever seen him. She had no idea what he could possibly be thinking when he said, 'Unquestionably.'

Once she did this, once she *showed* this, she could never take it back.

She reached out, very carefully, and touched his cheekbone. 'You and me,' she said, so quietly, as if her heart had already broken.

'You and me,' he agreed. 'Final count is forty-three.'

She nodded, feeling that odd power run through her, placid as ever. When she followed him down the stairs, she felt herself a girl again, following Severin into the basement. Kier's boots hit the dirt and the image flickered; the fire burned to nothing.

'Listen close and listen quickly,' Kier said. 'We don't have much time.'

The others stood awkwardly, weapons ready, confusion clear.

'We're completely surrounded,' he announced with the grim sort of cheer that came before a near-death experience – or death, she thought. 'Grey and I are going to do what we can. Brit, Ola, the second you hear anything, I want you running out the front and down the ridge, toward the sea. Eron and Sela, you ride Pigeon and seek shelter. The others will catch up. Get as far as you can. If we make it, we will find you. Do you understand?'

'But Captain—' Brit started.

'That's an order,' Kier said. He looked at Grey, his eyes heavy with longing, and she understood. He hesitated, scanning the others. 'I don't think I can say what an honor it has been to lead you,' he said, and she couldn't look at him, because if Kier was being soft like this, so openly – well, it really was the end, wasn't it?

The others put on their coats. Grey sheathed her sword at her hip, like a soldier – she needed her hands. 'Can you tell them apart?' she murmured to Kier as they crossed the front room.

'Yes,' he said. 'Do you trust *me*?'

She gave him a long look. If she did not trust him, they would've been dead a long time ago.

There was no sign of movement when they went out the door and shut it behind them. She had the impression of the artificiality of the night's stillness: no birds flew; no small creatures rustled in the grass. They went three paces from the door and stopped.

Grey faced Kier, watching the wind whip the stray curls over his forehead, tug at the bottom of his coat.

'If we live through this,' she said quietly, 'I want to bring back Locke.' She knew, with gripping certainty, that there was very little chance she would live through this.

The corner of his mouth tugged up, half scar, entirely hers. 'I'll meet you there,' he said.

Something moved in the grass beyond them. There was a signal, then an increase in the rustling. They did not have much time. Grey drew a breath, but she did not look away from her mage. Inside herself, she felt her own power, and she reached.

It was always meant to be this, she could see now, looking up at Kier and watching him look back. The two of them together, dying like this, so close that years from now, someone would come back to this place and find their bones locked together.

She wondered idly, on the edge of death, what had happened to her brother's body. *Severin,* she thought. *Severin, how could I ever forget you?*

She leaned forward before she could lose herself, already feeling the tugging in her middle. She pressed a hand to Kier's cheek to steady herself, then pushed to her toes and kissed him, once, her mouth to his in a move that was almost chaste. It was the only goodbye she could manage.

She broke away – and one of his hands was at the small of her back, pulling her hard against him. His hand found her hair, his fingers spearing through, thumb sweeping across her temple. Kier kissed her, *properly* kissed her as he never had before, and her heart ached with everything she would never have.

Maybe he did know. Maybe, after all this time, this was the one consolation he could give her.

He looked at her when she pulled away, brushing the hair from her forehead. 'Power in bravery,' he murmured, the motto of Locke.

He held his hands out, palms up. Grey placed hers on top of his, feeling the certain exchange of a closed circuit, of her power flowing into him and growing, growing, growing. She took all of the feelings that made her more powerful and swallowed them, not caring if they traveled through the tether. She faced the adoration and the devotion and the love, the jealousy and the agony and the longing. There was not a single word she could say to him to encompass it all, sixteen years by his side and the devastation of not having more.

She forced herself to focus on the pulsing well of power in her middle. She stretched and stretched, reaching, finding the other pulses surrounding them – and she *pulled*.

There was a gasp somewhere, then a cry. Another shout. Kier's eyes flashed open – the irises were not quite hazel, glowing in the gold that emanated from their palms – and there was another yell, too close, and he said, 'Grey—'

She felt the power sliding loose from the wells around them, the cries of horror as all were drained and left barren. It was too much, filling her as she pulled harder, stripping them, leaving them as defenseless against Kier's magic as common typics.

She took all of that power and pushed it at Kier.

The tether in her middle pulled taut, so tight she thought it would cleave her in half. She gritted her teeth against the pain, tears squeezing from her eyes, rolling down her cheeks. She hadn't remembered how much it hurt, to take so much power into herself, to pull it from the root.

It was like being drunk, to have so much at once, to command it. 'Take it all,' she said.

Kier listened. Grey felt the power leave her in one fierce swell even as more rushed in to replace it, and then there was more screaming, louder, from all around; she thought she was screaming, too, and maybe even Kier.

Grey detonated.

She was on her knees in the dirt. There was blood in her mouth. There was blood in her mouth and she was not quite down because there was something there; something had caught her and held her as the screaming around them cut off sharply.

Severin's hands on hers, bruise-tight—

There was nothing left. She was an empty vessel, lowered to the ground on her back. She stared up at the night sky for an immeasurable moment, choking on her own blood.

She felt it in her stomach, the shift of power, the moment her mother died—

Power in bravery. Grey's vision flickered, and she was only half aware of the voice calling her name. Quietly, she slipped away.

Part Three

A
Promise
of
Iron

interlude

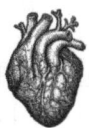

ON THE ISLE OF Locke, night had only just fallen when the ship arrived at the harbor.

In the old days – which really weren't that long ago at all – the child of the Isle who wasn't selected to inherit married based on letters and furtive meetings and discussions of the exchange of power and renewals. Such was the fate of Lady Wren, sent to Nestria to marry the week after her eighteenth birthday; such was the fate of Locke's aunts and uncles and great-aunts and great-uncles. Choice, their mothers and fathers always taught them, was an illusion. Though those on the mainland or in the villages could court and engage in dalliances and marry for want, that was not the role of the Isle, nor the role of its family.

No one was foolish enough to speak of love. Especially when whoever married Severin would not know if they were marrying the heir to the Isle and its power, or only their sibling.

'Choice,' Isaak Locke said to his son, as he swiped imaginary lint off Sev's shoulders, 'is your right.'

They stood in an upper room in the fortress, in the suite the family occupied for themselves. The candlelight burned warm against the frigid gloom – it was nearly spring, but that hardly mattered on the Isle, and wouldn't matter at all until summer came sweeping through Osar and Maerin and the Ghostwood and the Barrens for approximately three weeks before it went racing away again. Isaak had already dressed his firstborn son in one of his own doublets, picked through with shimmering golden thread in the shape of pears and cherries.

From the corner where she sat, Maryse said, 'This is boring.'

Severin shot her a glare. They did not often fight more than the usual bickering between children – after all, with seven years between the two of them, there was not usually much to fight *about*.

'*Gremaryse*,' Isaak sighed. 'Didn't your mother want to speak to you?'

'She already did,' Maryse said, curling back into the cushion she rested in on the floor. It was supposed to be for Markit, Severin's large hound, but Markit had been sent to the stables for the evening. She did not take well to visitors, which was usually fine, because the Isle received few of them – until recently.

'And?' Isaak asked. He glanced at his daughter, and Maryse was certain he saw how her braids had already started unfurling, and how curling into Markit's bed meant she was now covered in dog hair, her new dress wrinkled.

'She told me to behave,' she said primly.

Severin and his father exchanged a glance. Maryse sank deeper into her cushion and closed her eyes, lulled into peace by the scent of firewood and the low murmur of her father's voice.

'You don't have to make any decisions,' Isaak said, turning his attention back to Severin. 'That's not what this is about, not yet. I just want you to see if you take to her, if she is someone you would like to speak to again.' He went back to straightening Severin's clothes, then took a chain from the collection of jewels he'd brought, securing it across his son's chest. Maryse was pretty sure it had been a gift from Torrin to her father – the little stone pins at either side shone light blue. Scaelan colors.

'Is this because of Aunt Wren?' Severin asked. 'Because Uncle Pol is a cur and a brute and a tyrant.'

Isaak cleared his throat. He aimed a look at Maryse, who was watching the two of them through her eyelashes, feigning sleep – she had the feeling she wasn't meant to be here for this little speech, so she just snuggled deeper into Markit's bed, letting a contented smile creep across her lips.

'You did not choose to be born into this,' Isaak said. 'You didn't choose to be born Locke, nor to be a mage, nor to become a piece on the board. So the least I can give you is your freedom, even if your mother resents me for it.'

'She might say she does,' Severin said, stepping away from his father. 'But she doesn't. She married you for love, after all.'

'She married me for duty,' Isaak corrected. 'We just happened to be lucky that duty and love were not mutually exclusive.'

The plot was Isaak's idea, after all. Maryse had lurked in the halls as her parents fought in hushed tones (which was unusual for them) about the future of their children. Isaak was Scaelan and had married into the Isle; thus, Locke's customs probably still struck him as cold and unfeeling. After nearly a week of those hushed fights, and another week further of Maryse watching the stony silences between Isaak, Locke and Severin at family meals, they reached an agreement.

As a child of the Isle not born to inherit, Severin had to marry a noble from one of Idistra's other nations to protect the alliances between the nations, and to increase power. But Isaak was unhappy with the idea of arranging a marriage, no matter how much his wife reminded him of the customs.

In return, he asked for a compromise: from Severin's fifteenth birthday until the day he chose to marry, they would host one eligible noble for one week of every month. That allowed Severin to get to know each of them before he was old enough to marry, and write to the eligible girls to build a relationship over time. He would not be forced into a loveless marriage, as Maryse's beloved aunt was in her youth. He would still marry for power, still follow the rites of the Isle – but he would make his own choice.

When their grandmother heard of the arrangement, she was furious for weeks. The only thing that drew her out of her room when the first visiting noble from Nestria arrived was nosiness – which Maryse understood, because little else kept her from misbehaving.

Now, on the eve of the third visit, Maryse felt the whole business was growing rather dull. After all, how many girls were there in Idistra who would want to marry someone like *Severin*? Maryse loved her brother, but she could not understand someone else willing to love him unless they were forced to.

'Maryse,' Isaak said softly. She felt his hand on her cheek and opened her eyes. Her father stood above her, smelling of pine and the Isle's cold, like he always did (unless Uncle Torrin came to visit, in which case he smelled like wine, and sometimes Torrin's favorite dark liquor). His hair was nearly all gray now, his eyes lined but still joyful. When she thought of her father, she thought of him laughing. She glanced over his shoulder, at Severin studying his own reflection as he chose an earring.

'Yes?'

He gripped her hands, pulling her up to sitting as he squatted in front of her. Maryse turned her fingers to wrap around his hands, as always tracing his rings with her fingertips: one that showed his marriage to Locke; one that bore the crest of the Isle and his own signature as lord consort; and one that made her grandmother roll her eyes: a token from Scaelas as a show of gratitude.

'What else did your mother tell you?' he asked, his voice a bit more tense, a bit more urgent.

Maryse looked down at their linked hands, at the freckles that speckled her father's skin below the cuffs of his shirt. 'She reminded me of what to do,' she said quietly, 'when we have visitors.'

'Recite it for us,' Severin said from across the room. He had turned around to lean on the dresser, his arms crossed over his chest as he stared at his boots. Sometimes, when he stood like that, when she looked up at him, he was still a boy; but sometimes she registered that she was still a child, and he was very much not.

She chewed on her lip. She wished for a day when they could do this, go through these motions, without reminding her of the worst of it.

'If they draw arms,' she said, her voice high-pitched and nervous, 'I am to run to the cellar – not the nice cellar, but the root cellar below – and bar the door. There I am to await my guard. I am to wait, no matter what happens, for someone to come for me.'

'And?' Severin prompted, eyebrow raised.

'Whoever comes must know the recitation of the Isle's holy verses,' Maryse said. 'And I can't keep picking the twenty-seventh verse, just because I like it, as that makes it too easy,' she added.

'Very good,' Isaak said. He tugged on her hair. 'Your ribbons?'

She turned her head, swallowing hard. Her mother had done her hair herself. Isaak ran his fingers over the ribbons and the pearls threaded through them, which really were not pearls at all. They were poison.

'And your boots?' he asked.

She got up, using her father for balance as she turned and lifted her heels, showing him one boot heel, then the other. He tapped them, checking the knives.

'And Maryse,' Severin said. 'If one of them tries to kidnap you?'

She hated this question most of all. 'They are not to succeed,' she said quietly.

'Very good,' Isaak said, kissing her knuckles. He stood, knees creaking, keeping Maryse's hand in one of his. 'And Severin? If you're with her? If you are able to save her?'

A muscle in Severin's jaw tensed. 'I know what to do.'

It wasn't the third month they came for her, or the fourth, or even the fifth. It was the seventh month, weeks before the feast to celebrate Maryse's ninth birthday, when Isaak's desire to give his son a choice became the Isle's undoing.

In Retarik's temple in Osar, now a great hall, Severin and Maryse sat at the high table, awaiting their company. Maryse hated the cold, massive hall, and she was growing so tired of these monthly reception feasts, and Severin had stolen the last of her honey cakes. She sat pouting, arms crossed, as the courtiers in front of her danced. She did her best to avoid Locke's gaze; her mother was surely sending her a stern look to act in a way more befitting her station. To act like the heir to the Isle.

Before these monthly feasts began, Locke had so rarely hosted great dinners like this, so rarely called all the inhabitants of the Isle together for a feast – but now, seven months in, they too danced as if they were weary of the adventure.

Maryse wondered, kicking a wooden beam under the table, how long the treachery could endure.

Beside her, her brother slouched in his chair, one knee brought up to support his elbow. Their father kept darting reproving glances over at him, which Sev studiously ignored.

This was the seventh month – but it was the first time the visitor was a repeat suitor, specifically requested by Severin for a second visit.

It wasn't a wedding, but it wasn't an insignificant event, either. Maryse kept glancing over at Severin. He was only fifteen, but he would probably have to marry at eighteen, which wasn't really that far away – but at least he would be marrying someone he knew. Someone he chose. If she had to marry someone she'd never met before, like Aunt Wren had to, she supposed she would be terrified. She supposed she'd want three years of awful monthly parties to prevent something so heinous.

Maybe, she thought, if Severin made his choice now and focused on courting instead of meeting, the parties could stop, or at least slow down.

If anyone was left in Maerin that night, they would've noticed the shimmering of shields bending around ships, and the soldiers that unloaded from them after the lady was unhanded and taken up to the temple. They would've noticed as the forces moved swiftly through Maerin, then the little houses between Maerin and Osar, making tidy work of anyone who had stayed behind from the night's festivities. They would have noticed the cloying scent in the air – some drug only just discovered on the mainland, one that broke the tether between a mage and a well. One that rendered the warning system of magic between the guards and their High Lady unusable.

They would've noticed as the first of the houses began to burn.

In the great hall, the revelers came to a stop as the doors opened, and the citizens of the Isle melted away toward the walls, clearing a wide aisle between the doors and the head table.

Next to Maryse, Severin stopped his fidgeting. He did not look any less bored, but that in itself was a mask.

The knights came in four columns, their surcoats bearing the crest of Eprain: a boar, speared through, over a field of arrows. When they reached the head table, they split apart to reveal the girl. Last time, she had come with her father, Eprain's commander and Epras's younger brother; this time, she stood alone. She was dressed in pale pink silk, her blonde hair braided and pulled away from her face. She seemed to Maryse to be dripping in gems, from the heavy sapphires at her throat and ears to the pearl and diamond netting that covered her hair, as if she'd been dipped in the sea and had brought the shining remnants of the deepest blue with her.

Maryse wondered if any of her gems were poison, too.

The girl dropped to her knees before the table, her head bowed. 'Your majesty,' she said to Locke, a show of deference. Then, softer, 'My lord.'

Locke stood. 'Lady Polenna,' she replied, addressing the girl first before she nodded at the knights. 'How lovely it is to see you again.'

It was a lie. The last time, after Lady Polenna left, Maryse and her mother went on a spirited ride through the forest to practice Maryse's tethers under pressure, and at a distance.

I don't like her, Maryse had admitted to her mother as they tore through the forest. *I think she's dull.*

Locke had frowned, looking over at her daughter, and Maryse prepared for disapproval – but her mother's eyes sparkled, and she had only shaken her head. *I can't say I disagree*, she said finally. *But a dull wife is better than a dangerous one.*

There was no sign of that now. As usual, Locke greeted outsiders with a cool, lofty disinterest – maybe even superiority – that Maryse herself never managed, no matter how often she practiced the look and tone in the mirror.

'His Lord Epras apologizes for his absence, your majesty,' one of the knights said.

'I am dismayed to hear he could not accompany his niece,' Locke said. Maryse watched her mother's hand on her wine goblet. The silver seal ring tapped against the metal as she lifted it to her lips.

Something was wrong. Unlike Maryse, Locke *never* fidgeted.

'As is he, I assure you.'

Locke inclined her head.

Maryse shifted in her finery. She did not like the look in her mother's eyes – there was an anger there, simmering just below the surface. It was like when Maryse did something she wasn't supposed to in front of strangers and Locke had to keep her temper and not scold her until she they were alone. Maryse was very happy, in that moment, that the look was not directed at her.

'You've brought quite the force,' Locke said. 'Especially for a second meeting.'

The knight said nothing.

The girl, ignored until now, made her way toward the table and bowed her head to Severin. Severin inclined his as well, not as low as formalities would deem appropriate, but enough to acknowledge. Maryse saw her brother's hand by his side, clenched into a fist.

'Did you get my last letter?' the girl asked, her voice low and sweet.

'I did,' Severin said. Maryse did not really understand what they were talking about. She'd seen her brother blushing as he read parchment in the keep's library, but he always folded the papers and pushed her away when she came close. *None of your business*, he said when she asked what he was reading. He spent long hours in his room after the letters started arriving, his fingers stained more and more frequently with ink.

He was so nervous that his voice trembled. Maryse looked at him with something like wonder as Severin reached out to touch the girl's face, his own expression softening. Locke herself did not look at the couple; neither did Isaak. Both stared straight ahead as if daring their court to comment.

'How was the voyage?' Severin asked quietly.

The girl opened her mouth to answer – just as bells started outside. The tolling, Maryse knew, was the sound of alarm for when all other enchantments of warning failed.

Outside the hall, there was a shout. Maryse, paying attention again, felt a great wrenching inside her stomach as the drugs outside began to wear off, as she sensed the desolation unfolding across the Isle without their notice.

A ripple went through the crowd. Maryse heard someone shout, then Locke was on her feet. 'Guards!' she shouted.

Maryse tore her eyes from Severin – there were people falling all around the room, mages crumbling, wells standing shocked. She saw one of the girl's soldiers turn, plunging a sword into someone's stomach.

Severin moved so quickly that Maryse missed it. One moment he was standing still with the girl at his arm; the next, his dagger was through her heart, and she was falling to her knees before him, shock clear on his face.

Maryse stood watching, jaw dropped. For all her lessons, all her poisoned pearls and boots full of knives, Severin had been learning his own rites of protection over the Isle and his sister.

Severin had learned not to hesitate.

'Take her,' Locke said urgently, moving around Severin to Isaak as he rose.

Severin grabbed Maryse, his hands still slick with blood. It took Maryse a moment to realize she was sobbing, great racking cries tearing from her throat. Sev shushed her as he fled through the kitchens with her in his arms, then down a back passage into the cellar. There was another stairwell down that way that led to the sea – but when he wrenched the door open, they were greeted with a wall of flame. He slammed the door, coughing from the smoke.

He hesitated, and they both heard the boots on the floor above them.

'I thought you loved her,' Maryse cried, unable to make sense of it all. Upstairs, someone shouted – one of the cooks.

'I love you more,' Severin said fiercely. He set her down in the dirt and paced, pulling at his hair. 'I just – Retarik's bones, this wasn't supposed to happen. What do we do? What do we *do*?'

Maryse flinched when Sev swore on the name of the gods. She sat, her knees pulled to her chest. Upstairs, she could feel the push and pull of magic; she could sense the wells being extinguished like flames. She could not make herself reach for her pearls, nor her knives – not when she wasn't alone here, not when Severin had escaped too, not when it was actually happening.

'Is Locke living?' Severin asked, dropping to his knees in front of her.

She reached out – she was not good at it, unpracticed still, but she pressed. She tried to sense her mother in the battle above. There was a great flame in the middle of it, but it was waning.

'Yes,' she said. *But not for long*, something whispered in her mind. Severin must've read the look on her face.

He gripped both of her hands. 'I cannot protect you from this,' he said. He held her face, pressed her close to kiss her forehead. 'Don't be afraid, Maryse.'

'I'm not.'

He took a breath, the panic on his face clearing, resolving into a peaceful calm she did not understand. It scared her, then, how much he looked like their father. 'I need you to do something.'

She looked up at him, terrified. There were boots on the stairs, then fists slamming the doors. Severin looked up, over her shoulder, and sucked a breath through his teeth. 'We don't have much time.'

Agony tore through her. Maryse gasped, gripping her stomach as some great power extinguished. She screamed, trying to keep the pain at bay, but it was no use. She fell forward onto her hands. Severin caught her and held her close. He shook against her, and when she looked up, her brother was crying.

'Locke has fallen,' he said, reading the expression on her face. He closed his eyes for one brief moment. Maryse could not stop the sobs that racked her body, the keening noise coming from somewhere deep in her chest. There was a crackling sound behind them, and she sobbed harder as the door behind Severin smoked, then burned.

He shook his head. 'Stay quiet.'

She stayed quiet. He repositioned them so they sat on the floor, facing each other. She tried to wipe her nose, but he caught her hand and held it. He took her free hand with his. A closed circuit.

There was pounding overhead, pounding behind her, crackling flames behind him.

'You are Locke now,' Severin said, very quietly. 'Do you understand?'

She shook her head.

'I need you to do it, Maryse.' He did not explain, and he did not need to. He wanted her to do the thing she had been expressly told she mustn't do unless the Isle itself was at stake. He wanted her to do the thing that hurt more than anything else, the thing that felt the very best of all.

'I can't.'

'You *must.*'

'I—'

'Maryse, if they find you, if they *take* you, they'll get all the power of Locke. They will find a way to control it.' He spoke quickly, so quickly that his words were tangled, but she understood them all the same. It was the same thing her mother had always told her, had always warned her might come to pass.

'We can run. Together.'

'We *can't*,' Severin said, and now the tears flowed freely down his cheeks. 'If they take you, if you refuse to let them control you, they will make you bear an heir as soon as you're able. One who will hand over all the power, who they can control – and then they'll kill you anyway. I can't save you. You have to save your power, Maryse – you have to save yourself.'

She knew. She knew all of it, and what would happen to her if she didn't use her own power. She could barely breathe, choking on tears.

'After it's done, you have to run. You will live, Maryse, if you forget us.'

'No.'

'Do you promise,' Severin whispered, 'to let us go?'

'*No,*' she whimpered. She did not hug him; she did not break the circuit. He squeezed both of her hands, and it hurt.

'You have to,' he said.

As she sobbed, the door behind Severin exploded in a shower of sparks. They both ducked, but the hot embers showered down on Sev's body. Above her, he screamed in pain even as he shielded her. She felt the tether take, the most familiar sensation in the world.

'*Now, Locke!*' he shouted.

Maryse relented. She reached out, felt the swell of the island below her, felt the swell of the power as she stripped it from every other well on the Isle. It all rushed into her in one great torrent, so much power for such a small body, *too* much power. She pushed it at Severin even as he screamed.

Eyes shut, his hands gripped in hers, they detonated Locke and everything with it.

It is not a weakness, Alma – or should I only call you Locke now? – to love. I wish my own union had been as lucky, and frankly, I envy you. It is a mighty, powerful thing for someone to see your worst faults (and as your sister, I assure you there are many) and want all of you anyway.

Letter from Wren Locke Teinek to Alma, High Lady of Locke, 18 years AD

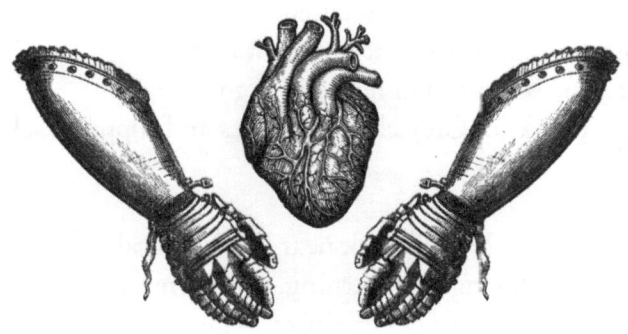

sixteen

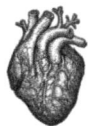

HER CHEST FELT LIKE it was splintering to pieces. Something warm was pressing on it, hard enough to break her. Her eyes were already open when she focused on the bleary shape above her. It was his hands on her heart, forcing it to beat.

'I have you,' he said. 'I'm not letting go.'

He didn't have to. Grey closed her eyes and slipped back under.

'Grey.'

She was back in herself, back near her own body, though she had no memory of leaving or returning. Her name was soft, insistent, in a voice she wasn't fully certain of – she was conscious that her head hurt, an endless beating pain behind her eyes. She hissed at the pressure of it, the wet heat of her mouth, the taste of metal. She did not think she could move – every limb was cemented, paralyzed, as if someone had draped a great lead-lined blanket over her and tied her to the ground.

Hands on her forehead, brushing her hair away – something cool. 'Grey,' they said again, then more distantly, 'Captain. She's stirring.'

'Our fucking luck to lose the healer,' someone else said. Brit.

'Go be unhelpful somewhere else,' Kier snapped.

Movement. More shuffling. Something warm and dry was on her cheek, then a door closed elsewhere. All other voices ceased – all other noises cut off. She stretched her hands and felt fabric underneath them; nice soft fabric, not the bedrolls they'd been using for the last two weeks.

The emptiness stretched out inside of her like a raw wound, like something had been cleft from within her, leaving her a bloody shell in its wake. She moved her hand to her stomach as if to prove it was still there – a hand caught hers and something tried to spark to life in that emptiness.

The migraine flared. She hissed against it. His lips brushed her forehead, and she sank back into nothing.

She came awake like a small vessel cresting over a wave. She sucked in a breath, asleep and screaming one moment and awake and screaming the next, her throat cracking and bleeding again, and the dark was so full and awful and complete—

Noises sounded in the other room, but in this one, she sat straight up into nothing. The fire ceased – Grey stopped screaming. She opened her eyes.

She didn't know where she was – an enclosed space, dirt floor, thatch roof. She was in a small room, alone, even though he'd promised she wouldn't be.

A shape darkened the doorway. She knew it as she knew her own heart. Kier stepped into the room clutching a magelight to his chest – not his, not without her; this one was pale green – and kneeled down before her.

'Are you here?' he asked, and she didn't understand. She reached for his face, ran her hand across the new beard and felt a deep, throbbing ache in her middle. The tether was limp and empty inside of her.

'I can't feel my power,' she said, unable to contain the edge of panic.

He shifted his weight to sit cross-legged next to her, drawing her out of the blankets and into his lap. 'It's okay,' he murmured. 'I feel it. There's just – there's so little left. You need time. We used . . . a lot.'

She buried her face in his chest, searching for memories, even as the dread rose like bile inside of her. 'What did I do?'

Kier paused. 'I don't know if—'

'Tell me.'

Pause. 'We killed them.'

'How many?'

Pause. 'Forty-three. All of them. Mages ... and wells.'

The breath left her in a whoosh – she remembered the catastrophic ache in her gut, the implosion of forty-three hearts at once, the massive death that drained her to the bone.

'I didn't know,' Kier said carefully, 'you could do that.'

'Mm.' She let her eyes slide closed, let that unspoken grief unfurl through the tether. He gripped her harder. 'Don't get used to it.'

'I won't.'

He was quiet for a moment and she listened to his heart, the beating of it, forcing herself not to think about forty-three lives lost in the blink of an eye, forcing herself not to think of the thousands who went down with her lost nation. So much destruction, so much *pain*, all because of her.

'Grey.' There was hesitation in his voice, and she wanted to weep. This was why she'd hidden herself for so long. She couldn't bear it, now he knew the truth of her. 'They never named the heir to the Isle, before it vanished. Because you weren't of age.'

She felt the fear in her chest – but this was Kier, and he already knew. 'No,' she said. 'They didn't.'

'Was Attis right, then? Did it pass to you when Severin died?'

Grey couldn't meet his eye. In her young life, her mother had one rule: do not reveal who is to inherit. Do not reveal who is a mage and who is a well. Do not reveal what power you do or do not hold. Even now, even though this was Kier, and she trusted him with her very soul, she did not know how to speak the words.

She remembered being eight years old, Lot and Kier both looking at her as they hatched a plan. She remembered the lie, like poison in her mouth.

But because it was Kier, she didn't need to lie.

'No,' she said.

'Severin was a mage, wasn't he?'

Grey squeezed her eyes shut. 'Yes,' she said.

'He was never the heir to Locke. It was always you.'

You lied to me, he did not say.

She didn't answer. There was no need to. The heir to Locke was always a well, and if the firstborn was a mage, or typic, then another child would take the Isle.

'Can I put you down? I want to see your face.'

She didn't want him to see her, but she needed to see his expressions. She needed to know how he looked, now that he knew she had kept this from him: this, the biggest secret of all. 'Yes.'

Kier shifted, laying her on her back. She missed the warmth immediately – she couldn't imagine sitting up on her own, let alone seeking him. Her spine felt oddly unarticulated.

He moved to press his hand to her cheek, stroking softly. 'Is that what happened?' he asked, so quietly it broke her heart.

She looked away, tears coming to her eyes despite herself. He didn't need to clarify. *Is that how you killed them all?* he didn't ask. *Is that how you destroyed Locke?*

'Yes,' she said, her voice breaking. She closed her eyes, wishing away the truth. 'They thought . . . they thought that if they controlled Severin, they could control power. And they tried to take him. But it was never my brother. They needed to control *me*.'

Kier took a breath. Held it. Then he nodded, and kissed her forehead. It took her a second to feel something odd, a pulse of light crawling up the tether – it was like warmth inside of her, nestling in that empty cavern where her power usually resided. She felt it, warm and glowing, a new sort of power, and her bones didn't feel quite like they were not where they were meant to be anymore. She opened her eyes.

'What was that?' she asked.

Kier gazed at her evenly. She felt the wall against her arm; she pulled herself up so she could lean against it.

'Where are we?' she asked instead, rubbing at her eyes. She wasn't wearing her shirt anymore, but rather a large blanket wrapped around her, and her vest underneath.

'Sorry,' he said, noting her gaze. 'You bled or vomited on everything else, so Ola gave up trying to keep you dressed. We're in another shepherd's hut, further down the valley. It seemed . . . safer.'

Grey nodded, taking in the small room. There was a bed frame against one wall, stripped metal, no mattress. This one had a real wooden door, too, but it was shut.

'Do they know what I am?'

Kier winced. 'They suspect as much,' he said.

There was no point worrying about that, so Grey forced herself to move past it, even as she felt her secrets unraveling beneath her. 'How long have I been asleep?' she asked.

'Two days. Nearly. You didn't even stir when we moved you. Scared the life out of Brit – they would've thought you were dead if you didn't make so much noise.' He winced. 'Not exactly the safest way to travel.'

She nodded. 'I'm sorry. I didn't mean to . . . go.'

Kier moved to her legs, stretching them out in front of her. His hands found her calf, massaging the place she was always sore. 'We're alive because of you.'

'That's not true. You did the magic.'

He shook his head, slow and reverent. 'That's not . . . Grey, surely you must know how impossible your power is.'

'Clearly not,' she said, leaning her head back against the wall. 'You know what I am. What that means. What that makes me.' She wanted to close her eyes and sleep for three more days, possibly forever. Kier's hand stilled, as if he could feel the self-hatred leaking through every pore. Yes, they lived – but for *what*?

'Grey.'

She opened her eyes. He sat very still in that way she could never manage – she always had to be moving. Even now, her fingers were caught in the blanket she wore, tangling in the edge. He swallowed hard, and she watched the movement of his throat. He was half the boy she knew, the boy she grew up with, modified with at least a quarter scar tissue and a new broken nose and beard, and yet . . . and yet he was the same. The same but different, and she could only feel an aching sadness inside of her when she thought about him growing older. She wanted to know the changes in him by heart.

'You nearly died,' he said.

'Yes.' There was no point in denying it. Even now, with every movement, she felt like she was one slip-up from the grave.

'And I . . . '

Grey swallowed back the lump in her throat. This was where it would come: this was where he would tell her that she had corrupted herself with that power. 'Yes?'

'I can't imagine . . . not having you.'

She smirked, the corner of her lip tugging up. A seed of bitterness sprouted in her stomach – she wondered if he couldn't imagine not having her, or not having her power. 'Retirement is coming soon, Captain,' she said. 'You're not sick of me yet?'

'That is absolutely not what I mean.'

She laughed, the sound aching inside of her. 'I'm your power. Too *much* power. If you lose me, you'll never do magic again.' She didn't know why she was saying this, why it hurt so much. She wanted to curl up here and for them to leave her alone, for her shame to consume her whole.

'You say it like that's all it is,' he said.

She stared up at the ceiling, thick thatch and mud. 'Isn't it? No matter what we are – you're my mage. I'm your Hand. Perhaps we were fools, all those years ago. It's a piteous thing, to only draw from one person forever and ever, to expect that.'

He paused. 'What are you doing?' he asked. 'Do you really think that? Do you really think *I* think that?'

She couldn't be certain where all this bitterness was coming from – maybe it was from death being such a close thing, the grip of it still cold on her neck; perhaps it was the memory of Locke behind her eyes, the press of Severin's hands in the moments before everything went dark. He'd only been fifteen when he died, still just a boy. He never grew up into anything because he tried so hard to save her, and what had she done? Killed him, just like she'd killed everyone else who ever loved her. All the power of Locke, and she'd squandered it – and for what?

Maybe it was because she knew in her heart that they could not retire to the countryside. There was no peaceful happiness in their future. She had never felt more certain of that fact, and she mourned the loss of it with a raw desperation she barely understood.

She was the heir to Locke, and she was bound to Kier, and she would drag him right down with her.

'Go away, Kier,' she said.

'Do you think,' Kier said, furious but level, 'that I regret binding to you? That I regret taking you as my Hand? That I regret all of the lives we've taken, so that we could survive? Do you think I don't know what it means to be yours?'

She opened her eyes, met his gaze. There was that anger again, so rare, so beautiful in vitality. She felt so lost and he was so goddam alive.

'No,' she said. She clawed for something, feeling desperately the weight of all those heartbeats silenced. She could not analyze the last part of his speech – it would be her undoing. 'You have seen the worst of me. You cannot . . . ' She couldn't finish the sentence.

Kier looked at her, and she felt something open up inside of her, something that made a flood of warmth bloom in her chest, that killed that sprout of bitterness. It took her a moment to realize that the emotion was coming from him, emanating from the tether. It was that earlier feeling, that warmth, but so much stronger. So much *more*.

She remembered the press of his mouth against hers, the desperation in his kiss when she was certain they were going to die.

'Kier?'

'Grey, beloved, you absolute fool – if that was the worst of you, then you remain a saint among us.' He shook his head wonderingly. 'And I have been trying to make you see me as more than your mage for six years now.'

She could not believe this. She could not understand the high color in his cheeks, the light in his eyes. He was so far away from her, the entire distance of her body, and it felt like miles. Even if she wanted to cross them, she wasn't sure her bones would agree, so she kept her cautious distance. She needed to know that she understood, that she wasn't scaring him into a confession he didn't mean now that he knew what she was capable of.

'I adore you,' he said, all in a rush. 'No – no. Listen. I . . . I'm in love with you. I've been in love with you for years, maybe forever. Sometimes it's all I can think about, and I can't breathe because it's so heavy on my chest that I . . . I might be holding it alone, the only thing about you I can't be certain of. It's agony, Grey, the not knowing.'

She could only stare at him blankly as the words clicked uselessly against her brain. She could not imagine it, him saying this to her, him thinking that she could not immediately feel the same.

Kier let out a breath. 'Okay. It's over. It's done. I will . . . go.'

He stood awkwardly, that knee giving him trouble, and despite the wrongness in her spine, Grey lunged forward and caught him around the waist.

'Captain Seward,' she said, holding fast as he dropped to his knees and turned to face her. He kept his other hand on her ribs for stability – she was grateful, because she wasn't sure how she'd remain upright otherwise. 'You fucking cretin.' Panic flickered across his face. 'Why didn't you tell me?'

He laughed, the noise more of a scoff, harsh and disappointed and maybe even disbelieving. 'You never kissed back,' he said.

She sucked a breath, the realization running straight to her stomach. He'd always been affectionate, yes – and she'd thought nothing of it. But every time he'd touched her, every time he'd kissed her forehead or her temple or the back of her hand, every time he'd folded himself around her . . . perhaps each moment had been its own confession.

And she, in her endless attitude of *I bet you say that to all the girls and at least half of the boys*, had utterly ignored it. She'd argued herself out of any possibility that even the most obvious sign was just another affection she didn't deserve.

'Fucking seas, Kiernan,' she growled. Grey leaned across the chasm between them, grabbed him by the lapels of his worn coat, and pulled his mouth down to hers.

They'd kissed before – not like this, never like this, not even when he had kissed her the other day – but his lips to her lips in a move she always wrote off as chaste. After battle, when they were alone again and alive, or sometimes before bed, when he'd kissed her temple and then her mouth. He probably imagined he was stealing those kisses, Grey thought desperately, before any thoughts washed away in the overwhelming headiness of him.

He pulled her into him like he could sink into her skin and become one body. His hands were on her waist, thumbs digging into her ribs, fingers against her vertebrae. She tangled one hand in his hair, the other on his shoulder, mostly for balance. Out of her blanket, there was so much of her skin against the fabric of his shirt and so little of his skin against hers. She scrabbled at the bottom of his shirt, pulling it untucked so she could slide her hands over the planes of his stomach, her thumb rubbing against his newest scar. She hissed as his lips went to her neck. Something opened within her, the slice of a knife in the bottom of her stomach, and she felt the smallest shift as thin, staticky power returned to her.

She dug her fingers in, holding him against her. He nipped her collarbone. 'Don't push yourself,' he murmured against her skin. He kissed the edge of her jaw, the crest of her cheekbone. 'You're still unwell.' He pulled away so he could look at her, and she shivered at the loss of warmth. 'And everyone is worried – I shouldn't keep you to myself.'

She moved her hands to his shoulders. 'You could, if you want.'

He laughed, leaning forward to kiss her with an exuberant joy that she felt through the tether. 'There will be time,' he promised.

But – as the ambush the other night handily demonstrated – there was no guarantee of that. Grey pushed down the rush of uncertain sadness and managed a smirk. 'I'm surprised we made it this long without interruption.'

'Ah, I gave *very* strict instructions.'

He helped her back against the wall and wrapped the blanket over her shoulders.

'Kier,' she said.

'Yes?'

'You don't hate me?'

'I could never hate you,' he said, so sincerely it physically hurt.

'I mean, even now you know what I am.'

He was silent for a long moment, watching her face. 'I've *always* known what you were,' he said finally, carefully. 'Perhaps I didn't always know what it meant, what it meant you could *do*, but it changes nothing.'

Grey nodded, letting herself relax. If Kier said it, above all, she believed him.

He stroked her hair tenderly, pausing after a moment, a smile spreading across his face. 'Hand,' he said wearily, 'do you ever *not* have blood in your hair?'

She tipped her nose up, grasping his hand. 'Perhaps I could be convinced to try harder. Maybe during retirement?'

He leaned down and kissed her once more, a promise of things to come. 'It can't happen fast enough,' he said.

It was Ola who came in first, Grey's healer's kit in hand. Her mouth was set in a grim line and she had dirt streaked across one cheek.

'Lie back, Captain,' she said. Grey did, sliding back on the tangle of fabric. She'd discovered after Kier left that it was a heap of coats protecting her from the wood floor, and had to bite her lip at the rush of emotion that came when she realized that everyone had donated their coat in this cold for the sake of keeping her warm.

She pressed her lips together as Ola moved down to palpate her abdomen. 'Was anyone else hurt? I can—'

'*Captain.*' Ola pinched her side. 'Stop being a hero and let us take care of you,' she said, exasperated.

Grey stopped trying to be a hero. She stared straight up at the thatch ceiling as Ola sat back on her heels to carefully brew a tea to ease her pain.

'Why "Captain?"' she asked, despite herself.

'Hmm?'

She propped herself up on her elbows, wincing, ignoring the scowl Ola aimed in her direction. 'You have been calling me Captain, not Hand. Pretty much since the inn. That's Kier's title, not mine.'

Ola blinked at her owlishly. She handed over the hot mug and

Grey propped her shoulder against the wall to give herself stability to drink. 'I suppose,' Ola said finally, 'we see you as equals. You and Kier.'

Grey gagged a little at the salty taste of the tea. 'Do we have anything to consume that isn't ghastly?' she muttered.

'You're lucky you missed dinner. Eron tried to be creative to make us all feel better.'

Grey sighed, but she forced herself to drink. There was a timid knock at the door, and she and Ola looked up as Sela peeked inside.

'Come in,' Ola said. 'I doubt we can do much more to offend Grey's modesty.'

Grey shrugged. After years living in shared tents, she didn't have much modesty to begin with. 'Kier mentioned something about clothes,' she said, glancing down. Her vest was different, and she didn't remember these breeches either – they weren't the black ones she'd been wearing on the road.

Ola and Sela exchanged a look. Three wells in a room, Grey thought neutrally, and two as good as useless.

'Your clothes caught on fire,' Sela said.

'Not *fire*, really—'

'What?'

Ola shot Grey a glare. Chided, she went back to sipping her tea. 'We didn't see the whole thing,' she said, 'and the captain is unwilling to give us details. But there was a great flare of light, and then you were screaming – Brit ran out to help because they're incapable of following orders.'

'You were on fire,' Brit said from near the wall. Grey hadn't even heard them come in. 'Sorry – I'm supposed to tell you Kier is relieving Eron on watch.'

'He shouldn't,' Grey said grimly. She set the empty cup down and pulled herself fully into sitting position. She felt mildly better and annoyed about it. Ola took the cup and set to brewing a new blend of tea and herbs.

'He has been . . .' Ola searched for a word.

'Unmanageable?' Brit offered.

'Unstable?' said Sela.

'*Stressed*,' Ola said, glaring at both of them. 'He has been *worried* about you. With good reason. Brit ran out, then they carried you back in, smoldering and naked, choking on blood, with a full company dead outside. Mages *and* wells.'

Grey winced. She accepted the full cup Ola offered and tried to sip without pulling a face. 'I'm sorry,' she said finally. 'I didn't mean for things to ... end like that.'

Ola sighed. 'Sela, sweetheart,' she said, turning to the girl. 'Can you go fetch Grey some bread?'

Sela nodded and went out. As soon as the door shut behind her, Ola leaned forward. Brit moved in front of the door, their shoulder pressed against it so they'd catch it when Sela came back.

'That's not normal power,' Ola said, an unsteady edge to her voice.

Grey was too tired for this. 'Kier and I are bound,' she said, as if that was explanation enough.

Ola shook her head. 'Magic can't kill wells, Captain.'

Grey met her gaze. She felt half-dead and exhausted, but the weight of Kier's confession had given her new buoyancy – perhaps, she thought, she was ready to gamble.

'If you're trying to say something,' she said, 'it's best to get on with it.'

'You knew Sela wasn't Maryse of Locke.'

At least that one was easy. 'Leonie left notes. I knew she was too young.'

Ola grimaced, pushing that away. 'Clever. But how did you know *for certain* that she wasn't a Locke? How did you have that much power?'

Brit crossed their arms. 'There are just a few things that don't add up,' they said apologetically. 'Nothing against you, Captain, but I've never seen Ola catch fire and burn all her clothes off.'

'You wish,' Ola muttered.

'It was a lot of power at once,' Grey said. 'I can't pretend to understand what happens when one uses that much power that quickly.'

Brit and Ola exchanged a look, as if holding some unspoken conversation. Brit raised an eyebrow and Ola shook her head; Brit seemingly disobeyed her advice. 'Why were you crying out for Severin of Locke?'

'What?'

'Severin. He was the heir, wasn't he?'

Grey clamped her jaw shut. Just barely, she remembered what Kier had said to her when she first woke up: *Are you here?*

Where had she been before? Or more accurately, *when*?

She shook her head. 'Can I have a shirt, please?'

'Sorry,' Ola said, handing her a soft gray one, too big, from Kier's bag. 'But Grey—'

'I'm not going to tell you anything that endangers you or the mission,' Grey said, struggling into the shirt. It hurt to pull anything over her head, hurt to move her arms like that. She knew, deep inside, that she should've been more alarmed: it could mean nothing good for others to know about her identity, and if Brit and Ola knew, then Eron probably did as well, and possibly even Sela. Sixteen years of hiding, all of it for naught.

But she didn't care. She couldn't find it in herself. All she felt was that empty hollow where her power used to rest, and the anxiety of being out of Kier's eyeline. 'We can talk later. After this is over,' she said eventually, when they wouldn't move from their tense positions. 'Is that answer enough?'

Ola and Brit exchanged a long look. 'Yes,' Brit said finally.

'Good.' Grey slipped down in her nest of coats. 'I'm going to sleep, then. Again. I've had enough of you lot for one day.'

Neither of them protested. Grey closed her eyes, pushed away the ache of her empty well and forced herself to sleep.

She woke again in the early hours of the morning to the pitch-dark hut. She sat up, relieved to find that her bones felt as they should and her skin was not aching in that oversensitive way it did when she'd used too much power. The only thing that hurt was her head, and that was to be expected after being unconscious for the better part of two days.

She squinted into the dark, making out two shapes nearby: Sela and Eron, she decided, so Brit and Ola were probably on watch duty and Kier was . . .

Anxiously, she reached through the tether, but she couldn't find him there. She got up, wobbling a little, holding to the wall for stability. She felt steadier by the time she reached the door, just barely ajar. She pushed through it.

The front room was smaller than the back: a worktable pushed against one side under the window, curtains drawn; two chairs beside it the only other furniture. Kier sat in one, hunched over the table, writing. A half-melted stub of candle was lit beside him, the light dim and flickering.

'Magelight would be more effective,' Grey said softly.

He looked up, an errant lock of hair falling across his forehead. His expression softened when he saw her standing, like that was a mighty, marvelous thing.

'I like the novelty,' he said. It was a bold-faced lie and she knew it – he couldn't make a magelight without her, and he wasn't going to draw from her. She reached within herself and felt the tether dormant.

'We used to do this back home,' she said carefully. 'Candles. Fires burning in the hearth.'

He raised an eyebrow. 'All that power, and you chose not to use it?'

It hadn't seemed like an abnormality when she was a child. In truth, the Isle of Locke was a cold and brutal place: fire warmed much more effectively than magelight, and she'd always preferred the flickering of candlelight over magelight's flat, unchanging glow; she suspected her mother was the same, and her grandmother. Her grandmother, Locke's own mother and the Locke before her, was still living when the Isle was conquered. Grey had not watched the old woman die. Now, she recalled her weathered, wrinkled hands holding a candle as it burned, then tipping it so the wax pooled neatly in the middle of the parchment. She was the one who had taught Grey the lineage of her mother's ancestors, guiding Grey's finger up the lines of the tree. Her husband, Locke's father, had been from Luthar, just as Locke's husband was Scaelan; it was the custom for the sovereign to marry within the other nation states to renew power there.

Grey pushed the memories away. Those dusty books, the family trees, her grandmother's body – all were lost to the sea.

'You can pull from me,' she said mildly. 'I'm okay.'

'You very nearly weren't.'

She shrugged, allowing this.

On her feet, removed from her cozy pile, she felt utterly filthy. Kier hadn't been lying earlier when he accused her of having blood in her hair. She was surprised he'd wanted to kiss her, but perhaps that was the thing about love. She didn't mind him filthy post-battle. The sweat, the dirt, the blood – it all meant he was still alive.

She spotted vats of water near the door, two full, one nearly empty. She retrieved a cup and filled it with water, using it to wash her mouth. She found a packet of tooth tabs in one of the packs and chewed the chalky tablet into a paste.

'What are you doing?' she asked Kier after she rinsed her mouth. She already felt vaguely more human. She found a bucket on the other side of the room, probably used to hold water or feed when the hut was in use, and checked to make sure it was clean.

He sighed, sitting back. 'Writing correspondence to Scaelas. I meant to yesterday, but you were . . . ' He trailed off, leaving the state of her up for interpretation. 'I keep crossing things out, rephrasing.'

She pulled off her shirt so she wouldn't get it damp. Grey retrieved the soap from Kier's shaving kit (his pack was much closer than hers, and his soap smelled nicer anyway) and poured a cup of water over her hair, leaning over the empty bucket. Her hair mostly contained, she started massaging the soap into it. It made a phenomenal mess, but at least she would be free of the filth of her sickbed.

'What are *you* doing?' Kier asked.

'Washing my hair.'

He sighed, the sound long-suffering. 'You're getting soap and water everywhere. Grey – how about I do that, and you can repay me by looking this over? Or write it yourself? I imagine you're far better at it.'

She looked up from her bucket, wet hair dripping day-old blood down her face. 'I'm a lady,' she said primly, 'in every definition of the word.'

That was enough to get a smile out of him. He slipped down onto the floor on the other side of the bucket, kneeling so his knees framed the wood. 'Just rest your chin,' he murmured, positioning her head where he wanted it. Grey relished the ache in her back, the dampness of her knees from the growing puddle, the cold of the water and the warmth of Kier's hands: all of it meant that she had survived, against the odds.

Kier massaged the soap into her scalp, his fingers deft and sure. She stifled a moan, turning her head and biting her lip.

'You know,' he said, taking the cup and pouring a stream of cold, clean water over her hair, 'I imagined telling you my feelings a thousand times, in a thousand different ways. And yet I never imagined the evening ending with your head in a bucket.'

She winced. 'Sorry.'

'Grey, if I don't spend the rest of my life washing gore out of your hair, then it's not a life worth living.'

She laughed despite herself, then closed her eyes, focusing on his hands on her scalp, rinsing out the soap.

'Hold still a second,' he said, and she heard rustling. He wrung out most of the water, then wrapped something around her head, lifting the mass of her hair. When a sleeve fell loose over her shoulder, she realized that he'd wrapped her hair in a shirt.

'Won't we need this?' she asked.

He shrugged. 'I've lost more clothing to you on this mission than during the entire war effort,' he said, resigned, and she noted with some glee that he hadn't realized just how many of his shirts she'd stolen.

'Kier,' she said before he could move away, even though there was a bucket of filthy water between them and she did need to clean the rest of her body before leaning further into any sweeping declarations. 'Did you mean it?'

He stopped ruffling her hair in the shirt and looked down at her. 'Which part?'

Grey chewed her lip. This whole afternoon felt like a fever dream, and to her credit, she wasn't entirely dismissing the idea that it *had* been one. 'That you want to spend forever washing viscera out of my hair.'

He laughed, warm and safe and familiar, and pressed a kiss to her forehead. 'I can think of no better way to spend our retirement.'

'But . . . our retirement.' She looked away, suddenly shy. 'You know what it means.'

He smiled, but it was a sad sort of thing, weighted with understanding. 'We have time to figure out what the future holds. Now come on, my lady. You foolish, courageous girl. Have a look at my letter.'

Grey released a breath. If he didn't want to talk about Locke now, and what she had to do, then she was fine to put it off.

She read his letter. She read it over and over, top to bottom, until the words bleared together, making corrections with his pen. Finally, she said, 'Give me a new sheet. My handwriting is better,' and he complied in an instant.

Halfway through, working on the phrasing of a line, she said, 'Brit and Ola suspect the truth.'

He looked up from his own letter – when she'd taken over the diplomacy, he'd started one to his mothers. 'I think Eron does as well. He said something about it when we were switching watch.'

Grey winced. 'Apparently I . . . made the fact obvious.'

'I tried to stifle it,' Kier said. 'Your screaming, I mean. I carried you when it got too bad, when Pigeon would go no further with you making such a racket on his back.' He sighed, putting his pen aside. 'I'm sorry. I should've thought of a better explanation than none at all.'

'It's not your fault,' Grey said, her brain caught on *I carried you.* How far? How long? 'Useless horse.'

'Mm.'

'What do we do?' She couldn't avoid the not knowing, no matter how much she wanted to.

'It's your call,' he said. She shot him a brief, withering glance. 'No, really – Grey, it's your life, your identity. This is not my mission, and even if it was, I would defer to you.'

Grey sighed, looking down at her letter. It had not come easily to her until she thought of her mother and grandmother, the lofty way they'd read her stories when she was a girl, and then it had seemed effortless. 'I think I need to stop running,' she said carefully. 'But I don't want to make that decision with an army at my back.'

Kier nodded, considering. 'Then we finish the plan as we've established it. We try for peace between Scaela and Cleoc Strata. Then you and me – and the others, if you desire it; if they too desire it – will go and try to figure out how to resurrect the Isle.'

She sat back, watching the light of the flickering candle. Her heart stirred with the anxiety of it, and something like hope. 'Okay,' she said.

'Do you know how to do it? How to bring it back?'

Grey chewed on her lip. 'Not exactly,' she hedged.

He raised an eyebrow.

'It can't be as easy as me just … going into the sea. Bleeding. Giving some sort of offering. Because we grew up on the coast, and gods know you and Lot and I put one another through more than enough bodily harm. I've bled into the sea a thousand times, and I've never raised the Isle with that alone.'

'Not that I can recall,' Kier agreed. 'There must be some other way to do it.'

'I suppose there must be.'

Under the table, his knee nudged hers. 'Does this mean I get citizenship?'

She crumpled one of the discarded pieces of paper and lobbed it at his head. 'Only if you're very, *very* good in bed.'

His eyes darkened, grin twisting with something that woke the tether up inside of her. They always flirted … but never with the potential of following through. 'My lady,' he said. He reached across the table for her hand, leaning to raise it to his lips. 'I look forward to the opportunity to prove myself.'

She kicked him under the table. He only laughed, leaving his hand twined in hers as they went back to their letters.

Solitude is the nature of Locke. Though it is the only nation in which the sovereigns sometimes share the title, the warm feelings of unity do not extend to the rest of Idistra: the Isle keeps its own secrets.

'Even the seas burned': A Brief History of the Rise and Fall of the Obsidian Isle by Bell Owndig, University of Isidar

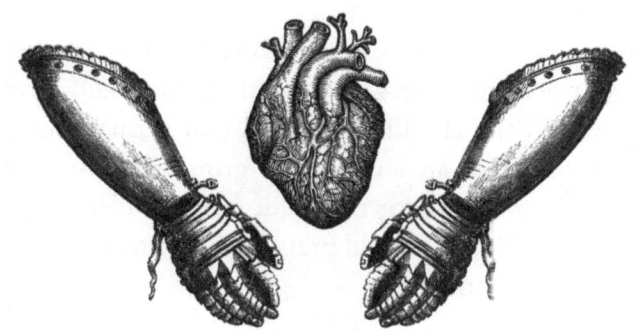

seventeen

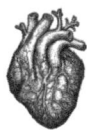

Despite grey's unsteadiness, even Kier agreed, when morning came, that it would be foolish to stay another day. So after she returned from her sunrise wash in the frigid stream, they dressed in what little clothing they had that wasn't covered in her blood, sweat or vomit, ate a quick and grim breakfast of jerky and dried fruit, and prepared for the road. Grey handed out the coats from her nest, wishing she could press the full extent of her gratitude into each and every one.

Kier stood over the table, tri-folding their letters one by one. 'Hold on,' Sela said, grabbing the two she'd written: the first to Cleoc, her mother; the second to Scaelas. Sela drew quick lines next to the names on the two pieces of parchment.

Grey peered over her shoulder; Kier peered over Grey's. 'What are those?' he asked.

'Diplomatic symbols,' Grey said. 'To ensure important letters reach the High Courts as quickly as possible. The second a rider sees them, they're to put down all other duties and travel straight to the recipient.'

'How did you know that?' Sela asked.

Behind her, Eron muttered, 'Told you so.' Kier shot him a

withering look before taking the envelopes from Sela and tucking them in his coat.

'Let's get going,' he said. 'Five days to Grislar at our pace, and I've requested a party to meet us at the encampment. Those letters will beat us there.'

They set off, sore and the worse for wear. Eron and Brit took the lead, Sela and Ola behind. Kier insisted that Grey should ride Pigeon, which she accepted with minimal complaint. Kier was content to stay back beside her, and Grey suspected it had something to do with her unsteady progress and the way he kept looking at her.

By mid-morning, they could see the edges of a city at the base of the mountains. Kier took Pigeon and his letters and rode while the rest of them ate dried fruit and complained about the drizzle. He returned nearly an hour later and confirmed that the letters had been sent with haste.

The landscape shifted again as they walked through the afternoon, the mountains behind them growing further and further away. This was the land Grey was most accustomed to, rolling hills and stands of skinny trees, intersecting dirt paths with grass growing down the middle. They walked and walked and walked, stopping for water or food more often than usual at Kier's insistence. This, Grey decided, was so she would not tire too easily on the road, or to force her back onto Pigeon if she was taking a turn walking.

At nightfall, they camped at the edge of a copse of trees, huddled together in the gloom as a storm rolled in. It was miserable and wet and cold, but Grey had the odd feeling that soon, they'd never be this way again. She tried her best to treasure it all, from Eron's shitty food to Sela's face as Grey taught her a new lesson while Brit tethered and created a pale green magelight with her power. She stored up Ola's laugh and Kier's bearded smile (she was surprised he still had the beard, but maybe it helped with the cold) and the swell of her own heart when she looked at them and knew that even if it remained unspoken, they understood the truth of her.

The next few days passed the same, but quieter. As the third day wore on, they could smell the salt in the air, growing closer and closer; the next morning, they could see the dark expanse of the sea on the horizon. They had to work to avoid the cities and villages now, but with more travelers on the road, it was easier to blend in. At night, they told stories and asked Grey cloaked questions about the Isle she'd once known, letting the open secret linger in the space between them until even Sela understood.

'I heard the children's godfather went searching for the son. That he got a letter from the boy,' Eron said one evening, idly sharpening a stick with one of his knives. 'Everyone was so certain that one of them lived.'

'He did,' Grey said, lying on her back, her head pillowed on Kier's thigh. 'No one thought it was a forgery.' It was the closest she'd ever come to a confession.

Eron made a low noise in his throat, nodding like that was a sensible thing to do.

On another night, Ola said, 'They say it's tradition to marry off as many of them as possible to those in other nations. That it renewed the wells in those places.'

'The last Locke's husband was Scaelan,' Kier said. 'That's why their godfather was, too. That's why we had more wells than other nations, when the Isle vanished.'

Grey only nodded. It was nice, sometimes, to let Kier answer the questions she couldn't stomach, and she found her thoughts turning to her father, Isaak. She remembered turning around, just as Severin led her away, to see a sword strike him in the arm, to see great gushes of blood flowing from his wounds.

It wasn't how she wanted to remember him, but it was the last image she had.

They continued their fireside questions, and she allowed it. Often, Kier would reach out during these times and squeeze her hand, or send reassurance through the tether: he knew, better than anyone, how closely she guarded her secrets, and how vulnerable she felt revealing herself.

And worst of all, she felt something changing within her, shifting. She stopped trying to push the others away.

She knew now, exactly, how Brit had three variations of their laughter, based on the appropriateness of any joke; and that they'd been paired with Ola for only two years, after their previous well had died in their arms; and that they were the oldest of four, and took more difficult assignments in order to keep their siblings out of the war. She knew that Ola was probably the best swordsman among them – in bored sparring sessions around the fire, Ola had laid her out on her ass more than once; and that her acid tongue hid the fact that she was incredibly easy to love, and fiercely protective of the people she cared about, which was a group that now included Grey herself. She discovered that Eron used to play the fiddle; that his father was Arkunish and had never returned from a visit to the continent when Eron was thirteen; that he'd started transitioning three years before and now loved and understood himself in a way he had only dreamed of before.

She even knew that Sela had no siblings but a slew of cousins who all threatened to kill her to take the title of Cleoc – jokingly, she insisted, at the quickfire glare that Ola aimed in a general northerly direction.

For all she learned, she knew they were watching her just as closely, *learning* her just as much. It was almost enough to make her uncomfortable – but then Eron handed Kier a warm compress for his knee without being asked one night as they sat around the fire, and Grey decided that it wasn't worth fighting her affection for these people when they were somehow tied to her.

An hour from nightfall on the fourth day, Kier made them stop at a stream because he was 'not bringing a filthy group of thieves into camp'. So they splashed in the water, Sela grim-faced at their lack of modesty; then they all turned around and dried and brushed their hair while she bathed alone. Grey glanced over at Kier and saw him shaving in his reflection on the water and sighed at the end of an era.

That night, after their watch, they lay nose to nose in their bedrolls while everyone else was asleep. After dinner, Sela had spotted a light in the valley below and Kier grimly informed her that it was camp: Grislar was in sight.

'Do you remember when we were here last?' Grey asked. She

reached her hand into the minuscule space between them. Kier laid his hand on top of hers.

'Of course,' he said. 'Our first assignment together.'

'I was so scared.'

'I know. I could feel it, even then.' He leaned forward and kissed her on the nose, then very gently on the lips. 'There's nothing to be afraid of this time.'

'Mm. You sure of that?'

'No,' he said, considering. 'What's the worst that could happen?'

Grey sighed. 'They could know, immediately, that I'm Locke.'

'How?'

She didn't know how to explain it. There was no way to know if reports of the company they'd slaughtered had reached Grislar, but if they had, that kind of power was out of the question for a normal well.

'Because I'm your Hand,' she said, which was somewhat convincing. 'I don't know. I look like my mother, kind of. If someone sees me, and associates me with that power . . . I don't know how to hide it, Kier. If I even can.'

'It will be fine,' he said. 'We'll protect you.'

She traced the line of his jaw with her fingertips. 'You can't protect me from everything.'

'Yes, well. I imagine I still have a few tricks up my sleeve when it comes to your safety. Even if it calls for . . . unsavory finagling.' He slipped his hand to rest on her waist. Since his declaration the other night, she'd developed a new personal obsession with all the ways he touched her during the day, the casual affection that remained unchanged from before, now heavy with meaning. She thought again of his challenge – his *promise* – and shivered with anticipation. It was almost convincing enough to be a result of the cold.

'You inspire confidence with every word, Captain Seward.'

He smiled, his teeth bright in the darkness. 'Just doing my duty to the nation, your majesty.' His hand slipped further – *cheeky bastard*, she thought – and she shimmied him off with a quiet laugh. It was so easy, with him, to pretend.

*

It was nearing noon the next day when they reached the edges of the city. Grislar was an old place, stone buildings crowding closer and closer until they reached the cliffs. The soldiers' quarters were on the far side of the city, close to the fortress that served as Scaelas's summer residence, pressed up against the sea. They'd sold Pigeon to a kindly farmer in the valley just after sunrise, so they walked into the city in a loose knot around Sela.

There was very little fanfare when they made it to the camp, but quite a lot of staring. There were whispers in town about the High Lord's approach the day before, unscheduled. Even more rumors circulated about a party with diplomatic immunity moving down from Cleoc Strata, and an armistice between the nations while the High Lord was in residence.

Grislar was one of the more established forts: real stone walls and a great tower looking out to sea, shining a light toward Eprain for any supply ships that entered the Bay of Locke. Grey paused on the hill that led down to the command building, staring out at the bay.

Home. She felt the press of it, the call of the sea, of the Isle that was once there.

Kier's hand graced her arm, barely a touch. She looked at him, the weight of his stare, as if he could ask if she was okay. She nodded, and they moved on.

They were hustled through corridors until they reached a nicely appointed office, usually reserved for the highest-ranking officer, who had been temporarily moved.

'Commander Reggin will be with you shortly,' the lieutenant said, before he left the group to wait.

'*Commander?*' Brit whispered when the door shut behind the man, leaving them alone.

Kier stood at rest, perfectly at ease near the window. Grey felt she could not mirror any ounce of his easy grace. 'I imagine they realize the importance of what is happening,' he said.

'But a commander?'

He shrugged. Scaelas had two commanders, one for the east and one for the west, the dual-headed authority of his military.

Commander Reggin, the eastern commander, generally operated out of the capitol.

Grey watched Sela, who kept looking anxiously at the door, then the window. The room they were in faced out to sea. Sela perched on the wide edge of the window, back flattened to the wall, as if she could see the cliffs of Cleoc Strata in the distance if she only looked hard enough.

Grey moved to lean against the wall next to her, then caught the girl's hand, lacing their fingers together. 'You have nothing to be afraid of,' she said quietly. 'I won't let anything happen to you.'

Sela looked at her for a long moment, and Grey thought she was going to claim she wasn't afraid. But then she shifted closer, resting her head on Grey's shoulder. 'Do you promise?' she asked.

Grey wrapped her arm more securely around her. 'I swear it.'

Kier came close, dipping his head toward Grey. 'Will Scaelas recognize you? If you look like your mother?'

Grey chewed her lip. 'It's not impossible.'

'Hmm.' He frowned. Before she could react, he pulled the tie out of her braid and arranged her hair so it fell around her shoulders, partially obscuring her face.

'Kier—'

He didn't wait for any further discussion; just moved off toward the other three, leaving Grey blinking after him. She did not hear what he said to them.

It was only a few more minutes of anxious shuffling before the door opened again, admitting a tall, stern man. The assembled guards straightened immediately; Sela did not move, other than to squeeze Grey's hand even tighter.

'Leave us,' Reggin said to the guards, who obeyed immediately, leaving the commander alone with the retinue.

Grey regarded him, from the gleaming polish of his boots to his salt-and-pepper hair, the serious set of his mouth, the absence of his sword. His Hand followed only a few steps behind, a young person with close-cropped auburn hair. The commander only nodded to the retinue as he went around the desk and sat down. Grey watched him watch them, then studied the way the Hand commander stared straight ahead, hands behind their back, firmly at rest. She wondered how such a young well had ended up at Reggin's side.

'Captain Seward,' the commander said finally, folding his hands on his desk. 'I have received . . . interesting reports from your journey.'

'We only did what we were told,' Kier said, slipping back into his captain voice. She hadn't realized how much authority he carried in these meetings, but it was all posturing. Even now, in worn travel clothes, he looked just as refined as the commander.

Reggin nodded to the chair in front of his desk. Kier sat down. Before Grey could move to her place behind him, Eron stepped forward, blank-faced. Grey froze, every muscle tensed as she watched him stand behind Kier and rest his hand on the captain's shoulder.

No one else moved. No one even looked surprised. Looking from face to face, Grey realized that they had *planned* this. She knew Kier well enough to understand: he would present Eron as his Hand when they met the High Lord too, allowing Grey to slip into the background, posing as a typic.

'Hand Captain,' Reggin said, nodding at Eron. Eron greeted the commander formally, in the perfect posture of a Hand. Grey squeezed Sela's hand back fiercely.

She never got to watch Kier's face in these meetings, since she spent most of them behind his back with her hand on his shoulder. Now she watched Eron – she hadn't realized before how similar they were in height and build, though Eron's skin was medium brown whereas Grey was pale, and his hair was black and curly against Grey's brunette.

But with only a name and rank and maybe a few statistics, who would know the difference?

'It's good that you left when you did,' the commander said, sitting back in his chair. 'Mecketer was attacked shortly after your departure.'

Grey's heart dropped. The others exchanged uneasy glances. They all had friends back at Mecketer, and though they were not planning to return . . . 'What happened?' Kier asked, obviously stressed. 'I left Lieutenant Chappelle—'

'Chappelle lives,' the commander said. 'As does most of your company. They fought well.'

Kier did not answer. *Most* did not mean *all*. Even now, death followed them, darkening every place they'd once been.

'I've received word from Scaelas that we're to host a convoy from Cleoc Strata – you must understand how much trouble it has been to prepare for such a change in plans – and though it's a shame we haven't found Locke, your diplomacy in this situation has been noted.'

'Thank you, Commander.'

So Reggin knew that they didn't have Locke. Grey let a pulse of relief slip free to Kier.

'If you will hand over the girl, we will make sure she is comfortable until the assembly from Cleoc arrives.'

Sela squeezed Grey's hand so tightly her nails dug into Grey's palm. Grey shifted, wrapping an arm around the girl's waist.

'I'm sorry, sir,' she said – she was never good at holding her tongue, but Kier would've wanted her to speak, she was sure – 'but if it's no trouble, we'd like to remain with Sela until then.'

The commander's eyebrow rose as he regarded her. 'And you are?'

'Officer Eron Fastria, sir,' she said. *That* was insubordination, but she was going to retire anyways. What were they going to do?

'Fastria,' he repeated. Grey did not look at the others, but she felt a pulse of warning down the tether. That muscle in Kier's jaw was tense again. 'Do you not trust my guards? I have hand-selected them for the task.'

Grey shook her head. 'It is not that, sir. But we all promised to keep Sela safe until we handed her personally into her nation's care. It would be disrespectful to my gods to leave her now.'

It was a lie, but so was her entire life.

'To ... your gods,' Reggin repeated slowly. Religion was not widespread in Scaela, but other soldiers had dedicated their lives at the knife-edge of death and remembered to stop at altars and pray for the rest of their lives, certain they had survived due to a deliverance. Perhaps he would think her a fool.

She shrugged. 'And as a matter of the captain's honor.'

Kier only sighed.

'Dutiful to the last, Captain,' Reggin said mildly.

'Unfortunately, Fastria is right. We would be honored if you would allow us to keep watch over Sela until we can hand her over. And we will, of course, ensure her safety.'

'I'm sure you will,' Reggin said, shuffling through papers on his desk. 'I'll allow it. If that's settled, there's one more matter at hand: Captain Seward, you have been put forward for promotion to master.'

Silence settled in the room, and now Grey *knew* the others were watching her face. She kept her eyes on Kier, watching as his hand twitched – it was his only break in composure. 'That's not what was agreed,' Kier said.

Reggin frowned. 'And what is it you have agreed to, then?'

'Papers, please?'

Grey reached into her jacket pocket, where she'd made sure the papers were this morning. She handed them to Eron, who gave them to Kier. 'Signed orders,' he said, putting them down a bit too force-fully in front of the commander. 'Hand Captain Flynn and I have been promised retirement.'

It would be a challenge, Grey thought grimly, to switch back now – but it was doubtful that the commander would meet either her or Eron ever again; and if he did, she was fairly certain her own position would be significantly different.

She glanced at Eron, who met her gaze. There was a twinkle in his eye and a smirk on his mouth, and she was fairly certain he wasn't mad at her for dragging his perfect record through the mud.

The commander read the letters and sighed. He looked back up at Kier – and Grey looked too. If he agreed to it, he'd be the youngest master in Scaela. Perhaps the youngest master *ever* in Scaela.

'Is there anything I can do to change your mind?' Reggin asked.

Kier said, 'Hand?' He glanced at Eron, but Eron let his gaze slip to Grey, eyebrow raised.

She nodded, the smallest movement of her chin. Even that was probably conspicuous, but right now, she didn't care.

'No,' Eron said, speaking as Grey. 'The captain and I are ready to go home, if you please.'

Her grandmother killed her own sons to give Cleoc's mother a direct line to the throne. Her mother murdered her father when it was found he was cheating the treasury. Cleoc has held her throne, avoided a civil war and even made peace with one of the five nations. Is it any surprise that they fear her as much as they love her?

Report from Merrick Porter, Scaelan spy in Cleoc Strata, undated

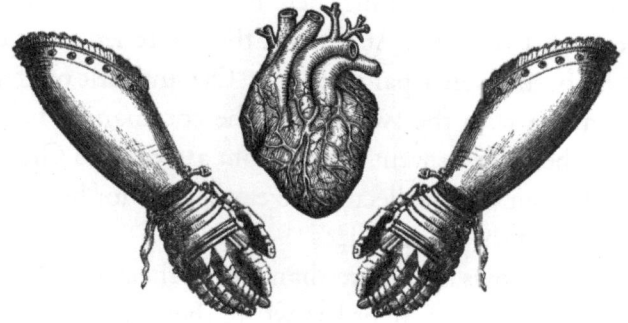

eighteen

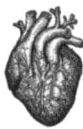

THEY AGREED THEIR LEAVE would start the following day –
first there was to be a dinner held in their honor, to thank them
for delivering Cleoc's heir. At the inn they were led to, they found
they had all been given separate rooms. Ola and Brit offered to stay
with Sela, along with the two guards the commander had insisted
accompany them. Eron went to the room assigned to Grey. No one
commented when Grey collected the clothes left for her from Eron's
room and moved them into Kier's.

But Ola's eyebrows said more than any of their mouths.

Once everyone was more or less where they were supposed to be,
Kier closed the door behind them. They stared at one another for a
moment, the silence desperately loud.

'How much time do we have?'

'Not much,' he said, unmoving. 'Cleaned up, dressed and downstairs for our escort before the hour.'

Grey slipped off her coat. He raised an eyebrow. She crossed the
space between them in three easy strides and pushed him against the
door. She rose on her tiptoes, leaning her weight against him, and
kissed him as sweetly as she could.

'And then,' she said against his mouth, 'after dinner?'

He laughed, warm and certain, his hands coming to her waist. 'I suppose I have a demonstration for the nation of Locke.'

She nipped his ear lobe. 'Not the whole nation, surely.'

He moved quickly, sliding his hands down to grip her thighs, pulling her up into his arms, turning them so she was the one against the door. Both froze as the wood clattered in the frame, waiting for someone to check on them – but nothing.

Grey sighed, relaxing against the door, locking her legs around Kier's waist. It felt so safe to be in the unyielding circle of his arms, his weight pressed against her, his focus hyper-fixated on the small section of skin where her neck met her shoulder and the span of her collarbone—

'Kier,' she said, tilting her head back to give him more access. But.

'Hmm?'

'Are you positive you don't want to be a master?'

He pulled back so quickly her back came away from the door – but she was safe in his arms, always; he would not drop her. He did set her down, very gently disentangling from her.

'Yes,' he said.

'But you always wanted it. Titles, promotions ... to be a commander. To go to unknown shores. To see the world.'

He laughed, looking at her with a bizarre incredulity. 'I always wanted *you*,' he said. 'And I still can't believe ... that I have you. I think I do.'

'You do,' she said, shy under the weight of his gaze.

He pushed her hair behind her ears. 'We can see the world together,' he said, kissing her forehead. 'We can be free together.' He kissed her nose.

'Is that freedom?' Grey asked.

He cupped her face in his hands. She rested hers on his chest, relishing the heat of his skin through his shirt, the beat of his heart against her palm.

'It is its own kind of freedom,' Kier said.

She wasn't sure about that, but it didn't matter because he leaned in to kiss her, pushing her a heady sense of certainty. 'We should clean up,' he said a few moments later. 'We can talk after.'

Grey raised an eyebrow. 'After the after. We have plans, Seward.'

'After the after,' he promised.

They separated. He called for a bath, then Grey went first into the small bathroom, washing for an inordinately long time because hot water was a luxury. She vaguely regretted not inviting Kier in with her, but it was good to have time alone, to think of nothing, to stare at the wall with a hazy sense of peace as the water warmed her cold bones.

She went out into the room wrapped in towels and shy, which was odd, because she'd just been thinking worse thoughts of him, and because they'd seen every inch of one another's bodies in a non-romantic context already (she'd *touched his intestines*, for sea's sake); but Kier was in a chair by the window, half-undressed, flipping through a book. Grey paused, shifting her weight from one foot to the other. She didn't think she'd ever stayed at an inn that had a bookshelf in every room. The High Lord had clearly spared no expense.

'What are you reading?' she asked. 'Does Scaelas stock anything saucy?'

'It's mine, actually.' To her surprise, he flushed. 'I, um, found it in a shop. In Pista.'

'What is it?'

He held it up, and Grey squinted at the title. It was, to her surprise, a book on the history and customs of the Isle of Locke.

'Kier . . . ?'

'I wanted to know everything I could,' he said quietly, not quite meeting her gaze. 'And I didn't want to burden you with the telling.'

She leaned back against the door. 'And have you learned anything?'

'A million things. But they left out the part about how astonishing you are.'

'Glad to see you're just as much of a shameless flirt as always, Seward.' She glanced down at herself, adjusting the towel. 'I've heard some astonishing rumors about you, too, truth be told. Care to prove their merit?'

He laughed, but he put the book pages-down on the windowsill and stood. He had the sinuous grace of someone who knew, deeply, how every muscle in his body worked. He came close and cupped her chin. 'We have thirty minutes, Flynn, and I need more time than that for what I'm planning.'

She laid a palm flat on his chest, fingers spread, over his heart.

Kier went to bathe, and Grey focused on finding something to wear. Scaelas had kindly provided a chest of formal wear for each of them, approximate in sizes, so she had more than enough options to choose from. She kneeled next to it, parsing through silk shirts and velvet vests and trousers and gowns. She found a deep navy gown, and though it wouldn't have been her first choice otherwise, something about the pattern of leaves and vines reminded her of a similar gown worn by her aunt, Wren, on one of the many occasions she'd brought her three boys from Nestria to Locke to spend time with their cousins.

At some point, Kier emerged in a cloud of steam, and she very conspicuously did not look at him as he started to dress.

That didn't stop him from glancing over at her in her chemise, his gaze scanning over the bare skin of her shoulders. 'This is unlike you,' he said, nodding to the dress cast over the bed.

'Unusual times call for unusual attire,' Grey said loftily, buckling one of her dagger holsters around her upper thigh.

'Indeed,' Kier said, moving behind her for the briefest moment to press his lips to her shoulder, his hand tracing the top of the leather buckle she'd just secured.

'Are you always this cheeky with your lovers?' Grey swatted his chest and spun out of his grip.

He caught her, drawing her back against his chest. 'No,' he said, leaning down to nip at her lower lip. 'I've never been with someone I loved before.'

She would never get used to this. She allowed it for only a moment, her heart warm with light – but then she pulled back, because he was correct: they did not have the time to get carried away.

Maybe nothing had changed – maybe she only noticed it more. But his fingers skimmed against her arm when he reached over her for his trousers hanging on the wardrobe, and he didn't brush past her without a touch to her waist or a kiss to her forehead. Maybe this was how he'd always been, a delicate ballet of stolen touches that she'd written off as his insistent grease-fire need for affection.

But now she was able to watch him with reckless abandon, without fear of him catching her – and truthfully, she could spend the rest of her days watching Kier doing the most mundane activities and still die happy. He'd cleaned up his patchy shave from the other day, so his jaw was pink and sharp; she longed to press her lips to the juncture just there, the soft shadow where mandible met throat, and she filed that away for later inspection. She leaned against the wardrobe, arms crossed over her chest, and watched as he pulled on a formal jacket. He had taken a cue from her, she suspected, and dressed in deep blue, his shirt unbuttoned a touch low in the fashion of the noblemen at court.

He was careful, straightening the cuffs at his wrists and the creases of his shirt, detail-oriented to a fault. When they were children, he used to redo the corners of her bedsheets because they were not crisp enough for his liking.

She wanted to run her hands over that careful work, mess him up. She wanted to *ruin* him.

'We're going to be late, Hand,' he said, not looking up from his ministrations, 'if you don't get your dress on.'

She sighed and pulled on the navy velvet, turning to the mirror and catching her own reflection as she braided her hair. Kier came without her asking and laced up the back of her dress. Grey watched his serious expression, then looked back at her own face. She pressed her lips together – she did not often see her reflection, and even more rarely did she see herself clean and finely dressed; she was both startled and unsurprised to find her mother looking back at her.

'You clean up nice, Fastria,' Kier said, hiding a smile as he tied his boots.

Grey rolled her eyes, straightening her skirts. He caught her a final time before they left the room. 'One more night,' he promised her.

'One more night,' she agreed, gripping his hair just hard enough to mess it up.

She had been to formal dinners before, honoring commanders and masters and marking high holy days, but she'd always been a guest at one of the far tables with Kier, watching their soldiers like hawks for any signs of childish misbehavior. They'd never been the guests of honor themselves, and the feeling was, frankly, startling.

They'd also never been in a diplomatic meeting-slash-hostage situation. Grey felt positively posed, her and Kier flanking Sela. Eron, still standing in as Kier's Hand, was on Kier's other side. Brit and Ola fidgeted next to Grey.

They waited in a reception room in Scaelas's summer residence in Grislar, overlooking the sea. Grey stayed closest to the window, drinking in the sight with a desperation that surprised her, seeking any trace of familiarity in that ever-changing ocean.

It was better than searching for familiarity in these rooms. She had been here, in this fortress-like palace, only once before, when she was a very, very little girl. She remembered how she'd spent most of the time being carried around on her father's shoulders as he laughed with Scaelas, while her mother, Locke, kept telling the pair of them to *just be serious; you're not boys anymore.* She kept catching the memory of her father's laugh, echoing in the corners of every room. If she was to make it through the night without breaking, it would be best not to think of that at all.

If only, Grey thought, they'd arranged this meeting within the military fort. She already knew there was nothing there to send her spiraling – she and Kier had worked at Grislar for nearly a year. They had spent so many nights on watch on the parapet, wind whipping their hair, listening to the call of the gulls and staring out into the emptiness of the waves.

The carpet was too soft, squishy and unstable under her boots. She kept shifting her weight anxiously, earning her a look from Kier over Sela's head. The retinue stood at rest, hand clasped over hand.

Grey glanced every so often at the clerk across the room. He sat reading a book, sheets of parchment and pens spread out in front of him. He was to take a transcript of whatever unfolded between the nations – after all, it was still a hostage situation, and a diplomatic one at that, even if it was disguised as a party. Two armored soldiers flanked the door, staring straight ahead at nothing.

Grey let her gaze slip to Sela. 'You okay, kid?' she murmured.

'Fine,' Sela said, her voice betraying her even if her posture didn't.

She looked impossibly different now with her dark hair washed and pulled away from her face, rouge on her cheeks and kohl around her eyes. A dress appropriate for her station flowed around her body, slate gray and structured on the shoulders, cut in at the hip in a fashion that was almost like armor. It made her look like a war hero in training, with her shoulders thrust back and her chin held at a severe angle – it reminded Grey of that night in camp, when she had gone to threaten the girl.

She broke rest to squeeze Sela's hand.

'What if she doesn't want me back?' Sela said very quietly, so the soldiers on the other side of the big room wouldn't be able to hear.

Grey broke fully, turning her head to look at her. 'Of course she wants you back,' she said.

'But when I went to Lindan ... She sent me. She didn't want me here.'

Grey thought of her own mother. Not her cool hands or the silver of her necklace, not the delicate kisses she pressed to Grey's temple. She thought of the blades Locke always wore, the poison she kept sewn into her hair ribbons. She thought of all the ways, from such an early age, she'd taught Grey to be on her guard.

The legacy of Locke, her mother had told her, brushing Grey's hair at night, *is blood and betrayal.*

'She was trying to keep you safe,' Grey said. 'I can guarantee it.'

A knock sounded on the door, two quick raps, and Grey squeezed the girl's hand once more before falling back into rest. The door opened, allowing for a sequence of guards; they were followed by a short, severe woman with ink-dark hair and a bear-like man with a red beard and russet hair, then eight more soldiers, who fanned out around the room, half of them keeping with the woman, the other half with the man. The woman paused three steps into the room, took an unsteady breath and pushed her shoulders back. She looked like she wanted to break into a run.

Sela broke first, staggering forward, then throwing herself at her mother – the guards moved to stop her, but Cleoc shot them a look so savage that Grey made a mental note to study it later, to figure out how to create the expression on her own face – and shuddered into her arms. The High Lady of Cleoc Strata pulled her daughter into her chest, her hand pressed firmly on the back of her head, holding her as close as she possibly could.

Grey noted Commander Reggin standing with the bear-like man – Scaelas, she knew; Scaelas, the High Lord, with his red hair.

Her father's voice: *Like when all the leaves go at once. We were boys together, you know – before I knew your mother.*

She couldn't run from the memory. Since she'd opened her heart to memories of Locke, they would not stop. She'd thought, after a whole childhood of keeping them at arm's length, they were gone for good, only for them to come bursting back in at the first glimpse of someone who had known her.

Scaelas, her own godfather, when she was Gremaryse of Locke; who had known her from the moment she was born to the moment Locke fell.

But he took no notice of her. She supposed this was something to be grateful for – if he looked at her straight on, she did not know how she would react. She could not fight the sense that she was play-acting.

'Is she whole and hale?' Scaelas asked the High Lady. She pulled back enough to look at Sela, to take her face in her hands. 'I hope you find her as promised.'

Cleoc said something to Sela that Grey could not hear, but the girl nodded. 'She is as promised,' she said, turning to Scaelas but keeping Sela in her arms as if she could not bear to let her go. 'We can proceed as discussed.'

'Excellent. I will draw up the agreed terms and meet with you back in the council chamber. I'm sure you want a moment with your daughter's rescu—'

He paused. He paused, and looked right at Grey, and Grey's stomach lurched. She met his eyes timidly, waiting, her heart in her throat.

'I'm sorry,' he said. He recovered himself, tearing his gaze from her. 'Please excuse my mind – always on the edge of something, you see.' More directly to Cleoc, he said, 'I will have my commander escort you to the appropriate room when you are done here, and we can finish this happy day with feasting and merriment.'

'Thank you. I hope we can find an agreement shortly,' Cleoc said. If she'd noticed the High Lord's oddness, she did not comment.

But Kier had noticed. As soon as Scaelas and his guards were out of the room, leaving the two original soldiers and the commander with Cleoc and her guards, he glanced at Grey with a brow raised.

She sent a quick jolt of assurance through the tether.

There was still the matter of Cleoc. She turned to them when the High Lord was gone, her eyes softer. 'You did not harm her,' she said. A statement, not a question.

Kier bowed his head, moving easily into command. 'I would never.'

A smile played on her lips, but it did not reach her eyes. 'Even though, I hear, it would've been force to equal what she dealt you, Captain Seward,' she said mildly. 'I know this is . . . a situation none of us expected. And you may see me as your enemy.'

'As you may see us,' Kier said.

'But let that not be anymore. From this day on – no matter what happens between our nations – you have a place at my table. Cleoc Strata will welcome you with open arms for the deeds you have done for my daughter.'

'It was an honor,' Grey said. She did not say, *Even though the First Daughter stabbed my mage,* because she was able to forgive and forget – mostly. Sela shot her a tight smile, as if she could read Grey's mind.

Cleoc went down the line to each of them, pressing a kiss to the back of their hands and handing each a silver pin embossed with an obsidian moon, matching the symbol on the crest of Cleoc Strata. 'An honor, in our nation,' she explained, 'for those who have exhibited true bravery.'

Grey didn't hesitate. She buttoned the little moon on her chest.

'Thank you for your kindness, your grace,' Kier said.

Cleoc nodded, then moved to wait by the door. Sela stayed back for a moment, her eyes wet, kohl streaked underneath. Grey leaned forward to wipe the streaks away.

'I'm sorry for all the trouble,' Sela said.

'Kid, you got me early retirement.'

'And six months of leave,' Ola said from the end of the line.

'And out of that fucking terrible encampment,' Brit added.

'Language,' Kier sighed, eyes rolling skyward.

'Will you visit?'

All hesitated. They'd been killing her countrymen for as long as they'd been fighting – but perhaps there was a way to move on from that.

'Yes,' she promised before the others could say no. She leaned in and kissed Sela on the cheek, then drew her into her arms.

Close enough that no one else could hear, with her face pressed into Grey's neck, Sela whispered, 'Will I see you on Locke?'

Grey's fingers dug into the girl's back, a warning and a thank-you. 'Maybe when you're older,' she murmured into Sela's hair.

They were not needed for the meeting between Scaelas and Cleoc, nor were they invited. One of the soldiers led them to the ballroom, where a party was already in full swing, the room crowded with officers and higher-ups from Grislar and surrounding camps and courtiers that Grey only vaguely knew the titles of. Despite the fact that the whole retinue was the reason for the party, people only wanted to talk to Kier, so she hung back with Eron as Kier drew his own little crowd.

'The captain looks handsome tonight,' Eron said, sipping his wine, leaning against her so no one could cut between them.

'He *always* looks handsome,' Grey lamented into her own glass. She glanced over the rim just in time to see Kier laugh, the dimple deepening in his cheek, and sighed.

'I'm sorry for any marks on your record,' she said after a moment.

Eron shrugged. 'I probably deserve it for feeding you poison for three weeks.'

'Fair point, well made.'

He hesitated, looking around, probably checking who was nearby; but he didn't realize that a crowded ballroom was sometimes the best place for secrets. 'Will you need help, Grey?'

'That's Eron to you.'

'My question stands.'

She shrugged. 'I don't know. I don't know what we're going to do, or how to do it, to be honest.' It was odd to talk about Locke so openly, even veiled as it was. But there was no hiding from the other three: they knew who she was, *what* she was, even if she herself would not put it into words.

'You know you have my sword,' Eron said quietly, 'should you need it.'

Grey glanced at him, registering the flush in his cheeks. 'Don't promise me that,' she said, reaching to lace their hands together. 'Take your leave, Eron. You owe me nothing – none of you do.'

He started to say something, but they were interrupted by an announcement from the master of ceremonies, signaling the arrival of the High Court and the start of dinner.

They hurried to their places of honor at the high table: Grey sat between Ola and Kier, across from Eron and Brit. Scaelas sat on Kier's other side, followed by Cleoc and Sela.

'Any good gossip?' Grey asked her mage.

'None. At least three marriage proposals, though. It's a tempting offer, to be a kept man.' Kier took a long sip of his wine. Grey pinched his thigh under the table.

'You're incorrigible.'

'Incorrigibly *handsome*.'

She barely managed to hide her smirk, glancing at him sideways. It was just . . . it was just, he was the same as always, her favorite person, her *beloved* person, and she could not fathom that he felt any fraction for her of what she felt for him, no matter how much he insisted he did.

She struggled to hide it, pushing away the heat in her stomach. Then, after a moment of thought, she tethered to Kier and pushed the heat toward him.

He blushed immediately, choking on his wine. When his eyes met hers again, there was a new, dark layer of want buried there.

'Timing?' he questioned. Under the table, his knuckles brushed the back of her hand.

'Mustn't ignore the High Lord,' Grey said smoothly, flashing an innocent smile, dismissing him to engage with his neighbor on his other side. Kier sighed and turned his attention to Scaelas.

Across the table, Commander Reggin was speaking to Eron, who he thought was Grey. 'I have already received requests for a transfer for you, Hand Captain Flynn,' he said, matter-of-fact, as the servers hurried to present the food while it was still hot.

Grey raised an eyebrow, eavesdropping. Kier tripped over a sentence.

'If you would be interested in remaining, I'm sure Captain Seward would understand.'

'You should think about it, Hand Captain,' Brit said, all mirth. They had, quite possibly, had too much wine. Grey kicked them under the table.

'Ah, I need a break,' Eron said. He looked at Grey, and she sighed – if she'd ruined his perfect performance record, he was taking her right down with him. 'And I'm terrible with a sword.'

The commander's eyebrows shot into his hairline. 'Your accomplishments say otherwise. And I do have some very tempting offers . . .'

Scaelas must've gone back to Cleoc, because Kier joined the conversation as plates were set down in front of them. 'Unfortunately, Commander,' he said with perfect politeness, 'they can't have my Hand.' His own hand went to Grey's knee, covered by the long draping of the table. 'We're retired.'

Have you written the words, in earnest, to Grace? If you two keep carrying on like this, you'll be making your confessions to her grave.

Letter from Lieutenant Lotrain Seward to Lieutenant Kiernan Seward, 9 years PD

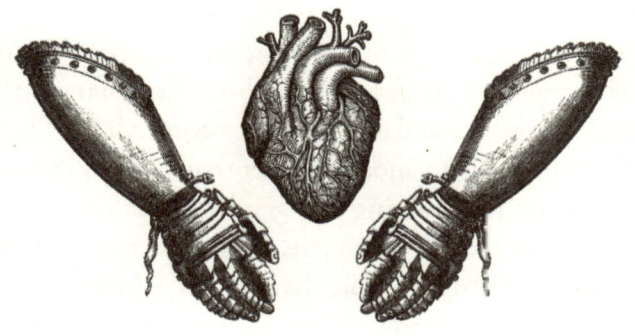

nineteen

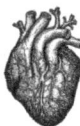

AFTER DINNER, SHE SUFFERED through a particularly dull (and possibly pointed) conversation with the commander about the importance of propriety and did her best to avoid Master Pickett, who she heard commenting to another officer that he must've misremembered the appearance, coloring and gender of the honored Captain Seward's Hand – though of course, he noted, two of those three factors could have changed. More than once, she looked up to see the High Lord's eyes on her, mouth furrowed into a frown within his red beard. When the dancing started, she was well and truly done – she suffered through one waltz with Eron before she threw caution to the winds and went to free Kier from his admirers.

It took her a moment to break through the circle to find him standing in the middle, sparkling wine in both hands. 'Captain,' she said, lowering her eyes demurely.

'Officer Fastria,' Kier said. He handed her one of the half-drunk glasses of bubbly wine; she brushed his knuckles with hers when she took it and flicked her eyes to the door.

'I believe you have duties yet, for the High Lady?'

'Ah, yes,' he said, easily slipping from the conversation. 'I did promise to speak to her. If you'll excuse me . . . '

They escaped from the circle, and Kier linked his arm in Grey's. They found Ola and Eron, drunk in a corner, watching Brit spin in circles with a mage from another encampment, with very different but equal versions of longing plainly written on their faces. Grey filed that detail away for later digestion.

She gripped Eron's chin in her hand. 'Please don't disgrace me,' she begged, before she kissed him on the cheek.

'I wouldn't *dare.*'

'Be safe,' Ola slurred gravely as Grey stepped back to Kier's side. 'In all ways that apply.'

'Still none of your business,' Kier said cheerfully. 'But I will take your suggestion on board.'

They slipped into the wet chill of the night, then into one of the dozens of carriages that waited outside. Kier gave the driver the name of the inn. They sat opposite one another, legs alternating, as they lurched into motion. Grey wanted very badly to grab him by his coat and pull him toward her, but they were in a windowed carriage, and perhaps she just wanted to look at him a little longer. His face mirrored the emotion she felt through the tether, something like awe and wonder and reluctant impatience. Her blood thrummed hot in her cheeks, in her stomach; her whole body felt electric and restless.

When they reached the inn, Grey stumbled out, feeling drunk on something other than alcohol. She kept her composure all the way up to their room, where her fingers fumbled with the key until Kier took it and slid it home.

Inside, door locked behind them, they regarded one another.

'So,' he said, carefully laying the key on top of the wardrobe.

'So,' she said, watching his every move.

They stared at each other. She didn't understand this shyness (hands in his intestines, etc.), but now that they were alone, she could not shake it. She inhaled sharply, unsteadily when he leaned forward to take her hand. He brought it to his lips, brushed a kiss on her knuckles.

'Is this more how you imagined it?' she asked.

Kier laughed. 'Grey, you're a treasure beyond any imagining.'

She raised an eyebrow. 'Captain Seward,' she said, because if she let herself believe him, there would be no recovery. 'I still have all my clothes on.' He moved to pull her closer, but she shook her head. 'Stand still.'

She brought her hands to his jacket, sliding under, pushing it over his shoulders. Grey leaned in to kiss that soft space at the edge of his jaw, the one she'd been so fixated on earlier, relishing his sharp inhalation. She pulled his jacket off and tossed it behind her, onto the bed.

'Grey,' he started. His hands went to her back, fumbling for the laces of her dress.

'Mm, no.' She pushed them away. She was dedicated to enjoying this, and she'd been imagining getting Kier's body under her hands for years. She would not be deprived of the joy of tormenting him.

He stood still, his breathing erratic, as she unfastened the buttons of his shirt. She ran her fingers along the obsidian of the moon. He watched her hungrily, hands clenched at his sides – he wanted to touch her, she knew, but even more, he wanted her to have her way.

She slid off his shirt, and the muscles of his stomach tensed as her hands skimmed over him. She kissed the line of his collarbone, flicking her tongue over the hollow of his throat, relishing the sound he made. Every single one of their sparring matches was written into his dense muscle; every battle showed on his skin. She swallowed hard, remembering all of them, a thousand recollections of his blood, his magic and her power, which had carved him from the boy she'd once longed for into the man she had now, under her hands.

'Do I get a turn?' he asked, amused, as she trailed her hands over the planes of his chest, the trail of fine dark hair from his navel, the scars on his abdomen.

'If you're good,' she said, skimming a thumb over his nipple, then drawing his mouth to hers to swallow his answering gasp. What a treasured thing it was, to hear that noise from him – to know it belonged to her and her alone.

'*Grey,*' he murmured against her lips.

She bit his bottom lip. 'Your turn,' she allowed.

Kier did not waste his time as he pulled her flush against him. He was insistent, undoing the laces of her dress with record speed, pushing it off her shoulders to pool at her feet. She tangled one hand in his hair, the other on his shoulder, half for balance. Her knees were unstable with the maddening slide of his tongue against hers.

He was still wearing too many clothes, which was a disaster, so her fingers went to the laces of his trousers as he wrestled her out of her chemise, breaking the kiss with a laugh. Then he was looking at her again, and the pure adoration on his face knocked the wind right out of her.

She fought the instinct to cover herself, keeping her shoulders square, her hands on his shoulders. He looked at her like he hadn't seen her skin a thousand times, every single day, in a million contexts. Like all of this was new – like he didn't know the shape of the scar on her ribs or the lines of her body. His hand cupped her breast reverently, one thumb sweeping back and forth over her until she ached with tension.

This time when she kissed him there was a new desperation. He stumbled, pushing her toward the window – thankfully he'd drawn the curtains before they left, or else those in the courtyard would be treated to a show – and boosted her so she was sitting on the wide windowsill, her back pressed to the fabric of the curtains. He rocked against her, still too many layers between them, but she felt him hard against her, and she groaned into his mouth.

He paused, pulling back just enough so he could see her, cupping her face with his hand. 'Is this what you want?'

She dragged his head down so she could nip at his ear. 'This is the *only* thing I want.'

He laughed, the sound warm and relieved. He hesitated for a second. As she started to ask if he was okay, he went for her pack. She watched him rummage for her healer's kit, then squint at the labels. He shook a measure of contraceptive herbs into his palm and took them with water, wincing at the bitter taste. She grabbed him by the hand and pulled him back, pausing to bite at his collarbone. 'Thanks.'

'Ola reminded me,' he said, running his hands up her back in a way that made her shiver.

'Please,' she said, pulling him down so she could kiss him on the mouth. 'Do not bring Ola into this.'

He laughed, warm and clear, then moved one hand toward the waist of her shorts. 'May I?'

'Please.'

He slipped his thumbs under the edge, then pulled them down, his hands skimming over her legs. His palms rested on her thighs for half a second before he pulled her legs apart.

'Kier—' She reached for him, but then he dropped to his knees and pressed a kiss to her inner thigh. She gasped, tangling her hand in his hair.

'I used to dream about this,' he murmured against her skin, hitching her thighs over his shoulders.

'Used to?' she forced herself to ask as he ran a hand from knee to hip. It was not worth telling him that she had imagined it too – her shyness was still cloying, even though she read the desire in his eyes when he looked at her. But it was hard for her to believe that he'd spent years sleeping by her side, orbiting her, thinking of her in this way, even *dreaming* of her, and nothing between them had changed until now.

'Mm. In my younger years, when I thought I could imagine the taste of you.'

Grey blushed, shy despite herself. She had never really spoken with past bedmates – it had been about relief, a mutually assured satisfaction, rather than genuine love or affection. Certainly, none of them had cared for her – not like this. 'How long?'

He skimmed his nose over her skin, sighing against it. 'Oh, just the better part of a decade.'

What absolute fools they were. All that time, and they could have been doing *this*.

She sucked in a breath as he kissed and bit his way between her legs, her head falling back when he put his mouth on her.

'How does it compare?' she barely managed to ask through the quiet supernova that erupted in her brain. It felt – it felt like magic, like power; it felt better than the swelling of heat when she found the power tethered around her and pulled.

Kier pulled back to kiss her hip. 'Infinitely better in real life.'

It was just— He ducked his head back down, his hands on her

hips, reacting to every gasp and breath. He was so confident, so sure of himself. He'd never been with her, but he *knew* her, knew her better than she knew herself. When he moved, it was exactly the right move at exactly the right time, like all of his imaginings of his mouth and hands on her body had perfectly prepared him to bring her as much pleasure as possible. Grey was caught in the tide of it, the grip of his hands and the soft murmur of his voice, his praise as she wound tighter and tighter under his touch. She felt the pleasure mounting, growing within her, the precipice looming; then he did something clever with his tongue and she came against him, tugging on his hair, his grip on her hips never easing.

It was just— He rose back up her body with steely determination, and she realized he still had trousers on – a *crime*, truly – and when she went to touch him, he said *please* in such a beautiful voice, but she pushed him away and moved to stand. She made short work of his clothes and pressed him into the chair he'd been sitting in earlier, his gaze on her molten hot as he watched her stand above him. For all of Kier's supposed fantasizing, she'd thought of *this*, too: taking him over, watching his hazel eyes go liquid and warm, waiting for her to possess him with a breath-catching stillness.

She moved to straddle him, her knees framing his hips. His eyes flicked shut as she stroked him, memorizing the velvety smoothness of his skin, the heat of him.

'Please,' he murmured again, his eyes nearly black when he opened them to gaze up at her.

It was just— When she shifted forward, positioned him with one hand while the other rested on his shoulder, when she sank down on him and he moved inside of her, it was as if the tether between them tightened, redoubled, exploded into something shivering and golden.

'Grey,' he sighed, her name the softest of exhalations. She felt the power of her pushing through the tether without her direction. She felt both in control and wildly out of it; both filled to the brim and needing more of him, as much of him as she could take, as soon as possible.

She moved against his body, slowly at first, getting used to the feeling of him inside of her. He shifted his hands to her waist, his gaze never leaving her face, as if he'd never get enough of the sight of her.

Grey could barely think as he moved, pushing up from under her. She leaned down to kiss him, taking his lower lip between her teeth. His grip tightened on her, and she rolled her hips against him, setting a faster pace.

'You are everything I've ever wanted,' he said, pressing his forehead to hers.

She shifted, giving herself more space to move against him, and he buried his face in her neck and kissed the juncture of her neck and shoulder until even that wasn't close enough. She ceded power, felt the echo of his magic as it fizzled against her skin. He moved his hands to her hips, pulling her up as he stood and pushed her back onto the windowsill, and she gasped at the change in angle as he paused and readjusted.

'*Yes*,' she moaned, biting his shoulder. She wrapped her legs tighter around his waist as he reached with one hand between her thighs, drawing circles with his thumb. She felt the tether inside of her, consuming, burning her alive. 'Kier, I need—'

'Let me,' he murmured, pressing his lips to her hair.

He increased his pressure until she had no thoughts; she was a creature of want and desire and nothing more. The wave crested, pulling her under, and she splintered apart with a half-sob against his shoulder. Kier made a low noise in his throat, breaking rhythm as he shattered inside of her.

She didn't move. She *couldn't* move. His fingertips skimmed up and down along her back, their breathing uneven but matched as they came back into themselves.

She kissed him on the temple, desperately, raggedly. 'Petition accepted,' she said into his damp hair.

'What?'

She leaned back so she could see his face – he was still inside of her, and she still throbbed with the aftershock of him. 'Congratulations. You're the first citizen of Locke.'

He laughed, burying his face in her shoulder. 'It's an honor,' he said, dropping to nip the top of her breast, 'to be yours, my lady.'

Time stayed syrupy and still. They cleaned up in the washroom, then she pulled on his shirt and crawled into bed, and he stretched out, still naked and uncaring, his hand skimming over her hip, her waist, the line of her thigh, like he was trying to memorize every part of her by touch. They talked about nothing, like they would any other day, but then she leaned in and kissed him, and he was there, warm and sure, and just as needy. Soon he was over her, his weight on his elbows, her leg hitched around his hip, and he was sinking into her all over again.

It wasn't like she'd imagined it would be, when she had allowed herself to imagine it. He was more certain than she'd anticipated, but he was eager for her to take the lead, to push him deeper into the bed and set her own pace. It was less of a battle for dominance and more of an understanding; him sinking into her as much as possible until she gripped his chin, then ceding power easily. Though she'd never been one to lead with previous partners, she loved controlling him, knowing that every breathy gasp was her doing, that every sharp sound, every profane word from his lips was hers.

After, they lay still, facing one another halfway down the bed. She was so languorously pleased that she could barely keep her eyes open. He was too warm for her to press against him – Kier always ran hot – but their fingers were tangled in the space between them. He did not seem to mind her fidgeting as she constantly knotted and unknotted their hands.

'Where should we go first?' she asked. It was long past dark now, and neither of them had bothered to turn any lights on besides the small golden magelight that Kier had summoned, which left the room mostly in shadow. She could still see every line of his face, though, mostly from memory. She lifted her free hand to run her little finger over the scar that always made his mouth do things it shouldn't. He turned his face to kiss her palm.

'Home first, I think,' he said, 'if you don't mind. It's been a while. I'd like to visit Lot.'

She nodded. Every time they went home, Kier kissed his ma and his mum and then went quietly out into the garden, kneeling at the foot of a tree, pressing his hand to the marker that bore Lot's name. He sat there for an infinite amount of time, talking softly to his brother of all that had passed in the months since he'd last been home. She understood from that initial visit after Lot died that the first trip to his grave, that great outpour, had to be done when Kier was alone. In the days following, she sat with him, gently running her fingers through the grass as they talked to Lot, in the way she used to run her fingers through his hair while they all lazed in the sun together.

'And Mum has been pressing,' he said. 'Ma hasn't been well – we should spend a few weeks, at least. Get our bearings. Make a plan.'

'I've been meaning to write to Imarta,' Grey said, feeling that familiar guilt – but it was easy to pick up when they saw each other. Every time she returned, her adopted mother looked up as she came through the door and said only, *Well? Where'd you go? No redactions, please* (even though there were always redactions; they were necessary), and fussed over her until she left again.

'I sent her a letter,' Kier said. 'Before we left camp.'

'Of course you did.' He was always better at being someone's child.

'And then?' he asked, genuine curiosity in his voice.

Grey sighed. *And then.* She rolled onto her back, staring up at the ceiling. 'And then, I suppose we need a boat.'

'I think we need more than a boat,' Kier said carefully.

'I don't know what the process is,' Grey confessed.

'I know. We have time to figure it out,' Kier said. 'But you're sure the bulk of it didn't . . . explode?'

'There were explosions,' Grey said, 'from the sheer force of power. But no, I don't think so. It's there, in the sea, waiting for me to come back.'

Kier thought on this. 'Maybe something will feel right when we get there. Or maybe your gods will give you the answer.'

'Maybe.' She closed her eyes, all desire for sleep erased by the memories that surfaced. She highly doubted her gods would want anything to do with her anymore. 'You never asked me how it happened. And even since . . . finding out about what I can do, you haven't asked how I did it.'

He was quiet for a moment. 'I didn't think it was my place.'

'And it changed nothing? Knowing I was the one who destroyed the Isle?' She opened her eyes, staring straight up, remembering how Severin grabbed her hand, then the two of them running, running, running.

'I think I've always known.'

She remembered the sweat on her back and the smell of burning wood, burning meat, burning hair – everything was aflame all the way up to the Ghostwood, then they were in the cellar and she couldn't see the fire anymore.

'You always thought so low of me? That I would kill my entire line? Destroy my home?'

He rolled over, drawing her close against his chest, shifting her to lie on her side. He stroked her cheek, his touch whisper-light. 'No,' he said. 'I always knew you were a survivor.'

She searched his face, uncertain what she was looking for. 'My father wanted Severin to have a choice,' she said, the words falling from her lips. 'They tried to protect us, protect my parents, when everything went so wrong ... Eprain sent a suitor, but it was just death in disguise. I remember her. Severin killed her himself, and I can't imagine how ...' She drew a shaky breath. 'Locke, my mother, rose like a storm cloud to face them, but it was too late. They used breakbloom to break the tethers.'

'Grey,' he said, so tenderly it hurt. 'You don't have to tell me this.'

She felt the tears on her cheeks, hot and endless. She couldn't remember the last time she'd cried. 'I remember the sound. Their boots. I remember their blood. Sev's hands – he held me so tight it left a bruise, the only thing left of him when I made it to Scaela.

'I know everyone thinks it was my mother who took the Isle down, but she and my father were already dead. I felt them the second they died, like great torches extinguished. And I think ... I think Sev knew what he was doing, what it would cost.'

'You were already Locke,' Kier said, understanding.

Grey nodded. 'And Severin knew what we could do together. So he told me to pull as much power from the wells around me as I could, and from the Isle itself. He shielded me, and I let the power explode. It was the only way to save Locke: to submerge it entirely. All three of them, Severin, Mam, Pa; and my grandmother, too. They all died so I could live.'

Kier wiped the tears away before they could collect in her hair. 'They did it because they loved you, Grey,' he said.

She looked up at his face, reaching to trace the line of his temple. 'But that's not the kind of love I want. I don't want sacrifice. I don't want anyone else to die for me.'

I don't want you to die for me, she did not say.

He leaned in to kiss her, tender and sweet. 'I'd happily perish for you any day of the week, Flynn,' he said, seeing right through her.

She moved her hand to the back of his neck, cradling his head. 'You're a fool,' she said very carefully, 'but if you insist on putting yourself in danger for me . . . I don't want you to be my mage.' His face immediately shifted into caution. 'No – not like that.'

'Grey?'

She wriggled closer, throwing her leg over his hip. His hand immediately went to her thigh. 'I want you as my commander, Kier. If we're able to resurrect the Isle, I want to know that it will be safe again, and I want it to be you.'

He studied her face. 'Any commander or master you want will come,' he said carefully. 'If you would have them. You could take from Cleoc Strata, from Scaela – gods, even Nestria would offer, if it meant a treaty.'

She shook her head. 'I don't care. I don't trust them. I don't trust anyone in the world like I trust you.'

He leaned forward to kiss her. 'I already have your name in my heart, Locke,' he said. 'It would be the greatest honor to carry your banner.'

'Are you sure you don't want to think about it?'

'No.'

She nuzzled into his chest, relishing the fact that she could just be here, against him, skin to skin as his arms folded around her. 'It's probably not the ideal retirement.'

He sighed, suffering as always, then rolled onto his back, tugging her along with him so she rested on his chest. 'We both knew from the start that retirement would be short-lived.'

'A hero and a genius, Seward.'

'I have other talents besides my bravery and intellect, you know.'

Grey bit gently at his collarbone. 'Oh? Can I get a demonstration?'

He paused as if thinking about it. 'Can I get a raise?'

'You don't even have a salary yet.'

His fingers traced down her hip. 'Not *yet*.'

She snorted. 'Bribery never suited you.' But she did not argue with his methods.

I'm sorry, my lord. We didn't get there in time – they'd already found Lady Wren and slaughtered her, her boys and the entire household. Please find enclosed her cloak pin bearing her House's seal. I will see her body safely delivered and laid to rest as her customs dictate.

Letter from Ikaaron Plides, Scaelan ambassador to Nestria, to Scaelas, 2 days PD

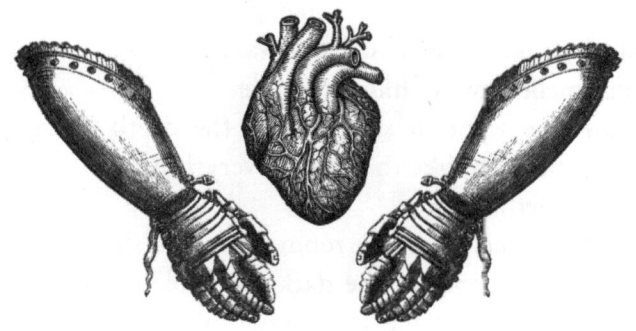

twenty

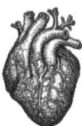

I N THE SMALL HOURS of the morning, Grey was roughly awoken
by something coarse and wet being pressed to her face. She inhaled sharply, pulling back, but there was a hand against her hair and
something smelled awful, like bitter bile.

She knew the scent. It smelled like the death of the Isle, like
screaming in her ears, like the end of everything.

'Kier?' she tried to say.

There was a sound across the room, a muffled shout – she couldn't
see anything but shapes in the dark, one holding a cloth over her
mouth, and the smell made something animal and furious rise up
within her. She struggled, but was held fast by strong hands. She bit
down, her teeth sinking through the towel into something fleshy
that swore and drew back. She sat up swinging, groping for her knife
under the pillow until her fingers closed on the hilt, mad and feral.

Her eyes were streaming, fuzzy; she couldn't see clearly – and she
couldn't feel Kier. She couldn't feel him beside her, or grappling for
her power in the tether that connected them as easily as breathing.

She slashed out and met flesh, felt hot blood on her hands. She
could only just see the shapes: three of them, large, looming over her.
More in the room where she couldn't see.

'She's armed,' one of them called.

'No one said they'd be *together*,' another seethed. She heard a strangled noise, a half-gasp across the room, the sound of something solid meeting flesh and bone. She knew the timbre of the noise even though she'd never heard that sound from him. *Kier.*

Grey fought. She slashed with her knife, connecting more than once, relishing the profanity that spilled from their attackers. The hand fell away from her face, but the damage was already done – no matter how she grappled with the tether, she was unable to feel Kier nearby, even though she heard him fighting just as surely as she was.

She knew the smell. They'd drugged her with breakbloom, a flower Eprain had found and cultivated for its abilities to dull magic, making it impossible for a mage to draw on their well.

It was the same drug, the same *poison* Eprain had used to splinter the tethers on Locke as they razed the Isle. The same poison that kept the High Lady from sensing the destruction they wrought.

But the men around her did not have the tight, fast Eprainish accents, nor lilting like Scaelan – their Idistran was broad and flat. Luthrite or Stratan, but she couldn't tell which. The people in the room with them were either typics, unaffected by the heady scent, or strong enough fighters without their powers – even a whiff of breakbloom broke every tether in the surrounding area for at least a few minutes. It was reserved for extreme situations.

Perhaps it was a comfort, Grey thought as she fought, terrified, that she and Kier were considered an extreme situation.

Then there was a knee heavy on her back, pinning her down. Fingers on that sensitive spot on her neck, the one that made her vision crowd with dots. A hand gripped her wrist, pressing hard.

'Stop fighting,' a voice growled in her ear, 'or I will kill you.'

She tasted blood and bitterness in her mouth. 'Kill me, then,' she snarled, and she swung again. The last thing she saw was a grim face through streaming tears, and the outline of her own mage on his knees in the corner with a blade to his throat.

Everything went black.

*

Grey came to an immeasurable time later, breakbloom cloying on her tongue. Her senses felt dulled, and she was still unable to feel Kier, but at least she could see. She choked on the gag, heavy on her tongue; there was too much saliva in her mouth, her chin wet with spit and blood. The gag itself had been soaked with the bitter floral solution.

Her hands were bound behind her back, the rope biting into her skin; her feet were bound too but they had long since lost feeling. She sat at an awkward angle. Her head rested on someone's shoulder. She lifted it with a jolt, coming to full consciousness.

'Mmph.' She followed the noise. It was Ola next to her, also bound and tied, a nasty-looking scratch running from her temple to the parting of her hair, jagged and bloody. She had clotted blood in her eyebrows, her eyelashes, crusted down the side of her face. Grey spotted Brit just past Ola. They were in a narrow stone room, cold and damp. She scanned the space – Eron was straight ahead of her, and then Kier ...

Kier.

He was bound similarly, lying on his side, dressed only in trousers and boots. His face was slack and he was covered in blood – for an awful moment Grey feared he was dead, until he took a quick, rasping breath. Judging by the bruising, she surmised that at least one of his ribs was broken.

Grey herself wore Kier's shirt and her own shorts, and Kier was similarly attired in the loose trousers he'd gone to sleep in – their captors had not bothered with providing coats or blankets, even though the cold chilled her to the bone.

Always the healer, she surveyed, taking stock: Ola's wound was ugly but hopefully not life-threatening; Eron was bleeding from his arm and had a black eye, but nothing further; Brit looked mostly fine besides a few scratches. She could not see the source of Kier's wound, which was worrying – if he'd been kicked unconscious, there was the potential for a concussion or brain damage, and that was something she couldn't stomach without some panic. But it was also possible that he was incapacitated by other means, and there was no way to know until she could see him up close.

For herself, the assessment was short: she'd been hit hard on the cheek by something, and she felt the hot, irritated swelling on the left side of her face. The breakbloom was heavy in her stomach and awful on her tongue, but she was otherwise all right. When she flexed her hands, she felt the crusted blood on them cracking, but she did not think it was her own.

She managed a look around their surroundings. There was a door in the corner, cloaked in gloom, with a knight on either side, standing guard silently. A high window let light into the room, but it would be impossible to reach, and it was covered in bars anyway.

She looked at Ola. Ola looked back, as if she could read Grey's mind, and shook her head. There was no way of escape. With the breakbloom on their tongues, none of them could tether – not that it would do Grey any good, with Kier unconscious.

Kier. She couldn't stop looking at him, her terror growing.

She couldn't say how long they sat bound in the dank, dark room. She tried to inch closer to Ola, to loosen the other well's bindings, but they were all tied so tightly it was impossible; besides, when one of the soldiers near the door saw her moving, he came and kicked her in the ribs.

She suffered the blow and did not try again. She cursed herself for letting her guard down, for going to sleep with only one knife, for not waking when Kier was apparently wrenched from her. She'd never slept so soundly in her life – Kier's arms around her must've lulled her into a false, deadly sense of security.

Some time later, he woke with a great exhalation and went straight to panic – it was agony to watch him, unable to move or speak words of comfort, though she tried to shuffle in his direction. When their eyes locked, she saw all the words he couldn't say there and tried to make her expression as calm as possible. *I'm alive*, she thought at him uselessly. *I'm alive and so are you, and though I cannot feel you, I can see you, and soon I will find a way . . .*

The door swung open, heavy wood hitting the wall. A retinue of guards entered, swords drawn, cautious. No surcoats. No crests. No way to tell which nation they fought for.

Enough guards streamed in for two to take each prisoner. Though she wanted to, Grey knew it was best not to fight, not yet; she could not guarantee that she could get everyone out safely if she did, and there was no point in getting killed for no reason. She did not resist as two of the guards grabbed her arms and hauled her down a stone hallway, toward a large atrium. She stumbled behind Ola, keeping tabs on Eron's ragged breathing behind her, and she could only just feel Kier. She still could not tether, not with the gag soaked in breakbloom, but she could feel the blunt edges due to their binding, and the headache was easing ever so slightly.

She grappled with her well, waiting for the instant they removed the gag, and found her power whole and sound. She gritted her teeth against the fabric. If anything went wrong . . . She remembered Severin gripping her hands. Then, he was nine years younger than she was now, and still so much braver.

In the atrium, they were shackled to the wall a few feet apart from one another. The guards were conversing now, in quiet tones – their accents sounded Luthrite, but she couldn't be certain. She shifted her weight from leg to leg, trying to keep herself from going numb. The stone against her back was wet with rivulets of water, chilling her further.

She leaned her head back anyway – Kier was chained next to her, just out of reach. The side of his head she hadn't been able to see was crusted with blood. He'd been hit by something – the hilt of a sword, she thought – and it looked like it hurt terribly.

If she could just tether to him, push some power into him, she could negate the worst effects – maybe put her hands on him, try to force a tether with contact, if that would keep him stable. But with the breakbloom on her tongue, she was absolutely useless.

A soldier walked into the room, dressed in armor. Not just anyone, Grey realized, taking in the embroidered sash he wore across his chest, over his breastplate and surcoat: a master at least, possibly a commander. She couldn't remember how many Luthar had, nor why they would take them prisoner.

No. Not Luthar. Grey squinted. Though the commander's crest was Eprainish, the guards that accompanied him wore a mix of Eprainish and Luthrite crests on their surcoats.

Eprain and Luthar were working together. She could not even begin to grasp the implications of that: if both turned on Scaela, using their combined forces . . .

She was not sure if an alliance with Cleoc Strata was enough to save them from that.

The commander paused, taking them in. Grey felt her muscles tense without being told, a shakiness in her thighs, a catch in her breath. Kier glanced over, and she felt the useless pull of him, trying to tether to her power, unable to.

'And this,' the man said, his eyes scanning over them, 'is the retinue that led the false Maryse of Locke across the country.'

They said nothing – they could say nothing, gagged as they were. But Grey took in Eron and Ola and Brit and Kier; perhaps they were fools for letting their guard down, for getting captured, but they were still broken and fierce and *hers*. She would die for every single one of them.

'Who is in charge of this operation?' the commander asked.

'The tall one, with the dark hair,' one of the soldiers said. Grey's head snapped in his direction, immediately sending her headache flaring, but she recognized the man who'd spoken. Though he now wore Luthrite garb, she was almost certain he'd been at the ball the night before. Judging by the way the blood drained from Eron's face, he must've recognized him, too. She remembered how drunk Eron was when she and Kier had left the night before – if the other man was a spy, searching for information, she had no idea what Eron had given up.

She could only trust that, even incoherent, he knew to keep his knowledge close to his chest.

Beside her, Kier stood straight and tall – a remarkable thing, to look so leaderly when he was dressed only in trousers, dried blood brown on his skin – and raised his chin at a defiant angle. The commander nodded to one of his soldiers, who stepped forward with a blade. Grey made a noise despite herself, struggling to move toward him – but they only cut his gag. It came away wet, and Kier spat a knot of thick blood out when they removed it. He had to have some other injury, something else that Grey couldn't see.

'And you are?' the commander asked.

But Kier only stared defiantly, insouciant to the last. Grey loved him with a fierce, unholy desperation – she wished, more than anything, that he could pull from her and decimate every person in this room.

After too long of Kier's silence, the soldier from the party spoke up. 'That's Captain Kier Seward, sir.'

'Seward.' The commander crossed his arms over his chest and stepped forward carefully. 'What are you?'

No answer from Kier, and the soldier didn't try to respond either. The commander's mouth twitched into a smirk. 'Fine,' he said. 'We'll do things your way.'

The guard next to Kier moved before Grey could react, before she could think, striking him square in the shoulder. Grey watched his quick, pained breath; she gasped herself as his collarbone cracked. She made a noise that sounded like an animal caught in a trap – the commander's eyes snapped to her immediately.

'You were the two found together,' he said, and Grey tried to focus as much hate as she could in her gaze. If only her gods had given her the ability to *do* something with her power, she would smite this man where he stood.

'Who is she?'

It wasn't like Grey could answer with the gag in her mouth anyway. Kier, too, said nothing.

The commander sighed. 'Bring in the prisoner,' he said over one shoulder. A few of the guards scurried away to follow his order. For a heartbeat, Grey panicked – had they found Sela, too? She thought it would be impossible to get past her guard, but . . .

He paced the stretch of stones in front of them. 'I'll make this quick. The girl you returned to Grislar was not Maryse of Locke, but you know that. What *I* know is that you managed to eviscerate an entire company of trained mages and wells without a single blade, which is, frankly, impossible. Unless one of *you* is a Locke.' He scanned their faces, lingering on each one. 'So who is it?'

Grey tried to breathe and tasted only poison. It was a mistake – it had all been a mistake. They never should've taken this assignment.

She and Kier shouldn't have stayed the night. They should have left the second they handed Sela over, taken their papers and *run*.

The guards returned with another person between them, their head and face covered with a dark hood. They wore the plain clothes and padded shirt that went under armor, caked in mud and dried blood.

'So nice of you to join us,' the commander said placidly, as if the prisoner had come willingly and not been dragged out of a cell.

There was no response. One of the guards discarded the hood, revealing her face. Hand Master Mare Concord stood looking dazed, gagged like the rest of them. Grey heard Ola draw a quick breath.

Mecketer was attacked shortly after your departure. That was what Reggin had told them – and none of them had thought to ask for a casualty list, had thought to check if Concord or Attis, who knew their mission and route and the details of their arrival, were safe.

Mare took in the group in front of her, and it was like the fight went out of her: her knees sagged, and she would've dropped to the ground if it wasn't for the guards holding her arms.

'Has she been drugged?' the commander asked.

'Yes,' one of the guards replied.

'Remove her gag.'

He cut it away, and Mare drew a heaving breath, her eyes tracing back and forth over the others with growing dread. They lingered for just a second on Grey before moving on. Her top lip was swollen and split, as was her left eyebrow. Grey surmised that she'd be a patchwork of bruises under her clothes: she'd clearly been beaten.

'Is this your retinue?' the commander asked.

'Yes,' Mare said, her voice raspy. Grey remembered her eyes, wild with fear, as she'd saved her from death years before.

'They have been . . . uncooperative. Would you do me the honor of naming those involved, and telling me their specialties?'

Mare licked her lips. She looked up and down the line. 'I don't know—'

'Don't toy with me, Concord.'

'I'm not. I only know Seward and Flynn's abilities. Captain Seward is an internal affinite.'

The commander looked at Kier for a long moment, eyebrows drawing together. 'Internal. The report on our company stated that it was clean work that killed our men. Some kind of effect on the hearts, forcing all to cease beating. Does that sound familiar?'

'I cannot say,' Mare lied. The commander rolled his eyes and gestured to one of the guards, who hit her so hard that her head twisted. She coughed, spitting a tooth out onto the floor. When she looked up again, blood dripped down her chin. Grey forced herself to watch despite her growing panic. It was the least she could offer her.

'Yes,' Mare said weakly. 'His speciality lies with the heart.'

'And Flynn?'

'His well.'

'On the end, sir,' the man from the party said, and Grey's blood ran cold. Eron had not betrayed her, betrayed *them*, but now he would take the fall for her, and she could not stomach it. One of the soldiers grabbed Eron's arm, following the gestures of the other, and pulled him forward.

'You're Hand Captain Flynn?' the commander asked.

Without hesitation, Eron nodded. Grey could have killed them *all*. She fought against her restraints, against her gag, causing a scene. One of the soldiers moved closer, gripping her hair, pulling it back. She snarled and tried to knee him in the groin, but he punched her in the stomach. She saw a blaze of white and curled around the pain for one second, two, waiting for it to pass.

'And who are *you*?'

'Officer Eron Fastria,' Kier said, the absolute *bastard*. 'She's a typic.'

With a raised brow, the commander nodded. Grey looked at Kier, desperate. He shook his head, just a fraction.

Don't. She read the directive clear on his face, and more than anything she wanted to fight it, but she knew better. She knew what was at stake.

'Though this has been . . . enlightening, it is not what I'm here for.' The commander resumed his pacing, and Grey wanted, so badly, to kill him. 'Who is the Locke?'

Kier's chin rose further, defiant. And the others . . . Though Grey glanced at them, not a single one looked at her. They all stared straight ahead, unreactive.

'*Who is it?*' he thundered, and Grey's heart pounded. She saw the soldiers move on Kier but he shot her such a murderous look that she only stood there in shock and horror, *damn* her, as one moved on him, slashing forward. The side of Kier's face that was already bloody ran red, and something wet fell to the floor – Grey couldn't contain her sob when she saw it was part of his ear. And he . . . he only made a gruff noise, the shudder traveling through his body.

'If you do not hand Locke over to me,' the commander said carefully, 'I will kill all of them and toss their bodies into the sea until one of them resurrects the Isle.'

'I don't think it works like that,' Kier said, his voice unsteady, a pain in the ass to the very end.

'I don't care. I will do it anyway, and we will have no power at all.'

Grey tasted bile mingling with the breakbloom, and she could not breathe. And then Kier looked at her, so beautiful even with the blood, even though he was about to hurt her; and last night he'd whispered in her ear, *You are going to ruin me.*

He was right.

'The girl, this time,' the commander said, and the guards stepped steadily toward her. Grey braced for pain, but Kier moved – not far, not with his restraints, but he angled himself so he was just in front of her.

'Wait,' he said, his voice not quite his own – there was blood in it, and fear, and she reached uselessly for his tether. 'Wait.'

The guards paused. She felt Ola looking at Kier, agony on her face, and then he straightened, wincing at the pain. Grey tried to lunge forward, to reach for him, to touch him in any way possible, but it was useless.

'It's not Maryse you're looking for,' he said.

Grey's brain screeched to a halt. Mare's face was absolutely unreadable.

The commander was almost lazy in his response, crossing his arms over his chest, moving closer to Kier as if to demonstrate that he did not fear him. 'Oh?'

The legacy of Locke is blood and betrayal.

Grey sucked in a breath, tasting blood and poison. She didn't know – she didn't know how she knew, but she could hear the words Kier was forming before he said them; she could feel the swell of apology through the weak, slippery tether as she tried to force through the effects of the breakbloom to no avail. *Don't do this*, she wanted to scream at him, but all that came through the gag was a muddled moan. *Do not do this to me.*

'It's me,' Kier said, calm and measured. 'I'm Severin, Heir to the Well, Lord of Locke, First Mage of the Isle. I'm the only survivor of the Isle's downfall.'

Your mother is not well. She sits in the garden for hours, under the tree where he lies. Imarta and I have tried everything, but she is inconsolable. The dirt is still a black spot on the lawn, as if nothing will ever grow there again.

Please, Kier. If you've ever listened to me at all, listen now: come home. I cannot bury both of you.

Letter from Laurella Seward to Lieutenant Kiernan Seward, 9 years PD

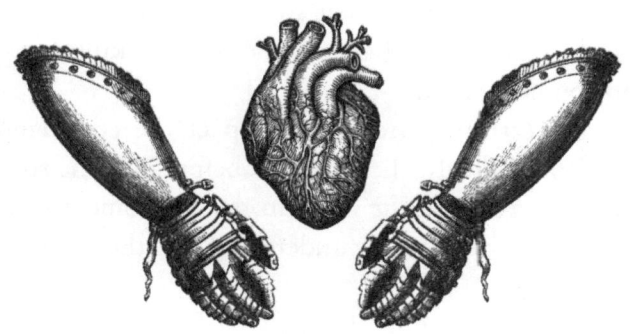

twenty-one

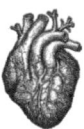

GREY FOUGHT.

She managed to knee the guard closest to her in the groin, then use his chin to push the gag low and out of her mouth. She couldn't do any more before one of the other guards caught her in the shoulder with the hilt of their sword and another kicked her to her knees, then there were hands in her hair, jerking her head up, and a blade on her throat.

She froze, breathing hard, gazing up at the commander with hatred. He moved slowly, then kneeled before her. She spat at him, but he threw up a shield – he was a mage, and someone else in this room was a well, and Grey now understood why the breakbloom was only on their gags.

'You were found with him, weren't you? Do you think of yourself as his knight? His protector?' The commander reached forward, tugging her hair. 'Or is it something else?'

'The girl is a fool. Obsessed with the captain and always has been,' Mare said, her voice flat and emotionless. 'Besotted.'

The commander laughed, like this pleased him. He moved the gag back into Grey's mouth, then gripped her chin in his hand. 'And are you just as besotted, Seward?'

A pause. 'She is nothing to me,' he said finally.

'And yet she was in your bed.'

'Do you care about everyone you take to bed?' Kier asked, that awful, devious insouciance creeping back into his tone.

Blood and betrayal. She knew he was doing it to save her, the *absolute bastard*, but it stung all the same.

'And yet she would die for you, it seems,' the commander said, standing and brushing his hands on his trousers, as if touching Grey had made him filthy. She felt the blade slip away from her throat, but the hand did not leave her hair, and there was another firm one on her shoulder, keeping her down.

'She's a fool. She's been nothing but trouble from the start,' Kier said, and there – there was just the briefest lapse into tenderness.

'Then enough worrying about the girl.' The commander looked at her over his shoulder, his gaze dripping with disdain. 'Knight, if you step out of line one more time, I will kill you. And that is a promise.'

'Please,' Kier said very quietly, only for her. 'Don't.'

She wanted to – gods, how she wanted to – but she was no use to anyone if she was dead. She sagged in the arms of her captors.

The commander turned his attention back to Kier. 'Severin, then. How can I be certain you're not just another imposter? That you are truly the heir?'

'I may be a mage, but I carry the dormant power of my mother's line. I can demonstrate it, if only you would allow me.'

'Not happening,' the commander said, arms crossed. 'You will remain drugged and powerless until I can trust you won't kill me, and I think that will take quite a while.'

'Then how can I prove who I am?'

'I'm sure you'll think of something.' The commander waved his hand, and Grey heard movement, then a muffled gasp. She glanced behind her to find the soldiers had moved, all of them holding blades to her companions' throats, all of them ready to deliver killing strikes.

Kier met his gaze and held it. 'It was Eprain,' he said quietly, 'who attacked. Who sent the ships. Who caused the death of Locke when they tried to take control of the Isle and its power.'

Grey drew a breath, tasting only the bitterness of the breakbloom.

She regretted telling Kier anything. One of the guards gasped; across the room, a few of the other soldiers eyed the commander warily. Even Mare looked surprised, her brows drawing together, as if she could no longer be certain she had made the right choice in protecting Grey.

But the commander only smirked. He looked Kier up and down. Grey didn't know what he was looking for – Kier was younger than Severin by five years, but with the gray at his temples and the impact of battles, he looked older than twenty-six. She wasn't sure how anyone else would know them: she and Severin had only been away from Locke a handful of times, and their parents were very careful about who could visit the Isle.

Only they weren't careful enough.

'Everyone else thought the elder Locke was the well,' the commander said after a moment. 'None but those in the Isle's confidence knew he was a mage, as is the way when there is more than one possibility for the heir. Did you know that?' he asked, pitching the question to the room. A few of the soldiers shook their heads, now looking uneasy.

The commander bowed his head, that grin spreading into a full, cruel smile. 'My lord,' he said, his voice heavy with faked deference, 'do you remember me? From your past life?'

Grey squinted at him. She could not place him.

He took a step toward Kier, his hand on his sword. A touch lower, he said, 'Do you remember my daughter?'

Her stomach dropped as it became clear: Lady Polenna. The girl who came with the ships, the girl Severin killed as his final act before he took Grey to safety. The girl who wasn't supposed to die – who was only meant to act as a decoy.

This was her chance. If Kier got it wrong, they would know he was not Severin. But, of course, he was too smart for that, because he was her other half and she had told him too much.

'I remember her death,' he said, his voice steadier now, back to his captain's manner. 'You may think her blood is on my hands, but you underestimated the Isle. Her blood is on *yours*.'

The commander's hand moved, almost too quick for Grey to

see – but she heard the sound of flesh on flesh; she watched Kier's head whip to one side. The commander's ring cut into his cheek, leaving a gash within the reddening skin.

'You know what I'm capable of,' Kier said, a deadly undercurrent to his voice.

The commander stepped back, recovering his composure. Flatly, he said, 'I do.'

'Then you know that if you do not safely release my companions, I can – and *will* – kill everyone here.' Kier's voice was smooth, deadly, beautiful. 'And then, when you are dead, I will find your family, Commander. Anyone and everyone you love. And I will look them in the eye and tell them exactly why they are sentenced to die. I will tell them how you sent your daughter to the slaughter; how you were so determined to kill my line that you did not care to spare her. I will find your High Lord, Commander, and end him too. You think the company you found was the worst of what I can do? I will make them all suffer, and I promise it.'

The commander regarded him. 'Pretty words, for a man who ran from his own dying family. You are just as guilty as I, and you have no power.'

Grey winced.

'But I will,' Kier said, moving forward until the restraints stopped him. She could not see his face, but she could see Mare's, and the Hand master looked like she had never really *seen* Kier before. 'Sometime soon, your guard will fail.' Somehow, impossibly, Grey felt the sensation of a thread from Kier, reaching out, pushing through the dullness of the breakbloom. He'd been ungagged long enough to be able to tether, but she was still drugged. She had no control of her power . . .

They were bound. They were bound, and she was Locke, and her power called to him. She felt the barest thread of a tether take, then the faintest trickle of power flowed from her stomach. He was *siphoning* from her.

A guard in the corner shouted out, gripping his heart. Before anyone could grab him, he fell. Another fell shortly after, and Grey felt the slice of pain in her stomach, the awful forced pull of power through the haze of drugs in her system.

Chaos fell over the room: the commander threw up a shield, the magic shimmering in the dimness, and two of the guards near Kier pushed him to the ground. Someone shouted, 'Flynn!' and another guard took down Eron, pushing his face into the damp stone. A few others gathered around their fallen comrades, attempting to revive them – but it was no use.

'You cannot draw from your well,' the commander snarled. 'That should be *impossible*.'

'I am Locke,' Kier seethed from the floor, his bloody side pressed down. 'I can draw any power. It is my *right*.'

It was a lie. A bluff. But he had them afraid, and Grey was terrified alongside them. With Kier on the ground, he was nearly close enough for her to touch. She sagged forward, trying to get closer, to give him any contact with her skin if that would get them free, but she was still too far away.

'*Enough*.' The commander's voice rang through the scuffle. 'I will free your companions, if I must. But you will stay, and you will resurrect the Isle. If you do not comply, Locke, I will not hesitate to kill you – and I will not use magic to do it. Is that understood?'

'Yes,' Kier said.

The commander spun on Mare next. 'You told me,' he hissed, 'that he was *bound* to his well. That they were useless without one another.'

Mare shook her head. 'I . . . I don't know. I only thought—'

'You are of no use to me anymore.'

Mare's eyes filled with fear. She looked at Grey – *they never need you as much as you need them*, she'd told her once.

'Concord—' Kier started, but it was too late.

One of the soldiers moved forward, quick as a viper, and cut Mare Concord's throat. Her eyes locked on Grey's face, Mare barely even flinched as the blade carved a deadly path.

Someone screamed, muffled by their gag. Grey watched, nauseous with fear, as the blood poured from Mare's throat, staining her shirt. She fell; the soldiers released her as she dropped to her knees, then her hands, then landed face-down. The pool of blood around her grew and grew.

We're all going to die in this armor. Grey closed her eyes.

'I will release your companions,' the commander said, 'but if you do not cooperate, Locke, I too will kill everyone you love. You are not the only one capable of threats.'

They were led away, Grey dizzy with the breakbloom and adrenaline and fear. Kier was taken with them down the hall, to a small room with a door.

'I would just like to say goodbye,' he said.

The commander shook his head. 'You ask for too much.'

Kier met his gaze, unfaltering. 'I am the High Lord,' he said loftily, daring the commander to protest. 'Would you not treat me in a way befitting my station?'

In the end, they let him say goodbye. They each were injected with a dose of breakbloom and given civilian clothes to dress in. Afterwards, they were taken to the entryway, and the supplemental guards backed to the wall, leaving the Lord of Locke to say farewell.

Grey could only stare at him, silent with anger, as he spoke to Brit and Ola and Eron, still held back by the guards. It was a death sentence, what he was doing. Finally, he turned to her, to where she glared at him.

'And you,' he said finally, so quietly it broke her heart. 'Would you leave without saying goodbye?'

He was three paces away, his own guards giving him healthy space even as hers didn't – it was as close as he could come to her before someone swung at them. They shifted uneasily as it was, and she hated him in that moment, more than she had hated anyone before. It was easy to hate him like this, when he was making sacrifices, because she could not look in his face and accept that she was about to lose him.

She wanted to curse him. She wanted to fight him. She wanted to kick him in the shin with her heavy boot. She would've, too, if her ankles weren't tied.

'Beloved,' he said, because he could not say any of her names without revealing the truth. She wanted to throw herself against his chest and beg him to never leave her – she wanted to hate him all the more for this. She made a sound that he seemed to interpret as *If you could try to tether, you could kill them*, because he said, 'It is too weak and there are too many.'

Grey bit the gag, a low and awful sound rising in her throat.

'Tell Lot I will see him soon, and give my love to our mothers,' he said, quiet and grave.

She could not respond, so she only glared, forcing as much emotion as she could into her gaze since she could not put it through the tether.

For a long time, he looked at her, as if he was trying to memorize her face. She could not force herself to do the same, not when he was half blood, not when he had betrayed her.

'We either release them or we don't,' one of the men behind Kier said sternly. 'Your call, Locke.'

Kier sighed. Leaned forward. 'You deserve to survive,' he said, very quietly.

Survival is not a meritocracy, Kiernan, she thought. Because if it was, Lot would be alive, and Severin, and her father, and all those who were so much better than her.

Then he stumbled, the move unlike him, and Grey felt something slip into her boot as he caught himself against her. The soldiers moved forward and he murmured, 'I'm so sorry.'

For an instant, she thought he'd smuggled a knife in – but the object in her boot was small and blunt.

'*Locke*,' the commander said, coming up behind them.

Kier nodded. He straightened, his eyes not leaving Grey's as he said, 'Take them away. And if any harm does come to them, I will keep my promise, Commander, and you know I will do it.'

That was it. They started to lead them away, and Grey fought with such ferocity that even Kier looked disappointed. She tried to do as much damage as possible until they finally drugged her, and as her eyes slid shut, she held his gaze and tried to convey with all of her might that she would never forgive him for this.

When Grey woke, she found herself slung across Ola's lap, her head pillowed on the other woman's thigh, Ola's fingers stroking her hair. She felt a surge of panic, then an unbelievable rush of bitterness. Her whole body was heavy, weighted, like she'd never move again. She kept her eyes closed.

Kier.

Above her, Ola was saying, '. . . and the closest encampment is Grislar, but I don't know where we are, and if we're in Luthar, it doesn't seem sensible to go asking.'

'Who would know the difference?' Brit asked from somewhere close by. 'Who would care? Let's head east, then follow the coast north.'

'We can't leave him.'

There was a silence, then, and Grey couldn't take it. She shifted, the others immediately focusing on her with a lot of soothing sounds that did absolutely nothing. She opened her eyes to find they were in a clearing surrounded by a dense wood of skinny, light-colored trees, in the middle of nowhere. Eron was pacing back and forth next to a magelight that Ola and Brit were maintaining. Grey felt the ache in every part of her body. She needed to speak, but the words were too heavy. They would not form. They would not come.

'Grey?' Brit was saying, looming over her. 'Did you hear me?'

She didn't. She couldn't. She tuned them out because nothing mattered, not anymore, not when Kier was gone and good as dead. She sat up, nearly hitting her head on Ola's chin, and hugged her knees to her chest. Ola's fingers were there on her back immediately, scratching down her spine.

'He did what he thought was best,' Eron said, and Grey wanted to *throw* something, because that sounded like Kier was already dead. Before she could stop it, a sob clawed its way out of her throat. She slapped a hand against her mouth, nails digging into her skin.

She wouldn't cry for him. Not when he'd done this to her. Not when he'd abandoned her, taken her name and her title and her heart and disappeared.

She could cry for Mare, who deserved it. For Kier, she would just remain angry.

'Fuck Kier,' she said, too loud, her tongue still thick with sleep. She lurched up, pushing off Ola and Brit, nearly careening into a tree with the unsteadiness of a monumentally pissed-off newborn deer.

'Grey!' Ola called after her. 'Where are you going?'

She didn't answer. She couldn't look at any of them, not with this anger brewing up within her. She pushed through the trees, wobbling unsteadily, breathing hard and grappling at the tether in her middle as if it would connect to Kier. She felt *nothing*.

An arm wound around her, right on her bruised stomach, pulling her against a chest – Eron, she realized. '*No*,' she gasped, grappling against his arm, but he said, 'We need you.'

She turned on him. 'What the fuck *was* that back there?' she demanded, the words clawing out of her. He gripped her wrists so she couldn't swing, accidentally pressing on the bruises left behind by her restraints. 'You just let him lie.'

'We can't lose you, Grey,' Ola said over Eron's shoulder.

Grey shook her head. 'You should've let me go. You should've let them take *me*.'

'Kier needs you alive and functioning,' Eron said firmly, 'and you are only doing half of that.'

She looked at him, the rage clear in every line of her body, even though it wasn't Eron she was mad at. She wished Kier was in front of her if only so she could shout at him, and the thought was so devastating and overwhelming that she did not know what to do with all the feelings she could not contain.

'*I'm* Locke,' she said, loud enough so the others could hear her as they moved toward her, unease on their faces.

'We *know* that,' Eron said. 'Now what are you going to fucking do about it?'

She stared at him, wordless. Kier was gone – Kier was in her place. But *she* was Locke, and Locke was her, and she was a well with the power to actually do something. Even now, she felt it, curling inside of her, vibrant and visceral with anger, a wounded animal ready to strike. She pressed one hand to her stomach as if she could grip the power in her fist and drag it out of her.

She sat down heavily on the forest floor. As she did, something in her boot pressed to her shin. She dug into the top and pulled out Kier's ring. She stared wordlessly at the silver in her palm, everything aching.

Not Kier's ring, not at first. Lot's ring. Lot, who had lied for her, who had died in the war the sovereigns started because she was not strong enough to tell the truth, to claim her Isle; Lot, who had died because she ruined everything.

'They're all dead,' she said to the others, to Kier, to no one. 'Do you know what that's like? Everyone who ever cared for me is dead.'

'You're not,' Ola said. 'We're not.'

'Not yet, but the odds aren't promising,' Brit pointed out. Someone hit them; they swore in response.

Grey looked up at the sky far above. It was impossible to tell where they were. Her heart, broken and bruised, had retreated somewhere deep inside of her.

'Locke,' Eron said, crouching so his face was level with hers. He had such kind eyes; she'd always envied the soldiers who'd kept any kindness after so much bloodshed. 'What are we going to do?'

Grey sighed. It wasn't the sacrifice that was the hard part; it was the running head-first off the cliff that she and Kier had always been so very good at. Perhaps it was the surviving that was worse. She remembered his face on the night she'd given him all the power she had, the flash right before he used it; she remembered his gaze last night, which now felt so long ago, the way he'd gripped her as he said, *You are everything I've ever wanted.*

She slipped Lot's ring onto her thumb, as it was too big for her other fingers. Grey stood up. She squared her shoulders, wincing at the ache even as she remembered Kier's broken collarbone, the echo of the pain she would've felt through the tether.

'Well?' Brit said. 'Are we marching into the sea?'

Grey was quiet for a long moment, turning over the rumors and her memories, examining each of them in turn. The truth was, she was one person, one sovereign without a nation, and she had gone so long without thinking about what that meant. She thought of Cleoc and that little obsidian moon, of Scaelas's hand in hers when she was only a girl.

'I think we need to speak to my godfather,' she said. 'Because there is an imposter claiming my title, and my commander has been taken captive, and we may still have allies yet.'

'Who is her godfather?' Brit asked.

'Contextually, I would assume it is Scaelas, you cretin,' Ola murmured back.

Grey ignored them, stretching out her hands, looking at the scars that marred them from fighting Scaelas's wars. 'I've given most of my life for him. The least he could give back is his protection.'

She started through the woods, not caring which way she was going – she would find her home; Locke was always there within reach when she went looking. 'Kier has made a mistake trying to save me. And we're going to find him and force him to his knees and make him fucking beg for forgiveness.'

'There she is,' Eron said quietly. 'That's our girl.'

'Going in the wrong direction, Locke,' Ola said, not unkindly.

It was hard to be the High Lady of Locke while traipsing through the mud without direction in borrowed boots, but Grey made the best of it. At the next village, they realized they were just over the Luthrite border, and though there were some close calls with patrolling forces, they made it safely into Scaela.

Getting into Grislar was another story.

'I'm Hand Captain Grey Flynn,' Grey hissed at one of the guards at the city's gate. The town was in lockdown due to the presence of both Cleoc and Scaelas, the gates guarded, the towers peopled with soldiers. She could see the streets of the city, the encampment spread far below, the rolling hills that dropped off at the cliffs. 'We need to speak with Commander Reggin.'

But the boy – he was a boy, dammit, probably barely older than Sela – said only, 'I have instructions to only allow in those who have papers.'

Grey very nearly punched him. Ola slid neatly in front of her and said, 'Do you know who you're talking to? Captain Flynn led the retinue that saved Cleoc's daughter.'

'Then she should have *papers*,' the boy said, exasperated.

Ola rose to her full height, still shorter than the guard, and pointed at Grey. 'She is a *war hero*. In two nations.' An icy pause swelled between Ola and the guard. 'And frankly, if I had *my* papers, I would shove them up your ass.'

'So close,' Brit murmured. 'So good, until the last moment.'

'I have orders,' the boy said.

Frustration welled up inside of Grey, fierce and insistent and— If she was going to be this, be *her*, then the least she could do was get through a fucking gate. 'I come with a message from the nation of Locke,' she snarled. 'And I require an audience. It's a life-or-death matter, and your commander needs to know about it immediately.'

The others looked at her with mixed expressions of pride (Ola) and consternation (Eron). She wondered how often she'd deferred to Kier, letting him lead as she worked quietly in the background.

The boy hesitated, an unknown emotion flickering on his face. 'The best I can do,' he said finally, 'is fetch my captain.'

'Then go *fetch your captain*,' Grey said through gritted teeth.

'Grey,' Brit said when the boy darted into the guard tower. 'Are you sure you want to do this?'

'There's no taking it back now,' Grey said. And more than that: she let the power slip over her, the strength of her mother's line running heavy in her veins; they were the only nation in which the founding family had remained in power, even after all this time, and she would not break that now. She had always been a Locke. She would always be a Locke. 'It'll be even more conspicuous when I raise a dead island if I don't claim it now.'

It didn't work quite as effectively as she'd hoped: they were taken to the boy's captain, who agreed to bring her to the commander because Grey was both of rank and part of the Stratan girl's retinue, though he only sighed when the guard said she had a message from Locke. He looked at her, then at the boy, and said, 'For a dead nation, I've been hearing quite a lot of it lately.'

They were taken to the commander, who looked almost chipper. His expression dimmed significantly when he took them in, their clothing and the blood on it, and the conspicuous absence of Kier. 'I was expecting Captain Seward,' he said, almost mournful. 'I thought he'd considered my offer.'

'Captain Seward is indisposed,' Grey said through gritted teeth. Even speaking his name hurt.

He shuffled through papers on his desk. His Hand stood resolutely behind him. Grey couldn't help her gaze flicking back to him, thinking with some grief of Mare Concord. How resigned they all were to being devoted and used.

But wasn't she the same? Here she was running into more danger after Kier. The difference, she supposed, was that Kier hadn't asked her to do it. In fact, he'd explicitly asked her *not* to do it. If he had his way, she'd be halfway to Lindan by now.

'Yes, well. Where did you go the other night? I haven't received Captain Seward's report.'

'Commander.'

Reggin looked at her, then narrowed his eyes. 'What happened to your face, Fastria?'

Oh, what a tangled mess they'd gotten themselves into. They'd be lucky, Grey thought grimly, to be granted an audience, let alone get out of Grislar without visiting the prison first.

'Flynn,' Eron corrected.

'Sorry?' Reggin's eyes flicked up, already impatient, like he didn't have time for them.

Grey sat heavily in the chair in front of his desk. She felt Ola and Brit move to flank her, Eron behind her. One of them touched her very lightly on the back, where Reggin couldn't see. She was grateful for this, that they stood by while she found the words. They let her lead in her own way. It was all or nothing – there was no backing down now.

'Captain Seward has been taken by a combination of Luthrite and Eprainish forces. I believe the two nations are allied, and they are convinced that Kier is Severin of Locke.'

She'd managed to stun the commander, who blinked at her owlishly. 'And why would they think that? He's a mage, yes, and a powerful one at that, but ... '

Grey stretched her hands out on her knees, twisting the silver ring on her thumb. 'They're not exactly wrong. Kier is a powerful mage, but it's only because I'm a powerful well.'

'But you're not a well,' Reggin said. His own well's hand tightened on his shoulder. 'Flynn?' he said, looking at Eron.

Eron smiled grimly. 'I'm sorry. I'm not Hand Captain Flynn – she is.'

Reggin blinked at them, confusion clouding his face, turning quickly to anger. They wouldn't have his attention much longer before they were all punished for insubordination.

Grey pressed on. 'The issue is, Kier is not Locke. I am. And I request an audience with Scaelas under the banner of my nation.'

'If you expect me to believe ...' Reggin started, that anger brewing.

Grey, hours removed from breakbloom and restored to her full power, shook her head. 'Believe me or don't. If you refuse, I will go to Cleoc, who *will* believe me. And unless you want to be at war again, I suggest you listen.'

He regarded her distastefully for a long moment, long enough that Grey started to doubt the merit of this idea. 'All I can do is ask. I cannot guarantee he will accept, Hand Captain Flynn.' He spat her name as if it was an insult.

For the first time since Kier was taken, Grey smiled, all teeth. 'He will.'

You don't *have* to marry her, you martyr. You could come home again, return to my side; we can continue like adventurers across the nation. If she's as fearsome as you say, then surely that's a better option.

Letter from Vearn Torrin to Isaak Masidic, 18 years AD

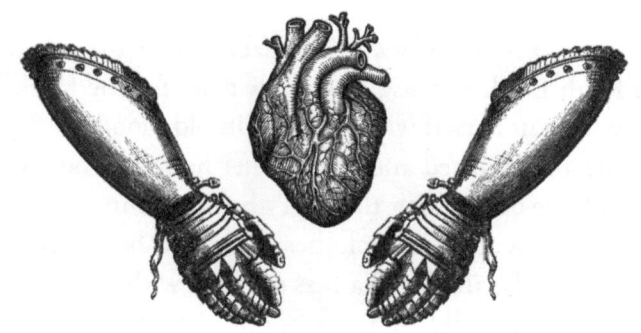

twenty-two

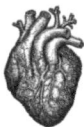

OLA INSISTED GREY WASH her face before the meeting with the High Lord, because it was not meet for the High Lady of a nation to present herself while crusted in old blood, so she washed her face. She also brushed and braided her hair, but there was nothing that could be done about the angry bruise around her eye, or her split lip. She dressed in clean clothes offered to her shyly by one of the younger guards, and let Ola fuss over her with salves as Brit and Eron watched. Ola undid all her work on the braid and arranged her hair so it fell over her shoulders ('It brings out the flecks of brown in your eyes, and besides, you look more like a lady and less like a soldier like that,' which was something Grey couldn't argue with). At least it hid some of the bruising.

'You have to look impressive,' Ola said, pacing back and forth across the small office they were installed in.

'I just have to look like me,' Grey said. 'Like ... my mother's daughter. My father's.'

'And that will be easy?'

Grey thought of the way Scaelas kept peering at her the other night at dinner, and her belly clenched with the pain of an old familiar wound. 'Yes,' she said.

She was acutely aware that every moment they spent doing this was another moment Kier was imprisoned, or worse. They were in one of the tower offices, reserved for high-ranking officials visiting Grislar, and she felt her gaze going to the sea more often than not, searching for a boat in the distant expanse of the bay.

To her surprise, when the door opened, it was not only Scaelas and his guard. Cleoc accompanied him, Sela on her arm.

Sela would speak the truth, and they would have to believe her. And though their beginning was rocky, Grey knew Sela would want to save Kier.

'Hand Captain Flynn,' Scaelas said as the combined guard filtered in, filing along the wall, the door shutting behind them. Cleoc moved easily to sit in an armchair by the fire, Sela standing at her side. Scaelas himself stayed in the middle of the room, dressed more simply today in a finely cut tunic with a waistcoat, breeches and boots. A single gem shone in his ear. On his left hand he wore the heavy gold ring of state. 'I was told you have an urgent matter to discuss.'

Someone must've informed him about Grey and Eron's switch, or maybe he just knew. When he looked, he looked at her.

'Where's Kier?' Sela asked, glancing around.

Grey stood. She looked at the High Lord. Vearn Torrin was his name, before he was Scaelas, before he had a nation under him; according to Grey's father, he hadn't gone by Vearn since he was in the nursery.

She had a speech ready on her lips, rehearsed with the others when they were alone, but now that he stood in front of her, the words fled. She looked at him, seeing his red hair and beard, remembering his hand in hers when she was barely up to his knee.

'I didn't want you to find me.'

Silence stretched over the room. Torrin staggered back as though she'd struck him. 'I . . .'

She squeezed her hands into fists, nails biting into her palms. Her voice was tight in her throat, raw and painful. She felt the burr of her old accent, her *true* accent, slipping in, as it always did when she was upset, like she couldn't hold the lilting Scaelan vowels on her tongue. 'After. When the smoke was still in the air. They say you searched for nearly a year for any sign of survivors, but I didn't want you looking for me. Severin told me not to, because there was no way we could be certain you'd keep me safe.'

His hand went to his chest, resting over his heart, as if she'd dealt him a fatal blow. He searched her face.

'I would have,' he said. 'I would've done anything in my power.'

Grey held her ground. 'You couldn't guarantee it.'

'Alma,' he said finally, the pain flickering on his brow so quickly she nearly missed it. 'You look so much like Alma. But you have Isaak's eyes.'

Grey did not allow her gaze to soften.

Torrin took one step forward, then another. Hesitantly, waiting for permission, he reached out. Grey inclined her head. He took her chin between his thumb and forefinger and gently moved her head so he could see the uninjured side of her face, then again, to study her bruise. She felt the rough fingers against her skin, his hands scarred with battle. He himself had been a soldier once, she knew – he'd fought in the wars, for the first decade; before his reign, he'd been in his father's army, alongside Grey's own father, before Isaak was married to Locke.

'Someone has harmed you,' he said quietly.

'Not for the first time,' Grey said.

He tilted her head back to face him straight-on. 'I did look for you, at first,' he said. 'And then the letter—' He drew a breath. 'The letter. It was you, wasn't it?'

No hesitation. 'Yes.'

He glanced away, at the window behind her head. 'Grey ... ' he murmured, looking at nothing. 'Of course, it's just another nickname.'

'Maryse would've been too obvious,' Grey said. 'Gremaryse was impossible.'

'And Flynn?'

Grey pulled back. Torrin's hand fell, fingers twitching. She crossed her arms over her chest. 'I was fostered by a widow, on the coast.'

'You were here, in Scaela, the entire time?'

She looked at him, her High Lord, the only person alive who

remotely resembled family. 'I have served you as a well and sword for eight years now,' she said. 'I have marched under your banner – and nearly died under it more than once.'

He stepped back. 'And now you come to me as a nation. Not as my god-daughter, I presume.'

Grey nodded slowly, ignoring the muttering from the guards in the background. There was no sound from Cleoc, no change; Grey wondered if Sela had already told her, or more accurately, if she had heard Sela's stories about their travels and guessed at the truth herself.

'I need your help,' Grey said.

In an upper room, they waited while Scaelas and Cleoc spoke to their necessary counselors. Grey, with no counsel of her own, kept an eye on the clock. Every second that passed could mean the end of Kier. She sat at a desk facing the window, writing two lists. The first was the names of those she trusted, those she knew she could rely on. Not all of them were physically close, which was an issue, but when she was back, and when she had Kier . . . The second list was her demands.

Behind her, Eron said, 'Attis is accounted for.' He was skimming through the casualty reports from Mecketer, recently delivered at Grey's request, searching for anyone else they knew who was missing or dead.

Grey swallowed hard, her pen pausing, remembering the spread of Mare's blood. 'Is she still at Mecketer?'

'I don't know. We'll need to ask.'

She had no loyalty to Klara Attis, but she could not imagine not being there if something happened to Kier. She would at least check in on the mage, at least tell her how her Hand had died.

Ola and Sela sat at a desk next to her, muttering over sketches. Grey did not have the mental capacity to understand what they were doing until Sela said, 'Grey, stand up,' and withdrew a length of measuring tape from somewhere on her person. Grey blinked up at her, bewildered.

She'd been surprised that Cleoc had allowed Sela to retire here, to this upper room, where Brit and Ola and Eron restlessly followed Grey's instructions as she tried to attempt to be the leader of a nation.

But Sela had said, 'Ma, they kept me alive for weeks,' so her mother had no choice, on the caveat that Sela brought a duo of guards to stand outside the door.

Grey regretted letting the girl join as Sela dragged her bodily out of her chair and pulled off her jacket. She announced measurements to Ola, who dutifully recorded them as Eron and Brit looked on. They all had work to be doing – Scaelas had provided Brit with a list of armory overages, with instructions for them to mark down what they could possibly use to outfit Locke; and before the casualty lists arrived, Eron was working out how many borrowed soldiers they would need to get Kier back, theorizing strategy with Grey when she was able to respond to him. Both were stationed by the window further down the room, where they could see the Bay of Locke clearly, watching for an enemy ship in case Luthar or Eprain moved early.

'What is all this?' Grey asked, allowing herself to be prodded.

'I've ordered you clothing,' Sela said. 'A gift for your new position.'

'Thank you,' Grey said quickly, 'but doesn't that feel . . . trivial?' She did not bring up the fact that it felt trivial because Kier was gone and he could be killed at any moment, and her nerves felt gnawed to the quick, because Sela already knew all of that; she probably also saw the growing panic on Grey's face the longer she was away from her task, her distractions.

Grey bounced up and down on the balls of her feet. Sela put her hands heavily on her shoulders to still her, like Grey was the child. 'You must look the part,' she said.

'I don't even know what the Lady of Locke is meant to look like,' Grey said.

'You're the only one who *does* know,' Sela said, 'but I can hazard a guess.' She removed her hands and wrapped the measuring tape back up. 'I've had Scaelas provide a list of tailors – I'll have at least half a wardrobe for you by daybreak. A shame we're not in Isidar – that's the capitol of Cleoc Strata, you know—'

'We *do*,' Ola muttered, 'as we are not uncultured *swine*.'

'—because I could certainly have a full wardrobe made for you overnight there,' Sela finished, barely missing a beat. She looked at Grey, the flicker in her eyes making something odd and vulnerable twist in her gut. 'Besides keeping me alive, you gave me time when you didn't have to. I owe you for that.'

Grey took a shuddering breath. Maybe that was what it meant to be the High Lady of Locke. What it took. Time, when she didn't need to, when it meant more to someone else than to her.

Kier, she thought, a little desperately. *If only we get more of it.* The tether ached within her, dormant and still, but at least she could feel its presence.

Time, and a bit of ruthlessness.

'Sela,' she said, reaching to grab the girl's hand. 'Promise me you won't come with us. You're welcome on Locke, but only when it's safe.'

Sela shrugged. 'I can only do what I'm told.'

A knock sounded on the door. They all jumped, too uneasy for this. Grey fussed, her hand instantly going to check her braids, but her hair was still down, and she only managed to hit herself on the bruised side of her face.

The others were looking at her. In a voice she hoped was chilly and regal, she said, 'Come in.'

It was one of the High Lord's house guard, one he'd brought with him from the capital. 'You have been requested, your highness,' he said with perfect formality. Grey sucked in a breath, her hand gripping Sela's for the barest second.

'Thank you,' she said. She looked back at the others. 'Can I bring my guard?'

Ola raised an eyebrow.

'Of course,' the man said. 'I will wait to escort you, if you would like to finish your business, your highness.'

Grey nodded, letting the door shut behind him, and released her breath. 'I don't mean it like—'

'No,' Ola said quickly, 'but you *should* have a guard.' She looked at Eron and Brit, something passing between them. 'And it makes sense, for now, as long as you're okay with it, that it should be us.'

Grey looked down at her hands, chipped nails, scarred from battles long since past. Who was she to think she could be sovereign? Could have a *guard*?

She ached for Kier. Longed for him in a space beyond thought, beyond words. It caught her every time she had one of these thoughts, every time she found herself needing counsel, or just someone else to tell her that she was not utterly ruining her namesake.

'I'll have you,' she said, 'if you'll have me.'

A hand gripped hers. She looked to find Ola there, sure as always, biting as always.

'We had you as our captain,' she said. 'It would be an honor to have you as our lady.'

'Okay,' Grey said. She took a second, forced herself to remain calm. 'Okay.'

With nothing left to discuss, they went out into the hall and followed the guard down the stone passageways and stairs. Grey walked with Sela, the others falling behind like shadows, in the same way Grey was taught to orbit Kier.

They arrived downstairs to a small, well-appointed meeting room dominated by a large table. It was one of the council chambers, Grey thought, based on the anteroom, which acted as a holding area for guests until they were admitted. Cleoc and Scaelas were already seated in the chamber beyond, a small retainer of guards blending into the shadows between each of them. The rest of their counselors had been dismissed – perhaps, Grey surmised, the other rulers were not quite ready to reveal Grey as Locke. She had seen herself in the mirror lately; she understood.

Sela nodded once to Grey and took the seat next to her mother. Though Grey was at rest and content to stand, Eron pulled out a chair to the other hand of Scaelas. He did something with his eyebrows, probably a reminder that she was now publicly the Lady of Locke, and she would have less trouble if she acted like it.

She sat and allowed him to adjust her chair, and did not look behind her as Eron, Ola and Brit faded like the other guards. It was a comfort to have them behind her, to hear their familiar breathing.

Cleoc regarded her with open curiosity. Here, unmasked, she was Locke uncontested. She folded her hands in front of her on the table, conscious of her lack of finishing; that she was battle-made and bruised and nothing like a High Lady should be.

In another world, she would've been raised to live up to her title. Once she was fully grown, it would've been announced that she was the heir instead of Severin; in the tradition of Locke, he would have then been able to leave the Isle, if he chose. Until that time, she would've been shaped by her parents into something hard as iron. She would've traveled, maybe – perhaps been trained for a year in Lindan, like Sela, or one of the other nations on the continent. Probably not, though, since Locke tended to keep to itself. But she would've been taught diplomacy and respectful negotiation and the means of survival in enemy courts. She would've learned the words to say, the expressions to make.

But Alma and Isaak were dead, and had been for sixteen years, long enough that Grey had learned very few lessons. She clung to the ones she had, the ones she remembered, squaring her shoulders and sitting ramrod straight like her mother always used to.

'You must know I believe you,' Scaelas said finally, breaking the silence. 'I'm just not certain how to convince my council.'

'You've already taken a risk on an imposter,' Grey said. 'At least this time you'd be correct.'

He inclined his head, allowing that.

She looked between Scaelas and Cleoc. 'What did you decide, then?'

'Why do you need to recover Captain Seward?' Cleoc asked.

Grey searched for a way to explain her relationship with Kier. 'He is my mage, your majesty.' She felt the tether inside of her, limp but there. She felt with an iron certainty that he was not dead. Harmed, maybe, but at least he was alive, and if he was alive, then she could still save him.

'Mages are replaceable,' Cleoc said, her finger dancing up and down the line of the pen in front of her. Grey did not know if Cleoc was a mage or well herself. Most of the sovereigns hid that information as if it was a weakness.

'It is non-negotiable. If you unite with me, you have me – and Locke, restored in full power – as your ally. Surely that is enough to entice you, even if you don't believe me fully. I will keep my word.'

'You're asking both of us to engage in open warfare with Luthar and potentially Eprain, if you are correct about their recent alliance,' Scaelas said, not meeting her eye. 'Along with any outside allies they may have.'

'You're already at war with both Luthar and Eprain.'

'*I* am not at war with Luthar,' Cleoc said. 'And tensions with Eprain are easing. Why would I endanger my nation, again, for your mage?'

Grey turned toward her. Cleoc wanted a confession, she could tell – she wanted to see Grey's weakness. She felt that simmering anger inside herself. She didn't want to proclaim her love for Kier to them, because it was *hers* and she was not willing for it to be a bargaining chip. She wanted to hold that love deep and protected in her chest, keep it where no one could see it or hear it or feel it, and protect Kier in the same way.

'He is my mage,' she said again. 'I know the old meaning of that does not persist on the mainland, but I am Locke, and it matters to me.'

Scaelas's eyes snapped to hers. Before he could say anything, Cleoc said, 'You cannot be both Hand and High Lady, loyal to your mage and your nation. There must be a choice there. It is easier to make it now.'

Grey stood, her feet moving before she had even fully made the decision to do so. 'If you refuse to do this, allow me to make things easier: I will not negotiate and there is no need for me to prove myself. Either you lend your forces and assist in the rescue of Captain Seward, or you do not. Either you unite with the nation of Locke and reap the benefits, or you do not. I cannot make that choice for you, but I will not stand here and listen to such distrust and doubt.'

'Hold on, Locke,' Torrin said wearily. 'That's not ... that's not what we mean. We have our nations to think about.'

'And I have mine,' Grey said.

'Then help us to help you,' Cleoc said. 'Give us a reason.'

She did not sit. Torrin looked at her, a strange expression on his face, until he said finally, 'Cleoc, if you will permit, I'd like to dismiss my guard and yours. Everyone in this room apart from the three of us.'

'Grey . . .' Ola started immediately.

'We have more to lose if she deigns to murder us in your absence,' he said, devoid of humor. He turned his attention back to Cleoc, quirking a brow. After a pause, a weighted moment, Cleoc inclined her head and waved a hand. Her guard shifted, looking uneasy, but they filed out with the Scaelans and Grey's own retinue. When Sela did not move, Torrin looked at Cleoc. 'Your daughter?'

'I am—'

'Go, love,' Cleoc said, squeezing her hand. Frowning, lodging a lingering glance at Grey, Sela went out after Ola.

Grey sat back down. The three of them were silent for a long moment, all eying one another, until Scaelas spoke.

'You and your mage are very powerful.'

Grey looked at him coolly. 'I am Locke,' she said. 'You did not have to dismiss our guards to tell me this.'

'That was what I thought, until today.' Scaelas spoke slowly. 'But another idea has occurred to me: that you are bound. I hope I am wrong, because surely, as Locke, you know the risks.'

Grey went very still. If Torrin was going to punish her for binding, scold her like a child, she was prepared to remind him that it would be overstepping on his part. She was no longer a Scaelan soldier, no longer within his control. There were no restrictions on binding on Locke itself.

'I don't see why it matters.'

Torrin winced. 'So you do not deny it?'

'No,' she said, without hesitation. 'I am bound to Captain Seward.' It was a relief to speak the words so openly, to claim them. To claim *Kier*.

'Maryse,' Torrin said, his eyes slipping shut. 'You didn't.'

'Can she not bind? She *is* Locke,' Cleoc said, looking between them.

'Don't speak to me as if I'm your child,' Grey said, her tone colder than she intended, but still not cold enough to encompass her emotions.

Torrin rubbed the bridge of his nose. 'We have a conundrum,' he said, meeting Cleoc's gaze in a way that Grey did not like. 'Whoever controls Locke controls power. Of course, when we thought Seward was just a mage, it did not matter if he was being sacrificed to resurrect the Isle. If they had him try to call it back from the sea, it would be unsuccessful.'

Grey winced. It *did* matter, but not for the reasons Torrin meant. 'It *will* be unsuccessful,' she said. 'Kier is not a Locke. He doesn't have the blood.'

'Ah, but that is where you are wrong,' Torrin said. Grey looked with alarm at Cleoc, but she looked just as confused as Grey herself felt, her lips pressed into a thin, grim line. 'When you bind to a mage, as a Locke, they take your power as their own. He is the blood of your blood now; you and he are one in a complete exchange of power. That is the way of the Isle, Maryse. Binding is a sacred act, a union even stronger than marriage.'

True names are for Hands and husbands.

Grey's heart thundered too loud in her ears. What else did she not know about her own nation's rites? 'So Kier . . . '

Torrin nodded. 'Kier is now a Locke himself, and has just as much claim to the Isle as you do. He doesn't need you. If he discovered the means to bring back the Isle, call it forth, Locke would rise to his command – granting Eprain and Luthar the Isle restored, and all power therein.'

Over the years, I have managed to learn something about our opponents. Nestria fight because they have to, but they would rather return to their ballrooms and parties. Cleoc Strata is just as vicious as its lady is rumored to be. Luthar is cunning, twisting our strategies into dust. And Eprain would rather poison you before battle than meet you on the field. Yet we are caught in the middle of them, forced to fight them all.

Journal of Hand Master Mare Concord, 7 years PD

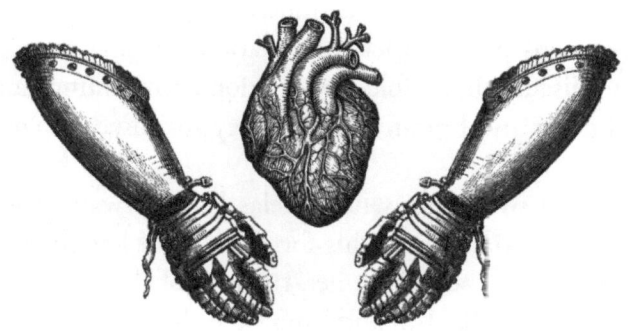

twenty-three

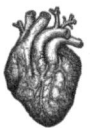

SCAELAS AND CLEOC, WORKING together after realizing the ruinous possibilities of the situation they found themselves in, decided the best course of action was to blast the entire business wide open. Grey helped as much as she could as they wrote to the sovereigns of the other three nations, urging them to come together to discuss the unfolding situation surrounding Locke. The letters to Luthar and Eprain were, as Grey surmised, diplomatically threatening.

After the missives were sent, Scaelas himself walked Grey to a room in the imperial wing of his fortress. Night had already fallen. She felt the ache of the day on her, the lack of sleep from the night before catching up. Ola, Brit and Eron were already sleeping in rooms near hers; Scaelas left his own guard to watch them overnight.

In the hall, Grey hesitated. She didn't know when she would next have the High Lord alone – she figured it was a rare occurrence.

'Why did you send that letter?' Torrin asked. 'Claiming Severin survived.'

There was no reason to keep it from him, not anymore. 'I was afraid,' she said. 'I was only a girl. The soldiers you sent to look were not kind or gentle. I didn't want you to find me.'

'Ah,' Torrin said, so quiet she barely heard.

'What do you know about the Isle's death?' Grey asked, since he had opened up the door to questions.

To her surprise, he answered immediately. 'Your father,' he said. 'He told me about the Isle's failsafe. He wasn't even supposed to know – it is the way of the Isle's sovereigns to keep their own secrets, even in marriage. But your mother loved your father – probably in spite of her upbringing.'

Grey pretended to be very interested in the stitches of the tapestry hanging on the wall near her rooms, running her fingers over the edge of the fabric. 'I know she did,' she said. 'And he loved her too.'

'More than life itself,' Torrin agreed. 'I never understood it – don't get me wrong, Maryse. I, too, adored your mother, when I got to know her, but I did it with a heavy measure of fear. She was a striking woman. She had this look, and when she turned it on you – well. One would wish they were dead rather than being on the receiving end of that look.'

'I remember,' Grey said; she herself had been on the receiving end of that look more than once. 'But he made her smile. She was always laughing, in private, when they were together.'

'Some would call that a weakness.'

Grey shrugged; she wouldn't. 'But the failsafe,' she said. She could not stand here talking about the love her parents once had for one another, remembering all the ways that love had led to their deaths.

'Yes,' Torrin said. He nodded to her room. They stepped inside, and he locked the door behind them. He went to the fire, burning with light violet flame, a static working from some unknown mage, and leaned against the mantle, staring into the flames. 'We were drinking together, late into the night, one evening when he came to visit – we did that more than I should admit, when we were reunited – and your mother had already retired for the night. Severin was just a boy; I don't remember if you were even born then.

'It's a protection from the Isle's gods. The risk of power is that it is coveted. It was understood that someday, others might turn on the Isle and all it stood for, so when each child in the direct line came of age, they were told the truth. If the Isle was ever set upon, if all hope was lost, there was a choice: the line could continue if all others died to save one. If they gave their lives, both their power and their magic, the one with the best chance of saving the line would survive.'

Grey stumbled back, her back hitting the poster of the bed. She had suspected as much, but she thought it had only been Severin who had given his life.

'All of them,' she said.

'Everyone on the Isle,' Torrin said quietly, 'died so you could live.'

She crossed her arms over her stomach as if there was any way possible to hold herself together.

'Do you wish it was him? After all this time, do you wish it was Severin who had lived?'

Torrin looked at her aghast. 'Gods, Maryse,' he said. 'How could you even ask me that?'

She didn't know. She couldn't speak. Some days, she herself wished it had been Severin who had lived instead.

Torrin crossed the room, taking her hand in his. He was tall, taller than her father had been, and broader in the shoulder, but there was something about him and his bearing that made her thoughts turn to Isaak the second she looked at him.

'I will do everything in my power,' he said, 'to make it up to you.'

'Do you know,' Grey asked, leaning forward despite herself, 'how to bring it back? How to resurrect the Isle?'

He sighed, his eyes flickering shut. He stepped back. 'I don't,' he said. 'I'm sorry.'

Grey nodded, trying to ignore the acid in her stomach. He wouldn't have known, she'd suspected, but that hadn't stopped her from hoping someone else held the answers for once.

'I should have forgotten that letter. I should've kept looking,' Torrin said.

Grey looked up at him. She had spent years of her life wishing she'd heard those words, but now that she did, they were empty. 'You should've,' she agreed. Except if he had, she never would've stayed with Kier. She looked away, swallowing down the lump that threatened her. 'You will tell me the minute you hear back?'

'Yes,' he said. 'And I will trust Cleoc for your benefit, though it makes me uneasy. We will do everything in our power to find him.'

Grey nodded. They had no other choice.

He took leave of her and she shut the door behind him. Though she was exhausted, she forced herself to bathe, to wash away the remaining grime and to apply more salves and ointments on her cuts and bruises. The one on her stomach was particularly nasty; her face looked worse than it felt. Once she was clean, she braided her hair and pulled on a nightdress someone had left for her, and let herself slip away to sleep.

That night, when she dreamed of the death of Locke, it was Kier's hands that held hers as the power rushed between them. Kier's bruises on her skin. Kier's body destroyed when the world exploded.

It was still dark when she woke to someone shaking her. She blinked up wearily to find Brit's form over her. They were already dressed, a magelight glowing blue between their fingers.

'Wake up. There's news.'

She hurried to dress, leaving her hair in its braid. Outside her door, Ola waited – 'Letting Eron sleep, though he might kill us for it,' she said through a grimace – and the three of them followed two of Scaelas's guards to a bigger council chamber than the one from the day before. There, Cleoc and Scaelas waited with their commanders and a number of other high-ranking officials. Grey wished, too late, that she had rebraided her hair.

'We've had news?' she said, accepting the bitter, dark coffee someone offered her. She glanced at a clock on the wall. It was just past four in the morning.

'Epras and Luthos have agreed to meet,' Cleoc said. 'You are right. They have allied.'

'And Nestria?'

'They remain silent, thus far.'

Grey nodded. She felt the eyes of the other knights on her; she could basically taste the confusion coming from Commander Reggin and his Hand. A few eyes widened when one of Cleoc's guards pulled out a chair and Grey slipped into it, as if they were expecting Ola or

Brit to claim the seat. Perhaps, Grey thought darkly, it was because both looked older, and had brushed their hair, and did not have a bruise covering half of their faces.

'We are to meet Eprain, Luthar and an ambassador from the continent in two hours' time,' Scaelas said. 'We have patrols on the sea, in case they attempt to do anything beforehand, and we have petitioned for the release of Captain Seward.'

Grey blanched. They often petitioned for the release of soldiers taken prisoner outside of the allowable context: more often than not, they were returned dead. And if Kier was killed for naught – if Kier was killed at *all* . . . she would raze the entire island. She would swallow it all with the sea in the depths of her grief.

'If I may, my lord?' Commander Reggin started. Scaelas inclined his head. 'Your highness,' Reggin said, turning to Grey. He said the title like it burned his tongue, but he continued all the same. 'We have arranged two companies from Scaela and have accepted two more from Cleoc Strata. These soldiers will accompany the High Lord and Cleoc as they negotiate the release of Captain Seward.'

Grey glanced over at Torrin. 'And I . . . ?'

'You will remain behind our forces, in the fortress and safe,' Torrin said firmly.

Grey scoffed. 'I have been *in* your forces for nearly a decade, and I have not died yet.'

'You will *not* risk yourself,' Torrin said, acting again like her father. If he was trying to make up for sixteen years of lost time, this was not the way to do it.

Grey felt Ola's hand heavy on her shoulder. Fingers dug into her flesh.

'Absolutely not,' she said. 'If you are meeting, I need to be there. If you are discussing my future, I need to hear it.'

'She has a point, Scaelas,' Cleoc said mildly.

'I will not reveal you as Locke,' Torrin said firmly. 'Not when they would accept Seward's death and leave you safe.'

Grey could not allow herself to think about the possibility. 'Then don't,' she said. 'Take me as your own guard. I will stand behind you and listen, but I will be there.'

'I cannot allow—'

'That is an acceptable compromise,' Cleoc said, sitting back in her chair, her gaze on Torrin cooling by the minute. 'And if he refuses to armor you, Locke, you may act as one of my guards.'

Torrin looked between the two of them, clearly furious, trying his best to tamp it down. It took all of Grey's focus not to smile sweetly at him.

'Then it is settled,' he said, shrugging. 'You will come, but not alone. Select one of your guard to accompany you.' He nodded to Reggin, signaling for him to resume his explanation of troop movements on the map.

'It is settled,' Grey agreed.

An hour later, Grey and Eron were lined up with the rest of Scaelas's guard, marching off to the meeting. Brit and Ola had protested, each volunteering in turn to accompany her, but if one of them perished, she could not imagine being responsible for splitting the pairing. For his part, Eron understood, reaching to squeeze her hand after the other two had stomped off to sulk.

With Grey's hair up and braided around her head, and dressed in Scaelan armor, she looked like any other guard. She felt the comfort of armor settling over her, the weight of it as familiar to her as the feeling of her own power.

Despite her anxiety, she had to appreciate the beauty of the coast as they rode to the meeting point. This close to Luthar, there were no beaches; the rolling hills went all the way to the cliffs, which fell away into the sea below. When she and Kier were children, Lot would take them to similar cliffs, and they'd take turns jumping into the waiting arms of the ocean below. When Imarta found out, she boxed all of their ears for making her panic, but she did not tell the boys' mothers.

'Gremaryse.'

She was brought out of her thoughts by Scaelas's voice, and looked up to realize he had fallen back, riding next to her. He, too, wore armor, but no helm. His own crest was embroidered in gold.

'Have you come to scold me more?' Grey asked. Eron, glancing over, slowed to give them privacy.

Torrin looked at her, frowning. 'I will not pretend,' he said. 'If I had my way, you would be locked in a tower until we figured out the safest way to do this.'

'You could try to keep me locked up, but you would fail.'

'You know,' he said, 'your father would not remain in a locked tower, either.'

Grey chewed her lip. She wasn't sure how he could bear it, talking about them like this, without the grief swallowing him whole.

'When he died,' Torrin said, 'I did not think I would make it. That first day, when the smoke hung heavy, I was certain— Well. We had not tethered in almost two decades, not since he was married and bound to your mother. But somehow, still, I knew.'

Grey forced through the panic rising in her chest. 'Are you telling me this because you think Kier is as good as dead?'

'I'm telling you this because I care about you.'

'You barely know me.'

He looked at her evenly. 'Does it matter?' he asked. 'Maybe that is true, or maybe I know you better than you could ever imagine, because you are their daughter, and you are just as fearsome as they could ever hope you to be.'

She couldn't go into this thinking of her parents and all the ways they never knew her. A beat of silence passed between them. Grey looked up ahead, catching sight of Cleoc, riding straight and tall among her guard. She wondered if she herself would ever emulate that instead of battle-worn stubbornness.

Finally, Torrin sighed. 'Do you promise to run at the first sign of trouble?'

'Absolutely not,' Grey said. 'Not without Kier.'

'I worried you would say that.' Torrin glanced at her sidelong. 'You're going to try to save him, aren't you?'

Grey looked at him evenly. 'I will do anything in my power to save him,' she said. 'I'm sorry, Torrin. I know it makes me sound young, or impulsive – I can't say I make a level ally. But if I had to choose between Kier and this whole sodding nation, I would always choose Kier.'

Torrin frowned. 'Well then,' he said. 'Whatever you do, I ask that you do it sensibly. I have already lost so many to this war, Maryse. And I ask that whatever you do, you don't do it alone.'

'You won't try to stop me? If I try to save him? If I do something foolish?'

He snorted. 'If you're anything like your mother, I don't see the point in trying.' He glanced up the column. 'Just do me a favor and don't tell Cleoc. It would be best if she only thinks *you* are a bad ally, and we leave me out of it.'

'I can do that,' Grey agreed.

They rode in silence for a few minutes longer, Grey's thoughts swimming with possibilities, with plans. As they crested the last rise, Torrin turned back to her. 'You matter more than your power, Maryse. I beg you to keep that in mind.'

Grey nodded, and did not say that she did not matter more than Kier. As they came over the hill, she could see the grassy area set up for the meeting. A murmur went through the guard as they spotted what lay beyond: Luthar and Eprain had brought nearly double the army of Cleoc and Scaelas.

'My lord,' one of the commander's squires said, riding close to Scaelas. 'Shall we call for reinforcements?'

Torrin stood in his stirrups, surveying the mass of Eprainish and Luthrite forces. He swore profusely – then sighed. 'No,' he said. 'At the first sign of skirmish, call for a retreat. I will not let this dissolve into yet another pointless battle.' He glanced over at Grey, lips pressed together, and nodded.

The party of Scaelas, Cleoc and their assorted guard split off from the soldiers and rode toward a small grouping in the middle of the field. Scaelas rode ahead, catching up with his guard, and Eron fell back in with Grey. It was a peaceful meeting – for now. At the first sign of harm, of attack by steel or magic, the guard was trained to surround the High Lord and get him to safety.

Grey surveyed the knot of people, her heart in her throat. There were about a dozen, all mounted – except for one. He stood between two riders – Grey thought it must be Epras and Luthos, unhelmed like Scaelas and Cleoc – dressed in all black. As they rode closer, she drank in the sight of him, the familiar bearing of his body, the wind rippling through his hair. One of his arms was in a sling, probably due to his broken collarbone, so at least he'd seen a healer. Next to her, Eron sighed in relief.

Kier.

She reached for the tether, struggling for any thread of him. She felt nothing, so he was still drugged. If they didn't have breakbloom on his person – and drugs were forbidden within the shield of a diplomatic meeting, so he must have been dosed beforehand – it would be at least twenty minutes, maybe more, before she'd be able to tether.

'He's alive,' she said, her throat tight.

'Of course he is,' Eron said, as if he had never doubted at all. He glanced over, offering her a crooked half-smile.

It took all of Grey's will to fall into line a few paces behind Scaelas with the rest of his guard; all she wanted was to race ahead, grab Kier and run from this place. He wore no armor, unlike Epras and Luthos, and carried no weapons.

He glanced up as Scaelas and Cleoc approached, something flickering on his face – and then he looked at the line behind the sovereigns, and his eyes lit on Grey.

She reached out, but she could not tether. Kier took a half-step forward before he remembered himself. Imperceptibly, he shook his head, grimacing.

'Luthos,' Cleoc said, nodding to the shorter of the two men. He had hair black as pitch and slouched in his saddle. 'Epras.' Epras sat straighter, his horse dancing under him. 'Locke.' She did not reveal a thing as she greeted Kier. 'You could have saved us a lot of trouble if we had spoken of this the other night, on different terms.'

It was a scolding, Grey knew, that was meant for her.

Kier shrugged with his good shoulder.

'It has been too long since we met like this,' Cleoc continued. 'Since we spoke sensibly and peacefully.'

'I have no interest in your speeches,' Luthos said shortly.

'Then present your terms,' Torrin said, 'and we can move on.'

Luthos and Epras exchanged a glance, and Grey was not sure what to read in it. She glanced at Kier again, but he was staring at the ground at her feet, his face unchanged. She reached for him with a tether, as if she could push all effects of the drug away with the force of her mind alone. She kept her hand resting lightly on the pommel of her sword, not quite able to calm her racing heart.

'We have found and recovered Severin, the lost heir to Locke,' Epras said. 'As such, the High Lord shall restore his Isle, take a consort from my court and continue the line of Locke in the name of Epras.'

Torrin looked at Luthos – who was much younger than the other sovereign, Grey remembered, only a few years into his reign. 'And you agreed to this?' he asked, incredulous. 'You allied with Epras, and yet will allow him to seize control of power?'

'Epras is capable of seeing reason,' Luthos said flatly. 'Unlike others.'

'All those years, and the heir was right under your nose,' Epras said, his tone dripping with contempt. 'All those years, and the power could've been yours.'

'It was never the power I wanted,' Torrin said.

'Gentlemen,' Cleoc cut in. She turned her gaze to Epras. 'It is not your role to rule Locke. He may be your prisoner now, but what happens if he kills your bride? Controlling power is not so easy.'

'Not if he's bound to his bride,' Epras said, 'as is the Isle's custom.'

Cleoc sighed. Grey tried again for a tether, forcing through the fog of the breakbloom that clouded Kier's system. Nothing.

'It looks like you have made up your mind, then,' Cleoc said. 'Locke shall be restored, and Epras shall rule. But I will raze your Isle. I will kill your bride. I will destroy everything you create, Epras.'

Cleoc had never reminded Grey so much of her own mother. Not for the first time, she wondered if this was what the throne did to women like them.

'Then I will remove your power,' Epras said.

Cleoc raised an eyebrow. 'How do you intend to do that?'

'Because,' Epras said, leaning forward, his smile poisonous, '*I shall control Locke.*'

'I believe we're getting off topic,' Kier said quietly. 'My lord, my lady, I have agreed to marry Epras's choice and name her my consort. I have agreed to restore the Isle. But I will do it only on the understanding that the fighting will cease and the united council will re-form.' He looked utterly resigned to his fate. 'There is no reason for the death to continue.'

'And you will restore power equally?' Scaelas asked.

A pause. 'I will equip Epras and Luthos with a renewal of power,' Kier said, 'since they have rescued me and restored me.'

Cleoc and Scaelas exchanged a glance. Grey drew a breath – so this was what they wanted. It was in Locke's power to distribute wells unevenly; because Grey's father had been Scaelan and their alliance was strongest, Scaela was the most power-rich nation when the Isle fell.

But now? Now it was all going to crumble. And Kier had agreed to it because he did not think he had the power for his promises to be fulfilled.

'We will not assent to that,' Cleoc said. As if sensing her unease, her horse danced under her. 'All power should be restored equally – you cannot convince us of this farce. Locke is your prisoner, not your ally.'

Epras smiled thinly. 'Semantics.' He nodded back to his soldiers. 'And it matters not – we have brought the festivities here. Our chosen bride waits, and we have agreed to this meeting so you can witness the marriage – and our alliance.'

Grey's heart dropped. Kier was still not looking at her, but it hardly mattered. She reached. She prodded. She *pushed*.

The thinnest thread of her power caught, and it held.

She pushed as much emotion his way as she could: love and apology and fury and relief, as much as she could muster. She was so busy pushing that it took her a moment to realize that the only feeling Kier was sending back was cold, hopeless dread.

'Eron,' Grey murmured. 'Something is wrong.'

'Besides everything?' he whispered back.

Grey focused on the tether, tuning out the meeting, which had devolved into bickering about land parcels and borders if an alliance was formed. She focused only on Kier, and the dread he was sending through the tether, and tried to answer with her own comfort.

She would not let him marry into Epras. She would not let him take this burden on – he could not even know, now, that he was truly a player in this game.

'If I do something reckless,' Grey asked, 'will you cover me?'

Eron sighed. 'Yes,' he said.

Grey turned back to the tether. She focused on Commander Reggin, imagining the firm lines of his face, trying to send the image to Kier. Kier frowned, glanced up. He looked at Grey, then at Reggin. Grey nodded, ever so slightly.

A pause. A beat. She felt the moment he started pulling from her – not enough to do any true harm, but enough to cause notice. Behind Scaelas, Commander Reggin straightened – then slumped in his saddle, sliding around. Not dead, but unconscious.

Scaelas turned, aghast. 'Did you just kill my commander?'

Grey was already moving. 'To Scaelas!' Eron cried, summoning the guard to close in around the High Lord, to protect him. 'They have attacked!'

'To Scaelas!' someone called back. The sound of metal on metal rang through the air as the field dissolved into chaos.

Grey took advantage of the confusion. Already, the guard folded around them, Reggin's Hand recovering his unconscious body. The guard raced away, bearing Cleoc and Scaelas off, as Luthos and Epras's guards scrambled to fold around their own sovereigns – leaving Grey an opening.

She tethered, pushing power at Kier. A scream as two of Luthos's guard fell with no apparent reason; Grey felt the slice of the deaths as Kier pulled from her. Behind her, she heard Scaelas calling for his forces to retreat. 'Go, Eron,' she urged – she would not risk him, too. He spared her only a glance before he shook his head. 'I'm commanding you to trust me,' she begged. '*Run.*'

He hesitated, looking at her for a half-moment more before he turned, following her order.

'*Get Locke!*' someone shouted. Grey nearly looked over her shoulder – but they were screaming about Kier.

Kier ducked out of the way of a Luthrite guard trying to grab him – she pushed another swell of power at him and felt the answering tug. And then she was over him, so close – she reached out her free hand and he grasped it, his foot finding the stirrup as he launched behind her onto the horse's back.

His arm wrapped around her, half hug, half for balance, and she felt his agony through the tether.

'What the *fuck* are you doing?' he snarled into her neck even as he pressed a kiss to the leather of her pauldron, as close as he could get to her skin.

'Saving your ass, as usual,' Grey said. He straightened and pulled from her, more easily now that they were in contact. She stripped power from the wells around her, trying her best to focus only on enemy forces – which was not difficult, as Luthos and Epras now directed their companies only at her. She turned the horse and rode back toward the sea, the cliff; back toward Scaela's retreating army.

'I love you,' Kier said against her skin, even as he ripped another rope of power from her middle. She hissed at the sensation – they could not keep going this recklessly.

'Save your declarations for when we're *off* the battlefield,' she said, wincing as he directed his power at another mage.

She focused on those wells, even though her head ached, and tore the power from the root. She tasted blood in the back of her throat as Kier cut them down.

'Grey,' Kier said, his voice bleak. 'Look.'

She did. From the top of the ridge, she saw Luthar and Eprain's full companies spreading out, forming an arc to cover every escape route – coming straight for them. She glanced on either side, but they were walled in, and faced with the cliffs behind them. The riders were bearing down on them, and *fast*.

'Do you have enough?' he questioned, testing the tether.

'No,' she said. She swallowed hard – even if she pulled from the other wells on the field, it wouldn't work. She was too tired, too depleted. If he tried to kill the riders who bore down on them, he might take her out, too.

She looked at him. 'Do you trust me?'

He grinned, the sight like a hot metal brand on her heart. 'Indubitably.'

She glanced at the cliff. 'It's time for us to get out of here.'

Kier dismounted, swinging Grey off with one arm as she dropped down, too. Like children, he gripped her hand as she turned to face the cliffs. She pulled off her helm, casting it aside. It wasn't high enough to kill them – only high enough to hurt.

Gremaryse, Grey thought to her patron namesake as they broke into a jog. *If you ever thought to claim me, now is the time to do it.*

Together they picked up speed, racing to the edge of the cliff. When the empty air came, Grey was ready for it.

They fell and fell, the air pushed from her lungs as they hit the surface of the water. The sea was merciless and terrible. As she dropped, falling through the dark, she clawed for any idea, any instinct of what she was meant to do – but she only felt her own cloudy terror. And now, still miles from the place where Locke once was, she felt the dark sea coming to claim her.

She reached for the surface, but she could not find it. She fought out of her armor, weighing her down, drowning her. She couldn't find Kier, either; she could only feel his pain and panic echoing in the tether like an animal cry. She opened her mouth, and the water swelled inside of her. She gasped, choking, and then she wasn't swimming at all.

Forget about us, someone called in the back of her mind.

She opened her eyes, the salt water burning, and tried to claw for air. 'I remember!' she shouted into the sea, where no one could hear her, where no one would watch the High Lady of Locke as she died. 'I will never forget.'

I gave everything for you. She heard Severin's voice, curling in the back of her brain. *I gave everything. And what would you give, to bring it back?*

Grey squeezed her eyes shut against the raging sea. *Take it*, she thought desperately, salt water invading her lungs. *Whatever you want. Whatever you need. Take it all.*

A hand grasped hers and tugged just as the sea started to roil.

And Retarik laid her hand upon Kitalma's breast. Between them, the power glowed with divine golden heat. The Isle shook as Kitalma spake, 'You are mine and I am yours, and let us never again be whole.'

Folklore recovered from the Isle of Locke, date unknown, author unknown

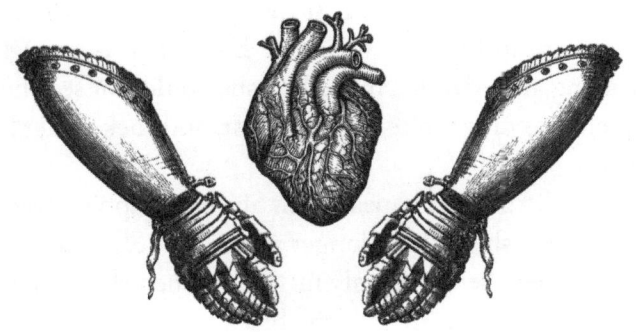

twenty-four

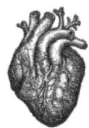

WHEN GREY WOKE, HER first thought was that her cantankerous grandmother who was once Locke had been right: there was something after death. Above her, she could not see the sky: on all sides there was only white swirling mist, and rock under her body.

She sat up.

There was solid ground beneath her. She was dripping wet, icy cold from the sea, but she was no longer *in* the sea. She was on a rocky cliff. Ahead of her there was only mist, but when she edged forward and looked down, she could see the black rock face, and more mist below. It had long been called the Obsidian Isle, and she felt the name curling around her now as she took in the inky darkness of the cliffs.

She sat back. To one side, through the gloom, she could just make out the solid stone walls of the fortress. Behind her, when she turned, the fog was ceding, slipping away from the skinny trees of the Ghostwood.

She stood. The cliffs of Locke were solid under her feet.

She turned in a slow circle, searching for – something. Unlike her, the ground was dry, as if the Isle had never been submerged at all.

There, at the edge of the wood, she spotted a shape. A body, face-down on the scrubby ground. She took two steps, three, and then she was running.

Protect me, Grey begged – she was not magic, nothing more than a mostly spent well of power, but she felt the island cave to her requests. She *felt* the tremulous safety of it.

And she could not think; she could barely breathe. Dripping salt-water and mud, she sprinted across the space between her and the wood and launched herself at that broken form, clad in black.

She threw herself to her knees in the dirt beside him, her hands going to his shoulders. She cursed herself, searching for the tether inside of her, but everything felt different here. She grabbed him by the shoulders and heaved, rolling him over.

Everything stopped. Went still as stone.

It was awful – because it was Kier, and for the first time in her life, he was unfamiliar to her. His skin was marred with purple splotches of bruises and part of his ear was missing and his eye was black and his arm had come loose from its sling so the broken edge of his collarbone pushed at his skin at an awkward, impossible angle.

How could he survive that? How could *anyone* survive that?

He did not move. He did not breathe. Her heart sank inside her like a stone when she realized that he *hadn't* survived it.

That was the unfamiliarity. The uncanniness. His face was lifeless, all spark of what made Kier *Kier* gone, lost to the sea and the cliffs and the air. Grey reached within herself for a tether that had snapped, torn from the root.

'Kier,' she pleaded, gripping his chin. She rolled him back to his side, not caring about his injuries, and pounded on his back. '*Kiernan*. Kier, please.'

Nothing. She pressed a finger to the space under his jaw. There was not even the trace of a pulse. The tether inside of her was gone, leaving only raw, aching emptiness behind. It had been years since she'd gone to reach for it and felt nothing at all, not even the suggestion of his existence. She hadn't felt this empty since before they were bound.

'Don't fucking *do* this,' she snarled, rolling him onto his back, pressing his chest in a measured pattern, as if she could force his heart back to beating. 'I won't love you if you do this,' she said, her throat thick with tears, forcing the lie through her lips. 'You can't make me love you if you're just going to . . . ' Her pattern faltered, and she pushed harder, feeling the ribs cracking under her hands. 'Come back to me, Kier.'

Nothing.

Grey couldn't breathe. She couldn't keep breaking him, couldn't keep doing this. Kier was dead, and there was nothing she could do to bring him back. She ran her hands up his soaked shirt, over the curve of his jaw, cradling his face. His skin was cold to the touch, clammy with seawater. Her hand trembled as she reached forward, running her fingertips over the curve of his lips, thumb skimming the cut of his scar.

All of it familiar – all of it devastating in its stillness.

She was the High Lady of Locke. The sovereign of the Isle, re-stored. The center and master of every bit of power that Idistra had to offer.

And yet there was not a single thing she could do with it, not on her own. She could not force his heart to beat again; she could not open him up and use the threads of her power to pull him back to-gether. Not if the life had already left him; not if there was nothing of him left to reach for.

For the first time in her life, sitting in front of Kier's body, Grey found that she was utterly powerless.

'You can't ask me to do this,' she said, her voice breaking. 'I can't do this without you.'

You can do anything you want to, with or without me, Kier would probably say. And she remembered the sound of his voice in the inn: *I always knew you were a survivor.*

Not this, Kier. She couldn't survive this. 'Please,' she begged, one last fruitless attempt to call him back from death.

But there was no response. Of course there wasn't – there would never be a response again. His voice would live on only in her memory.

She felt all previous versions of herself splitting apart and conver-ging again, all the decisions they had made: she was a girl of eight, taking his hand and pushing him her power; she was following him and Lot to a village with a letter in her hand; she was a teenager, pressing her fingers to her lips at night, trapping the feeling of the first time he had kissed her on a dare; she was fifteen, watching the determination form in his face as he made up his mind to save her; she was eighteen and his arms were around her, his tears hot against her neck; she was a dying light, a horrified shell of herself, and she was binding to him and changing him forever.

Every decision. Every sacrifice. All of it led to here, to now, to her on the edge of death and the edge of twenty-five, holding his body against her like that would bring him back.

In some world, some reality, there had to be a version of him that lived. A version of her that didn't make him die for her.

She wanted to take it all back, to claw back every year and every decision that had made them this version: the girl who lived turning into the woman who lived, who lured every person she loved into death by sacrifice.

She fell, her head landing heavy on his chest, and she wept over his body until the darkness claimed her.

Part Four

The Lady of Locke

I LOVE YOU, AND I'M SORRY.

Last words of Captain Kiernan Seward, recorded at Mecketer,
16 years PD

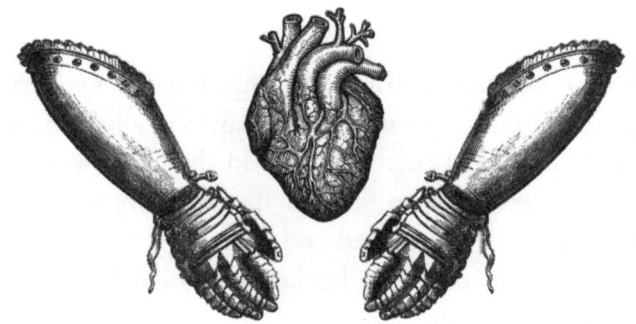

twenty-five

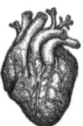

GREY DID NOT REMEMBER waking, but her eyes were open, and she was no longer on Kier's body. She jolted up, searching for him, but he was not there. She was in the Ghostwood now, surrounded by the skinny trees, just off the path. She knew where she was immediately – if she turned and walked in the other direction, she'd find the graves of all the Lockes who'd lived here before, and beyond that, the old abbey.

The first thing that came back to her was the grief. She felt it in every part of her body, the aching emptiness, the knowledge that with every second that stretched forward, she was living in a time in which Kier no longer existed. It was unbearable, the magnitude of that grief. She did not think she would ever find the bottom of it. She did not know, either, how she had moved from his body, or where his body had been taken.

She turned to find him, and froze, her heart in her throat.

Her mother waited, standing straight and tall as ever, the mist stirring near the bottom of her skirts. Locke had always had the unnatural, brutal beauty of someone who'd learned very early that to be iron strong, cruelty was its own kind of currency. Isaak walked from the mist behind her, his hand coming to rest on his wife's waist. Grey felt the bitter weight of them on her heart.

'You're here,' she said.

'We've been waiting,' someone said behind her. She turned – it was Severin. Severin, who'd grown nearly six inches in the summer before he died; Severin, with his mop of curly hair like his father's; Severin, who had held her hands and told her to forget. For one aching moment, Grey had hoped . . . but he was still fifteen, still as young as he was when they'd brought the Isle down.

He was still dead. They all were.

She rose slowly to her feet – she had never seen them from this height, never known that she'd grown to be taller than her mother. She was older now than Severin ever got to be. They spoke with the rounded vowels and smooth burr of the Isle, the accent that she herself had hidden over time, partially for protection. She spotted more shapes in the mist, more relatives that she only half remembered.

'You're not really here,' she said, laying her hand over her heart. She could not feel it beating. Perhaps this was death after all.

'No,' her mother said. She moved forward, the mist stirring as she walked. She did not look dead. When she reached up to touch Grey, the silver of her signet ring gleamed in the opaque light. 'You are Locke now.'

Before she could think better of it, Grey went to grab her mother's hand. Her own fingers went right through it – they both stepped back, as if burned.

Behind her parents, the mist was clearing. There in the meadow where the Lockes were buried, Grey could see someone else: in the rubble of the old temple, he sat on a sepulcher with his back to her, his black tunic sticking to his skin with the damp.

No, she realized. Not a sepulcher. The altar.

He wasn't alone – there was another person, a woman, standing beside him.

'Kier?' Grey asked, stepping forward. Her heart was again in her throat. Isaak looked over his shoulder, frowning at the place where Kier sat. Grey looked back at her mother. 'Is he . . . ?' She swallowed down any sign of her own weakness. She was Locke; she was born of these hard black cliffs and unforgiving sea. 'Is he dead?' she asked, forcing herself to be steady.

Alma looked over her shoulder, her face a mask of grief and regret. 'It required a sacrifice to save the Isle,' she said slowly. Grey remembered what Scaelas had told her. That they all died, so she could live.

'And it required a sacrifice to bring it back,' she said through numb lips.

Alma did not look at her. Grey felt her knees go weak; the very fabric of her world shredded around her. She stared at his back, but Kier did not turn to look at her, did not seem to hear.

In that moment, she understood the future. She would wake on this Isle, to a Locke resurrected, and she would find the bodies of her family. She would bury them. Kier's body would be there, too; he would join her family in death as he had never met them in life.

She would be Locke restored, and all of the power in the world would be hers. She could feel it now, thick in her stomach, waiting for her to call on it.

Without Kier, she was free to tether to anyone, if she chose. She would lead the forces and hold the Isle. She would power armies.

She would bury Kier, right here, on this Isle. The thought caught in her throat – she felt for a moment like she was choking, like she'd never draw breath again.

What she would give to see his face one last time, alive. His smirk – the light that came to his eyes when he saw her. How much she'd taken him for granted.

Her breath stuttered, her heart heavy in her chest – because she could not bear it. She could not bear a future that did not include him. She could not bear to stand on this Isle, the place where everyone she loved had died for her, and was still dying; she could not bear to do it *alone*.

But she was Locke, and this was *bullshit*.

'No,' she said. She stalked across the path, across the wood, toward where Kier sat.

'What do you mean, *no*?'

She whirled on her mother, her father, her brother; the three ghosts gathered behind her. 'I said *no*. I do not accept it. I will not let him be your fucking sacrifice. You can have your power – you can have the entire Isle. But I am taking Kier.'

'You cannot just take it back,' Severin said, reaching for her, as if that would do anything.

'Then I am going with him,' Grey said, her voice catching.

'You *can't*,' Alma said fiercely. She moved toward her daughter, but Grey twisted out of reach.

'I am Locke,' she seethed, feeling the power of the Isle rise up inside of her. 'I can do whatever I want.'

'Gremaryse Pellatisa, thirty-fourth daughter,' a voice said from somewhere behind the others.

Grey's head snapped up. She watched a figure come through the trees, wearing the old armor of the early Isle. She was utterly unfamiliar, with dark hair braided into an intricate formation that fell over her shoulders. She carried a jeweled blade in one hand. Her skin was alabaster pale, paler even than Alma's; her lips were too red to be real.

'And who are you?' Grey snapped.

'Do you not know me?'

Grey started to say no – but she did. She was utterly unfamiliar because she was real and human, looking like flesh and blood instead of a ghost or a saint. But when Grey focused, she realized that she'd seen her face on icons and tapestries, painted on the murals of the crumbling abbey, carved into the face of the tombs.

She hadn't recognized her because it wasn't possible to fully capture the awful, terrifying beauty of her, or the shade of her eyes, or the deep metal of her armor, set with details of birds and ivy.

This was Kitalma, the first of the Lockes, her great-ancestor many times over.

'If you're also here to tell me all the reasons I can't have Kier back, I don't care. I am taking him, and I will forsake this Isle and your power. I promise you.'

Alma winced. Grey wondered whether, if she'd grown into a woman under her mother's watch, she'd disappoint her as most daughters tended to do.

'Hold your promises, daughter of Locke,' Kitalma said, a smirk curling on those unnatural lips.

'Please,' Grey begged, barely recognizing the raggedness of her own voice.

Kitalma's face was unchanged. 'What's done is done,' she said.

But Grey would not accept that – she *could* not accept that. 'In the old stories,' she said shakily, 'the ones my mother used to tell, of the gods and their power. When you and your bride fought for the Isle, you won, but she perished. When Retarik fell – when she died – you did everything in your power to bring her back. You begged the sea for her life, and the sea listened.' A touch softer, she said, 'I am pleading now. I am calling upon you, in all of your power. Will you not listen to me?'

'I am here to give you the mantle of power, and you ask more of me?'

'I have given *everything* up for you and your power,' Grey said, her voice turning bitter. 'I have proven again and again that I would die for that power. Everyone I love died to protect it, to protect *me*. Even Kier. You cannot ask me to keep going without him.' But it felt fruitless, an eternity of bargaining that she would never find the end of. 'Please. He is all I ask for. His *life* is all I ask for.'

Kitalma watched her, her gaze other-worldly. 'You have made him one of my own,' she said finally. 'A sacrifice has been made, and a sacrifice must be kept.' Grey opened her mouth, already searching for words, but the goddess held up a hand. 'But I do pity you, daughter of Locke – 'tis a sorrowful thing, to be alone in the world.'

Grey regarded her warily, uncertain she understood, too heart-broken to hope.

'As such, I will offer you three choices. Under my terms.'

Grey's shoulders sagged. There would be terms – there would always be terms. She felt the weight of her exhaustion, tempered with grief. She just wanted to wake up. To wake Kier up. 'Of course,' she said. 'Just tell me what to do, and it is done. I will give up anything to bring him back.'

'The sacrifice has been made. I cannot just give him back to you without keeping something in return.' Kitalma spread her hands, the gleam of the dagger and its gems winking in the light. 'The first choice: I will keep the boy's life, and you will keep the Isle, as we stand now. Sometimes, daughter, the best way is to accept what has come to pass.'

'I will not accept it,' Grey said savagely.

'Very well, then. The second choice: I keep the boy, but only his freedom. You may have him as long as he remains here. Should he leave, his life again is forfeit.'

Grey stared at her, uncomprehending. 'What . . . what does that mean?'

'If I breathe life into him,' Kitalma said, her eyes gleaming – they were black as the Isle's cliffs, Grey realized. Black as the deepest part of the sea. 'He can never again leave this isle. He will be as he was, as long as he remains here until the end of his days.'

Grey sucked a breath through her teeth. Kier's freedom – she could not fathom cursing him like that, sentencing him to a life here, forever. 'I cannot give you that.'

'Then the third choice: he may have his life and his freedom, and leave this place as he wishes. In return, you surrender to me your power. It is your choice, Gremaryse, daughter of Locke.'

Grey's stomach dropped. Without her intending to, her hand went to her middle, palm pressed to her sternum, where she felt her power unfurling strong and true.

'Maryse . . .' Alma started.

But Isaak only watched her sadly. 'What is love without freedom?' he asked. 'Is that love at all?'

Grey met his gaze. It was like he had pulled the words directly from her own heart. 'I cannot give my power,' she said through numb lips. 'I am Locke. Kier isn't a well – he can't . . . There will be no grounding for the Isle.'

The old goddess raised a brow. 'Do you doubt me?'

'No.'

'All will be well, daughter. Your own heir will continue the line of Locke,' she said, as if it was a foregone conclusion that Grey would *have* an heir.

'But without my power—'

'I could just keep his life,' Kitalma said flatly. 'But the boy is already one of mine, by your own rite. If he lives, he would be connected to the very foundation of the Isle.'

Grey's heart sunk. Torrin was right – she had no idea what she'd done, how she had changed him, when she had bound to Kier.

'I have given you choices. If you want his life back, you must either give me his freedom, or hand me your power. Remember, this is a mercy – I could leave him free and dead, and your power intact. Those are my terms.'

Grey forced herself to breathe. Here she was, fighting with a goddess. No wonder she always got written up for insubordination.

'I would prefer he not be free and dead,' she said. The power mattered less; she could not imagine holding it without him. The very idea of tethering to someone else made her sick. She needed to think rationally, but she found it impossible – if she finished this conversation, she could have Kier back. Whatever followed was a matter for the version of her who didn't feel like this. 'And what ... When do I have to decide?'

Kitalma gazed up, as if she could see anything in the gloom. 'Keep the Isle, daughter. You may have one cycle of the moon, and then we shall meet again, at my altar, and I will need your answer. Until then, I will give your mage back to you and await your decision.'

Grey chewed her lip, but what else could she do? She could barely think past her own grief – she did not know how she would be able to make a decision with his body there, in front of her. She did not know how she could look upon him, dead, and not die herself.

'Thank you,' she said, 'for your mercy.'

'Very well. Go now,' Kitalma said, turning away. 'It is not safe here, in the between, for one who is yet so alive.' She glanced over her shoulder at Grey as the mist rose and thickened. 'Be careful, daughter. Iron, too, has its weaknesses.'

Grey turned to look at her mother, but she too was gone. They all were. She was alone in the misty wood.

'Grey?'

Her breath caught in her chest – not alone at all. She spun around to see Kier getting up from the altar, wincing at the way every movement jarred his broken bones. She stared at him, the words stuck in her throat, as he eyed her warily.

'Where are we?'

'We're in the Ghostwood,' she said, the words barely making a sound.

He looked around, taking it all in. 'I don't ... I don't remember getting here.'

Grey shook her head. She pressed a hand to her chest, as if she could stop the ache of losing him, as if she could rip it out of her. 'No,' she said, voice raw.

He stopped scanning and looked at her, his eyes warm and soft, his mouth tugging up into a relieved smile at the sight of her. He came close, his smile faltering as he reached very carefully to touch her face.

'My beautiful Locke,' he said, his fingertips only just brushing the bruise on her cheek. 'Does it hurt?'

She did not know how to stop the pain, even now when he was standing in front of her. 'Yes,' she said, the word sounding more like a sob.

She threw herself at his chest, not caring about the blood and dirt and seawater. He made a low noise in his throat – she was obviously hurting him, ruinously prodding his broken ribs, but he didn't care enough to push her away. His good arm wrapped around her, holding her tight, and it was as if the entire world made sense again.

His freedom or her power. She gripped him tighter, as if she could will the choice away.

'Are we home?' he murmured in her ear, his voice a raspy whisper. She squeezed her eyes shut.

'Yes,' she said, bittersweet. The relief was just as heavy as the power welling between them. She found the tether and locked into it, pouring so much power into him that he jerked. He shivered, then swallowed it down. She pressed her hand into his broken collarbone, forcing it back into place. He rested his head on her shoulder, breathing hard, as she finished her work and moved her hand to run her fingers through his wet, wild hair. 'We're home.'

When Retarik died defending the Isle, Kitalma laid her body over her wife's and wept, begging her life from Gremaryse, pleading with the goddess of sea and death for her mercy. After thirty days and thirty nights of weeping, Kitalma woke to her wife restored and blessed with an heir to carry on the line in the blood of Locke.

Folklore recovered from the Isle of Locke, date unknown, author unknown

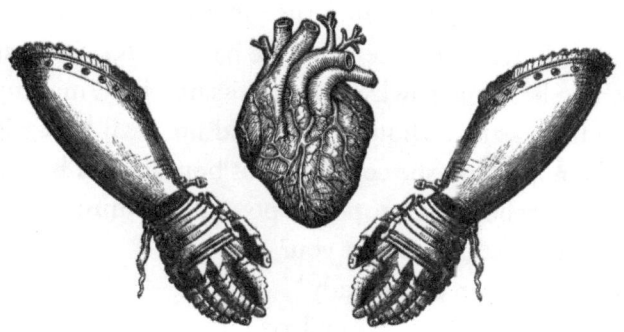

twenty-six

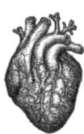

SAFELY TETHERED, GREY LED the way back toward the fortress at the highest point of the Isle. Her body moved without her telling it the directions, sinking into the inheritance of muscle memory her brain barely recalled. She kept one hand in Kier's, unable to let go; the other, she draped awkwardly across his chest, making sure his collarbone had healed. Though she could not heal him with power alone on the mainland, she could feel his bones under her hand now, knitting back together as her power poured into him.

'Do the others know? About you?'

'Brit, Ola and Eron did already.'

'I mean the High Lord. And Cleoc.'

'Oh. Yes.'

He glanced at her sideways. Grey only shrugged. She had too many emotions right now to deal with any of them, and the reality of being on Locke was closing in on her.

She could barely breathe with the crush of power swirling around the island. It was like pressure all about her – when she was young, she remembered it as a stomach ache, but that wasn't quite right. It was like electricity in the air, crackling through her lungs when she drew breath, sticky on her skin.

Kier was not unaffected either. He looked down at Grey, her hand on his chest as she poured power into him. 'I think . . .' He stopped, looking up at the fortress as they breached the edge of the Ghostwood, back out into the mist of the day. The fog rolled in, heavy from the sea. He frowned, and Grey treasured every expression his face made even as she wanted to rub her thumb across his lips to smooth away any unhappiness.

'You feeling okay?'

'I feel . . . like *everything* is trying to give me power,' he said. 'But that's . . .' *Impossible.* He didn't say impossible

'We have a lot to talk about,' Grey said. She did not think she could look into his eyes and tell him about his death, still cold on his bones and heavy on her heart, nor the decisions she had to make regarding it – but first, she had to tell him that he, too, was Locke.

They passed through the walls, under the open portcullis, to where the hulking stone keep waited. She sucked a breath through her teeth, staring up at the great doors.

'Is it as you remembered it?' he asked, his voice still rough with seawater.

'Yes,' Grey said. Kier looked at her. Very gently, he took her hand and removed it from his chest. He no longer bore any trace of unfamiliarity at all.

She was pretty sure his ribs were stable enough for now, his collar-bone mended. All over again, she was struck with the power of the Isle: it would've taken her hours, maybe days, to gradually do the same sort of work in Scaela, if she'd been able to do it at all.

'Are there bodies inside?' Kier asked, hesitating. Not fearful – just preparing.

'No,' Grey said, looking away. 'I don't know what's left of them, if anything. The feast was . . . in the town. Further down.'

He nodded. He pressed a hand to the solid wood of the door. The knocker in the middle was carved to look like a seabird, a ring of fire clutched in its beak. The door was untouched by rot or sea, as if it hadn't spent the last two decades submerged.

He offered Grey his other hand. She laced her bloody, wet fingers through his, then raised her other hand, set it beside Kier's on the wooden door. Together, they pushed it open.

The wood creaked, then gave, revealing a stone entry; all these years, it had been unlatched, as if waiting just for her. Grey took it in, gaze skating over the tapestries on the walls, untouched by age; the great stone staircase with the banister she and Sev used to slide down again and again until their grandmother scolded them. The sconces on the walls still bore fat, waxy candles, half-melted. She sucked a breath through her teeth, stepping into the home of her childhood like she was shedding time. She kept her fingers locked in Kier's as he followed a step behind her.

She walked carefully, wet boots squeaking on the stone floor. She led him through the entry, through an archway to the right: this was the dining hall, with its great windows looking out to the sea. She pressed her free hand to the cold glass. The fog still surrounded them on all sides, leaving the world white and formless.

'We won't be able to see anyone coming,' she said.

'I know. What do you think about this fog? Is it normal?'

Grey shook her head, thinking back to the Ghostwood. 'I don't know if the Isle is fully restored yet,' she said cautiously. 'We should have some time before we need to worry.'

'It feels like we're already shielded,' Kier said softly, curiously.

Protect me, she had asked the Isle, and it had listened. 'That must be the fog. I think it's only temporary,' she said. Even with just her power, she could feel that much.

'I can assess the shielding,' he said. He made a low noise at the force of power that hit him when he siphoned, wincing at it. 'Isn't that too much?'

Grey shook her head. She was not depleted in the slightest. 'Not here,' she said. 'Nothing is too much here.'

Kier was silent for a moment. She watched his face – *Do you know? Do you feel it in your heart? Does death still chill you to the bone?*

'I have so many questions,' he murmured finally, and Grey watched a second shield shimmer into existence. She felt it, strong and whole, a bubble of protection over only the fortress. Perhaps it would not hold, if anyone came in earnest, but it was a chance she felt safe taking. It was larger than any shield he'd cast before, by far – and it seemed to cost him nothing.

'It's temporary,' he said.

She turned back to him. Here, she felt oddly shy, as if he had not seen every part of her. Like this was the one thing she could not convince him to love.

What is love without freedom? She pushed the thought away before it could take root. There would be time to confront what she must choose. For now, she would revel in the simple fact that he was alive.

'Come on,' she said. She avoided the back parlor and kitchen and ballroom – there were too many memories to sort through, and she was not ready to deal with what she might find. Dull horror pounded in her heart. She was not ready. She could not face it.

Instead, she led Kier up the stairs, up and up and up, onto the turret roof where she and Sev used to greet the sunset. The wind whipped at their hair, and the roof of Kier's shield looked almost close enough to touch.

Grey sucked in a breath, taking in the Isle spread out below them. There was the sparse shadow of the Ghostwood, mist creeping through the trees, and on the cliffs at one edge, the crumbling remains of the old abbey. There, beyond the wood, she could see the small houses and great hall of Osar, some of them burned by Eprain's forces; then, further down, the harbor and the half-burned town of Maerin, and the remnants of the villages dotted between the two towns. To the far side of the Isle, she took in the Barrens, the uninhabited stretch of trees and mountains; the fortress was the highest point, but the Barrens were a close second. It was all still and silent, ghost villages for a phantom lord. From this height, she could see the entire Isle.

She turned away, back to the mist of the sea. A ruined Locke, but hers all the same.

'There will be time,' Kier said, gently touching her back.

She made him sit against the wall and removed his shirt. There, where she could see the whole Isle and all that surrounded it, where she could see the first sign of trouble, she called the power to her. She felt it moving from the Isle into her middle, then radiating outward, flexing all the way to her fingertips. When she pressed her hand to Kier's half-healed injuries, he flinched.

'That will take some getting used to,' he said, eyes sliding shut.

'Does it feel different?' Grey asked. It did to her, a bit – not in the feeling; power was power, even on Locke. It was the extent that had changed, and the quality of it. She didn't think she'd ever find the end of it, her own middle constantly refilled by the Isle around her.

'Very,' Kier said. He pressed a hand over hers – Grey had gone back to knitting the bones of his ribs back together. This, she mused, pushing the power into him as she tried to construct them in her mind, would be something she would not have the power, liberty or skill to do on the mainland. She nudged the threads of magic under his skin. His eyes slid open, pupils blown wide. He looked half-drunk.

'How so?' she asked.

'It feels . . . ' He considered this, gaze rolling back, staring at the misty white of the sky. His nose wrinkled, the effect only marginally ruined by the crookedness from the last time he broke it. 'It feels like you,' he said finally. 'All of it. I don't know if I can explain it better than that.'

She leaned against the stone next to him, her hand still tightly laced in his. She tried not to think of the moldering piles of bones and fabric that were waiting for them in Osar's hall – to think of that would be to think of what those bones had once been, and every time her thoughts edged along that, it did something very odd to her heart and throat and stomach and the relationship between the aforementioned organs.

They were here, waiting. They had always been here, waiting, every moment of the sixteen years she had spent away from this place; every single heartbeat in which she was alive and they were not.

She bit it all down in one clean slice, because once she started, she would not be able to stop.

'Can you try to explain?' she asked Kier, desperate for distraction.

He made a noise low in his throat, but he was breathing easier. She looked at him, double-checking his collarbone, then went to run her finger lightly near the collagen of his left ear, where the curving top had been cut off at a diagonal.

His gaze was fixed on her, utterly reverent. He was looking at her like she held all the magic in the universe. She knew Kier, and she knew in an abstract sense that Kier loved her, but until this moment, this look, she had not considered that he loved her more than he loved magic.

'I didn't know what it was about your power,' he said, 'until that time, before we were bound, when I didn't have you. I'd always taken you for granted – I was spoiled, growing up with you beside me, with the knowing. But ... with you – it has a scent. A feeling. It's sharp, and honed. It smells like the sea, mineral and clean, tinged with salt. I can almost taste the force of it – I can feel it in the back of my teeth.' He took in Grey's gaze and shook his head. 'I'm not explaining it right. Anyone else's magic is watered down. Tavern beer when the bills are catching up. But you're a shot of liquor. And here it's ...' He took a deep breath, eyes sliding shut, drunk on magic. 'It's in the air. It's in the land, the stones, the trees. And it's coming from you. It all feels like *you*. Gods, Grey, I've never felt so safe in my life.'

It took her a moment to recover. 'That's something,' she said finally, haltingly, 'considering there are warships from at least four separate nations bearing down on us.'

One of his eyes slipped open. 'But Scaela is still our ally?' he asked quietly, thumb skimming over the back of her hand, rubbing circles into her skin.

'And Cleoc Strata,' Grey said. 'As far as I know.'

He nodded, taking it in. She focused on the cold seeping through the stones, the wet shirt pressed to her skin under her battle padding, the breeze that slipped through the spell-slits in the walls.

'I'm so sorry,' Kier said finally.

'For?'

He chewed his lip. 'I didn't know ... I thought you'd listen to me, for once. That you would just let me do this. I didn't know I was forcing your hand, forcing you into reclaiming Locke.'

'You thought I would let you die?'

'I hoped you might,' he said, the faintest of smiles on his lips, and it made everything in her ache.

She shook her head, banishing Kitalma's words as she searched for her own. 'I would've come for you. I'd always come for you.'

'And I you,' Kier said.

'Then you should've known.'

'Maybe. But all I could think was ... Grey, I never wanted you to feel like that girl again. Alone. Abandoned.'

Grey looked at him, his long eyelashes and hazel eyes and the persistent stubble cropping up already on his jaw, the cut glass of his cheekbones, the stubborn silver on his temples. 'I need to tell you something,' she said.

She needed to tell him a great number of things, actually, but that was beside the point as she struggled to put the least of them into words.

He caught her hand. 'You can tell me anything.'

She took a breath, tried to school her features. The sky was steely gray, slipping toward darkness at the edges, a sunset without the presence of sun and gold and amber. The steady sort, like someone dimming a magelight until no glimmer of it remained. But it had been that way since they had arrived; the darkening sky had not darkened nor lightened; instead, it had stayed in transition. Grey realized, in the back of her mind, why the silence was so odd: there were no birds.

She felt the constant pull of Kier, the thrum of taking as he transformed her power into magic. The most familiar thing in the world.

She opened her mouth to tell him about it. About his death. About her choice. The words did not come – they stayed lodged in her throat, and Kier looked at her expectantly, and she could not do it.

Instead, she said, 'I didn't know, when we bound. That it would be different for you and me. But Kier – it has made you a Locke. That's why Scaelas and Cleoc came for you. Because if they risked you, if you figured out how to call Locke from the sea, it would've worked.'

That guarded look returned. 'But you are ...'

'I am still Locke,' she said. 'Still the High Lady. But you are a part of this Isle, too.'

He glanced away, shuttering any emotions. 'Do you regret it?'

'No,' she said quickly – *but I fear you will*, she did not say. 'I did not realize . . . I did not know then that it was that much of a union. In more ways than I suspected.'

His gaze softened, and there was something unfair about the way he looked at her, like she was the central point in his universe – she did not know how to convey, with word or look or deed, that he was the central point in *hers*.

He dropped her hand. His fingers moved along her jaw ever so carefully to cup her face. 'I knew, when we swore our bond,' he said, 'what I was doing. That I was giving all of myself to you. It's a gift, Grey – it's an inevitability, in some ways, that all I am would be yours.'

She shook her head – she could not tell him about his death; she could not reveal that she had stolen that, too. 'But that's not it. I have taken everything from you, even your family name. And now I've put a target on your back – they will want to kill you as much as they want to kill me.'

The light came to his eyes, the mirth etched into his jaw, looking insouciant in that way he always somehow managed to. 'They already want to kill me.'

'But now, it's *real*.'

'And you thought being the commander of Locke wouldn't put a target on my back? That mattering to you in the way I do would make me a desirable hostage?'

'Not in the same way.'

He pulled her close, nose touching hers. 'I am yours, Grey. If that makes you Seward, so be it. If that makes me Locke, then it is done. I am yours and I have been since the day we were bound, and even before that. I don't care for the name, or the title, or even for the power. I care for *you*.'

She took a shaky breath and leaned in to press her lips to his. Cold – they were both cold, so cold that she knew they were possibly in shock and definitely tripping head-first toward hypothermia, and she needed to face the rest of the rooms in the fortress and get a fire started in one of the big grates; but Kier was kissing her, and they were safe under the shield, and for right at this moment, that was enough.

She needed to tell him the truth. But the Isle was still around her, and safe, and she had not felt a safety like that in years. She let him kiss her; she did not think of the cold of his lips, the frigidity of his corpse, as she tried to force him to live again.

He broke away after a moment, breathless. 'What do we do now?' he asked.

Her numb fingers skimmed over the healed edge of his ear. 'Now, we do our best to survive.'

He kissed her again, tasting of blood and salt water. 'We've already made it this far.'

But not far enough.

Though the mist made her uneasy, she was glad of the time they had away from the rest of the world. She needed time alone to handle what needed to be done next – and because Kier already knew the worst parts of her, she could permit him to see it too.

Halfway down the stairs, she said, 'I think we need to start with the bodies.'

Her voice did not catch. She did not look at him over her shoulder. She only kept her eye turned down on the treacherous spiraling stone steps; and then briefly out of a passing window, where she could see the Ghostwood in the distance.

Kier's hand touched her shoulder. 'Let me,' he insisted.

She shook her head. 'I have to do it. But perhaps . . . Clothes first, I think.'

Procrastination. She did not know how her body would betray her when they walked to the hall in Osar where she knew her parents' bodies were, or the cellar below, to find the charred remains of Severin's. Then there was the household guard, who used to carry her on their shoulders when she was a child so she could see the storms rolling in; the cook, Kimbra, who used to slip her pastries while she studied with her mother, and made her buttery slices of bread with thick broth when she was sick; the people of Osar and Maerin, who called her Little Locke, who pressed kisses to her knuckles when she and Sev passed through the streets.

All of them were dead. Bodies. Rubble. Bones and decaying cloth.

'None of it is water-damaged,' Kier remarked as they passed through one of the upstairs rooms, one she knew was reserved for storage. He stopped to run his fingers over the carved wood of a dresser. 'It looks like it's just been here untouched.'

'I imagine it was bubbled somehow,' Grey said, pulling open the drawers. 'Maybe it's been shielded this whole time.'

It was an assortment of clutter, old furniture and boxes of molded, moth-eaten books and half-burned candles and discarded trunks full of everyday accoutrement that a long-established family discarded but did not dispose of, left in a room after decades and decades of use.

She felt oddly exposed, even though it was only Kier. She'd basically lived at his house as a child, Pia and Laurella putting her to bed alongside Kier and Lot so often that they procured an extra mattress, stored under Kier's bed and pulled out whenever she didn't leave when the sun went down. She'd known his grandmothers and grandfathers when they were alive, his aunts and uncles – she knew every bit of his family history as if it was her own. Perhaps his ma and mum had told it to her, filling her with some sort of family to make up for the fact that she apparently had none of her own. Imarta didn't mind: she welcomed the influence of Kier's family. She had no family left herself, and widowed as she was, it had always been just her and Grey.

But this was it, the real thing, the trappings of her life on Locke and those of her family before. She pulled out a moth-eaten tapestry from a trunk mottled with dust, rubbing her fingers into her family's sigil stitched into the cloth.

Would you give it all up for Kier's freedom?

Who would she be without her power, her birthright?

'This might be our lucky trunk,' Kier said across the room, going through another one of them. They were heavy and wooden, ancient, so much nicer than any of the trunks they'd been assigned on duty, or the inherited one Imarta kept in Grey's childhood bedroom. They were light wood, possibly cut from the Ghostwood or stock from the Barrens, carved with motifs from folklore that no one but Grey remembered.

He pulled out clothes much too big for her. She considered the shirts and trousers and socks and suspenders and leather armor as Kier cast off his own clothes and pulled on the replacements – she could not look at him, because if she did, she would see the scars and the bruises she had not yet healed, and she could not bear it right now – and said quietly, 'There are clothes in my mother's room.'

'Do you think . . .' He didn't finish the sentence, so she wasn't sure if he meant *Do you think you're ready for that?* or *Do you think you can handle the remnants of her?* or *Do you think that's a good idea?* All of it faded, and he just looked at her with an expression of open, plaintive care.

She chewed the nail of her thumb. 'I'll put on a new shirt. And there will be coats and cloaks downstairs. Then maybe we can investigate the rest later.'

He nodded, tossing her a shirt. She exchanged her sodden, bloody one for the old, soft, dry fabric. They left their wet things hanging over the railing and went downstairs. She felt like a child exploring a ruin, even though, despite sixteen years of separation, she knew the place like Kier knew every structure of her beating heart.

She hesitated on each landing, the rooms running through her head like the recitation of saints' names on the prayer beads in the ruin of the abbey that crowned the edge of the Ghostwood, the place where Kitalma's bones were laid to rest.

On the ground floor, she went to the cloakroom under the stairs and pulled out two of her father's big coats and waiting swords, handing one of each to Kier. 'I imagine we'll have to dispose of Eprain's bodies, too,' she said, strapping the sword to her belt, mostly out of habit. 'I don't want them buried with mine, but we should give them a respectful rest all the same.'

Kier nodded, looking at one of the tapestries over her shoulder. 'In Eprain, they burn their dead.'

Grey swallowed hard. She could remember, on their assignments on the coast, watching the smoke in the distance after the battles as the pyres were lit.

'Then we'll burn them,' she said. 'The tradition is similar for those on Locke who are not Lockes themselves. Their ashes are to be spread over the sea, reunited with the gods.'

'Then that's what we'll do.'

She nodded. It was the least she could offer, to follow the traditions of her own nation.

'Are there bedsheets to spare? To move the bones?'

'Probably,' Grey said, peering back into the dining room. 'Yes. First and third floors. There are linen closets by the stairs.'

She heard his boots on the stairs, his progress, a pause as he sorted through the linens. She pressed her face to the window in the dining room, but she could still not see past the misty white fog. The Isle remained cloaked. She could not see if warships waited for the Isle unveiled, nor what nations surrounded them.

Her fingers dug into the wood of the windowsill – despite the fact she'd been raised in Scaela, fought under Torrin's banner for nearly a decade and was his god-daughter, this Isle and all its power still instilled in her a sense of distrust. It would be easy for him and Cleoc to betray her, kill her or Kier or both, take the power for themselves and set the Isle ablaze again. Perhaps she was a fool to trust anyone at all with this power ripping anew within her.

'Grey?'

She turned to see him, linens piled high in his arms, and those thoughts crumbled. Perhaps she could not trust Scaelas or Cleoc, just as she could not trust the sovereigns of Eprain and Luthar and Nestria, but she could trust Kier.

She felt that echo inside of her, the acknowledgment of a devotion in the tether between them.

'Do you know how many there were, on the Isle?' he asked, setting the pile of sheets on the dining table.

She nodded, unable to speak. Her father's coat smelled of woodsmoke and sea air and the faint hint of sweat, and it was too much for her. She was a girl again. She was dying. She had never left.

Something flickered across Kier's face – she wondered if, on Locke, the emotions through the tether were that much stronger – and then he was in front of her, taking her hands in his. He did not say anything. He studied her like she was one of his maps, one of his diagrams of enemy movements, instructions handed down from higher command to be followed to the letter.

'You are here,' he said slowly, 'because you survived.'

Grey nodded. Forced herself to breathe. *But you didn't.*

She could not think it, or else she would lose any grip she had left on her sanity.

They found gloves and a cart in one of the work sheds outside, to avoid touching the rot with bare skin. Grey led the way down the little path toward Osar, avoiding the wider road that skirted around the Ghostwood – with the fresh memory of her ghostly family and Kitalma's bargain, she could not bear it yet.

Osar was not a big town. The entire population of Locke was less than five thousand: she hadn't understood the smallness of it until she'd arrived in Scaela, with a population in the hundreds of thousands. There had been more than five thousand soldiers at Mecketer alone. But now, faced with the reality of disposing of that many bodies, the number seemed staggering.

They reached the first of the empty streets. Grey did not look in the windows; she passed by all shadows without a second glance, focusing only on reaching the great hall at the far side, perched on the cliff.

It used to be a place of worship, an abbey to Retarik, Kitalma's bride. When worship of the old gods fell out of fashion, it became a ruin, much like its twin abbey across the Isle. Grey's great-great-grandfather revitalized it for use as a meeting place when the entire Isle was called to celebrate, like on the high holy days, to divert the crowds and better preserve the wards that protected the fortress itself.

Kier left the cart at the bottom of the steps and brought some of the linens with him. He followed her up the stairs, the pat of their boots on the stone the only sound. The gulls were still absent; with the thick fog, Grey couldn't even hear the sea crashing below.

The heavy doors were closed. Behind them, she knew, she would find carnage. She stopped at the top of the stairs, breathing hard, her heart pounding.

'We don't have to,' Kier said very quietly behind her. '*You* don't have to.'

The motto of her family, her house and her isle was *Power in bravery.* She did not feel brave, even with all the power of Idistra crackling in the air around her.

'I do,' she said.

Kier said nothing. He only put his hand on her shoulder.

Grey opened the door.

Iron to ashes, ashes to sea, sea to iron again. Let us rejoice at the memory of our victorious dead.

Funeral rites of the Isle of Locke

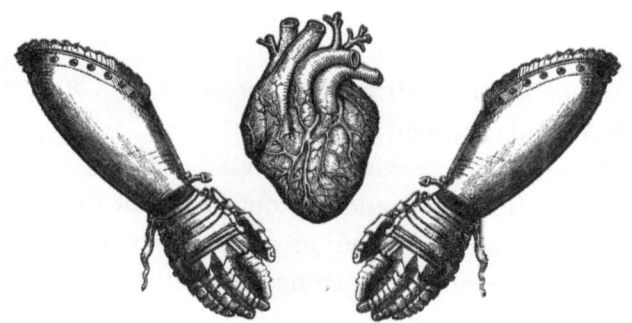

twenty-seven

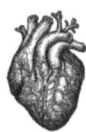

BEHIND HER, KIER SUCKED in a breath. Grey could only stare, her heart in her throat.

The door opened outwards, which was good, because the pile of bodies on the other side would've stopped it. But that wasn't what made her stand there unmoving in shock. Hazy sunlight streamed through the high windows, catching the dust motes in the air. The bodies were piled on the floor, over the tables, slung on chairs. Most of them had no visible injuries, nothing at all to say they were doing any more than sleeping. Some had clearly died in the struggle, run through with swords and stained with brown dried blood. She did not look to the front of the room, the dais.

It was all there, she thought with growing dread, as if time had not touched the Isle since the moment her power submerged it. She was a girl again, eight years old, waiting for death to catch her.

They were not bones, like she'd prepared for; not moth-eaten fabric and dust. They were flesh and blood, with open eyes and mouths and teeth and tongues, wearing masks of death and pain and fear. It was as if time had not touched the Isle in sixteen years, suspended forever in that awful night.

'Gods,' Kier said behind her. She heard the sound of metal as he drew his sword, but there was no reason for it. The assemblage in front of them was not simply sleeping, like the lost court in a fairytale. They all were dead.

Dread settled in Grey's heart as she stepped further into the room. She saw the soldiers from Eprain mixed among her own people, in various states of battle interrupted. The truth of it settled on her skin, a terrible realization sixteen years too late.

The battle hadn't killed them all. No, even with Eprain's soldiers, even after Locke herself had fallen, most of these people were still alive. It was something else that had ended them – a shock wave, a protection; the power of the Isle shutting down.

Grey had killed them. She remembered what Scaelas had told her: to save her, to save the line, it had required the sacrifice of everyone else.

She fell to her knees on the stones, narrowly missing the first of the bodies. 'I didn't know,' she said, helpless, because Kier must've gathered the truth of what he saw.

Behind her, he only sighed and sheathed his sword. She heard another sound, rustling and shifting, and came out of her horrified stupor to find him leaning over one of the fallen women, clad in a black gown as if already mourning. He shut her eyes carefully, then picked her up in his arms. Without another word, he turned for the door.

'What are you doing?' she asked, numb with agony.

He only looked at her. 'It's the way of Locke,' he said finally, 'to return their ashes to the sea.' There was no hatred in his gaze. No judgment. He turned and left, carrying his grisly cargo as carefully as he would his own bride.

She felt hours pass as they worked, separating the dead into two pyres. The larger pile, close to the cliffs, was for Locke's dead. The second, much smaller, was for Eprain's. Kier carried body after body out of the hall, shutting their eyes, laying them down in tidy rows in the same way he treated the dead after battle. He used his magic to help them, bearing most of the weight of the bodies, so it was as easy as moving stones around instead of grown people. Grey helped when she could, but she had to leave often to vomit, horrified all over again by the truth of what she'd done.

They did not approach the dais. She sensed that Kier was waiting for her to go first, but she could not do it. Not now. Not yet.

Outside, the mist did not change. The sun did not set. There were no gulls, and no waves. After a while, Kier, wiping sweat from his face with one filthy sleeve as he passed her on the stairs, said, 'I don't think time is passing.'

Grey looked up at the mist, the shield shimmering above. 'I think you're right.'

'For how long?'

'I don't know.'

They glanced at each other, uneasy. They were a quarter of the way through clearing the hall, Grey's body aching with the strain. There were a few hundred dead there, she thought; she was frightened to think of what the houses would hold, or to consider the grueling work of going through all of them.

'Are you tired?' she asked.

'No,' Kier said, his face uncertain. 'I'm not sure I feel . . . normal.'

Grey nodded. 'Then let's keep going.'

She lost herself in the awful work. She dragged the bodies through the hall, close to the door, then Kier came and took them to the pyres he was building. It would've been easier, she thought darkly, to have set the whole cathedral ablaze.

She found her grandmother unexpectedly, pulling the body of one of Eprain's soldiers by the arms to reveal the small woman crushed beneath him. She gasped, staggering back – Kier was there in an instant, reading the fear through the tether as if she was facing an unknown threat and not the gaping chasm of her own grief; his hands were on her shoulders before she could recover. She looked at the woman's pale, shriveled face, and the hands that had taught her to sew, and she turned and walked out.

Kier found her sitting at the edge of the cliffs, her legs dangling over the edge, tears cold on her face. She'd been sick again, but it didn't matter. She didn't think she'd ever stop being sick over this.

He didn't say anything until he was sitting next to her, his legs hanging alongside hers over the steep drop.

'Have I ever told you,' he said, 'that I'm afraid of heights?'

She squinted at him. 'No.'

'Good. It's because I didn't think I was until this very moment.' He looked down at the sheer drop in front of them and the gloom below, and his face paled.

'It was a mistake to come back,' Grey said.

He reached out and laid his hand over hers. 'There's nothing that can be done now. We'll get through the worst of it, and then we will keep on living.'

She winced. It cut too close to her own lies, and the truth she had not yet told him. 'They're all dead because of me.'

He did not deny it. 'There are hundreds of others in countries all over Idistra who are dead because of me.' *And you*, he did not say.

'But what did these people do, besides live here? They did not hurt me, nor fight me. Many of them would've fought *for* me, if given the chance.'

He nodded, the eerie silence like a blanket over them. 'You can do nothing to change that.'

She laughed bitterly. 'I could burn it all down. The entire Isle.'

'You could,' he said.

But you won't, he did not say.

She stared out at the mist, out at nothing. After a while, Kier got up and went to continue with the bodies. She did not know how long she sat there, motionless, before he came back behind her and said, 'I think I've found your parents.'

She got up and followed him back to the cathedral. She noticed a lone body lying away from the two organized pyres: it was her grandmother, set aside to be buried in the Ghostwood. She swallowed her bile down and did not ask Kier how he'd known.

The cathedral was nearly empty of bodies when she went back in, stepping carefully across the bloodstained stones. The table at the dais was in disarray: smashed goblets and dark wine stains on the tablecloth, mixing with the blood. Grey made her way to the stairs, Kier one step behind – and then she stopped.

Her mother was the one who had taught her to use her power, eking it out in tremulous threads from the time she was barely old enough to walk or speak full sentences. Though she had a reputation for swift justice, she was never cruel to her own daughter, who was often found clinging to her skirts. And Isaak, a mage from Scaela's noble class, used to make speckled magelights in the shape of constellations on the ceiling of her bedroom, then lie next to her and point out the names and shapes of each one.

They were now two bodies, eyes closed as if they were only sleeping, entwined in front of the tomb that was meant to hold Retarik's bones. Grey moved past the bodies that surrounded them in concentric circles, wrapped in thorny vines that pierced their flesh – whatever her father had done in his dying moments had flattened them all – and lowered herself very carefully beside them. She knew the dark green velvet of the dress, remembered the feeling of it on her cheek as her mother carried her to bed dozens of times. She reached out and ran her hand along the line of her father's sword, out of its scabbard, still clutched in his hand. The other hand rested on the dark velvet of her mother's waist. When Grey's eyes traced up to her mother's face, she saw what memory could not fill in, what she had not realized fully looking at her ghost with anger in the Ghostwood: she herself looked like a carefully made copy of her mother.

'I'm sorry,' she said, the grief bubbling up like it never had before. She couldn't breathe – all the magic in the world didn't matter; it wasn't enough. It couldn't bring them back.

She didn't hear Kier until he was behind her, kneeling, one arm snaking around her shoulders. She reached out to grip his forearm, nails digging in, and leaned back against him, unable to keep herself up, his other arm wrapped around her waist like he could protect her from all the awful things that had happened all those years before.

He didn't say anything. There was nothing to say. She tucked her head, hiding it in the shelter of his body, and sobbed.

When she was done, wrung out and exhausted, Kier was still there. 'I need to do it,' she said shakily, pulling away from the tangle of limbs.

He let her. He stood by as she took one of the linen sheets. Ever so carefully, she shifted her parents' bodies onto it. She recovered her father's sword and set it aside, her mother's silver necklace, the rings they'd inherited from Alma's parents and the signet ring of Locke. Once she'd folded the sheet over, she sat back on her knees and stared at the bundle of tidy white cloth, tied off and ready for the grave.

'Obsidian born and iron made,' Kier murmured. She used to say it to him, like a prayer, as she stitched his wounds together after battle.

She looked at him, something inexplicable rising within her. Perhaps all she wanted, after all this time, was to be soft.

The last body she needed waited for her in the basement. Kier followed her, quiet as a ghost, as she retraced the steps she'd run as a child. The stone chamber was a burned-out shell. There was no body where Severin had been – there were only shards and fragments, bones embedded in the walls, a tooth in one corner.

But she felt the spirit of him here, like a revenant, as if he'd been waiting for her this whole time. She sucked a breath through her teeth, certain she could hear her brother's laugh, that she could feel the press of his hand on hers.

'Sev?' she asked, turning, as if she'd catch the edge of his shadow on the wall.

But there was nothing. Only disaster. Only ash and bone.

The pyres crackled with unnatural mageflame as they set off back to the Ghostwood, the cart loaded with their grisly cargo. 'We should keep the ashes of Eprain,' Kier said, 'to return to their nation.'

Grey only nodded.

In the clearing where the Lockes were laid to rest, Grey picked up one of the shovels Kier had thought to bring. She found a spot unmarked by stones, past the line of graves, and started digging. Wordlessly, Kier took the other shovel and started on the other end. He seemed to understand that she needed the ache of this last task, that she had to do this. Carefully, they dug a grave for her parents and grandmother and what was left of her brother, for those who had sacrificed everything for her survival. When it was finished, they each took an end of the heavy tied-off sheets, the awkwardness of their weight, and laid them carefully in the open grave.

In another lifetime, if she had made another choice, she would be laying Kier to rest with their bodies.

She watched, kneeling at the edge, as Kier tipped in shovelful after shovelful of rocky dirt. For a half-second of unrepressed grief, she thought about climbing in with them.

She had to tell him the truth. She had to make him understand the decision she had before her. She opened her mouth, searching for words – then closed it. She could not do it.

A hand reached down when it was finished, caked in dirt and grime. 'Come on, Locke,' Kier said.

She took his hand. Side by side, they made their way home.

They share the title, you know. She thinks I can't hear her calling that smug little mainlander by *our* name, but I do. He wields her power and tells her he loves her, and the soft-hearted fool believes him. I worry what will happen if she passes the same attitude to the children.

Letter from Pellatisa Locke to Wren Locke Teinek, her daughter, 6 years AD

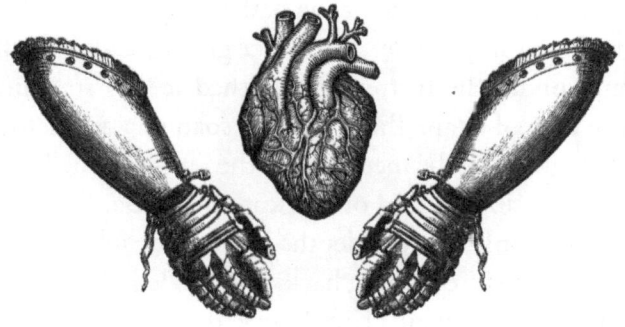

twenty-eight

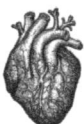

Upstairs, alone while Kier built a fire downstairs, Grey opened the taps on one of the bathtubs. It was run by a clever web of magic put in place by one of her great-uncles, which filtered the seawater under the fortress and turned it into steaming, clean water at the turn of a tap. There was still soap in a cabinet under the sink – she fought back the memories at the familiar smell of it, which she'd never been able to find or replicate in Scaela. She stripped off her clothes and sank into the depths of the tub, submerging herself fully for a second before coming back. She washed, drained the water, refilled it and washed again. Kier knocked once on the door just as she was getting out, wrapping herself in a fluffy towel she'd pulled from the linen closet.

'Are you okay?' he asked through the wood.

She took a shuddering breath. 'No, but I will be.' And she would. She had the oddest feeling that the bodies in the cathedral were the only ones left; that the Isle itself had protected her from any other casualties. It was as if everyone in that horrid hall had been there to guard their fallen lord and lady, even in death; and now that Little Locke was newly returned, safety was restored.

Despite the horrors of earlier, when she focused, she felt something

almost like peace. Like the very Isle had sighed in relief now that its
dead had been laid to rest.

She found thick socks and a dressing gown in the room next door,
which had once belonged to her aunt before Wren was sent to Nestria
to marry before Grey was even born. While Kier was bathing, she
went downstairs to search for provisions. He'd already lit a fire in the
great hearth in the dining hall, which brought a smile to her face,
despite everything.

In the pantry, the meat and produce was unrotten, the bread still
soft and fresh, but Grey could not bring herself to touch it. She found
a jar of honey and a bin of rolled oats. She took these, some spices
and a tin pot into the dining hall. Kier was back and dressed in clean
clothes, dragging in cushions and blankets from one of the parlors.

'What did you find?' he asked.

She held up her haul. 'Better than unflavored porridge and bits
of jerky.'

He snorted. 'I can't wait to tell Eron you did better with a sixteen-
year-old pantry than he did with provisions.'

'Eron could *never*,' Grey agreed.

Kier went back to the kitchen to fill the pot while Grey stoked the
fire and urged it to roaring warmth. When he returned, she made a
thick porridge and seasoned it with honey and cinnamon. It wasn't
much, but it was edible. They sat cross-legged in front of the fire,
draped with one of the big knit blankets, surrounded by the eerie
quiet of the Isle. She craved the sound of the wind and sea as much as
she feared it: in her heart, she knew that when those sounds returned,
so would the rest of her worries of the world beyond Locke.

'I'll only ask once more, then I'll leave it,' Kier said finally, setting
his empty bowl aside. 'Are you okay? Because we can go. We don't
have to stay; we don't have to do this.'

Grey swallowed hard, the porridge turning to dust in her mouth.
Your power or his freedom. For all she knew, if they left the Isle, Kier
would die – and that was not a reality she was willing to face. 'I'm
okay,' she said. 'I think that was the worst of it.'

He nodded. 'Then, the magic.' He turned so he was facing
her, close enough that his kneecaps brushed hers. 'I don't really

understand how you're doing this. It feels like I'm pulling a lot from you, and you're not even fazed.'

Grey set her own bowl aside with Kier's. 'On Locke – Locke *is* power. I am not just a well for power that can run out. I am a faucet, a doorway, a river. Power flows through me to you, but here, there is no end.' She coughed delicately. 'It's why the sovereign of Locke always marries a mage.'

Neither of them commented on that.

His eyes slipped shut. He hadn't untethered from her all day, and she realized that she didn't feel quite so ill. Perhaps that was the problem of Locke, too: it didn't ache so much when she had someone to share it with, when she had some way to direct the power rushing up through her from the Isle. 'Can I?' he asked, flipping his hands palm up, resting on their knees.

'Yes,' Grey said. She laid her hands flat on top of Kier's to close the circuit. He hummed, low in his throat.

'This will take some getting used to,' he said. A shudder rolled through his shoulders, down his back. 'I don't know how to control this much power,' he admitted.

'Better figure it out,' Grey murmured. 'We might be here for a while.'

The corner of his mouth quirked up. He leaned forward, just enough to steal a kiss before rocking back down.

'Can you ward some rooms?' she asked.

'Of course. Grey – if it's too much, we don't have to stay here. We could find our own place to settle, once everything is calm.'

They couldn't. The Isle was the only thing keeping Kier alive. The words were on her lips, but she could not say them.

She shook her head. Besides, this was her birthright, her home, the place she had raised with her own blood. It was all she had left of her family, of those who had died for her sake.

'Then we'll stay,' he said.

'It's not a cottage in the hills,' she said mildly, 'but perhaps it would be good to retire here.'

He laughed, sounding so well and normal that she felt the shadows fleeing the deepest caverns of her heart. 'I think we've retired from retirement,' he declared. He pushed to his feet, offering her a hand, and Grey was quick to follow. 'Give me a tour of our new home, and we can ward all the rooms you want.'

In a middle floor just off the tallest tower, she found a suite of rooms that had been unoccupied for ages, with a bedroom in the rounded turret that looked out to Scaela. She threw open the windows to let the sea air clear the room of stuffiness as Kier lit a fire in the grate. Grey found clean sheets and made up the bed, barely tutting when Kier straightened her corners.

'There's a free room down the hall,' she said, hesitating, 'should you want it.'

He raised a brow. 'I can take it officially,' he said. 'But if it is all the same to you ... I'll stay with you.'

'Then it can be yours officially,' Grey said, the corner of her mouth lifting.

There was no further consensus needed. She pulled on a thick winter shirt from the chest of drawers, full of old things; Kier found a rattling jar of tooth tabs in the small bathroom as they prepared for sleep. He drew the curtains, as dark had not yet fallen: the world was still misty and white, unchanged.

Kier set the pale golden magelight above the bed as they crawled in. She draped a leg over his hip – his hand went to her thigh, gripping tight.

She wasn't sure what reminded her, if it was his grip or something else, but she felt the ring around her thumb. 'This is yours,' she said.

'Mm.' He bent to kiss her hand, the ring on it. 'Keep it.'

'But it was Lot's.'

'If I'm to be your commander, I face too high a risk of degloving,' he said solemnly. 'Has no one in the army told you?'

She swatted his shoulder. 'Are you not even afraid? We might be at war tomorrow.'

'We've been at war our entire lives.'

It was true, but this felt different. It was *her* banner, *her* nation, *her* war – and she didn't want it.

'I want peace, Kiernan,' she said, running her fingers through the too-long hair that curled over his ears.

'I'll do my best to get it for you,' he murmured. 'I'll do my best to get you anything you want, Locke.'

Grey turned this over. 'What if I don't know what I want?' she whispered.

She had to tell him. The words were there, if she only just said them: *You died, Kier. You died and I fought the gods for you, and you're not even really living now. What would you choose? What would you want?*

His lips pressed to her temple. 'Then I'll wait for you until you decide,' he said. 'But we've been following everyone else's orders for so long – I want you to have a genuine choice, Grey. A future you have picked for yourself.'

She thought of him sacrificing himself for her, the look on his face when he had told her to say goodbye to his mothers.

The truth was: if she posed the choice to him, Kier would choose his own sacrifice. He would give up his freedom for her and leave her power. He would remain here on this Isle, growing older and more bitter, forced to accompany her all the way to her grave.

She rolled onto her back, staring up at the ceiling as his breathing grew even and his grip on her loosened. She could just ... not tell him. But it would be its own kind of betrayal, to keep the truth from him.

And yet.

He had run away for her, become a soldier for her, risen in rank for her, gone into battle for her, lied for her, nearly been killed for her, been kidnapped for her. He had *died* for her.

If he had the choice, he would always make the decision that saved her, that supported her. Maybe, for once, she wanted to make a decision to sacrifice for someone else, after he had given everything up for her. She could not bear to take more than that.

Scaelas, let me speak frankly: I know you are hurting, but we must move past this. If you cannot look past what was done to Isaak and the Isle, Idistra will never be at peace. We must move on, find a genuine solution, or we will all be at war.

Letter from Cleoc to Scaelas, 4 days PD

Then let us be at war.

Letter from Scaelas to Cleoc, 5 days PD

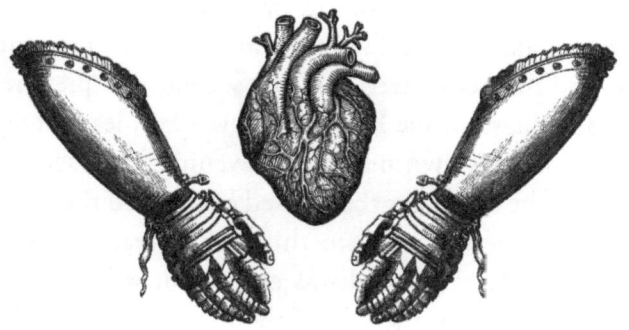

twenty-nine

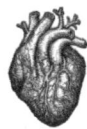

GREY DID NOT KNOW how much time did or did not pass as they readied the Isle. She measured the days in her own way as they worked until they were tired, then slept in her great bed, too exhausted for anything *but* sleep (or perhaps Kier was no longer interested in that kind of relationship; but he still kissed her at every chance, so she wondered at it). On the first day, they went through the armories, making note of weapons and supplies, preparing for an army that had not yet arrived. On the second, she prepared rooms for diplomatic guests while Kier walked the Isle, learning the lay of the land, making his own maps; that evening, they set up the war room in one of the chambers that looked out toward the rest of Idistra

She woke on the third day to thin light streaming in from the window. Kier's side of the bed was empty but still warm – she sat up to see his shadow on the side of the room. She rubbed her eyes, calmed by the sound of the gulls and the crashing of the waves, the shout of the wind; all the familiar sounds of Locke.

All the familiar sounds.

She froze. 'Kier?'

'I know.'

When she looked up at him, she realized that he was not dressing in the clothes they'd worn to work over the last few days; he was laying out his armor, dark gray as the banner of Locke, the rocks, the stormy sky. He was dressing for war.

'You can keep sleeping, love,' he murmured. 'I already went to the tower. We have time.'

She ignored him, slipping from the bed and going to the window. She squinted out at the bay, at the continent: she could only just see the coast. There were ships in the distance.

'I suspect we have an hour,' she said. She went back to the bed and sat heavily on the edge. It was no new sight, to watch Kier prepare for battle, his hair still wet from bathing in the early hours of the morning; but now it was her armor he wore, her crest of a blade over two linked rings embroidered on the surcoat draped over the chair, her battle he was preparing for. 'Maybe more. They'll worry for the shields. We should fly a banner for Scaelas and Cleoc, to let them know it's safe.'

'We should,' he said, but his voice had changed. Grey looked up – and felt the pulse of desire through the tether.

Something had caught Kier off guard when he glanced over at her. He crossed the room and dropped to his knees beside the bed, between her legs. His hands slipped around her calves. His eyes never left hers as he pressed a kiss just above her knee.

'It's just ... your *thighs*,' he confessed, almost mournful. As if to prove his point, he moved his hands upward, thumbs digging in, fingertips tracing the backs of her knees. 'I could write odes to your thighs. I might actually have dreams of your thighs.'

She raised a brow. 'Is that so?'

'They're perfect,' he lamented. She shuddered, watching the dimpling of his fingers into her flesh, falling back onto her elbows.

'You've never mentioned it.'

'A grievous error on my part.' He bent to kiss the freckle above her left knee.

'Kier,' she said, running her hands through his hair even as she knew it was a bad idea – but she hadn't been with him since Grislar, and even through the exhaustion, she *wanted*. 'We could be at war in a few hours.'

'Mm,' he hummed against her skin. Gently enough so it only just hurt, he bit the soft flesh of her inner thigh – the feeling went straight to her center. His hands came up, framing her hips. 'I'm aware.'

'I have to make you look like a commander,' she said, even as her head tipped back.

'Shouldn't take long. You never had trouble making me look like a captain.'

'And *I* have to look like a fearsome lady of an iron isle.'

'You *are* fearsome, even in only my shirt and your socks.' He rucked the aforementioned shirt up over her stomach.

'We shouldn't be distracted.'

He pressed a kiss up higher, at the soft fold where her thigh met her hip. 'Tell me to stop and I'll stop,' he said. 'But if this is the last morning of our lives, I want to spend it right here.'

She raked her nails over his scalp. 'And if I don't tell you to stop?'

His laugh was warm and smooth against her skin as his hand parted her thighs. 'Is that a yes?'

'*Yes.*'

Not much later, Kier went to the tower to raise the banner of Locke while Grey went into her mother's room. There, she found a sharply cut coat that looked more like armor than fashion and armored trousers that fit tight to her skin. She strapped her father's sword to her hip, scabbard shining in the first light of morning. Before she could think better of it, she slid the signet ring of Locke on her finger.

When they were ready for war, Locke and her commander walked together to the harbor in Maerin. The first of the ships had drawn closer, flying Scaelan colors, nearly within reach of the shield. The harbor was not big enough for warships, but it dropped anchor just outside the shimmering blue of the outer shield.

'They're launching a boat,' Kier murmured. They stood on one of the long docks, the wind whipping their hair. Above, the sky was steely and gray.

Grey watched the little boat as it drew closer, her breath catching when she made out the figures of the expedition party, their own retinue waving from the deck, relief swelling through her. They were close enough to hear the collective whooping from the occupants as the boat swept unharmed to the dock.

'They're safe,' she said, as if to convince herself. Kier moved, stooping down at the edge of the dock as Brit tossed him a line. He tied it off and helped to pull the boat in. Eron crossed over first, helped by Brit and Ola on one side and Kier on the other. His knee was bound and his arm was in a sling, but he was alive, and walking, and he hugged Kier fiercely before he moved on to Grey.

'What did you *do*?' she asked, her fingers digging into his back as she embraced him.

'You'll laugh.'

'I won't.'

He sighed. 'I fell from my horse, in the retreat.'

She had lied: she laughed. 'I'm sorry!' she said at his poisonous glare. But he didn't look *that* angry as he hugged her again.

'You fucking legend,' Brit said, kissing both Grey's cheeks as they too crossed to the dock. 'You absolute power-ridden bitch.'

'They mean that in a positive way,' Ola clarified, pushing past Brit. She gripped Grey's cheeks, pushing the wind-blown hair out of her face as she searched for any sign of strain. 'Love, how are you?'

Grey wanted to cave in to Ola. It was a triumph in itself that she remained upright. 'I'm here. We're alive.'

Ola's grin warmed as she looked to Kier, releasing Grey. 'Captain,' she said affectionately.

'Commander,' Grey corrected. Kier's hand tightened on her hip in response. She turned back to the sea, to the new boats launching, circling closer. She reached down, found his hand, and squeezed.

'Ready, Locke?' he murmured.

'As I'll ever be,' she said.

Boat after boat set off, unloaded and returned. Commander Reggin arrived with Cleoc's Commander Dainridge, a gray-haired woman in her forties with a glare as cold as ice, her skin tanned and wrinkled from years of wind and sunlight. They sent ambassadors, too: Ikaaron, from Scaela, and Yearna, from Cleoc.

'The High Lord plans to arrive this evening,' Ikaaron informed Grey after their introduction, when they'd moved off the dock to the paved area near the harbor. 'He wanted to come earlier, but we insisted he wait until the Isle is secure.'

'I'm sure he did,' Grey said drily. 'Commander?'

'Yes, my lady?' Kier replied.

'I will take my ambassadors to their rooms. Will you show those responsible for command our armories, then direct them into the war room and have their captains arrange their forces?'

'Yes, my lady.' He hesitated, for just a second. 'Will you take Ola and Brit with you?'

'I will, if you bring Eron.'

He nodded, and took leave of her without another word. Her new ambassadors did not seem to notice anything at all between Grey and her commander – she wasn't hiding their relationship, but she wasn't yet sure how she wanted to navigate it publicly.

They made their way up from the docks to the fortress. There, Grey showed the ambassadors the new war room and then the rooms she and Kier had prepared for diplomatic guests, where she left them to clean up and change.

They beat Kier and the commanders into the fortress. In the war room, without the others, Grey locked the door and turned to Brit and Ola. 'Okay,' she said. 'I don't know how much time we have, but what happened since we left? How long has it been?'

Ola winced. 'About two days. After you and Kier jumped, there were a few skirmishes, but no real engagement. Waiting to see what happened next, I suppose.'

Grey nodded. It had been longer than two days on the Isle, but she was glad for the time dilation and the reprieve it granted. 'Did you have the chance to see Scaelas?'

'Yes. He was furious at you.'

'They didn't really know what to do with us at first,' Brit said, leaning against the table, already spread with maps. 'Sela was with us for a bit and told us what she could, but otherwise we just kind of . . . watched. And waited. Pretty much as soon as you two jumped, there was this thick fog over the bay – both Scaelas and Epras sent ships, but it was the oddest thing. They came sailing back within the hour, turned around and redirected. No one could get the full way across, through the fog.'

Grey nodded. She had suspected some sort of shielding, some natural protection as the Isle came back into existence.

'We thought you were dead,' Ola said, not meeting her eye.

'You know me better than that.'

Someone tried the door, paused, then knocked. Grey sighed and reached for the handle. 'Let me,' Ola murmured, shooing her away. Grey went, taking her seat at the head of the table.

Ola opened the door to Kier, Reggin, Dainridge and a few other assorted masters and captains and their Hands. Grey watched as they filed in, seating themselves around the table: Kier to her right, Reggin and Dainridge close beside with Reggin's Hand behind them. In the absence of their sovereigns, Ikaaron and Yearna sat in the positions of Scaelas and Cleoc. Brit and Ola fell into position behind Grey; she presumed Kier had left Eron in charge of organizing the forces still assembling in the harbor.

Every eye was on her, expectant. After a beat, she turned to those around her. 'Commander Reggin, Commander Dainridge. Masters. Ambassadors. I welcome you to Locke, though I wish it was under better circumstances. This is Commander Seward, the head of my forces on the Isle.'

Beside her, Kier very nearly smiled. She couldn't tell if it was because she'd referred to him by his title, or because he was the entire extent of her forces on Locke.

'If we could be informed of the situation in Idistra, we can begin from there,' she said.

'Lady Maryse,' one of the Scaelan masters at the end of the table started, speaking out of turn. 'It appears that—'

'Locke.'

A silence spread over the room as every eye turned to Kier, Grey's included.

'Sorry, Commander Seward?' the master said. He was old enough to be Kier's father.

Kier raised an eyebrow. 'Would you call your own High Lord by name?' The silence was not broken; Grey forced herself to sit straight and tall, unflinching. 'She is Locke, Master.'

The master glanced at her, and to Grey's surprise, he did not look angry – he looked *ashamed*. They did not hate her.

They feared her.

'My apologies, your majesty,' he said.

'Thank you, Master,' Grey said, pushing away any lingering discomfort. She nodded to her allied commanders. 'Your reports, please.'

'Your majesty,' Ikaaron said, bowing his head. He glanced sidelong at Yearna, then launched into his explanation. 'Epras and Luthos have declared that their prisoner, Captain Kier Seward, was rightfully captured by their forces, and wrongfully freed by Scaelas. Now that your new Commander Seward has been revealed and is clearly not Locke . . .'

Grey looked at her hands, and did not correct them.

' . . . they have insisted that a repayment is due. In return, they have declared that the High Lady should accept the same terms Commander Seward agreed to: marry a suitor of their choice and restore power. If these terms are accepted, they will agree to a treaty with the Isle, and will cease their wars with Scaelas and Cleoc in return.'

Grey raised an eyebrow, trying to keep her features as cool as possible. 'They want to *marry* me?'

'Yes, my lady,' Ikaaron said. 'With you married and bound to their suitor, they will see a re-emergence of power simply by being aligned with you, and when you bear an heir, it would be in your line. It has been custom, as long as Locke has existed, to marry strategically for such redirections of power.'

Grey winced. 'And if I do not?'

He nodded to Commander Dainridge. Grey turned to face her.

'They have threatened to turn their combined forces on the Isle,' Dainridge said. 'Either to decimate everyone who remains here and take you prisoner, or to circle us until we starve.'

'Right,' Grey said flatly.

'You've been given three days to make your choice, and if you are not presented for marriage in that time, they will attack.'

She rubbed her temple. She reached through the tether to Kier, but found it curiously blank – he was holding back his own emotions until she made a decision without his influence.

'Those are the terms proposed,' Ikaaron said. He glanced at the others gathered, focusing for a second on Yearna. Cleoc's ambassador, before he continued. 'I have been instructed that we will assist you in defense of the Isle, if you choose to fight; but you could marry instead, if it pleases you. I recognize I am only the Scaelan ambassador and not your own adviser, but if my lord were here, he would offer this council: though marriage may seem a bloodless option, he personally would not advise it.'

She was growing quite tired of decisions like this, the choices predetermined and ironclad.

'I will *not*. That sounds like the fastest way to get killed in my own bed.' She felt an instant, undeniable rush of relief through the tether.

'I would think so too, your majesty,' Ikaaron said. 'With your permission, we will send a messenger with your response.'

'So we will fight,' Kier said, 'to keep the Isle.'

Grey got up and set to pacing. From here, she could not see down the Isle to Maerin, but she could see the choppy sea, and the ships that had started circling.

'Commanders, what do you propose?' she asked.

They argued over maps and troop formations for hours. If Eprain and Luthar were permitted onto her shores, they would not stop until Grey was dead, so they had to do everything in their power to hold the Isle, to ensure that didn't happen.

'Is there something we can do?' Reggin's Hand said when Grey's head had already been aching for the better part of an hour. 'A show of strength? A manipulation of power?'

Grey shook her head. 'I don't know what I *could* do.'

'Don't you control it?'

She looked at him, the boy whose youth she hadn't been able to see past when she first met him. Now, she wondered at it. She glanced at the list she had in front of her, of the names of those sitting before her: the commander's Hand was listed as *A. Reggin*. She would eat her own hat if he wasn't related to the commander, and something about that made her uneasy.

'We could send Locke back to Scaela,' one of the captains near the end of the table said. 'Or Cleoc, if they will have her. Just until the Isle is secure.'

Grey glanced at Kier. He looked like he was actually considering it.

'No,' she said. 'I will not leave again.' If she did, it would require her to leave Kier – and who knew if she'd be back before the next full moon, to tell Kitalma of her choice? She could not risk it.

They argued until the sun was high in the sky, at which point Grey ordered them to take a break. When she left the war room, she was surprised to find the Isle caught in a swell of activity. She told Ola and Brit to rest and eat, then set off for the highest tower.

No one had established a base there yet. She leaned against the crenelations, wind whipping her hair, threatening to tear it from its braid. At sea, the ships circled, but no one moved to attack.

There were soldiers camped in both Osar and Maerin, with tents pitched in the hilly fields and taking up the villages between. She could see the progress at the harbor, the workers small as ants, as little boats brought supplies ashore, which were then carted to the cities and the fortress. She watched the progress of those tiny people, of those great ships.

Boots sounded on the stairs; she did not turn. 'Why won't you consider going back to Scaela?'

She snorted. 'Not a chance.'

Kier came behind her, framing her hands with his, resting his chin on top of her head. 'It would be safer,' he said, but it was already a losing battle, and he knew it.

'Safety is overrated.'

He sighed. 'Spoken by someone who has never really known it.'

She turned in his arms, tracing the line of his healed collarbone. Safety was one thing – but freedom was another.

She realized that with the flurry of activity on the Isle below, the tenuous nature of her position, and the fact that other nations were already petitioning for her hand, she might not find more time alone with Kier.

Perhaps she had already missed her chance to tell him what she'd done. Perhaps she would never need to tell him at all – but that depended on the choice she still had not made.

'Kier,' she said, her fingers fussing with the curve of the crest on her surcoat. 'Would anything change, do you think, if I didn't have power?'

He laughed. 'Did Reggin's Hand get to your head?' He swept a hand over her hair. 'It's nothing to worry about. You won't lose your power – it's an impossibility.'

'But if, say, it happened.'

He rolled his eyes. 'It won't. It *can't*.'

'But if I chose to give it up—'

Now he looked at her, narrow-eyed. 'What are you thinking of?' he asked.

'Nothing,' Grey said, blush heating her cheeks. 'It's just speculation.'

He leaned close, kissing her forehead. 'Like I said. It's nothing to worry about – nothing will happen to your power. I won't let it.'

She could not meet his gaze.

'Scaelas and Cleoc should be arriving soon,' he said after a moment. 'Shall we go receive them?'

'It's probably best,' she said, pushing away all thoughts of what she was still considering.

She absorbed the changes in her Isle, the *life*, as they crossed the paths between the two towns. She was thinking of this when they passed a large stone house in Maerin with carts lined up outside the door. Leaning against one was a familiar figure, making marks in a notebook, her curly black hair secured on top of her head with a spare pencil.

Grey stopped short and felt her heart clench in her chest. 'Leonie?'

The medic looked up from her notebook. She was confused for the shortest span of a second before her eyes locked on Grey, then she'd set the notes aside and was walking as quickly as she could into the road. Grey didn't care for decorum; she *ran*.

Leonie caught her in her arms. She smelled of herbs and soap and lavender, and Grey buried her face in her neck.

'I didn't think I would ever see you again,' she admitted.

'Funny,' Leonie said, 'because I was explicitly named on your list.'

Grey laughed, pulling back to look her in the face. Leonie had a newly healing scar on the edge of her jaw, straight, from a blade. 'I didn't know you'd have time to get here, after Mecketer.'

Leonie shook her head. 'I was moved after the raid, shortly after you left.' She saw something over Grey's head and her smile grew even wider. 'Captain Seward – or Commander now, isn't it?'

'It is,' Kier said, leaning to kiss Leonie's hand. 'We're lucky to have you.'

'Ah, better than the last place I was in,' Leonie said. She gently slipped out of Grey's arms and went back to her list. 'It's good you're here, actually. For supplies, who do I ask?'

'Um. Me?'

'You're the High Lady. You shouldn't worry yourself with trivial matters.'

Grey looked at Kier, but he only shrugged. 'Report to me,' she said. 'If you come to the fortress and ask for me directly, I'll make sure they know to admit you.'

Leonie eyed her shrewdly over her notebook. 'Be careful who you tell that to, Locke,' she said. 'Or else you'll have everyone in the Isle asking for you.'

Grey rolled her eyes. 'I'll be back when I can,' she promised.

Scaelas and Cleoc did not linger at the harbor, but went into the war room for more arguing as soon as they reached the Isle. Though she had not been reunited with him long, with every look at Scaelas, Grey could tell with absolute certainty that he was furious, and she had little doubt as to the object of his anger.

They were served food as night fell, still debating strategy; as the hours crept on, one by one the captains left to assign watches and make sure their camps were properly established, followed by the masters, until only the commanders remained. It was nearing midnight when Kier finally said, 'There's not much more we can do tonight. Locke?'

She hated the uncertainty, but she agreed.

Reggin and Dainridge and their Hands moved to stand; Cleoc

and Scaelas did not move. 'If we may have a moment with the Lady?'
Scaelas said. At Kier's withering look, he sighed. 'Commander, you
may stay.'

The four of them lingered in the room. Cleoc said, 'It was a worrying decision, to directly attack one of your ally's commanders then
jump off a cliff.'

Grey crossed her arms. She would not be chastised like a child. 'I
saved your soldiers' lives.'

'Nearly at the risk of your own. It's like you learned it from Seward.'

She leaned back against the table. 'I did what I had to do.'

'You nearly *died*,' Scaelas said, his voice full of scarcely concealed
rage. 'That is certainly not what I agreed to. Now that we only just
have you, you threaten us with your death?'

Cleoc shot him a warning glare. 'It is more worrying for an ally to
make such rash decisions without consultation,' she said. 'I have put
my trust in you. Do not make me regret that.'

Before Grey could answer, Cleoc swept out of the room. The door
slammed shut behind her.

'Commander Seward,' Scaelas said quietly. 'A moment alone with
the High Lady?'

'Whatever you need to say to Grey, you can say to me.'

Grey sighed. 'Go, Kier. I'll be up soon.'

He paused for a second, two; then, seeing she wouldn't change
her mind, he too left. Grey turned to face Scaelas, her hands balled
into fists.

'I am not your daughter,' she said. 'You cannot come here to find
me, a grown woman, sovereign to my own nation, and deign to
parent me.'

'A *cliff*, Gremaryse?' Torrin seethed. '*A cliff?*'

'You told me I could save him!'

'I told you, whatever you did, to not do it alone.'

She threw up her hands. 'What else was I to do! Let Kier die?'

'You asked for my help, and then you did *that*! I don't know – you
could have followed the rules, for once in your life. Even if you ran
off with Captain Seward, you should've brought him back to the fort,
to your *allies*. We could've handled this correctly and safely.'

'I was doing what I thought was best.'

'You don't know anything about how this works,' Torrin snapped.

'You've made your stance on the matter very clear. But as I would remind you, your majesty – *you are not my father.*'

Torrin shook his head slowly. 'I am not,' he said. The fight went out of him; he, too, leaned on the table, his arm against hers. 'Do you feel them press upon your heart, Maryse?'

She felt her jaw tighten, the weight of them crushing down. 'Yes,' she said finally. 'Sometimes.'

'As do I.' He looked down at her – he was nearly a foot taller, built like one of his nation's hulking trees – and she saw the sadness in his eyes. 'Your father was like a brother to me. The first person in this world I ever knew. They say, in the old religion of Scaela, mages and wells were one soul cleft in two: if that was true, he was mine.'

'We don't have that story on Locke.'

'I know. Probably because it requires trusting another person.' *Blood and betrayal. That is your legacy.*

She pushed that aside. 'You're a well,' she said.

'Yes.'

'And my father's Hand, before he married my mother.'

Torrin looked away. 'Yes.'

'Did you love him?'

'Not in the way of you and your commander,' he said, considering. 'But in my own way. As, I suppose, we all do.'

Grey nodded. That she could understand.

'To lose you would be like knowing his death all over again,' Torrin said quietly. Behind them, the fire was crackling low in the grate; soon, it would be only embers. She did not move to prod it back to life.

'I am not yours to lose,' she said, but gently this time.

'I know,' Torrin said. 'That doesn't make it easier.'

Kier barely stirred when she finally came down from the tower, where she'd been pacing and watching the sea. She found one of his shirts, exchanged her own clothes for it and slid into bed. He immediately turned, pulling her against his chest.

'You're cold,' he said against her shoulder, adjusting her so her back was flush with his front, his legs pressed to hers.

'I wasn't ready for sleep,' she admitted. 'Did anyone question you, when you came to my rooms?'

'No. You have no guard. The others went to sleep hours ago.'

'Oh.'

He pressed a kiss to the space under her ear. 'Was he very disappointed? Scaelas?'

'No,' Grey said, unable to fully account for the lump in her throat. She laced her fingers with Kier's and pulled his arms even tighter around her. 'He told me about my father.'

Kier was quiet for a moment. 'Perhaps it's a good thing,' he said, 'to have some part of him. Of his memory.'

Grey nodded. 'Perhaps,' she said. But she lay awake in the dark for a long time after that, thinking of her ghosts.

Blood of my blood, soul of my soul, thine hand is over my heart. When you ache, then shall I ache; when you perish, then shall I perish. What is known to me is known to you. Let me not break this troth.

Verse 27, *The Holy Verses of the Isle*, often used in rituals of binding and marriage

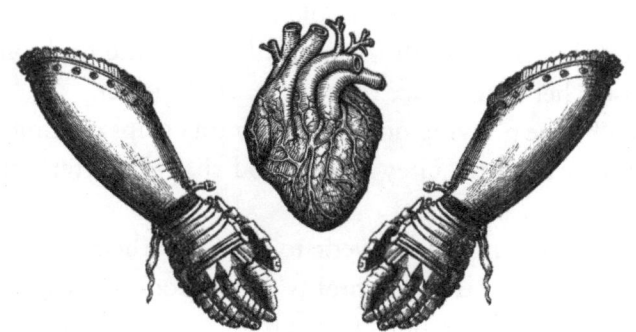

thirty

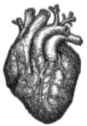

IT WAS DECIDED THAT Scaelas and Cleoc would provide enough soldiers to keep the Isle and hold it until they could force a surrender from Epras and Luthos – or until Grey could find some other way to assert her dominance over the nation's power.

Judging by the growing number of Eprain's ships circling, waiting for a sign of weakness, Grey understood that the latter option was the desirable one.

While Scaelas and Cleoc went to speak to their advisers, Grey left the planning in the war rooms to her commanders and went to check on how preparations were progressing. Kier sent a pulse of reassurance through the tether as she left the room; she ignored it.

One of Cleoc's attendants waited for her in a side room. She curtsied when Grey entered. 'Your majesty,' she said. 'Please accept this gift, from my nation.'

Grey crossed to the heavy wooden trunk and opened it. Inside, she found a number of rich, dark fabrics in shades of black and gray and navy with a few flashes of ivory silk. She sat back on her heels – it was the wardrobe that Sela had commissioned. On top, she found a letter, sealed with a modified Stratan crest pressed into the wax.

'Thank you,' she said to the attendant, forcing herself through speechlessness. 'I am immensely grateful to you, your nation and your lady.' *And its daughter*, she thought.

After the attendant left, she opened the letter.

My fearsome Lady Locke,

I am not allowed to join you on your Isle, and I am not as brave as you — you, for certain, would've found yourself a place on one of those ships, forbidden or not. I hope you do not think badly of me for my weakness.

Grey scoffed. If she had to worry about Sela on top of everything else, she might actually combust. She frowned, annoyed at herself for a moment, for finally understanding Torrin's healthy fear for her own safety.

I know this gift is small, and possibly insignificant. I cannot give you my sword or the promise of a nation I haven't yet inherited. I can barely help you. But you are the strongest person I know, and the strongest well. You will be okay. You have to be okay.

Thank you for your ruthlessness, Grey. It is its own kind of safety.

Yours,
W. N.

PS You can't die, because I've already started planning Locke's resurrection party, and the plans I have are in no way appropriate for a funeral.

She laughed, pushing away tears that threatened to overflow. She rifled through the fabrics, and was halfway through when she felt the press of cold metal. She frowned, pushing aside the top layer of clothes to reveal a set of cleverly made armor. It was dark silver, glimmering in the stormy light through the windows, overlaid with patterns of birds and ivy. It was, she realized with some awe, a twin to the armor Kitalma wore in the icons.

She clutched the metal, feeling the cold bite of it under her fingers. Ruthlessness was, she agreed, its own kind of safety.

That evening, while Kier and Dainridge and Reggin continued their planning, Grey took a candle and made her way through the dark halls to the administrative wing of the fortress. Cleoc and Scaelas and their various clerks and advisers had taken up most of the rooms, but, probably at Scaelas's instruction, Grey's mother's office was left free for her.

She hesitated at the door. It was warded – perhaps that was the true reason. Perhaps she was assigning kindnesses to Torrin that didn't belong.

The door opened easily beneath her touch, only creaking a little. She carried a leather satchel of documents over her shoulder, passed from the other sovereigns for her review. She set the documents on the carved wood desk and took the room in: the walls were covered with bookshelves, bearing old treatises and folklore alike. It was small, but far more nicely appointed than any commander's office she'd been in before. She could not say if it rivaled the luxury of Torrin's private office; she had never been there.

She lit the fire in the grate, then sat behind the desk. There was a stack of letters in the middle, seals broken, all bearing correspondence that was now worthless. She ran her fingers over the parchment to the other side, where her mother had been halfway through writing a response to Maerin's harbormaster. She read it over, but it was irrelevant: preparing for renovations to the port that had never happened.

She sighed and pulled out the documents from the satchel. Grey read the proposed articles of the treaty with Scaela and Cleoc Strata until her eyes were heavy with strain, until the door opened and Kier slipped through, his coat as dark and shadowed as the night itself.

He perched on the edge of the desk. 'It's late,' he said, his gaze careful. 'Tomorrow is our last day of peace before it all goes to shit, and you need to rest. You should come to bed.'

Grey glanced at the timepiece on his wrist. 'It's not that late,' she said. Not even midnight. 'And you can't order me around anymore.'

That got a smile out of him. 'Oh, I can try.'

She sat back, folding her hands over her lap. Her fingers were cold – she was not yet skilled at keeping fires going in the hearth. Kier must've noted the whiteness of her knuckles – he took her hands in his and rubbed the warmth back into them.

'Is it odd?' she asked. 'That no one thinks you have power over me anymore? That they no longer see me as just your well?'

Kier snorted. 'I never saw you as just my well.'

'Maybe not, but no one else asked my opinion.'

He thought for a moment, bringing one of her hands to his lips, then the other. 'It never mattered, what they thought,' he said after a moment. 'I always saw you as my equal. Every decision I made, it was with your council.'

Grey looked away. Kier misinterpreted her guilt – he took her chin in his hand, turned her face back to him. 'Nothing has changed, Grey. Not for me.'

She regarded him, studied his features. She nodded, and he nodded back.

'You should sleep when you can,' he said.

'I will, after I finish this. Half an hour more.'

He sighed, but leaned to kiss her forehead. 'I'm timing you, Locke.'

An hour later, the door opened again. Grey didn't glance up. 'I'm coming, I'm coming,' she murmured.

'Unfortunately, I don't think we can enjoy that kind of relationship anymore.'

She looked up, the pen falling from her hand, dripping ink across the note on tributes she was halfway through making. Leonie stood in the doorway, leaning on a cane. Grey frowned – she doubted the Isle's stormy weather was good for Leonie's bones.

'Please, sit,' she said, nodding to one of the chairs on the other side of the desk. Leonie crossed the carpet, leaving the door cracked behind her. 'To what do I owe the pleasure?'

'It's odd, hearing you talk like a noble.' Leonie smiled, easing herself into the chair. She wore a gray coat over her black skirt, and the sight of it brought a lump to Grey's throat. 'And it's to *whom*. It's the same answer as always, since neither of you is capable of looking after yourselves without the other getting involved. The commander sent me.'

'Ah.'

Leonie shifted her arm, and Grey realized she carried a basket. She drew out a bottle of wine and two glasses. 'Think it's still good?'

Grey snorted. There was no point explaining the time dilation, the unchanging nature of the Isle, the bodies. 'I suspect we're going to find out.'

Leonie's grin widened. She uncorked the bottle with a thin knife from her belt, then poured two glasses. 'Not too much,' Grey cautioned. 'I need a clear head, and Kier thinks I should go to bed.'

'I don't believe we need to heed his every word. After all, he also said Eron would beat Ola in a fight, and that's certainly false.'

'What kind of fight?' Grey asked, accepting the glass Leonie handed her, and the subsequent clink of their glasses as they toasted. She took a sip: the wine was rich and dark, probably plum. Probably a gift from Nestria sixteen seasons ago.

'Oh, you know. No magic, sparring, the usual.' Leonie sighed, sitting back. Grey watched the tension leaving her shoulders, and wondered if she herself would ever be able to relax again.

'You didn't have to follow me here.'

Leonie looked over her shoulder, watching the crackling fire. It was a novelty to the Scaelans, Grey supposed; even with its familiarity, it was a novelty to her, too. Magefire did not crackle like real flames; it did not smell like clean pine and woodsmoke.

'I told you I would be here if you had need of me.'

Grey closed her eyes. 'I do not want to bring people close to me if it's only sentencing them to death.'

'Do you really believe that's what this is?' Leonie said, taking another sip of her wine. Grey wanted to throw caution to the winds, drain the entire glass to the dregs and let her hair loose as she stood on the highest tower of her own Isle. 'Do you have so little faith that we may live?'

She swallowed hard, taking a mouthful of wine with it. 'They expect something great of me,' she said.

'Of course they do. You raised the Isle with blood and intention alone.'

Not alone.

'What?'

Grey looked up. She hadn't realized she'd said it aloud. But Leonie was watching her with care, and caution – and gods, she just wanted someone else to know about her decision. Not to help; but just to hold it, so she did not have to carry the weight of it alone.

'If I tell you something,' she said, running her fingertip along the rim of the glass, 'can I trust your confidence?'

Leonie snorted. 'I knew you were Locke for the better part of a year, and I said nothing then.'

Grey scrutinized her. Leonie only refilled her glass. 'You did?'

'With the way you manipulated power? With how you healed your captain? Of course I knew, Grey. I'm no fool.'

'Kier is dead.'

Leonie's hand slipped; she nearly dropped the bottle, but recovered quickly. She set it down, out of the range of the papers, as Grey took a long sip of her wine. 'Grey – I just saw him. He *sent* me. I told you.'

Grey shook her head. 'That's not what I mean.'

Leonie raised a brow and leaned in closer, her elbows on the desk.

'When we raised Locke,' Grey said miserably, the ache of it returning to her chest at even the slightest thought of it – she wondered if she would always have it, right there within reach, when she recalled the absence of his heartbeat. 'Kier . . . was not alive when we arrived on the Isle. I checked his pulse. I tried to bring him back. For a *while*, Leonie.'

Leonie nodded slowly, looking away. She knew Grey's training: if Grey had declared Kier beyond saving, if she had given up on him coming back, then he was surely dead.

'My mother appeared to me, and my father and brother, and the goddess Kitalma. They told me that to resurrect the Isle, a sacrifice was needed.'

'And that sacrifice was Kier,' Leonie said. 'But . . .'

Grey nodded, barely able to speak past the tightness in her chest. 'But.'

'He's walking now.'

'I was offered a trade. By the goddess.'

'Grey . . . '

She shook her head. She could not say it for a moment of quiet breathing, and then she forced the words out: 'I have time, yet. But I can either keep my power . . . or Kier can keep his freedom.'

Leonie sucked a breath through her teeth. 'And if you lose your power, will all power fade?'

'No,' Grey said, considering. 'The goddess said Kier will still be able to draw from the Isle, and my own heir will continue the line. So it is just . . . me.'

'And if Kier gives his freedom?'

'If *I* give it,' Grey corrected, feeling the distinction was important. 'Then Kier can never again leave the Isle. He will live the rest of his days here, and then he will die here.'

'He can never go home.'

'No,' Grey said.

Leonie nodded thoughtfully. She ran the tip of her finger over the wrinkled edge of the bottle's label. 'And have you decided?'

Grey rubbed her eyes. That was the question, wasn't it? Every time she opened her mouth to tell Kier, every time the words tangled on her tongue – because she had decided, and the decision made her ache.

'He's already given everything up for me,' she said, the words thick in her throat. 'I cannot take more from him.'

Leonie's hand stopped moving. 'So you would give it up? You would give away everything?'

'It's no more than he already sacrificed,' Grey said, the knot finally breaking. She took a ragged breath and wiped away her tears with her sleeve.

That was when she saw him, in the shadows of the doorway. He had one hand on the door still, frozen, halfway through pushing it open.

'Leonie,' Kier said. His voice was quiet, but the intensity of it made Grey's blood run cold. She reached for the tether – but in that very moment, Kier snapped it. 'If I may, I need to speak with the High Lady.'

Cold dread spread through her at the tone of his voice. She knew, with utter certainty, that she had made a grave mistake in not telling him – and there was absolutely nothing she could do about it, no defense she could use, no high ground she could take.

Leonie paled, turning to look at Kier. She twisted to look back at Grey, but Grey only shook her head. The damage was already done.

'Of course,' Leonie said. She left Grey one more lingering glance, took her bottle and the glasses and went out. Kier shut the door behind her.

He raised his eyes to Grey, finally. Only then did she see the full extent of his anger, written in the paleness of his face, the sharpness of his gaze, the ticking muscle of his jaw. She'd seen that expression before – but she'd never seen it directed at her.

He was still dressed, despite his earlier beckoning for her to come to bed – he had probably been working, too, at the desk in their room. Preparing for the battle to come. She regarded him, taking in the planes of his face in the firelight; she could not read him.

'What was I to do?' she asked, when she could not bear the silence anymore. She didn't know how long he'd been there, how much he'd heard, but he'd certainly caught the worst of it.

'You should've *told me*,' he said, his voice shaking with fury.

Blood and betrayal. That's the legacy of Locke.

She rose to her feet like a thundercloud. 'You cannot be mad at me for saving your life.'

'You didn't save my life!' Kier shouted. 'I *died*, Grey. Don't you think I deserved to know that?'

'I was going to tell you,' she said, fighting to keep her own voice level, 'once I decided what to do.'

'And you don't think I should get a say?' He whirled, finding an inkpot on one of the bookshelves. He threw it; she winced when it hit the stone wall above the fireplace and shattered in a spray of black drops and glass. '*Fuck!*'

'You have no reason to be furious about this,' Grey said, her nails digging into the wood of the desk. 'And if you insist on it, you can go home and be mad in your mothers' house. When this battle is over, you are free to leave, if you wish.'

He whirled on her, face blank for the barest second as he processed, then his fury intensified. His hands were clenched into fists at his side. '*You. Will. Not. Give. Up. Your. Power.*'

She stared at him, jaw throbbing from how tightly she was clenching it. When it was clear he was not going to say anything else until she did, she said, 'I will not take your freedom, Kiernan.'

'Give me that choice,' he hissed.

'I give you all the choices!' Grey shouted back. She wanted to throw an inkpot herself, but she did not.

He shook his head, the vein in his temple throbbing. He went over to the fireplace and picked up the biggest piece of ink-stained glass from the mantel before he threw it in the fire. 'I have never made a choice without consulting you,' he said, his voice pitched so low she barely heard it. Grey watched the fight run out of him as he gripped the mantel like it was the only thing that would keep him upright through this betrayal.

She swallowed, forcing the pain down. 'I love you. Every choice I have made, that I *am* making, is because I love you.'

His hand tightened on the mantel, knuckles going white. 'Why must you always sacrifice yourself, and call that love?'

She drew a sharp breath. It was a fatal blow, and they both knew it.

Kier did not look at her. He did not say anything as he turned away and went out, shutting the door behind him, leaving her standing in the wake of his destruction.

Grape –

Look after him. Please. I know he would die for you, but I think it's in all of our best interests if you don't let him. He has given up everything for you (and I support him in this decision), but I beg of you: don't let him give up his life.

Letter from Lieutenant Lotrain Seward to Grey Flynn, 7 years PD

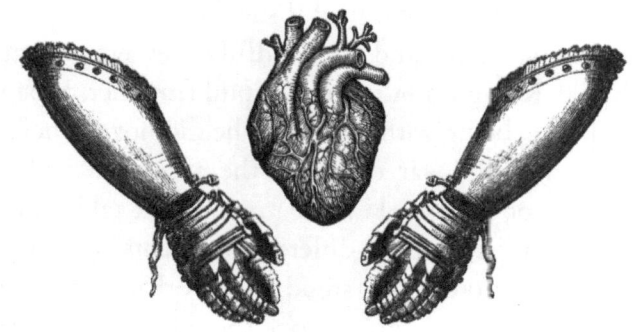

thirty-one

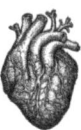

THAT NIGHT, GREY SLEPT alone.

She woke too early and returned to her office, working through treaties that would never be signed if she died. After, she fled to the infirmary, helping Leonie and her handful of healers prepare for the looming battle. Kier did not tether nor pull from her. If he found it an inconvenience, being without magic, he did not tell her.

She returned to the war rooms in the afternoon and took her seat between Cleoc and Scaelas. The maps on the tables were tidier, marked now with the bases for different regiments and the plans for attack, inked with notes. Kier stood at the other end of the table, leaning over them, with Reggin at one shoulder. Reggin's Hand sat in the chair his mage had previously occupied. Grey found her eyes often slipping to him, doing her best to distract herself from Kier's coldness with other thoughts, wondering at their relationship. Would her own father or uncle or brother drag her into war?

She felt Torrin's anxiety radiating off him. Perhaps her own was as thick, as noticeable – perhaps everyone misread the tension between Locke and her commander as concern for the battle to come.

'If you think you're ready,' Reggin was saying to Kier, 'then you should trust that instinct.' At Kier's nod, Reggin turned to the rest of the table. 'We will focus our forces here, and here, as Commander Seward has suggested.' Grey followed the indications on the map.

'Locke?' Scaelas said. 'What do you think?'

She thought her head was going to explode, and she did not have the brain for strategy. She knew, with perfect muscle memory, how to wield a blade, how to fight, how to defend. She couldn't keep looking at Kier and seeing the disappointment lurking beneath the surface. She glanced quickly at Scaelas, then used a line she'd heard from him more than once: 'I will defer to the wisdom of my commanders.'

The corner of Scaelas's mouth twitched up. Dainridge, Reggin and Seward were all in agreement: Kier would pull down the temporary shields and open the Isle to attack when their time was up, when Grey's final rejection of marriage was received.

'The only question that remains,' Dainridge said, pacing behind the table, 'is that of Locke.'

Grey's head snapped up. 'In what way?'

'Where will you be during the battle, your majesty?'

She glanced at Cleoc. '*I'll* be in the fortress, safe,' Cleoc said, perfunctory, her hands folded on the table. 'I am no soldier.'

Scaelas cleared his throat. 'And I will be with my forces. Fighting.'

Grey raised an eyebrow at him, daring him to tell her what to do – but he did not.

'Then Locke, too, will remain in the fortress,' someone said at the end of the table. One of Cleoc's masters, Grey thought.

'I will not,' she snapped. 'I will be fighting with—' She cut off, the thought interrupted before she could finish it: she'd been about to say, *I will be fighting with my mage.*

What had Cleoc said to her, on that day when they were trying to figure out the problem of Kier's imprisonment? She could not be loyal to both her Isle and her mage.

Across the table, she met Kier's eye. He was still angry – but there was surrender there. He would not offer counsel, not on her life; not when this decision mattered so much. He was watching her carefully, but he would not make nor unmake her decisions.

Perhaps, she thought grimly, it was payback for her making decisions without him.

'They're after *you*, Locke,' Commander Reggin said very carefully, as if urging her to consider her words when her own commander remained silent. 'If you are captured . . .'

'They are here,' Torrin said, not meeting her eye, 'to take you prisoner.'

Grey pressed her lips together. She looked at Cleoc, who did not want a rash, impulsive girl for an ally, who would not trust her if she acted out of hand; she looked at Scaelas, who would be fighting under his own banner, but who looked nauseous at the thought of her doing the same.

And then at Kier, who only waited. Who had already died for her once. She ached for all the things she should've done differently, all the words she should've told him before they'd gotten this far.

If she died in battle, she could not save him.

'I will be in the fortress,' she said, tasting bile in her mouth, 'helping as best I can.'

Kier let out a breath. She did not need to be tethered to him to sense his relief.

'But I refuse to be taken prisoner,' she said, folding her hands in front of her. She remembered the feeling in her stomach when her mother perished in battle. 'If I am to remain here, then I want poison or a blade. In case they take the Isle.'

Scaelas did not meet her eye.

But Kier did. When she glanced up, he was looking at her steadily. She had been such a fool, to try to make decisions like this without taking him into account. They always chose the cliff, the poison, the blade, to be the sacrifice – they always chose one another.

She remembered her mother braiding poison into her hair. Her father checking her boots for blades. Severin, not hesitating to kill the girl he thought he would marry. She thought of holding Kier's hand as they jumped. She felt, with bile in her throat, of how she had taken the choice of sacrifice or salvation away from him. And again, she thought of how she couldn't bear it – and how, if she took the choice away from him, he would be so much more likely to decide on his own sacrifice, without her.

'Then you shall have both, at your disposal,' Kier said.

*

When darkness finally fell, the eve before the battle to come, Kier was not in her room when she went upstairs to bed. The door to his own room, his *actual* room, was firmly closed. She had not been able to catch a moment with him before they were both pulled in different directions – and still, she was not sure what to say.

She left it. She bathed, sitting in the water with her knees pulled to her chest until it went cold. Then she dressed in warm clothes and a cloak, and left her hair wet down her back, though her grandmother always told her that would be the death of her. She walked through the fortress like a ghost, then up and up and up.

Alone, on the roof of Locke's tallest tower, she looked out at her Isle.

The stone of the crenelations was frigid under her hands. The torches in the harbor glowed with violet magelight, a warning to any ships that sailed too close. There were a few lights spread around the Isle as soldiers from each camp kept watch. Far offshore, the ships circled. She did not know how much longer they would keep their distance, treating her like prey.

There were boots on the stairs behind her. Grey stiffened, expecting Kier – but it was only Ola who came, wrapped in a blanket, her hair loose over her shoulders. She moved next to Grey and let her head fall on her shoulder.

'I imagine you're not here of your own free will,' Grey said bitterly.

'Would you believe me if I said I was?'

Grey shot her a scathing look.

Ola sighed. 'You're a good one, Flynn. If you must know, the commander came into my room in a rage the other night and demanded that I make sure you actually went to sleep tonight.'

Damn him.

'You fought.'

It wasn't a question, so Grey did not answer it. 'Do you think we'll survive tomorrow?' she asked instead, desperate to think of anything else.

'Who knows,' Ola said. 'But there have been many days when I've asked that question, so it's not much of a change.'

Grey snorted. 'I have never felt so powerless in my life,' she said finally. 'Everyone here seems determined to die for me. And I – I don't know, Ol. There has to be something I can do, something that will save them.'

'You've been determined to die for everyone else, Grey,' Ola said mildly.

'It's different,' Grey insisted.

'Is it?'

She didn't answer. The only noise was the waves crashing below as she considered this. 'I might understand why Kier is angry,' she said finally. 'But that doesn't explain why everyone else is willing to die.'

Ola chewed on her lip. 'If it helps, it's not about you at all. Locke was always the linchpin in the middle of a complex set of treaties. It benefits Scaelas and Cleoc to return to that.'

Grey put her elbows on the stone and rested her head in her hands. It did help, and she did know that, though it was easy to forget. It was almost a relief to know they were following her for her political significance rather than her personality. 'And there's been no word from Nestria. They hope to remain neutral, to fall in with the favor of whoever wins.'

'Lucky bastards,' Ola said simply, rubbing Grey's back. 'I envy them. If only someone would do the work for *us.*'

They stood in silence for a while, listening to the wind, growing progressively more damp as the clouds spat down their drizzle. Grey watched the warships out at sea.

She flexed her fingers, checking in on her well, and the gentle pull of the power from the Isle. Now, days into her position as Locke, she understood it further. It was like a mapwork of light inside of her: she could feel the strongest tether, between her and Kier, shining golden and strong; there was another flow of power too, a doorway between her and the Isle.

But something had changed, since time started again. She felt pinpricks within her of all other wells. Before, when she'd reached for someone's power on the battlefield, to rip it away, it had been there when she'd looked for it. Now, she didn't even need to look. She could see the connections, like silvery threads of power, winding from Locke to those who carried its riches.

'I think they expect something impressive of me,' she said quietly.

Ola scoffed. 'You're Locke. You brought back an entire *island*. How much more impressive do you need to be?'

Grey sighed. 'I don't know. And I don't know *how*. I barely have a grip on my own power – I've only been here for a few days. But I have to do something.'

'Like what?' Ola asked. 'Blow up the Isle?'

Grey elbowed her arm. 'I don't know,' she said. 'Bigger than that, even. It seemed like when they presented their choices, there were only two: marry or fight. But what if there's a third choice? One of my own making? One that does not force so many to their deaths?'

'Any ideas? Happy to brainstorm.'

Grey laughed without humor. 'I don't think it's that easy.' She stretched her hands, feeling the power of the Isle running through her. 'Do you remember, in the valley, when we thought we were going to die?'

'How could I forget?' Ola said. 'I would count it among the finest hours of our friendship.'

Grey shifted her weight, the thoughts crystalizing. 'I've been thinking,' she said. 'Back there, I . . . ripped the power away. It hurt, but I did it.'

'It didn't just hurt, Grey. It nearly killed you.'

She inclined her head, allowing that. 'But what if I could do it on a larger scale?'

Ola was quiet for a moment, considering that. 'I think,' she said carefully, 'you would be showing your hand, and demonstrating that you have a control of the power that . . . puts you more at risk.'

'I agree.'

'And if it nearly killed you last time to pull the power from a few dozen wells, I can't imagine the catastrophic disaster to your own body to pull it from *thousands*. Can you even do that, at a distance? How would it work?'

'I don't know.' Grey pressed her lips together. She had known for long enough that it was very possible she'd become a casualty of this war herself. 'I'm not worried about dying,' she lied.

Ola rolled her eyes. 'Well, it makes things a lot easier if you *don't* die,' she said.

'It would save lives. If I could do it.'

'But what if you can't, and you die too?'

Grey shrugged. There was no way around it, and Ola was right: it was possible she could pull that much power, but there was very little chance of her own survival if she did. Besides: 'I think, if I did it. If I pulled the power. I think everyone would hate me. Or fear me, at the very least.' She chewed her lip, her eyes watering in the frigid wind. 'I have no desire to flex my hand and control the nation.'

'Even if it saves lives?' Ola said, flipping her own argument back on her.

Grey had nothing to say to that.

Ola snuggled in closer, stealing Grey's warmth. 'You know how I envy Nestria? Because they get to watch how everything plays out, before they decide?'

'Yes?' She didn't know where Ola was going with this.

'Well, I absolutely, positively do *not* envy you.'

Kier had not warded his door.

It was too soon to make up, and his anger was probably still burning bright like a live coal, but they would be back at war very soon, so she did not have time to give him to cool down.

She thought again of choices yet unmade. There had to be a third option to save the Isle, one that did not guarantee the loss of her freedom or the death of everyone she loved.

But she already had three choices to save Kier's life, or take it, and she did not think she would find a loophole, nor seek another. What she had to do was work within the choices she was given — what she had to do was speak to the only person who knew her at all.

He slept curled on his side, as always, dimly outlined by the embers of the fire dying in the grate. Grey shut his door behind her and took off her boots and crawled into his bed with her damp clothes still on. He woke up instantly, pulling her close out of muscle memory before he remembered his fury. He released her, blinking warily.

'I'm sorry,' Grey said, kneeling in the space next to him. 'You're right. I should have asked you.'

He sat up, rubbing his eyes. The blankets fell to his hips, revealing his bare stomach, his back. 'You should've,' he agreed.

She looked at him unhappily. In six years, they had not gone longer than hours talking to one another, let alone days. 'I don't want to fight anymore,' she said quietly.

He regarded her, seeing past all her protections, as he always did, then nodded, seemingly coming to some decision. She was not yet forgiven, but he was no longer irate.

He hesitated, then took her hand and raised it to his lips. 'Have you slept?' he asked.

'No.'

'You should.'

'This is more important.' She drew a breath. 'Kier, I would give everything in the world for you. Without a second thought.'

He leaned forward, moving his hand from hers to cup her cheek. 'I know you would,' he said solemnly, 'but you do not allow me to do the same.' His thumb skimmed her cheekbone. She turned her head to press a kiss to his palm.

'What is love, without freedom?' she murmured against his skin.

He leaned close to kiss her shoulder, then to whisper in her ear. 'What is life, without you?'

She swallowed down the lump in her throat. She gripped Kier's shoulders, strong and scarred, and pulled him against her. She kissed him hard, fitting her body to his. He was hesitant for the barest second before he rose up to meet her. She worshiped him with lips and teeth and tongue, breaking the kiss only long enough for him to pull her shirt over her head before his mouth was back against hers. She wrestled out of the rest of her damp clothes, fighting to get as close to him as possible.

She could barely think as he flipped them, pressing her back to the bed with his full weight. His hand slipped between her thighs, and she groaned as his teeth found her shoulder; she twisted her hands in his hair and pulled.

'Promise me,' he said as he positioned himself, the weight of his hips pressing hard against hers as he drew her knee up.

'Promise you what?' she gasped, digging her nails in, arching closer as he hesitated the barest distance from burying himself inside of her.

He leaned up onto one elbow so he could see her face. 'Do not give up your power for me,' he murmured, and she felt every muscle in his body still as he waited for her answer.

She ghosted her thumb over the scar on his lip, up over the ridge of his crooked nose, then under his eye. 'I will not give up my power,' she said, the words catching in her throat.

He kissed her, bearing her down into the bed, and there was nothing further left to say.

'Will you tell me how it happened?' he murmured against her skin. His head rested on her breast, her fingers carding through his hair. They both needed to sleep, but she couldn't bear the idea of closing her eyes. 'When I died?'

She swallowed hard, fighting against the instant lump in her throat, but she owed him this. 'What do you want to know?' she asked.

He ran a hand along her side, trailing over her waist, her hip, her thigh. 'I want to know whatever you will tell me. What you *can* tell me.'

She stared up at the ceiling, the shadows of this room as familiar to her as anywhere on this Isle was – which was to say, as familiar as her own heart, and just as painful.

'You deserve to know it all,' she said. So she told him – she told him about how the sea tore them apart, and how she called for her gods. She told him about waking on the shore, and trying to force his heart to beat, and breaking his body in the process. The only reason she finished her sentences was because he grasped her in his arms and whispered, *I'm here, I'm here, I'm here* into her hair, and she felt the steady thrum of his heart under her fingertips, and the healed bones beneath her hands, the echoes of her power still singing inside of his body. She told him about Kitalma and the Ghostwood. Her mother's face. Her father's warning. The shape of his body on the altar.

'Three choices,' Kier repeated once she was finished. 'Three different sacrifices. My freedom. Your power. My life.'

'Yes,' Grey said. They were sitting up now, his back to the head-board, Grey cradled in his arms.

He sighed, pulling her closer. His lips grazed her temple as he said, 'And I don't suppose you would just . . . let me die. Return everything to normal.'

Icy dread pooled in her stomach, and she sent the full force of her grief down the tether. Kier drew a sharp breath, catching the brunt of it, his hands tightening on her arms. 'Don't you dare ask that of me,' she said. 'Don't go making a martyr of yourself. *That* is not a viable option.'

'We might still die tomorrow,' he reminded her.

'Then we'll do it together,' Grey said fiercely. She levered up, turning around, moving a leg over his hip so she was facing him. She cupped his chin, forcing him to look at her. 'I am not choosing an option that guarantees your death, Kier. I have already lost everyone. You cannot ask me to give you up, too. You said—' She broke off, the grief too thick. Kier wrapped her tighter in his arms, but he waited for her to finish.

Grey recovered. 'You said that the only love I know is sacrifice.'

He winced. 'It was not my finest moment.'

'No, maybe not. But perhaps you're right. Everyone I've ever loved has died for me, or tried to. But Kiernan, I want to love you without fearing that you will die, too. I want to love you knowing that I'll wake up in the morning and you'll still be here. That you won't go racing into the next battle to save me, facing the next obstacle without me, because you're trying to protect me.

'We buried my *parents*. My last memory of this place was bring-ing it down, taking Severin's hands in mine and detonating him to save myself. That is the kind of sacrifice love has made for me – that love has made me bear. You saw what it was like down there – what happened. What I *did*. You know that they died for me, that Sev did, that this whole Isle gave up its life so I could survive. I cannot lose you, too. And if that means I will lose my power—'

'No,' Kier said. 'That is not a viable option, either.'

'Kier—'

'Listen to me.' He cupped his hands around her skull, cradling

her head. 'You *are* Locke. The nation – the whole of Idistra – is too
unstable to continue without you being in control. *Totally* in control.
You are too valuable for that kind of sacrifice. I would never ask you
to make it, and if you chose to do it on your own, you would never
find the end of my fury.'

Grey turned her face away.

Softer, he continued, 'Take my freedom, Grey. Everything I have
is yours. Everything I *am* is yours. Take my freedom, and keep your
power, and keep my life. If you are here, I want to live. Even if it
requires haunting this godforsaken rock for the rest of my life, never
being more than an hour's walk from you at any time – because,
honestly, that's how we would be anyways.'

'I can't,' Grey said. 'I can't.'

'You can, and you will,' he insisted. 'It's yours, Gremaryse Locke,
High Lady of the Isle and keeper of my heart, just as I am yours.
Take it. Take it all.'

She couldn't speak. She leaned down, pressing her lips to his, sur-
rendering even as she sent her worry down the tether. 'Win me my
Isle,' she said against his mouth, 'and it is done.'

He pulled back for just a moment, studying her face. Kier, *her*
Kier, with his uneven handsomeness, and the glimmer in his eye,
and that serious line sprouting up between his brows that deepened
with every passing day. What a beautiful thing it was, to watch him
grow older. To watch him live.

'Then it is done,' he agreed, pulling her back down.

'Commander?'

Kier shifted behind her, his skin pressed to hers. He sighed against
her hair and she felt him move, drawing the quilt up to cover her
where it must've slipped in the night.

She opened her eyes to find pale blue magelight filling the room,
deepening the shadows. As her eyes adjusted, she could make out
one of Kier's new squires, already dressed. He was not looking at her,
either out of propriety or because he found the hard lines of Kier's
body far more interesting than hers.

'What is it?' Kier asked, sitting up.

'A boat has been spotted drawing near to the beach, sir. The ships are lowering more. They are shielding, so we cannot tell how many there are. We think they mean to attack before first light.'

'Very well. Thank you, Nahir. Have you told anyone else?'

'You're the first, sir. I went to wake Locke before you . . .' He trailed off, not willing to point out that Locke was here. Grey bit her lip to keep her expression blank.

'Please wake Reggin and Dainridge, if they're not already up. Scaelas, too; and Cleoc for good measure.'

'Yes, sir.'

Kier was out of bed before the squire was fully out of the room. Even though he slept in Grey's room most nights, they'd had the foresight to keep some of his clothes here; he pulled power from Grey and lit the room with a magelight as he quickly dressed.

She sat up, letting the blankets fall. Groggily, she found a sachet of his contraceptive herbs in the table by his bedside and took a measure of them dry. If they survived this, she would have to see Leonie about a more permanent measure.

'Are you going to the war room?'

'Yes,' he said, fastening his trousers. He poured her a glass of water from the ewer on his dresser; she accepted it gratefully. 'Then onwards from there, I suspect.'

She nodded. She would be needed in the war room, too; then Kier would go, and she would stay, and she would feel every single second as an hour.

He came close as if reading her thoughts and dropped next to her on the bed. He cupped her chin in his hand. 'I won't fault you for leaving the fortress, for fighting, if that's what you choose.'

'I haven't decided,' she admitted. Then, 'Are you afraid?'

'Petrified,' he said cheerfully. He rested his forehead against hers. Then, haltingly, he said, 'Locke will not fall again, Grey. I swear it to you: there will be no second death.'

She brushed her knuckles over his cheek, feeling the drag of the stubble on his jaw. 'I trust you,' she said.

He leaned in to kiss her tenderly. There would be no further time for goodbyes, in the war room, in front of the other sovereigns and their military leaders. 'Please don't die again,' she whispered when he broke free.

She felt his smile against her lips. 'And miss my chance to make myself insufferable? I think not.'

He kissed her once more, and then he was gone.

You are not, in any circumstances, to abandon your mage. Without you, they are as good as dead.

Wielding Power, Volume 1: Third Edition, revised PD

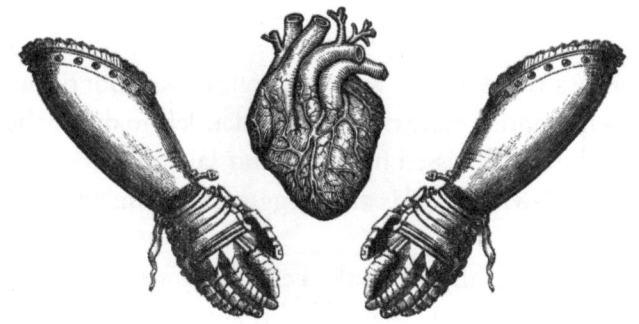

thirty-two

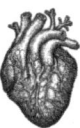

THEY WERE ONLY IN the war room long enough for the lookouts to give their reports before the commanders left to direct their forces. Kier bowed his head, kissed her hand and said a gruff 'My lady,' and then he was following Scaelas and Reggin and Dainridge into battle.

Without her.

Ola and Brit were already in the field. Eron, still injured, had been ordered by Leonie to stay away – and that meant he was assigned to stay with Grey.

She kept a thought on Kier, feeding him power as he moved down the Isle. He sent her a swell of reassurance and love and the promise that he would be back soon.

'Well, Locke,' Cleoc said when the war room was clear of all but her attendants and Eron. She nodded to the padding Grey wore, the same she would wear under her armor. 'Are you going, then?'

Grey chewed her lip. 'Would you think less of me if I told you I still haven't decided?'

Cleoc's sharp look softened. Grey wondered, then, how old Cleoc was: old enough to have Sela, but she didn't know much beyond that. She didn't even know who she had been before she carried her nation's title, or how long she had had it.

Cleoc turned to Eron, offering him her arm. She started out of the room; Eron, confused, went with her, followed by Cleoc's attendants. 'Let me know when you *do* decide,' she said breezily. 'Though it would disappoint my daughter if you died. She is quite taken with you and the commander both.'

Grey stood blinking in surprise. It took her a second to realize why Cleoc had taken Eron with her: Cleoc suspected that he would stop Grey if she did something ill-advised.

She was halfway up the stairs to her room when she felt the tug on the tether. She pushed power at Kier without thought; immediately, she felt the carnage as he began to wield his magic.

She stopped at her rooms only long enough to secure her armor and grab her father's sword and strap it to her hip. Then she was racing to the tower, pushing her way through the door as pinpricks of death continued to erupt all over the Isle. She felt every one like a blow.

Gasping, she grabbed the edge of the crenelation and looked out.

There were hundreds of soldiers on the beaches below Osar. That was what she noticed first: how the fighting congregated there, how she could see the orderly lines of the bodies even from here. There was more fighting in the harbor as boats landed, spilling forces into the town. Just past the harbor, one of Eprain's ships burned with blue fire, downed by one of Cleoc's mages.

She knew, in some distant way, that they'd been prepared for this. That this was exactly what they'd expected. But she also knew the awfulness of battle, and she could not stay here in the fortress while others were dying for her.

No one took any notice of her, in the mess of it. She slipped through the Ghostwood like a wraith, only stopping to drive her father's sword through a Luthrite mage who would've otherwise cut her down. She'd memorized the path Kier was meant to take, and she tried her best to follow it. She was gripped with a sudden, awful fear that he was going to die, and she would be nowhere near him.

She'd been a *fool* to let him go alone.

She felt the tether grow stronger as she drew near the company

Kier led. She almost stumbled over the first of the bodies as she entered the thick of the fighting, the smell of blood and magic and sweat mixing. A Hand captain from Eprain nearly ran her through before she raised her own sword and drove it up through their sternum. She felled three more opponents and took a hit to her side, protected by her armor from anything more than a bruise, before the battle shifted and she spotted Kier. He wielded magic carefully, cutting down a soldier in front of him even as he deflected a blow to his side with a shimmering gold shield; he called something to Brit, who fought to his side with Ola at their back.

All of his castings were gold now, she noticed with a rush of adoration.

She pushed a heavy knot of power at him. His expression shifted, concentration rippling for only one second, and then his eyes were on hers and there was a wicked smile curving across his face.

'Watch my back?' he called.

'Always,' she agreed, fighting her way to his side.

'Welcome to the party, Hand Commander,' Ola grunted, dodging a sword before Brit aimed a spray of metal pellets at the attacker.

Kier pulled another knot of power from her. She felt vital, like she would never run out of the warm, golden power. Even with each quiet explosion within her, she felt more rushing up to replace it.

'How are we doing?' she asked, in the faintest lull.

Kier made a low noise, dodging another hit. 'Not as well as we could be,' he admitted through his teeth. He turned, just enough to catch her eye. 'Grey, I'm glad to see you, but you shouldn't be here.'

Her answering smile was hot as live steel. 'It's a good thing you don't outrank me.'

They pushed back, but it didn't take Grey long to realize that the tide of soldiers from the beach was endless and growing, and their own force of ten thousand was dwindling. With blood leaking from his newly rebroken nose, Kier angrily ordered his regiment to pull back, closer to the Ghostwood.

'Grey,' he said after a while. Her arms were exhausted, every muscle aching with the strain of keeping them alive. She was bleeding from a split lip and a cut across her eyebrow, and she'd lost sight of Ola and Brit. 'We're losing ground. If they push us through the Ghostwood, we'll be cut off from the other regiments.'

Grey swiped the blood out of her eyes with the edge of her surcoat. The horror of war, the blood and the bile, the fear and the hate – it was all hot on her tongue. She couldn't remember why she'd wanted this, why she'd left the fortress at all. She watched as one of the Stratans was disemboweled, falling to his knees as his insides slipped out, slippery and red and purple. The swordsman, a Luthrite Hand, turned toward Grey with murder in his eyes.

She froze. Felt the power rising up within him, this man in front of her, who carried the power of her own nation. She felt it as it slipped down the thread to his mage, fighting a little ways away; felt it as it was directed at her. It glanced off her, because a well could not be harmed by magic, but it didn't matter.

This was the truth of power.

She reached out, felt the power in the snarling well before her and pulled. His face went blank with shock as he reached for his power – and felt nothing.

'Grey!' Kier shouted, feeling the pull and realizing what it meant: his lady was revealed. Grey's brain faltered, realizing that she'd pulled the power with barely a thought, like a reflex, as easily as she fed power to her own mage.

'*LOCKE!*' the soldier shouted, lunging toward her. Kier threw a shield to protect her a half-second too late: the sword bit into her side and pierced her armor. The soldier dragged the blade to the side to do as much damage as possible before Kier's shield caught it, lodged in her flesh. Not even the mostly decorative armor of Kitalma could save her as she looked up at the shocked face of the man before her and saw death staring back. She only barely saw a sword cut him down as she fell to her knees.

It was like time slowed down, her very own dilation.

'Grey.'

Kier caught her as she fell, shielding both of them without a second thought. She pressed a hand to his face, leaving a print in blood behind. Her vision was crowding with dots – behind him, she thought she saw the goddess at the edge of the Ghostwood, surveying the destruction Grey had wrought on her very own Isle.

She felt the deaths, every single one. Perhaps that, too, was what it meant to be Locke: even as she felt her own heart stalling, even as she felt the weight of her soul caught in the balance, she knew the dance of the battle in the pit of her stomach. She felt it in every strong thread of power tethering her soldiers to their mages; she felt it in the broken cords of tethers as Hands lay dead and dying.

They were hers, all of them; she felt every single life on her shores. Some of those lives were familiar, like Kier's in the center; or like Leonie, her well of power waning as she fought to keep Grey's army alive. She felt pain from somewhere close, from someone she loved – Ola's name flickered briefly, like a dying light, before Grey felt herself again unsettled.

She reached for them, those she loved, and there were no words that came back: only a rush of agony, the sear of determination. She felt like she was outside of her body as the lights she held inside of her flickered out one by one, as she felt the power in the Isle tightening and receding.

And above it, all around her, she looked up, and she saw him.

'I'm sorry,' she said. She tasted blood, which meant nothing good for her wound.

'*Grey*,' Kier said, his face wavering in her vision. 'Don't—'

The Isle is not the root of power – it is in the hands of the figure Locke, not the nation. Control the person, you control the power. Kill the ruler – and, well.

Goodbye, power. Goodnight, magic. Farewell to Idistra, and all you once were.

Letter from Wren Locke Teinek to Scaelas, undated

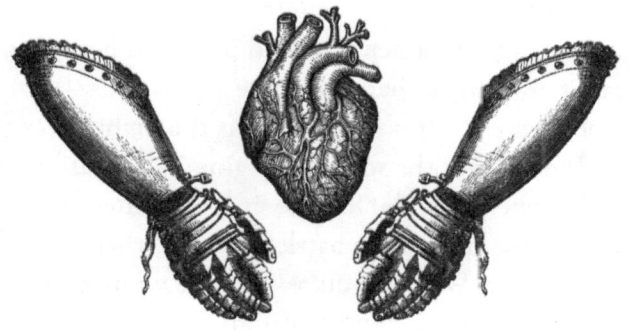

thirty-three

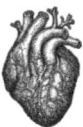

'GREMARYSE.'

Her own name, in the old vowels of the Isle, spoken in its true form – the Scaelan tongue couldn't quite master the vowels and syllables, except for her father, who had practiced her name until he could speak it as neatly as her mother.

She opened her eyes. It was the same as the nightmares she'd had of Severin. Then, it was the screams ringing in her ears as she woke, the smell of smoke; now, she felt the lingering aftershocks of battle as an echo. She was still on the battlefield, still where she had fallen, but it was . . . empty. Well, not quite – an uneasy mist crept through the trees of the Ghostwood in the distance, and the space between her and the wood was criss-crossed with threads of multicolored light. The one nearest and brightest was shimmering gold, so close she could almost grasp the threads in her fingers. So close it was too bright to take in.

Something ached in her stomach. At first, she thought it was her own well, run dry, but that was an impossibility on Locke. She pressed a hand to her side and looked down at it, frowning when it came away dripping in gold.

She closed her eyes against the brightness.

Someone crouched next to her, hands pulling aside her helm, then fingers brushed back her sweat-damp hair. Someone leaned to kiss her forehead, the cold metal of their necklace trailing over her nose. She caught a familiar scent – woodsy and warm, like cloves, with the barest hint of nettlewren, the little purple flowers that grew over the Isle in the summer.

It was her mother's perfume.

When Grey opened her eyes this time, her mother's face hovered above her.

'Ma,' she said. She scanned over her, taking in the dark green velvet of her dress, the necklace she wore around her throat, the intricate braids in her hair. She was dressed the same as she was for her death. 'Locke,' Grey corrected.

Alma looked away. 'Not anymore,' she said, the faintest smile tracing her lips.

Grey looked at the shining threads, at the mist creeping from the Ghostwood. 'Am I dead?' she asked.

'Not quite,' Alma said. Her fingers continued tracing through Grey's hair as if the movement was compulsive, beyond her control. Grey remembered a thousand moments like this, on the edge of falling asleep as her mother told her a story.

Maybe that was what death was like. Maybe this was a mercy, and it would be like falling asleep, safe, in her mother's arms.

'Come here,' Alma said, dispelling the illusion. She reached down to link her hand in Grey's, tugging her to sit up. Grey gasped at the pain in her middle, radiating out. 'I need you to stand, little bird. Can you do that?'

Her breath caught in her throat at her nickname, the one only her parents used for her, too painful to confront in even her memories. She knew, then, that she could not be hallucinating.

'I can try,' she said through gritted teeth. She let her mother pull her, both of them shining with that odd gold. At first, Grey thought it was power, since it was coming from her stomach, but with this much pain, it could only be blood. In this version of time, her blood shone gold as the magic emanating from that figure in front of her, who could only be Kier.

'What is this?' she asked when she was standing, holding tight to her mother's arm to stay upright. Alma turned them toward the Ghostwood, leading Grey through short, stuttering steps.

'You only received half of your inheritance,' she said. 'I died before I could show you the rest.'

Grey looked at her sideways. Alma walked with her head held high, but she was fuzzy at the edges, half remembered, half constructed. Grey recalled trying to touch her in the Ghostwood, when she'd bargained for Kier's life, and how her hand had gone right through her.

It could not bode well, now, that she could walk by her side, using the ghost for support.

'What is it?' Grey asked.

Alma waved a hand broadly, showing her the threads. 'Do you see it?'

'The lights?'

'Yes. That,' she said, not slowing, 'is our power. That is who we are and what we are, as Locke. There has long been the truth known that whoever we marry and bind to, we bestow power upon that nation in a show of favor and gratitude. But it is also true that we can take power away, just as easily.' She stopped next to a knot of the threads, shining dimly in technicolor. Reaching forward, she ran her finger along one of them. 'As the High Lady, Maryse, you are not just the channel for power. You are the root of it. You can do with it what you will – you can bestow it upon whom you wish, and you can remove it from whom you wish.'

Grey sucked a breath through her teeth. 'So I can take the power from Epras and Luthos.'

Alma looked at her, her gray eyes solemn. 'You can take the power from *Eprain* and *Luthar*, Gremaryse. All of it.'

'But that's—'

'Awful? Treacherous? Unfair?' Alma laughed, short and harsh. She resumed walking, Grey struggling to keep up with her. They passed through the first trees of the Ghostwood, into the mist. 'So is dying, love.'

'I can't do that,' Grey said. 'Tactically, maybe it buys us time, but realistically, it's a nightmare for—'

'It can be temporary,' Alma said. 'Take it. Get what you want. Give it back.' She turned, gripping Grey's hands in both of hers, her gaze as fierce as Grey had ever seen it. '*Live*, little bird. It's all we've ever wanted for you.'

Grey drew a breath. They were nearly to the cemetery in the Ghostwood, nearly to the old temple. She let Alma lead her through the graves to the altar, the same one she had seen Kier's body on as she'd bargained with the goddess.

'Reach for it,' Alma said.

Grey felt for those thin strands of light. She felt, very keenly, the threads of magic tangled in a web over her isle, the tethers held and caught and lost and dropped, the snuffed-out deaths of wells firing all over. She felt them on the sea, in their boats; she felt them far, far away, across Scaela and Luthar and even Nestria, as far as her power could reach. She felt each and every one, the hearts and fear and joy and love and hate of thousands and thousands, all touched by her power.

How many of them had died for her? How many were yet to perish?

Ruthlessness, Sela had reminded her, was its own kind of safety.

Grey swallowed, tasting blood in her mouth. She had the feeling her time here was winding down, and she needed to come to some decision – a decision that would save Kier, and maybe the other people she loved. Maybe even herself. Too slow, her hand came to her side, pressed to the place the sword had been drawn out, as if she could hold her life inside that wound.

'Okay,' she agreed. 'Show me how to do it.'

Alma led her to the altar. She helped her onto it, helped her lie down – even in this in-between, she must've been worried about Grey's strength failing – and clutched her hand. She taught her how to reach with her power, how to sense the allegiances, how to read the intentions in each of those threads en masse.

'And now,' she said, when Grey had them all. 'Now, you take it all back.'

Grey felt the tethers in her stomach, the thousands and thousands of them belonging to those who fought for her death, and she snapped them all at once. It was oddly easy to separate them, those who had clamored to her shores to bring her down – easy as if she was looking at a map of multicolored forces, like the ones Kier presided over in her war rooms. She took the power, all those thousands and thousands of threads, and she *pulled*. They clung to her, a cauterized wound.

She gasped, arching at the pain of it. Alma's hands were there to catch her, to soothe her, as she screamed at the agony of it all rushing back.

When she could feel again, when she could see past the pain, she was lying flat on the altar slab with her mother standing over her grim-faced. 'It's done,' Grey said, her voice hoarse from screaming. 'And now?'

'You have a choice,' Alma said.

Grey closed her eyes. She was growing quite tired of choices. 'Go on,' she murmured.

Alma reached forward with a kerchief, swiping the blood away from Grey's forehead. 'You could come with me,' she said softly. 'You could stay with us.'

Grey didn't trust the softness. Her mother had been many things, but she had rarely been soft. She caught Alma's hand, lacing their fingers together. Alma squeezed as tight as could be, as tightly as Severin had held her on the night he gave his life for hers.

Grey opened her eyes. 'You don't want that,' she said.

'Part of me does,' Alma replied. 'No one else knows what it is, to be Locke. The weight of all that power, of all those choices – you could give it up. Set it aside. Let those fools reap the consequences of what they did to us – what they're still doing to you. Aren't you *tired*, Maryse?'

She *was* tired. She was exhausted, actually. Tired of running, of fighting, of sacrificing.

'There is another who could carry the line, thanks to your devotion,' Alma said, her gaze on Grey's face. 'Leave him the Isle. Leave him his life. Come with me and rest.'

Kier. Grey chewed her lip, looking away. 'And my other options?'

'Go back and face your fate – but I cannot guarantee you will survive it.'

She closed her eyes. That was it, wasn't it? If she was here, she was already on the edge of death. What her mother offered her wasn't a kindness, but rather an illusion of choice. 'I'm as good as dead already,' she guessed.

'Unless you have a very talented healer and a lot of luck,' Alma said softly, 'then yes.'

'And the battle?'

She looked away. 'I don't know,' she said. 'I can only hope it is enough, what you have done. If you go back, you are not returning to any guarantee of victory, or peace.'

Grey nodded, taking this in. 'Were you afraid? When it was over?'

'Of course I was,' Alma said. 'But being afraid is better than being hopeless.'

'And will it hurt? If I go back?'

Alma smoothed her thumbs over Grey's hands. 'Of course it will,' she said. 'Living always will.'

Grey swallowed hard, battling past the pain. 'And dying?'

'That's its own kind of pain,' Alma said. 'And its own kind of peace.'

Grey looked at her mother, at the coolness of her eyes and the lines of her face. She, too, looked older than her years – and Grey wondered what it would be like to look in a mirror and see *this* version of Alma staring back at her. To grow older all on her own.

She brought Kier back, didn't she? What a terrible thing it would be, to bring him back only to leave him to mourn her. To abandon him. To condemn him to stand before Kitalma at the full moon and declare the choice as if it had been his own. Or perhaps her sacrifice would save him entirely.

But perhaps it wouldn't – and perhaps she was tired of making decisions without him.

And after all, she did have a very talented healer.

Grey leaned down. Kissed the back of Alma's hand, leaving a smear of golden blood on her skin. 'I wish I had grown to know you better.'

'I wish I had lived to see you grow,' Alma responded.

Grey lay back on the altar. Alma got up, going around to her head, combing her fingers through Grey's hair. She moved Grey's hands, folded them over her chest, like a body prepared for the tomb.

She leaned down and pressed her lips to Grey's forehead once more. 'Goodbye, Locke,' she said. '*Wake up.*'

I have a difficult time with the balance of it all: as Locke, it is my decision who gets power, and who does not. As Alma, I would like to bless those I like, but that is not always fair, is it? I don't know if there is an answer. I don't know if fairness should factor into it at all. But perhaps it should not all be based on my own thoughts and whims.

I hope, when I pass this title on, my child has a better idea of it. So far, I feel as if I am just making more of a mess.

Letter from Alma, High Lady of Locke, to Wren Locke Teinek, her sister, 18 years AD

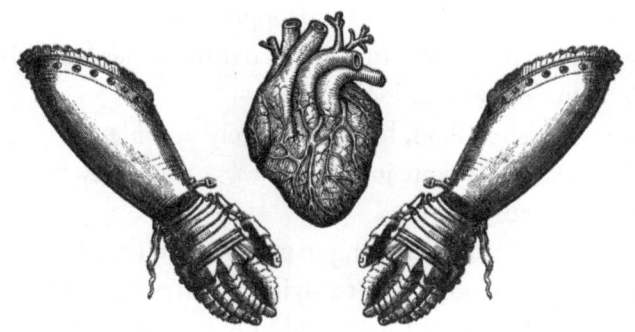

thirty-four

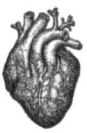

'Grey.'

Her name again, this time on Kier's lips. She felt the pain first, the blaring agony of it; then the wet heat of her blood. Something seemed to be shifting inside of her, something that shouldn't have been moving in the first place.

She heard the clatter of his helm dropping to stone, then his sword. 'Grey,' he said again, the warmth of his palms on her face. She forced herself to open her eyes, to look at him.

'Did we win?' she asked, her voice barely audible.

'You disappeared – you just *vanished* – the wells from Eprain, Luthar, some of our own . . .'

'Kiernan,' Grey said, struggling to get through this. He was already wrapping his arms around her, readying to carry her back to Leonie, to safety, to a world of pain she could only imagine. *'Did it work?'*

He pressed his lips together. 'It worked,' he said. 'Whatever you did, it worked. They're retreating as we speak, and we're rounding up prisoners on the beach.' He glanced down at her – she felt him moving below her, walking as fast as he could to get her back to the fortress without disrupting her wounds too much. She let her head lean, the leather of his pauldron soft, though a bit blood-soaked.

'It worked,' she sighed, letting her eyes slip shut.

'And if it worked at the cost of your life,' he said through his teeth, 'I will not forgive you. I thought you said you weren't going to sacrifice—'

'I'll live,' Grey mumbled against his shoulder, 'just to spite you. There's nothing I love more than proving you wrong.'

He laughed, but there was an edge of panic to it. 'Then *live*, Locke,' he pleaded. He said more, but no matter how much Grey desperately wanted to hear it, it wasn't enough. She slipped, and this time, nothing caught her when she fell into the darkness.

She woke in her own bed.

She sat up and immediately regretted it, gasping at the starburst of pain that erupted from her middle. Hands were on her shoulders in an instant, pushing her down. 'Stay down, Locke,' Leonie said above her.

As usual, Grey didn't listen. She winced as she propped herself on her elbows. She wore a loose shirt, and underneath, she could see the bandages that wrapped her middle. Every part of her ached.

Leonie was alone in the room with her, sorting medication on a table someone must've dragged in from Grey's private sitting room. She ran her fingers over one of the pestles and asked, 'Are you in pain?'

'Manageable,' Grey lied. 'Water?'

Leonie was there in an instant with a glass, one hand behind Grey's back to help her up, the other holding the glass so she could drink. Grey sipped greedily, spilling half of it down her shirt and barely caring. When she was finished, Leonie brought her another glass and set it on the nightstand, before sinking into the chair by Grey's bedside. 'The commander is going to be furious he wasn't here when you woke,' she said, brushing the hair away from Grey's forehead. Grey could see the end of her own braid draped over her chest; she was unsurprised to see bits of gore and mud in the brown strands.

'Where is he?' she asked hoarsely. Leonie leaned forward to adjust her pillows, helping her sit more comfortably.

'Dainridge sent for him. It couldn't wait.'

Grey nodded, the press of too many questions on her tongue. She remembered herself floating, untethered from her body – she felt the sum of all those souls. 'I took the power away,' she said slowly. 'Didn't I?'

Leonie hesitated.

'If you don't answer, I'll ask Kier, and I'm certain *he* will.'

'Then yes. You took the power away. From all of Eprain and Luthar, it looks like.'

Grey nodded, chewing her lip.

'And they still don't have it back.'

She pressed a hand to her middle, where the stomach ache throbbed. 'Right.'

'Can you . . . ?'

She shot Leonie a look. 'Yes,' she said, feeling the weight, and the phantom tethers leading to the owners of the power she now held. 'But this is something that I only want to do once, and as such, I would *like* it to be an effective threat.'

Leonie nodded slowly. 'That is . . . '

'Ruthless,' Grey said.

'But sensible.'

'Perhaps.' She glanced at Leonie, remembering the stress radiating off her in battle. 'But . . . we won.'

'Yes,' Leonie said. She set down the tincture she was mixing – probably something awful she was going to force Grey to drink sooner rather than later. 'The Isle was defended. And because of the total loss of power and magic with it, there have been appeals for peace. For treaties.'

Grey couldn't begin to think of peace or treaties. She couldn't think of anything past the next few seconds. She let her eyes slip shut for only a moment, but she couldn't be sure it was actually a moment when she opened them again. 'And the damage?'

'We lost two thousand of our ten thousand. Eprain and Luthar lost four and a half, but they sent more, and Cleoc's navy did major damage in the bay.'

So many lives lost, all because of her. She could not focus on that – if she did, she would lose it, and she could not afford to do that right now. 'And . . . Scaelas? Our allies? My friends?'

'I hear Cleoc and her attendants had a lovely afternoon,' Leonie said wryly. 'Eron is fine – he's with Kier. Scaelas is injured, but he will live. He has threatened to stay with you until he is healed, though, and teach you how to act like a noble.'

Grey winced. He must've heard that she'd joined the battle – but he was still not her father. 'A fine threat indeed,' she said.

'Brit is fine. Ola is . . .' Leonie hesitated, and Grey saw the flicker of uncertainty – her stomach seized at the thought. In an awful moment, she remembered that grasp of pain, when she was out of herself, but then . . . 'She'll live, if I have anything to say about it,' Leonie said finally, seeing Grey's look. 'She will lose the arm.'

'Ah.' But she was alive. She was alive, and she would live. As soon as she was able to stand, Grey would find her, even if she had to fight Kier and Leonie both to do it. 'And our commanders?'

'Dainridge sustained minor injuries. Commander Reggin perished protecting the harbor.'

Grey closed her eyes. 'And his Hand?'

'Living, last I knew.'

'And Seward is fine,' Kier said, coming in, nodding to Leonie with some coldness – he still had not quite forgotten that she knew of his death, Grey realized. 'Though he *is* annoyed, as he gave direct orders to be sent for immediately if Locke woke in his absence.'

Leonie rolled her eyes. 'Oh, shut up, Kier. I was going to send for you as soon as I answered Locke's questions.'

He sighed, but his shoulders relaxed. He perched on the side of Grey's bed, resting a hand on her knee over the covers. 'I see that you have viscera in your hair again.'

Grey managed a smile. 'You're the one who wanted a lifetime of washing blood from my person.'

Leonie got up, gathering her things. 'You two have the *weirdest* relationship.'

Neither denied it.

When her bag was packed, she said, 'Seward, I expect you to keep her in bed – not like that, you deviant. Cleoc and Scaelas will want to see her, but Scaelas is also forbidden from moving, so Cleoc will have to manage going between their sickbeds one at a time. And I swear to you, Grey, I do not care if you are my High Lady – I will not hesitate to maim you if you pull out your stitches.'

Grey raised an eyebrow. She was more used to Kier being on the receiving end of Leonie's threats. 'Right you are,' she said.

As soon as Leonie left, Grey sighed. She pressed a hand to her stomach, assessing. 'How bad was it?'

Kier winced. 'Bad.'

'Run through?'

'Edge of death, Flynn.' He kept his voice light, but he still gripped her knee with a fear that she understood. She was usually the one feeling that fear for *his* life.

'Mm.' She swung her legs over the bed, gasping at the rush of pain. Kier was there in an instant, his hands fluttering, searching for somewhere to push her back down that would not hurt. 'What are you doing?'

'The Isle won't run itself,' Grey said, wincing in pain.

He settled for her shoulder, grasping it and pushing her carefully down to the pillows. She sucked in a breath at the pain, and he pulled back immediately, as if burned. 'I'll call Leonie back,' he threatened.

'Kier . . .'

'I'll get you Cleoc and Ikaaron,' Kier said, stepping back, 'so you can at least feel useful. But so help me, gods, I *will* put Eron in charge of feeding you until you are better if you try to leave this room.'

Grey narrowed her eyes. 'You wouldn't.'

'Don't try me, Locke,' he said on his way out.

The combined efforts of Kier and Leonie only managed to keep her in bed for two days before Grey rose in the middle of the night, slipped away as Kier slept and crept downstairs and into her office. Scaelas's guards saw her as she passed, but they only sighed and shook their heads – their own High Lord had performed a similar maneuver in the hour before, and he hadn't even had to sneak past a commander in his bed.

She'd only been behind her desk for half an hour before a soft knock sounded on her door. She looked up as the High Lord slipped inside, limping heavily, favoring his right side.

'You too?' she asked, brow raised.

He nodded, taking the chair across the desk. 'That medic of yours is ...' he trailed off, searching for a word that fit before he settled on 'persistent.'

'She's *your* medic,' Grey said, turning her attention back to one of Cleoc's treaty amendments. 'Leonie is Scaelan.'

Torrin sighed. 'Ah, I don't think so. Not anymore.'

Grey's eyes flicked to his. 'I can't steal all your best soldiers.'

'You should have people here you trust, Maryse,' he said softly.

She set the amendments aside, chewing on her lip. 'We should get Cleoc,' she said darkly. 'Since they won't let us meet otherwise.'

Scaelas quirked a brow. 'I can send for her, if you want.'

'I don't know what I want.' She sat back in her chair, trying not to wince as her stitches tugged. 'I don't know how to reward anyone. How to thank anyone. How to make up for the lives lost, or the power I've taken.' She rubbed her brow, wishing she could find the answers on the backs of her eyelids.

'Ah. Epras and Luthos grow restless.'

'They've asked for treaties. For peace. For alliances.'

'Then you are in a privileged position. You have the power to end all conflict in Idistra, if you so choose.'

Grey couldn't fathom that kind of responsibility. But there was a question that came before that of peace. 'Do you think I should give them their power back?'

Torrin hesitated. 'You should not ask me that, Maryse. I am not your ally on paper yet; I have the interests of my own nation to keep in mind. And my own nation has been at war with both of them for a long, long time.'

'What would Cleoc say?'

He scoffed. 'The same, probably; but I suspect she would put half of them to death, just to even the score.'

Grey didn't want to put anyone to death. 'Then I will ask you as my godfather,' she said, peeking at him sideways.

He sat in silence for a moment. The candles on her desk flickered dimly; she wished she'd lit the fire on the way in, but she hadn't wanted to alert too many people to the fact she was awake and working.

'I think,' he said slowly, 'that you have proven your point. That your power has been sufficiently flexed.'

She nodded. It was what she had thought too, lying awake in her bed, staring at the ceiling. 'I don't want to be feared,' she said. 'Just . . . respected.'

Torrin sighed. 'Bring us peace, Locke, and you might find yourself beloved.'

She managed a smile. 'If you want me to do that,' she said, 'I fear we must wake Cleoc.'

They had a treaty by dawn. Peace terms were delivered to Eprain and Luthar by evening, and to Nestria the following day; within a week, all six nations had reached an uneasy agreement. Two weeks after the restoration of Locke, the wells of Eprain and Luthar woke to find their power restored and strengthened, as if nothing had changed at all.

The pyres burned for days on the coasts of Idistra as the dead were returned home. Despite the growing chill of winter, when she couldn't sleep, Grey spent a few hours of the night on the roof of the fortress, watching the smoke, letting the horror settle and wane. Most times, she was not alone in her grief. She was joined by Ola, who tried to understand the new shape of her body; by Brit or Eron, who were happy to talk or let her be silent as her moods changed; and sometimes by Kier, who was content to just stand by her side.

On Locke, a new life was beginning. It was agreed that anyone who'd defended the Isle would be welcomed with open arms, if they chose to stay: nearly two thousand soldiers and their families relocated there. The High Lady of Locke held a reception in one of the old market halls near the port every morning, greeting her new countrymen as one of their clerks recorded the newcomers in the census.

In the weeks that followed, she fell into a new routine. In the mornings, she woke with the dawn and sat with Ola in her room until she was well enough to fight; then, they met in one of the private courtyards at the back of the fortress. They sparred, Ola straining with the effort as she learned to fight with her left hand instead of her right. After Grey had bathed, she went to the harbor; then, in the early afternoon, she met with her ambassadors and continued to establish her council. Some days she had tutors in to try to fill the gaps in the knowledge she otherwise would've had as High Lady. She spent the rest of the day in appointments, or going between her office and the one next to hers, where her commander worked. If her advisers were wary of the fact that Locke's commander knew every bit of business that came across their lady's desk, they had the sense not to protest it to her.

She was in her office, signing off on supply requests, when Cleoc and her attendants came to the door. Grey stood immediately, no longer wincing; her stitches had been pulled out a few days before, and Leonie had given her a clean bill of health.

'I think it's time for me to take leave of you, Locke,' Cleoc said, inclining her head.

Grey stayed standing; after all this time, she did not know what to say. 'I can't even think how to thank you,' she said finally.

The edges of Cleoc's severe mouth turned up in a smile. 'You owe me nothing,' she said.

Grey moved around the desk to grasp the woman's hand. She was surprised when Cleoc pulled her into a tight, fierce hug.

'I will never forget,' she said, 'what you did for my girl.'

Grey closed her eyes, letting herself lean into the embrace. The business with Sela felt like a lifetime ago.

When Cleoc pulled away, she pressed something into Grey's hand. Grey looked down to find the small obsidian moon from their first meeting in Scaela resting in the middle of her palm. 'I thought it was lost,' she said.

'Be safe, Locke,' Cleoc said, leaning in to kiss her quickly on the forehead. 'I will be waiting for your letters.'

As the first month of peace drew to a close, there were plans for a great feast on the Isle to celebrate its successful resurrection. Grey found it a welcome distraction; she was trying very hard not to watch every change of the moon as the days leading up to her next meeting with Kitalma slipped by.

Ola told her excitedly of the preparations happening in Osar, led by an overambitious ex-captain from Cleoc's army; the same evening, Brit and Eron separately complained to Grey about how Ola was annoyingly and unexpectedly in love with an overambitious ex-captain from Cleoc's army.

Later, in bed, Kier asked if she'd heard of the preparations. It was a rare night in which they'd both gone to their rooms before the early hours of the morning (only for Kier to slip into hers very shortly after); with her responsibilities as Locke and his efforts to stabilize their new home, they barely had time alone.

'They were mentioned to me,' she said.

'And your thoughts?'

She kissed his chest, then bit gently at his ribs. He had only recently stopped treating her as if she was made of glass, and now he kept his dark eyes on her as she slipped lower. 'If there's a party, not a single person on this Isle will need us. We could make our own plans.'

'They'll notice if you're not there,' he murmured, eyes slipping shut as she kissed his hip. 'It's *your* resurrection.'

'I don't care,' Grey said, before demonstrating exactly what they could be doing instead.

Grey sat in the chair in her office and watched the sea below her window. Her desk was piled with correspondence. At least two messages bore Imarta's careful handwriting – she was due to arrive from Scaela when the Isle was safer, for the feast that Kier insisted Grey couldn't skip.

The door to her office opened. She turned, expecting one of her new cooks with questions about dinner, or Eron with a note about supplies needed for the armory, or Leonie asking for more medical provisions. But it was Kier, dressed simply, smelling of rain. He'd just come in from the cold – he was negotiating the delicate process of rebuilding the shield and setting up a static warning system that couldn't be disrupted by breakbloom. He found it easiest to do this alone, in the ruins of the abbey to Kitalma on the edge of the Ghostwood. Grey did not examine the complicated feelings she had every day when he went there.

One more day, and then she would need to go to the wood herself and declare her choice to the goddess. One more day before Kier was no longer a free man.

He, too, had his nose buried in correspondence, and more stacked on the table he'd dragged next to her desk the week before. Though his own office was next door, he'd spent so long hunched over her shoulder or sitting on her floor as they discussed what to do, she'd just given him a space in here permanently.

It was better this way, when they could be in the same room.

'Ma wrote,' he murmured, perching on the arm of her chair. She kissed the bend of his elbow, more out of habit than anything else, though the desperate appeal of regular physical affection was not lost on her. 'There was a well born, in Scaela.'

'We can't verify it,' Grey said, leaning forward to read over his arm. 'It's difficult to detect aptitude in a baby.'

'Difficult,' Kier agreed, 'but not impossible.'

'And it's only rumor until we hear it from Scaelas.'

'Who should probably return to his own nation,' Kier said darkly. He folded his letter and tossed it onto Grey's desk. 'What are you reading?'

She sighed, waving the paper in his direction. 'Requests from our new Nestrian ambassador, ahead of their arrival. It's tedious business. Hurts my head.'

'They don't think enough of the state of your head,' Kier agreed, bending low and somewhat awkwardly to kiss the top of the afore-mentioned oft-neglected subject.

'Sela wrote too. She wants to hold a unity ball in Cleoc,' Grey said.

'Ah.' The sound came from low in Kier's throat. She felt the immediate stiffness in every line of his body. 'In Cleoc?'

'Yes. But the letter came from Sela and not her mother, so.' She sat back in her chair, twisting the signet ring on her finger. 'A large party, full of nobility who were our enemies only weeks ago . . . it sounds like an invitation for an assassination attempt. I've written back that we are, possibly, not quite stable enough for that yet.'

'Diplomatic to the last,' Kier said, his breath ruffling her hair.

She tugged his arm and pulled him down with her. With a bit of reconfiguring, he'd slipped under her and lifted her into his lap. His arms wrapped around her, safe and strong as always. She watched the movement of the sea through the window over his shoulder, the crash of the waves against the cliffs below, the rising of the tide.

'We've received further petitions for citizenship,' he murmured against her collarbone. 'It would be worth figuring out how to go about that.'

'It would be,' Grey said. Though she wanted to close off the Isle, to keep those already here, those she loved, close to her, she knew the error in that: Locke's isolation had led to so much fear and betrayal before. She could not allow it to happen again.

A knock sounded on the door. Grey made to move, but Kier's arms did not release her. It was inappropriate, perhaps, for the Lady of Locke to be found in the arms of the nation's commander, but the follow-up thought to that was that anyone who'd gotten past the guards at her door (which she protested, but both Kier and Scaelas vehemently agreed she should keep them; Kier and Torrin rarely agreed, but when it came to matters of her safety, they were a force to be reckoned with) was already quite aware of their relationship.

'Yes?' she called, shifting to be slightly less entwined.

It was Leonie, bustling in with a list of provisions needed, Brit on her heels. 'It's not an easy task, rebuilding a hospital,' she said, all business, even as her eyebrow raised and her lips quirked at the sight of them.

Brit threw themself in the chair in front of the fireplace. At Grey's look, they waved a hand. 'Ola's with her captain again,' they said darkly.

Now Grey did push up to take the list from Leonie. She skimmed over it, chewing on her thumbnail as she focused. 'I'll pass it to Ikaaron. See if Scaela can help.'

'And in return? You're going to be drowning in favors by the year's end,' Kier said. His eyes were shut, his arms spread on the arms of the chair, like he was waiting for the moment she sat again so he could wrap them around her.

'I don't think sixteen years of reparations have been paid back to us just yet,' Grey said mildly. She put the list on her desk and started to copy it down.

'Also,' Leonie said, 'I have cleared Scaelas for travel. He can leave as soon as he wishes.'

Grey ignored Kier's sigh of relief. 'Is he going, then?'

'Soon. Tomorrow, probably.'

Grey straightened slowly, her thoughts a jumble. Though Torrin's presence made Kier antsy – she knew, though he didn't admit it to her, that even though it was their fault that Torrin had given up his search for his god-daughter, Kier resented him for it simply because it had hurt her feelings – she would be sad to lose his guidance.

'You can go with him if you want,' she said.

Brit and Leonie only blinked at her. Finally, Brit said, 'What?'

Grey paced, struck with new conviction. 'You don't have to stay if you don't want to. Eron and Ola, too. You're Scaelan – I don't want to force you to be here.'

'We're all here because we want to be here,' Leonie said firmly.

'Speak for yourself,' Kier said, but he was ignored. Grey shot him a dark glare.

'What even are we?' Brit mused. 'Lockians? Lockstrian? Keys?'

'*Brit*,' Leonie murmured, rubbing her temple.

They waved a hand. 'And you can ask them, but Ol and Er will tell you the exact same thing. We're staying, Grey. If it means Scaelas has to sell you our contracts, then so be it. But we're staying.'

She hesitated, still uncertain. She wondered when, if ever, the worst of the uncertainty would fade.

'But you should pay me,' Brit said. 'Just saying.'

Grey sighed, and made a note to herself to review her own treasury, and to have a discussion about salaries with her commander.

In the evening, she and Scaelas dined alone. He imparted as much wisdom as he could to her, but in the end, he just kissed both of her hands and said, 'Obsidian born and iron made, Maryse. Gods, they would have been proud of you.'

It took her a long time to swallow the lump of sorrow in her throat.

After dinner, she dressed in a nondescript outfit of black trousers, a blue tunic and a heavy cloak, slipped past her guard and set off for one of the newly reopened pubs in Osar. There was a woman waiting for her in a shadowy back corner, sipping ale, with a frosty second glass waiting at the empty seat. She'd arrived earlier on the ship that came to take Scaelas away and had sent word through Eron.

'Master Attis,' Grey said, slipping into the other side of the booth. 'I'm glad you could get away.'

Attis studied her. The space under her eyes was dark and shadowed, as with grief. She opened her mouth to speak, swallowed and looked away. 'I just want to know,' she said, 'that she wasn't alone.'

Grey shook her head. 'She was not.'

Attis's eyes slipped shut. She took a long breath, held it, then another. She was trying very hard, Grey could tell, not to cry.

'Will you tell me how it happened?' she asked.

Grey nodded. Though there had been so much horror, so much terror, it was the least she could do to put Mare to rest.

She was too lost in memories to go to bed, so she went to her tower, where the winter wind whipped her hair. She did not look out to sea, but to the harbor, where the ship was being prepared to take Torrin back. She was turning to scan the sea when she noticed a small, dimly golden magelight glowing on one of the cliffs. She squinted down at it.

There was a path that went all the way down the cliffs; when she was a girl, Grey was told it was to receive shipwrecks or retrieve bodies. She and Sev had used it for crabbing. There was a deep ledge halfway down, shielded from view from all but those on this very tower. It was about the size of Grey's courtyard. Sometimes, when she was younger, she and her father used to sit there to watch the storms roll away from the Isle, protected from the weather with the cliff at their backs.

There, one could sit very quietly, unseen, and look out at the shores of Scaela in the distance, without judgment.

It took her twenty minutes to get down, but Kier was still there when she reached the ledge. He sat with his knees tucked to his chest, his arms around them. She hesitated when she saw that his cheeks were wet.

'You can join me,' he said gruffly – of course he'd known that she was there.

She stepped carefully and lowered herself to the ground next to him. His magelight glowed dim and golden; his magelights were always golden now.

She did not ask. After an immeasurable moment, the sea crashing on the cliffs below, Kier said, 'I was just thinking that I would never see Lot's grave again, or the tree behind our house, or the village square, or that awful yellow kitchen.'

Grey stayed still as a stone, the grief like a vise on her heart.

'I will never go to Lindan, to see what their magic is like, or Nisielle, or even Nestria,' he said slowly, 'or anywhere at all.'

'No,' she said slowly, swallowing down her own tears. He was silent for a long moment. The wind whipped his too-long hair.

'You're not going to try to run?' Grey asked.

He snorted. 'I'm dead the second I leave the Isle, Grey, and your gods won't give my life back twice.'

She chewed her lip. They had not spoken much of the decision since that night, before the battle; any time she brought it up, Kier just sighed and told her again that they were choosing the only viable option. It was not a small thing, to give up his freedom – and though they both knew why the choice had to be made, it hurt her deeply. 'What if you get tired of me?' she asked.

'I won't,' he said, his voice softening.

'But what if you *do*?'

He sighed, long-suffering. 'Then I'll die, I guess. Or you can go away and leave the Isle to me.'

'You'll never have space away from me.'

She saw the flicker of the curve of his smile, disrupted by his scar. 'A burden, to be sure, but I will bear it.'

'I'm serious.'

'As am I, Grey.' He shifted, folding around her, bringing her to sit between his legs with her back to his chest. He wrapped his arms around her; it was much warmer buried with him in his heavy cloak. 'You've already fought death and your gods for me. I would do the same for you, though let us hope it doesn't come to that.'

She was quiet for a long moment. It wasn't fair at all, what he was doing, what she was making him do. But perhaps love was a little bit of sacrifice, after all; and perhaps a bit of sacrifice could be allowed, as long as they were together.

'Kier,' she said.

'Yes?'

She found herself suddenly without words. So she gripped the tether, pushing as many warm feelings of thanks and love and adoration at him as she could. She heard his sharp indrawn breath; then he was burying his face in her hair, his lips pressing to the crown of her head, then her temple, then her neck. *I love you. At the end of it all, I love you*, she thought at him with every emotion she showed him.

'As do I,' he promised.

You would like him, I think. He would sacrifice the world for her – I suppose we all would, in the end.

Journal entry from Vearn Torrin, High Lord of Scaela, addressed to Isaak Masidic Locke, in memoriam, after the resurrection of the Isle

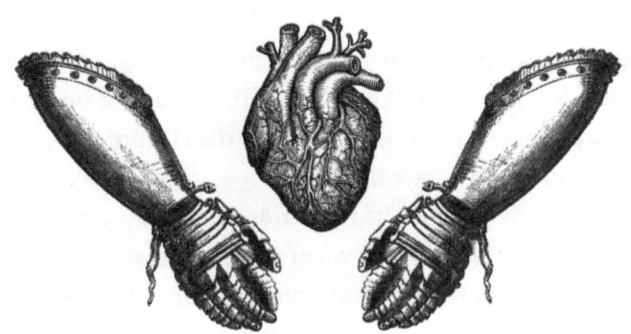

thirty-five

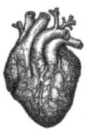

THE WIND WHIPPED THROUGH the Ghostwood, screaming in the trees. It was a sound Grey knew as well as the beat of her own heart: so many years, she'd tried to recall the timbre of it, to recollect the background noise of her childhood.

She wore a heavy cloak, fastened at the throat, with the hood pulled up to obscure her face. It wasn't often that people came to pray at this abandoned altar, but if anyone did, she did not want them reporting that the Lady of Locke and her commander had been seen here in the dead of night.

'Stop fidgeting,' Kier said to her. 'You're making me anxious.'

She was only shifting her weight from foot to foot, standing before the moonlit altar, but she tried to school her body into obedience.

'Are you not afraid at all?'

Kier grimaced. 'If I think about it, it means acknowledging the fact that I might anger your god, who holds my life in her hands. So really, I'm trying to avoid thinking about it at all.'

He was kidding, but the truth of it made Grey's stomach feel like it was full of heavy stones. She reached out, crossing the gap between them to take his hand. 'She made no mention of your behavior factoring into the deal,' she said, trying to keep her tone light. 'Which is good, for obvious reasons.'

Kier didn't answer. He was looking straight ahead, at the altar. It looked more like a tomb – and Grey suspected it was, the stone container the final resting place for Kitalma's bones. She wondered if Retarik was laid there as well, or if she really was interred in her own ruined abbey across the Isle. If the gods had been separated in death, by some mortal's choice.

Kitalma's temple had fallen into disrepair too. The wall behind the altar, which once held thick glass windows, had half crumbled into the sea at some point during the reign of one of Grey's ancestors. Now, they looked at the roaring waves and the spray that kicked up as the waves crashed against the cliffs. It was a rare clear night, and the moon shone over the sea, casting Kier's face in shadowed silver.

'It's not too late,' she said, 'to change your mind.'

He looked at her askance. 'You can't get rid of me that easily.'

Before she could respond, the air in front of them shifted, shimmered – and then Kitalma was there, standing before the altar, where before there had only been moonlight. She wore her simple dress and armor, a medallion hanging from a chain around her neck. She was just as Grey remembered her: a fierce warrior goddess, a queen in her own right. A reckoning.

'Oh,' Kier said, his voice soft – as if, even knowing what he knew, he did not fully believe in the goddess himself.

'Daughter of Locke,' Kitalma said, turning her face to Grey. She looked at Kier, her expression unchanging. 'Boy.'

Grey bit her lip. She inclined her head in reverence, making the sign of appreciation with her right hand. She'd been taught it as a girl, mostly as a joke – in Grey's childhood, they believed in the gods, but they did not keep their customs.

'You have come with your decision?' the goddess asked. The moonlight seemed to move through her, as if she was not fully real. Grey wondered what would happen if she reached out and touched her – if her hand would move right through the goddess's image, if she would dissolve into nothing.

'We have,' she said. It was her job to speak the words, to take from

Kier what he wanted to give. She wished her mouth did not feel so dry, her throat so sore. She wished she didn't feel like she was ruining him. 'I will keep my power.'

'And I will surrender my freedom,' Kier said.

Kitalma looked between the two of them. For a moment, Grey wondered if she was judging them, but who could understand the judgment of the gods? After all, it was Kitalma who stole the heart of her lover – or was given it, depending on which version of the story Grey chose to believe. Perhaps the goddess understood Kier's sacrifice, and the necessity of it, better than anyone.

Kitalma reached forward, her hand gaining solidity the closer it got to Kier's body, until she pressed it flat to his chest. Kier sucked in a breath. Grey watched something gold and formless stir, running from Kier's body into Kitalma's. The goddess glowed for a moment with startling light, the medallion on her chest glowing brightest of all. For the barest fraction of a second, Grey was certain she saw someone else behind her, the impression of a hand on Kitalma's waist, the glint of armor and a billowing mass of tangled red curls – but she could not fully make out the shape of the other woman. She only saw her impression, and her smile, and then she was gone.

'Then it is done,' Kitalma said. She took Grey's hand and pressed it to the medallion. It was warm to the touch. 'You belong to the Isle, and to its daughter. May your union be sweet and long in its years.'

Before either of them could respond, the goddess faded away as quickly as she'd appeared, leaving the moonlight, and the sea, and the altar behind.

'Well.' Kier blinked, long and slow. 'That felt ... official.' He glanced at Grey, some odd mirth playing across his face. 'Did that feel like a marriage ceremony to you, or was that just me?'

'I don't know?' Grey said, pitching it as a question. She flexed her hands. She felt oddly bound to Kier, even more than their official binding ceremony had made them. 'Do you feel okay?'

He pressed his hand to his chest, rubbing the spot where Kitalma had touched him, where she'd pulled some physicality of his freedom away. Grey covered his hand with her own, as if she could heal the invisible wound that lurked under the surface.

'I feel fine,' he said, but there was that trace of sadness. Perhaps it would always be there. Grey thought about all the years she had been separated from her own home, severed at the root, missing something that no longer existed.

'You're astonishing,' she said

The sadness dimmed, just enough. Kier called forth a golden magelight, glowing faintly in the seaside. 'Astonishingly handsome,' he said.

Grey elbowed him between his ribs. 'And more annoying by the day.'

He laughed, the sound of it brightening the gloom of the temple. He slung an arm around her shoulders, steering her back toward the Ghostwood, back toward the fortress, back toward the rest of their lives. 'Then you'd better get used to it,' he said. 'You're stuck with me. Forever.'

Grey turned her head to kiss his shoulder, seeking shelter from the freezing wind and rain that pelted them. The Isle was always mercurial with its weather, at odds with the warmth glowing within her chest. 'I can tolerate forever,' she said.

epilogue

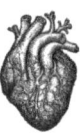

O N A NIGHT THREE months after the resurrection, the Isle sparkled with pale golden magelights. The boats had been arriving for nearly two days, pausing off the coast so the visitors could admire the glimmering new shields, before depositing guests in the harbor. For the first time in Grey's memory, Maerin and Osar were both full to bursting, loud with sounds of mirth and happiness and laughter.

Grey was in her rooms, getting ready for the feast, the second event in a week-long festival. They'd already spent most of the afternoon in Osar: everyone wanted to bow to Grey, or kiss Kier's hand or cheek (which was, frankly, a reaction she understood very well), or throw flowers at both of them and Grey's close group of guards and advisers.

Pia, Kier's ma, was behind her, pulling her corset strings tight as Laurella, his mum, absolutely destroyed her son at a game of cards. Imarta perched on Laurella's chair, commenting on her cards in a way that made Kier more and more frustrated.

'I told you not to play with them,' Grey said, breathless, running her hands over the boning of her corset as Pia tied it off. 'You always lose, and you're always cross about it.'

'I don't *always* lose,' Kier grumbled.

There was a knock at the door. Pia, who cared more for Grey's modesty than Grey did, threw a dressing gown over her shoulders. Tress, one of Grey's new attendants, pushed inside. 'The ship from Cleoc has arrived, your majesty,' she said.

'Oh,' Grey said, relieved. 'Can you send for the others? They all can come here. I'll meet them in my sitting room.'

'Yes, your majesty.'

'I'll never get used to that,' Pia muttered when the girl was gone.

'Just wait until you hear what they call Kier,' Grey said.

'I've heard *jackass* bandied about a bit down in town,' Laurella offered. There was a low noise of irritation from the table as she beat him at another hand.

Imarta moved to Grey's dresser, going through her earring collection. Most of it had been taken from her mother's rooms. She settled on a pair of garnets, which she handed to Pia.

'I can put on my own earrings,' Grey said, taking them herself. 'And get dressed. Truly, you're all clucking over me like hens.'

'I'm not,' Laurella protested.

'No, but you're putting Kier in a mood, and *I'm* the one who has to spend the evening by his side.'

There was no protest at that, but they also didn't let Grey put her hair up herself. Finally, she waved them off, asking if they would *please* go to Osar ahead of time to make sure everything was to their liking. Imarta paused after Pia and Laurella left, her hand pressed to Grey's cheek. Over the last two days, during long walks along Locke's paths, Grey had told her everything – with no redactions.

'I'll make your excuses,' she said, dropping a kiss on Grey's forehead.

'Thank you,' Grey said, squeezing Imarta's hand once more before she went.

Kier came to her back as she pulled on her heavy dress, his hands pushing hers aside to do up the little buttons. She knew he was annoyed, because he did not press a kiss to her bare shoulder blade or the curve of her neck.

'I told you not to,' she said, unable to hide her smile as he met her gaze in the mirror.

'Oh, shut up.' Buttons done, his hands fell to her waist, tightening around her. 'You look exquisite tonight.'

She studied him in his formal suit, gray and black and severe, making him equal parts fearsome and handsome; his hazel eyes were clear and startling in their depth. 'As do you,' she said, her smile deepening. She turned in his arms and leaned up onto her toes, gripping the back of his neck, pulling him down to kiss her.

'We can't,' he said after a moment, pulling away. 'Places to be, and so on.'

'We could skip,' Grey murmured, kissing his jaw.

'We shouldn't. It's in your honor.'

'And yours,' she protested. 'If I recall, it's also to celebrate the shields. And the Isle wouldn't be back and safe without you.'

'Your majesty?' Tress had returned, hesitating at the doorway, eyes lowered.

Grey stepped away from Kier. Though some who worked in the fortress had guessed the nature of the commander's relationship with the Lady, she liked to keep it protected, close to her chest – she worried that, someday, someone might see Kier as her weakness.

It was a feeling she was trying very hard to get over.

'Your guests are in the sitting room,' Tress said, curtsying.

'Thank you,' Grey said, nodding to dismiss the girl. She moved quickly, keeping her eyes down. According to the rumors, much of Locke still feared her for her power – but that, too, was something she was trying to get over; and late at night, when it worried her, Kier told her over and over again all the reasons why a healthy dose of fear was a good thing.

They went into the sitting room. Eron had already found the wine Grey kept for guests and was pouring a round, passing glasses to Brit and Ola. Near the door, Sela paced; when she saw Grey, her eyes lit up, and she flung herself at her. Grey caught her with a huff as Sela squeezed her even tighter than her corset.

'You're wearing the dress,' she said against Grey's shoulder. 'It's my favorite.'

'I love it,' Grey said. She pulled back to study the girl's face, noting the dark marks of sleeplessness under eyes. 'The whole wardrobe has been invaluable.'

'The armor did fail, though,' Kier said, smirking, as he took Sela from Grey's arms for his own hug.

'It was decorative!' she protested.

'First lesson of working with Flynn? Anything that looks like it could be fought in *will* be fought in.'

Sela sighed, but she didn't maintain a frown for long. She sat between Grey and Kier on one of the plush sofas, kicking her feet up to rest on the edge of the little table. Grey accepted the wine from Eron and took a sip. 'We can't stay long,' she said sadly. 'At any moment, any number of clerks or guards or attendants could burst in and demand my attention.'

'We get it,' Ola said, shifting her weight. She kept her right arm tucked tight to her chest, the shirt pinned just under her elbow. 'You're important.'

Grey winked at her. 'But never too important for *you*.'

Ola scoffed. 'Tell that to your damn guard. I swear, I tried to come see you the other day, and that burly one with the eyebrows—'

'Rabbit?' Kier offered helpfully.

'What kind of fucking name is Rabbit?' Eron said.

'Nickname,' Kier explained. 'Big as a tree? Curly hair?'

'Well, fucking *Rabbit* told me I didn't have the clearances. The clearances! Gods alive, Grey, the fact that I was turned away by some brute called *Rabbit*.'

Grey sighed. 'I'll have a word,' she said, letting her head fall back on the cushions. Only months ago, the three of them had been her only guard, but she had forced them to take the six months of leave they'd been promised for delivering Sela. If they chose to return to her service after that time? Well, Kier would have space for them.

And if they chose to do anything else, go anywhere else? That was fine, too.

In the meantime, it made it easier for Grey to keep slipping her guard if they were strangers.

Brit was waggling their eyebrows at her; for her part, Grey was doing her level best to ignore the question in their eyes.

'Good. Because the next time I see your bunny, I can't promise what my hand will do.'

'He's not that bad,' Kier murmured. 'And he keeps Grey safe.'

'Oh, shut up, Kier,' Ola sighed without heat.

'Eron?' Grey said, shifting her gaze. 'Any grievances to air, while we're here?'

'None at all,' Eron said primly. He was, Grey had discovered recently, spending a lot of time in the kitchens. She did not know if it had to do with the fact that he was now interested in the art of cooking, or because there was excellent food there at all hours.

'Brit?' she said, wincing.

The mage only looked at her, taking a long sip of their wine. 'Oh,' they said, 'you know. Feeling a little ... burdened with anticipation.'

Grey raised an eyebrow. 'Perhaps,' she said slowly, 'that is something we can discuss tomorrow.' She had taken a risk, trusting Brit with a secret – she trusted Brit with a lot, but secrets were an entirely different territory – and she wasn't going to let them ruin it now, mere minutes before she shared it with Kier.

They flashed her a bright smile. 'Excellent news. I will be up at dawn waiting for your summons.'

Grey rubbed the bridge of her nose. On Sela's other side, Kier looked a little confused, but he was smirking, as he always did when they didn't feel so keenly the weight of their new roles.

'We *should* go, though,' Eron said sadly. 'Yearna had some very pointed threats for me if we kept Sela away from her guard for too long.'

The others shuffled to prepare, pulling on jackets and finishing their wine. Kier moved to follow them out the door, but Grey grabbed his arm and held him back. 'We'll meet you there,' she said to Ola, who shot her a questioning glance. Brit only smiled; Ola shook her head and muttered something under her breath about other rabbits.

'What's wrong?' Kier asked, moving to adjust one of the jewels that had shifted in Grey's hair.

'Nothing. Just a surprise.'

He raised a brow, but did not ask for further clarification.

Grey pulled on her cloak and led him out. When she dismissed her guard, telling them to go to the feast without her, they protested. 'I'm with the commander,' she said. 'I will be fine.'

'Sir?' one of them said tentatively. He never unmade her decisions – but he did push for her safety.

Kier only shrugged. 'Go on, then.' Grey couldn't fight her wicked smile as they left.

She pulled Kier across one of the courtyards, down through the fortress and toward the walls. There, he lifted the gate with magic, and quietly drew a golden magelight as Grey led him toward the cliff-side path. She barely noticed the power he pulled from her now; in her mother's journals, she came to understand what Torrin had been trying to tell her. It was the nature of the sovereigns of Locke to not always be bound and married, but always tethered. After all, it was Kier who maintained the shields, Kier who kept the golden magelights burning, Kier whose wards guarded her door. There was power flowing through him constantly since the night months ago when they'd stood before Kitalma at her altar and given his freedom away.

'I suppose I don't get to ask what this is,' he said, his arm looped through hers.

'We're almost there,' she promised.

He sighed, looking down at her hem. 'You're going to get your dress all muddy.'

She shrugged. It was all posturing anyway; she was used to being covered in mud, and nearly everyone on the Isle had seen her in far worse shape. The finery was an active disruption from her usual state of disarray.

They rounded the hairpin turn on the path, and Grey's stomach pulsed with anticipation. Beside her, Kier paused, drawing a quick breath.

'Grey,' he said, her name barely a sound in the dark. He stopped. She watched his face carefully as he swallowed unsteadily. She felt suddenly full of hollow anxiety, as if she could've made the wrong decision in giving him this.

'It's yours,' she said.

Kier nodded, but he did not let go of her; he just moved to hold her hand and brightened the magelight. She kept a step behind him down the last bit of the path toward the ledge, protected from the worst of Locke's winds.

The little cottage was pale bluish-gray stone, the same shade as the clapboard houses on Scaela's shores but sturdier, nestled in with one wall built against the cliff. Kier hesitated for just a second before he opened the door. They stepped into the kitchen, painted pale yellow, and he gripped the back of a chair for support as he looked at it in wonder.

Grey said nothing.

He moved through the rooms: the kitchen, then the parlor, with its great fireplace and cushioned chairs and sofas. She had selected everything with comfort in mind, writing to Laurella and Pia when she was stuck. In their final letter before coming to Locke, Laurella had included a sketch she'd done of Lot and Kier when the pair were boys. He held it now, his face unreadable as he took the frame from the mantel. He studied it for a long moment, unreadable, then put it back and moved up the stairs.

He peered in at the bathing room, the two bedrooms ('For your mothers, and anyone else you want to visit,' she told him quietly) and the study, before he went up the final set of stairs. There, on the top floor, he found a bedroom with a wide bed and a trunk, and a great window looking out at Scaela. At his home.

He sat down hard. It was lucky, she thought, that the bed was there to catch him when his knees went weak.

She sat carefully beside him on the floor, resting her head on his knee. A very Locke quiet settled over them as they stared out to sea. Even the crashing waves and the shouting wind did not seem all that loud when they were in this little haven.

'*Grey*,' Kier said quietly, his voice breaking.

She looked up to see tears on his cheeks. She pushed herself to her knees and took his face in her hands, wiping them away with her thumbs.

'Is it okay?' she asked.

He drew a breath, looking at the window over her shoulder. 'It's . . . I don't think I have words,' he admitted. He brought his hands up, covering hers. 'How did you do all this?'

Grey chewed her lip. 'Brit and Ola,' she admitted. 'I was sure they would spoil the surprise.'

Kier laughed, breathy and uneven. 'Fucking materialists,' he said, looking around the space in wonder, taking in the dark beams that crossed the ceiling and the quilt on the bed. His smile quirked up; he must've recognized that the quilt was one his mothers had brought from home.

'No one else knows it exists,' Grey said.

He looked at her, realization dawning. 'And you asked me to shield and ward this path so you and Ola could spar in peace . . .'

'Yes.'

'So no one else can come down here.'

'Yes,' she said, her own grin widening.

'And you warned me of loose rocks on the cliff so I wouldn't come here alone.'

'I'm sorry. I didn't want you to see it until it was finished.'

Kier shook his head in astonishment, sitting back, taking it in. 'A house,' he said.

'A cottage, really. An apology, for ruining your retirement.'

'Grey . . .'

She looked away then, letting her hands fall into his lap. He put his own over hers. 'I want to be clear,' she said. 'This is *your* house, Kier. Not mine. I will not come here unless you invite me. It is your place, and yours alone. I cannot give you your freedom back, but I can give you your space.'

He was quiet for a moment. When she looked up, she found him studying her face. He moved his thumb to tilt her chin up, bringing his magelight closer so he could see every detail of her face. Then he shifted, kneeling carefully in front of her. He traced his fingers across her collarbone – she was unable to suppress her shiver – and bent to kiss her, very gently.

'Will you stay the night, if I ask it?'

'That defeats the purpose of your own house.'

He nudged his nose against hers. 'What if I ask very, very nicely?'
'Yes.'

Another soft kiss, like the press of his golden light. 'And we don't
have to go to your party?'

She smiled, feeling his lips curve up in response. '*Our* party,' she
said, her fingers moving up his sides and across his chest, skimming
over the details of his coat. 'I might have . . . already asked Imarta to
give our regrets, if they didn't see us in half an hour,' she admitted.

Kier laughed, his eyes sparkling. 'Oh, Locke,' he said, moving his
hands to grip her waist, his fingers digging in between the boning of
her corset. 'Your foresight remains astonishing, as always.'

She kissed his nose. 'The nation of Locke accepts your com-
pliments, but suggests you support your declarations with action,
Commander.'

He twined his fingers through hers. 'And am I not Locke, too?' he
asked, the barest hint of hesitation in his voice.

'If you wish it?' she asked. She did not dare to hope.

That hesitation did not fade. 'If *you* wish it.'

Far below, the waves crashed on the rocks, the sea rushing against
the dark cliffs of the iron isle. She skimmed her fingers across his
cheek, searching his face, the grin spreading across hers before she
could stop it. 'That you are, Locke,' she said.

acknowledgments

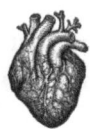

What an odd journey this has been, and what a joy.

To my editor, Nadia Saward: thank you for seeing something in me, this book and this world. It has been an honor and a delight to work with you, and I am so lucky to have you both as an editor and a friend. I don't think there's space for the amount of sappiness I have to unleash upon you so in no particular order, thank you for your insightful edits and guiding hand, your compassion when it felt like the world was crumbling and your endless support during the entire process.

My thanks to the entire team at Orbit UK who made this book happen: Anna, Joanna, Nazia, Jenni, Emily, James, Serena, Ella, Madeleine, Tom and everyone else who had a hand in it. Thank you to Rebecka for bringing Idistra to life (I love my little serpent dragon friend) and to Jane for catching all of my worst typos. A huge thank you to Anna Moshak for creating such wonderful art for the cover.

Thank you to Uwe and Amelia for bringing this one over the line, and to the team at Triada US for the support.

Thank you to Maddy Belton for taking a chance on me and to the team at Madeleine Milburn for bringing this book to readers around the world. To Maddy, Valentina and everyone else on the team: you have changed my life.

My admiration and thanks to the teams at my international publishers, who brought this book to new readers: Il Castoro in Italy, Piper in Germany and Umbriel in Spain. Thank you to Madeleine Colavita, Grace Fischetti, and the entire team at Grand Central who brought this book stateside: my parents are in your debt (though they are only allowed to read the redacted version).

This idea was nurtured by early readers: a huge thank you to Caitlin, Debbie, Emma and all others who read early drafts and cheered for Grey and Kier along the way. Tasha, thank you for a) literally teaching me how to write for adults, b) letting me have at least three meltdowns on your couch and c) accepting it without argument while I wrote book two in your inbox (more on that later). Knights knights knights forever and ever. Georgia, thank you for dealing with every single one of my mental breakdowns and debating the most effective ways to kill love interests. To Kat, Saara, Karin, Cherae, Sam, Alice and all other writing friends, thank you for Dishoom breakfasts and writing sessions and many discussions that should not be held in public but inevitably are. Existing in a space with such amazing creative individuals has changed everything about the way I write. To Becca and Shakira, thank you for letting me rant about the general chaos of publishing. To Katie Moss and Carly Suri, thank you for your endless wisdom on armor, weaponry, and various other intricacies.

To the Illumicrew: I love each and every one of you (though I am terrified to go through names and miss someone) – you make the book world so much more fun. Thank you for your support and excitement over the years. Daphne, you have made my life better in a million ways – thank you, above all, for being a wonderful friend. To Davi and Cat, there are no other raccoons I'd rather share a trench coat with. Also to the team at Illumicrate: thank you for bringing this gorgeous edition to life. Katie, Yas, Layla: you are wizards; and thanks for naming your cat after my book, Akash.

To Adam Roberts and Prudence Bussey-Chamberlain: this book wouldn't exist without you (and neither would the unpublished one before). Thank you for your patience and guidance over the last few years. Thanks, too, to my students, who make me think (read: spiral) about world-building and conventions of fantasy on the regular.

Thank you to all the readers, bloggers, bookstagrammers, TikTokkers, reviewers and beloved publishing professionals who supported this and previous books. It has been an absolute joy to meet so many of you over the years. Particular shoutouts to Lili, who has been there since book one and is such a delight; and to Charlotte, who did not let me pass out at Comic Con on one of the most surreal days of my life.

As always, I would be nowhere without my family. To my parents, Jane and Vic, thank you for loving me, supporting me and attempting to understand publishing. My love and thanks to Lex and James, Dana and Tony, and all members of my family and my in-laws who have been so supportive over the years. Thanks to all Bovalinos, Robinsons, Stewarts, Andersons, Weavers, Mosses, McKenzies, Mutchells and other assorted family members. Sir Gordon, my tiny cat, I hope you find my work satisfactory as usual.

And finally, Matt: you make the world brighter and I love you for it. Without you in my life, there would be no more love stories.

about the author

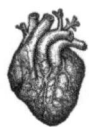

V. L. Bovalino (she/her) is originally from Pittsburgh, Pennsylvania and now lives in the UK with her partner and their very loud cat. She holds a PhD in English and splits her non-writing time between publishing and academia. She also writes books for young adults as Tori Bovalino, including *My Throat an Open Grave* and *The Devil Makes Three*. Tori loves scary stories, obscure academic book facts, and impractical, oversized sweaters. She can be found on Instagram as @toribovalino.

Find out more about V. L. Bovalino and other Orbit authors by registering for the free monthly newsletter at orbit-books.co.uk.

CW01501310

*FAIRS, MARKETS
AND THE
ITINERANT BOOK TRADE*

PUBLISHING PATHWAYS
PREVIOUS TITLES IN THE SERIES

EDITED BY ROBIN MYERS & MICHAEL HARRIS

EDITED BY ROBIN MYERS, MICHAEL HARRIS & GILES MANDELBROTE

FAIRS, MARKETS
AND THE
ITINERANT BOOK TRADE

Edited by
Robin Myers, Michael Harris
and Giles Mandelbrote

OAK KNOLL PRESS
&
THE BRITISH LIBRARY
2007

© 2007 The Contributors

First published 2007 by
Oak Knoll Press
310 Delaware Street
New Castle
DE 19720
and
The British Library
96 Euston Road
London NW1 2DB

Cataloguing in Publication Data
A CIP Record for this book is available
from both The British Library and
the Library of Congress

ISBN 978 15845 62009 (Oak Knoll)
ISBN 978 07123 4984 0 (BL)

Typeset by Ella Whitehead
Jacket design by William Reiner and Mark Parker Miller
Printed in the United States of America by Sheridan Books, Ann Arbor

Contents

Introduction

DEALERS IN BOOKS, as with most other commodities, have operated from a variety of locations, ranging from large, well-stocked emporia to the smallest, ramshackle or temporary premises. Books have also been bought and sold at fairs and markets and by itinerant traders, alongside clothes, food and other products. Nowadays, most of the printed material sold in markets is confined to boxes of shiny paperbacks or piles of dog-eared magazines on stalls selling miscellaneous bric-a-brac, although in Cambridge and one or two other towns occasional regular bookstalls are still to be found. It is a far cry from the heyday of the fairs of Frankfurt or Leipzig, which formed part of the infrastructure of the pan-European distribution of new and secondhand books, central to the sixteenth- and seventeenth-century wholesale and retail book trade. By the early eighteenth century the international marketing of new books was increasingly done by other means, though antiquarian and secondhand books continued to be sold at the long-established fairs. In England town markets, controlled by a variety of grants and licences, helped to accommodate the buyers and sellers of books, but it was not until the second half of the twentieth century that there were regular assemblies of provincial and metropolitan booksellers in specialist antiquarian book fairs.

The present volume is based on papers given at the 27th annual conference on book trade history, sponsored by the Antiquarian Booksellers' Association and held, in 2005, at the Society of Antiquaries. It explores some of the ways in which the open-air book trade contributed to the cultural life of Europe. The contributors show how the early 'Latin' trade in learned books flourished at the urban fairs, while cheap popular books were spread through the countryside by pedlars and hawkers. At the same time, small books and broadside ballads were also distributed within urban areas by street traders, balladeers and the so-called 'walking stationers', who operated from makeshift stalls and barrows.

While the fairs and markets established a clear line of commercial activity outside the formal boundaries of the shop, much open-air trading took place in the streets and public spaces. The itinerant members of the trade, visible mainly through prosecutions and punishment, kept the wheels of commerce turning at a popular level through their ubiquitous buying and selling and by acting as a pool of casual labour. The over-lapping activities of street trader, hawker and pedlar formed part of a complex economic system across Europe which has yet to be brought clearly into view.

John Flood gives a lively account of the Frankfurt Fair, making use of a wide range of sources to provide a clear view of the rise and fall of a great commercial enterprise. Although there were other rival fairs, most notably — especially for the German book trade — the important Leipzig fair held twice a year, Frankfurt was ideally situated at the junction of trade routes, with waterway access via the Rhine and the Main for the bulk transport of books and other heavy merchandise. At its peak in the sixteenth and seventeenth centuries, the Frankfurt fair had become a hive of international bookselling, with permanent shops lining the streets which surrounded the stalls of the central fair. Each year, in spring and autumn, booksellers, printers and bookbinders from all over Germany, France, the Netherlands, Italy, England and the Baltic converged on Frankfurt to buy and sell learned books and to arrange credit in an age when there were few easy or safe ways of settling accounts at a distance. The Frankfurt fair also provided crucial encouragement and competitive stimulus to booksellers such as Georg Willer, who began the practice of issuing catalogues of the latest publications sold there. But the Thirty Years' War cast a long shadow and by 1749 the Frankfurt fair had petered out, only to be revived as an international publishers' fair 200 years later in 1949.

Clive Griffin describes the role of the itinerant book trade in Spain and Portugal in the sixteenth and seventeenth centuries. Most of the travelling booksellers, printers and bookbinders were immigrants, many of them from France or Flanders. They covered a wide area of the peninsula, selling mainly imported books and commodities, and they also sometimes travelled with printing presses. Their books were often only a sideline: as foreigners, they had to be prepared to turn a hand to anything to earn a precarious or even perilous living, and they ran the risk of being denounced to the Inquisition as purveyors of heretical or subversive material. Inquisition records provide the primary source material for the sometimes heart-rending stories of the dangers faced by these unfortunate individuals.

By contrast with these small-time dealers in popular literature and ballads, Ian Maclean's case study of the international Latin trade is concerned with the chaotic affairs of the once prominent and prosperous

Symphorien Beraud, a bookseller who was murdered in the streets of Lyon in 1585. Beraud left a tangle, in France, Italy and Spain, of unsettled finances and warehouses crammed with books, some decaying, whose value it was almost impossible to assess. Maclean weaves his way through a mass of confused evidence, offering a detailed commentary on the inventory drawn up in 1591 of the stock of Beraud's former associate, Etienne Michel. The legal documents associated with this case provide a unique insight into the trade in learned books in southern Europe in the late sixteenth century.

The other papers in the volume deal with the itinerant and street trade in the seventeenth, eighteenth and nineteenth centuries. Jeroen Salman describes the early stages of a large-scale research project to quantify the role played by pedlars in the distribution network for printed materials in the Netherlands between 1600 and 1850. The Netherlands at this period were much more urbanized than Britain and Salman's particular focus is on a neglected figure, the urban pedlar. Consequently his picture of the itinerant book trade is very different from that provided by the late John Morris for Scotland, where hawkers and pedlars traversed the eighteenth- and nineteenth-century highlands and lowlands. Morris has brought together much valuable information about these obscure traders, some of whom left evocative memoirs of their hard lives, trudging hundreds of miles in all winds and weathers, carrying heavy packs of books and other goods, and sleeping rough in barns or under hedges. David Stoker's study of distribution networks for books and newspapers in rural Norfolk, Suffolk and Cambridgeshire sets the itinerant book trade in the broader context of the development, in the early eighteenth century, of established local bookshops, the rise of the newspaper press in Norwich, Cambridge and Bury St Edmunds, and the introduction of book auctions. He describes the network of hawkers, usually accompanied by a horse or cart, and pedlars, who carried their wares on their back, together with the regional markets and fairs at which books were sold, most notably the celebrated Stourbridge Fair held annually near Cambridge.

In his account of the street trade in the poorer areas and open spaces of London from the seventeenth to the nineteenth century, Michael Harris draws on evidence from Old Bailey trials and from Henry Mayhew's monumental *London Labour and the London Poor* — rich but often overlooked sources for book trade history. As well as investigating the character and organization of the London street trade, he also introduces us to the distinctive and colourful cast of eccentric traders who flitted through the London streets.

Robin Myers
Michael Harris
Giles Mandelbrote

London
December 2006

Contributors

JOHN L. FLOOD is Emeritus Professor of German in the University of London. He has written extensively on the history of the book in Germany. His publications include *The German Book 1450–1750* (edited with W. A. Kelly, 1995), *Johannes Sinapius (1505–1560)* (with D. J. Shaw, 1997), and a four-volume handbook, *Poets Laureate of the Holy Roman Empire* (2006). He is a Past President of the Bibliographical Society.

CLIVE GRIFFIN is the Fellow in Spanish at Trinity College, Oxford. His main research interest is the history of the book in Golden-Age Spain and his most recent book is *Journeymen-printers, Heresy, and the Inquisition in Sixteenth-Century Spain* (Oxford, 2005).

MICHAEL HARRIS is the co-founder (with Robin Myers) of the annual London conferences on book trade history and was formerly Reader in Media History at Birkbeck College, University of London. His research and publications are mainly concerned with newspapers and the book trade in London during the seventeenth and eighteenth centuries.

IAN MACLEAN is Professor of Renaissance Studies in the University of Oxford and Senior Research Fellow at All Souls College, where he is also Fellow Librarian. His main research interest in the history of the book is the trade in learned books in Europe in the sixteenth and early seventeenth centuries.

The late JOHN MORRIS was Assistant Keeper in the British and Antiquarian Department of the National Library of Scotland. He was editor of the *Armorial of British Bookbinding* on CD-Rom and of the Scottish Book Trade Index. He has written on the relationship between chapbooks and ballad sheets and the Scottish oral tradition.

JEROEN SALMAN is research fellow at the Utrecht Research Institute for History and Culture in the Netherlands and teaches at the Utrecht University College. His main research interests are popular printing, the itinerant book trade, almanacs and children's literature in the seventeenth and eighteenth centuries. He has recently co-edited (with Marieke van Delft and Frank de Glas) *New Perspectives in Book History. Contributions from the Low Countries* (Walburg Pers, Zutphen, 2006).

DAVID STOKER taught in the Department of Information Studies at the University of Wales, Aberystwyth. He has published extensively on the history of the Norwich and East Anglian book trade and has edited *The Correspondence of the Reverend Francis Blomefield (1705–52)* (Bibliographical Society, 1992).

List of those attending the Conference

Hugh Adlington
King's College, London

Barry Benster
Bookseller

Leo Cadogan
Bookseller

Kenneth Charlton
Retired academic

Melissa Cook

Timothy Cutts
National Library of Wales

Carlo Dumontet
National Art Library,
Victoria & Albert Museum

Judy Edwards
18th-century theatre studies

Christine Ferdinand
Fellow Librarian,
Magdalen College, Oxford

Margaret Ford
Christie's

Alice Ford-Smith
Wellcome Library

Jane Francis
Retired librarian

Victoria Gardner
D.Phil. student,
St John's College, Oxford

Dr Jacqueline Glomski
History Department,
King's College, London

David Hall
Wolfson College, Cambridge

Jane Haslam
University College, London

John Hewish
Retired librarian

Sheila Hingley
Durham University Library

Judith Hodgson
Bookseller

Jonathan Hopson
National Art Library,
Victoria & Albert Museum

Ashley Huish
Retired librarian

Nancy Ives
Researcher. Low Countries
Research Association

C. R. Johnson
Book collector

Kenneth Karmiole
Antiquarian bookseller

Bill Lavin
Assistant librarian (rare books),
University College, London

Christopher Lee
Independent scholar

Colin Lee
Book collector

Elisabeth Leedham-Green
Darwin College, Cambridge

Bill Lehm
Special Collections,
University College, London

Karen Limper
Curator, British Printed
Collections, British Library

Anita McConnell
Independent scholar

Dr Warren McDougall
Book trade historian

Christina Mackwell
Librarian,
Lambeth Palace Library

Alexander Malcolm
Book collector

Keith Manley
Institute of Historical Research,
University of London

John Martin
Mayfly Ephemera & Books

Howard Mather
Bookseller

Miriam Miller
Retired librarian, Ph.D. student,
University College, London

John Mooney
Head of Conservation,
British Library

Leslie Morris
Librarian, Houghton Library,
Harvard University

Michael Mulcay
Senate House Library,
University of London

Jennifer Murray

Alan H. Nelson
Professor Emeritus, University of
California, Berkeley

Deborah Novotny
Head of Preservation,
British Library

Charles Parry
National Library of Wales

Michael Perkin
Retired special collections librarian

Sue Petrie
Ph.D. student, University of Kent

Nicholas Pickwoad
University of the Arts, London

Susannah Randall
Research student, Trinity College,
Cambridge

Professor Graham Rees
School of English and Drama,
Queen Mary, University of
London

Julian Roberts
Emeritus Fellow, Wolfson College, Oxford

Uta Schumacher
Bibliographer and book collector

Andrew Serjeant

Bernard J. Shapero
Bookseller

Julianne Simpson
Wellcome Library

Junie Sinson
President, Caxton Club, Chicago

Eric Stockdale
Retired judge and author

David Stoker
Department of Information Studies, University of Wales, Aberystwyth

Matthew Symonds

John Symons
Retired librarian, Wellcome Library

Christine Thomson
Bookseller

Jean Tsushima
Archivist Emeritus, Honourable Artillery Company, Editor H.A.C Biographical Dictionary Trust

J. J. van Heel
Museum Meermanno-Westreenianum, The Hague

Stijn van Rossem
University of Antwerp

Lisa Vine
Independent researcher

Dr Maria Wakely
School of English & Drama, Queen Mary, University of London

Anne Watts
Publisher

Veronica Watts
Bookseller

Susan West
English Heritage

Clare Wikeley
Research student, University of Southampton

Margaret Willes
Retired publisher

'Omnium totius orbis emporiorum compendium': the Frankfurt fair in the early modern period

JOHN L. FLOOD

BETWEEN 19 AND 23 October 2005, 284,838 people descended on the exhibition grounds at Frankfurt am Main to visit the annual Frankfurt Book Fair, the most important regular event in the publishing world's calendar. The association of publishing with Frankfurt has a long history — though not quite so long as one might imagine. Indeed, given the city's important role in the book trade, especially in the sixteenth century, it seems almost a paradox that it was such a relative latecomer as far as the introduction of printing was concerned. Leaving aside the short-lived press of Beatus Murner in the Franciscan friary at Frankfurt in 1511/12, the first printer in the city was Christian Egenolph who arrived from Strasbourg in December 1530, to remain until his death in 1555.[1] This was three quarters of a century after the earliest printing at nearby Mainz, and in the meantime printing had established itself in many major German cities and abroad, beginning with Bamberg (c.1459), Strasbourg (1459/60), Cologne (1464/5), Rome (1467), Augsburg (1468), Venice (1469), Basle (1468/70), Nuremberg (1470), Paris (1476) — and even distant London. Only after Egenolph established the first long-term printing shop in Frankfurt did others recognize its favourable position; it then eclipsed the previous centres of the German book trade like Augsburg, Nuremberg, Basle, Strasbourg and (since the 1520s) Wittenberg in importance. Frankfurt really came into its own as a printing and publishing centre only in the second half of the sixteenth century, and already soon after 1600 it was overtaken by Leipzig. Among the men who made Frankfurt what it was were, besides Egenolph, Peter Braubach, Hermann Gülfferich, the publisher Sigmund Feyerabend and a bevy of printers associated with him, and André Wechel, a refugee from France following the 1572 St Bartholomew's Day massacre.[2]

Although, like most German cities, Frankfurt was a small place, with 15,000 inhabitants in 1475, it had long been an important town. The medieval kings and emperors, who had no fixed capital, are known to have visited it some 300 times before 1378, and right down until 1806 it was here that the election of the emperor generally took place, and from 1563 onwards he was crowned here, too. In 1372 it had become an imperial free city, owing allegiance directly to the emperor and with the right to levy its own taxes and make its own laws. Its convenient location enabled it to become a centre of trade at an early date. A market is attested already in the eighth century. A privilege was granted for an autumn fair in 1240, though its origins probably go back even to the twelfth century, and a charter for a spring fair was granted by Emperor Ludwig IV (Ludwig der Bayer) in 1330. Frankfurt's chief asset was its location in the centre of Germany, almost equidistant from Lübeck, Venice, Vienna, Lyon, Paris, Antwerp and Amsterdam; no wonder, then, that merchants preferred to meet on the banks of the Main, rather than travel in person all the way to the extremities of Europe. Frankfurt lay on major trade routes linking Lüneburg, Hamburg and Lübeck, with Scandinavia and the Baltic beyond, with Nuremberg and Prague in the east, Regensburg and Vienna on the Danube, and Augsburg, Venice and Italy in the south. Nevertheless, road transport was difficult and slow — five miles a day is said to have been average for a heavy wagon, and even sending a letter by messenger took many days: it counted as exceptionally fast for a letter to take only nine days from Frankfurt to Lübeck, and three weeks would have been more usual.[3] Crucial to Frankfurt's commercial importance was its favourable position on the chief waterways, close to where the River Main joins the Rhine. On the Main lie the ecclesiastical centres of Bamberg and Würzburg and the small imperial free city of Schweinfurt. The Rhine links Basle, Strasbourg, Worms, Mainz, Cologne and the Netherlands, and affords access to the North Sea. Water transport was ideal for heavy barrels of books. Christopher Plantin, for instance, would send his books by wagon from Antwerp to Cologne, where his colleague Maternus Cholinus would arrange onward transport up the Rhine to Frankfurt.[4] On arrival at the Main quayside they could be rolled to the nearby Buchgasse or Büchergasse ('Book Lane') (Fig. 1), a name first attested in 1518, between the river bank, the city walls and the church of St. Leonhard.[5] (Fig. 2)

Yet, for all its convenience, transport on water was still difficult and hazardous and hampered by restrictive practices which would only be abolished through the efforts of Napoleon and Prussia in the nineteenth century. In the early modern period Germany was not the unified country it is today. The Holy Roman Empire comprised a multitude of small

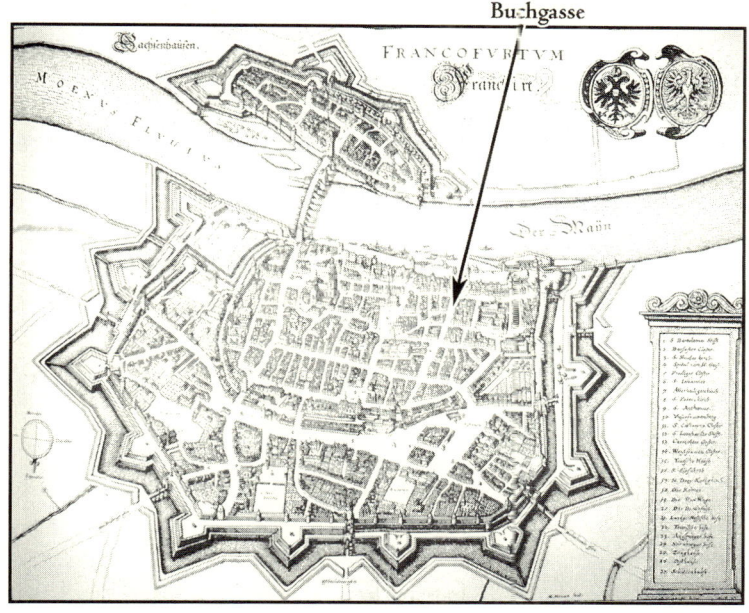

Fig. 1. Map of Frankfurt by Matthaeus Merian (1646?), showing the location of the Buchgasse. From *Topographia Hassiae et regionum vicinarum* ..., 2nd edn, Frankfurt am Main, 1655

states: merely travelling from Bamberg to Frankfurt involved passing through nine separate territories, and on the stretch from Miltenberg to Frankfurt it was obligatory to use Miltenberg boats.[6] On the Rhine, tolls were exacted at 31 points between Basle and Cologne.[7] Going overland from Nuremberg to Frankfurt, a couple of hours by train today, took six days, involved passing through six separate territories, required four changes of escort,[8] while tolls and levies were exacted at every border, the amount charged often being set arbitrarily. On average it seems that the cost of transporting goods from Nuremberg to Frankfurt added a quarter to the price of the goods themselves.

The Frankfurt fair was only one of many. Towns large and small throughout Europe held fairs on a regular basis.[9] They would develop at places where trade routes intersected, where goods had to be loaded on to or off ships, and at places where rivers were crossed by bridges.[10] Leipzig, where the fair can be traced back to 1268, lay on the intersection of two major trade routes, the so-called *Via Regia* from Frankfurt via Erfurt to Leipzig and on to Breslau and Poland, and the *Via Imperii*, leading from Venice, Verona, across the Brenner to Innsbruck, Augsburg, Nuremberg, Leipzig, Wittenberg, and on to the Hanseatic cities of Lübeck and Hamburg and beyond to Scandinavia. The Leipzig fair became even more important as German expansion eastwards continued in the later Middle Ages. Although itinerant traders could theoretically turn up anywhere at any time, it was in the interests of purveyors of bulky or heavy goods to go where people congregated. We need to remember that places we think of as major European cities today were, by our standards, very small in the early modern period: even Vienna's population was only about 20,000 in 1500. Merchants' travel plans were largely dictated by the dates of the fairs. At Vienna there were two major fairs: at Ascensiontide and around St Katharine's Day (25 November), each lasting for two weeks before and two weeks after the religious festival itself. At Krems they had the St James's Fair on 25 July and the Sts Simon and Jude Fair on 28 October.[11] At Linz, where the fairs can be traced back to the thirteenth century, there was the Easter Fair, lasting two weeks, and the St Bartholomew's Fair which lasted for four weeks around 24 August.[12] At Leipzig the Spring Fair started on the third Sunday after Easter (*Jubilate* Sunday) and ran for a week until *Cantate* Sunday, while the Michaelmas Fair began on the Sunday after Michaelmas (29 September) and ended the following Sunday.[13] At Friedberg in Hessen (20 miles north of Frankfurt) there were two fairs, each lasting a fortnight, one starting on St Walpurgis' Day, 1 May, and the Michaelmas fair beginning on 29 September. As for Frankfurt itself, the dates of the Lenten (Easter, Spring) Fair varied considerably over time, and precise details are now hard to determine. From 1366 it lasted two weeks, from *Oculi* (the fourth Sunday before Easter) until *Judica* (Passion Sunday, the second Sunday before Easter); the fair proved such a success that from 1384 to 1394 it was extended to almost four weeks, from *Oculi* until the end of Holy Week, much to the wrath of the ecclesiastical authorities; in 1399 it was agreed that, as from 1400, it should run from *Oculi* to the Friday before Palm Sunday, thus lasting just under three weeks. However,

Fig. 2. The Main Quay (Mainkai), Frankfurt am Main, drawn by Matthaeus Merian the Elder in 1646, from *Topographia Hassiae et regionum vicinarum* ..., 2nd edn, Frankfurt am Main, 1655. The legend implies that the barrels in the foreground are wine barrels.

in practice merchants often did not, or could not, adhere to the official dates: much depended on whether Easter was early or late and on what travel conditions were like — ice on the rivers and flooding often affected transport arrangements, and much confusion resulted. In 1502, for example, the fair began in Holy Week (when it should have ended) and ran for two weeks after Easter. In the seventeenth century it generally ran from *Judica* (Passion Sunday) to Easter Tuesday.[14] From 1710 it commenced on the first Sunday after Easter, not least because the weather was generally better then, but this had the consequence of forcing traders to choose between Frankfurt and Leipzig; Frankfurt soon realized its mistake, and in 1726 an imperial edict decreed that the Frankfurt fair should begin on Easter Tuesday — but it was too late: the fairs still overlapped and Leipzig had already gained the upper hand.[15] The Frankfurt Autumn Fair was originally held around the time of the feast of the Assumption (15 August), then was moved to the period 24 August–8 September, but in

1349 it was decreed that it should run from 15 August to 8 September, then from 15 August to 22 September, but from 1394 it was determined that it should end a week after the Nativity of the Virgin (8 September), thus on 15 September. In the late sixteenth century the Autumn fair, lasting three weeks, always began on a Monday between 6 and 12 September; the precise date depending on what day of the week the Nativity of the Virgin was celebrated: if this fell on Monday, Tuesday or Wednesday, the fair began on the Monday falling between 6 and 8 September; if it fell on Thursday, Friday, Saturday or Sunday, it would begin on the Monday falling between 9 and 12 September.[16]

The fairs were obviously hectic places, and seeing that they tended to follow one another in different places in quick succession there were inevitably sometimes mishaps. The inexorable calendar of events meant that printers would be under pressure to have a book ready for a certain deadline. After all, the fairs provided almost the only possibility for publishers to sell books in large quantities, particularly to other book dealers. To cite one example: the Zurich publisher Christoph Froschauer took 2,000 copies of his folio and octavo editions of Joachim von Watt's *Epitome trium terrae partium* to the Frankfurt fair in 1534 and managed to sell half of them.[17] Obviously, therefore, it was vital to have one's books ready in time. If you missed one Frankfurt fair you had to wait six months for the next. A good instance of the importance of keeping to the schedule is furnished by Johann Schönsperger the Younger, who entered into an agreement with the Augsburg parchment-maker, paper merchant and publisher Peter Aprell to bring out an edition of 1,000 New Testaments on paper with six copies on vellum for Frederick the Wise, Elector of Saxony. However, according to Schönsperger, Aprell let him down badly: not only was he not able to supply sufficient vellum of a suitable quality, which meant that he incurred the wrath of the Elector, but the printing of the thousand copies on paper was delayed, too, so that he missed the deadline for the Frankfurt fair and lost money thereby.[18] Many contemporary books show evidence of the pressure under which printers and publishers were working. For instance, the corrector of Jacob Wimpheling's *Epitome rerum Germanicarum*, Strasbourg: J. Prüss, 11 March 1505, apologises for any errors by saying that they had been forced to print the work quickly because of the imminent Frankfurt fair: *Coacti sumus ob imminentes nundinas Francofurdenses intra brevissimum tempus id opus formis excudere.*[19] And we know that when Luther's New Testament translation was being printed in the summer of 1522, extreme measures had to be taken by the printer Melchior Lotter at Wittenberg to ensure it was ready for the Leipzig Michaelmas fair. Another rush job is reported by Euricius Cordus, Professor of Medicine at Marburg, who compiled a treatise on the English Sweating Sickness, a terrible epidemic ravaging Germany in the summer of 1529: writing on Thursday, 2 September that year, he says his Marburg printer was anxious to get his book to Frankfurt, about 100 km away, for the fair that began on 6 September; the book was printed on Saturday, 4 September.[20] In 1557 we find a Leipzig bookseller having to defend himself before the authorities for selling an objectionable political pamphlet, offering the plausible excuse that he and his colleagues had not actually read the book while they were in Frankfurt because the fair was so hectic; they had merely glanced at the title, purchased a few copies and packed them up and sent them to Leipzig for resale, not realizing what the contents of the books were until they unpacked them again.[21] Another kind of pressure resulting from the fair is exemplified by the Augsburg bookseller Georg Willer. In October 1559 he was in prison because of his involvement with sectarian printers. His wife pressed for his release on the grounds that the books he had bought in Frankfurt were expected imminently and, if they were impounded, not only would Willer himself suffer because he would be unable to supply his customers, who were already waiting for them, but the books themselves would be useless because, being calendars, practical handbooks and the like, they had a short shelf-life and would soon be obsolete.[22]

Given the difficulties and hazards of travel it was not possible for every merchant to attend every fair in person. Some might make a point of attending a particular fair, at Frankfurt, for example, on a regular basis, or at least ensure that they were represented — Plantin, for instance, would send his son-in-law Moretus. Or they might concentrate on the fairs in a particular area — booksellers from southern Germany in particular regularly visited fairs at the towns on the Danube, with Linz proving an important venue for booksellers from Poland, Germany and Italy.[23] Another Austrian venue was Hall in Tirol, on the north/south trade route, where a fair was established in 1356 and which in the sixteenth century became an important outlet for south German booksellers.[24] This doubtless explains why this area was targeted for an inquiry into what kind of books were owned by the local population by the commission instituted by Archduke Ferdinand of Tyrol in 1569, as they were suspected of possessing many Protestant books.[25] As an alternative to visiting the fairs in person a merchant might employ the services of an agent living locally or indeed he might choose to have himself represented at the fair by an agent not himself resident in the fair town. The Lyon printer Sebastian Gryphius, for instance, marketed his books at Frankfurt through the Basle printer Andreas Cratander: nearly all of Gryphius's books of scholarly interest, more than 140 titles, are listed in Cratander's 1539 catalogue of the books available through his Frankfurt depot.[26] Later, Plantin, too, would represent other publishers on a commission basis, their goods being held on sale or return.

There was rivalry between the fairs, and regulation became necessary, for the establishment of a fair in one place could have a serious impact elsewhere. Thus the development of the Leipzig fairs resulted in the banning of smaller fairs in the bishoprics of Magdeburg, Halberstadt, Meissen, Merseburg and Naumburg, as confirmed by Pope Leo X in 1514. As early as 1469 Emperor Frederick III banned the New Year's Fair at Halle since it rivalled the New Year's Fair at Leipzig whose charter he had confirmed in 1466.[27] And in 1488 the Leipzig Council stripped Leipzig merchants of their citizenship who maintained outlying branches at Halle and Naumburg.[28] In 1497 Emperor Maximilian I granted the Leipzig fairs the status of imperial fairs, which meant that towns within a radius of fifteen German miles (about 70 English miles) were forbidden to hold rival markets. At a later date, in 1675, Duke Rudolf August of Lüneburg and Braunschweig petitioned Emperor Leopold I to allow Braunschweig to hold two fairs like Frankfurt and Leipzig; both these cities protested vehemently.[29]

*

Over time the Frankfurt fair's European importance grew to such an extent that Henri Estienne II (1528/31–1598) eulogized it in his *Francofordiense emporium* (1574) as 'Omnium totius orbis emporiorum compendium', 'the sum of all the fairs of the whole world'.[30] His account tells how all kinds of goods were traded there. Augsburg sent cloth, Ulm linen, Nuremberg's craftsmen their metal-ware. Wine and clothing came from the Rhine area, dried fish, horses, hops and furs came from the north, glass from Bohemia, ironware from Styria, silver and pewter from Saxony, copper from Thuringia. Estienne describes it as 'a veritable workshop of war', so many and varied were the weapons on display. Then there were vast numbers of fine horses for sale, and he enthuses about the succulent

Fig. 3. The fair in the late seventeenth century, from *Warhaffter und eigentlicher Schau-Platz der weitberühmten Franckfurter Mess*, n.pl., 1696. The picture shows the area in front of the Römer, the fourteenth-century city hall.

Westphalian hams, sufficient to feed an army on. Then there were luxury goods: spices, clothing, items of gold, silver and bronze, iron kitchen equipment, *objets d'art*, Dutch paintings, pottery, fine vases and painted earthenware. Only then does he come to what he calls the second fair, the book fair, which he calls an 'Academy of the Muses', for the Muses assemble their printers and booksellers there and order them to bring with them the books of the poets, the orators, the historians and the philosophers, not only of Greece and Italy, but of every land the Muses have touched. For Estienne Frankfurt had become what Athens had once been, and this idea is reflected in a German poem published in 1596 in which the author, Konrad Lautenbach, marvels at the wide range of scholars of all lands and disciplines who patronized the fair:

> Hie findst Geistliche und Juristen,
> Medicos und Alchymisten:
> Berümbte gewaltige Doctores
> Vornehmer Schulen Professores;
> Von Marpurg, Leipzig, Wittemberg,
> Tübing, Basel, Heidelberg.
> Wie auch von Löwen in Holland
> Ochsenfurt in Engelland
> Padua in Italien,
> Und von Cantabrigien.
> Also auch von Geneve, deßgleich
> Von Parise auss Franckreich.[31]

Here you'll find clerics and lawyers, medics and alchemists, famous authoritative doctors, the professors of distinguished academies, at Marburg, Leipzig, Wittenberg, Tübingen, Basle, Heidelberg, as well as Louvain in Flanders, Oxford in England, Padua in Italy, and Cambridge, from Geneva, too, and Paris in France.

The book fair had developed out of a general trade fair. Evidently manuscripts were sold there in the fourteenth century, for Gerhard Groote (1340–84), founder of the Brothers of the Common Life, is already reported to have preferred to buy his books at Frankfurt.[32] Printed books were being sold at the Frankfurt fair certainly by 1462. Indeed, it is worth recalling that the earliest reference we have to Gutenberg's 42-line Bible relates to Frankfurt around the time of the autumn fair 1454. In a letter of 12 March 1455 to the Spanish Cardinal Juan de Carvajal, the humanist Enea Silvio Piccolomini, the later Pope Pius II but at the time secretary to the Holy Roman Emperor Frederick III, reported that while he had been attending the Imperial Diet at Frankfurt in October 1454 — he is known to have been there from 5 to 31 October — he had seen samples of a printed Bible 'that could be read without glasses', produced for inspection by 'a marvellous man'. Whether this was Gutenberg himself or, perhaps more likely, his associate Peter Schöffer, we do not know, and although these samples were more probably displayed in the context of the Imperial Diet rather than at the trade fair, it is intriguing, even significant, that they were exhibited at Frankfurt during or very close to the period of the fair.[33]

The fair seems quickly to have established itself as something members of the book trade from near and far should attend. Thus we know that the Basle printers Johann Amerbach and Michael Wenssler were at the fair in 1478.[34] It attracted not only booksellers, but paper merchants, type-founders, bookbinders, and printers hoping to dispose of some of their products through an agent. Also there would be many scholars wanting to relieve themselves of their stock of complimentary copies of their own works in exchange for other books, and authors touting manuscripts, promising potential publishers large sales and profits in this life and a heavenly reward in the next. A measure of the growing trade is that already on 24 March 1485 Berthold von Henneberg, Archbishop of Mainz, demanded of the Frankfurt council that it should examine the books offered for sale at the Lenten fair.[35] Already in 1488 printer-publishers accounted for one-twelfth of the rental income for stalls at the fair.[36] Perhaps the earliest reference we have to the Frankfurt fair and the trade with England is in a letter written in London on 8 August 1495 by Andreas Ruwe, probably a Cologne merchant who describes himself as a German bookdealer, to Johann Amerbach (from Basle) at Frankfurt at St Leonhard's at the sign of the swan. He asked Amerbach to supply 50 copies each of Augustine, *Super Johannem*,[37] *De civitate Dei*[38] and *De Trinitate*,[39] Robert Holkot's *Super librum sapientiae*,[40] the works of St Ambrose,[41] and St Bernard's *Liber meditationum*,[42] plus various other books.[43] But it seems to have been the presence of Italian humanist publishers from the late fifteenth century onwards that made the German scholarly world aware of the fair.[44] The first Venetian printers appeared at the fair in 1497.[45]

Frankfurt provided the necessary conditions for the development of trade. The city authorities supported the development of commerce. They controlled prices charged for food and lodging, tolls on the movement of goods were light, and trading was generally relatively free of restrictions, while safety was, if not guaranteed, then at least reasonably assured, merchants coming to and leaving the city being provided with armed escorts. Robbers and highwaymen were generally not particularly interested in books,[46] though this did not mean that consignments of books were safe. Thus Anton Koberger reported to Johann Amerbach on 9 July 1506:

I am sorry to say that when the carrier came via Wimpfen, he was waylaid. The robbers led the carrier together with the wagon off the road into a wood where they broke into the barrels and looked for money. Later it rained and half the books in the three barrels were drenched and damaged. There went my profit.[47]

The opening of the fair was announced by the ringing of the church bells, the imperial flag was flown from the towers, and shields bearing the city arms were hung from the gates for the duration of the fair. A particular feature was that there was a special court to deal expeditiously with disputes between merchants; Henri Estienne was effusive in his praise for the court's impartiality.[48] The second week of the Frankfurt fair was the week when merchants settled up (in so far as they did in cash[49]) with one another, not only finalizing business concluded at Frankfurt itself but settling their accounts for transactions agreed elsewhere. Merchants from Italy, Basle, Augsburg and Nuremberg would meet here with merchants from the Hanseatic cities in the north. The custom developed for them to give credit from fair to fair, that is, on a six-monthly basis, accounts being reckoned in Rhenish Goldgulden (gold florins), but customers with large accounts and in good standing would sometimes be given a year's credit. Late medieval merchants were not usually in a position to pay cash on the spot, so credit and trust were important. The use of letters of credit, promissory notes and bills of exchange enabled them to operate without openly transgressing religious sanctions against usury, and payments would be made through a network of business contacts, friends and mutual acquaintances. Sellers and buyers would agree a time when payment would be made. Indeed Frankfurt was the principal place for completing financial transactions.[50] Only later did the fair at Lyon become another alternative.[51] But there were still many uncertainties and difficulties, as is evident from a letter written by Anton Koberger to Johann Amerbach on 1 March 1500:

There is no need to write much except that I'm afraid that I cannot come to Frankfurt for I do not want to put myself in such danger and I am also sure that no reliable and trustworthy person from here [Nuremberg] will come through with whom I can make arrangements or payment to you at Frankfurt. Therefore I am sending you this special messenger to inform you in good faith that you should not come to this Lenten fair at Frankfurt for my sake, for I cannot make payment to you; but I will arrange for the 1000 Rhenish florins due you and Master Hans to be paid at the Lyons Easter fair that takes place a little after the Frankfurt fair through my cousin Hans Koberger, and I hope and trust that you are not annoyed about it for I assume that it will not cause you or Master Hans any loss. You may bring the money more safely from Lyons to Basle than from Frankfurt to Basle [...].[52]

On 20 July 1504 Koberger wrote to Amerbach expressing the fear that, because of military conflicts in the area, the Frankfurt Autumn fair might even be cancelled and that a large sum of money he had expected to receive after the Easter fair at Lyon would have to remain there until the August fair since no one was willing to transport the money to Nuremberg because of the war.[53] Paying money at a distance was a complex and hazardous affair. Thus Andreas Ruwe, writing from London to Johann Amerbach on 8 August 1495, said,

I have already sent you three letters to inform you that you would receive the money you lent me via two merchants of Cologne. As I understand it, they have cheated both of us. Now I am appointing yet a third merchant from Cologne, Hermann Blitterswich. If I am not mistaken, he or one of his agents will pay you in my name and I will no longer be in arrears.[54]

Booksellers could take only part of their stock with them, so often they would leave supplies in the hands of agents or in storage from one fair to the next.[55] Anton Koberger of Nuremberg in 1506 established a warehouse at Frankfurt at which he could leave his stock, and later Christopher Plantin similarly had a warehouse there, where after the Lenten fair 1579, for instance, he held 11,617 books, representing some 240 different titles.[56] Although the focus of the book trade in Frankfurt was around the Buch-gasse and St Leonhard's church very few precise addresses seem to be known. Johann Amerbach, from Basle, had his Frankfurt depot at the sign of the swan, and Jorg Aschenburger, attested from 1500 to 1513, had his at the house Alte Burg near St Leonhard's.[57] Hans Scherpf, a Frankfurt resident, was the official representative of the Venetian printer Bernardinus Stagninus (Stanquino) from 1505 to 1508; Stagninus often came to the fair in person and stored his books at the house Rustenberg (Rüstenberg).[58] In 1518 Thomas Anshelm from Haguenau (near Strasbourg) had his store in 'Her Brünnen Hauß bey sant Lienhart'.[59] In the mid-1520s Hans Moreller had a house in the Gelnhäuser Gasse where he represented the interests of his father-in-law, the Strasbourg printer Hans Knobloch.[60] These storage depots are described as vaults. We can imagine that the title-pages of the latest publications and poster-style catalogues were affixed to the outer doors and windows to attract customers to come inside to examine the wares. Books which might be suspect to the authorities would probably be hidden in dark corners or on high shelves, away from prying eyes. Only the merchants themselves would know what books they had in their stores at any one time.

These depots might sometimes develop into outlying branches of a major firm. Thus the Augsburg printer Johann Schönsperger the Younger not only established a branch of his business at Zwickau in 1523 but also had depots in Nuremberg, Frankfurt, Linz, Vienna and Speyer. The book-seller and publisher Paul Brachfeld, originally from Antwerp, who maintained branches of his business at Frankfurt am Main, Leipzig and Frankfurt an der Oder, mentions in the prefaces to his own catalogues (produced from 1595 to 1598) that in Frankfurt am Main he had a shop that was open throughout the year, not just at fair times.[61] The Strasbourg bookseller Lazarus Zetzner (*fl.* 1585–1616) also had shops in Cologne and Frankfurt: Frankfurt was a Lutheran city, Cologne was Catholic, so Zetzner was clearly trying to have the best of both worlds (a safe Cologne imprint could help facilitate sales in Italy). A catalogue of the books he offered in his Frankfurt shop in 1606 survives in the form of a broadside poster, headed *Catalogus Librorum Francofurti in Taberna Lazari Zetzneri Bibliopolae Argentinensis publice prostantium, anno millesimo sexcentesimo sexto.*[62] It lists some 122 books, arranged alphabetically, with formats but no dates or prices.

*

This brings us to the question of the fair catalogues. The book trade was centuries ahead of any other trade in issuing catalogues of its wares. Lists of books issued by individual printer-publishers are known from the late 1460s, and by the early sixteenth century it became increasingly necessary for publishers to issue catalogues of their stock. These would be distributed by the publishers or agents at the fairs, much as happens today, but in due course a general catalogue listing the new books on sale at the fairs became desirable. These comprehensive fair catalogues were in effect the fore-runners of national bibliographies; indeed, as recently as 1931 the *Deutsche Nationalbibliographie* superseded what had originally been the Leipzig fair catalogues.

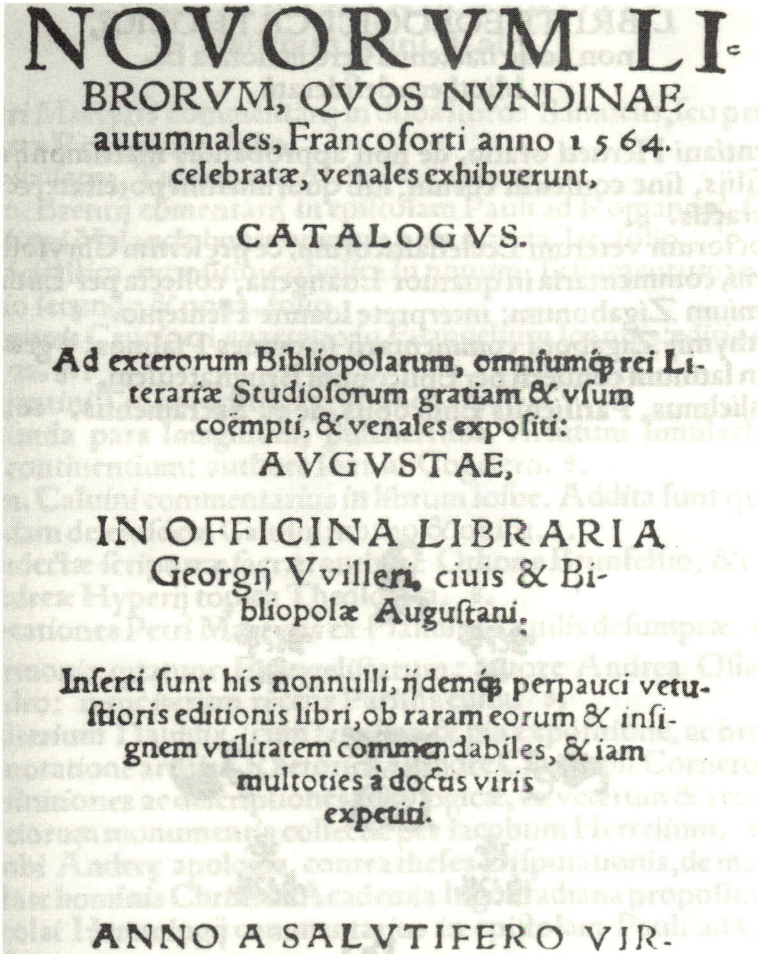

NOVORVM LI=
BRORVM, QVOS NVNDINAE
autumnales, Francoforti anno 1 5 64.
celebratæ, venales exhibuerunt,

CATALOGVS.

Ad exterorum Bibliopolarum, omnsumǽp rei Li-
terariæ Studiosorum gratiam & vsum
coëmpti, & venales expositi:

AVGVSTAE,

IN OFFICINA LIBRARIA
Georgij Vvilleri, ciuis & Bibliopolæ Augustani.

Inserti sunt his nonnulli, ijdemǽp perpauci vetu-
stioris editionis libri, ob raram eorum & insi-
gnem vtilitatem commendabiles, & iam
multoties à doctis viris
expetiti.

ANNO A SALVTIFERO VIR-
ginis partu, M. D. LXIIII.

Fig. 4.   Willer's first catalogue, Autumn 1564

The initiative for bringing out a general listing came from the Augsburg bookseller Georg Willer (active from 1548 to 1593) who produced the first such catalogue in the autumn of 1564; thereafter it appeared twice yearly. Surviving copies have been reproduced in facsimile by Bernhard Fabian.[63] Willer's first catalogue, *Novorum librorum, quos nundinae autumnales Francofurti anno 1564 celebratae venales exhiberunt, catalogus* (Fig. 4), was a small quarto of 22 pages listing 252 books classified by subject (basically following the order of precedence of university faculties: theology, law, medicine, the liberal arts), as follows:

> Catholic theology 'not new but hitherto in demand in our bookshop'[64]
> Protestant theology in Latin
> Catholic theology in Latin
> Civil and canon law [in Latin]
> Medicine in Latin and Greek
> Sacred and secular history in Latin
> Philosophy [including dialectic, rhetoric, grammar]
> Poetry [in Latin]
> Astrology and mathematics [in Latin]
> German books on the Scriptures and Protestant theologians
> German books on Catholic theology
> German books on the law and on writing [i.e. drawing up legal documents]
> German books on medicine
> German books on history
> Miscellaneous German books [these include titles such as *Reynicke Fuchs* and
>   Brant's *Narrenschiff,* a book of pictures from the Bible, and books on
>   mathematics and geometry]

With only minor modifications such as the addition of a section on music books already in the Spring 1565 catalogue and a separate section for Calvinist and Zwinglian theology in 1576, this arrangement continued throughout the sixteenth century and beyond.[65] Another section of interest is the long list of maps from Venice in the Autumn 1573 catalogue. With regard to law books, the remarks of a contemporary are worth noting. When in 1580 the Frankfurt patrician Nikolaus Rucker edited a volume of legal opinions by the Italian lawyer Johannes Baptista Zilettus, he observed in the preface that such books, especially from Italy, were in such demand that at recent Frankfurt fairs nearly 200 publications of this type had been on offer.[66]

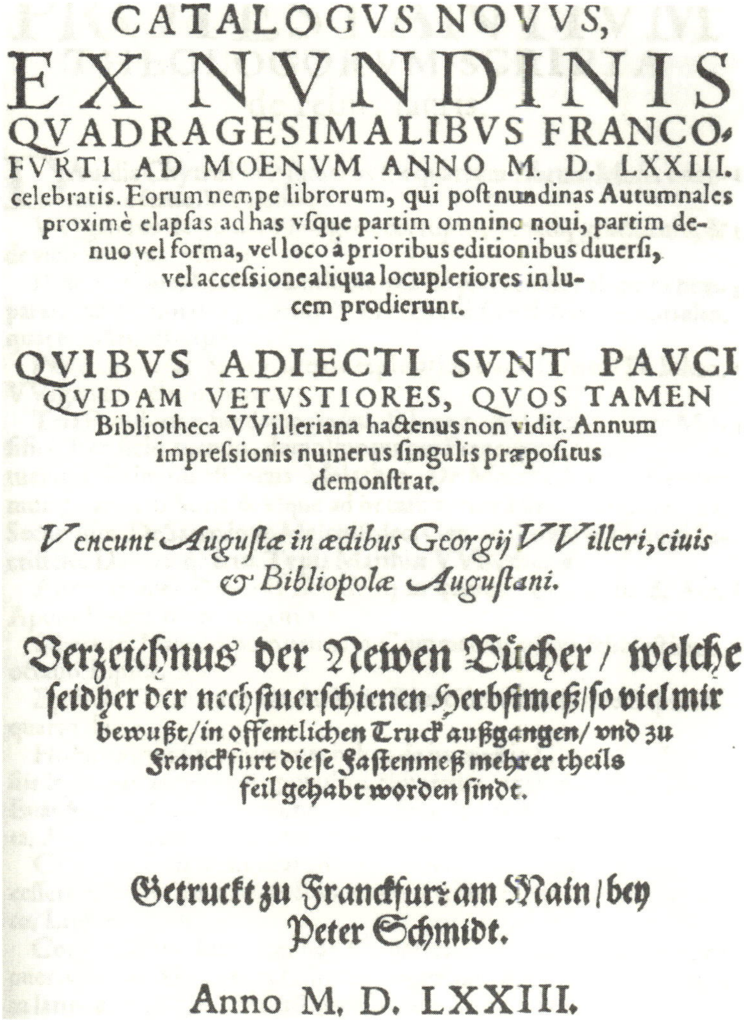

CATALOGVS NOVVS,

EX NVNDINIS

QVADRAGESIMALIBVS FRANCO-
FVRTI AD MOENVM ANNO M. D. LXXIII.
celebratis. Eorum nempe librorum, qui poſt nundinas Autumnales
proximè elapſas ad has vſque partim omnino noui, partim denuo vel forma, vel loco à prioribus editionibus diuerſi,
vel acceſsione aliqua locupletiores in lu-
cem prodierunt.

QVIBVS ADIECTI SVNT PAVCI
QVIDAM VETVSTIORES, QVOS TAMEN
Bibliotheca VVilleriana hactenus non vidit. Annum
impreſsionis numerus ſingulis præpoſitus
demonſtrat.

Veneunt Auguſtæ in ædibus Georgij VVilleri, ciuis
& Bibliopolæ Auguſtani.

Verzeichnus der Newen Bücher / welche
ſeidher der nechſtuerſchienen Herbſtmeß / ſo viel mir
bewußt / in offentlichen Truck außgangen / vnd zu
Franckfurt dieſe Faſtenmeß mehrer theils
feil gehabt worden ſindt.

Getruckt zu Franckfurt am Main / bey
Peter Schmidt.

Anno M. D. LXXIII.

Fig. 5. Willer's Easter 1573 catalogue

Willer stressed the fact that most of the books he listed were available in his shop at Augsburg. Initially he listed only the titles of German and foreign books which he had bought in Frankfurt for reselling, but from 1573 (Fig. 5) he included books that he knew only from information supplied by publishers or dealers. To ensure that the catalogues were as up-to-date as possible, from 1567 he had them printed at Frankfurt,[67] apparently so that he could sell copies at the fair itself and thus attract customers who would be unlikely to order books from him at Augsburg afterwards. His earliest catalogues did not include publishers' names, but from Autumn 1568 just over half the entries include this detail, fairly regularly but by no means consistently. Otherwise, however, no information is given — no date, no pagination, no price. Only from Autumn 1567 was the date of publication helpfully given in the margin so that one could see at a glance which were the latest books.[68] Figure 6 shows a page from Willer's 1592 catalogue with the year and place of publication,[69] publisher and format all clearly set out, with Latin titles in roman and German ones in gothic.[70] No prices were given because a fixed book price did not yet exist. Amongst themselves booksellers would agree special rates, the so-called Frankfurt *Tax* ('Frankfurt rate'), whereby in the case of books smaller than folio the price would be set according to the number of sheets involved. As booksellers would have to explain to their customers, these prices were not retail prices but a kind of net price to which transport, packing, customs and other charges had to be added; costs could depend on the number of copies purchased, the distance they had to be transported, and even the state and safety of the trade route along which they had to pass.[71]

That catalogues such as Willer's really were needed is shown by the fact that he soon had his rivals. In 1577 a similar catalogue was issued by another Augsburg firm, Johann Georg Portenbach and Thibaus (Tobias) Lutz, and continued by them and their successors until 1616.[72] By the 1590s there were others, too.[73] This situation prompted the Frankfurt Council on 10 August 1598 to ban the publication of private fair catalogues and to institute its own official one,[74] a sensible precaution given the existence of the Catholic-orientated Imperial Book Commission (established in 1569 to prevent the circulation of seditious and defamatory material). Frankfurt had been officially Lutheran since 1535.[75] The institution of an official catalogue enabled the Council not only to demonstrate to the Emperor that it was being vigilant but helped it to enforce stricter control of the trade, keep a check on the observance of printers' privileges

CATALOGVS AVTVMNALIS
MVSICI LIBRI DIVER-
farum linguarum.

1592. I Sagoge ad artem Muficam ex varijs auctoribus collecta,
pro tyronibus. Huic adiectæ funt fugæ aliquot fuauiores.
Item Harmonia carminum vfitatiorum , facro contextu
dulciffimæ, à Ioanne Crufio Halenfi felectæ & in lucem edi-
tæ. Noribergæ apud Lochnerum & Hofmannum. in 8.

1592. Triciniorum facrorum, quæ moteta vocant , omnis ge-
neris Inftrumentis muficis & viuæ voci accommodatorum
liber vnus. Ioanne à Caftro authore. Antuerpiæ apud Pe-
trum Phalefium. in 4.

1592. Hortulus Citharæ vulgaris, continens Phantafias, Paffo-
mezes, Paduanas, Gailliardas , Almandes, Branles , Voltes,
&c. Antverpiæ excudebat Petrus Phalefius, fibi & Ioanni
Bellero. in 4.

1592. 𝕹𝖊𝖚𝖜𝖊 𝕿𝖊𝖚𝖙𝖘𝖈𝖍𝖊 𝖂𝖊𝖑𝖙𝖑𝖎𝖈𝖍𝖊 𝕷𝖎𝖊𝖉𝖊𝖗 𝖒𝖎𝖙 𝖋ünff 𝕾𝖙𝖎𝖒𝖒𝖊𝖓/
𝖜𝖊𝖑𝖈𝖍𝖊𝖓 𝖟𝖚𝖒 𝖊𝖓𝖉𝖊 𝖟𝖜𝖊𝖞 𝖒𝖎𝖙 𝖘𝖊𝖈𝖍𝖘 𝕾𝖙𝖎𝖒𝖒𝖊𝖓 𝖍𝖎𝖓𝖟𝖚 𝖌𝖊𝖘𝖊𝖙𝖙/
𝕯𝖚𝖗𝖈𝖍 𝖁𝖆𝖑𝖊𝖗𝖙𝖎𝖓𝖚𝖒 𝕳𝖆𝖚ß𝖒𝖆𝖓𝖓. 𝕹ü𝖗𝖓𝖇𝖊𝖗𝖌 𝖎𝖓 𝖛𝖊𝖗𝖑𝖊𝖌𝖚𝖓𝖌
𝕬𝖓𝖉𝖗𝖊𝖊 𝖂𝖔𝖑𝖈𝖐𝖊𝖓. 𝖎𝖓 4.

1592. Fafciculus nouus felectiffimarum cartionum, 5.6.& plu-
rium vocum , nunc primùm in lucem editus. Authore Ot-
thone Sigfrido Harnifch. Helmftadij apud Iacobum Lu-
cium. in 4.

1592. 𝕷𝖆𝖚𝖙𝖊𝖓𝖇𝖚𝖈𝖍/ 𝖉𝖆𝖗𝖎𝖓𝖓 𝖛𝖔𝖓 𝖉𝖊𝖗 𝕿𝖆𝖇𝖚𝖑𝖆𝖙𝖚𝖗 𝖛𝖓𝖉 𝖀𝖕𝖕𝖑𝖎𝖈𝖆𝖙𝖎𝖔𝖓
𝖉𝖊𝖗 𝕷𝖆𝖚𝖙𝖊𝖓/ 𝖌𝖗ü𝖓𝖉𝖙𝖑𝖎𝖈𝖍𝖊𝖗 𝖛𝖓𝖉 𝖛𝖔𝖑𝖑𝖊𝖗 𝖁𝖓𝖙𝖊𝖗𝖗𝖎𝖈𝖍𝖙: 𝕾𝖆𝖒𝖕𝖙 𝖆𝖚ß-
𝖊𝖗𝖑𝖊𝖘𝖊𝖓𝖊𝖓 𝕻𝖔𝖑𝖓𝖎𝖘𝖈𝖍𝖊𝖓 𝕿ä𝖓𝖙𝖊𝖓/ 𝕻𝖆ß 𝖒𝖊𝖟𝖊𝖓/ 𝕲𝖆𝖎𝖑𝖑𝖎𝖆𝖗𝖉𝖊𝖓/ 𝖗𝖈.
𝖋𝖑𝖊𝖎ß𝖎𝖌 𝖟𝖚𝖌𝖊𝖗𝖎𝖈𝖍𝖙. 𝕯𝖚𝖗𝖈𝖍 Matthæum VVaifelium Barten-
fteinenfem. 𝕱𝖗𝖆𝖓𝖈𝖐𝖋𝖔𝖗𝖙 𝖆𝖓 𝖉𝖊𝖗 𝕺𝖉𝖊𝖗/ 𝖉𝖚𝖗𝖈𝖍 𝕬𝖓𝖉𝖗𝖊𝖆𝖒 𝕰𝖎𝖈𝖍-
𝖍𝖔𝖗𝖓. 𝖎𝖓 𝕱𝖔𝖑𝖎𝖔.

𝕯𝖊𝖗

Fig. 6. A page from Willer's Autumn 1592 catalogue

and ensure that the required copies of books were deposited.[76] The Council was concerned not least to ensure confessional objectivity; nevertheless, even the official catalogue was soon the cause of complaint to Emperor Rudolph II: already in 1602 Nikolaus Stein (Stain), a Catholic printer at Frankfurt, sought an imperial privilege to produce a Catholic catalogue because the official one was allegedly biased against Catholicism.[77] The booksellers and publishers were required to register their wares with the authorities:[78] in 1686 (presumably confirming previous practice) it was specified that details had to be submitted between Monday and Wednesday of the first week of the fair, so that the catalogue could be available at the latest on the Monday of the second week. This catalogue appeared — latterly somewhat fitfully — until about 1750. By the mid-seventeenth century the Frankfurt catalogue alone had a print-run of 1,200 copies, costing 1 Gulden for five copies.[79]

At Leipzig, too, a fair catalogue was produced, but whereas Frankfurt would have its official catalogue, in Leipzig it always stayed in private hands.[80] The first Leipzig catalogue was issued by Henning Grosse in 1594 and it remained in the hands of his successors until 1759.[81] From 1598 to 1619 a second catalogue was produced by Abraham Lamberg, and from 1620 Grosse and Lamberg issued the catalogue jointly. Because the Leipzig fairs followed those held at Frankfurt the Leipzig catalogues largely contained the same books as in the Frankfurt ones, though they often included a (sometimes substantial) section of 'books not shown at Frankfurt'. In 1637 the spring books from Frankfurt arrived late in Leipzig, with the result that only one catalogue was produced in Leipzig that year, claiming to cover the spring and autumn books from both centres.[82]

Over time the catalogues changed in character. In the earliest Willer listed the books he could supply *from* the fair; later they listed all the books available *at* the fair. The earlier catalogues included not just new publications but older books too. In the seventeenth and eighteenth centuries, on the other hand, they often included books that had not yet appeared, some of which indeed never appeared. Sometimes titles would change, one instance being that of Joachim von Sandrart, 'the German Vasari's', *Teutsche Academie* (Nuremberg, 1675) which was first announced in the Michaelmas 1672 Leipzig catalogue under the title *Academia Universale della Pittura, Scultura & Architectura: Oder: Gründliche Beschreibung der edlen Mahlerey/Bildhauerey und Baukunst* ..., while in the Frankfurt Autumn 1675 catalogue the same book, now at last available, appears under the title *Teutsche Academie der Edlen Bau- Bild und Mahlerey Künste*.[83] Overall it has to be said that the catalogues have their limitations as reliable sources of information inasmuch as they record only a proportion of the books produced at the time — it is reckoned that only about 20–25 per cent of the books available were actually listed in the catalogues.[84] Primarily they focus on books of scholarly interest, especially in Latin, with a potential for wide geographical dissemination. Hence small works, books of sermons, prayer-books, university theses, calendars and the like scarcely feature. Nevertheless, as long as we remember that the catalogues' purpose was to advertise and to generate interest, not to serve as comprehensive bibliographical aids, they must be considered invaluable and indispensable sources, giving a reasonable picture of the German and international book trade of the early modern period.

As the first regularly appearing current awareness bulletins, these catalogues long remained essential reading for scholars and bibliomanes. Already in 1611 Georg Draud, a Lutheran pastor, attempted comprehensive compilations based on the individual catalogues.[85] The catalogues' importance as sources of bibliographical information is shown by the fact that in July 1615 the curators of the Bodleian Library agreed to meet within a week of the arrival of the Frankfurt fair catalogues to select books, and from 1617 they seem to have used the London bookseller John Bill's own English version of the Frankfurt catalogue which appeared from 1617 to 1628 (STC 11328–11331.2);[86] Bill's lists contained only selections from the latest issue of the Frankfurt catalogue, omitted all books in German, and added some older titles still available in London. In 1685 Jean-Paul de La Roque, editor of the *Journal des savants* in Paris, in welcoming the founding of the German periodical *Acta eruditorum* in 1682, specifically remarks that until then German books had been known in France only through the Frankfurt fair catalogues.[87]

One indication of the centrality of the book fairs in the marketing strategy of German publishers is the fact that many books, irrespective of where they were actually produced, bore the words 'Frankfurt und Leipzig' on their titlepages, a phenomenon which has caused bibliographers and cataloguers much confusion; 'Frankfurt und Leipzig' often meant nothing more than that these were the places where the books were traded, or else was intended to imply something about the quality of the book (rather like our own claim that a particular work is 'available from all good bookshops'); it is possible also that it was intended circumspectly to conceal the true place of printing.[88] As the importance of the Frankfurt fair grew, the more the local book trade benefited. Frankfurt printer-publishers waited for the world to come to them, though doubtless they, too, would arrange to be represented at Leipzig and elsewhere. It is likely that Frankfurt publishers brought out certain titles specifically to catch the biannual fair trade, though as far as I know this aspect has not yet been properly researched. A prime example is the *Historia von D. Johann Fausten*, the first Faust book, which seems to have been quite a sensation at Autumn fair in 1587. This anonymous Lutheran tract, which the printer, Johann Spies, referred to as 'this modest fair ware' (*geringer Meßkram*) in his preface dated Monday, 4 September,[89] was an instant success: at least four unauthorized reprints are known from the same year, Spies himself brought out an expanded version in 1588, and the total number of authorized and unauthorized reprints, adaptations (for instance, a Catholic version and a verse version) and translations the work experienced from 1587 into the 1590s is impressive, to say the least.[90] The English translation, *The Historie of the Damnable Life and Deserved Death of Doctor Iohn Faustus*, made 'according to the true Copie printed at Franckfort' and published in 1592,[91] served as the basis for Christopher Marlowe's *Tragical History of Doctor Faustus*.

Even more interesting perhaps as products specifically brought out in connection with the fair are the so-called *Meßrelationen*. These newsbooks, generally quartos of about a hundred pages, gave a digest of current affairs, mostly political and military events and commercial news but sometimes also sensations, comets and the like. They have sometimes been seen as forerunners of newspapers, but in fact they were very different. Whereas early newspapers appeared weekly and later even more frequently, the *Meßrelationen* were published biannually in connection with the fairs. Nor can they be seen as direct forerunners of the periodical press because whereas the *Meßrelationen* were first issued in the 1580s, the first proper periodicals in Germany date from nearly a century later.[92] Several *Meßrelationen* appeared at Cologne in the 1580s and 90s, one was published at Strasbourg in connection with the fair there in the autumn of 1590, and the first Frankfurt *Historische Relation* appeared for the Lent fair 1591, with others at Magdeburg around 1600. At Leipzig the first came out for the Spring fair 1605 and the last appeared around 1730.[93]

For information as to who attended the Frankfurt fairs we are dependent on such correspondence, account books, and lists that have chanced to survive.[94] We know the names of a few publishers from such places as Mainz and Basle who attended in the fifteenth century, and the rich correspondence relating to Anton Koberger of Nuremberg shows that between autumn 1493 to spring 1509 he visited the fair in person on at least fifteen occasions and was represented by others at least five more times.[95] The prolific publisher Giovanni Battista Ciotti (1560–after 1625) of Venice regularly visited the Frankfurt fair from 1583 onwards. In 1587 he had a book printed there by Johann Wechel. Ciotti books are recorded at Frankfurt in 1594 (3 titles), 1599 (7), 1600 (45), 1601 (40), 1602 (26) and 1605 (3).[96] The London printer and bookseller John Bill, who was active from 1604 until his death in 1630, was a regular annual visitor to the fair. He was an agent for King James I, Sir Thomas Bodley, the 9th Earl of Northumberland and others. Another regular visitor to the Frankfurt fair in the third quarter of the seventeenth century was the Copenhagen bookseller Peter Haubold who also listed 56 titles in the catalogue between 1667 and 1682, missing out only 1679 while his colleague Daniel Paulli announced 117 titles over the same period, missing out only 1674.[97]

A good example of the rare surviving documentation records the Frankfurt publisher Sigmund Feyerabend's sales at the Spring fair 1565. He sold books to a total of 106 booksellers. Sixty-one of these, who accounted for 1403 books, came from southern Germany (i.e. from south of the Main); 36, buying 983 books, came from northern Germany. Three booksellers from Antwerp bought 83 volumes, three from Switzerland 23, two from Paris 17, and one from Venice 57. In addition he sold 69 books to unspecified individuals.[98] A list of all the booksellers and publishers who visited the Autumn fair in 1579 has survived.[99] This records 70 printers and publishers, 30 booksellers, and also names twenty men not actually present at that time but who normally came. Altogether 36 different towns are mentioned.[100] Among the people mentioned are several who did not produce books themselves but were exclusively booksellers. Between 10 and 16 September 1579 these traders were all questioned by three named officials, being required to produce, where applicable, their imperial privileges (the only form of copyright then in force), to show that the copies they were required to deposit with the authorities had in fact been supplied, and to provide lists or catalogues of their books.

That Frankfurt was very much a hub of the book trade is revealed by an analysis of Sigmund Feyerabend's customers in his records for the years 1590–97. There were approximately 350 customers from 110 different places. Of these only 10–15% were individual readers; the overwhelming majority were trade customers. About two thirds of them were from major commercial centres or from university towns. Apart from Frankfurt itself, the towns most strongly represented were Nuremberg and Cologne, then Stuttgart, Strasbourg, Leipzig and Augsburg, followed by Wittenberg, Jena, Leiden, Antwerp, Venice, Magdeburg, Heidelberg, Tübingen, Ulm, Worms, Basle and Schwäbisch Hall; then came Zurich, Braunschweig and Hamburg. Dealers from some of these places will have sold their books on to customers further afield; thus a bookseller from Nuremberg may well have found customers in Bohemia and one from Leipzig customers in Poland. And Georg Willer in Augsburg is known to have covered fairs and markets all over southern Germany down to Lake Constance, Bavaria south of the Danube, Lower and Upper Austria, Styria, Carinthia as far as Lubljana, and the Tyrol down as far as Bozen (Bolzano).[101]

Business at Frankfurt was not necessarily always as lucrative as some might have hoped. Take the case of Casiodoro de Reyna, a Spaniard who in 1567 had advanced 400 Gulden to the famous Basle printer Johann Oporinus to print 1,100 copies of the first Bible in Spanish.[102] Oporinus died deep in debt in 1568, and his private library had to be sold off to satisfy his creditors. This took several years to arrange, but at last in 1574 the whole collection was knocked down for 800 Gulden to Casiodoro de Reyna. Casiodoro had the books sent to Frankfurt where he hoped to get better prices for them than in Basle. However, things were not as easy as he imagined: at the next Frankfurt fair he sold barely 60 Gulden worth, though in the long run things turned out well enough: he found favour as a supplier of books to the court libraries at Heidelberg and Kassel, and in 1575 he had a book published at his own expense in which he described himself as 'Genius Bibliothecae Oporinianae' ('genius of the Oporinian collection').[103]

The growth in importance of the Frankfurt fair was due in part to the general increase in the demand for books. German universities were increasing in number and size;[104] greater prestige and value was attaching to the possession of books; the educational book market was changing; and the cosmopolitan nature of the Latin book trade were all significant factors.[105] But already by the end of the sixteenth century the glory days were past, and a long decline set in. There was a downturn in the number of Latin books advertised after 1630, and the commercial attractiveness of Frankfurt declined after it was besieged by the Swedes under King

Gustavus Adolphus in 1631, when other publishing centres, notably Leipzig and Leiden, began to come to prominence. Commercial greed and sharp practice had their part to play also, but the factors were many.[106] Important firms such as those of Wechel and Zetzner were laid low because the supply of books exceeded demand. Another factor was the institution of the Imperial Book Commission in 1569. In principle the city authorities had been bound by the Archbishop and Elector of Mainz to censor the books on offer at the fair, but they showed themselves so tolerant in such matters that eventually Emperor Maximilian II instituted a commission with the duty during the fair of inspecting the booksellers' stands, examining the privileges and the catalogues, and seeking out objectionable books.[107] The Imperial Commission lay largely in the hands of the Jesuits who made of it a rigorous instrument for furtherance of the Counter-Reformation. Given that Frankfurt at this time had four times as many Protestants as Catholics, the Commission's partisan and arbitrary censorship inevitably led to the decline of the book trade. The difficulties were compounded in 1597 when Emperor Rudolph II appointed two commissioners whose task was to exercise *permanent* oversight over the book trade, not just at fair times. In 1605 this commission was also charged with inspecting books on behalf of papal authority too. The rigorous manner in which the commissioners performed their duties and especially their zeal in rejecting Protestant publications, not to mention their rapacious demand for free copies,[108] contributed not a little to the ruination of the Frankfurt fair, even though the city still retained a leading position in the production and marketing of types and the design and printing of illustrated books. Whereas in 1650 twice as many books were on offer at Frankfurt as at Leipzig, by 1670 the numbers were more or less equal, and by 1700 Frankfurt's share was less than half that of Leipzig.[109] The Venetians and the Dutch had stopped coming, and by 1720 the number of Leipzig firms coming to Frankfurt was down to five, falling later to two. The table on the next page illustrates the decline of the fair as an international event.[110]

Even though the absolute number of titles traded steadily increased between 1564 and the outbreak of the Thirty Years' War (1618) and, after a decline, recovered to some extent after the war, the proportion of foreign books as a percentage of all the books on offer declined inexorably from almost 40 per cent in the 1560s to less than 21 per cent in 1618, less than 12 per cent in 1660, and dwindled to virtually nothing by 1700. Indeed

Number of titles listed in the fair catalogues 1564–1709, by decade
(boxed figures relate to the Thirty Years' War period)

	1564–69	1570–79	1580–89	1590–99	1600–09	1610–19	1620–29	1630–39	1640–49	1650–59	1660–69	1670–79	1680–89	1690–99	1700–09
German-speaking countries	1225	2967	4196	5645	10228	12300	9480	5996	7581	7269	7068	7204	7460	9499	11494
France	152	438	464	394	564	918	562	252	75	128	81	40	57	13	2
Italy	381	614	492	536	1082	559	286	34	75	40	16	10	23	6	4
England	0	21	27	10	36	151	77	15	7	27	3	2	33	0	0
Antwerp and southern Low Countries	247	411	349	363	619	781	740	486	522	474	123	6	1	1	12
Amsterdam and northern Low Countries	2	4	48	226	384	798	416	665	826	865	727	326	336	247	22
TOTAL	2007	4455	5576	7174	12913	15507	11561	7448	9086	8803	8018	7588	7910	9766	11534
Foreign imports as percentage of total	*39.0*	*33.4*	*24.7*	*21.3*	*20.8*	*20.7*	*18.0*	*19.5*	*16.6*	*17.4*	*11.8*	*5.1*	*5.7*	*2.7*	*0.3*

Italian books have almost disappeared by 1630 and French books by 1640, while English books barely have a toe-hold at any time, not least because of the high prices charged for them.[111] The only area of significant growth is in books from Amsterdam which increase steadily from about 1590 to 1660. The collapse of supply from the southern Low Countries is linked to the decision by Plantin's heirs and their Antwerp colleagues in 1660 not to attend the fairs, and even though books from Amsterdam and the northern Low Countries continued for a while longer, their numbers dwindled too, especially as Frankfurt declined and the importance of the less internationally oriented Leipzig fair increased around 1700.[112] The effect of the Thirty Years' War on the German book trade is illustrated also by Neddermeyer's statistics of books on history and classics published from 1600 to 1709. Taking the years 1610–19 as = 100, he arrives at the following percentage values.[113]

1600–09	1610–19	1620–29	1630–39	1640–49	1650–59	1660–69	1670–79	1680–89	1690–99	1700–09
86	100	78	40	47	77	95	73	55	97	123

The Thirty Years' War (1618–48) had terrible consequences for Germany. Although Frankfurt itself was at first less affected than some other towns, the fundamental changes that occurred in the social, political, cultural and economic life of Germany in the later seventeenth century had such serious effects on the traditional book trade that the fair inevitably suffered, though the situation at Leipzig seems to have been even worse.[114] The impact of the war is highlighted in the graph on the next page, contrasting the number of titles listed in the fair catalogues with book production in Britain.[115] Although, strictly speaking, we are not comparing like with like (a better comparison would be total book production in Germany rather than the number of titles in the catalogues, but these figures are not available), the graph shows rather dramatically how — decade by decade — the number of titles in the catalogues declined after 1620, reached its low point in the 1630s, and even after the end of the war stagnated for 40 years, whereas by contrast British book production consistently outstripped the fair catalogue figures from the 1630s onwards.

Many dealers, especially foreigners, did not bother to resume their activities in Frankfurt after the Treaty of Westphalia in 1648, the restrictions imposed by the Imperial Book Commission being a serious disincentive. Between 1680 and 1690 publishing at Frankfurt collapsed, and thereafter the centres of book production in Germany were predominantly in the centre and north rather than as previously in the south. In particular, north German Protestant presses flourished. Leipzig moved quickly into the forefront of the German book world, and its book fair outstripped Frankfurt's in importance. Leipzig was favoured by its accessible position in central Europe, the privileges that the Saxon government bestowed on the trade fairs and the liberality with which the city council interpreted them, as well as by the importance of its university, and above all the business acumen of members of the book trade there.[116] It was a member of the Leipzig trade, Philipp Erasmus Reich (1717–87), a partner of the firm of Weidmann (founded in 1682), who in effect put an end to the Frankfurt fair by closing his Frankfurt warehouse in 1764 and encouraging others to do the same.[117]

According to Paul Raabe, it was only in 1765 that the number of titles published in Germany (1,517) reached the level of 1600 again.[118] In the last quarter of the eighteenth century German book production increased rapidly: from 1,800 titles a year in 1770 to 3,500 in 1790 and more than 4,000 in 1800.[119] During this period also the balance between Latin and German books shifted significantly. The ratio of Latin to German books listed in the Frankfurt and Leipzig catalogues was 71:29 in 1650, 38:62 in 1700, 28:72 in 1740, and 4:96 in 1800.[120]

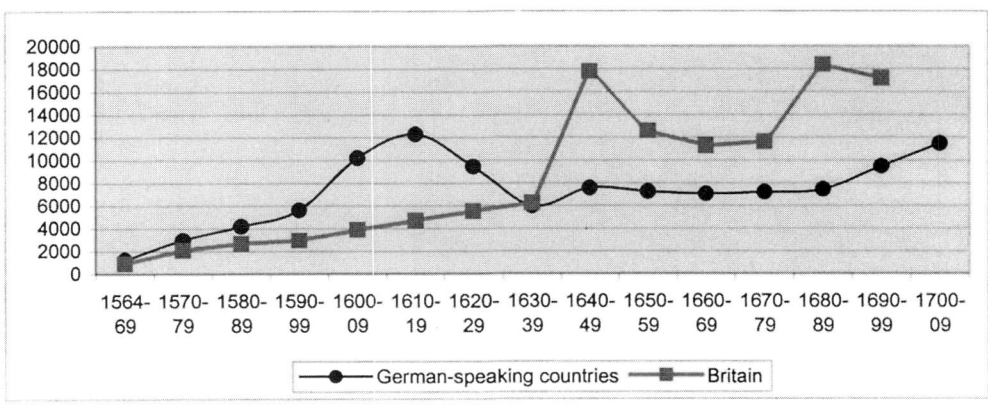

NUMBER OF TITLES LISTED IN THE FAIR CATALOGUES 1564–1709 COMPARED WITH BRITISH BOOK PRODUCTION FIGURES (ten-year totals apart from 1564–69)

Frankfurt's loss was, then, Leipzig's gain. During the first decade of the eighteenth century four times as many publications were listed in the Leipzig catalogue as in that of Frankfurt. Details are naturally hard to come by, but in 1741 312 firms from 106 different towns were represented at the Leipzig fair. Of these 152 came from 60 towns in north Germany, 119 from 29 towns in southern Germany, while 41 firms came from 17 towns in other countries (several of them from Switzerland).[121] In contrast, at Frankfurt ever fewer books were exhibited from year to year, and the fair ceased entirely in 1749, ironically enough in the very year of the birth of Frankfurt's most famous son and Germany's greatest writer, Johann Wolfgang Goethe. A few years later, in 1765, Goethe went as a student to Leipzig. When he arrived at Michaelmas the fair was in full swing, and he records in his autobiography, *Dichtung und Wahrheit* (Part II, Book 6), with what interest he wandered amongst the stalls; he was particularly impressed by the exotic visitors from Poland, Russia and Greece. From a few years later, we have the reminiscences of Magnus Swederus (1748–1836), bookseller in Uppsala from 1775. In his autobiography he boasts of having been the first Swedish bookseller to visit the Leipzig fair, where his Swedish origin aroused such attention that he received about 150 visitors in four days; he sold 20 to 50 copies of some of his books to several firms and established accounts with more than 130 colleagues all over Europe. He notes that German booksellers granted six months' credit together with a 10 to 25 per cent trade discount, whereas he received a meagre 5 per cent discount 'for prompt payment' in London.[122] But Leipzig never attracted foreign booksellers and publishers on the scale that Frankfurt had done in its heyday: Leipzig was essentially a German, rather than an international, fair.

However, although the Leipzig fair attracted few booksellers from abroad, this does not mean that foreign books were not to be found there. Let us consider the case of English books. In the Frankfurt catalogues relatively few English books were listed: 36 in the first decade of the seventeenth century, 151 during the second, and 77 during the third, with virtually nothing in the English language thereafter.[123] (The significant increase during the second decade Blum attributes to growing interest in the fair by English booksellers following the marriage of James I's daughter to the Elector Palatine Frederick V in 1612.) It is only in the eighteenth century, in the Leipzig catalogues, that books by English authors begin to appear more regularly.[124] In 1733 Henning Grosse, bookseller and publisher of the Leipzig fair catalogue, offered Isaac Newton, in a Latin edition produced in Amsterdam. But in the catalogue for Michaelmas 1737 Grosse advertised the availability of 26 works in English, including John Dart's *History and Antiquities of the Cathedral Church of Canterbury* (1726), Alexander Pope's *Literary Correspondence* (1735–7), and *The History of Poland under Augustus II* (1734), John Stacie's translation of the work by Jean Baptiste Desroches de Parthenay. In the Michaelmas 1755 catalogue, another Leipzig bookseller, Johann Wendler (1713–99), listed editions of a number of literary authors including Thomas Gray, Milton, Pope, Thomson, and Young, and moreover Wendler mentioned that he was issuing a special catalogue of English books free of charge — unfortunately no copy of this seems to have survived.

*

In conclusion, a word about the Frankfurt and Leipzig fairs today. Despite the retention of the traditional name, Frankfurter Buchmesse, the Frankfurt book fair cannot really be seen as continuing the old tradition. When after a break of 200 years it was established in 1949, after the Second World War and the sealing of the division of Germany, it was initially intended to be an internal German affair, rather than an international showcase. Accordingly just 200 German publishers and booksellers exhibited there that year. But already in 1950 publishers from other countries were attracted to it, and steady growth continued thereafter — in 2004 6,691 publishers from 110 countries exhibited 350,619 titles.

The Leipzig trade fairs were the international showcase of the former German Democratic Republic and as such were regularly celebrated on postage stamps. Today the Leipzig Book Fair continues to be held over four days in March each year, but it is a markedly smaller affair than its Frankfurt counterpart. In 2005 there were 2,142 exhibitors from 31 countries, and the event attracted only 108,000 visitors, almost 50 per cent of whom came from Leipzig and within a 100 km radius.

References

1. See Günter Richter, 'Christian Egenolffs Erben 1555–1667', *Archiv für Geschichte des Buchwesens*, 7 (1967), cols 449–1130.
2. For further information on these see, respectively, Herwarth von Schade, 'Peter Braubach in Frankfurt (1540–1567). Ein Werkverzeichnis', *Archiv für Geschichte des Buchwesens*, 21 (1980), 849–964; Imke Schmidt, *Die Bücher aus der Frankfurter Offizin Gülfferich – Han – Weigand Han-Erben. Eine literarhistorische und buchgeschichtliche Untersuchung zum Buchdruck in der zweiten Hälfte des 16. Jahrhunderts*

(Wiesbaden: Harrassowitz, 1996); Heinrich Pallmann, *Siegmund Feyerabend, sein Leben und seine geschäftlichen Verbindungen*, Archiv für Frankfurts Geschichte und Kunst, n.F. 7 (Frankfurt am Main: Völcker, 1881); Ian Maclean, 'André Wechel at Frankfurt 1572–1581', *Gutenberg-Jahrbuch*, 63 (1988), 146–76.

3. Claus Nordmann, *Nürnberger Großhändler im spätmittelalterlichen Lübeck*, Nürnberger Beiträge zu den Wirtschafts- und Sozialwissenschaften, 37/38 (Nuremberg: Krische, 1933), p. 142.

4. For the Lent fair 1579 Plantin sent six barrels containing 5,212 copies of 67 different titles. Cited by Colin Clair, *A History of European Printing* (London: Academic Press, 1976), p. 223. Cholinus (d. 1588) was official printer to the city of Cologne and member of the city council. For full details of shipping and road transport routes to Frankfurt in the early modern period see Alexander Dietz, *Frankfurter Handelsgeschichte*, 5 vols (Frankfurt am Main, 1910–25), III, 287–360.

5. The 'Buchgaß' is mentioned several times by the Frankfurt poet Konrad Lautenbach in his *Marckschiff oder Marckschiffer Gespräch von der Franckfurter Meß* (1596). (On this see note 31 below.)

6. Nordmann [note 3], p. 137.

7. Pierre L. Van der Haegen, *Der frühe Basler Buchdruck*. Schriften der Universitätsbibliothek Basel, 5 (Basle: Schwabe, 2001), p. 75.

8. Gerald Strauss, *Nuremberg in the Sixteenth Century* (Bloomington: University of Indiana Press, 1976), p. 132. Nor could the escort be relied upon. As Anton Koberger explained to Johann Amerbach in a letter of 14 February 1502, he did not expect to attend the Lenten fair at Frankfurt because 'the princes will not ride escort, so it does not seem to me a good idea to put myself in danger and ride there without escort', cited from *The Correspondence of Johann Amerbach. Early Printing in its Social Context*, selected, translated, edited, with commentary by Barbara C. Halporn (Ann Arbor: University of Michigan Press, 2000), p. 241, after *Die Amerbachkorrespondenz*, ed. Alfred Hartmann and Beat R. Jenny, 10 vols (to date) (Basle: Verlag der Universitätsbibliothek, 1942–), I, no. 148.

9. For an early account of fairs and their role see Paul Jacob Marperger, *Beschreibung der Messen und Jahr-Märckte* ... (1711, repr. Frankfurt/Main, 1968) (Klassiker der Betriebswirtschaftslehre, 2). (A slightly earlier edition, of 1710, is in Munich, Bayerische Staatsbibliothek: Res.Merc.141.)

10. The Danube provides a good example: bridges were built at Vienna in 1439, at Krems in 1463 and in 1497 at Linz.

11. Likewise there was a Simon and Jude fair at Basle (see Oscar von Hase, *Die Koberger* (Amsterdam and Wiesbaden, 1967), p. 306). Other important fairs were at Nördlingen where, even though this was principally a wool and cloth fair, we hear of a literary manuscript being bought in 1458, the Augsburg printers Johann Bämler and Jodocus Pflanzmann selling 20,000 indulgences (Hans-Jörg Künast, *'Getruckt zu Augspurg': Buchdruck und Buchhandel in Augsburg zwischen 1468 und 1555* (Tübingen: Niemeyer, 1997), p. 153) and the Strasbourg printer Adolf Rusch selling scholarly works in 1470 (von Hase, p. 307). Strasbourg itself had fairs at Shrovetide and St John's Day (von Hase, p. 307). In general, because of its fortunate location Strasbourg proved a very convenient place at which to transact business, especially for merchants from Basle,

Lyon, and Nuremberg (on Koberger's use of Strasbourg see von Hase, pp. 307–9). Strasbourg also played a major role in shipping on the Rhine.

12. Norbert Bachleitner, Franz M. Eybl and Ernst Fischer, *Geschichte des Buchhandels in Österreich*, Geschichte des Buchhandels, 6 (Wiesbaden: Harrassowitz, 2000), p. 11.

13. Elector Frederick II later established a New Year's fair at Leipzig, too. This was confirmed by Emperor Frederick III in 1466. On the Leipzig fairs see von Hase [note 11], pp. 310–16.

14. The literature reveals much uncertainty over the dates of the Frankfurt Spring Fair. The details given here are from Dietz [note 4], I, 37–8. See also Friedrich Kapp and Johann Goldfriedrich, *Geschichte des Deutschen Buchhandels* (Leipzig, 1886–1913), II, 221, 225. Künast [note 11], p. 162, note 316, says it began on *Oculi* Sunday (the third Sunday in Lent), and ended on the day before Palm Sunday.

15. Kapp/Goldfriedrich [note 14], II, 222, 225.

16. Dietz [note 4], I, 40. According to von Hase [note 11], p. 331, the Frankfurt Autumn fair began on 20 September, the eve of St Matthew's Day.

17. Cited by Clair [note 4], p. 221. The British Library has copies of both the folio and the octavo editions (pressmarks 566.i.26 and 793.b.2, respectively).

18. Hans-Jörg Künast, 'Johann Schönsperger d. J. und seine gescheiterten Unternehmungen in Sachsen', *Leipziger Jahrbuch zur Buchgeschichte*, 8 (1998), 297–318, here p. 300 and p. 317f. for the relevant documentation. The New Testament (VD16 B4323) did eventually appear, in 1523, presumably in time for the autumn fair.

19. Kapp/Goldfriedrich [note 14], I, 455.

20. See John L. Flood, '"Safer on the battlefield than in the city": England, the "Sweating Sickness", and the Continent', *Renaissance Studies*, 17 (2003), 147–76.

21. They had 'solch buch zu Frangkfurt nicht gelesen, sondern wie es pflegt inn Messen in gedreng und eil zuzugehen, nicht mehr dann den Titel gesehen, und ein anzahl Exemplaria hingesetzt und alsbald eingeschlagen und aufladen lassen, und nicht eher inn erfarung kommen seind, was inn gemeltem Buch stehet, bis das sie die Buecher anher gebracht, und aus den Fassen genommen'. Cited by Reinhard Wittmann, *Geschichte des deutschen Buchhandels* (Munich: Beck, 1991), p. 59, after Kapp/Goldfriedrich [note 14], I, 470.

22. Künast [note 11], p. 162, esp. note 317.

23. Heinrich Grimm, 'Die Buchführer des deutschen Kulturbereichs und ihre Niederlassungen in der Zeitspanne 1490 bis um 1550', *Archiv für Geschichte des Buchwesens*, 7 (1967), cols 1153–1772, here col. 1741; Bachleitner [note 12], p. 10.

24. Helga Noflatscher-Posch, *Die Jahrmärkte von Hall in Tirol. Ein Handelszentrum Tirols in der frühen Neuzeit* (Hall/Tirol, 1992).

25. John L. Flood, 'Subversion in the Alps: Books and Readers in the Austrian Counter-Reformation', *The Library*, VI, 12 (1990), 185–211.

26. Günter Richter, 'Buchhändlerische Kataloge vom 15. bis um die Mitte des 17. Jahrhunderts', in Reinhard Wittmann (ed.), *Bücherkataloge als buchgeschichtliche Quellen in der frühen Neuzeit*, Wolfenbütteler Schriften zur Geschichte des Buchwesens, 10 (Wiesbaden: Harrassowitz, 1985), pp. 33–65, here pp. 54–5. The sole surviving copy of Cratander's 1539 catalogue is in the Austrian National Library,

Vienna (Richter, p. 37, note 15). This arrangement serves to illustrate the important role played by Basle as a channel for cultural exchange.

27. Von Hase [note 11], p. 310.

28. Von Hase [note 11], p. 312–13.

29. Their protests are printed in Ernst Hasse, 'Notizen zur Geschichte des Verfalls der Frankfurter Büchermesse', *Archiv für Geschichte des Deutschen Buchhandels*, 4 (1879), 221–3.

30. Henricus Stephanus [= Henri Estienne], *Francofordiense emporium sive Francofordienses nundinae* (Geneva, 1574), p. 15. This text is also available in *The Frankfurt Book Fair: The Francofordiense Emporium of H. Estienne*, edited with historical introduction, original Latin text with English translation on opposite page and notes by J. W. Thompson (Chicago: Caxton Club, 1911; repr. Amsterdam, 1969). For the history of the book fairs generally see Kapp/Goldfriedrich [note 14], vols I and II, *passim*; Alexander Dietz, *Zur Geschichte der Frankfurter Büchermesse 1462–1792*, Schriften des Frankfurter Messamts, 5 (Frankfurt am Main, 1921); and especially Rainer Koch (ed.), *Brücke zwischen den Völkern. Zur Geschichte der Frankfurter Messe* (Frankfurt am Main, 1991), comprising three volumes: 1. *Frankfurt im Messenetz Europas – Erträge der Forschung*; 2. *Beiträge zur Geschichte der Frankfurter Messe* (pp. 195–203 deal with the book fair); 3. *Ausstellungskatalog zur Geschichte der Frankfurter Messe* (pp. 190–210 relate to the book trade). See also Michael Rothmann, *Die Frankfurter Messen im Mittelalter*, Frankfurter historische Abhandlungen, 40 (Stuttgart: Steiner, 1998), and Sabine Niemeier, *Funktionen der Frankfurter Buchmesse im Wandel — von den Anfängen bis heute*, Buchwissenschaftliche Beiträge aus dem Deutschen Bucharchiv München, 68 (Wiesbaden: Harrassowitz, 2001).

31. *Marckschiff oder Marckschiffer Gespräch von der Franckfurter Meß. Darinn alles, was in derselben Meß namhafftes und seltzames zusehen, beschrieben ist durch Marx Mangold* [= Konrad Lautenbach (1534–95)]. The complete text is printed in Julius Ziehen (ed.), *Der Frankfurter Markt oder die Frankfurter Messe von Heinrich Stephanus* (Frankfurt am Main: Diesterweg, 1919), pp. 45–78.

32. Kapp/Goldfriedrich [note 14], I, 449.

33. On the Gutenberg Bible at Frankfurt, see Martin Davies. 'Juan de Carvajal and Early Printing', *The Library*, VI, 18 (1996), 193–215.

34. Van der Haegen [note 7], p. 70. For other early visitors to the fair, see von Hase [note 11], pp. 316–32.

35. Kapp/Goldfriedrich [note 14], I, 453.

36. Von Hase [note 11], 1967, p. 318.

37. Amerbach's edition is unsigned but was probably published in 1490 (London BL: IB.37461).

38. Amerbach published editions in 1489 (London BL IB.37313) and 1490 (London BL: IB.37328).

39. Amerbach published editions in 1489 (London BL IB.37313(2)) and 1490 (London BL: IB.37328(2)).

40. Amerbach's edition appeared in 1489 (London BL: IB.37324).

41. Amerbach's edition appeared in 1492 (London BL: IB.37347).

42. Amerbach's edition appeared in 1492 (London BL: IA.37349).

43. Halporn [note 8], pp. 86–9; *Amerbachkorrespondenz*, I, no. 38.
44. Von Hase [note 11], p. 376.
45. Kapp/Goldfriedrich [note 14], I, 457. The Venetian printer Baptista de Tortis attended both Frankfurt fairs in 1498 (see *Archiv für Geschichte des Deutschen Buchhandels*, 4 (1879), 215–16).
46. 'Es tuen die Straßenplacker den Buchführern nichts, lassen sie ziehen, weil die Juden auf Bücher das allerwenigste Geld geben. Manche Reiter aber nehmen ein Büchel an, das man ihnen verehrt.' Cited by Grimm [note 23], col. 1171.
47. Halporn [note 8], p. 269, after *Amerbachkorrespondenz*, I, no. 306.
48. Estienne [note 30], pp. 9–10.
49. In the early period booksellers usually bartered books in sheets against equivalent sheets of other publications, so-called *Tauschhandel*. While this helped dealers with their cash-flow problems and ensured diversification of stock, it had the undesirable side-effect of encouraging unscrupulous publishers to produce sub-standard works which they exchanged for works of higher quality. This eventually led leading publishers, such as Philipp Erasmus Reich (1717–87), co-owner of Weidmann's at Leipzig, to demand cash payment or six-monthly settlement with a discount. Opponents such as Johann Thomas Edler von Trattner (1717–98) in Vienna resorted to ruthless piracy of Leipzig publications, which led to their exclusion from the Leipzig fair, to which they responded by selling their wares through itinerant booksellers and pedlars. See Richard Mummendey, *Von Büchern und Bibliotheken*, 2nd edn (Darmstadt: Wissenschaftliche Buchgesellschaft, 1964), p. 313.
50. On this particular role of Frankfurt see von Hase [note 11], p. 328, who observes that Koberger might sometimes have money collected at fairs in Lyon and Leipzig, but always took care to despatch money to the home addresses of individuals at Basle or Strasbourg if he could not meet them at Frankfurt.
51. The Lyon fair can be traced back to 1420. Initially there were three fairs a year, each lasting twenty days, but in 1463 Louis XI granted *lettres de franchise* for four fairs annually, each of two weeks. One was held in August, another at All Souls'. Merchants of all nationalities were admitted, apart from the English, 'noz ennemis anciens'. From 1484 until 1498 the fairs were suppressed, allegedly on account of the nearness of Lyon to the frontier which had resulted in the perpetration of frauds, but in 1498 Louis XII confirmed the four fairs with their privileges, and these were reconfirmed in 1514, 1547 and 1559. Among the firms that established branches of their business at Lyon were the Giunta family. For recent work on the book trade at Lyon see contributions in *Le Berceau du livre: autour des incunables. Etudes et essais offerts au professeur Pierre Aquilon par ses élèves, ses collègues et ses amis, Revue Française d'Histoire du Livre*, 118–21 (Geneva, 2004).
52. Halporn [note 8], p. 230, after *Amerbachkorrespondenz*, I, no. 110.
53. Halporn [note 8], p. 259, after *Amerbachkorrespondenz*, I, no. 231.
54. Halporn [note 8], p. 87, after *Amerbachkorrespondenz*, I, no. 38.
55. The larger firms would hold supplies of books in major towns all over Europe, and only the owner would know what he had in stock and where at any given time. Such stocks were valuable assets, though their worth would decline with age (diminished topicality) and physical condition (damage through damp, mice, worms). Books that

were not selling might be reissued under a new titlepage, creating the impression of a new edition, but in reality such methods were but desperate attempts to dispose of dead stock.

56. Cited by Clair [note 4], p. 220.

57. Grimm [note 23], cols 1490–8, details bookdealers resident in Frankfurt itself.

58. Grimm [note 23], col. 1492.

59. Kapp/Goldfriedrich [note 14], I, p. 455.

60. Grimm [note 23], col. 1492.

61. Richter [note 26], p. 54. Rudolf Blum, 'Vor- und Frühgeschichte der nationalen Allgemeinbibliographie', *Archiv für Geschichte des Buchwesens*, 2 (1960), 233–303, here p. 237, states that this first permanent bookshop was established in 1597.

62. The only known copy, measuring 380 x 305 mm, is in Milan, Bibl. Ambrosiana (S.M.L.IV, 25/4). See Christian Coppens, 'Five unrecorded German bookseller's catalogues, end 16th–early 17th century', *Archiv für Geschichte des Buchwesens*, 54 (2001), 157–69. Zetzner's catalogue is reproduced on p. 162. On Zetzner see Ian Maclean, 'Mediations of Zabarella in Northern Germany, 1586–1623', in Gregorio Piaia (ed.), *La presenza dell'aristotelismo padovano nella filosofia della prima modernità* (Rome and Padua: Antenore, 2002), 173–98, here pp. 177–80.

63. Bernhard Fabian (ed.), *Die Meßkataloge des sechzehnten Jahrhunderts*, 5 vols (Hildesheim and New York: Olms, 1972–2001). Vol. I covers Autumn 1564 to Autumn 1573 (with the exception of Easter 1566 and Easter 1567, for which no catalogues seem to have been produced), vol. II Easter 1574 to Autumn 1580, vol. III Easter 1581 to Autumn 1587, vol. IV Easter 1588 to Autumn 1592, and vol. V Easter 1593 to Autumn 1600 but lacks Autumn 1598, for which no copy has been found. On this see David Paisey, 'German Book Fair Catalogues', *The Library*, VII, 4 (2003), 417–27. See also Bernhard Fabian (ed.), *Die Meßkataloge des sechzehnten, siebzehnten und achtzehnten Jahrhunderts. Microfiche-Edition* (Hildesheim and New York: Olms, 1977–86), covering the Leipzig catalogues from 1594 to 1860. A study covering the catalogues over a long period and attempting a statistical analysis is Gustav Schwetschke, *Codex Nvndinarivs Germaniae Literatae Bisecvlaris: Meß-Jahrbücher des Deutschen Buchhandels von dem Erscheinen des ersten Meß-Kataloges im Jahre 1564 bis zu der Gründung des ersten Buchhändler-Vereins im Jahre 1768* (Halle, 1850–77; repr. Nieuwkoop: de Graaf, 1963). Paisey, *op. cit*, p. 426, voices justifiable reservations about the reliability of Schwetschke's statistics, noting, for instance, that he offers no figure for pre-1601 publications from Cambridge even though STC 25363, 25368, 25367 (all listed in Willer) and 17121 (listed in Portenbach/Lutz) are known to have been available at Frankfurt. See further Wolfgang Borm, *Catalogi Nundinales 1571–1852. Die Frankfurter und Leipziger Messkataloge der Herzog August Bibliothek Wolfenbüttel* (Wolfenbüttel, 1982). For the catalogues' importance as forerunners of a national bibliography see Blum [note 61].

64. 'Libri theologici catholici, non noui; hactenus verò in nostra Bibliotheca desiderati'. Four titles only.

65. For an analysis of the books on music see Albert Göhler, *Verzeichnis der in den Frankfurter und Leipziger Messkatalogen der Jahre 1564 bis 1759 angezeigten Musikalien* (Leipzig: Kahnt, 1902). See also Stephen Rose, 'The mechanisms of the music trade in

central Germany, 1600–40', *Journal of the Royal Musical Association*, 130 (2005), 1–37, esp. pp. 5–12 on 'Music at the Book Fairs'.

66. Karl Schottenloher, *Die Widmungsvorrede im Buch des 16. Jahrhunderts*, Reformationsgeschichtliche Studien und Texte, 76/77 (Münster, n.d.), pp. 153–4. The book in question is Rucker's edition of *Matrimonialium consiliorum tomi duo … per Joannem Baptistam Zilettum …*, Frankfurt am Main: M. Lechler for S. Feyerabend, 1580.

67. See Oliver Duntze, 'Die Frankfurter und Leipziger Meßkataloge als buchgeschichtliche Quellen', *Buchhandelsgeschichte*, 2002, no. 1, pp. 10–18, here p. 18, note 48, says they were printed by Martin Lechler, but as Fig. 5 shows, by 1573 they were being printed by Peter Schmidt.

68. Virtually all the books were very recent publications, though Paisey [note 63], p. 418, noticed one title dating from 1513.

69. Frankfurt does not dominate in any way. From outside the German-speaking area there are many books from Venice, Paris, Antwerp, Rome, Lyon, some from Prague, Vilna, Cracow, even Coimbra, and a handful from London, Oxford, Cambridge and Edinburgh.

70. On the use of gothic types by German printers as a Protestant manifesto see John L. Flood, 'Nationalistic currents in early German typography', *The Library*, VI, 15 (1993), 125-41.

71. The uncertainty of the transport also added to the cost. Thus Anton Koberger in Nuremberg complained to Johann Amerbach on 1 March 1500: '[…] Those barrels have still not all arrived and some of those that did arrive are completely soaked. Please have thick, strong barrels made and pay more for them so that the books are better protected' (Halporn [note 8], p. 229; *Amerbachkorrespondenz*, I, no. 110). Again, on 9 February 1503, he complained: '[…] five barrels arrived, all five wet and completely soaked. Please see to getting good barrels and especially when you are sending me the manuscript exemplars in them' (Halporn, p. 250; *Amerbachkorrespondenz*, I, no. 182). And yet again, on 17 June 1504, he complained that the barrels Amerbach used were 'very thin and weak' and 'completely unsuitable for long-distance shipping [from Basle to Frankfurt]' (Halporn, p. 258; *Amerbachkorrespondenz*, I, no. 229).

72. The British Library holds an incomplete set of these (pressmark C.107.bb.3), covering the years 1577–97, beginning with *Catalogus nouus nundinarum autumnalium Francofurti anno M.D.LXXVII. celebratarum*. For some notes comparing Portenbach/Lutz's catalogues with those of the same years by Willer see Paisey [note 63], pp. 423–4.

73. These included one by the Frankfurt publisher Sigmund Feyerabend for the Lenten fair 1584, one by Peter Schmidt in 1590, and several by Peter Brachfeld issued from Spring 1595 to Spring 1598. For a fuller account see Graham Pollard and Albert Ehrman, *The distribution of books by catalogue from the invention of printing to A.D. 1800* (Cambridge, 1965), pp. 79–84.

74. The decision is recorded in Bürgermeisterbuch 1598, fol. 84, in the Stadtarchiv, Frankfurt am Main. See Richter [note 26], p. 54, note 98. The titlepage of the Autumn 1598 catalogue is illustrated in *Lexikon des gesamten Buchwesens. LGB²*, ed. Severin Corsten *et al.* (Stuttgart: Hiersemann, 1987–), V, 156.

75. For a sketch of the history of Frankfurt within the Empire and further literature on the city's history see Gerhard Köbler, *Historisches Lexikon der deutschen Länder*, 6th revised edn (Darmstadt: Wissenschaftliche Buchgesellschaft, 1999), pp. 175–6.

76. Examples of privileges are discussed by Ian Maclean, 'The market for scholarly books and conceptions of genre in Northern Europe, 1570–1630', in Georg Kauffmann (ed.), *Die Renaissance im Blick der Nationen Europas* (Wiesbaden: Harrassowitz, 1989), pp. 17–31, here pp. 22–3.

77. See Wolfgang Brückner, 'Eine Messbuchhändlerliste von 1579 und Beiträge zur Geschichte der Bücherkommission', *Archiv für Geschichte des Buchwesens*, 3 (1958), cols 1629–48, here col. 1641. For the subsequent history of these rival catalogues see cols 1642–8. The Catholic catalogues were published at Mainz from 1606 to 1614, then at Frankfurt until 1619, and from 1625 to 1627 in parallel at Munich and Frankfurt. See Pollard/Ehrman [note 73], pp. 80–2. Paisey [note 63], p. 423, also mentions short-lived catalogues from Heidelberg and Munich.

78. See Albrecht Kirchhoff, 'Beiträge zur Geschichte der Preßmaßregelungen und des Verkehrs auf den Büchermessen im 16. und 17. Jahrhundert, II: Zur Geschichte der Kais. Bücher-Commission in Frankfurt a. M.', *Archiv für Geschichte des Deutschen Buchhandels*, 4 (1879), 96–137, here pp. 129–30.

79. Dietz [note 4], III, 60–1. Richter [note 26], p. 51, note 81, gives the price as 1 Schilling a copy in 1590.

80. See Duntze [note 67], p. 11.

81. On the Leipzig catalogues see Albrecht Kirchhoff, 'Die Anfänge des Leipziger Meßkatalogs,' *Archiv für Geschichte des Buchhandels*, 7 (1382), 101–22; and 'Weiteres über die Anfänge des Leipziger Meßkatalogs,' ibid., 8 (1833), 22–7. See Gernot Gabel (ed.), *Der erste Leipziger Messekatalog aus dem Jahr 1595. Faksimileausgabe nach dem Exemplar der Universitäts- und Stadtbibliothek Köln* (Cologne, 1995). After the Leipzig catalogue was taken over by the Weidmann'sche Buchhandlung in the later eighteenth century, it was thoroughly reorganized by Philipp Erasmus Reich who gave up the traditional subject classification in favour of an alphabetical listing. In this form the catalogue continued until 1860 (see Duntze [note 67], p 11). On Grosse see *Lexikon des gesamten Buchwesens* [note 74], III, 283–4.

82. Paisey [note 63], pp. 424–5.

83. See Susanne Meurer, 'The Composition and Context of Joachim von Sandrart's *Teutsche Academie*', Ph.D thesis, University of London (Warburg Instute), 2005, pp. 151 and 158.

84. On the problems presented by the fair catalogues see Peter Düsterdieck, 'Buchproduktion im 17. Jahrhundert. Eine Analyse der Meßkataloge für die Jahre 1637 und 1658', *Archiv für Geschichte des Buchwesens*, 14 (1974), cols. 163–220; David L. Paisey, 'Literatur, die nicht in den Meßkatalogen steht', in Paul Raabe (ed.), *Bücher und Bibliotheken im 17. Jahrhundert*, Wolfenbütteler Schriften zur Geschichte des Buchwesens, 6 (Hamburg: Hauswedell, 1980), pp. 115–25; and Duntze [note 67]. Further literature of relevance is cited by A. H. Laeven, 'The Frankfurt and Leipzig book fairs and the history of the Dutch book trade in the seventeenth and eighteenth centuries', in *Le Magasin de l'Univers. The Dutch Republic at the Centre of the European*

Book trade, ed. C. Berkvens-Stevelinck, H. Bols *et al.* (Leiden, 1992), pp. 185–98, here, p. 189, note 10.

85. *Bibliotheca Classica, Siue Catalogus officinalis: In Qvo Singvli Singvlarum Facvltatvm Ac Professionvm Libri, Qvi In Qvavis Fere Lingva Extant, Qviqve Intra Hominvm fere memoriam in publicum prodierunt, secundum artes & disciplinas, earumque titulos & locos communes, Authorumque Cognomina singulis classibus subnexa, ordine alphabetico recensentur* (Frankfurt am Main: N. Hoffmann for P. Kopff, 1611), and *Bibliotheca Librorvm Germanicorvm Classica. Das ist: Verzeichnuß aller vnd jeder Bücher, so fast bey dencklichen Jaren in Teutscher Spraach von allerhand Materien hin vnd wider in Truck außgangen, vnd noch den mehrertheil in Buchläden gefunden werden: Darinnen nicht allein Jedere Facultet in jhre besondere Classes der gestalt ist abgetheilet daß so wol die Materien, als auch die Autores ... sampt Anzeigung wann, wo, vnd in was Format oder Grösse ein jedes getruckt, ganz leichtlich vnd ohne besondere Mühe zu finden ...* (Frankfurt am Main: J. Saur for P. Kopff, 1611). British Library pressmarks: 820.e.24 and 820.e.25, respectively.

86. *The Cambridge History of the Book in Britain*, IV: *1557–1695*, ed. John Barnard and D. F. McKenzie (Cambridge: CUP, 2002), p. 160. On Oxford and Bill see also Maclean [note 76], p. 27, and particularly Julian Roberts, 'Importing books for Oxford, 1500–1640', in James P. Carley and Colin G. C. Tite (eds), *Books and Collectors 1200–1700. Essays presented to Andrew Watson* (London: British Library, 1997), pp. 317–33, especially pp. 328–9, where he notes the puzzling rarity of copies of the Frankfurt (not to mention the Leipzig) catalogues in Britain.

87. *Journal des savants*, Année 1685 (Amsterdam: G. P. and J. Blaeu, 1686), 'Au lecteur'.

88. On 'Frankfurt und Leipzig' see *Archiv für Geschichte des Deutschen Buchhandels*, 4 (1879), 223.

89. *Historia von D. Johann Fausten. Text des Druckes von 1587. Kritische Ausgabe*, ed. Stephan Füssel and Hans Joachim Kreutzer, Reclams Universalbibliothek, 1516 (Stuttgart: Reclam, 1988), p. 6. In one of the episodes Faust himself visits the Frankfurt Lenten fair (p. 100).

90. Fairly full details of all the early *Faust* editions may be found in Hans Henning, *Beiträge zur Druckgeschichte der Faust- und Wagnerbücher des 16. und 18. Jahrhunderts* (Weimar, 1963), and Füssel/Kreutzer [note 89]. For the expurgated Catholic version see Peter Amelung, 'Ein unbekanntes Faust-Buch von 1588', *Gutenberg-Jahrbuch*, 63 (1988), 177–82, and for the verse version, produced by Tübingen students, see *Der Tübinger Reim-Faust von 1587/88*, ed. Günther Mahal (Kirchheim/Teck: Schweier, 1977).

91. The edition printed by Thomas Orwin in 1592 (STC 10711; British Library C.27.b.43) was possibly not the *editio princeps*. See John Henry Jones (ed.), *The English Faust Book* (Cambridge: CUP, 1994), esp. p. 146.

92. The first periodical published in Germany was Otto Mencke's *Acta eruditorum* (1682), inspired by the *Journal des savants* and the *Philosophical Transactions* of the Royal Society in London.

93. On these see *Lexikon des gesamten Buchwesens* [note 74], V, 157–8. For a fuller account, with reference to much secondary literature, see Ulrich Rosseaux, 'Die

Leipziger Meßrelationen 1605–1730. Ein Beitrag zur Medien- und Kommunikationsgeschichte der Frühen Neuzeit', *Leipziger Jahrbuch zur Buchgeschichte*, 12 (2003), 11–31. An old but still valuable treatment of the subject generally is Felix Stieve, 'Ueber die ältesten halbjährigen Zeitungen oder Messrelationen und insbesondere über deren Begründer Freiherrn Michael von Aitzing', *Abhandlung der Historischen Classe der Königlich Bayerischen Akademie der Wissenschaften*, 16, 1 (Munich, 1881), pp. 177–265. For a checklist see Klaus Bender, *Relationes Historicae. Ein Bestandsverzeichnis der deutschen Meßrelationen von 1583 bis 1648* (Berlin: de Gruyter, 1994).

94. Examples include the correspondence of Amerbach and Anton Koberger, the account books of Froben and Episcopius (see Rudolf Wackernagel, *Rechnungsbuch der Froben & Episcopius, Buchdrucker und Buchhändler zu Basel, 1557–1564* (Basle: Schwabe, 1881)), the Frankfurt publisher Sigmund Feyerabend (see Pallmann [note 2] and also note 98 below), and Michael Harder (see Ernst Kelchner and Richard Wülcker (eds), *Mess-Memorial des Frankfurter Buchhändlers Michael Harder, Fastenmesse 1569* (Frankfurt am Main and Paris: Baer, 1873)), and the official lists of booksellers attending in 1569 (see Kapp/Goldfriedrich [note 14], I, 661ff. and 772ff.) and 1579 (Brückner [note 77]).

95. Von Hase [note 11], p. 320–1.

96. Dennis E. Rhodes, 'Some neglected aspects of the career of Giovanni Battista Ciotti', *The Library*, VI, 9 (1987), 225–39, here p. 228. See also Maclean [note 62], p. 177.

97. See Ingrid Ilsøe, 'Bøger og boghandlere under Christian V.', *Fund og Forskning*, 25 (1981), 19–46, here pp. 30–1. Haubold and Paulli were the first to publish annual lists of Danish books.

98. See Heinrich Pallmann, 'Ein Meßregister Sigmund Feyerabend's aus dem Jahre 1565', *Archiv für Geschichte des Deutschen Buchhandels*, 9 (1884), 5–46.

99. Brückner [note 77].

100. These are: Cologne, Strasbourg, Augsburg, Nuremberg, Mainz, Frankfurt, Basle, Zurich, Lausanne, Antwerp, Heidelberg, Wittenberg, Leipzig, Jena, Tübingen, Erfurt, Magdeburg, Vienna, Bamberg, Speyer, Neustadt an der Haardt [now Neustadt an der Weinstrasse], Hildesheim, Braunschweig, Helmstedt, Ursel, Paris, Venice, Lyon, Turin, and Geneva. Towns mentioned as not being represented at the Autumn 1579 fair include Ingolstadt, Marburg, Trier, Prague, Dinkelsbühl and Würzburg.

101. Hilkert Weddige, *Die 'Historien vom Amadis auss Franckreich'. Dokumentarische Grundlegung zur Entstehung und Rezeption* (Wiesbaden: Steiner, 1975), pp. 121–2.

102. Carlos Gilly, *Die Manuskripte in der Bibliothek des Johannes Oporinus*, Schriften der Universitätsbibliothek Basel, 3 (Basle: Schwabe, 2001), pp. 18–19. Oporinus died before printing could be put in hand.

103. Gilly [note 102], pp. 21–4. The book in question is Jean Boulaise, *Tabula chronographica* (Frankfurt am Main: N. Basseus, 1575), published 'impensis Genii Bibliothecae Oporinianae'.

104. Foundation dates of universities in the Holy Roman Empire: Prague 1348, Vienna 1365, Heidelberg 1386, Cologne 1388, Erfurt 1392, Würzburg 1402/1582, Leipzig 1409, Rostock 1419, Greifswald 1456, Freiburg 1457, Basle 1460, Ingolstadt 1472, Tübingen 1477, Mainz 1477, Graz 1486, Wittenberg 1502, Breslau 1505, Frankfurt

an der Oder 1506, Marburg 1527, Königsberg 1544, Jena 1548, Strasbourg 1566/1621, Helmstedt 1576, Giessen 1605, Rinteln 1621, Altdorf 1622, Kiel 1665, Halle 1694, Göttingen 1737, Erlangen 1743. Frankfurt am Main itself did not have a university until 1914.

105. For an analysis of the changing market for scholarly books see Ian Maclean [note 76].

106. For an illuminating discussion, based on an analysis of posthumous editions of Melanchthon, see Ian Maclean, 'Melanchthon at the book fairs, 1560–1601: editors, markets and religious strife', in Günter Frank and Kees Meerhoff (eds), *Melanchthon und Europa, 2. Teilband: Westeuropa*, Melanchthon-Schriften der Stadt Bretten, 6 (Stuttgart: Thorbecke, 2002), pp. 211–32.

107. Maclean [note 2], pp. 155–6, reprints Wechel's own handwritten catalogue of 1579, preserved among the papers of the Imperial Book Commission at Vienna. On Wechel's catalogues see also Maclean [note 76], p. 24. On the Wechel business generally see R. J. W. Evans, *The Wechel Presses: Humanism and Calvinism in Central Europe, 1572–1627* (Oxford: Past and Pesent Society, 1975).

108. Originally two copies had to be deposited at Frankfurt, but this was increased to five in 1570, reduced to two in 1608, increased to three in 1621 and to five in 1650. In 1678 the commissioner Georg Friedrich Sperling demanded seven: five for the Emperor, one for the Elector of Mainz as Archchancellor of the Empire, and one for himself. See Hans Widmann, *Geschichte des Buchhandels vom Altertum bis zur Gegenwart*, revised edn (Wiesbaden: Harrassowitz, 1975), I, 89; Adalbert Brauer, 'Die kaiserliche Bücher-kommission und der Niedergang Frankfurts als Buchhandelsmetropole Deutschlands', *Genealogisches Jahrbuch*, 19 (1979), 185–99, here p. 194. Brauer's article traces in detail the relations between the city council and successive commissioners. On the Imperial Book Commission generally see Ulrich Eisenhardt, *Die kaiserliche Aufsicht über Buchdruck, Buchhandel und Presse im Heiligen Römischen Reich Deutscher Nation (1496–1806): ein Beitrag zur Geschichte der Bücher- und Pressezensur*, Studien und Quellen zur Geschichte des deutschen Verfassungsrechts, A, 3 (Karlsruhe: C. F. Müller, 1970). On its arbitrary workings and ultimate failure see Stephan Fitos, *Zensur als Mißerfolg. Die Verbreitung indizierter deutscher Druckschriften in der zweiten Hälfte des 16. Jahrhunderts* (Frankfurt am Main etc.: Lang, 2000).

109. These details from Laeven [note 84], p. 187.

110. These figures, somewhat simplified, are taken from Laeven [note 84], p. 191. Based on Schwetschke and Kapp/Goldfriedrich, they conflate the Frankfurt and Leipzig catalogues. The boxed figures relate to the war period.

111. On the high prices of English books see *The Cambridge History of the Book in Britain, IV: 1557–1695* [note 86], p. 736. Paisey [note 63], pp. 419–23, makes a provisional listing of some 60 pre-1601 books from Britain in the Frankfurt catalogues. Among them are 3 books published by John Legat at Cambridge, 2 from Henry Charteris at Edinburgh, 2 from Joseph Barnes at Oxford, and the remainder from London (including 8 published by George Bishop, 3 by John Day, 9 by Thomas Vautrollier, and 13 by John Wolfe). Moreover, Paisey notes several items which appear not to be recorded in STC, as well as 22 recorded by Willer with dates between one and four years later than those listed in STC, possibly indicating reissues intended by the

original British publishers for supply to Frankfurt. See also Max Spirgatis, 'Englische Litteratur auf der Frankfurter Messe von 1561 bis 1620', *Beiträge zur Kenntnis des Schrift-, Buch- und Bibliothekswesens*, 7 (Sammlung bibliothekswissenschaftlicher Arbeiten, 15; Leipzig, 1902), pp. 37–89; Irene Wiem *Das englische Schrifttum in Deutschland von 1518–1600*, Palaestra, 219 (Leipzig, 1940). There is no evidence of books in German by London printers in the sixteenth century, but some books in other languages, particularly Italian, were produced for the continental market and appear in the Frankfurt catalogues, e.g. books by John Wolfe with false imprints (STC 17161, 15414.6, 19911, 19913; see Paisey [note 63], p. 421).

112. Laeven [note 84], p. 192.
113. Uwe Neddermeyer, *Von der Handschrift zum gedruckten Buch*, 2 vols, Buchwissenschaftliche Beiträge aus dem Deutschen Bucharchiv München, 61 (Wiesbaden; Harrassowitz, 1998), I, 417, table 6 (a). The boxed figures relate to the war period.
114. Widmann [note 108], I, 88. On Frankfurt in the Thirty Years' War see Dietz [note 4], IV, 1–17.
115. The figures for Britain are derived from the statistical tables compiled by John Barnard and Maureen Bell, in *The Cambridge History of the Book in Britain*, IV: *1557–1695* [note 86], pp. 779–84.
116. For the workings of the book commission in Leipzig see Albrecht Kirchhoff, 'Die Kurf. sächsische Bücher-Commission in Leipzig', *Archiv für Geschichte des Deutschen Buchhandels*, 9 (1884), 47–176.
117. See S. H. Steinberg, *Five Hundred Years of Printing*, new edition, revised by John Trevitt (London: British Library, and New Castle DE: Oak Knoll, 1996), p. 94.
118. Paul Raabe, 'Der Buchhändler im achtzehnten Jahrhundert in Deutschland', in Giles Barber and Bernhard Fabian (eds), *Buch und Buchhandel in Europa im achtzehnten Jahrhundert: The Book and the Book Trade in Eighteenth-Century Europe*, Wolfenbütteler Schriften zur Geschichte des Buchwesens, 4 (Hamburg: Hauswedell, 1981), pp. 271–91, here p. 275.
119. Raabe [note 118], p. 282.
120. Figures from Steinberg [note 117], pp. 54–5. It is noted there that, naturally enough, Latin predominated longer in university towns such as Jena and Tübingen than in mercantile centres like Hamburg.
121. These statistics, cited by Thomas Bürger, 'Aufklärung in Zürich', *Archiv für Geschichte des Buchwesens*, 48 (1997), 1–278, here p. 143, are based on the *Verzeichniß der meistlebenden Herren Buchhändler, Welche Die Leipziger und Franckfurther Messen insgemein zu besuchen pflegen* (1741) (Deutsches Buch- und Schriftmuseum Leipzig: Bö C VIII, 28).
122. Sten G. Lindberg, 'The Scandinavian Book trade in the Eighteenth Century', in Barber/Fabian [note 118], pp. 225–48, here p. 232. The source is Magnus Swederus, *Biografiska Småsaker til minnes för efterlefwande, 2. stycket* (Uppsala: Bruzelius, 1832).
123. Blum [note 61], p. 256. Paisey [note 63], p. 424, reports that the earliest book in the English language he has found in the catalogues is Thomas Bilson's *The True Difference between Christian Subjection and Unchristian Rebellion* (Oxford, 1585) (STC 3071, in the Portenbach/Lutz catalogue for Autumn 1586).

124. The following details derive from Bernhard Fabian, 'Die Meßkataloge und der Import englischer Bücher nach Deutschland im achtzehnten Jahrhundert', in Reinhard Wittmann and Berthold Hack (eds), *Buchhandel und Literatur. Festschrift für Herbert G. Göpfert zum 75. Geburtstag am 22. September 1982*, Beiträge zum Buch- und Bibliothekswesen, 20 (Wiesbaden: Harrassowitz, 1982), pp. 154–68.

Itinerant Booksellers, Printers, and Pedlars in Sixteenth-Century Spain and Portugal

CLIVE GRIFFIN

IN THE SIXTEENTH CENTURY Spain and Portugal were on the margins of the European book industry. Those countries did, of course, have active centres of printing, and, indeed, the number of Iberian presses seems to have grown towards the end of the century, but they could not rival the size and output of printing-houses in the major centres of France, Germany, Italy, Switzerland, or the Low Countries. Spain's situation was not dissimilar to this country's, with the important difference that, whereas printing in England was concentrated on London, in Spain — which was at this time composed of several distinct kingdoms — it was geographically dispersed in a series of centres: Alcalá de Henares, Barcelona, Burgos, Madrid, Salamanca, Seville, Toledo, Valencia, Valladolid, and Zaragoza, as well as many smaller towns.

One traditional explanation for the relative underdevelopment of Iberian presses was that in northern Europe Protestantism encouraged reading while in southern Europe Catholicism blighted it, leading to low demand and production. This theory can no longer be accepted: indeed, the level of literacy seems to have been high in Spain, even in the countryside, yet a large proportion of the consequent demand for printed material was supplied by imports.[1] The weakness of the Spanish printing industry, which was unable to meet this domestic demand, is best attributed to a series of interconnected causes, among them the absence of investment in the presses, which was blamed by contemporary printers on a dearth in Spain of consortia of merchant-publishers willing to lay out the large sums required for major projects; the shortcomings of local paper production; and the scarcity of trained typographers.[2]

The result was that books flooded into the country, particularly copies of what could be termed 'international editions', that is to say Bibles, the classics, works of theology, jurisprudence, medicine, philosophy, and similar subjects, all printed in Latin. For their part, Spanish presses tended to concentrate on more popular editions in the vernacular languages of the

Iberian Peninsula. From the 1540s onwards foreign publishers based in cities such as Antwerp and Lyon were breaking into even this market and exporting books of ballads, fiction and popular history to the Peninsula. There is plenty of evidence of these imports, large shipments of books flowing into Spain along well-established routes. Some were dispatched from Antwerp, travelling down the English Channel and through the Atlantic to Spain's largest city, Seville; from mid-century, Flemish book-sellers maintained agents there, at least in part because Seville was the major port for dispatching goods to the Spanish colonies in the Americas.[3] Others were shipped from Lyon down the Rhone to the Mediterranean and then on to Barcelona and Valencia, in both of which cities local book-sellers commissioned editions from Lyon publishers.[4] Yet others were transported from Lyon by barge and cart to the Atlantic port of Nantes, thence by ship through the Bay of Biscay to the north coast of Spain, and overland to the university city of Salamanca as well as to the fairs which were held twice yearly in the nearby town of Medina del Campo which constituted the hub of the Iberian book trade. All this is to say nothing of large consignments of books dispatched direct to the Iberian Peninsula from Italy.

This export trade to Spain was dominated by multinational publishers and booksellers: the Giunti family of Florence, Venice, and Lyon had branch offices in Spain; the great Low Countries printer and publisher Christophe Plantin employed Jan Poelman as his factor at Salamanca; a less important Lyon printer and publisher, Charles Pesnot, had an office at Medina del Campo run by his nephew Pierre Landry who published many leading Spanish authors.[5] It was not generally in the interest of the principal merchant-booksellers in Spain, who often had family ties with the multinational publishing businesses, to foster local Spanish production since most of their profits came from the import trade.[6] Lack of investment meant that local Spanish presses were not large or well equipped enough to deal with surges in demand like the one created for new service books in the aftermath of the Council of Trent. Large contracts for liturgical edi-tions went abroad to the Antwerp printer Christophe Plantin.[7] Foreign publishers even employed agents in Spain who looked out for manuscripts they could send to be printed in major European centres and then import the books back into Spain.

There were, then, merchant-booksellers in Spain who were operating on an international scale. At a more modest level, there were settled booksellers who plied their trade in Spanish towns and cities. We can discover their names and learn something about the volume of business that passed through their hands by examining the accounts left by their suppliers. For instance, the debts recorded in the will of a leading member of the trade, the German Jacobo Cromberger who founded a dynasty of printers, publishers and booksellers in Seville at the beginning of the sixteenth century and died in 1528, shows us that he dispatched books wholesale to booksellers in centres like Alcalá de Henares, Burgos, Córdoba, Granada, Lisbon, Toledo, Valencia, Valladolid, and Seville itself as well as sending large numbers of books to booksellers at the Medina del Campo fairs. But he also supplied small-scale booksellers in less important provincial towns and even villages throughout Spain and Portugal: places like Ayamonte, Évora, Jaén, Jerez de la Frontera, Málaga, Mérida, Oporto, Plasencia, El Puerto de Santa María, El Pueblo de Santa Olalla, Zafra, and Zamora.[8]

There were, however, yet humbler members of the trade in Spain. These were the itinerant booksellers, pedlars, and also the travelling typographers who tend to go unnoticed in histories of Spanish printing and bookselling. The reason that I have been interested in these obscure figures is that I have been piecing together the story of the Spanish and Portuguese Inquisitions' pursuit and breaking up of an informal network of immigrant printing-workers, booksellers, and pedlars who were accused in the 1560s and 1570s of sympathizing with the Reformed religion. The principal sources I have drawn upon for this research are what remains of the Spanish and Portuguese Inquisitions' papers.

(a) *Itinerant Booksellers*

A typical example of these booksellers was a man who went by various versions of his name, but was probably called something like Enrique Borceller or Bruselete. Sixteenth-century Spain was underpopulated and suffered severe skill shortages, acting as a magnet for traders, artisans, and labourers from north of the Pyrenees in search of work, or better paid work, there. Borceller was clearly one such immigrant; some witnesses testified before the Inquisition that he was of German origin, others that he was a Fleming, and yet others that he was from Lyon.[9] He was fluent in several languages, and spent his life shuttling between Germany, France and the Iberian Peninsula. As a young man he had been in the employ of a French bookseller based at Salamanca called Jacques Boyer, the older brother of the more famous bookseller Benoît Boyer who was a major player in the book trade at Medina del Campo.[10] By at least the 1560s, when he appears in the papers of the Spanish Inquisition, Borceller had left settled employment at Salamanca and owned some sort of a shop or warehouse at Toledo, but spent most of his time on the road, buying and selling books in Salamanca, Valladolid, the Medina del Campo fairs, and north of the Pyrenees. As he journeyed through Castile plying his trade he spread Reformist ideas among the foreign workmen and booksellers he encountered. Unfortunately, I have found no record of the sort of books he distributed, but accounts of his activities nevertheless provide evidence that itinerant foreigners with a training in the trade were travelling the roads of Spain dealing in printed material. Informed speculation does, moreover, enable us to hazard what sort of wares such travelling booksellers handled.

In 1539 simmering resentment between humble workers and merchants in the small Castilian town of Membrilla (in the province of Ciudad Real) came to a head when some of the former gathered to listen to an antisemitic pamphlet which was being read out loud to them. They chose to interpret this tract as referring to the local merchants, consequently jeering at them and insulting them as unchristian. The incident gave rise to a court case during which evidence was provided about how copies of the inflammatory printed pamphlet had been acquired: one had been brought back to Membrilla from a recent fair, and had doubtless come from a travelling bookseller who had set up a stall there selling popular little works of this nature.[11]

The Inquisition's papers I have read record the names of many such itinerant booksellers; they were all foreigners, mostly French in origin, and were either mentioned in passing in Inquisitional trials or appeared in person (or in effigy) at Spanish *autos de fe* in the early 1570s. I have found very little precise information about them, but some were certainly humble members of the trade who brought their wares to Spain from France, while others were agents or family members of well-known Lyonnese printing-houses who travelled round Spain presumably seeking contracts to supply booksellers there.[12] One such party of agents from Lyon was expected in Spain in 1564 and was described in some detail by a small-scale Burgundian bookseller arrested by the Holy Office. The party was eventually tipped off that the Inquisition was preparing a reception committee, and that they would be arrested as heretics. They prudently decided to remain in France.[13]

Enrique Borceller was principally a bookseller who occasionally dealt in other sorts of merchandise.[14] Some other foreigners sold books as a side-line. Two such men appear in the papers of the Lisbon Inquisition. They were both French, Jean de Lyon and Pierre d'Altabel, who had at one stage been active in eastern and southern Spain but, by the time one of them was arrested in 1565, were selling books in Portugal. Jean de Lyon was primarily a book-binder who had worked at his craft in France, Spain, and Portugal, as well as travelling to Italy where he may also have bound books. He had fought in Picardy on the Huguenot side during the first French War of Religion. D'Altabel, for his part, was an apothecary by trade who had accompanied Jean de Lyon in his travels through Spain, but was primarily based at La Rochelle on the Atlantic seaboard of France. He frequently appeared in Lisbon supplying Portuguese colleagues with med-icinal drugs, but he would also take with him small shipments of books, which Jean de Lyon would then distribute.[15] We know that some of those books would have had to be sold under the counter in Portugal because they were editions of the psalms translated into French by Marot and De Bèze; other works they dealt in were similarly proscribed by the Holy Office.[16]

These two Frenchmen realized that there was good money to be made from importing books into Portugal, where local presses could not supply demand, and in 1566 they took ship for La Rochelle to have a book printed there in Portuguese. They even recruited itinerant typographers to accompany them from Lisbon, doubtless because they knew how difficult it was proving at that time to find skilled men to work in the presses at La Rochelle. The edition they intended to finance and print for export back to Portugal was one of the great staples of the book trade in the Iberian Peninsula: a thoroughly orthodox book of hours which was not only the only book owned by many a Spanish or Portuguese family, but was also widely believed to have talismanic powers if carried about the person.[17] Unsurprisingly, when Jean de Lyon and Pierre d'Altabel sought a licence in La Rochelle for their book of hours to be printed there, the local Huguenot authorities declined. Nothing daunted, the two French entre-preneurs turned instead to another good money-spinner, a grammar book by Despauterius which would find a ready outlet among Portuguese students.[18]

This example of bookselling as a side-line for men engaged in other activities is only one among many I have encountered. For instance, a Fleming, who was probably called Hendrik van der Loe in his native

Antwerp, had worked since childhood in Flemish, French and, in particular, Spanish printing-houses. In the years before the Inquisition started to take an interest in him, he had been based in the main in the Alcalá de Henares printing-houses, but he had always spent part of the year on the road looking for work with printers in other regions of Spain. The Inquisitorial papers normally refer to him as a typesetter, but on occasion they also add that he dealt in printed material; I suspect that, as he travelled from centre to centre, he would take a small supply with him which he would sell as he went.[19] In this he was not untypical of peripatetic printing-workers who would turn their hands to other activities when they were on the road or when work was difficult to come by. This willingness to take on a variety of jobs was not untypical of skilled printing-workers, who earned their keep as servants, retailers, or soldiers when times were hard.

I have divided itinerant foreigners involved in the book trade into booksellers, pedlars and printing-workers. However, the career of Hendrik van der Loe indicates that such categories overlapped: he was principally a typographer, but dealt on a small scale in books and so could be considered an occasional travelling bookseller or even a pedlar.

(b) *Pedlars*

My second category is, indeed, pedlars, several of whom appear in the papers of the Inquisition as well as in other Spanish archives. One such man from Antwerp was known in Spain as Pedro de Güerta or Pedro Flamenco. He was picked up in a small village south of Toledo as the result of a denunciation made by a fellow-Fleming who suspected Güerta of having an affair with his wife. There seems to have been no substance in this accusation, but the two men had nevertheless come to drunken blows shortly beforehand, and they clearly disliked each other. Both would end up at the stake. Pedro de Güerta had long travelled the roads of Spain selling a variety of goods, including printed matter. He was at one stage in partnership with a Frenchman and they had a depository in Valladolid as well as going to northern Europe to purchase merchandise which they peddled in Spain. When he was arrested in the late 1560s, the stock Güerta was carrying with him was inventoried. It included over a hundred printed woodcuts and some ninety pictures of St Veronica's headcloth with the image of Christ's face impressed upon it. One of the witnesses at his trial maintained that Güerta had confided in him that, although he lived from their sale, he believed such printed images to be worthless trash.[20]

Oddly, there is no mention that he carried in his pack any of what were known in Spain as 'nóminas'. These were strips of parchment or, more frequently, paper on which were written or printed the names of saints or short prayers guaranteeing protection from the evil eye, or crop failures, and aiding women in labour; indeed, before giving birth some mothers would ingest the strip of paper in the hope that their pain would be eased. Such 'nóminas' were the stock in trade of pedlars in Spain, and we find enormous numbers of sheets of them in the inventories of contemporary printers' warehouses; not a single copy seems to have come down to us.

A fuller inventory was drawn up in 1575, on the death in the village of Villerías de Campos, near the city of Palencia in northern Spain, of an anonymous pedlar described simply as 'a poor man'.[21] Included in the stock he transported on his donkey were, again, printed pictures of religious subjects as well as the blank notebooks which many customers bought to record their household or business accounts.[22] He also had small number of books which he peddled round the villages: a copy of *La Magalona* (a very popular work among sixteenth-century Spanish readers which was a translation of the medieval French *Pierre de Provence et la belle Maguelonne*); a life of the saint called San Alejo, which was enormously widely read in Spain; four volumes of collected ballads; and one copy of what is recorded as 'Agamenón': not Sophocles's tragedy but *La venganza de Agamemnón* (or *Agamemnon's Revenge*) by the Spanish playwright Hernán Pérez de Oliva.[23]

More striking than these single copies, though, were 85 printed sheets. Many of these were ballad broadsides. The ballad tradition was central to Spain's literary culture from the Middle Ages onwards, and ballads permeated all levels of Spanish society. They are, for instance, Cervantes's target in the early chapters of *Don Quixote* before he turns his attention to another genre strongly promoted by Spanish publishers, the romances of chivalry, which were similarly read or listened to by both the educated and the illiterate.[24] It is not surprising that the anonymous pedlar should have been carrying, on the one hand, a few copies of the more expensive collections of ballads in book form and, on the other, a large number of single-sheet publications which would have contained a single, or just a handful, of these songs. This is testimony to the trade's supplying the same, or similar, texts in editions tailored to a variety of markets, rather than to its providing different texts for different readers according to their social class. The unfortunate pauper who died in Villerías de Campos was carrying ballads to suit different pockets.[25]

Ballad broadsides were printed in industrial quantities; pedlars distributed them to all corners of the country; and the ships leaving Seville for Mexico or Peru transported thousands of these ephemeral publications to the Spanish colonies where they were, in turn, distributed by pedlars.[26] Foreign visitors to Spain in the sixteenth and seventeenth centuries considered these broadsides typical of the country. Samuel Pepys, for instance, visited Cadiz and Seville in the winter of 1683/4, once he had fulfilled his official duties at Tangiers. He returned to England from his short stay in southern Spain with a collection of printed items he had picked up in those cities. Unsurprisingly, it included what he listed as a 'Bundle of Ballads'. These turn out to be 75 contemporary chapbooks consisting of both traditional ballads dating from the fifteenth century and modern poems and songs composed in the metre and rhyme scheme popularized by the medieval Spanish ballad.[27] Seville was famous for the production of such broadsides and chapbooks, but the anonymous pedlar who worked the villages round Palencia would have obtained his supplies of such cheap publications further north from the nearby city of Burgos where the local presses similarly specialized in such editions for the mass market.[28]

There was an enormous production in Spain of printed broadsides containing ballads and other songs. The inventories of printers' warehouses invariably contain tens, and sometimes hundreds of thousands of copies. This production seems to have had two principal outlets in sixteenth-century Spain. First, there were the pedlars like Pedro de Güerta or the anonymous man who died in Villerías de Campos. They travelled the countryside selling their wares, or plied them on city streets. Some of these ubiquitous pedlars are mentioned in the will of the Seville printer Jacobo Cromberger where, for instance, we find a reference to a debt owed him by an unnamed 'very weather-beaten man who sells thread, ribbons, and books at the city's Arenal Gate' (that is to say in the red-light quarter of the city down by the docks and shipyards on the banks of the river Guadalquivir). 'Cortes, the bookseller, who plies his trade in country villages' could have been either a general pedlar or an itinerant bookseller.[29] Second, there was the veritable army of blind hawkers. They bought ballad broadsides from printers, and would then peddle them round the city streets and villages. The usual way these blind men would attract customers was to sing the ballads to a crowd and then offer the printed version for sale.[30] The fascinating study of a sixteenth-century author of popular ballads who was tried by the Spanish Inquisition provides a vivid account of how those writers (commonly known as *ruiseñores*, or nightingales) would pay for their compositions to be printed as broadsides, and then school a group of blind hawkers to sing them, before the blind men set out to peddle the printed version.[31] The practice of blind men singing the songs they peddled continued in Spain right up to the early twentieth century, mixing the traditional medieval ballads with lurid rhymed accounts of recent crimes and even stories of Napoleon and nineteenth-century Spanish heroes.[32] These popular, and often bloodthirsty, ballads are termed 'literatura de cordel' or 'cord literature' by cultural historians. This is because the pedlars would advertise copies of the printed ballads by hanging them on strings supported by a framework, rather like a portable washing line. The selling of cheaply printed broadsides and chapbooks by pedlars who have first sung them to potential customers continues to the present day in some parts of Brazil. The Australian travel writer Peter Robb recounts his recent impressions of Recife, the old colonial city on the Atlantic coast of northeast Brazil. There, by a bus stop, he heard a man intoning a ballad to the sounds of an acoustic guitar wired up to a car battery:

On the corner, a few yards away, another man was squatting by a display of leaflets. There were dozens of them and they were the words of songs like the one being sung. At once crude and beautiful, the long rhymed ballads were hand-set in ancient, irregular letterpress, printed on folded sheets of the cheapest pulp paper. Some of the libretti were laid out on the ground and others were held up for sale on a frame strung with clothes-lines, to which they were pegged and fluttering like drying underwear or trapped birds, with a crude and vivid woodcut on the cover... I bought a ballad about a girl who turned into a snake and another on the arrival in hell of Lampião — the outback bandit who wore steel rimmed glasses and an outback leather hat studded with silver medallions, and was the greatest of the northeast's primitive rebels. I unpegged the story of a boy who didn't know how to make love to girls and the account of a football match in purgatory. The black man and the rubber tapper. The boozer and the believer.[33]

(c) *Itinerant Printers*

My third category of travelling working men is printers. As has been seen, however, such categories are not watertight. For example, a terrified French compositor was tried by the Toledo Inquisition in the late 1560s. In Spain he was known as Juan Franco, or John the Frenchman, and, by the time he was arrested and tried for heresy, he had been a printing-worker in Spain for some sixteen years. He had married a Spanish woman who lived in Salamanca, where they had their home, although he would still take to the road to seek work in other towns. When the Holy Office arrested a suspect, an inventory would be drawn up of his or her possessions. It transpires from Juan Franco's trial that when the Inquisition's agents inspected his home, they found thousands of needles, dozens of spoons and brushes, as well as a good deal of cloth, thread and ribbons. It is quite possible that he supplemented his wages in the presses by running a small shop or stall, or that his wife did so in her own right. On the other hand, the needles, thread and ribbons were typical of a pedlar's wares. Printing-workers engaged in a range of economic activities to make ends meet in hard times, and Franco may have worked as a pedlar when travelling through Spain in search of work.[34]

Men we could loosely call 'printers' certainly joined pedlars and booksellers on Spanish roads. Two sorts of peripatetic printer should, however, be distinguished. On the one hand, there were master-printers who would travel to small towns, often with a single printing-press, where they had been commissioned to produce a specific edition or series of editions. The case of early printing in the Andalusian town of Baeza is a case in point. In the 1550s a new university had been founded there. Soon afterwards a series of small and somewhat crudely printed works of devotion appeared in the town. The printer did not sign them, but the sort of books he produced closely followed the spiritual concerns being promoted by the new university of Baeza. It can be safely assumed that he was commissioned to set up his press and print works for that university. As far as can be deduced from his output, he would either have worked alone at half-press or with one assistant. When the commission was completed, he dismantled his press and moved on.[35] This was characteristic of the jobbing-printers who formed the often unrecognized backbone of the Spanish printing industry.

On the other hand, there was the army of itinerant printing-workers (the beaters, pullers, compositors, type-casters, and those engaged in related crafts like book-binding) who travelled from press to press in sixteenth-century Spain and Portugal, sometimes being employed by a master-printer for a matter of a few weeks, sometimes working in the same press for more than a year. These are the men whom I have followed most closely in the Inquisitional archives, and a study of their trial papers has produced surprises. The industry in the Iberian Peninsula seems to have been dominated by immigrants, in large part from France, but with a good number coming from the Low Countries, Switzerland and Germany. The sources I have used may exaggerate the proportion of itinerant foreigners working in Iberian presses because the Inquisitors were particularly interested in Protestants, so Frenchmen suspected of Huguenot tendencies were bound to figure largely in their case load, as did workers coming from other countries infected — as the Holy Office put it — with the plague of heresy. Nevertheless, it is evident that there was a large network of such foreign artisans in the Iberian Peninsula who constituted an informal and mobile craft community constantly working together, bumping into each other on the road, and drinking together in taverns throughout Spain and Portugal. Indeed, there is evidence that there were so many foreigners in the industry that French was the working language of the presses in some Spanish cities. These foreign artisans were attracted across the Pyrenees by the lure of relatively high wages, the stability Spain offered at a time when France was racked by the Wars of Religion, as well as by the lack of any guilds in the Spanish printing industry which meant that many of them who had been too poorly qualified to find work in their native France were immediately employed once they reached Spain. This in turn may be a factor in the generally mediocre quality of Spanish printing in the latter half of the sixteenth century.

Some of these workers put down roots in the Peninsula, while others came and went over the Pyrenees depending upon the work available, upon the situation in their homelands, or upon their wariness of the Holy Office. Colleagues would warn them when the Inquisition started to take an interest in them, and they would then either try to leave the Peninsula, or would change their identities. Occasionally one of these itinerant crafts-men managed to settle in an Iberian city and acquire a press of his own, thus fulfilling the ambition cherished by so many journeymen of becoming masters in their own right. One such case was the Norman compositor Pierre Régnier who trained in Rouen, and worked his way as a journeyman round north-west France before coming to London in 1554–5 when

Prince Philip of Spain was in England for his marriage to Mary Tudor at the time of the Catholic Restoration. Régnier was employed in London by the printer Jean le Roux (John de Rouse) who lived in Shoe Lane but, when the situation of sympathizers with Reformist ideas became too precarious in London, Le Roux took fright and fled to Antwerp taking his workers' wages with him. Pierre Régnier had no alternative but to return to northern France where he went from press to press until he eventually found steadier employment for a few years at Lyon. In the late 1550s he was recruited there to go to Barcelona where he worked as a compositor until he was commissioned by a group of local booksellers to set up a new press in the Catalan capital. Over the next few years he gradually bought out these booksellers' interest in this press and became his own master, training apprentices, and employing other French workers, until the Inquisition eventually apprehended him. Its investigations into his and his wife's Reformist beliefs led her to the stake and him to be chained to the oar in the living hell that was Spain's galley fleet at the time of the Battle of Lepanto in 1571. Many itinerant printing-workers as well as booksellers and pedlars condemned as heretics must have had the dubious honour of rowing as galley slaves in that famous Catholic victory over the Turk.

* * *

Some of the men I have discussed were printing-workers like Pierre Régnier. Some, like Pedro de Güerta, were pedlars. Others were booksellers like Enrique Borceller. Yet others like Juan Franco or Hendrik van der Loe seem to have played a variety of roles in the book trade as pedlars, printing-workers and booksellers. What they all had in common was that they were foreign and itinerant. This was a dangerous combination in the 1560s and 1570s because the Spanish and Portuguese Inquisitors were not only in xenophobic mood, but were suspicious of anybody who had lived and worked in Reformist centres north of the Pyrenees where they could have imbibed heretical opinions. As several of those Reformist centres had active printing industries which had employed workers who subsequently sought their livelihood in the Iberian Peninsula, those artisans were especially vulnerable to the Holy Office when they reached Spain or Portugal. As the Inquisition's archives provide most of the information for this study, I have good reason to be grateful to the conscientious bureaucrats who staffed that institution. Those unfortunate members of the book trade who found themselves up before the Inquisitors may well have taken a different view.

References

1. Sara Tilghman Nalle, 'Literacy and Culture in Early Modern Castile', *Past and Present*, 125 (1989), 65–95; Trevor J. Dadson, 'Literacy and Education in Early Modern Rural Spain: The Case of Villarrubia de los Ojos', in Nigel Griffin, Clive Griffin, and Eric Southworth (eds), *The Iberian Book and its Readers: Essays for Ian Michael* (special double issue of the *Bulletin of Spanish Studies*, 81:7–8 (2004)), pp. 1011–37.

2. Clive Griffin, *Journeymen-Printers, Heresy, and the Inquisition in Sixteenth-Century Spain* (Oxford: Oxford University Press, 2005), pp. 78–9 160–1.

3. The Antwerp and Liège printers, publishers, and booksellers the Bellères (or Beelaerts) employed Juan Lippeo (or Jan Lippens) as their agent in Seville; he distributed books which the Bellères had acquired not only in Antwerp but also at the Frankfurt book fairs, through their wide network of contacts in northern Europe, and then forwarded to him in Spain. See Klaus Wagner, 'Flamencos en el comercio del libro en España: Juan Lippeo, mercader de libros y agente de los Bellère de Amberes', in Pedro M. Cátedra, María Luisa López-Vidriero, and Pablo Andrés Escapa (eds), *El libro antiguo español VI: de libros, librerías, imprentas y lectores* (Salamanca: Universidad de Salamanca, Seminario de Estudios Medievales y Renacentistas, 2002), pp. 431–86. Seville booksellers involved in the colonial trade obtained much of their supply from foreign merchant-booksellers based in northern Castilian centres such as Salamanca and Medina del Campo who had, in turn, imported it from abroad; see Carlos Alberto González Sánchez and Natalia Maillard Álvarez, *Orbe tipográfico: el mercado del libro en la Sevilla de la segunda mitad del siglo XVI*, Biblioteconomía y Administración Cultural, 78 (Gijón: Trea, 2003), p. 72.

4. Manuel Peña Díaz, *Cataluña en el Renacimiento: libros y lenguas (Barcelona, 1473–1600)* (Lleida: Editorial Milenio, 1996), 96–103; Philippe Berger, *Libro y lectura en la Valencia del Renacimiento*, Estudios Universitarios, 19 & 20, 2 vols (Valencia: Institució Valenciana d'Estudis i Investigació/Edicions Alfons el Magnànim, 1987), I, 272–3.

5. Mercedes Fernández Valladares, *La imprenta en Burgos (1501–1600)*, 2 vols (Madrid: Arco Libros, 2005), I, 154–72; Wagner, 'Flamencos en el comercio del libro en España', p. 431; Christian Péligry, 'Les Éditeurs lyonnais et le marché espagnol aux XVIe et XVIIe siècles', in Manuel C. Díaz y Díaz, *et al.*, *Livre et lecture en Espagne et en France sous l'Ancien Régime: colloque de la Casa de Velázquez* (Paris: A.D.P.F., 1981), 85–93 (p. 87).

6. In 1530, a short-lived company of booksellers had been established at Salamanca and Medina del Campo along the lines of the Grande Compagnie des Libraires at Lyon. But this Spanish company merely imported books wholesale from abroad, frequently looking to Lyon for their supplies; see Marta de la Mano González, *Mercaderes e impresores de libros en la Salamanca del siglo XVI*, Acta Salmanticensia, Estudios Históricos & Geográficos, 106 (Salamanca: Universidad de Salamanca, 1998), pp. 107–249 (especially pp. 210–13, 254); and Vicente Bécares Botas, *La compañía de*

libreros de Salamanca (1530–1534), Serie Inventario, 1 (Salamanca: Seminario de Estudios Medievales y Renacentistas/Sociedad de Estudios Medievales y Renacentistas, 2003), pp. 10, 17. It is true that a member of the Giunti dynasty, Juan de Junta, owned a press at Burgos from 1527, and another at Salamanca from 1532, but the 1557 inventory of his Burgos warehouse shows an overwhelming number of imports in his stock; see William Pettas, *A Sixteenth-Century Spanish Bookstore: The Inventory of Juan de Junta*, special issue of the *Transactions of the American Philosophical Society*, 95:1 (1995).

7. The traditional assertion that Philip II awarded Plantin a monopoly on the printing of the post-Tridentine service books for Spain and its colonies in the New World is incorrect. Some Spanish presses had a share in their production, but the Antwerp printer was nevertheless commissioned to print enormous numbers of such books which he shipped to Spain in the 1570s; see Vicente Bécares Botas, *Arias Montano y Plantino: el libro flamenco en la España de Felipe II*, Humanistas Españoles, 19 (León: Universidad de León, 1999), pp. 98–112.

8. José Gestoso y Pérez, *Noticias inéditas de impresores sevillanos* (Sevilla: Gómez Hermanos, 1924), pp. 43–53. Zafra, for example, had a population of only about 1,000 souls; see Juan Gil, 'Extremadura en sus páginas', in Juan Carlos Rodríguez Ibarra *et al.*, *Extremadura en sus páginas: una exposición del papel a la web organizada por la Consejería de Cultura de la Junta de Extremadura*, 2 vols (Badajoz: Junta de Extremadura, 2005), I, 11–140 (p. 68). Antonio de Guevara, the unreliable author of the *Golden Book of Marcus Aurelius*, a best-seller throughout Europe, confirms the existence of booksellers at Zafra (see Gil, 'Extremadura en sus páginas', p. 85).

9. Griffin, *Journeymen-Printers*, pp. 127–8.

10. Vicente Bécares Botas and Alejandro Luis Iglesias, *La librería de Benito Boyer (Medina del Campo, 1592)*, La Imprenta, Libros y Libreros, 1 (Salamanca: Junta de Castilla y León, Consejería de Cultura y Turismo, 1992).

11. Antonio Castillo Gómez, 'Leer en la calle: coplas, avisos y panfletos áureos', *Literatura: Teoría, Historia, Crítica* [Journal of the Departamento de Literatura de la Universidad Nacional de Colombia, Bogotá], 7 (2005), 15–43. The pamphlet in question was the notorious *Alborayque*, normally issued in 4° and consisting of 3 folded sheets, with a woodcut illustration on the titlepage; see Clive Griffin, 'An Unlucky Number of Seville Imprints', *Gutenberg-Jahrbuch* (1999), 146–55 (pp. 147–8).

12. For example, a Frenchman known in Spain as Juan Temporal was burnt in effigy at the Toledo *auto de fe* of 4 June 1571, the indictment reading: 'Frenchman, book dealer from Toulouse, sold books at Alcalá, [condemned] as a notorious heretic, Lutheran, burnt in effigy, possessions confiscated'; or Juan de Perusa, 'Frenchman, book dealer from Toulouse, sold books at Alcalá, [condemned] as Lutheran heretic, burnt in effigy, possessions confiscated'. See Sebastián de Horozco, *Sebastián de Horozco (¿1510–1581?): relaciones históricas toledanas*, introduction and transcription by Jack Weiner, Vestigios del Pasado, 8 (Toledo: Instituto Provincial de Investigación y Estudios Toledanos, 1981), p. 231.

13. The Burgundian bookseller, Gaspar de la Vega, who traded in Alcalá de Henares and Toledo, identified one of the party as 'Carlos Pesnot [the Charles Pesnot mentioned

above], printer at the sign of the Salamander [at Lyon]' (Griffin, *Journeymen-Printers*, p. 121n.).

14. Even the Bellères' agent at Seville, Juan Lippeo, handled Flemish textiles, clothes, etc. as well as books (Wagner, 'Flamencos en el comercio del libro en España', p. 441).

15. A recent study of the shipment of books from Seville to the Spanish colonies in the New World during the seventeenth century provides evidence of general traders who exported printed material (often printed religious pictures, ephemera, and other cheap, popular editions) as a side-line; see Pedro J. Rueda Ramírez, *Negocio e intercambio cultural: el comercio de libros con América en la Carrera de Indias (siglo XVII)* (Seville: Diputación de Sevilla/Universidad de Sevilla/CSIC, 2005), p. 193.

16. French cloth traders and pedlars of Protestant persuasion who travelled to the Iberian Peninsula selling their wares would sometimes conceal prohibited books in their bundles of merchandise; see Werner Thomas, *Los protestantes y la Inquisición en España en tiempos de Reforma y Contrarreforma* (Leuven: Leuven University Press, 2001), pp. 419–49.

17. For the magical properties of such books see Pedro M. Cátedra, *'Historia y prophetía de la Sibilla erithrea de la noche de la Natividad' por Toribio Ruiz (Orense, 1544) ahora publicada por Pedro Manuel Cátedra García con motivo de la celebración del IV Congreso de 'Lyra minima' cuyo programa va añadido al fin* (Salamanca: Seminario de Estudios Medievales y Renacentistas/Sociedad de Estudios Medievales y Renacentistas, 2004), pp. 29–32.

18. Griffin, *Journeymen-Printers*, pp. 211–13.

19. It has even been suggested that printing-workers in Spain would sell ephemera they had set up and run off on their own account after working hours; see Ángel San Vicente, *Apuntes sobre libreros, impresores y libros localizados en Zaragoza entre 1545 y 1599*, 3 vols (Zaragoza: Gobierno de Aragón, Departamento de Cultura y Turismo, 2003-   ), I, 9.

20. Griffin, *Journeymen-Printers*, p. 246.

21. Luis Antonio Arroyo Rodríguez, 'Las mercancías de un vendedor de pliegos de cordel de la segunda mitad del siglo XVI', *Bulletin Hispanique*, 101:1 (1999), 247–51.

22. On the sale and use of blank account books in Spain see Antonio Castillo Gómez, *Entre la pluma y la pared: una historia social de la escritura en los Siglos de Oro*, Serie Historia Moderna, 248 (Madrid: Ediciones Akal, 2006), pp. 70–80.

23. Fernández Valladares, *La imprenta en Burgos*, nos. 200 and 240, records editions of Pérez de Oliva's play printed much earlier in the century at Burgos in the form of chapbooks. The anonymous pedlar's copy would have come from a later reprint. On the important role of Burgos in the production of chapbook drama see Mercedes Fernández Valladares, 'Un taller de imprenta para la *Farsa llamada dança de la muerte*: Burgos como foco difusor del teatro de cordel en el siglo XVI', *Revista de Filología Románica*, 20 (2003), 7–23.

24. Roger Chartier, 'Del libro a la lectura: lectores "populares" en el Renacimiento', *Bulletin Hispanique* (special number entitled *Les Livres des Espagnols à l'époque moderne*), 99:1 (1997), 309–24 (p. 312).

25. For a discussion of the Spanish trade's reasons for, and strategies of, creating and supplying different markets for ballads see Chartier, 'Del libro a la lectura', pp. 313–14,

319–20. It has been roughly estimated that one and a half million copies of poetic broadsides were printed in sixteenth-century Spain; given the wide audience each copy could reach through the practice of reading aloud, few Spaniards could have been untouched by them; see Víctor Infantes, 'Las ausencias en los inventarios de libros y de bibliotecas', *Bulletin Hispanique* (special number entitled *Les Livres des Espagnols à l'époque moderne*), 99:1 (1997), 281–92 (p. 291).

26. Rueda Ramírez, *Negocio e intercambio cultural*, pp. 194–202.

27. E. M. Wilson, 'Samuel Pepys's Spanish Chap-Books', *Transactions of the Cambridge Bibliographical Society*, 2:2 (1955), 127–54; 2:3 (1956), 229–68; 2:4 (1957), 305–22.

28. In her excellent recent history and catalogue of sixteenth-century printing at Burgos, Mercedes Fernández Valladares lists over 200 editions, for which she has found firm evidence, of just the poetic broadsides (ballads, etc.) among these products designed for a mass market. Given the ephemeral nature of copies of such material, this is a remarkably high figure. Almost half of all sixteenth-century editions printed at Burgos lack colophons giving details of date, printer, place of printing, etc., a sure indication of the popular nature of that city's production. Fernández Valladares has carried out the Herculean task of identifying their origin and assigning them an approximate date of production (*La imprenta en Burgos*, I, 81n, 265–70; II, 1523–33).

29. Gestoso y Pérez, *Noticias inéditas*, p. 49.

30. Antonio Rodríguez-Moñino, *Nuevo diccionario bibliográfico de pliegos sueltos poéticos (siglo XVI)*, 2nd edn, rev. by Arthur L.-F. Askins and Víctor Infantes, Nueva Biblioteca de Erudición y Crítica, 12 (Madrid: Castalia/Editorial Regional de Extremadura, 1997), pp. 85–125. Rodríguez-Moñino conjectures (pp. 19–20) that printers sold these broadsides not individually to pedlars and blind singers, but wholesale by the 'mano' (25 sheets) or by the ream.

31. Pedro M. Cátedra, *Invención, difusión y recepción de la literatura popular impresa (siglo XVI)*, III Premio de Investigación Bibliográfica 'Bartolomé José Gallardo' (Mérida: Junta de Extremadura, Editora Regional de Extremadura, 2002), pp. 79–98.

32. Julio Caro Baroja, *Ensayo sobre la literatura de cordel*, Colección Fundamentos (Madrid: Istmo, 1990).

33. Peter Robb, *A Death in Brazil: A Book of Omissions* (London: Bloomsbury, 2005), pp. 21–2. If, as I suspect, the snake girl was a descendant of Melusine, a twenty-first-century Brazilian workshop was reprinting a legend that had poured off European presses in pamphlet form ever since the fifteenth century.

34. I have no concrete evidence that Franco dealt in printed books, but he certainly held a large stock of blank paper. At one stage he formed a partnership with a fellow-compositor at Salamanca to produce packs of playing-cards. This was not his usual work, but indicates that he was prepared, or obliged, to be entrepreneurial; playing-cards would also have been a useful addition to a pedlar's stock. I am indebted to Vicente Bécares Botas for informing me of this partnership which he discovered in the Archivo Histórico Provincial de Salamanca too late for it to be included in his *Guía documental del mundo del libro salmantino del siglo XVI*, Libros Singulares 7 ([Salamanca]: Junta de Castilla y León/Fundación Instituto Castellano y Leonés de la Lengua, 2006), which will prove an enormously useful tool for future researchers into the world of the book at Salamanca and elsewhere in Spain.

35. Pedro M. Cátedra, *Imprenta y lecturas en la Baeza del siglo XVI*, Inventario, 2 (Salamanca: Seminario de Estudios Medievales y Renacentistas/Sociedad de Estudios Medievales y Renacentistas, 2001), pp. 15–23.

Murder, Debt and Retribution in the Italico-Franco-Spanish Book Trade: the Beraud-Michel-Ruiz affair, 1586–91[1]

IAN MACLEAN

THIS PAPER OWES a great deal to various scholars: to my colleague Clive Griffin, who passed on to me a document that was puzzling his colleague Anastasio Rojo Vega; to Anastasio Rojo Vega, who introduced me to the archive in Valladolid in which much of the material on which the paper is based is to be found; to my wife Pauline, who negotiated for me with the staff of the archive, and helped me decipher and translate the documents we found there; and to Henri-Louis Baudrier and Henri Lapeyre, two meticulous scholars respectively of the Lyon book trade and the Spanish merchant Simon Ruiz. I was attracted to the subject because it seems to me to reveal quite a lot about the intimate workings of the world of learned books; but it also features a murder, and it is with that I shall begin.[1]

On 30 September 1586, Symphorien Beraud, a prominent Catholic merchant publisher, who was already the Recteur de l'Aumône and together with this honour was on the point of becoming an échevin and thereby acquiring noble status, was murdered in the streets of Lyon; according to the records that survive, this happened a day after he had broken off his three-year-old commercial association in the book trade with another Lyonnais merchant publisher, Etienne Michel. He was not interred until 18 November, in the Eglise Notre-Dame de Confort, which was the burial place of his former employer and later commercial partner Filippo Tinghi, whose heir he was.[2] Beraud left a horrendously complicated estate; before coming to that, I should first say something more about the man and his untimely end.

Beraud's parentage does not seem to be known: he is first mentioned in documents (together with his brother Jean) in 1570, as being in the employment of Filippo Tinghi, whose factor he became, and thereafter, in 1572, his heir. This occurred eight years before Tinghi's death, and should surprise us, given Tinghi's numerous Italian family, with whom he was on good terms: it certainly surprised them, and they made strenuous attempts to have the will annulled.[3] One might be inclined to speculate that there was a blood relationship between the two, although that cannot be more than a surmise, even if hinted at by one contemporary.[4] Beraud strengthened his ties with the book trade by marrying as his first wife a daughter of Charles Pesnot, whose family were prominent book merchants in Lyon, with strong commercial links in Spain; but they were not as well connected as Filippo Tinghi. His uncle was a member of the powerful Giunti dynasty, which was active as publishers in Venice, Lyon and Florence and as booksellers in Spain as well, and involved in a number of publishing companies in Lyon about which I shall have more to say.[5]

Tinghi was a shrewd and energetic publisher, who had begun his career as the factor of his uncle. Even before he became independent, he kept his eyes open for developments in the market for learned books, and exploited them: he it was, for example, who saw the future in publishing collections of letters by prominent physicians, a practice begun by his colleagues in Basle, and he arranged for the first compendium of these to be lavishly (and profitably) produced by the Giunti presses in 1556–7, with a long introduction in which he carefully constructs the image of the humanist learned publisher whose role is to be at the service of scholarship throughout Europe.[6] He also saw the benefit of the privilege system, by which books were protected in given jurisdictions, and was hard-headed enough to use the French royal privilege against his own family and former employers, the Giunti. He taught Beraud a number of trade practices which were to bring him success: one of these was the practice already mentioned of introducing books in the persona of the learned publisher whose principal aim was to serve the scholarly community;[7] another was direct recourse to the Paris Parlement and the king rather than the local Lyon Sénéchaussée court to secure privileges or endorsements for activities which were forbidden to publishers by the city authorities in Lyon, such as the use of Lyon titlepages for books printed in Geneva for a great deal less money, often on inferior paper.[8] Tinghi also passed on to his heir an extensive network of wholesale and retail booksellers in Spain, Portugal and Italy, through whom he kept stocks of his books abroad. When Beraud inherited Tinghi's estate, he had to collect debts from booksellers in Florence, Naples, Saragossa, Siena, Turin, Venice, Piacenza, Barcelona, Milan, and no doubt many other places.[9] Yet another beneficial practice was the use of agents and the storage of books at the great northern fairs and at Medina del Campo; one of the agents of Beraud and Michel at the latter place was Jean Boyer, a nephew of Benoît Boyer, the largest bookseller in the city,[10] who had been an associate of Tinghi; another was Mathieu Nesme; we will hear about both these men again. A third contact in Medina was Pierre Landry, who had also been connected both with Tinghi, and the Pesnot family, and had many dealings with booksellers throughout Spain.[11] Tinghi also had recourse, as would his heir, to commercial association as a cure for difficulties of cash flow; this led the Giunti family to enter into an association with Beraud in 1577 (he was given leave to market on their behalf the immense dormant stock they held, and to mark it up by 12% for his own profit). Beraud also saw the benefit of sharing risk: this was no doubt the motive which led him to associate himself commercially with Etienne Michel, with whom he constituted a formal partnership in July 1583.[12] He certainly gave and accepted printed sheets in payment of debts to and from other publishers, and may also have engaged in *Tauschhandel,* that is, the practice of exchanging unbound stock on an agreed basis (usually, printed sheet for printed sheet) with other publishers at book fairs; this would have caused his stock of books to become diversified, and developed his role as bookseller.[13] In virtue of his activities, he formed part of an international network of merchants accepting (and sometimes refusing) each other's promissory notes (cédulles) and bills of exchange, and pursuing each other's debts and obligations by the use of local proxies. Like Tinghi, he produced what Baudrier calls 'éditions rafraîchies' or reissues. His estate was valued by Baudrier at 65,000 écus (195,000 livres); it consisted very largely of unsold books, shares in publishing enterprises, and multifarious credits; he also owned a number of houses and a book warehouse, mentioned in other deeds. The estate was very difficult to settle.[14]

It does not seem from the documents that survive that Beraud was more at risk of assassination than any other member of the book trade in Lyon, although he certainly had enemies (not least the Lyonnais printers whom he undercut) and creditors, and there is some history of sanguinary instincts in members of the publishing world associated with Beraud, inspired by confessional allegiance.[15] At some point after his death, a suspect emerged: Giovanni Maria Cio[n]nacci, a Florentine merchant with whom Tinghi, Michel and Beraud had had commercial dealings: he had represented the interests of the Giunti against Beraud in the disputed Tinghi inheritance in 1582. He was tortured in late 1586, refused to confess, and on 8 August 1591 submitted to the estate of Beraud a claim for 500 écus damages plus interest, which I compute at about 15% compound: in all 893 écus 11 sous 1 denier — an early example of criminal compensation. The Sénéchaussée of Lyon upheld it; the administrators of the estate unsuccessfully appealed against the sentence in the Parlement de Paris, and then agreed to pay the sum in four instalments at the Lyon fairs.[16] It is noteworthy that a Florentine merchant, described as 'noble' in at least one document,[17] holding a fairs privilege in Lyon, was put to the question; for this to happen under French law, there had to be a 'forte présomption' or the testimony of two unimpeachable witnesses (possibly, given Cionnacci's later claim against the Beraud estate, these were the two persons acting on behalf of the heirs, Jean Compère and Julien Regrey). I believe it to be unusual for someone of this rank to be so treated;[18] and it would be interesting to know on what evidence he was tortured. In continental criminal law of the time, a 'strong presumption of murder' (which, without a voluntary confession, only justified flogging or some minor physical punishment, not execution), was defined as follows: someone is seen by two independent witnesses of unimpeachable character leaving a house with only one exit, looking pale and distressed, carrying a sword dripping blood: inside there is no person other than the freshly murdered corpse of the victim.[19] So Cionnacci must have been denounced, and the evidence of the witnesses must have persuaded a magistrate that he would be likely to confess under duress.

Baudrier does not record any suspicion falling on Etienne Michel, although he had broken off commercial relations with Beraud, which should have lasted until June 1587, 'pour plusieurs causes et raisons' a day before the murder.[20] Like much in this case, however, this document, which is dated 20 December 1586, three months after the murder, may not be what it seems: there is some chance that it is a legal fiction enacted to allow various parts of the Beraud estate to be liquidated (notably, the 'Grande Compagnie des libraires lyonnais', in which Beraud, Michel and Sybille de la Porte had shares). It does not seem that in 1586, Michel had a particularly bad reputation, although he was quickly to acquire one: but he certainly had led a somewhat adventurous or unstable career as a publisher. He was born in about 1550 into a Lyon family which seems to have been linked to the book trade: his brother was to become a printer, and his widowed mother's second husband was the prominent merchant publisher Thibaud Payen. When Payen died in 1570 or 1571, her son Etienne inherited

Payen's business, and adopted his printer's device; a symbolic act of some importance, as Tinghi's controversial decision to have his use of the Giunti device ratified by the French king shows.[21] It is clear that he suffered from insufficient capital from the beginning, which he tried to palliate by sharing risk. Although by all accounts himself a Catholic, he entered to this end into association with Protestants or families having strong links with Geneva: Louis Cloquemin from 1572 to 1577, and Barthélemy Honorat and Sybille de la Porte from 1579 to 1583.[22] With them he became a speculative publisher of books across a wide range of disciplines which had first been produced elsewhere.[23] Michel published both under his own name, and conjointly with his associates: he presumably marketed these books in different places. Like Beraud, he reissued under his own name books that he had acquired through exchange or in settlement of debt.[24]

I pass now from the murder to the estate of Beraud, and the problems of succession, which were to drag on for more than ten years, and led to three imprisonments for non-payment of debt, one in Lyon and two in Medina del Campo. Beraud left four heirs, each having an equal part: his wife and three surviving children. His daughter Marguerite was married to Alexandre de Villeneuve (or Vilanueva, or Villanova), a Lyonnais merchant grocer, who took an active part in the recovery of the monies of the estate. Its administration was handled by two prominent citizens of Lyon: Jean Compère, Docteur en droit, an advocate, who was tutor to the orphans, and Julien Regrey, a merchant draper, who was the godfather of Sibille Beraud. In July 1590, they were joined by Alexandre de Villeneuve, who was given the task of liaising with one of the most powerful Spanish merchants of the time, Simon Ruiz of Valladolid. He eventually agreed to become involved in the affairs of the succession through their mutual connection with Francisco (François) de Castro (Castres), a member of a Lyon mercantile family probably of Spanish origin: his actions were crucial in bringing about the settlement of the estate. The administrators began by establishing the outstanding debts and credits, and arranging to dispose of the stocks of books which were mainly, but not exclusively, stored in Lyon. For the Lyon stock, Beraud's former associate Etienne Michel initially offered 21,000 écus, an offer he raised before 5 July 1587 to 23,500 écus to match that of a bookseller in Salamanca called Claude Curlet; his offer was accepted on 16 December 1586, and he gained possession both of Beraud's keys to the store or stores where the stock was kept, and the Company's account books which would permit him to collect debts owed to the estate by bookseller clients.[25] Also in 1587, he entered into an association with Adrian Périer, a Parisian bookseller recently arrived in Lyon, and became co-owner with him of a share in the Grande Compagnie des libraires lyonnais, which had first been owned by the Giunti, then Filippo Tinghi, then Symphorien Beraud, and then Etienne Michel; Sybille de la Porte and Barthélemy Honorat also held shares in the Company, which they disposed of in April and November 1589 respectively.[26] He seems to have paid about 5,000 écus on account soon after his acquisition of Beraud's share.

In mid-1587 Michel left Lyon, and by March 1588 was in Medina del Campo to collect the monies owed there by the Boyers to the estate of Beraud (some 46,000 réaux or reales: about 4,000 écus). Boyer was later (in December 1590) to act for the estate against Mathieu Nesme in Medina del Campo (Nesme was mentioned by Alexandre de Villeneuve to Ruiz as a possible source of Michel money through garnishee). Michel appeared next in Venice, where on 8 August 1588 he executed a deed consigning books to a client (a member of the Giunti family) to the value of 248 écus which he held in common with two Lyonnais publishers with whom he constituted a company between 1579 and 1583: 11 of the 54 titles, which were apparently never delivered, were probably part of the stock of the Grande Compagnie de libraires lyonnais to which Michel still had access.[27] These journeys show Michel to be in financial difficulty; Baudrier says that he was declared bankrupt in the course of 1587, and that in 1588 his wife obtained a 'séparation de biens' to relieve her of responsibility for his debts. But he was still apparently on good terms with Compère in March 1588, who agreed at that time to be the godfather of his son; and he was still active as a speculative publisher, for he was reported as being in Paris in 1589, where he attempted to publish with a Parisian colleague a controversial work by Roberto Bellarmino, and was prevented from doing so by the Procureur général.[28]

It seems that at some time before January 1589, Compère and Regrey stopped trusting Michel and started pursuing him in law; Compère and Regrey first appointed a canon of the cathedral of Medina del Campo as their proxy in a bid to recover 18,000 écus from Nesme, who was holding some of the stock of Beraud books kept in the city.[29] He was apparently ineffectual, because some eighteen months later, they switched from him to the powerful merchant Simon Ruiz.[30] At some point before 23 July 1590, Michel had gained the reputation of being devious, dishonest and ruthless;

he was suspected of hiding sums of money from the administrators of Beraud's estate.[31] In Alexandre de Villeneuve's letter of that date to Ruiz, he calls him 'un cattivo homo et de malla fede'. Villeneuve must have feared the effect of Michel's silver tongue on Simon Ruiz, because in succeeding letters he continues to denounce him in ever more emphatic terms, and ends up in July 1591 calling him 'el mas mal hombre que sia en el mondo'.[32] In Villeneuve's entreaty to Ruiz, he stressed both his friendship with François de Castres,[33] and the Christian duty incumbent upon Ruiz to protect the widow and orphan. Accompanying Villeneuve's letter was a notarial document dated 13 July 1590 giving Ruiz leave to have Michel imprisoned for non-payment of a debt of 18,600 écus, where Mathieu Nesme was to join him: at the same time, another proxy, Gianpietro Homodeo, was authorized to pursue Michel, seize his person, and bring him back to Lyon to answer to his creditors.[34] Michel was probably not apprehended until 1591; in the course of that year, Ruiz caught up with him, and had him thrown into jail in Medina del Campo. René Postellier, a prominent Lyon merchant publisher acting for the Beraud administrators, was given the power to release both Michel and Nesme on 10 October 1592;[35] this was reissued (for Michel alone) on 11 January 1593, and again on 12 November 1594, at which time he was offered, and apparently accepted, release on condition that he returned to Lyon to settle his affairs.[36] The voluminous correspondence between Alexandre de Villeneuve and Ruiz is also concerned with the recovery and liquidation of Michel's stocks of books in Medina del Campo, and a number of other dealings. Meanwhile, in November 1590, Périer, Michel's current commercial partner, was imprisoned in Lyon at the request of the administrators of the Beraud estate. He argued that he would be unable to recover any monies from inside the prison, and was not only allowed to be released by Compère and Regrey, but even given bed and board by the latter. In January 1591 Périer tried to find out through a proxy where Michel was, and once located, to make him come back to Lyon so that their association could be dissolved; this suggests that Michel was not yet detained in Medina del Campo. Périer himself then fled from Regrey's house shortly thereafter 'usant de mauvaise foy'; Regrey had him caught and consigned to prison again, and forced him to liquidate some of his assets at ruinous rates; he also caused the share owned by Michel and Périer in the Grande Compagnie to be separated from the rest of the stock.[37] It was this share which was inventoried in December 1591, and seized with Périer's consent by Regrey and Compère. Alexandre de Villeneuve and the administrators of Beraud's estate had already seen it, because it is described in a memoir of December 1586 as 'many bales and piles of books'.[38] What its relationship is to the stock valued at 23,500 écus is unclear: but it seems to have been part of it. Périer was to remain in prison for 18 months, and on 20 March 1592 made a public declaration of his 'mauvais mesnage' with Etienne Michel, who had promised Périer when he left Lyon in July 1587 that he would send him bills of exchange to enable him to settle his debts, which of course he did not do. Périer must have deeply regretted his association with Michel. He eventually returned to Paris, whence he had come in 1586 or 1587, in 1596.[39] After his return to Lyon in 1594 or later, Michel himself apparently published only one more book in his name (associated with that of Hugues Gazeau), in 1597;[40] but although probably bankrupt, he is still described as a 'libraire de Lyon' in an act of 1602, which confirms, by reference to the 'séparation de biens' with his wife, his continued precarious financial situation.[41]

The liquidation of the assets of the Beraud estate was to take a further five or so years; but I can omit this rather tedious part of the story. I wish now to turn to the inventory of 27 December 1591 which valued the Lyon book stock of Périer and Michel. The surviving, certified, copy was sent to Ruiz by Alexandre de Villeneuve in January 1592. Its preamble runs as follows:

An inventory of 545 bales of printed books found in two stores in this town of Lyon near the Church and Convent of the Jacobins, called la Compagnie, which 545 bales have been handed over by Etienne Michel merchant publisher of Lyon to Maître Jean Compère tutor of the children and heirs of Symphorien Beraud and Julian Regrey administrator of the goods and faculties of the said children to be surety and mortgage for part of the sum of 18,600 écus which Michel and his compagnon and associate Adrian Perier owe to the said heirs of Symphorien Beraud by contract dated 5 July 1587 received by Maître Jean Gravier Royal Notary in Lyon, as the said Compère and Regrey have made disclosure to us: at whose request the present inventory has been made to value the books for the case between the said Compère and Regrey and the said Etienne Michel pending against Etienne Michel in the towns of Medina del Campo and the royal chancery in Valladolid in the country and realm of Spain. This inventory has been made in the presence of Maître Pierre Austrein Conseiller du Roi Lieutenant particulier in the Sénéchaussée and Presidial Court of Lyon.[42]

It is tempting to try to imagine the scene in the two stores, one of which is described in another document as so damp that the papers kept there were deteriorating,[43] in the dead of a Lyon winter. Four colleagues of Michel were able to see exactly what his claims for solvency were based on; a humiliating experience, even in absentia, for Michel, as he had confidently stated that the stock was worth the full sum that he owed to the Beraud estate.[44] Even the notarial description of 1586 refers to the implicit disorder in the warehouse by mentioning 'piles of books' as well as those stored in bales; Villeneuve scornfully referred to them as 'libri imperfetti et ingarbullati con molto di modo'.[45] As well as computations to the half-folio, there are quite a few errors in calculation (about 13% of the figures are wrong, as well as the sum of one of the pages); this cannot be put down to fraud, as Périer and Michel had two representatives present as well as the Beraud heirs; the task of counting and recording over 2,800,000 printed sheets, some of which were up to 70 years old, could not have been easy. It appears that most of the books were collated into single copies, which was of some assistance to the auditors of the stock: but reference to books 'by alphabet' suggests that there were also uncollated sheets.[46]

It is possible to identify with some certainty many of the books listed, as their format and collation are given, and as nearly all were said to have been published in Lyon, with the imprint of one of the Giunti family, or of Tinghi, Beraud, Beraud and Michel, Périer and Michel, or of Honorat, Cloquemin, Thibaud Payen, or other Lyonnais publishers with whom the Compagnie had close links, such as Sebastianus Gryphius and Hugues de la Porte: some seem to have been the result of exchange or settlement of debt, or were acquired speculatively at some point by the Grande Compagnie des libraires. They reflect the cultural capital on which the success of this part of the Lyon book trade was based. The largest component of the stock consists of standard folio works of law; many of these are named in the privilege that Tinghi sought and obtained from the French crown in 1578.[47] This list contains all the major texts of Roman and Canon Law, all the standard glosses, a high proportion of the best-known medieval commentators, and one or two moderns (Andrea Alciati, Giulio Clari): a vast and ambitious publishing programme, of which Tinghi and Beraud between them only completed a small part. It is not clear to me whether the doctors of Canon Law whom Tinghi planned to reprint were any longer as much in demand after the Council of Trent as before; like the breviaries and missals which no longer had validity in the post-Tridentine world, and the schoolbooks of Gryphius which had passed out of fashion, this part of the inventory has the decided feel of dead stock.[48] There is quite a lot of Catholic pastoral theology and preachers' aids; a few retained authors, such as Francesco Giuntini and Crisostomo Javelli; some standard reference works (such as Calepino, and Cartari's *Imagines deorum*); also a certain amount of literature in the vernacular (popular romances such as *Amadis de Gaule*, translations of Plutarch, Lucan, Livy, Pliny and Dioscorides); some speculative large-scale publication of standard texts such as Aristotle and St Thomas Aquinas; and an illustrated Bible. Interestingly, hardly any of the medical books published by Beraud and Michel are to be found here.[49] In the list there are reissues of earlier texts with new titlepages, and reprinting of works from jurisdictions which did not extend to Lyon.[50] Together with these titles are found Michel's new ventures, not yet ready for release: a new edition of Seneca, some new legal authors, a speculative reprint of Galen.[51] But even with these newly printed works, apparently stored as uncollated sheets rather than completed books, the stock cannot have been a very reassuring sight to the creditors.

At the end of the inventory are the signatures of the booksellers chosen by each side to agree the quantities and valuation: these are René Postellier and Jean Huguetan (for Périer acting as Michel's proxy); and for Compère and Regrey, Jean-Baptiste Regnaud and Pierre Cavellat. Of these, at least one (Jean Huguetan) was a prominent Huguenot, while Périer himself was almost certainly a Catholic, for he married the widow of Gilles Beys who was also Christophe Plantin's daughter.[52] There does not seem to be any separation of the religious communities in the publishing world. They agreed the value to be 12,812 livres 8 sols 7 deniers: 'reduitz en escus sol d'or 4,270.16.2': still over 14,000 écus short of full satisfaction of Michel's debt, in spite of his assurances to the administrators of the Beraud estate that the stock in question was worth enough to act as guarantee for his full debt to them.

This is a copy of the deed, and it ends with a certification in both Latin and Italian, with notarial and other witnesses. Many of the documents relating to the case are multilingual: the Bonvisi bank at Lyon represented Ruiz, and wrote to him in Italian; Villeneuve wrote to him in both Spanish and Italian (and sometimes a mixture of the two); a Latin translation attested by a notaire is found on several of the documents, as on this one. Ruiz apparently could not read languages other than Castilian, for

Villeneuve apologized to him for failing to send the inventory in that language, and invites him to have it translated in Medina. It is accompanied by a copy of the dissolution of the association between Symphorien Beraud and Etienne Michel dated 20 December 1586. The valuation was computed by the printed ream: books printed in Lyon between 1520 and 1560 are given a value of 20 sous the ream; between 1560 and 1579 45 sous the ream; and between 1579 and 1589, 55 sous the ream. Incomplete books were given a value of 10 sous a ream. As a rough guide, paper prices at the time, which depended on weight, varied between 25 sous and 40 sous the ream.

The relevant figures are as follows:

1520–60   565 reams 6 quires 13 sheets (10% of the stock inventoried)
1560–79   328 reams 12 quires 2 sheets (6%)
1579–89   4049 reams 2 quires 13 sheets (71%)

There were 745 reams 3 quires of imperfect copies (both new ventures not yet completed, and defective copies: 13% of the total). The inventory does not identify the books which fall into these categories, except in the case of imperfect copies and very old stock, where the entry contains the word 'noir' (presumably gothic letter) or 'viel'.[53] This practice, which is found also in publishers' and booksellers' catalogues at the time, as a means of disguising those elements of the stock which were not recently printed but which might be candidates for reissuing with new titlepages,[54] makes the attribution of date to the various items very difficult. On the basis of surviving editions that I have been able to identify, there seem to be many more books dating from before 1560 than the calculation suggests. This could with some plausibility be attributed to the failure of editions, on a large scale, to survive to the present day; but it may also be that others had been supplied with new titlepages and dates, as it is known from the evidence of colophons which do not match the imprint that a certain number of titles had already been reissued.[55] The discrepancy may also indicate that those engaged in the inventory were happy with approximations of date. In any case, it is necessary to suppose that many of the works for which I can find only editions in the earliest period were later reissued or reprinted. Whether the booksellers charged with the inventory took account of this is not clear, but I rather doubt it. How far the books were marked down in value can be assessed from records of retail prices for some of the titles: the *Corpus Iuris Canonici*, for example, here valued at

1 livre 8 sous (703 sheets), appears with a price of 15 livres in the documents associated with Cloquemin.[56] On this basis, Michel's claim that his books were worth 18,000 écus is made to seem more plausible.

The stock, including the incomplete books, was later seized, and there is evidence that 60 to 80 bales of the most presentable volumes were sent to Medina to be distributed to booksellers and sold at the October fair.[57] Other books were distributed to the creditors over the period 1592 to 1598. These, together with the new ventures, were reissued with new title-pages and preliminaries.[58] Two beneficiaries already in the book trade were Pierre Landry and Jean-Baptiste Buysson: but the merchant grocer Alexandre de Villeneuve was not. When he eventually received part of the settlement of the estate in the form of sheets (of the very popular sermons of Luis de Granada), he reissued them in his name *qua* publisher.[59] A number of titles also appear from this inventory (as well as from other warehouses in which Beraud must have kept books) with the imprint 'heirs of Symphorien Beraud'.[60]

I should like now to highlight a number of features of the trade in learned books which are revealed by this affair and the inventory which records it: the first concerns collaborative ventures. As is clear from this example, it was extremely difficult to liquidate assets in the book trade. This is partly because stock was dispersed across Europe, and left in the hands of retail booksellers who would not necessarily settle accounts on a regular basis, and partly because many booksellers and publishers held shares in jointly-owned companies whose assets were principally in the form of book stocks. Tinghi was in three of these: the Compagnie des libraires de Lyon, the Compagnie des héritiers de Jacopo Giunti, and the Grande Compagnie des libraires de Venise, founded by Lucantonio Giunti I, not to be confused with the exporting association called the *Societas* through which a number of Venice and Padua printers and publishers sent books to Frankfurt in the last years of the sixteenth century.[61] There are other associations we have already met, which can be recognized on imprints by combinations of names: Beraud and Michel is one, Michel and Cloquemin, Michel and Honorat, and Michel and Périer yet others. Very often, when an edition of some great work was undertaken (such as the *Corpus Juris Civilis*, or the Summa of St Thomas Aquinas), the imprints carry the names of individuals acting as members of the Compagnie with which they were associated; they can also bear the name of the printer rather than that of the publisher. Both practices can wrongly give the impression that there were multiple editions and great popular demand, whereas the contrary implication (that there was the need to spread risk because the market was not assured) seems to me more plausible. An example in the inventory which poses this problem is afforded by Domingo de Soto's *De iustitia et iure* (appendix, no. 13); this appeared in 1582 with no fewer than six different imprints.[62]

The role of factors is of interest. One Lyon publishing family (the de Gabianos) were known to train these, and release them for employment elsewhere;[63] but the majority remained in the same business, where they became in due course full partners, either by promotion or, more commonly, by marriage to the widow of their employer (Beraud is an example of the former case; there are many examples of the latter). Yet others went on to become independent booksellers and publishers in their own right, as did Gilles Beys, the son-in-law of Christophe Plantin who acted as his factor in Paris from 1564 to 1577 before striking out on his own.[64] Those who did this often changed the policy of their previous employer, in the belief that they had perceived an error in his strategy, or a new niche in the market. Beraud took over the Giunti stocks because he believed that he could sell them more successfully than they could in Spain and Italy; Michel clearly also thought that there were unexploited markets in the same geographical areas, and sought to exploit the gaps left in various regions by reprinting works that he knew had sold well elsewhere. For his part, Gilles Beys seems to have thought that very small formats and translations into the vernacular of natural philosophy would be profitable. These and other strategies were often unsuccessful. Some publishers such as Périer put their failure down to external factors, such as the religious wars in France;[65] but it is possible to identify a reason internal to the book market itself, namely its progressive saturation. This can be seen most clearly in the crisis suffered by the learned book trade in the late 1610s and 1620s which is marked by a number of bankruptcies and distressed sales of large stocks; eventually even ruthless exploiters of the collapse of rivals (such as the Wechel family of Frankfurt) became the victims of the excess of supply over demand.[66]

There are various noteworthy aspects of the financial and commercial arrangements of the book trade revealed by the case under discussion. The evidence of the agreements between Beraud and the Giunti, and of the stock of books held by Michel, suggests that sales of learned books were very slow, and that throughout the century estimates of market uptake were very optimistic. These books sat in locked warehouses all over Europe; how many there were in any given store was a secret known only to members of the Compagnie who owned them, and they were very loath to reveal what their assets were, as is clear from the lengths the administrators of the estate of Beraud and other litigants had to go to obtain account books and keys to the warehouses. The bales of printed sheets were respected as assets, because they could be used as security for debts, and as forfeit for bills of exchange; but as the inventory of 1591 shows, their values declined, their preliminaries and final gatherings suffered destruction, and they deteriorated because of moisture and worms.[67] If placed in small numbers with booksellers, they seem not to have been paid for until a sale was achieved. Publishers were often asset-rich, but the goods they held were illiquid, and this led to problems of cash flow. One paradoxical effect seems to have been greater and greater speculative exposure to the market: the only way they perceived to stay in business was to take more and more risks with slow-selling products, thereby contributing to market saturation. Through this practice, publishers, although on occasions technically bankrupt, continued to be active in their trade, having presumably made an assessment of their rate of return on investment, and the delays in the recovery of liquidity they would have to endure. As is well known, double-entry book-keeping was taken up by merchants in the course of the sixteenth century throughout Europe, having been a sort of trade secret known to the Italians before that;[68] it may have facilitated some of the calculations merchants had to make which previously had been difficult to compute, but as it was principally aimed at supplying information on an individual basis about transactions with a given client, it did not easily yield up information about profit and loss. Leon Voet has shown by a meticulous study of accounts of Christophe Plantin that he recovered the costs of an edition on average over three years, and thereafter showed a profit; but this calculation does not seem to be recorded anywhere by Plantin himself.[69] Various commercial pressures, including the stipulation made at some book fairs that only new editions should be advertised there, encouraged the reissue of existing stock with new titlepages;[70] I believe that such reissues are another factor which has led book historians in the past to overestimate the size and vigour of the book market. They also reveal that some names in imprints are not those of publishers at all, but rather creditors seeking to realize some money from recovered goods.

A different picture emerges from the publication of religious service books, and of official legal documents. Plantin is known to have had the privilege (but not the monopoly) of printing missals and breviaries for Spain, and no doubt made a very great profit on them.[71] But even here too rosy a picture of returns can be produced. Lapeyre discovered in Ruiz's papers a commercial assessment relating to liturgical books. It was computed in this document that there were about 50 bishoprics in Spain, each with a need for 1500 breviaries, not counting the needs of monks and nuns (put at about 500); about double this number was thought to be the requirement for missals and *diornales* (sorts of breviary). It was estimated that 40 presses could be established to provide in one year 40,000 breviaries and the same number of missals. The cost of production and the tax were computed (including the capital outlay for presses and paper); and from that the profit could be ascertained (about sevenfold, without labour or distribution costs).[72] Interestingly, it was not sufficient to persuade the merchant for whom the document was produced to become involved in a publishing enterprise. He may have been looking for a far greater return; but he may also have noticed the flaw in the estimates, namely that there would be a very active market in secondhand missals and breviaries which would make it very difficult to maintain the rate of production. It is interesting to note that the first formal auction catalogues of secondhand books occur quite late (in the last decade of the sixteenth century, in the Netherlands), but it seems reasonable to suppose that the secondhand market must have played a role in the difficulties experienced by the learned book market from the 1520s onwards.[73]

If the associations or companies of publishers had to be terminated because of death or disharmony, the resulting legal actions seem often to have been highly complex and expensive, and can be misleading. I am fairly certain that the dissolution of the association between Beraud and Michel, which was dated in a document after Beraud's death to the day before his death, is a legal fiction allowing for their association to be brought to an end in the neatest and most efficient manner; but it may lead to the suspicion that Michel was complicit in some way in Beraud's death, although no-one seems to have suggested this at the time. The fact that the associates had to proceed by letters of credit, often through proxies, led to a great deal of suspicion of dishonesty: the internal regulation of financial disputes through arbitrators who were colleagues and publishers (and who in turn, because of fundamental disagreement, were themselves forced in some cases to appoint an arbitrator to settle the matters they had been appointed to deal with[74]) only worked if both parties engaged in the arbitration in good faith, which seems not always to have been the case. Non-appearance at agreed meetings and non-compliance with court orders seem to have been as common a feature of commercial life as no doubt they are today.[75] The issue of good and bad faith, both between merchants and between merchants and their factors, is an important facet of the anthropology of trade at this time; it also reveals how alive its participants were to its operation and regulation, and should deter us from assuming that mercantile activity in the past was in some way less sophisticated or complex than that of the present. The laws relating to the settlement of disputes were clearly very sophisticated; the international nature of mercantile exchanges (multi-lingual documents and even versions of names, the use of proxy) is also very striking. So was the ability of merchants to act at a distance to enforce their rights and interests. In the present case, Compère and Regrey were able to have Michel and Nesme apprehended in Medino del Campo through a third party, whose involvement in the affair began with the husband of one of the heirs of Beraud calling in a debt of friendship.

The case of Beraud also reveals the relationship between commerce and confession at this time. There can be no doubt as to Tinghi's and Beraud's membership of the Catholic community of Lyon; and no doubt either of their commercial ties with Protestant Geneva. Clearly, religious affiliation did not get in the way of trade, even though after 1563, the town council of Lyon seems to have been very intolerant of Protestants, and regretted that printing workers who sought employment in Geneva because of the downturn in the printing trade in Lyon very often slipped into heresy (as they perceived it) as a result.[76] Nor, in the case of Beraud, did loyalty to the commercial community of Lyon stop him consorting with Genevan printers. A notable feature of this collaboration is the practice, engaged in by Tinghi first, then by Tinghi, Beraud and Michel under letters patent from the king, of having titlepages separately produced with Lyon imprints for Geneva-printed books.[77] Baudrier even says that these books, which were stored in warehouses outside Lyon, were sold in bound form.[78] The Consulat (the council of twelve of Lyon) forbade this practice; they attributed the decline of the Lyon printing industry directly to it. On 14 July 1588 they summoned Pierre Landry, Guillaume Rouillé and Jean-Baptiste Regnaud, with a number of other prominent merchant publishers, to answer the charge that they had severely damaged the printing industry in Lyon by using Genevan printers and adding to their products a Lyon address, to ensure that their works could be sold in Spain and Italy, causing an emigration of compositors and other print workers to Geneva. The merchant publishers replied that they had been forced to do this by the high costs and restrictive trade practices of the Lyon printers, who retorted in turn that they had been forced to put up their prices because of the rising cost of living.[79] The dispute raised the issue of jurisdiction; did letters patent from the king or the Paris Parlement override the decisions of the various competent authorities in Lyon (the Sénéchaussée and the Tribunal de conservation des privilèges royaux des foires de Lyon)?[80] This question gave rise to the widespread practice of having recourse to a variety of courts at this time, and shows the uncertainties in the minds of litigants about the precedence of one jurisdiction over another, and their willingness to be opportunistic for commercial advantage.

Another aspect of the confessionalization of the book trade which might be mentioned here is censorship. Ruiz decided in 1572 no longer to deal in books imported from France, as 'so much corruption comes from that country that they are rightly examined very carefully before being allowed in [to Spain]'.[81] But Ronald Truman has found a document of 1629 which suggests that the censorship in Spain was nothing like as efficient as is suggested by Ruiz's remark;[82] and the few book inventories in notarial documents in Valladolid which I have seen suggests the same.[83] It appears that the frontier between Spain and Northern Europe was more porous than has sometimes been believed. I do not think however that Beraud or Michel were engaged in any publishing enterprise which would have exposed them to the rigours of censorship or Inquisition. Both seem to me to be interested in making money out of the book trade in ways which did not fall foul of such regulation; as the printing of a book in Geneva with a Lyon address shows, this not only enabled the publisher to save money, but also prevented the contents from being suspected of heresy. Some of their books also advertised the fact on their titlepages that they had been scrutinized by the Church before publication.[84]

A final point I should like to make is that commercial imperatives seem often to have over-ridden confessional interests. Religious tensions in Lyon were high, after the turbulent period of Protestant domination in the early 1560s and with the violent events which occurred there after the St

Bartholomew's day massacre in Paris in 1572; one would expect the book trade to be very cautious about collaboration across the confessional divide, but this does not seem to have been the case. One does not find cases of Catholic printers and publishers producing overtly Protestant material, but the reverse is quite common.[85] After the introduction of the Index in Spain and Italy, even Protestant authors writing on religiously neutral topics were condemned under a blanket act of censorship, as were publishers in suspect printing centres, such as Geneva and Basle;[86] the use respectively of Lyon and Cologne imprints allowed publishers such as Michel and Beraud, who engaged in speculative publication of works which had succeeded commercially in other places, to exploit parts of the book market which otherwise would have been closed to them, at least in open trade. Vestiges of the same practice may be found in the activities of Jean Mareschal, the Lyon bookseller who fled to Heidelberg, and in that of Giovanni Battista Ciotti of Venice and Lazarus Zetzner of Strasbourg, who caused books they commissioned from printers in Frankfurt to appear with a Cologne address, and even in Geneva booksellers such as the Chouets issued the same book with different titlepages for different confessional markets.[87] The case of Michel also shows this practice of disguising the true provenance of a book could be used for reissuing and pirating books; Michel in particular seems to have had a very clear view about the zones in which the activities of various publishing centres were efficient and profitable, but as his unsold stock shows, his strategy did not always work. This is another reason why we should be very wary of attributing market demand to works which are printed at many publishing centres. Any attempt to interpret the data about learned book publication at this time quantitatively must, I believe, be engaged in with great caution.

References

1. Anastasio Rojo Vega is a distinguished historian of the Spanish book; see *inter alia* his 'Les livres des Espagnols à l'Epoque moderne', *Bulletin hispanique*, 99 (1997), pp. 193–210 and his *Impresores, libreros y papeleros en Medina del Campo y Valladolid en el Siglo XVII* (Salamanca: Junta de Castilla y León, 1994). The documents referred to in this article are to be found in the Archivo Histórico Provincial de Valladolid, Archivo Simon Ruiz, caja 246 (hereafter AHV 246, with the date of the document); Henri-Louis Baudrier, *Bibliographie lyonnaise: recherches sur les imprimeurs, libraires, relieurs et fondeurs de lettres de Lyon au XVIe siècle, publiées et continuées par J. Baudrier*, 12 vols, (Paris: F. de Nobele, 1964–5); Yvonne La Perrière, *Supplément provisoire à la "Bibliographie lyonnaise" du président Baudrier* (Paris: Bibliothèque Nationale, 1967);

also Sybille von Gültlingen and René Badagos, *Bibliographie des livres imprimés à Lyon au seizième siècle* (Baden-Baden, V. Koerner, 1992–); Henri Lapeyre, *Une famille de marchands: les Ruiz. Contribution à l'étude du commerce entre la France et l'Espagne au temps de Philippe II* (Paris: A. Colin, 1955).

2. Baudrier, *Bibliographie lyonnaise*, IV, p.125; V, pp. 40–52, 77; VI, p. 442.
3. Ibid., VI, p. 442.
4. Ibid., V, p. 51; the source of the rumour, Francesco Giuntini, an author of astronomical works published by both Tinghi and Beraud, claimed diplomatically to have lost the letter which might have revealed the reason for Tinghi's choice of heir and not to have read it, when asked to reveal its contents to a Lyon notary.
5. On the Giunti, see ibid., VI, *passim*, and William A. Pettas, *The Giunti of Florence: merchant publishers of the sixteenth century* (San Francisco: B. M. Rosenthal, 1980).
6. *Epistolae medicinales diversorum authorum, nempe Ioannis Manardi Med. Ferrariensis, Nicolai Massae Med. Veneti, Aloisii Mundellae Med. Brixiensis, Io. Baptistae Theodosii Med. Bononiensis, Ioan. Langii Lembergii Med. Principum Palatinorum Rheni. Adiectis indicibus duobus, quorum prior Epistolarum argumenta, posterior rerum ac vocum toto opere memorabilium elenchum continet* (Lyon: heirs of Jacopo Giunti, 1556), *1r; his model for the 'hoc epistolarum genus' is Giovanni Manardo (1462–1536), *Epistolae medicinales* (first edn, 1521), which Michael Isingrin of Basle published in 1540 with a similar publisher's preface to that of Tinghi. Both books were lavishly produced in folio.
7. One of Beraud's prefaces of this kind may be found in the *Communium opinionum syntagma* of 1581 (*2r–v). It is dated 31 August 1580. In it, he pays tribute to Filippo Tinghi, who had died shortly before, as a tireless servant of the republic of letters, who devoted his own financial resources to the production of useful works of legal scholarship which gave efficient access to the best authorities by publishing them together in a convenient form; he refers to him as someone he loved as though he were his own father, and undertakes to continue his work.
8. Baudrier, *Bibliographie lyonnaise*, VI, p. 440, says that production costs in Geneva were a third less than those of Lyon, which publishers complained were artificially high because of restrictive trade practices: see also ibid., IV, p. 125, VII, p. 206. On the relationship of the Sénéchaussée and the Paris Parlement, see Timothy D. Watson, 'The Lyon City Council, c.1525–75: politics, culture, religion' (unpublished D.Phil. thesis, Oxford, 1999), pp. 73–101.
9. Ibid., VI, pp. 436–59; V, pp. 34–52.
10. Vicente Bécares Botas and Alejandro Luis Iglesias, *La Librería de Benito Boyer (Medina del Campo, 1592)* (Salamanca: Junta de Castilla y León, 1992); Cristóbal Pérez Pastor, *La imprenta en Medina del Campo* (Madrid: Sucesores de Rivadeneyra, 1895), p. 262.
11. For an example of the storage of books in fair cities and outside Lyon, see Baudrier, *Bibliographie lyonnaise*, V, pp. 300–1, VI, p. 441; on Nesme and Boyer, see ibid., V, pp. 34–52; on Landry, see ibid., V, pp. 294ff, 396ff, and Pérez Pastor, *La imprenta en Medina del Campo*, pp. 232, 237–8, 242, 251, 444, 447, 450, 452, 456, 497.
12. Ibid., V, pp. 44; La Perrière, *Supplément provisoire à la "Bibliographie lyonnaise"*, pp. 131–6.
13. Baudrier, *Bibliographie lyonnaise*, V, p. 43.

14. Ibid., V, pp. 76–89, 487–9.
15. Alessandro Marsili sought remuneration for having a protestant beheaded in the unrest in Lyon following the St Bartholomew's Day massacre in Paris: see ibid., II, p. 158.
16. Ibid., V, p. 47; VI, p. 84.
17. Ibid., VI, p. 354.
18. See John H. Langbein, *Prosecuting crime in the Renaissance: England, Germany, France* (Cambridge, Mass.: Harvard University Press, 1974); id., *Torture and the law of proof: Europe and England in the ancien régime* (Chicago: University of Chicago Press, 1977).
19. Julius Clarus, *Liber quintus receptarum sententiarum*, in *Opera* (Frankfurt: ex officina Wolfgangi Richteri, impensis omnium heredum Nicolai Bassaei, 1604), p. 38: (q. 20 n. 4) 'Ad torturam etiam quae indicia sufficiant, non potest dari certa doctrina: sed pariter relinquitur arbitrio iudicis [...] Ad condemnandum vero gravissima indicia requiruntur, et (ut Dd. appellant) indubitata, prout potest poni exemplum infra [q. 21 n. 40]. Scias tamen, quod in hoc articulo Doctores multum varie loquuntur. Nam aliqui dicunt, quod regulariter ex praesumptionibus violentis, vel indiciis quantum-cumque indubitatis non debet aliquis in causa criminali condemnari [...] Alii dicunt, quod si agatur ad poenam pecuniariam, potest reus ex indiciis indubitatis etiam criminaliter condemnari. Et ita communiter teneri attestatur Grat. *cons 136 num 22 libr. 1* secus autem si agatur de poena corporali. Alii dicunt, quod ubi ex praesumptionibus proceditur, multum debet Iudex temperari suam sententiam, et maxime ne condemnet, nisi raro et modice ad poenam non pecuniariam, nec corporalem [...] Alii dicunt totum contrarium [...] Alii dicunt, quod quando indicia sunt indubitata, semper potest deveniri ad condemnationem, maxime in delictis occultis, et difficilibus probationibus, et tractatibus secretis, et in quib[us] veritas clarius haberi non potest [...] Et haec op[inio] nos servatur, quantum ad hoc, ut ex praesumptionibus deveniatur ad condemnationem, nam quotidie ex indiciis et prae-sumptionibus rei per Senatum condemnantur, non quidem in poenam mortis, neque poenam ordinariam ipsius delicti, sed in poenas etiam corporales, puta triremium, fustigationis, ictuum funis, et huiusmodi, et in specie ita servatum fuit in quodam Antonio Maria Fayta, qui cum esset indiciis indubitatis gravatus de homicidio, fuit per decennium ad triremes condemnatus [...]'; ibid., p. 150: (q. 21 n. 40) 'Si aliquis visus est ex aliquo domo cum gladio sanguinolento, et cum facie pallida, quae domus non habeat nisi unicum ostium, et intus reperiatur homo mortuus, tale indicium est sufficiens ad condemnationem. [...] Ego in practica semper vidi servari, quod hoc positum sit in arbitrio Iudicis. Nam aliquando vidi reos, contra quos extabant huiusmodi gravissima indicia, graviter torqueri, aliquando etiam vidi eos condemnari, non tamen poena ordinaria delicti, sed extraordinaria, iuxta ea, quae dixi supra [q. 20 n. 5]. Et ideo Iudex, considerata qualitate facti et personarum, amplecti quam opin[ionem] maluerit.'
20. Baudrier, *Bibliographie lyonnaise*, V, pp. 77–8.
21. Tinghi's permission to use the Fleur de Lys of Florence (a printer's mark otherwise exclusive to the Giunti) was successfully opposed by Giovanna Giunti in the Lyon courts in March 1578; Tinghi's two royal letters patent date from 5 July 1578 and 5 July 1580: see ibid., VI, pp. 438–59.
22. Ibid., IV, pp. 113–26, 408; VII, p. 348.

23. One might cite his speculative reprinting of natural philosophy (Girolamo Cardano's *De subtilitate* in 1580, using as copy the Rouillé edition of Paris, 1559), of law (Matthäus Wesenbeck's *Paratitla* in 1583, previously published in Basle by Episcopius and Nicolai in 1563), of medicine (Johannes Jacobus Wecker, *Medicinae utriusque syntaxes* also in 1583, previously published in Basle by Episcopius and Nicolai in 1576) and of humanist writing (Marc-Antoine Muret's *Orationes xxv* in 1583, previously published in Paris by Loqueneulx in 1577): see La Perrière, *Supplément provisoire à la "Bibliographie lyonnaise"*, pp. 147, 153.

24. For an example see Gérard Morisse, 'Blas de Robles (1542–1592) primer editor de Cervantes', in *El libro antiguo español VI: de libros, librerías, imprentas y lectores*, ed. Pedro M. Cátedra, María Luisa López-Vidriero and Pablo Andrés (Salamanca: Universidad de Salamanca. SEMYR, 2002), pp. 285–320 (pp. 308–9). The edition in question of José Anglés's *Flores theologicarum quaestionum in secundum librum Sententiarum* was reissued by Jean-Baptiste Buysson in 1595–6; he may have been a creditor of Michel who received the sheets in settlement of debt. I am grateful to Clive Griffin for this reference.

25. Beraud, *Bibliographie lyonnaise*, V, p. 78; IV, p. 408, 122, gives the name variously as Curlet, Curla or Carlet, see ibid., I, p. 354 and VI, p. 452 Pérez Pastor, *La imprenta en Medina del Campo*, p. 455 records it as Curlet, and gives the place of residence. See also AHV 246, letters of Alexandre de Villeneuve dated 16.12.1591 and 14.1.1592.

26. Baudrier, *Bibliographie lyonnaise*, II, pp. 210–17. La Perrière, *Supplément provisoire à la "Bibliographie lyonnaise"*, p. 139, records that he was summoned with other merchant publishers to appear before the Consulat in Lyon on 12 July 1588, but there is no evidence that he was present in Lyon at the time.

27. Ibid., p. 137.

28. Ibid., pp. 138–48.

29. In a letter of 26 August 1591 (AHV 246), Villeneuve tells Ruiz that Nesme has 'muchas ballas', as well as a cédulle worth 9,600 écus from Benoît Boyer: see also ibid., the letter of 20 October 1591, and Baudrier, *Bibliographie lyonnaise*, V, p. 487. On the non-delivery of the consignment of books, see La Perrière, *Supplément provisoire à la "Bibliographie lyonnaise"*, p. 140.

30. Baudrier, *Bibliographie lyonnaise*, II, pp. 211–12; V, p. 80 (the first proxy was a canon of the cathedral at Medina called Juan de Valencia; according to Villeneuve's letter of 4 April 1591, his powers were revoked before that date); La Perrière, *Supplément provisoire à la "Bibliographie lyonnaise"*, p. 140.

31. AHV 246, letter of Villeneuve dated 29 July 1591.

32. Ibid. On 16 December 1590, he warned Ruiz not to 'attendare alle buone parolle del detto Michel'; on 4 April 1591, he describes Michel as 'l ombre muy malo et qual non tiene conscientia alguna'. In his letter to Ruiz of 10 February 1592, Villeneuve expressed the view that Michel deserved to be condemned to the galleys.

33. This seems not to have gone as Villeneuve hoped, as Castres did not release monies given by Ruiz to him to hand over to the Beraud administrators until a debt to him from the estate had been settled: see Baudrier, *Bibliographie lyonnaise*, V, p. 88. Villeneuve refers in a number of letters to Castres as a person who did not seem to be worthy of the description 'honrable hombre'. The number and whining tone of

Villeneuve's letters must have irked Ruiz, because he did not bother to reply to them all.

34. La Perrière, *Supplément provisoire à la "Bibliographie lyonnaise"*, p. 140.

35. Villeneuve had urged Ruiz not to authorize Nesme's release until he had handed over the cédulle from Benoît Boyer in favour of the Beraud estate. See also Baudier, *Bibliographie lyonnaise*, I, pp. 352–6. Postellier was the brother-in-law of Charles Pesnot.

36. Ibid., II, p. 212; V, p. 80.

37. Ibid., II, p. 213.

38. AHV, 246, sent with the letter of Villeneuve dated 16 December 1591.

39. Baudrier, *Bibliographie lyonnaise*, II, p. 210.

40. Giacomo Menochio, *Commentariorum de praesumptionibus*: see appendix, no. 4.

41. It was still possible in France to be active as a publisher and be bankrupt, as the case of Toussaint du Bray shows: see Roméo Arbour, *Un éditeur d'oeuvres littéraires au XVIIe siècle, Toussaint du Bray, (1604–1636)* (Geneva: Droz, 1992), pp. 137–56.

42. See appendix for the French text.

43. La Perrière, *Supplément provisoire à la "Bibliographie lyonnaise"*, p. 137.

44. AHV 246, letter of Villeneuve dated 14 January 1592.

45. Ibid., letter of 16 December 1590; similar comments appear in the letter of 16 December 1591.

46. See appendix, nos. 24, 121.

47. Baudrier, *Bibliographie lyonnaise*, VI, p. 453: 'spéciallement toutes les oeuvres de Albericus de Rozate, toutes les lectures et conseilz d'Alciat, toutes les oeuvres de Bartole, toutes les oeuvres de Balde, toutes les oeuvres de Petrus Paulus, Parisius, Consilia Bertrandi, Consilia Cornei, toutes les oeuvres de Philipus Decius, toutes les oeuvres de Bartholomeus Socinus, les oeuvres de Marianus Socinus, Consilia Barba[t]iae, le Cours civil avec les glosses, le Cours canon avec les glosses, Christophorus Portius super Instituta, les oeuvres de Ludovicus Romanus, les oeuvres de Jason Maynus, Consilia Ruyni, toutes les oeuvres de R[i]m[in]aldus, toutes les oeuvres de Turrecremata, toutes les oeuvres de Felin, toutes les oeuvres de Joannes Faber, les oeuvres de Dominicus de Sancto Geminiano, les oeuvres de Henricus Brichus, les oeuvres de Hippolytus de Marsiliis, les oeuvres de Joannes de Imola, les oeuvres de Lucus de Pena, les oeuvres de Mathaeus de Afflicitis, les oeuvres de Rippa, toutes les oeuvres de Paulus de Castro, les oeuvres de Bartachinus, les oeuvres de Salicel, les oeuvres de Hostiensis, les oeuvres de Azo, les oeuvres de Zabarelle, le grand volume des Répetitions de divers autheurs, le grand volume des Grandz traictés de divers autheurs, les oeuvres de Cynus, la grande glosse ordinaire Singularia omnium doctorum, toutes les oeuvres de Julius Clarus'. See also above, note 21.

48. See appendix, nos. 37, 62, 65, 68, 75, 79, 99.

49. There are exceptions, but from the earliest period of the stock: see nos. 109 (*Antidotarium*) and 95 (Brasavola's two books with the title *Examen*). But the commercially successful authors Laurent Joubert and Guy de Chauliac, published by Beraud in more than one edition, do not figure in the inventory.

50. For examples, see appendix, nos. 15, 57.

51. For examples, see appendix, nos. 84, 128, 129.

52. See Baudrier, *Bibliographie lyonnaise*, II, p. 210; IX, pp. 330–7.
53. For examples, see appendix, nos. 48, 117, 120, 135.
54. See G. Richter, 'Bibliographische Beiträge zur Geschichte buchhändlersicher Kataloge im 16. und 17 Jahrhundert', in *Beiträge zur Geschichte des Buches und seiner Funktion in der Gesellschaft: Festschrift für Hans Widmann* (Stuttgart: A. Hiersemann), 1974, pp. 183–229; R. Engelsing, 'Deutsche Verlegerplakate des 17. Jahrhunderts', *Archiv für Geschichte des Buchwesens*, 9 (1969), 217–338; *Bücherkataloge als buchgeschichtliche Quellen in der Frühen Neuzeit*, ed. Reinhart Wittmann (Wiesbaden: Harrassowitz, 1984); Graham Pollard and Albert Ehrman, *The distribution of books by catalogue from the invention of printing to A.D. 1800, based on material in the Broxbourne Library* (Cambridge: Roxburghe Club, 1965).
55. For an example, see appendix, no. 32.
56. Baudrier, *Bibliographie lyonnaise*, IV, p. 41.
57. AHV, 246, letters of Villeneuve to Ruiz dated 1 April 1592 and 29 April 1592.
58. For examples, see appendix, nos. 4, 24, 26, 87.
59. See Baudrier, *Bibliographie lyonnaise*, V, p. 489–91; by November 1595, he had fallen out with René Postellier, who accused him of sequestering both the keys to the bookstore and the account books, against the interests of Adrian Périer: ibid., p. 488.
60. See appendix, nos. 20, 129; R. Arbour, *L'Ere baroque en France: répertoire chronologique des éditions de textes littéraires*, vol. 1 (Geneva: Droz, 1971), p. 183 (no. 1593/1451) lists also Pierre de Boaistuau, *Le theatre du monde*, Heirs of Symphorien Beraud, 1593.
61. Baudrier, *Bibliographie lyonnaise*, VI, p. 443; references to the *Societas* of Venice are found in the Frankfurt book fair catalogues in the 1580s and 1590s.
62. Ibid., VI, p. 442.
63. Ibid., VII, p. 207.
64. See Ian Maclean, 'The readership of philosophical fictions: the bibliographical evidence', in *Philosophical fictions of the French Renaissance*, ed. Neil Kenny (London: Warburg Institute, 1991), pp. 7–15.
65. See Baudrier, *Bibliographie lyonnaise*, II, p. 216.
66. See Ian Maclean, 'The market for scholarly books and conceptions of genre in Northern Europe, 1570–1630', in *Die Renaissance im Blick der Nationen Europas*, ed. Georg Kauffmann (Wiesbaden: Otto Harrassowitz, 1991), pp. 16–31.
67. See above, note 43.
68. See Yasuhiko Kataoka, *The first manuscript in the world on double-entry bookkeeping written by Benedetto Cotrugli* (Tokyo: Institute of Business Research, Daito Bunka University, 1998) on Cotrugli's *Della mercatura et del mercante perfetto*; its author died in 1468.
69. Leon Voet, *The Golden Compasses: a history and evaluation of the printing and publishing activities of the Officina Plantiniana at Antwerp*, 2 vols (Amsterdam and London: Vangendt, Routledge and Kegan Paul, 1969–72), II, passim.
70. See Maclean, 'The market for scholarly books'.
71. Voet, *The golden compasses*.
72. Lapeyre, *Les Ruiz*, pp. 571–3.
73. See Pollard and Ehrman, *The distribution of books by catalogue*.
74. For a case of second-order arbitration, see Baudrier, *Bibliographie lyonnaise*, V, p. 587.

75. For examples, see Baudrier, *Bibliographie lyonnaise*, V, pp. 86, 587, and above, note 26.
76. Ibid., V, p. 298.
77. Ibid., VI, p. 440 (joint submission with Sébastien Nivelle of Paris); ibid., VI, p. 459 (letter patent from the king addressed to Tinghi, Beraud and Michel of 5 July 1580).
78. Baudrier, *Bibliographie lyonnaise*, VI, p. 441.
79. Ibid., V, p. 298.
80. For evidence of appeals to this body, see ibid., VII, p. 214, and La Perrière, *Supplément provisoire à la "Bibliographie lyonnaise"*, pp. 136–7.
81. Quoted by Lapeyre, *Les Ruiz*, p. 570: 'que como bien tanta corruzion desa tierra, mirase mucho primero que se pasen y con rason'.
82. Ronald W. Truman, 'Fray Juan Ponce de León and the seventeenth-century *libreros* of Madrid', *Bulletin of Spanish Studies*, 81 (2004), 1091–107.
83. See Rojo Vega, 'Les livres des Espagnols à l'Epoque moderne'; AHV Protocolos 1629.
84. E.g. Giuntini's *Speculum astrologiae* of 1581 and 1583, which has as part of its rubricated title the phrase 'omnia sub censura Sancti Eccesliae Catholicae Romanae' prominently displayed in red.
85. Although not universal: witness the attempts by the Genevan consistory to suppress the publication of certain scholastic theologians: see Baudrier, *Bibliographie lyonnaise*, VI, p. 448.
86. *Index des livres interdits, ix: Index de Rome 1590, 1593, 1596. Avec étude des index de Parme 1580 et Munich 1582*, ed. J. M. de Bujanda *et al.* (Quebec: University de Sherbrooke/ Droz, 1994).
87. Dr Dennis Rhodes is preparing a bio-bibliography of Ciotti; see also his 'Some neglected aspects of the career of Giovanni Battista Ciotti', *The Library*, 6.9 (1987), 225–39; on Zetzner and Mareschal, see Ian Maclean, 'Mediations of Zabarella in Northern Germany, 1586–1623', in *La presenza dell' Aristotelismo padovano nella filosofia della prima modernità*, ed. Gregorio Piaia (Rome and Padua: Antenore, 2002), pp. 173–98. The Chouets and other Genevan publishers very often use the Latin form 'Aurelia Allobrogum' in an apparent attempt to disguise the provenance of their wares.

APPENDIX

The Inventory of Etienne Michel,
27 December 1591

This transcription presents the entries in the inventory (but not the accompanying text) in bold; the proposed identification of the books and any notes appear in Roman and italic. Each entry in bold contains information in the following order: number of bales; title, or author, or both; format; number of copies per bale; number of printed folio sheets per copy; the total in terms of reams, quires and folios. In the transcription, the same abbreviations are used as in the manuscript: b for bale; f for feuille (folio sheet); r for rame (ream); m for main (quire); do (for ditto) appears in place of the format, but there are cases where it cannot be correct. { indicates that the works named are bracketed in the text as being part of the same bale. The total number of copies of any given work can be computed by multiplying the number of bales by the number of copies per bale, and adding this figure to any other occurrences of the same title: e.g. for Cartari, *Imagines deorum*, there are two entries: one bale of 64; three bales of 110, making 394 copies *in toto*.

I have supplied numbers to the entries; where the same work occurs later in the inventory, it is given the earlier number, and the notes are not repeated. The letters A, B, C, i attached to the number refer respectively to the date ranges given at the end of the inventory (1520–60; 1560–79; 1579–1589; 'imparfait'), which determine the value of the folios in the bale. As no indication of date is given (except 'viel'), I have been unable to identify with certainty the quantities recorded at the end of the document in each category, except in the case of imperfect copies, but even there I have had to assume an error in calculation. An asterisk indicates that the folio count given in the inventory matches the page, folio, or collation count of the edition cited.

In the notes, the identifications cite the following sources:

A: Herbert Mayow Adams, *Catalogue of books printed on the continent of Europe, 1501–1600, in Cambridge libraries* (Cambridge: Cambridge University Press, 1967)

Bau: Henri-Louis Baudrier, *Bibliographie lyonnaise: recherches sur les imprimeurs, libraires, relieurs et fondeurs de lettres de Lyon au XVIe siècle, publiées et continuées par J. Baudrier*, 12 vols (Paris: F. de Nobele, 1964–5)

Baus: Yvonne La Perrière, *Supplément provisoire à la "Bibliographie lyonnaise" du président Baudrier* (Paris: Bibliothèque Nationale, 1967)

BL: British Library, London

Bod: Bodleian Library , Oxford

CCF: Catalogue Collectif de France

CranzS: F. Edward Cranz, *A bibliography of Aristotle editions, 1501–1600*, rev. Charles B. Schmitt (Baden-Baden, Koerner, 1984)

Gültlingen: Sybille von Gültlingen and René Badagos, *Bibliographie des livres imprimés à Lyon au seizième siècle* (Baden-Baden, V. Koerner, 1992–)

HAB: Herzog-August-Bibliothek, Wolfenbüttel

HPB: Consortium of European Research Libraries Hand Press Books Database (followed by the library)

KVK: Universität Karlsruhe, Universitätsbibliothek, Karlsruher Virtueller Katalog (followed by the library grouping)

PBN: Paris, Bibliothèque Nationale de France

Discrepancies in addition and in format are noted, but otherwise descriptions are kept to a minimum. The place of publication is Lyon except where otherwise stated. In cases of reprintings (which may also include reissues), I have accepted the later date. The name of the publisher appears in the usual vernacular form (where the printer also is named, this appears as on the imprint). The pagination given in bibliographies and library catalogues is indicated by f(olios), col(umns) and p(ages).

Inuentaire de Cinq cens quarante cinq balles, Liures imprimez trouué [*sic*] dans deux magasins en ceste ville de lyon pres l'Eglise et couuent des Jacobins appellé [*sic*] La compagnie, lesquelles Cinq cens quarante cinq balles Livres ont esté remises par Estienne Michel Libraire dudit Lyon a Me Jehan Compere tuteur des enfans et heritiers feu Simphorien Beraud et Jehan Regrey administrateur des biens et facultez desditz enfans pour leur seruir d'ypotheque asseurance et risgarda de partie de la Somme de dixhuit mil et six cents escus en laquelle ledit Michel et Adrian Perier son compagnon et associé sont tenuz et obligez ausdicts heritiers Beraud par obligation du Cinquiesme Jour du moys de Juillet mil cinq cens quatre vingts et sept. Receue par Me Jehan Grauier Notaire Royal audit Lyon, ainsi que lesditz Compere et Regrey nous ont fait apparoir, a la requeste desquels a esté fait ledit present Inuentaire aux fins de faire estimer apprecier et esualuer les Livres imprimez contenuz audit present Inuentaire pour leur seruir et ualoir ce que de raison, mesmes contre ledit Estienne Michel au proces qui est pendant d'entre lesditz Compere et Regrey en ladite qualité demandeurs contre ledit Michel deffendeur ez villes de Medina del Campo que reale chancellerie de Vallidoly pays et Royaume d'Espagne, lequel Inventaire a esté faict en consequence des actes et procedures faites par deuant Me Pierre Austrein Conseiller du Roy Lieutenant particulier Ciuil et Criminel en la Seneschaussée et Siege presidial dudit Lyon.

1C. **deux b.**   **Amadis de Gaulle 16e.–19e voll. a deux cent vingt la b. f.20**

r 17 m 12

Bau 5.39 *Le dix neufiesme livre d'Amadis de Gaule*, trans. Gabriel Chappuys, Jean Beraud, 1582, 16f, 447f, 3f. Bau 4.59 records another edition trans. Jacques Charlot, Louis Cloquemin, 1581, 16f, 445f, 2f. According to the entry for the former of these editions in *Index Aureliensis; catalogus librorum sedecimo saeculo impressorum* (Baden-Baden: Heitz, 1962–), i.454, no. 104.460, 447f=461f, which would make the whole work 480f, for which the correct inventory entry would be 30f.; this may not be a complete edition, but has been taken to be such in the inventory.

2B*. **une b.**   **Amadis in 16. 17e voll. a deux cent la b. f.27½**   **r 11**

Baus 145 *Le dix septième livre d'Amadis de Gaule*, Etienne Michel, 1578, 15f, 440f.

3B*. **une b.**   **Raymundus Sebond. De nat. hominis 16. a cinq cens la b. f.13   r 13**

Bau 4.247, 288 Raymond Sabunde, *De natura hominis*, Thibaud Payen, 1568, 411p, 2f.

4C. **trois b.**   **Menochius de praesumptionibus. fol. a trente la b. f.110   r 19 m 16**

Baus 157 Giacomo Menochio, *Commentariorum de praesumptionibus pars prima*, Etienne Michel, 1588, 32f, 486p, 1f. The collation does not match. The edition must have been published in Michel's absence. There are references to a later edition: Bau 5.336–7, Pierre Landry, 1593.

5C*. **une b.**   **Decisiones Pedemontan. Fol. a quarante la b. f.136   r 10 m 17 f 15**

Bau 6.479 Octavianus Cacheranus, *Decisiones sacri Senatus Pedemontani*, Filippo Tinghi, 1579, fol, 4f, 480p, 28f.

6A. **cinq b.**   **Anania super decretales. do. a dix la b. f.318   r 31 m 16**

A A.1008 Joannes de Anania, *Super primo [-quinto] Decretalium*, 4 vols, excud. Petrus Fradin, 1553. Pierre Fradin printed for the Compagnie des Libraires.

7A. **trois b.**   **Odoffredus do. a quatre la b. f.800   r 19 m 4**

A O.68–79 Odofredus, [various commentaries on the *Corpus Juris Civile*], 10 vols, excud. Blaisius Guido, Petrus Compater, Franciscus et Claudius Marchant fratres, Joannes Pullon, Per Georgium Regnault, 1550-2.

8A. deux b.   **Fulgosij Lectura do. a six la b. f.597**   **r 14 m 6 f 14**

Bau 7.317; Raphael Fulgosius, [various commentaries on the *Corpus Juris Civile*], 3 vols, Hugues de la Porte and the heirs of Aimon de la Porte (excud. Stephanus Rufinus and Joannes Ausultus; excud. Claudius Servanius), 1546 ; A F.1143–4 *In primam Pandectarum partem commentariorum tomus primus*, Compagnie des Libraries (excud. Claudius Servanius), 1554.

7A. une b.   **{Odoffredus do. a trois. f.800}**   **r 7 m 10**

9A*.   **{Angelus s. Instituta do. a six f.185}**

HPB (BVB) Angelus a Gambilionibus, *In institutiones commentarii*, Compagnie des libraires, 1557, 357f, 21f.

10A*. une b.   **{Consilia Oldradi do a trentesix f.80}**   **r 8 m 3 f 20**

Bau 6.268 Oldradus a Ponte, *Consilia*, heirs of Jacopo Giunti, 1550, 162f.

11A*.   **{Anania Super 5o decretal. do. a neuf f.135}**

Bau 7.402 Joannes de Anania, *Super quinto libro Decretalium*, Jacques et Jean Senneton, 1546, 270f.

12C*. une b   **{Soto de natura et gratia fol. a vingt f.48}**   **r 10 m 18 f 15**

A S.1497 Domingo de Soto, *De natura et gratia*, Giovanna Giunti, 1581, 183p.

13C*.   **{-idem de iustitia et Iure. fol. A unze f.185}**

Bau 5.62–3; Baus 152; A S.1487–92 Domingo de Soto, *De iustitia et iure*, Symphorien Beraud and Etienne Michel, 1582, 24f, 344f; also with the addressses of Barthélemy Honorat, Giovanna Giunti, Alessandro Marsili, Charles Pesnot, Guillaume Rouillé, 1582. An example of an edition shared beyond the membership of the Compagnie des Libraires.

14C*.   **{Summa de exemplis. 4o. a trente. f.85}**

Bau 5.72 Joannes de Sancto Geminiano, *Summa de exemplis et rerum similitudinibus locupletissima, verbi dei concinatoribus, cunctisque literarum studiosis maximo usui futura*, Symphorien Beraud and Etienne Michel (in off. Q. Philippi Tinghi), 1585, 10f, 330f.

15C*. une b.   **{Cardanus de subtilitate 8o. a trente f.48½}**   **r 13 m 6 f 12**

Baus 147 Girolamo Cardano, *De subtilitate*, Etienne Michel, 1580, 718p, 1f, 28f; a speculative reprinting using Guillaume Rouillé, 1559, as copy, possibly printed in Geneva.

16C*.   **{Responsa Philippi. fol. a vingt f.70}**

Bau 5.56–7 Joannes Philippus, *Responsa*, Symphorien Beraud and Etienne Michel (in off. Q. Philippi Tinghi), 1584, 10f, 226p, 19f. Michel held the privilège, dated 14 June 1579.

17C*. **{Paratitla Wesenbecii 4o a quarantesept f.81}**

Baus 153 Matthäus Wesenbeck, *In pandectas iuris civilis et codicis Iustinianei lib xii commentarii ... illi sub paratitlorum nomine iam saepius prodeunt*, Etienne Michel and Symphorien Beraud, 1585, 8p, 494p, 34p, 100p, 10p; earlier editions by Louis Cloquemin and Etienne Michel in 1576 and by Michel alone in 1583. KVK (SWB), Hugues Gazeau and Etienne Michel, 1597, variously 296p, 1434p.

18C*. **{Roland furieux 8o et suitte a soixantecinq f.74}**   r 15 m 2 f 15½

Bau 4.144–5; Baus 150, 152 Ludovico Arioso, *Roland furieux*, trans. Gabriel Chappuys, Etienne Michel, 1582, 8f, 702p, 1f; id., *La suite de Roland furieux*, Etienne Michel 1583, 4f, 408p; both editions shared with Barthélemy Honorat. The correct total for the whole bale is r 14 m 18 f 15½.

19C*. **{Mondes de doni 8o a quarantesept f.56½}**

Bau 4.145; Baus 152 Antonio Francesco Doni, *Les mondes celestes*, trans. Gabriel Chappuys, Etienne Michel, 1583, 12f, 735p, 122p, 21p; an edition shared with Barthélemy Honorat.

20C*. **une b. Histoire de Lutius florus 8o a deux cens vingtquatre la b. f.28½**
                                                                r12 m 15 f 9

BL; KVK (RERO) Publius Annius Florus, *L'histoire romaine* [...], trans. L. Constant, Geneva [de l'imprimerie de Jacques Berjon], 1580, 28f, 198f, 1f; heirs of Symphorien Beraud, 1609, 198f. Possibly printed in Geneva on commission for Etienne Michel or Symphorien Beraud.

20C*. **une b. -idem a deux cens quarantequatre la b f.28½**   r 13 m 18 f 4

21B*. **deux b. Repetitio Gutterij fol. a quarantesept la b a 46 la b. f.140**
                                                                r 25 m 15 f 5

HAB Joannes Gutterius (Juan Gutierrez), *Repetitionum et allegationum novum commentarium*, Salamanca, Juan de Canova, 1570, 4f, 494p, 29f. The correct figure is 47, not 46, per bale.

22C*. **une b. {Concordantiae Bibliae. 4o. a vingtneuf. f.136½}**   r 10 m 14 f 16½

Bau 9.396 *Concordantiae Bibliae*, Guillaume Rouillé [and Jean-Baptiste Regnauld], 1586, 548f.

23C*. **{Decisiones diversorum. tom. primus. fol. a seize f.88}**

Baus 156 *Decisiones gravissarum et subtilissimarum quaestionum quae in utroque foro versantibus occurrunt a variis auctoribus collectae*, 3 vols, Etienne Michel 1588; vol 1, 4f, 357p.

24C*. **une b.** **{Tractatus de Coniecturis. fol. a vingttrois f.178}**   **r 12 m 5 f 4**

Bau 5.73; 5.329, 333, 336 Franciscus Mantica, *Tractatus de coniecturis ultimarum voluntatum*, Symphorien Beraud and Etienne Michel (in off. Q. Philip. Tinghi), 1585, 6f, 346p, 29f; Pierre Landry, 1590, 6f, 646p, 27f reissued in 1592 and 1593).

13C*.   **{Soto de iustitiae et Jure. fol. a unze f.185}**

25C*. **une b.** **{Thesaurus bibliorum 8o. a cinquanteneuf f.55}**   **r 14 m 8 f 10**

HPB (ICCU Rome) William Allot, *Thesaurus Bibliorum*, Symphorien Beraud and Etienne Michel, 1584–5, 418p, 22p. Other editions listed include one in 1580 by Alessandro Marsili and another in 1583 by Ludovicus Garanaeus (a Saragossa printer, giving Lyon as the address: Bau 1.174–5). The total for the bale should be r 13 m 10 f 4 (see below, 26).

26C*.   **{Sylva Granatensis 8o. a trenteung f.57}**

Bau 5.75–6; A G.990 Luis de Granada, *Sylva locorum communium*, Paris, Adrian Périer, 1586; Savinianus Pesnot, 1586; KVK (HBZ) Symphorien Beraud and Etienne Michel, 1586; Bau 5.335, Pierre Landry, 1592, 8f, 868p, 6f. The multiplication of the sheets has been done on the basis not of 31, but 39, to achieve the total count for the bale.

27C*.   **{Summa sacramento. a victoria 16o a centtrentequatre f.13}**

Bau 2.169 Franciscus a Victoria, *Summa sacramentorum Ecclesiae*, Alessandro Marsili, 1583, 390p, 13f.

28C. **une b.** **{Tite live en fra. fol. a trois f.336}**   **r 10 m 15 f 13**

PBN Livy, *Les decades*, 2 vols, Paris, a shared edition by Nicolas Chesneau, Abel L'Angelier, and Jacques Dupuis, 1583.

29B*.   **{Pline en fra. fol. a dix f.438}**

Bau 7.429–30; A P 1594 *L'histoire du monde*, 2 vols, Claude Senneton, 1562, 6f, 678p, 1f, 84f; 16f, 745p, 1f, 52f.

30C*. **une b.** **{Opera Junctini. fol. a quatre f.633}**   **r 11 m 16 f 24**

Bau 5.60–1; A J.435–6 Franciscus Junctinus, *Speculum astrologiae*, 2 vols, Symphorien Beraud, 1581, 1583 (a reissue), 10f, 1313p, 3p; 1170p, 20f. Previously published by Tinghi in 1573, 1575 and 1577 (Bau 6.459–60, 464–4, 470–2).

31C*.   **{Imagines deorum 4o. a soixantequatre f.53}**

Bau 4.139; Baus 149, Vincenzo Cartari, *Imagines deorum*, trans. Antoine du Verdier, Etienne Michel, 1581, 359p, 28f; an edition shared with Barthélemy Honorat. The calculation should read r 34 m 19 f 15.

32C*. **une b.**   **Dioscorides en fra. 4o a septante la b. f.74**   **r 10 m 7 f 5**

Bau 4.58 Dioscorides, *Les six livres de la matiere medicale*, Louis Cloquemin, 1580 (a reissue of an earlier edition by veuve Arnoullet), 8f, 574p, 1f.

33. **une b.**   **Horae Romanorum in 16o a cinq cens nonante et ung la b f.12½**

                                                             r 14 m 15 f 12½

Bau 4.234; Hanns Bohatta, *Bibliographie des livres d'heures* (Vienna: Gilhofer and Ransch-burg, 1909), H 89, *Hortulus animae, denuo purgatus in quo horae beatissimae Virginis Mariae secundum usum Romanorum continentur*, Thibaud Payen, 1546, 20f, 215f, 4f; Thibaud Payen, 1553 (Rosenthal cat. 64, no 817). I am grateful to Cristina Dondi for this reference (see also below, 50).

34C. **une b.**   **{Consilior. Rol. a valle tom. 3 fol. a vingt et ung f.106}**

                                                             r 14 m 8 f 21½

Bau 5.69; Baus 157 Rolandus a Valle, *Consilia sive responsa*, 4 vols in 2, Symphorien Beraud and Etienne Michel, 1585, 1588.

35A*.   **{Alciatus super Codice. 8o. a quarante neuf f.46½}**

HPB (ICCU Rome) Andrea Alciati, *Index super commentariis Codicis*, Jacopo Giunti, 1536, 40p, 700p.

36B.   **{-idem in Pandectas 8o. a trentequatre f.41½}**

HPB (ICCU Rome) Andrea Alciati, *In Digestorum seu Pandectarum librum xii commentarii*, Jacopo Giunti, 1547, 387p, 21p.

37A*.   **{Paraphrasis in vallam 8o. a soixante f.13½}**

CCF (Marseille) Desiderius Erasmus, *Paraphrasis seu potius epitome in Elegantiarum libros Laurentii Vallae*, Sebastianus Gryphius, 1556, 199p, 8f. The Erasmus Online Catalogue records an edition by Thibaud Payen in 1551.

38A*.   **{Alciatus de rub. iuris Canonicj. 8o. a seize f.31}**

HAB Andrea Alciati, *Commentarii in rubricas Iuris Canonici*, Jacopo Giunti, 1542, 8p, 416p, 164p.

39B. **une b.**   **{Rudimenta medic. ab Anguilera. fol. a trentehuit f.83}**

                                                             r 11 m 14 f 14

Bod Antonius ab Aguilera, *Praeclarae rudimenta medicinae*, Alcalá, Juan Villanueva, 1576, 164f. The correct figure for the bale should be r 11 m 13 f 9. This bale is possibly the product of *Tauschhandel* or debt settlement.

40B*.   **{Martines de anima fol. a cinq f.155}**

Bod Petrus Martinez de Toledo y Brey, *In tres Libros Aristotelis de anima commentarii*, Sigüenza, excud. Joannes Gratianus, 1575, 10f, 561p.

41A*.　　　**{Sauonarola in Ruth. 4o. a vingt f.76}**

HPB (ICCU Rome) Girolamo Savonarola, *Homiliae in totum libellum Ruth* […], Salamanca, Juan de Canova, 1556, 300p.

42B.　　　**{Zegobiensis in euangelia. fol. a ung imparfait f.130}**

Bod Johannes Segobiensis, *De praedicatione evangelica*, Alcalá, excud. Joannes Gratianus, 1573.

43B*.　　　**{floresta en espagnol. In 12o. a quinze f.17}** /2/

Melchior de Santa Cruz de Dueñas, *Floresta española de apothegmas*, Toledo, Francisco de Guzmán, 1574, cited by Pedro M. Cátedra and Anastasio Rojo Vega, *Bibliotecas y lecturas de mujeres, Siglo XVI* (Salamanca: Instituto de Historia del Libro y de la Lectura, 2004); another edition, Salamanca, Pedro Lasso, 1576, +^{12} A–Q^{12} (see Lorenzo Ruiz Fidalgo, *La imprenta en Salamanca (1501–1600)* (Madrid: Arco Libros, 1994), II, 824.) I am grateful to Clive Griffin for these references. Also Bod Alcalá [por Gaspar de Ortega] impressa por Sebastián Martinez, 1578, 204f (Tabla 2f).

44A*. **deux b. Baduellus in Ciceronem pro Milone. 8o. a deux cens quarante la p f.25**　　　　　　　　　　　　　　　　　　　　　　　　　　　　**r 24**

Bau 8.258 Claude Baduel, *Annotationes in Ciceronis Pro Milone* […], Sebastianus Gryphius, 1552, 394p, 1f.

45B*. **quatre b. facius De rebus gestis Alphonsi. 4o a cent vingt la b f.57**
　　　　　　　　　　　　　　　　　　　　　　　　　　　r 54 m 14 f 10

Bau 8.297, 304 Bartholomaeus Facius, *De rebus gestis ab Alphonso primo Neapolitanorum Rege commentariorum libri x*, heirs of Sebastianus Gryphius, 1560, 1562, 312p, 8f, 4f, 106p, 5f.

46A*. **deux b. Ferrarius super feudis. 8o. a deux cens la b. f.29¾**　　**r 11 m 18**

Bau 8.276–7 Joannes Ferrarius Montanus, *In usu feudorum*, Sebastianus Gryphius, 1555 452p, 4f. The correct figure is r 23 m 16; only one bale has been counted.

47A*. **une b. Axiomata legum 8o. a deux cent octantecinq f.17½**　**r 7 m 19 f 2½**

Bau 8.210–1 [possibly Matthaeus Gribaldus], *Axiomata legum*, Sebastianus Gryphius, 1547, 279p. The correct calculation should be r 9 m 19 f 12½.

48A. **cinq b. Corpus Canonicum do r.n. viel a cinq la b. f.706**　　　**r 35 m 6**

Corpus iuris canonici; r.n. is presumably rouge et noir (i.e. rubrication): Hugues de la Porte made a speciality of publishing this (multiple editions by him between 1535 and 1560: Bau 4.304ff.). Bau 7.341 says that some copies of the edition of 1572 'portent la marque de la Compagnie des libraires'.

49B*. deux b.   Socinus Junior in secund. partem lib primi decret. a trentequatre la b. f.223   **r 30 m 2 f 14**

HPB (Jesus College, Oxford) Mariano Socino, *Super secunda parte libri quinti Decretalium*, Parma, Seth Vioti, 1574, 14f, 397f. The correct calculation should be r 30 m 6 f 14.

50. une b.   Horae S. Johann. Hyerosolimit. 16o. a cinq cens treize la b. f.10
                    r 10 m 5 f 5

Bohatta, *Bibliographie des livres d'heures*, 1476: *Hore beate Marie virginis secundum usum Hierosolymitanum*, Lyon, 1516, 8vo, a–m^8 (the only known surviving copy of this recension of the book of hours). Cf. below, 79.

51B. douze b.   Socinus in Ciuile do. A douze la b. f.269   **r 77 m 9 f 11**

Bau 1.35 Bartolomeo Socino, *Ad ius civile commentaria*, ex off. Matthaei Bernardo et Stephani Servanii, 1564. 'do' does not refer to 16mo but fol.

52A. six b.   Decretum do. r n. vieil a douze la b.   **r 39 m 9 f 3**

Decretum Gratiani; See above, 48; possibly by Hugues de la Porte, who specialized in the printing of canonical legal texts.

52A. une b.   -idem contenant neuf rames   **r 9**

53A*. une b.   Nouuella super sext. do. a quarante quatre la b f.72   **r 6 m 6 f 18**

Bau 6.266 Joannes Andreae, *In sextum Decretalium librum novella commentaria*, heirs of Jacopo Giunti, 1550, 131f, 1f, 10f.

54A. une b.   Ancharanus super Clementinis. do. a soixante la b. f.51
                    r 6 m 2 f 10

KVK (BVB) Petrus de Ancharano, *Super Clementinis*, heirs of Jacopo Giunti, 1549, 93f.

55A. une b.   Geographia Ptolemej. fol. a vingtdeux la b. f.122   **r 4 m 16 f 14**

Bau 12.256 Ptolemy, *Geographia*, Hugues de la Porte, 1541, 149p, [1]p, 50 maps, 50f, 48f. The calculation should read r 5 m 7 f 9.

56A*. six b.   Jacobus de Arena. do. a vingt la b f.170   **r 40 m 16**

HAB Jacobus de Arena, *Commentarii in universum ius civile.* Hugues de la Porte, 1541, 309p, 30p.

57A. six b.   Cronica volaterranj fol. a trentehuit la b. f.162   **r 73 m 17 f 11**

Bau 8.259 Raphaele Maffei Volaterrano, *Commentariorum urbanorum*, Sebastianus Gryphius, 1552, 18f, 1218p, 1f.

58C. huict b.   Opuscules de Plutarque fo. E. Michel. a vingtquatre la b. f.243
                    r 93 m 6 f 6

Baus 146 Plutarch, *Œuvres morales et meslees*, trans Jacques Amyot, Etienne Michel, 1579, 4f, 842p, 1f, 82f.

59C*. deux b.   Images des dieux fra. 4o. a septante la b. f.85½   r 24 m 14 f 20

Bau 4.140–1; Baus 150 Vincenzo Cartari, *Les images des dieux des anciens*, trans. Antoine du Verdier, Etienne Michel, 1581, 8f, 637p, 21f; an edition shared with Barthélemy Honorat. The correct calculation should be r 23 m 18 f 20.

60C* cinq b.   Imagini di Dei do. ytal. a cent septante la b. f.33½   r 56 m 19

Bau 4.140; Baus 149 Vincenzo Cartari, *Le imagini de i dei de gli antichi*, Etienne Michel 1581, 28f, 47[6]p; an edition shared with Barthélemy Honorat.

31C*. trois b.   Imagines deorum 4o. lat. a cent dix la b. f.53   r 34 m 19 f 20

61C*. trois b.   Blason des Armoiries. fol. a cent vingt la b. f.65   r 46 m 16

HPB (Yale) Jérôme de Bara, *Blason des armoiries*, Barthélemy Vincent, 1581, 12p, 248p, 2p.

62A*. une b.   Ovidij amatoria. 8o. a deux cens trentehuit la b. f.25   r 11 m 18

Bau 8.271–2 Ovid, *Amatoria*, Sebastianus Gryphius, 1555, 397p, 1f.

63B*. une b.   Andria Terentij latfra. 8o deuxcent quarante la b. f.27   r 12 m 19

Bau 2.282 Terence, *Andria*, Thibaud Payen, 1561 427p, 2f. The calculation should read r 12 m 19 f 5.

64. une b.   Breuiar. Roman. Pii quinti 8o a centdix la b. f.56   r 12 m 4 f 20

The breviary of Pius V was not published before 1568.

65A*. une b   Dialectica Aristotelis 8o a cent octante la b. f.34   r 12 m 4 f 20

CranzS Aristotle, *Dialectica*, Sebastianus Gryphius, 1554, 541p.

66A*. une b.   Pandectae medicinae. fol. a soixante la b. f.90   r 10 m 16

Bau 4.225–6 and Bau 6.194 Matthaeus Silvaticus, *Pandectae medicinae*, Thibaud Payen and Jacopo Giunti, 1541, 180f.

67A*. une b.   {ferrarius super instituta. 8o a cinquante la b. f.31½}   r 10 m 7

Bau 8.268 Joannes Ferrarius, *In IIII Institutionum libros annotationes*, Sebastianus Gryphius, 1554, 470p, 16f, 1f. The correct calculation should read r 10 m 1.

68A*.   {Physica Aristotelis. 8o a quarante la b. f.50}

Bau 8.270; CranzS Aristotle, *Physica*, Sebastianus Gryphius, 1554, 1559, 800p.

69A*.   {Bellum Gramaticale 8o. a cinquante la b. f.[1]2½}

Bau 4.239; 8.110, 123 Andreas Guarna, *Bellum grammaticale*, Thibaud Payen, 1548, 39p; previously Sebastianus Gryphius, 1538, 1539, 39p; also Jean II Frellon 1551. Although the '1'of '12½' appears to have been struck through, the calculation has been based on 12½f, not 2½f.

70B*.   {Lucanus in 8o a cinquante la b f.17}

Bau 8.302 Lucan, *De bello civili libri decem*, Sebastianus Gryphius, 1561, 269,1f.

71i. une b.   {Cicero pro domo sua 4o a cent cinquante f.7}   r 11 m 2

72i.   {-idem de legibus 4o a deux cent cinquante f.9}

73i.   {-idem ad Brutum 4o a deux cent cinquante f.9}

PBN Probably three parts of Cicero, *Opera*, Sybille de la Porte, 1588. Although not described as such, calculated as 'imparfait'.

74A*. trois b.   Loriotus de apicibus Iuris. fol. a soixante la b. f.98
                                                                          r 35 m 5 f 15

Bau 8.280 Petrus Loriotus, *De iuris apicibus tractatus viii*, Sebastianus Gryphius, 1555, 18f, 708col, 1f.

75A*. une b.   Ovidij epistolae. 8o a quatre cent la b. f.14   r 11 m 4

Bau 8.136 Ovid, *Heroides Epistolae*, Sebastianus Gryphius, 1540, 223p.

14C*. six b.   Summa de exemplis 4o a septante la b. f.85   r 71 m 8

76C*. trente b.   Regulae Iuris fol. a seize la b. f.389   r 373 m 8 f 20

Baus 155 *Regularum utriusque iuris tam civilis quam pontificii tomus primus*, 2 vols, Etienne Michel, 1587, 2f, 792p, 592p, 84f.

30C*. trente et une b. Iunctini opera fol. a dix la b. f.633   r 392 m 9 f 5

77B. une b.   Tractatus cautellarum. fol. a cinquante la b. f.134
                                                                          r 13 m 8

Bau 6.473–4 *Tractatus cautelarum omnium*, Filippo Tinghi, 1577, 4f, 4[47]p, 22f. The collation does not match.

78B*. trentesix b. Summa hostiensis. fol. a dixsept la b. f.191
                                                                          r 233 m 15 f 17

Bau 6.467 Henricus de Segusio, Cardinal Hostiensis, *Summa aurea*, Filippo Tinghi, 1576, 386f. The calculation should read m 233 m 17 f 17.

78B*. quatorze b.   -idem.fol. a dixhuit la b. f.191   r 96 m 5 f 7

78B*. une b.   **-idem fol. a quinze la b. f.191**   **r 5 m 14 f 15**

78B*. une b.   **-idem fol. de douze et deux rames et demye**   **r 7 m 1 f 17**

It is not clear what the reference to 'deux rames et demye' is; possibly 750 sheets constituting incomplete copies? If so, they do not seem to have entered into the calculation of 'imparfait'.

79A. douze b.   **Missale S Iohan. Hyersolo. fol. a vingt la b. dix rames**
                     chasq. balle   **r 120**

Bau 6.255; Lyon, Bibliothèque Municipale *Missale S Ioannis Hierosolymita*, heirs of Jacopo Giunti, n.d. (possibly 1551), 22f, 374f; heirs of Jacopo Giunti, 1553.

80C*. huict b.   **Breuiari. predicatorum. 8o a cent dix la b. f.57**   **r 100 m 6 f 10**

A L.974 *Breviarium Praedicatorum*, Symphorien Beraud and Etienne Michel, 1586 (ex off. Q. Philippi Tinghi), 440f. The collation does not quite match.

81C*. unze b.   **Quaestiones disputatae D. Thomae fol. a quarante la b. f.175**
                     r 154

Bau 5.75; 6.332; Baus 1586 St Thomas Aquinas, *Quaestiones disputatae*, Symphorien Beraud and Etienne Michel, 1586, 4f, 346f; previously published by the heirs of Jacopo Giunti.

82C*. unze b.   **Tractatus de Attentatis. fol. a quarante la b. f.161**
                     r 141 m 13 f 15

HPB (ICCU Rome) Robertus Lancellotus, *Tractatus de attentatis*, Symphorien Beraud and Etienne Michel (in off. Q. Philippi Tinghi), 1585, 12p, 546p, 98p.

34C. seize b.   **Consilia Rolandj a valle. fol. a quatorze la b. f.366**
                     r 163 m 19 f 9

83C. une b.   **Dictionar. puerorum 4o latfra. a nonante la b. f.69**
                     r 12 m 8 f 10 /3/

Baus 146 Orazio de Toscanella, *Dictionariolum puerorum*, Etienne Michel, 1578, 405p. The collation does not match.

84i. dixneuf b.   **Opera Senecae. in 8o imparfaictz. a cinquantecinq la b. quatorze**
                     rames la balle   **r 266**

Bau 5.90–1 Seneca, *Scriptorum quae extant*, 2 vols, heirs of Symphorien Beraud, 1592.

85C*. trois b.   **Emanuelis Costae opera. fol. a trentesix. la b. f.180**
                     r 38 m 17 f 15

Bau 5.66 Emanuel Costa, *Opera*, Symphorien Beraud and Etienne Michel, 1584, 720p.

86C. **quatre b.**   **Pline en fra. fol. a douze la b. f.438**   **r 42 m 14**

A P.1594 Pliny, *L'histoire du monde*, 2 vols, Charles Pesnot, 1581. The calculation should read r 42 m 0 f 24.

87C*. **huict b.**   **Sermones Granatensis. 8o tomus primus. a cent soixante**
                        la b. f.38   **r 97 m 5 f 15**

Bau 5.68; 5.489–90 Luis de Granada, *Conciones*, 4 vols, Etienne Michel and Symphorien Beraud, 1585; National Library of Scotland tomus primus, 1585, 573p; 8 vols, Alexandre Villeneuve, 1598.

88C*. **quatre b.**   **Opuscules de Plutarque. fol. grosse lettre. a quatorze la b. f.360**
                                                                              r 40 m 2 f 10

Baus 55; Bau 5.90 Plutarch, *Œuvres morales et meslees*, Etienne Michel, 1587, 7f, 674f, 44f ; heirs of Symphorien Beraud, 1592, 2f, 674f, 24f. Not 58 (see collation). 'grosse lettre' presumably refers to a larger point size.

89C*. **trois b.**   **Consilia Grammatici. fol. a quarante la b. f.162   r 38 m 17 f 15**

Bau 5.66 Thomas Grammaticus, *Consilia et vota, seu iuris responsa*, Symphorien Beraud, 1584, 665p; previously published by the heirs of Jacopo Giunti in 1550.

90B. **six b.**   **Breuiar. Carmelitarum. 8o a nonante la b. f.71½   r 77 m 4 f 10**

HPB (ICCU Rome) *Breuiarium Carmelitarum*, Venice, Giunti, 1568, 64p, [887]p, [1]p, [112]p.

68A*. **trois b.**   **Aristotelis physica Argiropilj. 8o deux b. a cent douze et une**
                        balle a 89   **r 22 m 8**

The bale at 89 has not been included in the total.

25C*. **une b.**   **Thesaurus bibliorum. 8o a cent dix la b. f.55**   **r 12 m 2**

91C*. **deux b.**   **Toletj dialectica. 8o a cinq cens la b. f.14**   **r 28**

Bau 2.170 Petrus Toletus, *Opera*, Alessandro Marsili, 1586, 224p (the first part of *Opera* has the title *Introductio in Dialecticam*).

92C. **une b.**   **Quadrains de Pibrac en musicque. 4o a cent la b. f.60   r 12 m f**

Georg Draut, *Bibliotheca exotica* (Frankfurt: Balthasar Ostern, 1625), p. 210: Paschal de L'Estocart, *Cent et vingt six Quadrains du sieur de Pibrac mis en musique*, Lyon, 1582.

93C. **une b.**   **Figures de la bible. 8o a deux cens quarante la b. f. 31**
                                                                              r 14 m 18 f 21

Bau 4.143; Baus 151 Gabriel Chappuys, *Figures de la Bible declarees par stances*, Etienne Michel, 1582, 114f; id., *Figures du Nouveau Testament declarees par stances*, Etienne Michel 1582, 46f; an edition shared with Barthélemy Honorat, 1581. The calculation is correct for 241 copies, not 240.

94A. **une b.**   **Ephemerides Taboetij. in 4o a cent soixante huit la b. f.49**
$$r \ 16 \ m \ 9 \ f \ 7$$

Bau 4.278 Constantius Taboetius, *De quadruplicis Monarchiae primis authoribus ... Ephemerides historicae*, Thibaud Payen (sumpt. Francisci Pomani), 3 vols, 1559, 52p, 40p, 40p. As the collation does not match, it is possible that there is a confusion here with Franciscus Junctinus, *Ephemerides Ioannis Stadii*, Symphorien Beraud and Etienne Michel, 1585 (Bau 5.70), but that collation also does not match.

94A. **une b.**   **-idem 4o a centcinquante la b. f.49**   **r 14 m 14**

95A*. **une b.**   **Antonij Musae examen. 16o 2 volls. a centsoixante trois la b. f.44½r**
$$14 \ m \ 16 \ f \ 3½$$

Bau 2.235–6 Antonius Musa Brasavola, *Examen omnium simplicium, quorum usus publicis est officinis; Examen omnium syruporum, quorum publicus usus est*, Antoine Vincent and Jean II Frellon, 1556, 2 vols 862p, 33f, 281p, 3f. The calculation should be r 14 m 12 f 13½.

96A*. **une b.**   **Biblia Pagninj. fol. a trentehuit la b. f. 160**   **r 12 m 3 f 5**

Bau 7.312 *Biblia sacra ex Santis Pagnini tralatione*, Hugues de la Porte, 1542, 6f, 267f, 38f.

97A. **une b.**   **{Pandectae Legis euangelicq. 16o a centsoixante trois la b. f.19}**
$$r \ 6 \ m \ 8 \ f \ 11$$

Bau 8.215, 234, 262 Simon du Corroy, *Pandectae legis evangelicae*, Sebastianus Gryphius 1547, 1549, 1555, 313p, 24f. The calculation works if there are 169 in the bale.

94A.   **{Ephemerides Taboetij. 4o a trente f.49}**   **r 2 m 18 f 20**

98A. **une b.**   **Rogerius de testamentis. fol. a trentehuit la b. f.170**   **r 12 m 18 f 10**

KVK (BSZ) Constantius Rogerius, *In aliquot iuris civilis Pandectarum titulos commentarii eruditissimi: de testamentis* [...], Thibaud Payen, 1552, 8f, 127p, 18f, 410p, 11f, 233p.

99A. **une b.**   **{Missale Romanoru. 4o vieil a cinquante deux f.67}**   **r 11 m 14 f 14**

Thibaud Payen published a number of 4to Missals (e.g. Bau 4. 233 (1546) 4.261 (1555)). These would presumably be unsellable because of the revisions made at the Council of Trent.

100A*.   **{Melchior Super decretales. 8o a octantecinq f.28}**

Bau 6.273 Melchior Kling, *In praecipuos secundi libri Decretalium titulos commentarii*, heirs of Jacopo Giunti, 1557, 20f, 202f, 2f.

38A. **une b.**   **{Alciatus de rubricis Juris Canonici. 8o a cinquante sept f.31}**
$$r \ 3 \ m \ 10 \ f \ 17$$

101B*.   {-idem in pandectas. 8o a dixhuit f.41½}   r 1 m 9 f 22

Bau 6.264 Andrea Alciati, *In secundum tomum Pandectarum iuris civilis* [...] *commentarius,* heirs of Jacopo Giunti, 1550, 595p, 73p.

102A*.   {-idem de rebus creditis. 8o a vingtsept f.25½}   r 1 m 7

HPB (ICCU Rome) Andrea Alciato, *In Dig. librum xii De rebus creditis,* Jacopo Giunti, 1547, 387p, 19p.

103A.   {-idem de rubricis Juris Ciuilis. 8o a quatorze f.33}   r 0 m 18 f 12

Gültlingen, 4.40 (336) *Index locupletissimus in rubricas iuris civilis,* Jacopo Giunti, 1546, 32f (possibly attached to *Lectura super secunda parte Digesti novi in tit. De verborum obligationibus,* Jacopo Giunti, 1546, 646, 48p).

104A*.   {Aristotelis rhetorica hermolaj Barbarj. 8o a quarantecinq f.23}
                                                                                   r 2 m 1 f 10

Bau 4.277 Aristotle, *Rhetorica,* trans. Hermolaus Barbarus, Thibaud Payen, 1558, 359p, 4f.

105A*.   {faber in logicam. 8o a cinquante sept f.34½}   r 3 m 17 f 13

KVK (BSZ) Jacobus Faber Stapulensis (Lefèvre d'Etaples), *Introductiones artificiales in Logicam,* ed. Judocus Clichtove, Jacopo Giunti, 1545, 274p. The correct calculation for this number of copies should be r 5 m 2 f 11½; or if the calculation is correct, there should only be 44 copies in the bale.

106A*.une b.   {de rat. conscrib. Epistolas. 8o a cent quarante f.21}   r 5 m 17 f 15

Bau 4.272 Desiderius Erasmus, *De conscribendis epistolis opus,* Thibaud Payen 1557, 335p; previously published by Sebastianus Gryphius and Thibaud Payen (Bau 4.231, 8.124, 134, 162, 176).

107A*.   {corona florida. 8o a ~~septante~~ huict f.26 [a 48 la b.]   r 2 m 9 f 23

Bau 6.194; 12.434; HPB Antonius Gazius, *Corona florida medicinae,* Jacopo Giunti, 1541, 8f, 198f, 2f. The number in the bale has been corrected.

108C*.   {Epigrammata Verderij 8o a octante deux f.11½}   r 1 m 17 f 18

PBN Claudius Verderius (Du Verdier), *Peripetasis epigrammatum variorum* [...], Paris, Mathurin Prévost, 1581, 182p.

109B*.   {Antidotarius medicinae 16o a cinquante f.13}   r 1 m 6

Bau 4.283 *Antidotarium sive de exacta componendorum miscendorumque medicamentorum ratione,* Thibaud Payen, 1561, 398f, 9f.

53A*. une b.   {Nouella Johan. Andreae s. sexto. do. a vingtsept f.72
                                                                                   r 3 m 17 f 19

56A*.	{Jacobus de Arena do a huit f.170}	r 2 m 14 f 10

110A. **une b.**   {Practica Petri Jacobi 8o a vingt f.33}   r 1 m 6 f 10

Bau 6.184 Petrus Jacobus, *Practica*, Jacopo Giunti, 1539, 16f, 263f, 1f.

111A*.   {De bona curso. 8o a centquarante six f.19   r 5 m 10 f 24

KVK (GBV) Hubertus de Bonacurso, *Preludia et exceptiones*, Jacopo Giunti, 1543, 4f, 144f, 4f.

53A*.   {Nouella Johan. Andreae. 8o. a vingtsept f.29½}   r 1 m 11 f 8

The calculation should be r 1 m 14 f 16½.

112A.   {Laurentius Valla 8o a trente six f.35}   r 2 m 6 f 10

Bau 2.269 Lorenzo Valla, *Elegantiae linguae latinae*, Thibaud Payen, 1554, 552p, 19f. Frequently published by Sebastianus Gryphius (Bau 8.65 etc.). The calculation should be r 2 m 12 f 15.

94A. **une b.**   {Ephemerides Taboetij 4o a cinquante trois f.49}   r 57 m 3 f 22

113C*.   {Consilior. Feudal. tom. secundus fol. a cinquante deux f.98}
                                                                r 10 m 3 f 21

Bau 5.68–9 *Consilia feudalia , ex variorum doctorum scriptis dilgentissime collecta*, Symphorien Beraud and Etienne Michel, 1585, 4p, 303p, 14f, 72p, 5f.

114C*. **quatre b.**   Lexicon theologicum. fol. a trentequatre la b. f.170
                                                                r 46 m 4 f 20

HPB (St John's College, Oxford) Joannes Altenstaig, *Lexicon theologicum*, exc. Joannes Symonetus, 1580, 4f, 670p, 1f.

79B. **cinq b.**   Tractatus cautellarum. fol. a cinquante la b f.134   r 67

13C*. **sept b.**   Soto de iustitia et Jure. fol. a trente la b. f.185   r 77 m 14 f

115C. **sept b.**   Javelli opera fol. a quatorze la b. f.461   r 88 m 13 f 23

Bau 5.57 HPB (ICCU Rome) Chrysostomus Javellus, *Opera*, 3 vols, Symphorien Beraud, 1580; published in the same year by Charles Pesnot (Bau 3.148) and Antoine de Harsy.

116C*. **deux b.**   Bannes. In primam et secundam d. Thomae fol. a vingtsix
                       la b. f.267   r 27 m 15 f 9

Baus 156 Domingo Bañes, *Scholastica commentaria in primam [secundam] partem angelici doctoris d. Thomae*, Etienne Michel, 1588, 14f , 880 col, 12f; (vol 2) 4f, 1070 col, 18f. Vol 2 fits the collation.

116C. **huict b.**   -idem in secundam fol. a cinquante la b. f.145   r 116

117A. **deux b.**   **Decius in Ciuile. In 4o petit papier viels contenant les 2 b. dixhuit rames**   **r 18 /4/**

Bau 2.268 Philippus Decius, *Commentaria in prim. et secund. Dig.*, Jacopo Giunti, 1550, but folio, not 4to. The 'petit papier' may indicate small sheets, and explain the attribution of format.

118i. **une b.**   **Tractatus de pignoribus. fol. Imparfaitz. a vingtsix la b. f.175**   **r 9 m 2**

Bau 5.73–4, *Tractatus de pignoribus et hypothecis, ex diversis u.i. doctoribus decerpti*, Symphorien Beraud and Etienne Michel, 1585, 724p; previously by Filippo Tinghi in 1575 and 1578 (Bau 6.465–6), and by Giovanna Giunti in 1579 (Jesus College, Oxford).

119i. **une b.**   **Calepinus. T. Linguarum. fol. imparfaitz contenant sept rames la b.**   **r 7**

Baus 155 Ambrogio Calepino, *Dictionarium decem linguarum*, Etienne Michel 1586; previously published by Sebastianus Gryphius in 1553 (Bau 8 67), Thibaud Payen in 1565 (Bau 2.286), and Filippo Tinghi in 1578 (Bau 6.474).

119i. **une b.**   **-idem contenant six rames quatre mains**   **r 6 m 4**

119i. **une b.**   **-idem contenant six rames dix mains**   **r 6 m 10**

119i. **une b.**   **-idem contenant six rames six mains**   **r 6 m 6**

119i. **une b.**   **-idem contenant six rames**   **r 6**

120i. **deux b.**   **Corpus Ciuile fol. noir a porta. Imparfaitz du volumen. contenant dix rames la b.**   **r 20**

Corpus iuris civis: multiple editions by Hugues de la Porte and Antoine Vincent between 1538 and 1572 (Bau 7.305ff.).

121i. **douze b.**   **Decisiones Neapolit. De afflictis. vn alphabet. chasque b. contenant vnze rames**   **r 132**

Bau 6.460–1, 482 *Decisiones sacri regii consilii neapolitani ab Matthaeo de Afflictis, Antonio Capycio, Thoma Grammatico collectae*, Filippo Tinghi, 1581, 4f, 863p, 43f; previously published in 1574. 'alphabet' may signify not yet collated into single copies.

121i. **trois b.**   **-idem. fol. per. alphab. contenant les trois b. vingthuit r. treize mains quinze f.**   **r 28 m 13 f 15**

see note above.

89i. **une b.**   **Sermones Granatensis. 8o imparfaitz. a vingtsix la b. rames 12**   **r 12**

122i. **une b.**   **Aristotelis opera. fol. imparfaitz. contenant huit rames**   **r 8**

Bau 4.139; Baus 146, 149 Aristotle, *Opera*, Etienne Michel, 1578, 2 vols 1581; edition shared with Barthélemy Honorat.

123i. **une b.**   **Deffectz Summa Sti Thomae. fol. contenant huit rames**   **r 8**

Bau 4.142; Baus 150 St Thomas Aquinas, *Opera*, 3 vols, Etienne Michel, 1581; an edition shared with Barthélemy Honorat. Previously published by Filippo Tinghi in 1575 and 1577 (Bau 6.464–5, 472–3).

24C. **sept b.**   **Regularum Juris to. tertius fol. Per alphab. a douze rames la b.**
                                                                                r 84

Baus 155 Etienne Michel (see above, 76). This is a new volume in the process of being printed.

124C. **quatre b.**   **-idem 3us tomus. fol. contenant trentequatre rames les quatre b.**
                                                                                r 34

114i. **une b.**   **Lexicon Theologicum. fol. imparfaitz. contenant neuf rames**   **r 9**

125i. **quatre b.**   **Decisiones Canonic. fol. cayers apart. contenant neuf**
                        rames la b.   **r 36**

Bau 6.477 Aegidius Bellamera, Gulielmus Cassiodorus, Capella Tholosana, Joannes Mohedanus, *Sacrosanctae decisiones canonici*, Filippo Tinghi, 1578, 786p. Possibly a new edition in the course of being printed.

125i. **cinq b.**   **-idem contenant quarante sept rames les cinq b.**   **r 47**

23i. **unze b.**   **Parties Decisiones diuersorum. fol. contenant dix rames la b.**
                                                                                r 110

23i. **six b.**   **-idem tertius tomus. fol. Contenant dix rames la b.**   **r 60**

23i. **deux b.**   **-idem tomus primus. fol. Contenant dix rames la b.**   **r 20**

126A. **une b.**   {**Lectura Cornej do. a deux f.318**}   **r 5 m 5 f 11**

A C.2662 Petrus Philippus Corneus, *In primum [secundam] Codicis partem; in secundam Digesti veteri partem*, heirs of Jacopo Giunti (excud. Jacobus Faure), 1553.

{divers liures vieilz. contenant quatre rames}

127A. **une b.**　　**Albericus, Immolensis et Baldus do. contenant quatre rames**
　　　　　　　　　　　　　　　　　　　　　　　　　　　　　　　　　　　　　　r 4

The Giunti presses printed a number of editions of Albericus a Rosate, Baldus de Ubaldis
and Johannes de Imola in the 1540s and 1550s. All three names are cited in the Tinghi royal
privilege of 1578.

128i. **dixhuit b.**　　**Cayers divers de Galeni opera. fol. commencé a imprimer**
　　　　　　　　　　　　contenant six rames la b.　　　　　　　　　　　**r 108**

128i. **cinq b.**　　　**-idem contenant quarante neuf rames les cinq b.**　　　**r 49**

52A. **une b.**　　　　**Socinus in Ciuile. do. contenant six rames**　　　　　　**r 6**

129i. **quatorze b.**　　**Decisiones Boerij. fol. commencé a imprimer. contenant cent**
　　　　　　　　　　　　trentequatre rs. les 14 b.　　　　　　　　　　　　**r 134**

Bau 5.91 Boerius, *Decisiones burdegalenses*, heirs of Symphorien Beraud, 1593, 4f, 867p, 21f.

130i. **unze b.**　　　**Surij tomus tertius. fol. commencé a imprimer. contenant**
　　　　　　　　　　　　douze rames la b.　　　　　　　　　　　　　　　　**r 132**

Possibly Lorenzo Surio, *De vitis Sanctorum* (Venice, 1581, in multiple volumes; an epitome
was published at Lyon by Thomas Soubron in 1594: Bau 4.358); less likely id., *Tomus
tertius conciliorum omnium* (Cologne, 1567).

131i. **une b.**　　　　**Summa syluestrina. 4o Imparfaitz. contenant douze rames**
　　　　　　　　　　　　　　　　　　　　　　　　　　　　　　　　　　　　　　r 12

Bau 5.63 Sylvestro Mazzolini, *Summae Sylvestrinae*, 2 vols. Symphorien Beraud, 1585.
Previously published by other members of the Compagnie des libraires.

132i. **une b.**　　　　**Pintj opera fol. Imparfaitz contenans dix rames**　　　**r 10**

Baus 154; A P.1262–3 Hector Pinto, *Opera omnia latina*, Etienne Michel, 1584;
Barthélemy Honorat, 1584; heirs of Barthélemy Honorat, 1590.

121i, 133C. **une b.**　　**Decisiones Neapolitan. fol. et Stella in Lucam. Imparfaitz de**
　　　　　　　　　　　　dix rames la b.　　　　　　　　　　　　　　　　　**r 10**

Bau 5.58, 65; 6.381; Baus 152 Diego de Estella, *In sacrosanctum Jesu Christi evangelium
secundum Lucam enarrationum libri duo*, Symphorien Beraud, 1580; Etienne Michel,
Giovanna Giunti, 1583.

14i. **une b.**　　　　**Summa de Exemplis. 4o imparfaitz de neuf rames la b**　　**r 9**

123i. **une b.**　　　　**Opuscul. Sti Thomae. 1a secundae. fol. imparfaitz de dix**
　　　　　　　　　　　　rames la b.　　　　　　　　　　　　　　　　　　　**r 10**

123i. **une b**	**Summae Sti Thomae pa secundae. fol. impartfaictz de dix rames la b**	**r 10**
89i. **une b.**	**{Consilia Grammatici. fol. imparfaitz neuf rames}**	**r 9**
85i.	**{Opera Emanuelis Costae. fol. imparfaitz}**	
30i. **une b.**	**Speculum Junctini. fol. Imparfaitz de sept Rames la b.**	**r 7**
83i. **deux b.**	**Tractatus de Attentatis. fol. imparfaitz. contenant unze rames la b.**	**r 22**
83i. **une b.**	**-idem. fol. imparfait. de neuf rames cinq mains la b.**	**r 9 m 5**
134i, 123i. **une b.**	**Feuilles diuerses de Pinellj opera. fol. et Summa Sti Thomae. fol. de douze rames**	**r 12**

HPB (ICCU Rome) Aires Pinhel, *Omnia opera*, Filippo Tinghi, 1576.

134i, 123i **une b.**	**-idem contenant dix rames**	**r 10**
135A. **une b.**	**Fulgosius, Socinus, Riminaldus, Corp. Ciuile et Canon. Noir. fol. vielz. de six rames**	**r 6**
119i. **une b.**	**Parties diuerses de Javelli opera. fol. imparfaitz de unze rames**	**r 11**
81i. **une b.**	**Parties de quaestiones disput. D. Thomae. fol. dix rames**	**r 10**
81i. **une b.**	**-idem imparfaitz contenant neuf rames**	**r 9** /5/
134i. **deux b.**	**Parties diuerses de Pinelli opera. fol. contenant dix rames la b.**	**r 20**
122i. **une b.**	**Deffectz de Aristotelis opera. fol. contenant sept rames la b. r 7**	
117A. **deux b.**	**Decius in Ciuile. 4o petit papier vielz contenant dix rames la b.**	**r 20**

135C. **six b.**	**Bible en fra. fol. a rigletz. Beraud et Michel a douze la b. f.337**	**r 48 m 10**

Bau 5.70 *La saincte bible contenant le vieil et nouveau testament*, 3 vols, Symphorien Beraud

and Etienne Michel, 1585, 8f, 637p, 1f, 504p, 295p, 25f. The collation does not match. 'a rigletz' means ruled.

r	95	m 10	f 14
r	1253	m 6	f 1
r	1280	m 18	f 12½
r	2072	m 0	f 14½
r	356	m 9	f 5
r	5688	m 4	f 22

[These are the totals for pages 5, 4, 3, 2, 1 of the document respectively, which appear at the bottom of the relevant pages. The third figure should read 1281 m 2 f 12½; the fourth figure has been mistranscribed, and should read r 2702 m 0 f 14½.]

Nous soubsignez Jehan Baptiste Renault Rene Postelier Jehan Huguetan et Pierre Cauellat marchants libraires a lyon nommez conuenuz et accordez, sçauoir nousditz Baptiste Renault et Pierre Cauellat de la part de Me Jehan Compere aduocat ez Cours de Lyon tuteur des enfans et heritiers feu Simphorien Beraud viuant marchant libraire audit Lyon et Julien Regrey administrateur des biens et facultez desditz enfans et nousdits Rene Postelier et Jehan Huguetan de la part d'Adrian Perier libraire audit Lyon compagnon associé d'Estienne Michel et son procureur, suyuant le pouuoir à nous donné et la nomination faite par laquelle nous auons estez commis et le serment par nous presté et fait paradeuant Me Pierre Austrein Conseiller du Roy Lieutenant particulier ciuil et criminel en la seneschaussée et siege presidial de ceste ville de Lyon ainsi qu'il appert par les actes et ordonnances de iustice, du septiesme, dixiesme et douziesme du present moys de decembre 1591 pour apprecier et eualuer les liures imprimez contenuz au present inventaire desquels nous auons exactement veuz et visitez ensemblement, et consideré la qualite, defectuosité et imperfection d'iceulx, et des temps et annez de leurs impressions, lesquels nous auons reduitz a la Rame, esualué et apprecié unanimement a la forme et maniere que s'ensuit,

Liures de lyon imprimez depuis l'année 1520 iusques a l'année 1560 contiennent Rames	565 m 6 f 13	prisé la Rame vingt sols	565. 16s 6
Et depuis l'année 1560 iusques a l'année 1579 r.	328 m 2 f 21	prisé la rame quarante cinq sols	739. 8. 9
Et depuis l'année 1579 iusques a l'annee 1589 r.	4049 m 2 f 13	prisé la rame cinquante cinq sols	11135. 1. 10
Et les liures imparfaitz lesquels ne se peuuent parfaire contiennent Rames	745 m 3	prisé la rame dix solz	372. 11. 6
			12812. 8. 7 d

Laquelle somme de douze mille huit cens douze liures huit solz sept deniers a quoy nous auons estimé et eualué lesditz liures reduitz en escus sol dor montant la somme

4270. 16. 2 dor

Et ainsi le certiffions par nos seings manuels cy mis ce iourd'huy vingtseptiesme iour dudit moys de Decembre mil cinq cens quatre vingts et unze.

[signatures of Pierre Cavellat, Jehan Huguetan, Rene Postelier and Jean-Baptiste Renault]
[new hand]

coram me petro delaforest auctoritatibus appostolica et regia notario tabellione publico et ciue lugduni subsignato et testium /6/ subscriptorum comparuerunt suprascripti D. Petrus Cauellat Johannes Huguetan Johannes baptista Regnaud et reneus postellier mercatores librorum D. lugduni qui dixerunt et declarauerunt medio eorum iuramento virtute auctoritate eis attributa debitae apreciauerunt et estimauerunt in eorum conscientiis mercantias librorum supra declaratas prout in cartis et paginis supra descriptis continetur recognouerunt et recognoscunt fecisse eorum manibus propriis subscriptiones et chirografa suprascripta et apposita, De quibus declarationibus et iustifica[ti]o[n]ib[us] suprascripti D. Johannes Compere et Julianus regrei D. n. petierunt instrumentum q[uo]d obtuli et confeci sub hac forma eis valeturum tempore et loco opportunis. Actum et datum lugduni in officina dicti notarii a meridie die octaua mensis januarii millesimo quingentesimo nonagesimo secundo presentibus petro et iohanne forestano clericis dicti lugduni testibus voccatis et rogatis.

[signature of Pierre Delaforest]
[new hand]

Noi sotto scripti faciamo fede coma il soprascritto m°. Piero delaforesta e notaro reale di questa citta di lione et a le sue scriture si da plena et indubitata fede in indicio et fora questo di 10 di genaio 1592 in lione a circonsitione

[signatures of Aless[and]ro Scarlatti and Stefano Bonvisi] [Bau 6.249 records an Alexandre Salotti as the representative of Filippo Tinghi in 1573.]

'To all Booksellers, Country Chapmen, Hawkers and Others': how the population of East Anglia obtained its printed materials

DAVID STOKER

Introduction

This paper surveys the evidence for different forms of bookselling activity in one English region during the early modern period (approximately between 1570 and 1800), including both 'established' tradesmen who operated from shops and members of the itinerant book trades who might visit the regular markets and periodic fairs. In particular, it will seek to highlight the changes that took place during the eighteenth century, following the introduction of provincial newspapers into the region, largely between 1701 and 1717. This seems to have been a catalyst for the growth of different forms of bookselling and associated trades, or has at least resulted in the preservation of more documentary evidence of its activities. Yet, there were also fundamental changes taking place in the economy of the region at the same time.

East Anglia (consisting of the historical counties of Norfolk, Suffolk and Cambridgeshire) represents about 9% of the English mainland, and at the beginning of the eighteenth century was the most densely populated and economically developed region of the British Isles. Norwich, with a population of around 30,000 in 1700, was easily the largest provincial city and manufacturing centre in England, and the nearby port of Great Yarmouth was then ranked sixth.[1] The university town and inland port of Cambridge and the important seaports of Ipswich, and King's Lynn would also have featured among the 20–25 most populous towns in the country.[2] Bury St Edmunds lay not far behind in size and importance as a social and regional centre and an assize town. The region could also boast two important ecclesiastical centres based on the cathedrals of Norwich and Ely, and about 60 market towns. Eighty-five percent of East Anglians travelled less than ten miles to their nearest market, whereas only 50% of Midlanders could do the same. The average figure for all England was 61%.[3]

The region particularly benefited from a long coastline, which defined its eastern and northern boundaries, and its access to the fenland waterways to the west. Three important sea-ports (Great Yarmouth, King's Lynn and Ipswich) dealt with coastal trade to London, north-east England and Scotland, overseas trade to the Low Countries, Scandinavia and the Baltic, and provided access to the network of inland waterways. Daniel Defoe who visited King's Lynn in the 1720s, claimed it had 'the greatest extent of inland navigation of any English port outside London', providing access to navigable waterways supplying 'six counties wholly, and three counties in part'.[4] Heavy goods could therefore be transported by sea or by river to all the major towns in the region.

Book trade activity in the region
There is plenty of evidence of book trade activity in the three county towns of the region well before the period under review. The trades of stationer and bookbinder are recorded in Cambridge from the thirteenth century and in Norwich from the fourteenth century. The first recorded 'booksellers' were in Cambridge by 1502, in Ipswich during the 1530s, and in Norwich in the 1550s.[5] The trades of bookseller and bookbinder were not always clearly distinguishable from one another, but by 1570 bookshops were recognizable as a permanent feature in each of these towns. Bookbinders were poorly rewarded compared to booksellers but required far less capital to start up in business. Sixteenth- and seventeenth-century bookbinders often aspired to become booksellers and those who continued to practise binding alone were usually poor men. For example, Anthony Nicholson of Cambridge, who succeeded his father in 1666 and practised until his death in 1680, left an inventory valued at only £2 12s. 8d.[6] Michael Crotch worked only as a bookbinder in Norwich between 1631 and at least 1664. One of his sons, John, was still trading in the eighteenth century, but the family seems never to have established a prosperous business in the city.[7] A few bookbinders are recorded in market towns of East Anglia from the end of the seventeenth century, although at times only on the basis of a single inscription in a binding — such as John Tompson of Harlestone in 1694.[8]

East Anglia also saw some of the earliest printing in England, with the trade introduced to Cambridge in 1505, Ipswich in 1547, and Norwich 1567.[9] Yet these were only brief interludes, and it was only after 1583 that printing became established in Cambridge when Thomas Thomas was appointed University Printer and set up a press. The work of the Cambridge printers in the century and half before the university managed to establish its own press in 1696 has been recorded in detail elsewhere. Much of this story relates to their struggle with the Stationers' Company to assert the right to print profitable works such as the Bible, in addition to academic works required by the university. They undertook some local jobbing work and produced almanacs during the seventeenth century, but apparently did not print ballads (which would have infringed the rights of the Ballad Stock), newsbooks, or the popular works that were the staple reading matter of most people in the region.[10] In common with most of England, the counties of Norfolk and Suffolk had to wait until the beginning of the eighteenth century, after the lapse of the licensing act, before printing was established.

Printing was re-introduced in Norwich by Francis Burges in September 1701, after nearly 130 years. Two months later he began printing the *Norwich Post*, which is usually acknowledged as the earliest provincial newspaper.[11] Within the next five years there were three presses and as many newspapers operating in the city.[12] Printing spread to Bury St Edmunds around 1711 when William Thompson and Thomas Bailey, two printers from Stamford, set up a press.[13] By 1717 they were publishing a newspaper, the *Suffolk Mercury*. Likewise John Bagnall opened a printing office in Ipswich in 1717, issuing his newspaper the *Ipswich Journal* in 1720. It was not however until the mid-1740s that the printers of Cambridge considered it worthwhile to establish a newspaper.[14]

Thereafter the spread of printing in the region was somewhat slower. Commercial printing reached King's Lynn about 1740, when William Garratt, a bookseller from Boston (Lincolnshire), established a small jobbing press in the town. His activities are known only from the survival of one or two minor publications and playbills.[15] Printing had spread to Wisbech in Cambridgeshire by 1770, and Woodbridge in Suffolk by 1773.[16] Great Yarmouth, owing to its proximity to Norwich, was relatively late to have its first commercial press. In the late 1770s the Norwich printer John March set up a press in King's Street, followed soon afterwards by another Norwich printer, William Payne.[17] By 1780 printing had spread to thirteen towns in the region; twenty years later this number had doubled as commercial printing also spread into the smaller market towns.

Papermaking was introduced to Barnwell near Cambridge in the 1550s, close to the site of Stourbridge fair, but there is no evidence that the paper was ever used by the local printers and the mill was disused by the mid-seventeenth century.[18] It was not until after the 1690s that the trade was re-established at Castle Rising and Taverham in Norfolk, and a decade later in Suffolk at Sudbury and Long Melford.[19] By the end of the eighteenth century there were 24 mills in the region with plenty of evidence of the manufacture of printing and writing papers.

Bookselling in East Anglia[20]

Bookselling businesses in the towns of East Anglia during the seventeenth century varied considerably in terms of their size and prosperity. Because of the business provided by the University, the booksellers of Cambridge tended to operate on a larger scale than their contemporaries elsewhere in the region and there were more of them. Cambridge typically had nine booksellers in business at any time throughout this period,[21] some of whom were able to amass considerable estates valued in many hundreds of pounds. For example William Morden, who traded from 1652 until his death in 1679, left substantial bequests; William Graves, who with his son traded from 1631 to 1686, left goods to the value of £667.[22] Initially the earnings of the Cambridge booksellers were based on retail sales of books from London and overseas, but increasingly towards the end of the century they became involved in the financing and distribution of their own publications, either printed locally or in London. Thus in 1683 John Creed was able to include a list of seventeen titles 'printed for' him on the final page of one of his books.[23]

Norwich was a significantly larger city than Cambridge, but could only support between four and six booksellers at any time during the century, almost all of whom traded as bookbinders as well; several others undertook sidelines such as the sale of patent medicines or agencies for the supply and provision of news. Thus in 1684 William Pinder advertised 'all Sorts of Bibles Common-Prayer Books, Testaments, &c. As cheap as any man in Norfolk can sell, and your Books well bound, and claspt, and Money for old Books'.[24] He avoided the expense of purchasing his freedom in 1670 by performing services for Norwich Corporation (taking a poor boy as an apprentice without any premium and binding books to the value of 20s.).[25] One successful Norwich bookseller, Thomas Gilbert, who traded between about 1569 and his death in 1603, left an estate valued at £166 3s. 4d. including stock and tools of £120. At the other extreme Thomas James, who traded for seven years until his death in 1629, was able only to amass goods to the total value of £18, of which only £8 came from his stock and bookbinding tools. During the later years of the century, booksellers appear to have fared better; thus the inventory of William Oliver, who traded between 1662 and 1689, was valued at £451, including stock worth £235 and good debts of £100.[26]

The main obstacle for any new bookseller wishing to set up in business was the capital needed for the stock. Samuel Selfe, who set up in business in Norwich in 1700, did so with £200 of his own and £200 worth of stock on credit from London booksellers.[27]

As with Cambridge, the more successful Norwich booksellers began to play a part in the publication of small works with a local interest from the second decade of the seventeenth century, and the numbers of such publications grew rapidly, particularly after 1670. During the 1680s, Norwich booksellers such as William Oliver, George Rose, and Edward Giles were able to publish greater numbers of increasingly substantial works.[28] Twenty-eight titles were listed in 'A Catalogue of Books, Printed for and are to be Sold by Edward Giles, Bookseller in Norwich, near the Market Place', in 1692.[29]

Although Ipswich had some of the earliest printers and booksellers in the region, only about seven booksellers are recorded there throughout the whole of the seventeenth century, indicating that there was rarely more than one operating in the town at any time. One notable tradesman, William Weekly, was sufficiently successful, however, to be able to publish a list of five titles in 1655.[30]

Bookselling gradually spread from the county towns to the other urban centres in the region, and was recorded in King's Lynn in 1617, Bury St Edmunds in about 1637, and Great Yarmouth in 1658. In each case, those concerned appear to have been established tradesmen operating from bookshops: men such as Jeremy Bromley, who served an apprenticeship and began his bookselling career in Norwich before moving to Lynn in 1617. He was succeeded by his son Edward about 1635 who went on to serve as the mayor of the borough.[31] Samuel Woomock is known only as the distributor of a volume of local sermons published in Bury St Edmunds in 1651,[32] whereas John Tuthill, who purchased his freedom of Great Yarmouth in 1658, was the undertaker of at least four works by the famous local preacher John Brinsley between 1661 and 1664. He continued in business until the 1680s, and was succeeded by his son who was in business for at least another decade.[33]

The last quarter of the seventeenth century also displays the first evidence of part-time bookselling in some of the market towns — men such as Samuel Burroughs, and Henry Younge, both grocers of Stow-market who died in 1676 and 1680 respectively, or John Whiting of Lavenham who died in 1686. In each case their probate inventories list primers, grammars, and other books for sale.[34] One Bury St Edmunds bookseller, John Marston, is also recorded as having traded in Sudbury in 1685, although he probably operated from a market stall in the town rather than a bookshop.[35]

It was during the eighteenth century that the trade of bookselling really began to develop in East Anglia. The numbers of booksellers recorded by the *British Book Trade Index* indicate a four-fold growth in tradesmen throughout the region. Similarly, the number of towns where booksellers are recorded increased from nine to 44.[36] From the 1720s there is ample evidence of country booksellers, based in one of the many market towns in the region. Their names may be recorded in a number of sources, including newspaper advertisements, imprints, prospectuses, subscription lists, or in later years, directory entries. It should not be assumed, however, that all such names were professional members of the book trade, as sometimes an author would recruit his friends and acquaintances in the countryside to help distribute a work. Francis Blomefield, for example, made use of a combination of established booksellers, itinerant hawkers, and brother clergymen to distribute the printed parts of his history of Norfolk throughout the region.[37]

The imprints of local publications, such as the accounts of notable trials, can be useful for identifying country booksellers. Thus *The trial of John Shilling, for the wilful murder of Mr. John Raven, of Burnham Westgate, carrier,* held at Thetford in 1786, was printed in Bury St Edmunds, but named booksellers in Norwich, Dereham, Swaffham, Lynn, Docking, and Fakenham.[38] Other imprints might include sweeping statements such as 'the booksellers of Norwich, Cambridge, Lynn, Wisbech, Yarmouth, Downham, Ipswich, and the counties of Norfolk and Suffolk in general'.[39]

Country booksellers would almost certainly have been following other trades at the same time. William Gilbert of Halesworth advertised his 'old established' business in the *Ipswich Journal* in 1804 as 'Bookseller, book-binder, stationer, cutler, ironmonger, and brazier', and Richard Leatherdale of Hadleigh, who died aged 70 in 1804, was described as 'a book-seller, stationer, linen and woollen draper'.[40] William Page, of Holt, is listed as 'Bookseller, stationer, hairdresser, and perfumer' in *Bailey's British directory* for 1784 and as 'bookseller, toyman and ironmonger' in John Pendred's *London and Country Printers, Booksellers and Stationers Vade Mecum* of 1785. A brief survey of the secondary trades undertaken by men describing themselves as booksellers in the region also includes the trades of newspaper agent, collector of stamp duties, hardware seller, grocer, draper, schoolteacher, and from the 1780s, that of printer. Towards the end of the eighteenth century a few country booksellers also ran circulating libraries. Thus a trade card in the John Johnson Collection refers to J. Erratt, of Holt, 'Bookseller, stationer, printer, bookbinder, proprietor of Erratt's Circulating Library, hardware and glassman'.

Local booksellers might also become involved in the distribution of goods. Thus when John Fenn was arranging with his London publisher to correct the proofs of his first volume of 'Paston Letters' in 1786, he requested that they be included in the weekly parcels sent to his local bookseller, William Barker of Dereham, by his London correspondents, Messrs Sawbridge and Law.[41] Barker is an interesting example of a new generation of country bookseller in the final decades of the eighteenth century. He served an apprenticeship with Martin Booth, bookseller of Norwich, and his name is first found as an independent trader in the imprint of one of Booth's catalogues in July 1777.[42] He opened a new shop in the market place of East Dereham in January 1778 and became local agent for the *Norwich Mercury*.[43] Around 1790, he acquired a press and also became a jobbing printer.[44] The business was continued by his son until at least 1817.

Part-time bookselling might be conducted in a market town by a tradesman based in a larger town in the vicinity. David Samuel, bookseller, stationer, and bookbinder in the High Street of King's Lynn during the 1730s, maintained a market stall and lockup in the town of Swaffham which traded on Saturdays, the local market day. Another King's Lynn bookseller, William Whittingham, did the same in Fakenham and Downham Market during the 1780s. David Samuel's business is of interest because there was an unusually detailed inventory taken at the time of his death in 1739, listing almost every item he had in stock.[45] The inventory corresponds with the arrangement of stock in his shops, and the second part lists the materials held at Swaffham (about 600 recently published titles, in formats of octavo or smaller). He also maintained a basic stock of stationery items, shop books, paper, quill pens, spectacles and so on in Swaffham, together with various unspecified bundles of pamphlets, primers, engravings, as well as a reference to '14 dozen Chapman', presumably referring to chapbooks.

The itinerant book traders

The various distribution mechanisms for printed matter during the seventeenth century were listed in Roger L'Estrange's *Considerations and proposals in order to the regulation of the press*, in 1667. Established tradesmen included, 'the Printers themselves, stitchers, binders, and stationers', but he also included a host of itinerant traders and those involved in the transport and distributive trades, such as 'hawkers, mercury-women, pedlars, ballad-singers, posts, carriers, hackney-coachmen, and mariners'.[46] Since there is no concrete evidence that bookshops existed outside the six largest towns in the region at this time, one must assume that readers in the villages and market towns were often reliant on itinerant traders, who travelled across the country between fairs and markets.

Ballad singers would travel from town to town performing their songs and selling printed copies. Their subject matter included murders, executions, monstrous births, disasters, battles, miraculous occurrences, and unrequited love. Many early titles with regional connections are now known only from entries recorded in the Stationers' Company registers, such as 'A dolefull discourse of a lamentable spoile done by ffyer in the town of East Dereham' in 1581, or 'God's mercy showed to the poor at Orford and Aldborough in Suffolk shewinge the soden growth of peaze upon a sea rock' (in 1596), although these probably represent only a small proportion of those actually produced. There are also a few survivals, such as two accounts of a fire at Beccles in Suffolk in 1586, each of which was printed in London but with a Norwich bookseller Nicholas Colman named in the imprint.[47] There are very few surviving black-letter ballads printed in East Anglia itself.[48]

There was doubtless a healthy trade in the sale of ballads from the mid-sixteenth until the end of the seventeenth century. Robert Scott of Norwich (who is otherwise known as a grocer, but also appears to have been supplying members of the itinerant book trade) sold several thousands of 'Odas vocatur Ballades' between July 1568 and November 1570, in addition to many hundreds of other small books including almanacs, primers, horn books, plays and jest books.[49] Tessa Watt published some of the entries relating to ballad sellers from the Norwich Court books prior to 1640.[50] There is likewise plenty of evidence from the end of the seventeenth century. Thus in 1681 John Taylor of Eye in Suffolk, and his wife, 'produced a licence from the Master of the Revells to sing and sell Ballads'.[51] In 1690 Robert Woollans and Henry Martyn were allowed to 'sing read and sell ballads for the space of a week behaving themselves civilly', and Richard Welly and his wife were allowed to sing ballads and sell pamphlets for fourteen days 'at the pump in the market and not elsewhere'.[52]

Strictly, a pedlar sold small goods, including printed pamphlets, on foot, whereas a hawker sold them from horseback or from a horse and cart. The difference is sometimes noted in the records. Thus, in 1679 Laurence White was allowed to 'Read and Sell pamphlets on horse-backe until next Wednesday next' in Norwich.[53] However, the two terms were also used interchangeably.

With the arrival of printing throughout the region in the eighteenth century, there begins to be evidence of the publication of other forms of sensational news publications, intended for sale by both the established and itinerant trades. The staple diet of these was similar to that of the ballads: disasters — such as a fire at a puppet show at Burwell in Cambridgeshire; freaks — such as 'the merry facetious dwarf of Botesdale'; monstrous births — an account of the famous rabbit woman of Godalming was printed in Ipswich; and there were periodic accounts of bloody crimes — such as that of the murderer Robert Boon of Great Yarmouth.[54]

The one context in which there are many contemporary references to pedlars selling publications was at the scene of public executions, which always drew large crowds from miles around. On several occasions the reports of these provided an opportunity to air disputes between rival printers. One dispute between the Norwich printers Henry Crossgrove and William Chase, relating to the accuracy of the latter's broadside sold at the execution of William Morris in September 1734, has been described elsewhere.[55] The following August the dispute flared up once again, when Crossgrove declared:

It is generally expected that Ward and Mann, the Two Maleafactors condemned here the last Assizes, will be Executed this Day ... They are Two wicked and ignorant poor Wretches, whose ages together can't make 43; they own the Facts they are to suffer for, and they have been very idle wicked Lads; and if any Papers should be published to catch the Penny, under Title of their Dying-Speeches and Confessions, (as was done last Year by Richard [sic] Morris, tho' he solemnly declared with his last Breath at the Gallows that he had made None) I do assure the

Publick they will not be of my Printing, and that I will never be any ways concerned in such Grub-Street Undertakings.[56]

On the same day Chase advertised just such a publication in his own newspaper, guaranteeing its veracity, on which Crossgrove inevitably poured scorn the following week.[57] Such exchanges were not uncommon during the middle years of the century and show the local printers exploiting any means of reaching a popular market and employing a network of itinerant tradesmen to sell their wares.[58]

The trade of 'chapman' is frequently noted in the records as a collective term for pedlars, hawkers and other itinerant merchants. The *Oxford English Dictionary* defines 'chapman' as 'A man whose business is buying and selling; a merchant, trader, dealer' as well as a pedlar, and their wares were by no means limited to printed materials.[59] Very little is known about the everyday operation of these traders. There is conflicting evidence as to the numbers of itinerant tradesmen operating in East Anglia at the end of the seventeenth century. Several chapmen are recorded in the *British Book Trade Index*, but it is not certain that they were associated with the sale of reading matter. Margaret Spufford analysed the numbers of pedlars' licences issued in 1697 in her study of seventeenth-century popular fiction and found to her surprise that relatively few licences were issued in East Anglia compared with other areas of England.[60] This observation is supported by the lack of survivals of such works printed in the region, or with the names of East Anglian distributors, before the turn of the eighteenth century. There are a few references to itinerant book tradesmen other than ballad sellers in the records of the Norwich Mayor's Court, but these tend to relate to the suppression of vagrancy rather than the regulation of trade. Thus 'John Tonge, a seller of Almanacs taken vagrant in this city is ordered forthwith to depart and not to return to make the like sale within this city at any time hereafter' in January 1634.[61]

Chapbooks are notoriously difficult to define in a sufficiently inclusive manner, but were usually small books (both in terms of their printed format and the fact that they would be printed on one or at most two sheets) which were sold unbound by chapmen and other itinerant traders. The production of these small books was initially centred in London, but with the spread of printing moved into the English provinces. Victor Neuberg noted their production in Newcastle, York, Birmingham, Northampton, Sheffield, Worcester, Tewkesbury, Leicester, Banbury, Nottingham, Carlisle, Coventry, Manchester, Durham, Whitehaven, and

Bath, and Stockton — but not one town in East Anglia.[62] There are surprisingly few surviving references to the sale of these books in the region after about 1720.[63]

That the itinerant bookselling trade did exist in East Anglia at the beginning of the century may be inferred from some of the earliest local newspaper advertisements in the region. Thus, within two weeks of setting up his shop in Norwich in 1706, the printer Henry Crossgrove was advertising:

To all Booksellers, Country Chapmen, Hawkers, and others, this is to give notice that they may at the Printing Office in Magdalen Street, in a short time be furnisht with all manner of little Novels, Histories, Poems, Romances, Story-books, Riddle-Books, Song-Books, Jest books, Broadsides, and Ballads, they shall all be printed on good Paper and a very fair Character, and sold very Reasonably, especially to those who shall buy to sell again.[64]

Likewise Crossgrove's rival Elizabeth Burges advertised

… to all booksellers, country chapmen & others that at the Printing-house near the Red-Well, Norwich they may be furnish'd with all sort of history-Books, Song-Books, Broad-sides &c.[65]

John Bagnall, the first printer in Ipswich, advertised to 'booksellers, chapmen, hawkers, peddlers or others' in the *Ipswich Journal* in January 1721,[66] although thereafter such advertisements became increasingly rare; further evidence for the sale of this type of literature in East Anglia after this date, other than the brief reference in David Samuel's inventory, is sparse. This is surprising since the middle years of the eighteenth century were the heyday of the chapbook, as the format began to replace the traditional black-letter ballad as the principal vehicle for the dissemination of popular literature.

Evidence of the involvement of traders such as carriers and mariners in the distribution of printed publications in East Anglia comes from court records and relates to exceptional circumstances, such as the suppression of 'seditious publications' in the 1630s. One example occurred when a cargo of publications was found on the ship 'Jewel' in Yarmouth harbour, having been imported from Rotterdam.[67] Investigations into the distributors of William Prynne's controversial publication *Newes from Ipswich* during 1637 identified a number of named individuals including one puritan minister,[68] but whether the remainder were part of the regular book trade is open to doubt.

The postboy was an important element in the distribution network to the market towns and villages, and on one occasion Henry Crossgrove sought to recruit letter carriers to carry his newspaper.[69] The role of the postal service in the distribution of news and other current publications was shown by the complaints made by three Norwich tradesmen (at least two of whom were established booksellers) in March 1656 concerning the increased costs of receiving small packets of news and the decline in reliability of the service.[70]

Following the Restoration, Roger L'Estrange was awarded a monopoly on the publication of printed news, which had the effect of encouraging the growth of manuscript newsletters, distributed by the postal service. What little evidence there is of the existence and popularity of newsletters comes from the larger towns. Sir Thomas Browne of Norwich makes frequent reference to newsletters in his correspondence, on one occasion referring to them as the 'coffie and common newes letters' as they circulated in coffee houses.[71] The Norwich bookseller William Nowell was involved in supplying local news to the compilers in London and in providing copies of their letters for the local authority.[72] On more than one occasion the Norwich town clerk attempted to censor their contents.[73]

The one area where there is a good range of evidence concerning the workings of an itinerant trade is newspaper distribution in the eighteenth century. Those concerned are usually referred to as hawkers, and no doubt covered considerable distances each week. These traders may have distributed other products prior to the arrival of the newspapers, and the proprietors probably made use of existing networks. In addition to delivering the newspapers, they would also act as agents for the proprietor to collect advertisements, or sell other products published by them. Thus John Crouse and William Stevenson advertised their *Norfolk and Norwich Memorandum Book* as available both from their Medicinal Warehouse in Norwich market place and also from the hawkers who delivered the *Norfolk Chronicle*.[74] Similarly, the imprint of the rival *Chase's memorandum book* for 1781 indicates that it was sold by eighteen named booksellers in nine East Anglian towns, as well as 'the Distributors of the Norwich Mercury'.[75]

Newspaper hawkers presumably operated on commission as well as employees and sometimes acted as informal letter carriers and miscellaneous delivery men in their own right. There is an interesting series of letters between two sisters, Barbara Kerrich and Elizabeth Postlethwaite, who through marriage found themselves living at opposite ends of Norfolk. They were able to maintain a regular correspondence between 1733 and 1751 as both their husbands subscribed to William Chase's *Norwich Mercury*. They each paid the hawkers a small bonus to hand over their letters to a colleague covering their sister's round. The imminent arrival of Mr Chase's newsman is therefore given as an excuse for closing several of the letters. When at one point the proprietor found out about this informal delivery network, the hawker concerned made it abundantly clear that this was one of his perquisites and 'that he might carry his papers himself if he discouraged people from sending letters by him'.[76]

There were occasional difficulties between newspaper proprietors and their hawkers. Michael Harris briefly referred to a dispute between the Norwich newspaper printer Henry Crossgrove and a lame newspaper hawker in 1718.[77] Likewise in April 1749, Crossgrove's successor Robert Davey found that his hawkers were helping themselves to the half-sheet of songs given as a free gift with this paper, and warned his readers to ensure they received a copy.[78]

East Anglian markets and fairs

The commercial activities of both itinerant and established book traders usually centred on the many markets and fairs in the region, as these provided a place for open yet regulated retail trade, rather than private bargaining. A market may be defined as a central place for the regular sale of goods and services from the surrounding area. Markets are primarily outlets for local produce, by contrast with fairs which frequently attracted tradesmen from a much wider area. There was a wide range of different-sized markets, some specializing in products such as fish, oysters, meat, butter, hay, horses, leather, or fabrics, depending upon their situation and the size of the local population.

During the seventeenth century there were about 75 markets taking place each week in the three East Anglian counties. Every major town in the region had its market place or places, and markets were also held in many smaller 'market towns', the presence of which distinguished them from surrounding villages. Most markets were held weekly, but in the larger towns they might be held semi-weekly or more often. Ipswich had five markets each week for different produce. Bury St Edmunds had four markets held at different locations for the sale of horses, butter, fish and cattle as well as the Great Market for other produce.[79]

By far the largest market in the region, and indeed in provincial England, during the seventeenth century was that held twice weekly at Norwich. This dated from Saxon times, although the present site, described in the 1740s by Francis Blomefield as 'the grandest market-place' and 'the best single market in all England', was established by the Normans.[80] It was organized according to the produce on sale, but there are no records of any members of the book trade selling from the stalls.[81] An illustration, taken from a watercolour by John Cotman in the first decade of the nineteenth century, shows the market largely as it was throughout the previous two centuries except for the absence of an elaborate market cross which was demolished in the 1730s.[82] This structure seems to have been a place where ballad singers and other itinerant trades were permitted to sell their wares. One bookshop is visible in Cotman's illustration, that of William Booth, on the upper walk adjacent to the market place, in a row of shops that appears to have been continually occupied by at least one bookseller's business from the beginning of the seventeenth century or earlier.

A fair is an occasional gathering of buyers and sellers, in a place and at a time ordained by charter or statute or by ancient custom. Although primarily commercial in origin, fairs would often include shows and other social entertainments. In addition to local tradesmen, they would frequently attract traders from across the country, as foreigners would be permitted at the fair whereas there might be restrictions on trading at the market. They might last a day or two, or two weeks or more. The exact number of fairs taking place at any one time in East Anglia is difficult to determine as country fairs might come and go and different sources give significantly different numbers. According to *Jarrolds almanac* for 1822 there were 204 fairs per year in 148 towns and villages in Norfolk and Suffolk alone. Many towns and even some villages might have two or three fairs each year. Potential traders could be informed of their timing by trade directories such as *The chapmans and travellers almanack*, which claimed to contain a list of all the fairs in England, Scotland and Ireland.[83]

Among the more important fairs in the region were those held at Ely, St Faith's (near Norwich), Great Yarmouth (a herring fair), and King's Lynn. For most of these there is little evidence of book trade activity, although the records of the Beccles fair contain a reference to a chapman and bookseller renting a stall.[84] In addition to these, there were two fairs of national, if not international, importance which were held in the region each year, those at Stourbridge near Cambridge and at Bury St Edmunds.

Bury Fair was renowned for the sale of luxury items, a contemporary description noting 'Several rows of haberdashers, milliners, mercers, jewellers, silversmiths and toy shops'.[85] The entry in *Magna Britannia* (1721) described it as 'famous all over England, not so much for merchandises as for the company'.[86] It even had a well-known country dance named after it.[87] John Macky visited Bury Fair in the early years of the eighteenth century:

The Fair lasts a Fortnight, and all the neighbouring Nobility and Gentry come there every afternoon, where they divert themselves in Raffling till it is time to go to the Comedy, which is acted here every Night; and afterwards go to the Assemblies, which are always in some Gentleman's House or other, during the Fair. I must own I never saw a fairer Assembly of Beauties in any Part of the World than at this Fair; which seldom concludes without some considerable Matches or intreagues: And indeed it is more a Market for Ladies than Merchandizes.[83]

The preoccupation with match-making and sexual liaisons also features in a contemporary poem

> Where Suffolk claims the circumjacent Fields,
> And pleasing sites and beauteous Prospects yield;
> There stands a Town, Bury St Edmond's nam'd,
> Much for its Men, more for its Women fam'd;
> This place for such Increase is so renown'd,
> That for five Beaus, ten lovely Belles are found;
> Th' unequal lot down thro' the Vulgar runs,
> And thrice ten Dorothys for twenty Johns.[89]

The atmosphere of the fair at the end of the seventeenth century, with many different tradesmen crying out their wares, and the disreputable behaviour of some of its visitors is described in Thomas Shadwell's play *Bury-Fair* in 1689. However, the only reference in the text to printed matter is when two Jack Puddings or Jesters hand out papers advertising:

A most delicious dainty monster, the most delightful monster, the prettiest monster ever was seen! The most admirable! The most incomparable monster!

Despite its reputation and the patronage of the nobility, Bury Fair could not rival Stourbridge or Stirbitch Fair, which Defoe considered to be the greatest in the world. This was a medieval fair, held in a field adjacent to the river Stour, a tributary of the river Cam on the edge of Cambridge. By the fifteenth century it was of national rather than regional significance owing to its strategic position in the network of inland waterways, attracting both the wholesale and retail trades. Barges transported goods to and from the fair ground via King's Lynn to other parts of the country. By the end of the seventeenth century the fair was at its height as a commercial event, and it is believed to have been the model for Bunyan's 'Vanity Fair' in *The Pilgrim's Progress*. Contemporary descriptions talk of vast quantities of crops, wool, textiles, and animals traded. In addition there were large numbers of luxury trades including milliners, cabinet makers, perfumers, and toymen.[90] Stourbridge was also an important social as well as economic event, although in Macky's opinion, it did not compare with Bury 'for Beauties, or the fineness of Company; although it much surpassed it in Cattle and Other Merchandizes'.[91] The satirist Ned Ward, writing in his *A Step to Stir-Bitch-Fair* in 1700 gives a detailed account of the fair at this time:

Stir-Bitch-Fair, where Vice, Merchandise, and Diversion, draw the Cambridge-Youth, London-Traders, Lyn-Whores, and abundance of Ubiquitarian-Strolers, into a promiscuous Assembly, all contributing something to either the Pleasure or Profit of one another; some coming to spend Money, others to get it:

... such a Number of Wooden Edifices, and such a Multitude of Gentry, Scholars, Tradesmen, Whores, Hawkers, Pedlars, and Pick-pockets, that it seem'd to me like an Abstract of all sorts of Mankind, drawn into a lesser Body, to show the World in Epitomy.[92]

Stourbridge Fair was also known for the sale of books, although it could not compare with the great European book fairs at Frankfurt and Leipzig. Booksellers from both London and Cambridge are known to have traded at Stourbridge from the mid-sixteenth century and probably before. At the end of the seventeenth century John Dunton spoke of the London bookseller William Shrewsbury as a regular attender and the only bookseller that 'understands FAIR-KEEPING to any advantage'.[93] Ned Ward wrote of

... a Place call'd originally Cooks-Row, but now more properly Cuckolds-Row, from the great Number of Booksellers that are now crept into Possession of their Greasinesses Division; this Learned part of the Fair is the Schollars chief Rendezvouz, where some that have Money come to buy Books, whilst others who want it, take 'em slily up, upon Condition to pay if they're catch'd, and think it a Pious piece of Generosity, to give St. Austin or St. Gregory Protection in a Gown Sleeve till they can better provide for 'em.[94]

A plan of the fair ground, drawn about twenty years later, shows that the booksellers still had a specific area to themselves close to the main road, then known as 'Booksellers Row'.[95]

The growth of established book trading and its spread into the countryside appears to have been matched by the beginnings of a decline in the two great East Anglian fairs and their transformation into largely social and leisure events. These changes were chronicled by Charles Caraccioli in his *An historical account of Sturbridge, Bury, and the most famous fairs in Europe and America*, published in the early 1770s, at a time when their extent had become apparent, but there were still a few who might remember them in their heyday. Bury Fair, had then been decreasing in size for 40 years, and had 'become rather a Place of Amusement than a temporary Mart, as most of the Merchandises now brought thither are chiefly Articles of Luxury and Curiosity'.[96] His account stressed the signicance of the assemblies, concerts, theatre performances and book auctions, which had existed in the seventeenth century, but which were now the centre of attraction.

Caraccioli also noted that Stourbridge Fair had been declining for twenty years and had been abandoned by booksellers. He offered a series of economic reasons for its decline.

A heavy Load of Taxes entailed upon People ever since the last War, the extortionate Price of Provisions, the easy Communication with all commercial Cities and Manufacturing Towns, the great Increase of Land Carriages, the Navigable Canals lately cut, and the Number of Riders from the Capital and other trading Places, who take Orders for all Kinds of Merchandise all over the Kingdom, have ruined all the Fairs.[97]

Yet in spite of his pessimism for the future of the Fair, it would continue to thrive as a social occasion for a further century and a half.[98]

In the Burney Collection there are several volumes of printed playbills from East Anglian theatres dating from the 1780s, which provide evidence of the significance of both fairs as social events.[99] On 30 September [1782?] an unnamed company performed at the Stourbridge Theatre 'A tragedy called the Fair Penitent'. At the end of the play there was a comic dance entitled 'The Drunken Swiss' and a new pantomime entertainment

'Harlequin's Trip to Stirbitch-Fair'; after the pantomime the audience were shown 'A Perspective View of Stirbitch fair'. A fortnight later (17 October) 'His Majesty's Servants from the Theatre Royal Norwich' performed 'A tragedy called the Roman Father' at Bury St Edmunds. At the end of the second act there was another 'Comic Dance called The Drunken Swiss' and a new pantomime, 'Harlequin's Trip to Bury-Fair' followed by 'A Perspective View of Bury-fair'.

East Anglian book auctions

The first recorded book auction in the region was held at an inn at Trumpington near Cambridge in May 1686, organized by the London bookseller Enoch Wyer.[100] Later in the same year, that 'most famous Auctioneer of all Great as well as Little Britain', Edward Millington, held the first of a regular series of auctions at Bury and Stourbridge Fairs which were to continue into the eighteenth century.[101] Soon afterwards he began to organize auctions in some of the larger towns of the region, either at local bookshops, as in Norwich in 1689 and 1693, or else in coffee houses, as in Lynn in 1694.[102]

Ned Ward gave an amusing account of Millington in action at Stourbridge Fair, who 'sells Books by the Hammer, and gives the Scholars as merry an Entertainment, as a Mountebank and his Andrew'.

Here's an Old Author for you, Gentlemen, you may Judge his Antiquity by the Fashion of his Leather-Jacket; herein is contain'd, for the Benefit of you Scholars, the Knowledge of every thing; written by that famous Author, who thro' his Profound Wisdom, very luckily discover'd that he knew nothing? For your Encouragement, Gentlemen, I'll put him up at two Shillings, advance 3 Pence; Two Shillings once: What no Body bid? The Bidder advances 3d. Two and 3d. once: Gentlemen, Fye for shame, why sure Men of your Parts and Learning, will never suffer the Works of so famous an Author to be thus undervallued: If you'll believe me, Gentlemen, he's worth more to a Powder-Monkey to make Cartridges of, than what's bid: Two and three pence twice? What no Body amongst you Gentlemen of the Black Robe, that has so much respect for the Wisdom of our Ancestors, as to advance t'other 3d? Well Sir, I find you must have him at two and three pence, Knock, and now you've bought him: Sir I must tell you, you'll find Learning enough within him, to puzzle both Universities: And thus much I promise you further Sir, when you have read him seven years, if you don't like him, bring him to me again, in Little Brittain, and I'll help you to a Man shall give you a Shilling for him, to cover Band-Boxes. At this sort of rate he banters the young Students; and whatever they purchas'd, gave 'em a Jest into the Bargain.[103]

The annual book auctions at Stourbridge might last for a week or more whereas those at Bury Fair were not so large but seem to have featured sales of luxury goods as well, in keeping with the different nature of the event. One book auction in Bury in 1689 also included the sale of roses, perfumes, together with 'Hungary water, chocolata, best Spanish snuff, essences, and all sorts of powder for the hair'.[104]

The death of Millington in 1703 encouraged provincial booksellers to embark upon this form of trading. In November 1704 Thomas Goddard, a young bookseller in Norwich, issued the first of a series of catalogues.[105] He modelled himself on Millington, whom he had seen in action in the city during the 1690s, with lofty addresses 'To the Most Curious of the Inhabitants of the City of Norwich'.

Gentlemen, &c. I Here present you with a Catalogue of Books which I intend to dispose of by Auction, which should I commend, you'd say 'tis Interest, so I shall submit it to your determination, leaving the Catalogue to speak for itself. Only this must be Allowed, that he who most Undervalues them, does least Understand them.[106]

By 1708 Goddard's auctions had become sufficiently renowned in the city to be the subject of a satirical poem by one of his rivals:

Upon my Word, (which I ne'er falsifie
But when there's Need, or I have a mind to lie)
With best of Books I here stand now invested,
And all in Order readily digested:
Here's for the Learned deep Philosophy,
And for the Pious sound Divinity:
Here's Bunyan's Progress of the last Edition,
And Daniel Burges of the Jews Condition;

Here's Baxter's Thrust at us poor heavy Sinners,
His Now or Never if we would be Winners:
Come who bids up, I'll set it at a Shilling,
Tho' to give two I know ye all are willing;
Come bid apace, and ne'er suspect a Cheat;
The Books brand new, I'll swear 'tis dainty Meat.
Nor are they all, for I have Numbers more,
Such worthy Books I never sold before.

Now for the Scholar, here's most noble Feasting,
(Believe me, Sirs, this is not merely Jesting)
Here's Metaphysics, Physick, and Geometry,

Opticks, nay Ethicks, with Astronomy.
Here's Homer, Virgil, and that Rhiming Crew;
Ovid's Epistles, Ladies, really new.
Come ne'er suspect the Book that I commend,
Your Interest only is what I intend.

Nor are all these with which I can supply
Your various Fancies: Here comes History;
Here's Rauleigh's Deeds, the Life of Captain Drake,
Whose Acts to read will make your Hearts to quake:
Next here's St. George, our famous English Champion;
That worthy Sir Bevis of Southhampton:
Here's fam'd Parismus, Parismenides;
Noted Tom Thumb, and valiant Hercules;

Billy of Bilricay the Vealshire Knight,
With fam'd Don Quixot, who did Windmills fight,
And Sancho Pancha his most trusty Squire:
Nay Granny Shipton, with her Nose all Fire.
Here's nimble Jack, who oft made Giants rore:
Here's Crispin's Life: The Death of poor James Shore.
Here's Warwick's Guy, who did strange Monsters fight,
And last of all, here's the brave Red Rose Knight.[107]

Within a decade he was also auctioning other products in addition to his
regular book auctions.[108]

Booksellers from outside the region clearly saw East Anglia as an
important potential market for travelling book auctions. Francis Hubbert
(also known as Hubbard) from London organized two auctions at King's
Lynn in 1713 and 1717 respectively[109] and an unnamed bookseller advertised an auction of books at the Kings-Head Inn in Beccles, in 1710.[110] In
1720 Henry Wilson from Boston in Lincolnshire brought a collection of
'choice books in most faculties', one third of them new books, to auction
at the Town-Chamber on the Quay in Great Yarmouth.[111] However, the
prime location for book auctions was the city of Norwich, particularly
during one of the assize weeks when it was full of the gentry from the
surrounding area.

For seventeen years Thomas Goddard had a monopoly of book
auctions in Norwich, but during the summer assizes in 1721 he faced
competition from his own former apprentice William Chase.[112] The following November Henry Wilson, an auctioneer from London, brought a

collection of books to be sold at 'Mr Holland's the Hatter in the Close in Norwich'.[113] Goddard, who was now threatened with the loss of another of his most profitable enterprises, attacked the interloper in the local press and organized his own rival auction at his 'Paper Warehouse' in the basement of the Guildhall in Norwich market place.[114] For the next three years Goddard and Chase were left alone to enjoy their duopoly. A further attempt at opening up Norwich auctions to new traders took place when the London bookseller Edmund Curll joined forces with the Norwich bookseller James Carlos to hold a sale during the November assizes of 1724.[115] Goddard and Chase therefore agreed to combine their resources and in future hold joint auctions which would overshadow any competition.[116]

By 1726 they were promising their customers

above all, to divert and entertain our Friends, it will be in Part an Auction, and in Part an Oratory; the latter Part if we can't perform to the Satisfaction of our Customers, we'll endeavour to procure one that can: The whole Performance shall be (as Mr. Browne has intitled his Works) both serious and comical, and we shall for every Night have a different Subject.[117]

The subject of the oratory on 19 November was 'the Antediluvian World; the Flood, and the Alterations this Terraqueos Globe suffer'd thereby', and the following week was 'the noble Appendage of the Earth, the Atmosphere, with something about Meteors'.[118]

A final attempt at dislodging Chase and Goddard came in April 1730 when the London bookseller John Oswald and the auctioneer John Dansken rented one of the upper rooms in the Norwich Guildhall for a fortnight during assize week to hold a massive book auction. As soon as they knew of these plans, the two Norwich tradesmen inserted an advertisement in Chase's newspaper:

Whereas we have received information of a foreigner designing to sell books by auction in this City. This is to acquaint our fellow citizens & friends, (who we hope will discourage all Foreign interlopers) That we will, at the same time he begins, open our Auction & Oratory at the Guildhall Warehouse in the Market, with a ... good collection of valuable books: of which, from time to time notice shall be given in this paper. T. Goddard   W. Chase.[119]

Thus in April 1730 there were rival book auctions taking place on different floors of the Norwich Guildhall. Goddard and Chase's plan seems to have succeeded, for the following week Oswald and Dansken were advertising that 'if better incouragement be not given the sale will end on Tuesday night' and a week later the sale was advertised as having moved to Bungay.[120] Both William Chase and Thomas Goddard were to die wealthy men, in 1742 and 1750 respectively, largely as a result of the wide range of their bookselling activities.[121]

By the 1740s book auctions were no longer merely a feature of fairs and assize weeks and were appearing throughout the region, particularly following the death of local book collectors.[122] The Cambridge bookseller William Thurlbourn organized a series of auctions in the town between 1742 and 1760, beginning with a sale of duplicates from the Royal Library at Cambridge. After 1748 his auctions were held in association with another Cambridge bookseller, Thomas Merrill.[123]

A decade later book auctions were being held in the larger towns and some market towns. John Shave of Ipswich held an auction at Sudbury in 1760; Henry Keymer held another at Dereham in 1762, and William Eaton yet another at Yarmouth in 1763.[124] Meanwhile Joseph Finley of Bury was advertising a collection of books for sale at the fair in 1755.[125] However, the emerging auction houses in London were always on the look-out for the real treasures. Thus following the death of the antiquary Thomas Martin of Palgrave, Suffolk, in 1771, his pictures and coins were auctioned locally, and his huge collection of printed books was purchased by the Norwich booksellers Martin Booth and John Berry, who disposed of them in a catalogue sale. Yet his priceless collection of manuscripts was taken up to London where it was auctioned in two sales by Baker and Leigh.[126]

During the 1760s and 1770s the range of commodities appearing at East Anglian auctions had grown enormously to include household effects, pictures, land, houses, ships, horses, wine and the stock of bankrupts. Catalogues might be available from a host of inns and tradesmen throughout the region.[127] Some established booksellers even abandoned their original trade to specialize as full-time auctioneers, such as Jonathan Gleed of Norwich. But it could be risky to be over-reliant upon a new trade such as auctioneering, and Gleed went bankrupt in 1766.[128] The trade of auctioneer was then beginning to emerge independently of bookselling. Some auctioneers such as William Seaman, who sold a number of ships in Yarmouth c.1783–5, clearly had no connection with the book trade.[129]

Some East Anglian booksellers preferred to buy up the libraries of book collectors and then sell them by means of priced catalogues. William

Thurlbourn of Cambridge published two such catalogues in 1728,[130] and the Norwich booksellers followed suit soon afterwards. By the mid 1730s and for the remainder of the century, catalogue sales were more popular than book auctions as a way of selling secondhand books, and their frequency and scale increased markedly during the 1760s.[131] The Norwich bookseller Martin Booth's catalogue of 1777 contained more than 7,500 titles, as well as coins and medals, and that advertised by the bookseller Christopher Berry in 1794 claimed to include 30,000 volumes.[132]

Conclusion

By the 1780s printed matter in many different formats was far more widely available throughout East Anglia than at the beginning of the century. The established book trades in particular appear to have been thriving and adapting to new economic opportunities as they arose. Bookselling had also spread into the market towns of the region, albeit on a part-time basis in association with other trades. The itinerant trades were still important, but relatively less than they had been a century before. The great fairs had also declined as trading events and had been transformed into social gatherings. The book trades in the three counties would continue to expand and prosper until the end of the century and the impact of the Napoleonic wars.

Two of the catalysts for these changes appear to have been the introduction of printing to the region (outside Cambridge), which took place during the first two decades of the century, and the growth of provincial newspapers. Newspaper publishing appears to have grown far more rapidly in East Anglia than in other parts of the country. Of the 38 English titles listed by R. M. Wiles before 1720, ten were from East Anglia.[133] However, these developments should also be seen in the context of the wider economic growth and social developments within England. The first half of the century saw the development of an economic infrastructure, including financial services such as credit and banking, together with a growth in overseas trade. There were also significant improvements in both road and water communications.[134] Levels of literacy and general education among the populace also increased markedly.

East Anglia fared well during the eighteenth century where, as a result of increased prosperity, there was a development of retail trading, the increased sale of luxury goods and the introduction of new trades. However, elsewhere in England even more fundamental economic changes were beginning to take place, which would see East Anglia lose its preeminence and its relative prosperity. The emerging Industrial Revolution was centred on the midlands and the north, so that by the 1801 census Norwich had fallen to seventh place among provincial cities, Ipswich had fallen to thirty-seventh and Cambridge to forty-eighth. By the middle of the nineteenth century the region had become an economic backwater.

References

1. Penelope Corfield, 'From second city to regional capital', in Carole Rawcliffe and Richard Wilson (eds), *Norwich since 1550* (Hambledon & London, 2004), pp. 139–66, p. 144 and p. 158.

2. Based on the figures in John West, *Town records* (Chichester, 1983), which places them all in the twenty most populous towns, whereas Penelope Corfield uses a different methodology counting contiguous urban areas (e.g. Rochester/Chatham) as one unit.

3. Alan Everitt, 'The marketing of agricultural produce', *The agrarian history of England and Wales*, vol. 4 ed. Joan Thirsk (Cambridge, 1967), pp. 466–592, p. 538.

4. Daniel Defoe, *A tour thro' the whole island of Great Britain*, 4th edn, 4 vols (London, 1748), I, p. 76.

5. Based on entries in the *British Book Trade Index* (hereafter BBTI) http://www.bbti.bham.ac.uk/.

6. George Gray and William Palmer, *Abstracts from the wills and testamentary documents of printers, binders, and stationers of Cambridge, from 1504 to 1699* (London: Bibliographical Society, 1915), pp. 121–2.

7. David Stoker, 'The Norwich book trades before 1800', *Transactions of the Cambridge Bibliographical Society*, 8 (1981), pp. 97–8.

8. Tompson is named as the binder of a Bible in the Norfolk Record Office (N.R.O.), PD 119/182.

9. See David McKitterick, *A history of Cambridge University Press*, vol. 1 (Cambridge, 1992), William Sessions, *The first printers at Ipswich in 1547–1548 and Worcester in 1549–1553* (York, 1984), and David Stoker, 'Anthony de Solempne: attributions to his press', *The Library*, 6th ser., 3 (1981), pp. 17–32.

10. McKitterick, *A history of Cambridge University Press*, vol. 1, p. 385; Cyprian Blagden, *The Stationers' Company: a history, 1403–1959* (London, 1960).

11. David Stoker, 'Printing at the Red Well: an early Norwich press through the eyes of contemporaries', in Peter Isaac and Barry McKay (eds), *The mighty engine: the printing press at work* (Winchester, 2000), pp. 29–38.

12. David Stoker, 'The establishment of printing in Norwich: causes and effects 1660–1760', *Transactions of the Cambridge Bibliographical Society*, 7 (1977), pp. 94–111.

13. For example, they printed Edward (Ned) Ward, *A satyr against wine* (Bury St Edmunds, [c.1712]).

14. R. M. Wiles, *Freshest advices: early provincial newspapers in England* (Columbus, Ohio, 1965), appendix C.

15. See David Stoker, 'The early booksellers and printers of Kings Lynn', in *Studies in the provincial book trade of England, Scotland, and Wales before 1900: papers presented to the British Book Trade Index Seventh Annual Seminar, Aberystwyth, 1989* (Aberystwyth, 1990), pp. 76–125. There also was a private press in the Norfolk village of Fersfield in 1736, set up by the historian Francis Blomefield.

16. BBTI.

17. Frank Farrell, *Yarmouth printing and printers* (Yarmouth, 1910), p. 9. Payne is not noticed by Farrell, but he printed Thomas Howe, *Virtue and patriotism founded on religion* (Yarmouth, 1780). There had previously been a private press in the town operated by the antiquary John Ives about 1772 (ibid., pp. 7–9).

18. McKitterick, *A history of the Cambridge University Press*, p. 456.

19. David Stoker, 'The early history of papermaking in Norfolk', *Norfolk Archaeology*, 36 (1976), pp. 241–52.

20. The careers of booksellers operating in Cambridge, Norwich and Ipswich during the seventeenth century, have been discussed in detail elsewhere, see McKitterick, *A history of the Cambridge University Press*, vol. 1, Stoker, 'The Norwich book trades before 1800', and Tony Copsey, *Book distribution and printing in Suffolk 1534–1850* (Ipswich, 1994).

21. Figures calculated from BBTI entries for booksellers in each town for the first year in each decade, after removal of duplicates.

22. McKitterick, *A history of the Cambridge University Press*, pp. 367–8, and Gray and Palmer, *Abstracts from the wills and testamentary documents*, pp. 118–19 and 124–5.

23. John Jewel, *Apologia ecclesiae anglicanae* (Cambridge, 1683), and McKitterick, pp. 367–8.

24. From a printed advertisement pasted in the back of the Colman Library copy of Alexander Neville's *Norfolk furies* (London, 1623).

25. N.R.O., Norwich Mayor's Court Book, 26 October 1670.

26. N.R.O., Norwich Consistory Court Inventories, INV 653/3, 23 June 1689. See also Ursula Priestley and Alayne Fenner, *Shops and shopkeepers in Norwich 1660–1739* (Norwich, 1985), pp. 19–20.

27. Lawrence Stone, 'Libertine sexuality in post restoration England: group sex and flagellation among the middling sort in Norwich in 1706–7', *Journal of the history of sexuality*, 2 (4) (1992), pp. 511–26, p. 512.

28. David Stoker, 'Norwich "publishing" in the seventeenth century', in John Hinks and Catherine Armstrong (eds), *Printing places* (London, 2005), pp. 31–47.

29. *A Brief and plain discourse upon the decrees of God* (London, 1692), pp. 8–9.

30. Printed at the end of Alexander Pringle, *Mish'am. A stay in trouble or The saints rest in the evil day* (London, 1657).

31. Stoker, 'The early booksellers and printers of Kings Lynn', p. 86.

32. Edward Willan, *Six sermons* (London, 1651).

33. Tuthill is last known *c.*1680 when his name appeared on an advertisement for a patent medicine and on *Proposals for the works of Isaac Barrow* (London, 1682). Zech Tuthill, bookseller of Great Yarmouth, sold copies of Charles Peter, *New Observations on Venereal Disease* (London, 1695).

34. Copsey, *Book distribution and printing in Suffolk*, pp. 34, 104 and 106.

35. Henry R. Plomer, *A dictionary of the printers and booksellers who were at work in England, Scotland and Ireland from 1668 to 1725* (London, 1922), pp. 198–9.

36. Some caution needs to be applied when using statistics generated from a collaborative and as yet incomplete database such as the BBTI. For a discussion of its potential use, see John Hinks and Maureen Bell, 'The Book Trade in English Provincial Towns, 1700–1850: an evaluation of evidence from the British Book Trade Index', *Publishing History*, 57 (2005), pp. 53–112.

37. David Stoker (ed.), *The Correspondence of the Reverend Francis Blomefield* (London: Bibliographical Society, 1992), pp. 50–4.

38. *The trial of John Shilling* (Bury St Edmunds, [1786]).

39. *The trial of Joseph Wakefield and Henry Smith ... At the Lent assizes 1788, ... at Thetford* ([Bury St Edmunds, 1788?]).

40. Copsey, *Book distribution and printing in Suffolk*, pp. 53, and 69.

41. David Stoker, '"Innumerable letters of good consequence in history": the discovery and first publication of the Paston Letters', *The Library*, 6th ser., 17 (1995), pp. 107–55, 129.

42. Martin Booth, *A catalogue of a large and valuable collection of books* ([Norwich?], 1777).

43. *Norwich Mercury*, 6 June 1778.

44. William Cowper, *An hymn, written by William Cowper, Esq. to be sung after the sermon for the benefit of the children of the Sunday-schools* (Dereham, [1790?]).

45. N.R.O., Norwich Archdeacon's Court Inventories, 1739, no. 8. Reproduced in Stoker, 'The early booksellers and printers of Kings Lynn', pp. 90–105.

46. Roger L'Estrange, *Considerations and proposals in order to the regulation of the press* (London, 1667).

47. Thomas Deloney, *A proper newe sonet declaring the lamentation of Beckles a market towne in Suffolke* (London, 1586) and D. Sterrie, *A briefe sonet declaring the lamentation of Beckles* (London, 1586).

48. The only surviving exception was an execution broadside, *Certayne versis writtene by Thomas Brooke* (Norwich, 1570). Anthony de Solempne's press in Norwich ceased working soon afterwards.

49. From the records of a case heard in the Court of Common Pleas (The National Archives, CP 40/1297 membrane 1668) brought by Abraham Veale, a wholesale stationer in London, briefly described by H. R. Plomer in 'Some Elizabethan book sales', *The Library*, 3rd ser., 7 (1916), pp. 318–29.

50. Tessa Watt, 'Publisher, pedlar, pot-poet: the changing character of the broadside trade, 1550–1640', in Robin Myers and Michael Harris (eds), *Spreading the word: the distribution networks of print 1550–1850* (Winchester, 1990), pp. 61–81, p. 70.

51. N.R.O., Norwich Mayor's Court Book 25 (1677–1695), f. 85.

52. Ibid., ff. 264, and 272.

53. Ibid., f. 37.

54. *A narrative of the sudden and surprizing fire which happen'd at the puppet-show at Burwell, in Cambridgeshire ... 8th of September, 1727* (Bury St Edmunds, [1727]), *The Suffolk wonder: or, the pleasant, facetious, and merry dwarf of Bottesdale* ([Ipswich?], 1755), *The wonder of wonders: or, a true and perfect narrative of a woman near Guildford*

in Surrey, who was delivered lately of seventeen rabbets (Ipswich, 1726), *An account of Mr. Boon's confession: together with the last passages of his life* (Norwich, 1704).

55. David Stoker, 'Prosperity and success in the eighteenth-century English provincial book trade: the firm of William Chase & Co.', *Publishing History*, 30 (1991), pp. 31–88 (pp. 38–40).

56. *Norwich Gazette* 1506, 16 August 1735.

57. *Norwich Mercury*, 16 August 1735, and *Norwich Gazette* 1507, 23 August 1735.

58. Chase and his successors also printed *A Calendar or, list of the several prisoners to be tryed at the Assizes*, ostensibly for the use of the authorities, but which would also be advertised for sale to the visiting gentry who wished to attend the trials.

59. The *Concise Oxford English Dictionary* has 'chapman' as synonymous with pedlar, which corresponds with Cotsgrove's *Dictionary of the French and English Tongues* (London, 1611), which defines a chapman as 'a paultrie pedlar, who in a longe packe or maunde (which he carries for the most part open and hanging from his necke before him) hath Almanacks. Bookes of News, and other trifling ware to sell'. Technically these definitions refer to a 'petty chapman'. Some of the chapmen whose wills are recorded in the Prerogative Court of Canterbury or the Norwich Consistory Court were far from being 'paltry pedlars' and the ready reckorers in *The English chapman's and traveller's almanack* at the end of the seventeenth century imply they were buying and selling on a far greater scale than might be encompassed in a pedlar's pack.

60. Margaret Spufford, *Small books and pleasant histories* (London, 1981), pp. 118–19.

61. N.R.O., Norwich Mayor's Court Book 16 (1624–1634) f. 462.

62. Victor Neuberg, 'The Diceys and the chapbook trade', *The Library*, 5th ser. (1969), pp. 219–31, pp. 225–6.

63. The author of this paper has never seen an example of a chapbook either printed in East Anglia, or with the name of a distributor from the region. This does not mean that they never existed, but the notable lack of survival from this one region requires further investigation. One of the reasons why the chapbook trade was so healthy in the lowlands of Scotland, continuing well into the nineteenth century, may have been because there were so few newspapers in this region. Perhaps the opposite applied in East Anglia?

64. *Norwich Gazette* 3, 21 December 1706.

65. *Norwich Post* 257, 3 May 1707.

66. Copsey, *Book distribution and printing in Suffolk*, 24.

67. *Privy Council Registers, preserved in the Public Record Office*, 12 vols (London, 1967–8), ii, pp. 385, 442.

68. *Calendar of state papers, domestic series, of the reign of Charles I*, 23 vols (London 1858–97), 10 (1636/7), pp. 427 and 487, and J. Browne, *The history of Congregationalism in … Norfolk … and Suffolk* (Norwich, 1877), pp. 95–7.

69. 'If any Post-men, or letter carriers have a desire to sell the Weekly News in any Market-Towns or Villages in their respective Walks, they may be furnisht with the Norwich Gazette on very advantageous terms', *Norwich Gazette* 2, 14 December 1706.

70. N.R.O., Norwich Mayor's Court Book 23 (1654–1666), f. 28.

71. British Library, Sloane MS. 1847 f. 137, and *The works of Sir Thomas Browne*, ed. G. Keynes, 4 vols (London, 1964), iv, p. 119.

72. *Calendar of state papers, domestic series, of the reign of Charles II*, 28 vols (1860–1938), 6, 29 September 1666, and N.R.O., Norwich Mayor's Court Book 23 (1654–1666), f. 202, 31 October 1663.

73. R. Hill, *The correspondence of Thomas Corrie* (Norwich, 1956), p. 12.

74. *Crouse and Stevenson's Norwich and Norfolk memorandum-book, for the year* [1775–1789] (Norwich, 1774–88).

75. *Chase's Norwich Memorandum-book, or gentleman and tradesman's daily journal, for the year, 1781* (Norwich, 1781).

76. Nigel Surry (ed.), *Your affectionate and loving sister: the correspondence of Barbara Kerrich and Elizabeth Postlethwaite* (Dereham, 2000), pp. 114–15.

77. Michael Harris, 'A few shillings for small books; the experiences of a flying stationer in the 18th century', in Robin Myers and Michael Harris (eds), *Spreading the word*, pp. 83–108, p. 86.

78. *Norwich Gazette*, 23 September 1749.

79. St Edmundsbury District Council, 'The History of Bury St Edmunds Markets', http://www.stedmundsbury.gov.uk/sebc/visit/markethistory.cfm.

80. Francis Blomefield, *An essay towards a topographical history of Norfolk*, 5 vols (Fersfield, Norwich and Lynn, 1739–75), ii, p. 647.

81. Ursula Priestley, *The great market* (Norwich, 1987), p. 8.

82. A lithograph by H. Ninham, based on Cotman's watercolour is reproduced in Priestley, *The great market*, p. 18.

83. *The Chapmans and travellers almanack* (London, 1693–5); other examples included *The English chapmans and traveller's almanack* (London, 1702) or *The traveller's and chapman's daily instructor* (London, 1705).

84. Spufford, *Small books and pleasant histories*, pp. 118–19.

85. Charles Caraccioli, *An historical account of Sturbridge, Bury, and the most famous fairs in Europe and America* (Cambridge, [1773?]), p. 16.

86. Thomas Cox, *Magna Britannia et Hibernia, antiqua et nova*, 6 vols ([London], 1720–7), v, pp. 253–4.

87. *The dancing-master: or, directions for dancing country dances*, 17th edn (London, 1721), p. 207.

88. John Macky, *A journey through England*, 4th edn, 2 vols (London, 1724), i, pp. 27–81.

89. *Bury-Fair* (London, 1689).

90. A detailed account of the fair in the late sixteenth century is given in M. C. Siraut, *Some aspects of the economic and social history of Cambridge under Elizabeth I*, University of Cambridge M. Litt. thesis, 1978.

91. Macky, *A journey through England*, i, pp. 138–9.

92. Edward (Ned) Ward, *A Step to Stir-Bitch-Fair with remarks upon the University of Cambridge* (London, 1700), pp. 3, 14.

93. John Dunton, *The life and errors of John Dunton late citizen of London* (London, 1705), p. 299.

94. Ward, *Step to Stir-Bitch-Fair*, p. 15.

95. *Bibliotheca topographica Britannica*, v (London, 1790), opposite p. 73.

96. Caraccioli, *An historical account of Sturbridge, Bury, and the most famous fairs in Europe and America*, p. 16.

97. Ibid., p. 38.

98. See Tania McIntosh, *The decline of Stourbridge fair, 1770–1914* (Leicester, 1998). Bury Fair likewise survived as a fun fair into the twentieth century.

99. British Library, 937.f.2, 4 vols (1780–88).

100. *A catalogue of choice books* ... ([London], 1686), *English Short-Title Catalogue* (hereafter ESTC) t64485.

101. John Lawler, *Book auctions in England* (London, 1906), pp. 70–3. Several of the catalogues are recorded in ESTC. See also Robin Myers, Michael Harris and Giles Mandelbrote (eds), *Under the hammer: book auctions since the seventeenth century* (London & New Castle, DE, 2001).

102. *A catalogue of valuable books ... which will be sold by auction ... at Mrs. Elizabeth Oliver's house on Monday the 16th of December, 1689* (London, 1689), *A catalogue of ancient and modern books ... which will be sold by Auction ... at Mrs Olivers House, on Monday the tenth of July 1693* (London, 1693) and *A catalogue of ancient and modern books ... Which will be sold by auction ..., at Mr Ferrour's coffee-house [Kings-Lynn] ... 26 of March* (London, 1694).

103. Ward, *Step to Stir-Bitch-Fair*, pp. 15–16.

104. For example, *A collection of choice books, ... will be sold by auction ... at St. Edmonds-Bury Fair on ... 23d of September 1689 ... by Edward Millington* ([London], 1689).

105. *A catalogue of books of the Reverend Mr Hannott. Which are to be sold by auction, being the 20th Nov., by T. Goddard* (Norwich, 1704).

106. *A catalogue of books both ancient and modern ... Which will be sold by auction, ... on Monday the 31th [sic] of December instant, ... By Thomas Goddard of Norwich, bookseller* (Norwich, 1705).

107. *The auctioneer, a poem. By Mpqr Dkbyq, the Man in the Moon* (Norwich, 1708). The poem was written by the printer Henry Crossgrove and was bound in a volume of his newspaper, the *Norwich Gazette*. It was written after Goddard set up a printing office and began to produce the *Norwich Post-man*. The only known copy was lost in a fire in Norwich Central Library in 1994, but a microfilm copy survives.

108. 'A catalogue of an auction of cloths etc to be had at Mr Tho. Goddards booksellers', advertised in the *Norwich Gazette* 532, 19 January 1717.

109. *A catalogue of choice books in Greek, Latin, and English ... Which will be sold by auction, ... in Lynn–Regis ... 9th of February, 1712/3* (London, 1713) and *Bibliotheca Willisiana, &c. being the libraries of the learned Sir Thomas Willis, Knt. ... which will be sold by auction at Lynn Mart, on Friday the 7th of February* (London, 1717).

110. *Norwich Gazette* 180, 18 March 1710.

111. *A catalogue of choice books ... to be sold by Auction, ... at the Town-Chamber on the Key in Great Yarmouth* (Norwich, 1720).

112. *Bibliotheca miscellanea: or a catalogue of choice books. ... Which will be sold by auction, ... during the ... assizes ... Monday the 31st of July, at the Guild-Hall, ... by W. Chase* (Norwich, 1721).

113. *Norwich Gazette* 787, 4 November 1721.

114. *Norwich Gazette* 788, 11 November 1721.

115. *Norwich Gazette* 945, 14 November 1724.

116. *A catalogue of books, both antient and modern, ... which, ... will be sold by auction, at the Guild-hall Warehouse ... on Monday the 6th of December ... by T. Goddard, and W. Chase* (Norwich, 1725).
117. *Norwich Gazette* 1048, 5 November 1726.
118. *Norwich Gazette* 1050 and 1051, 19 and 26 November 1726.
119. *Norwich Mercury*, 28 March 1730.
120. *Norwich Gazette* 1227 and 1228, 11 and 18 April 1730.
121. Stoker, 'The Norwich book trades before 1800', pp. 90–1 and 103–4.
122. For example, *A catalogue of the remaining part of the library of the Reverend Dr. Andrew Snape, ... and the entire library of the Rev. Mr. Henry Brearey, ... to be sold by auction, Monday Nov. 7th* (Cambridge, 1743), or *A catalogue of the library of the Rev'd Thomas Everson ... to be sold at the Bell Inn Thetford* (Cambridge, 1749).
123. A number of Thurlbourn and Merrill's catalogues between 1742 and 1761 are recorded in ESTC.
124. *Ipswich Journal*, 18 October 1760; *Norwich Mercury*, 29 January 1762; *Norwich Mercury*, 3 December 1763.
125. *Ipswich Journal*, 4 October 1755.
126. David Stoker, 'The ill-gotten library of "Honest Tom" Martin', in Robin Myers and Michael Harris (eds), *Property of a Gentleman: the formation, organization and dispersal of the private library 1620–1920* (Winchester, 1991), pp. 91–112, p. 105 and n. 52.
127. For example, *A catalogue of the genuine, modern, and elegant houshold furniture, and other effects, belonging to Francis Laprimaudaye, Esq. at Drinkston, within eight miles of Bury* (Norwich, 1771).
128. Stoker, 'The Norwich book trades before 1800', p. 103.
129. A series of Seaman's catalogues is recorded in ESTC.
130. *Bibliotheca Banesiana; or, a catalogue of the library of the late Reverend Mr. Matthew Banes, of Fen-Ditton in Cambridgeshire, ... To be sold, on Monday the 12th day of February, 1727–8. ... By William Thurlbourn, bookseller in Cambridge* [London?, 1728], and *A catalogue of a curious and valuable collection of books in most languages and faculties* [Cambridge, 1728].
131. Trevor Fawcett, 'Eighteenth century Norfolk booksellers: a survey and register', *Transactions of the Cambridge Bibliographical Society*, vi (1972), pp. 1–18, pp. 6–7.
132. *A catalogue of a large and valuable collection of books* (Norwich, 1777), and *Norwich Mercury*, 8 March 1794.
133. See Appendices B and C in *Freshest advices*. This figure includes two 'Great Yarmouth' editions of the early Norwich newspapers, which have not survived. In addition there was at least one other short-lived Norwich newspaper not mentioned by Wiles (see Trevor Fawcett, 'Early Norwich newspapers', *Notes and Queries* (1972), pp. 363–5).
134. See Nicolas Barker, 'The rise of the provincial book trade in England and the growth of a national transport system', Frédéric Barbier, Sabine Juratic, and Dominique Varry (eds), *L'Europe et le livre: réseaux et pratiques du négoce de librairie XVIe – XIXe siècles* (Paris, 1996), pp. 137–55.

Watching the Pedlar's Movements: itinerant distribution in the urban Netherlands

ITINERANT SALESMEN, also called pedlars, street vendors, hucksters and ballad singers, are considered to be the most important distributors of popular printed matter in Europe. The pioneering studies of Margaret Spufford and Laurence Fontaine and the follow-up studies of many others in England and France, have highlighted the need for a Dutch contribution to the European debate on the itinerant book trade.[1] An important step is a recently started Dutch research project, entitled 'The pedlar and the dissemination of the printed word'. One of the aims of this project is to make a detailed comparison of the Dutch and the English itinerant distribution networks in the period 1600–1850.[2]

Why these two countries? The assumption of this project is that in the highly urbanized Netherlands the itinerant trader functioned as a crucial extension of the established booksellers in the towns. The pedlar contributed to a distribution network that effectively reduced the gap between the established bookseller and the more modest consumers in town and countryside. Therefore in this project a distinction will be made between itinerant trade in a mainly rural society (England) and in a more urban one (The Netherlands). Although for a large part of the research period this distinction is real, the growing urbanization in England in the course of the eighteenth and nineteenth century must also be taken into account.[3]

The Netherlands form a good starting-point for offering a new perspective on the itinerant book trade. Recently I have challenged the persistent assumption that the high degree of urbanization and the distribution of established booksellers in the Netherlands would have made an itinerant book trade largely superfluous. By the end of the eighteenth century, for instance, only 10% of the inhabitants of the cities of Middelburg and Zwolle patronized the bookshops there.[4] Considering the high level of book production, the relatively high standard of living and the high literacy rates, it is more than likely that a large proportion of the urban population bought their printed matter in the streets. In cities like Utrecht

137

and Amsterdam, research has revealed that there certainly was an extensive network of pedlars selling printed matter both inside and outside the towns.[5] So, even in the Dutch Republic, where the economic position of the official book trade was relatively strong, itinerant bookselling played a crucial role in the distribution of print in villages as well as in towns.

The project has been divided into three closely connected parts: 1) social and economic research of the entire distribution network; 2) the process of pictorial representation; 3) the itinerant dissemination of printed news.[6] Within the borders of the Netherlands, the project will concentrate on two cities and their surrounding countryside. The first is Amsterdam, the city which may be taken as the centre of book production in the period under review, and which because of its size and infrastructure is best suited for research into the urban street trade in books. The second city is the provincial town of Utrecht, which served as a centre of distribution at regional level. There were few other printing towns in the province of Utrecht. Outside the borders of the Netherlands a thorough comparison will be made with two English cities, the national printing centre London and the provincial town of Exeter, and their respective surrounding countryside.

Three questions guide the project: To what extent were the itinerant and established book trade in the Netherlands and in England interconnected in the research period? What is the relationship between the social position and the image of pedlars as well as the materials they supplied? What was the market share of the itinerant traders in the dissemination of printed news?[7] In this essay I will restrict myself to the first question and give some points of departure, methodological possibilities and a few preliminary results. The Netherlands are at centre stage here. Reconstructing the distribution network will be done in four steps: the scale of the trade, the social stratification of the pedlars, trade practices and supply of printed matter.

Numbers, names and professions
By the scale of the trade we mean the total number of itinerant tradesmen operating either within the city, or using it as a base. The aim is to arrive at some indication in quantitative terms of the degree to which the itinerant trade was part of urban book culture. In our search for relevant sources in the Netherlands, however, we are confronted with some complicating factors. Official ordinances in England and France against pedlars have formed a rich source to estimate the range of itinerant trade in towns and

villages. Together with complaints from local organizations, such as guilds, they give information on where and how chapmen travelled through the country. In the Netherlands, however, there were not many commercial obstacles. A recent study shows a decentralized, ineffective, and mildly repressive censorship.[8] So in this country we will not find an equivalent of the English legislation which in 1699 required that all pedlars should be licensed.[9] Therefore the number of pedlars has to be configured with the aid of a multitude of more or less indirect sources such as tax data, trade licences, patents, book bans, market registers, town tolls, criminal sentences, and other incidental forms of registration, including the Napoleonic surveys of 1810–13.[10]

The results of some first explorations indicate at least a strong presence of itinerants in Amsterdam and Utrecht during the whole research period. In the last two decades of the eighteenth century, for example, about one third of the local book traders in the city of Utrecht can be identified as itinerant.[11] For Amsterdam the provisional figures are more random. What we know for certain is that in this Dutch centre of the printing press the number of regular booksellers was large. In 1690 there were 146 regular booksellers and publishers. On the basis of one source, the criminal records, we know that at least seven itinerant traders (c.5%) sold their printed wares in Amsterdam in that same year.[12] Sometimes we come across an exceptionally rich source of information. From the administration of the *Amsterdamsche courant*, for instance, we learn that between c.1767 and 1795 approximately 50 street sellers distributed the weekly newspapers.[13] A totally different source, namely tax data, reveals that in 1749 at least five people distributed newspapers in Leiden.[14]

The large group of vagrants, beggars, unskilled and irregular labourers, which included pedlars, constituted between 10 and 20% of the working population of an average Dutch town in the seventeenth and eighteenth century. Depending on the economic circumstances, the number could fluctuate widely.[15] Although this still does not give us an exact indication of their numbers, it does illustrate that the overall economic situation was an important contributory factor towards the number of street hawkers. When times were hard, the urban retail trade was sometimes the only alternative to begging.

A growing need for regulation and restriction of street trade can thus be regarded as a symptom of economic recession. This was the case in Utrecht around 1760, when the provincial authorities introduced a system of annual permits for pedlars who wanted to travel the surrounding countryside with their goods. These pedlars sold a variety of wares such as lottery tickets, needles, pins, yarn, combs and spectacles. Some of them also had schoolbooks, newsletters, religious books, prints, ballads and almanacs in their packs.[16]

Politically turbulent times can be considered as creating a demand for urban street hawkers. For example during the Peace of Munster (1648) or the War of the Spanish Succession (1701–14), there was more than enough work for the sellers of pamphlets.[17] The street vendor and author of the autobiographical work *De ongelukkige levensbeschryving van een Amster-dammer* ('The unhappy life and times of an Amsterdam bookseller') [1775], probably Harmanus de Koning, a bookseller and news vendor on the side of the revolutionaries, described his personal experience of the phenomenon. In the tumultuous year of 1747, when William IV had just been appointed stadtholder of Holland, he wrote:

In those days, there was a great circulation of all kinds of lampoons, with which several booksellers made good money. I myself took a rich share. I laid my hands on them, and with one or two brothers in the trade we would go to the coffee houses to sell them.

At that time De Koning sold, for instance, the sought-after anti-Orange pamphlet *De weergaloze Amsterdamsche Kijkkast* ('The unparalleled Amster-dam goggle-box'). The author Arnoldus Olofson was sentenced to three years in prison for this publication. De Koning wrote with some regret in 1749: 'Everything started to stagnate again, and the lampoons disappeared, so that making a living was getting more difficult.'[18]

This example also makes clear that much information can be gleaned from the occasions when street vendors were confronted by the legal author-ities. Pedlars could be arrested for different sorts of offence, commercial as well as political. In their sometimes desperate attempts to earn a living, they often acted against the local rules for the book trade, fervently defended by the local booksellers' guilds. They sold their sometimes illegal wares at the wrong moments, in forbidden places and below the market value. Authorities time and again took action against hawkers who distrib-uted immoral and subversive books and prints. Pedlars might also be jailed for crimes that were not related to their trade, such as robbery, burglary, adultery, and assault.

For the research in Amsterdam our starting point will be a database which was the outcome of an already completed legal history project by a Dutch researcher, Sjoerd Faber, in which he collected 19,035 breaches of the law in Amsterdam in the years 1680–1810. This database, available on the Internet, was compiled from books of confessions, gaolers' bills and sheriffs' rolls. It incorporates, among other things, entries for names, professions, and offences.[19] The period 1680–1730 is not entirely covered however; Faber only examined the books of confessions in the years 1680, 1690, 1700, 1710 and 1720. In our own project we are going to explore the years in between and stretch the research period at the beginning (from 1600) and at the end (towards 1850).[20]

The Faber file contains 269 itinerant traders for the entire period covered by the research. Within this group however, there are many pedlars and street vendors whose wares are not identified. In the group whose goods are mentioned, among the sellers of matchsticks, potatoes and sea fish, 22 vendors of printed matter can be distinguished. Eleven of these specialized in the sale of current and topical material such as lampoons, libels, news, magazines and songs. Contrary to what the objections of the guild would suggest, most of these were inhabitants of Amsterdam, not strangers. Also contrary to what might be assumed, itinerant booksellers were no more prone to confrontation with the legal authorities than members of the regular book trade, quite the reverse: about 46 offenders called themselves bookseller, printer or binder during questioning.

The fact that the suspects themselves often described their profession may actually obscure the picture, especially if they thought that a higher social status would be to their advantage. In 1690 Dominicus Garsie, for instance, called himself a bookseller although he was really a street vendor. He was unable to find work as a typesetter, and that was why he had been vending 'nieuwe tijdingen' ('new tidings'), contrary to the statute. The example shows that we should subject all self-styled booksellers in this type of database to closer scrutiny. At the same time, it is another sign that the borderline between the official and the itinerant book trade was rather fuzzy.

Besides the number of pedlars we should also look at the duration of their activities. Recidivists, who appear frequently in the confession books, indirectly supply information about the terms of their ambulant trade. We know that Gijsbert Pietersz Vroom worked in Amsterdam between at least 1689 and 1694 as a 'pedlar with books', because he was repeatedly arrested for irresponsible bidding to inflate prices at a public sale, molesting a woman, causing a fight in an inn, and for theft and handling stolen goods.[21] In 1690 the chimneysweeper Robbert Janse earned some extra money by selling 'nieuwe tijdingen' and 'nouvellen' ('newsletters') on the streets of Amsterdam, for which he was reprimanded. This appeared to be no isolated incident, since he had been doing this for at least twelve years.[22] Sometimes the interrogation not only gives information about the duration, but also the location of their activities. In the 1690s the ballad singers Neeltje Claas and Appolonia Jacobs had their regular base at the 'Nieuwebrugh' in Amsterdam.[23] Two unknown ballad singers sold their songs on the Spaarndammer Bridge for nearly twenty years.[24] From guild protests we learn that in the 1750s Barbara Breuk (or Brink) had a book-stall somewhere in Amsterdam.[25]

Life and work
Unlike England and France, the Netherlands still lack a social classification of the pedlars based on a range of social and economic sources. To accomplish this, we will first have to explore evidence about possessions and income, inferred from tax data, probate inventories, histories of habitation, poor records and genealogical data. Other less obvious sources, such as criminal records, may also yield this kind of information.

An interesting and at the same time complicating element is the fact that some pedlars carried on several commercial activities at the same time, or changed from one job or position on the social ladder to another. At the beginning of the seventeenth century Lenaert Diericks van Tetrode was known as a publisher and bookseller in the city of Gouda, but he also had a market stall in Leiden town hall and at the governmental centre, the 'Binnenhof', in The Hague.[26] If the aforementioned Harmanus de Koning really was the author of *The unhappy life and times of an Amsterdam bookseller*, then in him we find a colourful combination of apprentice boy, street vendor, stallholder, printer of lampoons and prohibited books, maker of newspapers, and a member of the booksellers' guild.[27] Another pedlar, Egbert Koning, who lived in a small village in Noord-Holland at the beginning of the nineteenth century, not only sold printed books, but also had a grocery store, became a butcher and worked on a farm.[28]

Trade practices comprise all the activities undertaken by pedlars in acquiring trade goods, financing, transporting and selling them. In ascending order of specialization we distinguish the occasional trader, the pedlar of printed matter and other goods, the pedlar selling printed matter exclusively, and the pedlar selling specialist printed matter.

The occasional trader, the first category, is in most cases a local city hawker who combined different jobs and sold printed matter for only part of the year. His core business was printing newsletters and pamphlets, but also seasonal categories such as almanacs, prognostications, new year prints ('koningsbriefjes'), Christmas songs and so on. Robbert Janse, mentioned above, fits well into this category. There were also semi-professional distributors. In December 1668 the Amsterdam publisher Jacob Stichter advertised in the *Opregte Haerlemsche courant* that the new militia almanac for 1669 was going to be distributed by the militia drummers (tambours).[29] At the end of the seventeenth century pedlars like Hendrik 't Water combined the packing of herrings with the selling of pamphlets.[30] Neeltje Claas was a silkwinder but in 1697 sold songs on the Amsterdam bridges instead, probably because of lack of work.[31]

The second type of pedlar sold printed matter and other goods at the same time. Those who mainly travelled the countryside sold books as a by-product of their often diverse merchandise. They bought their stock in the city, travelled from village to village and therefore could not 'refresh' their supply easily. As for the range of printed products, this long-distance pedlar avoided great risks and resorted to steady sellers such as schoolbooks, bibles, almanacs and history books. In Utrecht pedlars such as Johannes Krul are examples of this type. In 1789 he got permission from the Court of Utrecht to travel the surrounding countryside with children's books and schoolbooks, as well as plasters, small images, combs, linen and yarn.[32] Other combinations of merchandise included books sold with stockings, handkerchiefs, writing paper, sealing wax, perfume and snuff. In the Netherlands there seemed to be no great interdependence, as Spufford discovered for England, between the itinerant trade in books and textiles.[33]

The pedlar selling printed matter exclusively could be someone with a market stall near the town hall or on a bridge, as well as a small travelling trader with only a basket or a barrow. In the first case the range of products could be more extensive and the books more sizeable. Around 1800 the Amsterdam publisher Johannes Allart faced protesting colleagues because he paid his creditors in books, when he knew that these books were sold on the bookstalls for reduced prices.[34] A residential bookseller as well as a travelling bookseller could own a market stall. In the last case they were considered a nuisance because of their low prices, the bad quality of the books, and the fact that they did not pay the (high) membership fees of the booksellers' guild. Another complaint was that their stock was too extensive.

In 1765, the Amsterdam booksellers' guild complained that 'nowadays the number of market stalls is easily the same as that of bookshops'. The guild found reason to refer to the regulation that stated that 'the sale of books, newspapers, news sheets or songs, [...] on markets, bridges, streets, the Exchange or in other public places, was strictly prohibited.'[35] In eighteenth-century Leiden, this problem of secondhand or old books was partly solved by giving the 'old-booksellers' a special position in the guild.[36]

Within the category of the specialist pedlar, besides the seller of pamphlets, catchpenny prints and schoolbooks, the most appealing representative is the ballad singer. Ballad singers belonged to the poorest category of street vendor. If these people did not manage to scrape a living by selling songs, nothing was left other than to beg for charity or go thieving. In the Amsterdam confession books we find several examples of stealing, begging and vagabond ballad singers. Antonij Sluijter, for instance, who became a ballad singer after his (failed) career as a soldier, was imprisoned for burglary in 1688.[37] When the Amsterdam police interrogated Matthijs Helmans in 1710 he called himself a sailor, a beggar and a ballad singer.[38] In the eighteenth century the members of the criminal gang called 'Hees' committed crimes in Holland, Zeeland and Utrecht. They were described as vagabonds and ballad singers.[39]

The content of a song or the performance of the ballad singer could also be a reason to be arrested on the street, as Jeremia Isaacs Sel experienced in 1740. According to the authorities his songs were rude and obscene. He was sentenced to fourteen days with only water to drink, to think over his sins.[40]

Specialists and supply
An intriguing question relating to trade practices is what kind of networks existed between pedlars and their suppliers. Was there a Grub Street publishers' community in Amsterdam or elsewhere that provided the street vendors with their wares? And the other vital question is: what did the pedlars and street sellers carry in their packs?

Licences which were issued often stipulated the types of printed matter that could be sold. Registered pedlars in eighteenth-century Utrecht sold schoolbooks, history books, prints and newspapers in the countryside. The Court of Utrecht did not provide a permit however for distributing a newspaper, the *Antwerpsche courant*. Later I will explain why this publication was so controversial. Protests by guilds indicate what kind of pirate editions pedlars were selling, and which books were sold below the fixed prices. Besides the guild protests, bailiffs' lists and books of confession also show which pamphlet titles street hawkers were offering illegally.

By reconstructing the goods and the itinerant network step by step we will be able to identify a group of publishers who specialized in pedlars' goods.[41] In England such a distinction in book production already existed in the seventeenth century. From 1620 the London ballad partners dominated the market for broadside ballads, aiming at pedlars as distributors for them. One of the London specialists, the bookseller Charles Tias, sold thousands of chapbooks through pedlars in the 1660s.[42]

In France a similar development occurred in the eighteenth century. Centres for itinerant trade, like the fair of Caen, became especially significant from the 1760s. Fontaine calculated that tens of thousands of chapbooks and prints, intended for itinerant distribution, were traded there. Avignon on the other hand became a production centre for pictures, prints and playing cards that were distributed throughout the countryside by alpine pedlars.[43]

Did the Dutch Republic have certain regions, provinces or cities that specialized in books for the itinerant trade? So far we have found no such geographical concentration as in France. Perhaps there was no great need for it, because of the strong urbanization and wide dissemination of residential book traders in the country. Pedlars could stock up at several nearby cities. Therefore it seems more fruitful to investigate whether there was a division within the cities themselves.

According to contemporary, but subjective, sources, such as a satirical pamphlet from 1690, the Amsterdam publishing business was indeed divided into large, respectable bookshops on one side, and publishing houses and small despised printers and street vendors on the other. The latter were tolerated as long as they stuck to their disreputable books. They were not allowed in the domain of exclusive and scholarly works.[44] The names of the 'second-class booksellers' mentioned in this pamphlet were not fictional. (Gijsbert) de Groot, Johannes (I) Stichter and Gerrit Ewouts or/and his widows were indeed running bookshops in Amsterdam during this period. Furthermore the pamphlet lists five street vendors who sold allegedly trashy books on bridges and locks. It is interesting to see that some of them were not solely itinerant, but had a small bookshop or a minor publishing house.[45] This category could have formed an important bridge between the official and the marginal book trade.

A severe problem is our lack of knowledge of small bookshops and booksellers in villages and small cities. An interesting exception is the prosperous village shop run by Lijsbeth de Bije in Maassluis in 1696. De Bije also had tools for bookbinding, a chest with bibles, psalm-books and other religious texts and a large quantity of chapbooks and 262 rather valuable books. The cheap books that were bound were schoolbooks, riddle books, history books and popular stories. Furthermore she had about 500 songbooks and jest books in stock. De Bije probably bought her stock from the Dordrecht bookseller Johannes de Geer.[46] She may have provided several pedlars with books, but it is not unlikely that she hawked her books in the surrounding villages herself. Around 1675, in a small village called Graft, Gerrid Hermansz seemed to be a baker and a bookseller as well. Unfortunately we don't know if he went from door to door.[47]

I will give two more detailed and eye-catching examples of Amsterdam specialists of popular printing, who can be defined as suppliers of pedlars. The first is the catholic publishing house Stichter, which has a long history in Amsterdam. All sources seem to indicate that this firm was an important production centre for pedlars' goods. For more than two centuries, they had wide fame because of their varied assortment of almanacs.[48] Secondly, the imprint of a seventeenth-century songbook called *De nieuwe Rotterdamse nachtegael* ('The new Rotterdam nightingale'), attributed to Jacob Cornelisz Stichter (1650–72), had the telling formula 'printed in partnership for the pedlars' ('gedruckt in Compagnie voor de Kramers').[49] During the 1680s Johannes (I) Stichter was convicted for illegally reprinting almanacs and for the printing and distribution of lewd pamphlets and songs. These activities must have been one of the reasons why the Stichter family was added to the list of second-class publishers.[50] In the eighteenth century this publishing house produced almanacs as well as catchpenny prints, jest books, newspapers, songbooks, print books, catholic church books, and schoolbooks.[51] A combination of these books and prints would conventionally be found in a pedlar's basket.

Fig. 1. De nieuwe Rotterdamse nachtegael ('The new Rotterdam nightingale') [1650–75], Amsterdam, Jacob Cornelisz Stichter. This titlepage has the formula 'printed in partnership for the pedlars'. (The Hague, National Library)

The Stichters used a publishing strategy for almanacs that became very popular from the last quarter of the seventeenth century and lasted for the entire eighteenth century. It was a strategy that must have supported the pedlar trade. I refer to the growing importance of a typical by-product of the almanac: booklets with all sorts of content that were intended to be bound together, sometimes at the request of the individual customer, with the smallest almanac formats. Booklets like this which became very sought-after were the so-called jest books. These were originally published in octavo, but for this new purpose the content was compressed and the size reduced to a sextodecimo format. As a supplement to the almanacs this genre could reach a much wider reading public. That the Stichters family contributed strongly to this popularization is confirmed by an inventory of their printing house from 1716. In that year the firm not only had a large quantity of almanacs in stock, but also 73,000 printed sheets to make up transport books, songbooks and history books.[52]

The second example of an Amsterdam specialist is the van Egmont family. Like the Stichters, the van Egmont firm seemed to have everything a pedlar might need. To start with, Jacobus (I) van Egmont was known as a notorious printer of pirated editions. In 1715 he produced an illegal edition of an originally English pamphlet entitled *Het gedrag van den hertog van Ormond* ('The behaviour of the Duke of Ormond'). The pedlars arrested for hawking this title assured the prosecutor that selling pirated editions on the street was the usual business of van Egmont. The publisher even made booklists of the illegal material available in his shop.[53] He also used the pirated edition of the *Antwerpsche courant* to advertise his other publications.

This *Antwerpsche courant*, with its shady reputation, is for several reasons an interesting publication. It was in fact a cheap compilation of other newspapers and had various local editions in Amsterdam, Haarlem, Rotterdam and The Hague. Publishers of the *Antwerpsche courant* paid lower taxes than the publishers of the more respectable newspapers in Amsterdam or Haarlem. Probably the reason was that the *Antwerpsche courant* appeared irregularly. The retail prices were very low: in Rotterdam people paid two pennies ('duiten') per copy.[54] The Amsterdam hack writer and journalist Jan van Gysen (1668–1722) was held responsible for its content. Because of its political comments and alleged catholicism the *Antwerpsche courant* was considered a subversive medium by the Utrecht and Holland authorities.[55] The satirist Jacob Campo Weyerman for instance,

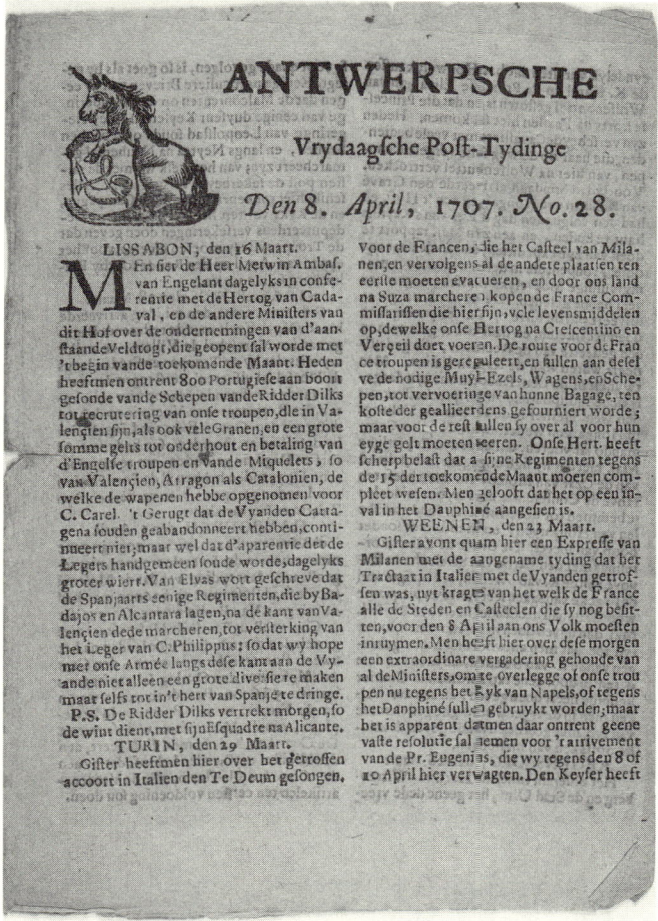

Fig. 2. Antwerpsche Vrydaagsche post-tydinge ('Antwerp newspaper') [*c.*1707], Amsterdam, Jacob Brouwer (Amsterdam, University Library)

blamed van Gysen for his reprehensible position over the war of the Spanish Succession (1701/2–1713). Weyerman probably had the small, political poems of the author in mind.[56]

Developments in French newspapers at the end of the seventeenth century seem comparable to the Dutch origins of second-class newspapers. According to Laurence Fontaine these 'changes reveal a pursuit of lower costs and a closer fit with the style of the pedlar selling the newspaper.'[57] In other words: some occasional newspapers were becoming typical pedlars' wares. The *Antwerpsche courant*, produced in the Northern Netherlands, fits remarkably well in this development and also seems largely to have depended on the itinerant trade. In Amsterdam at the beginning of the eighteenth century, a small network of publishers, bookshops and pedlars clustered around this newspaper. The street seller Philip Pieterse, hawking them in 1707 in the streets of Amsterdam, purchased his stock from the shop of Cornelis van Hoogenhuysen, who also published this newspaper.[58] Van Hoogenhuysen's shop was in those years an important address for political writings and was regularly visited by pedlars. It cannot be a coincidence that van Egmont had been his apprentice.[59] The fame of these suppliers of pedlars' material reached beyond the city walls of Amsterdam. In the 1740s the pedlar Cornelis Hartman purchased his pamphlets in Amsterdam from Jacobus (II), the son of Jacobus (I) van Egmont, and hawked them in the streets of Utrecht.[60]

Another joint production of van Egmont and van Gysen was the so-called *Weekelyksche Amsterdamsche mercuuren* ('Weekly Amsterdam mercury', 1711–22). In this periodical van Gysen commented in a 'burlesque way' on topical matters in the regular newspapers.[61] Just like the *Antwerpsche courant* the *Amsterdamsche mercuuren* will have found most of its purchasers through the street vendors. In some editions van Gysen tells us in detail about his experiences with the itinerants. In 1716 for instance, he complained that everybody expected him to supply his newspapers, but nobody took account of the fact that his wife had just died. He grumbled that the vendors were complaining and the printers were angry because he could not meet their expectations.[62] And after a commercial conflict with van Egmont he warned the public that street sellers were spreading a pirated edition of his *Amsterdamsche mercuuren*. Later he denounced the lack of discretion of the vendors in spreading scandal about his financial situation.[63]

JAN van GYSENS
WEEKELYKSCHE
AMSTERDAMSCHE
MERCUUREN;

Verhalende op een Boertige wys, 't voornaamſte
Nieuws door heel Europa. Beginnende met den
18. September, 1710., en eyndigende
den 7. September, 1711.

EERSTE DEEL.

t'AMSTERDAM,
Gedrukt by JACOBUS van EGMONT, Boekdrukker en Boekverkoper
op de Reguliers Breeſtraat, in de Nieuwe Drukkerŷ, MDCCXI.

Fig. 3. *Weekelyksche Amsterdamsche mercuuren* ('Weekly Amsterdam mercury'), 1710/1711,
by Jan van Gysen, Amsterdam, Jacobus van Egmont (The Hague, National Library)

The van Egmonts were also celebrated for their catchpenny prints, a category of print that could be produced with very low cost and effort. Investment was small because they often used old woodblocks, acquired from former publishing houses. The widow of Jacobus (I) van Egmont produced traditional titles such as: *Leven en Daden van Thyl Ulenspiegel* ('The life and deeds of Thyl Ulenspiegel'), using the sixteenth-century woodblocks of Jan van Ghelen from Antwerp.[64] In later years they applied a lucrative combination of these penny prints and print books, thereby responding to a whole new market for children's literature. They published a picture-book for children (*Extra fraai Kinder-Prent-Boek*) in the 1770s, for example, which was compiled entirely from former separately published prints. The fact that these prints were never intended for children seemed to be no objection.[65]

In the first decades of the eighteenth century Jacobus (I) van Egmont was one of the most interesting innovators in his field. He was, as far as I know, the first publisher who systematically produced titles which were explicitly issued for pedlars. In his publications he played with the image of these street vendors. In the years 1714–22 he put a songbook on the market that was entitled *Kleyn Jans konkelpotje, of het pleyzierige en vermakelijke vossenburgje* ('Little Jan's gossip pot'). This songbook was said to be printed for the ballad singer Pieter de Vos, alias Klein Jan ('Small Jan'), who also wrote the words. Another product of van Egmont was a spectator-like periodical called *De Amsterdamsche mars-drager* ('The Amsterdam pedlar'). In this periodical a pedlar gave his views on current events and on more general issues. Being a clever businessman van Egmont did not omit to publish a stock-list of his songbooks on the last page. He also used this periodical for advertising other apparently pedlar publications such as *Apollo's prullekraam* ('Apollo's knickknack stand'), *De zingende Kramer* ('The singing pedlar') and *Mars-dragend hondje* ('The basket-carrying dog').[66]

Conclusion

Mapping the Dutch itinerant network provides an insight into the multi-faceted distribution of books in a strongly urbanized country with an advanced publishing industry. Amsterdam publishers and booksellers were very aware of the need to use street vendors to reach a large reading public. In this early phase of the research we cannot say much about how extensive the itinerant network actually was, who was part of it and how it functioned

Fig. 4. *De Amsterdamsche mars-drager* ('The Amsterdam pedlar'), 1720, no. 18, Amsterdam, Jacobus van Egmont (The Hague, National Library)

from day to day. Furthermore, the source material so far used is one-sided. Focussing on criminal archives naturally leads to a negative view of the role of the itinerant trade in society. The books of confession do not show a representative part of the itinerant trade in a large city like Amsterdam. For the people who remained on the straight and narrow we have to explore other sources, such as local licences, immigration registers, and market registers.

Still, as we look at how the itinerant and regular distribution network interacted in Amsterdam, we must conclude that, at first sight, there seemed to be no long-term relationships between regular booksellers and pedlars, of the kind Laurence Fontaine described for France. Agreements were flexible and contacts were ephemeral. On the other hand, at the beginning of the eighteenth century there seems to have been a specialist network of pedlars, publishers, booksellers and typical pedlars' products in Amsterdam. The *Antwerpsche courant* and the *Amsterdamsche mercuuren* may serve as examples of the type of printed matter that was not only distributed by the street trade, but in fact constituted some of its products.

Evidently the main questions cannot yet be answered at this early stage. In five years' time, however, I hope we can present a new urban model for studying the dynamic interaction between the itinerant and regular book trade and between popular culture and learned culture.

References

1. Margaret Spufford, *Small books and pleasant histories* (London, 1981); *The Great Reclothing of rural England: petty chapmen and their wares in the seventeenth century* (London, 1984); Margaret Spufford, 'The pedlar, the historian and the folklorist: seventeenth century communications', *Folklore*, 105 (1994), pp. 13–24; Laurence Fontaine, *History of pedlars in Europe* (Cambridge, 1996); *Colportage et lecture populaire. Imprimés de large circulation en Europe XVIe–XIXe siècles*, ed. R. Chartier and H.-J. Lüsebrink (Paris, 1996); *Spreading the word. The distribution networks of print 1550–1850*, ed. R. Myers and M. Harris (Winchester, 1990).

2. The Netherlands Organization supports this VIDI project for Scientific Research (NWO). This article is one of the first publications from the project.

3. At the end of the eighteenth century 40% of the Dutch population lived in towns of over 2,500 inhabitants (in the province of Holland even 60%). The percentages in Germany (17%) and France (12%) were much lower. Even in strongly urbanizing England the percentage at that moment was about 25%. Jan de Vries and Ad van der Woude, *Nederland 1500–1815. De eerste ronde van moderne economische groei* (Amsterdam, 1995), pp. 82–95; Joost Kloek and Wijnand Mijnhardt, *1800: Blauwdrukken voor een samenleving* (Den Haag, 2001), p. 38.

4. P. Hoftijzer, 'Leesonderzoek in Nederland over de periode 1700–1850. Een stand van onderzoek', in *Bladeren in andermans hoofd. Over lezers en leescultuur*, ed. Th. Bijvoet and others (Nijmegen, 1996), p. 171.

5. Jeroen Salman, '"Vreemde loopers en kramers." De ambulante boekhandel in de achttiende eeuw', *Jaarboek voor Nederlandse boekgeschiedenis* 8 (2001), pp. 73–98; J. Salman, 'Peddling in the past. Dutch itinerant bookselling in a European perspective', *Publishing History* 53 (2003), pp. 5–19.

6. For the process of representation: Jeroen Salman, 'Between reality and representation. The image of the pedlar in the 18th century Dutch Republic', in *New Perspectives in Book History. Contributions from the Low Countries*, ed. Marieke van Delft, Frank de Glas and Jeroen Salman (Zutphen, 2006), pp. 188–202. For the itinerant dissemination of printed news: Jeroen Salman, 'Het nieuws op straat. Pamfletten en couranten in het vroegmoderne distributienetwerk', in *Het lange leven van het pamflet. Boekhistorische, iconografische, literaire en politieke aspecten van pamfletten, 1600–1900*, ed. M. Meijer Drees, J. de Kruif and J. Salman (Hilversum, 2006), pp. 56–67.

7. A postdoctoral researcher will investigate the representation of the pedlar; a PhD student (Roeland Harms) will carry out the research into the distribution of news. As project leader I will carry out the research into the itinerant distribution network as a whole.

8. I. Weekhout, *Boekencensuur in de Noordelijke Nederlanden. De vrijheid van drukpers in de zeventiende eeuw* (Den Haag, 1998).

9. Spufford, *The Great Reclothing*, pp. 14–18.

10. Only 33 'pedlars with books' ('colporteurs') were registered in these Napoleonic surveys because they only counted the ones who sold books exclusively. B. P. M. Dongelmans, *Van Alkmaar tot Zwijndrecht. Alfabet van boekverkopers, drukkers en uitgevers in Noord-Nederland 1801–1850* (Amsterdam, 1988), pp. 9–25; J. D. Popkin, 'The book trades in Europe during the Revolutionary Era', *Papers of the Bibliographical Society of America* 78 (1984), pp. 407, 413.

11. Salman, '"Vreemde loopers en kramers"', pp. 79–80.

12. The figures of regular booksellers are based on *Thesaurus 1473 – 1800*, available in the electronic book historical system *Bibliopolis* (www.kb.nl\bibliopolis), consulted 09-03-2006. This *Thesaurus* is based on titlepages, so small printers and booksellers who did not publish books themselves, are absent. The information from criminal records is partly based on the database of Sjoerd Faber (see www.stimore.nl).

13. I. H. van Eeghen, 'De Amsterdamse courant in de achttiende eeuw', *Jaarboek Amstelodamum* 44 (1950), pp. 44–5. According to the *Thesaurus*, in the period 1760–1800 472 people were running publishing houses and bookshops in Amsterdam.

14. Salman, '"Vreemde loopers en kramers"', p. 78.

15. De Vries and van der Woude, *Nederland 1500–1815*, p. 648.

16. Salman, '"Vreemde loopers en kramers"', pp. 76–7.

17. M. van Otegem, 'Tijd, snelheid, afstand; de mechanica van het pamflet', *De zeventiende eeuw* 17 (2001), nr. 1, pp. 56–7.

18. *De ongelukkige levensbeschryving van een Amsterdammer* ('The unhappy life and times of an Amsterdam bookseller'). First published in 1775 by Harmanus Koning. Reprinted with an introduction by Marius J. Dekker (Amsterdam, 1965), p. 88.

19. See www.stimore.nl. Consulted 09-02-2006.
20. With Roeland Harms I am currently going through the years between 1690 and 1700 and between 1720 and 1730.
21. Gemeentearchief Amsterdam (GAA hereafter), RA Confessieboeken, Inv. nr. 335, fol. 21, dd. 8-9-1689; inv. nr. 335, fol. 130, dd. 29-8-1690; inv. nr. 337, fols. 165-6, dd. 16-01-1692; idem fol. 169, dd. 25-1-1692; inv. nr. 338, fol. 215.
22. GAA, RA, Confessieboeken, inv. nr. 596, fol. 118, dd. 14-6-1690. M. M. Kleerkooper and W. P. van Stockum jr., *De boekhandel te Amsterdam voornamelijk in de zeventiende eeuw. Biographische en geschiedkundige aantekeningen* (Den Haag, 1914-16), pp. 1255–6; P. J. Verkruijsse, *De marskramer. Verslag van een onderzoek naar de marskramer in archivalia* [unpublished research record, University of Amsterdam, supervised by P. J. Verkruijsse] (Amsterdam, 1994), pp. 11–14; GAA, NA, inv. nr. 446.
23. R. Dekker, L. van der Pol, '"Wat hoort men niet al vreemde dingen…"', *Spiegel Historiael* 17 (1982), pp. 486–94.
24. Kleerkooper and van Stockum, *De boekhandel te Amsterdam*, vol. I, p. 314. See Verkruijsse, *De marskramer*, 48.
25. GAA, Boekverkopersgilde, inv. nr. 52, 'Notulen gehouden bij de overluyden' (microfiche 2), dd. 18-8-1756. Extracted from A. Baggerman, *Een lot uit de loterij. Familiebelangen en uitgeverspolitiek in de Dordtse firma A. Blussé en Zoon, 1745–1823* (Den Haag, 2000), p. 91.
26. D. van Heel, *De Goudse drukkers en hun uitgaven*, 12 (Gouda, 1951-3), vol. 4, pp. 13–14; E. F. Kossmann, *De boekverkoopers, notarissen en cramers op het Binnenhof* (Den Haag, 1932), pp. 77, 78, 194.
27. *De ongelukkige levensbeschryving van een Amsterdammer.*
28. *Ware beschrijving wegens den levensloop van mij Egbert Koning, door wie dit boek zelf is gemaakt en uitgegeven in den ouderdom van 68 jaar* (Z.p. 1860) (University Library Leiden, BGWMNL).
29. *Oprechte Haerlemsche Courant* (OHC) ('Haarlem Newspaper'), dd. 18-12-1668.
30. GAA, RA, confessieboeken, inv. nr. 338, fol. 62, dd. 27-08-1692.
31. Dekker and van de Pol, 1982, '"Wat hoort men niet al vreemde dingen…"', pp. 487-8.
32. Utrechts Archief, Hof van Utrecht, inv. nr. 135–1, 135–2, *Lijsten van personen, aan wie vergund is hunne nering ten plattelande uit te oefenen* 1763–1808, dd. 10-12-1789.
33. M. Spufford, 'Drukwerk voor de armen in Engeland en Nederland, 1450–1700', in *Bladeren in andermans hoofd*, pp. 74–5.
34. Baggerman, *Een lot uit de loterij*, p. 93.
35. *De ongelukkige levensbeschryving van een Amsterdammer*, pp. 86, 236.
36. H. van Goinga, *Alom te bekomen: Veranderingen in de boekdistributie in de Republiek 1720–1800* (Amsterdam, 1999), p. 197.
37. GAA, Justitieboek, inv. nr. 594, dd. 29-1-1688/ 31-1-1688.
38. GAA, RA, Confessieboeken, inv. nr. 361, dd. 15-3-1710.
39. F. van Egmond, *Op het verkeerde pad. Georganiseerde misdaad in de Noordelijke Nederlanden 1650–1800* (Amsterdam, 1994), p. 83.

40. Lotte van de Pol, *Het Amsterdams hoerdom. Prostitutie in de zeventiende en achttiende eeuw* (Amsterdam, 1996), p. 333.

41. Salman, 'Peddling in the past', p. 14.

42. Tessa Watt, 'Publisher, pedlar, pot-poet: The changing character of the broadside trade, 1550–1640', in *Spreading the word*, ed. Myers and Harris, p. 68.

43. Fontaine, *History of pedlars in Europe*, pp. 40–3, 190–1.

44. The title of this pamphlet is *Relaas van de beroertens op Parnassus* ('The Story of the Disturbance on Parnassus'). See Salman, 'Peddling in the past', pp. 14–15.

45. Among these vendors were (Johannes) van Lamsveld, (Klaas) ter Loo and (Niklaas) Neus. Two booksellers called 'Tjercken' and 'Hooft' are not in the *Thesaurus* (www.bibliopolis.nl).

46. H. C. Dibbits, *Vertrouwd bezit. Materiële cultuur in Doesburg en Maassluis 1650–1800* (Amsterdam, 1998), pp. 218–22.

47. A. Th. van Deursen, *Een dorp in de polder. Graft in de zeventiende eeuw* (Amsterdam, 1994), p. 139.

48. I. H. van Eeghen, 'Ambachten en beroepen voor almanakjes en kinderprenten van de Erven Stichter 1769–1800', *Jaarboek van het Genootschap Amstelodamum* 74 (1982), pp. 105–30; I. H. van Eeghen, 'De Stichter's Enkhuizer almanak en Amsterdam', *Jaarboek van het Genootschap Amstelodamum* 75 (1983), pp. 23–4.

49. *De nieuwe Rotterdamse Nachtegael* [c.1650–75] Den Haag Koninklijke Bibliotheek 174 H 10.

50. Van Eeghen 'De Stichters Enkhuizer almanak en Amsterdam', p. 38.

51. Van Eeghen, 'Ambachten en beroepen voor almanakjes'.

52. J. Salman, *Populair drukwerk in de Gouden Eeuw. De almanak als lectuur en handelswaar* (Zutphen, 1999), pp. 234–5.

53. I. H. van Eeghen, *De gilden: Theorie en praktijk* (Bussum, 1974), pp. 124–5; I. H. van Eeghen, *De Amsterdamse boekhandel, 1680–1725* (Amstercam, 1960–78), vol. 3, p. 133; Kleerkooper and van Stockum, *De boekhandel te Amsterdam*, vol. I, pp. 848–9.

54. Van Goinga, *Alom te bekoomen*, pp. 38–9.

55. Salman, 'Het nieuws op straat', 65.

56. These were also published separately: *Jan van Gysens alle de gedichten welke gediend hebben tot verciering van de Antwerpsche Courant, zedert den 21 December 1706. tot den 24 Mey 1707*. Cornelis van Hoogenhuysen, who also brought this newspaper to the market, published this book (University Library Leiden, 1199 E 12).

57. Fontaine, *History of pedlars*, pp. 195–7.

58. Van Eeghen, *De Amsterdamse boekhandel*, vol. 3, p. 161; Verkruijsse, *De marskramer*, pp. 9–10.

59. Van Eeghen, *De boekhandel in Amsterdam*, vol. 3, 161; Kleerkooper and van Stockum, *De boekhandel te Amsterdam*, vol. II, p. 1256; Verkruijsse, *De marskramer*, pp. 8–14.

60. A. W. E. Daniëls, *Het toezicht op de publicatie van drukwerk in de stad Utrecht, 1597–1749* (unpublished doctoral thesis, University of Utrecht, 1997), pp. 52, 60, 67–8.

61. Rob Beentjes, 'En de man hiet Jan van Gyzen' Een verslag van twaalf jaar lief en leed in Jan van Gysens Weekelyksche Amsterdamsche Merkuurer (1710–1722)', *Mededelingen van de Stichting Jacob Campo Weyerman* 17 (1994), pp. 3, 7.

62. Beentjes, 'En de man hiet Jan van Gyzen', p. 11.

63. Beentjes, 'En de man hiet Jan van Gyzen', pp. 12–13.
64. M. de Meyer, *De volks- en kinderprent in de Nederlanden van de 15e tot de 20e eeuw* (Antwerpen-Amsterdam, 1962), p. 487.
65. P. J. Buijnsters and Leontine Buijnsters-Smets, *Bibliografie van Nederlandse school- en kinderboeken 1700–1800* (Zwolle, 1997). See no. 1618 and 1619 with a third edition from *c.*1775.
66. Salman, 'Between Reality and Representation', pp. 195–9.

The Scottish Chapman

JOHN MORRIS

'WHAT IS A CHAPBOOK?' Most people who have had their attention drawn to this strange corner of bibliography probably define chapbooks as badly printed little books on abominable paper on one of a number of popular subjects and probably with crude cuts, the verse ones of eight pages, the prose ones perhaps twenty-four. But why chapbooks? The books themselves never talk about chapbooks — 'books for chapmen and hawkers' once or twice, 'histories' and 'garlands' quite commonly, but never in my experience 'chapbooks'. *The Oxford English Dictionary* definition runs as follows:

> Chap-book [from chap in CHAPMAN + BOOK] A modern name applied by book-collectors and others to specimens of the popular literature which was formerly circulated by itinerant dealers or chapmen, consisting chiefly of small pamphlets of popular tales, ballads, tracts, etc.

The first recorded use of the word was in 1824, in Thomas Frognall Dibdin's *Library Companion* (p. 238): 'It is a chap-book, printed in rather a neat black letter....'. *The Oxford English Dictionary* further defines 'chapman' as a man whose business is buying and selling, and notes that the usage is obsolete. Walter Chepman who brought printing to Edinburgh was of course a man engaged in buying and selling, or as we should now say a merchant. The chapmen with whom we are concerned, however, were the petty chapmen, itinerant dealers who travelled about from place to place selling or buying, keeping booths (in Scotland 'crames') at markets, hawkers or pedlars.[1]

Here is a romantic view from the 1870s:

> Old Dauvit was a middle-sized, broad-shouldered man with a keen, pawky eye, and a very sleek, worldly face. He was always clad in a blue coat like a large surtout, with big metal buttons, homespun grey vest and trousers, while his head was surmounted by a huge broad bonnet with a red top; round his neck he wore a green and yellow Indian neckerchief, which encircled his unbleached shirt collar. The lappels of his coat and vest pockets were the only fanciful part of his dress; his pack was tied in a linen table-cover, and slung over his shoulders, but Dauvit strode on as

if he felt no burden, planting his staff firmly on the ground, and keeping a sharp eye on business. His stock consisted, perhaps, of hardware goods, comprising *five bawbee* knives, needles, pins of all sizes, from the small 'minikin' to the large 'Willie Cossar;' thimbles, scissors, bone combs, specks; also ballads, such as 'Gill Morice' and 'Sir James the Rose', or four and eight page pamphlets generally comprehending among the number 'John Cheap the Chapman,' 'The King and the Cobbler,' and 'Ali-Baba, or The Forty Thieves,' Dauvit had his regular 'rounds,' which he traversed twice, or it might be many times a year; usually contriving at nightfall to reach some friendly farmhouse, where the cog of porridge and bed of straw were cheerfully given in return for his budget of news, his packet of chapbooks, or small parcel of tea and sugar, bespoken on his last visit. Every person, from the peer to the peasant, welcomed and encouraged Dauvit to castle and cot. When he entered a house he always had a suitable remark to set off his rustic bow, and confident familiar smile. 'Uncommon fine weather, mistress,' was his favourite salutation, varying the 'fine' with 'coarse,' 'cauld,' 'dry,' 'wat,' or 'changeable,' to suit the weather. Then followed some complimentary remark, such as- "I needna ask if ye're weel the day, for ye're the very picture o'health;" or some decidedly pleasant observation, especially to the young lasses, as "fair fa' your bonny face, I haena seen your match in a' the borders;" or, "Eh, now! but a sight of you's a gude thing; I wonder if I ha'e ony nice ribbon in my pack for you the day," with, it might be, "Ye're a comely lassie. I wish he saw you, the noo, that likes ye best." Of course, after such flattering speeches Dauvit was asked to lay down his pack and give them his news, and then he, nothing loath, opened up his budget of information, told the mistress when he last saw her married daughter, and how she was looking; delivered the message to Jenny the kitchen-maid, received from some far away brother; or told the master all about the various 'craps' upon the different farms he passed through, generally ending with — "I ha'e seen nae pasture to compare wi' your ain," or, "Ye've braw corn, maister, in the park down there." He was generally asked to join the family of the small farmer at meals; but he was a very moderate eater and well bred in his own fashion, handing all the plates of bread to the company at table till told again and again "that he was eatin' nane his sel' but only watchin' other folk." Dauvit learned about all the marriages likely to take place, and, throwing himself in the way of the bridegroom or bride, would make him or her a present of a ribbon or neckerchief; then, after a joke and an encomium on the absent one, expressing his certainty that two such "weel-doin' industrious young folk couldna but be happy," he would inform them that "he was aye at hame frae the last Monday o' the a'e month to the first Monday o' the other; or, if they wad either write what they wanted or come owre, he wad gi'e them some grand bargains," adding "that he wad tak' the siller as they could gi'e him it." But Geordie Johnston o' the Shaw remarked, after doing, as he termed it, a "gude stroke wi' Dauvit," that "he wasna sae accommodatin' as he made believe." When business

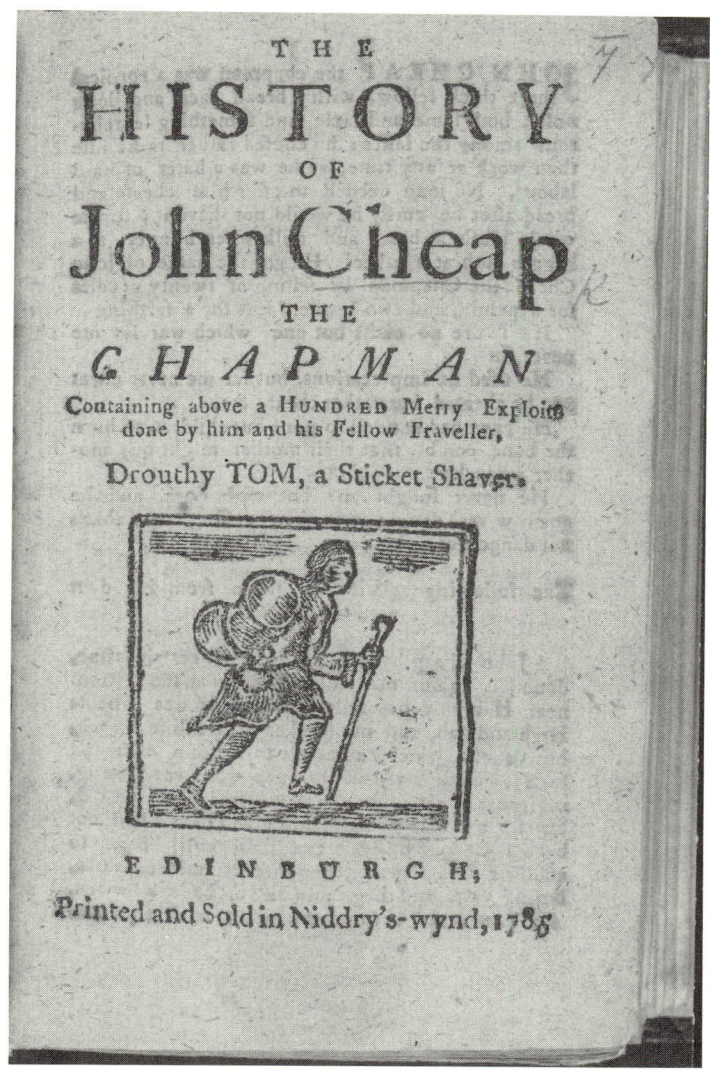

Fig. 1. The history of John Cheap the chapman was published in numerous editions from 1772 onwards. Most have a rough woodcut illustration of a chapman on the titlepage.

was over, if he could reach another farm-town before dark, he would roll up the pack, and wishing them all 'a gude afternoon,' speed on his way; but if it was near nightfall, he remained and spent the evening, sitting with the assembled household round the fire, retailing his news.[2]

This passage is said to be from a novel and gives a fine romantic description of a well-to-do chapman with a regular clientèle. Note that he was always at home, replenishing stocks and doing other business one week in the month, and no doubt followed a regular and fixed circuit the rest of the time. However chapmen were not in general so popular with the country folk, and had an uphill job to ingratiate themselves with their customers, very necessary if they were to sleep in comfort or even eat. They were considered lazy, cheats, and on the make by those who laboured on the land. Fairly typical was the countryman who told John Cheap:

If I should ly in his midden-dib [muck-heap], I should get no quarters from him that night; a wheen lazy idle villains rins a' to be chapmen, comes through the country fashing fouks, ay seeking quarters; the next day ye'll be gaun wi' a powder'd pirrywig, and a watch at your arse, and winna let fouk stand afore your chap-doors, ye'll be sae saucy.[3]

The sources for our knowledge of Scottish chapmen are of three kinds. First the records of the various chapmens' societies with which Scotland was well endowed. Secondly, the personal reminiscences of chapmen, one of the richest sources, but particularly difficult to find, and many apparently hopeful titles on examination are very disappointing. William Glover's *Journal through the counties of Berwick, Roxburgh, Selkirk, Dumfries, Ayr, Lanark, East, West, & Mid Lothians, in the year 1817*, typically reads 'I left Haddington at 9 o'clock and arrived at Edinburgh at 2.30 p.m.'. This is then followed by a 30-page description of Edinburgh taken from a named guidebook, and an account of the state of the Sunday schools there. This pattern he follows throughout the whole work remorselessly, place after place, never mentioning what he did or whom he saw, except for the sermons he attended.[4] Even less readable are *Some account of the travels of John Magee, pedlar and flying stationer, in North and South Britain, in the years 1806 and 1808* and the same author's *An account of many wonderful instances of Divine Providence which have occurred to John Magee*. Magee was a religious maniac with a persecution complex. Most of his two books are devoted to his fanaticism, though he does have the odd remark about dogs and the hardness of a pedlar's lot.[5]

The third type of source consists of casual or oblique mentions of chapmen that occur in other books or records, together with a few drawings and photographs of chapmen and hawkers, or legal reports of chapmen murdered for the contents of their packs, newspaper cuttings, and Acts of Parliament. These have one thing in common, that their primary purpose was not to tell us about the chapmen trade, and yet they often provide details we could find in no other way. There have survived a few business records of chapmen, including a nearly complete set of books for John and William Morison, chapmen of Glasgow for 1761–73, which is among the Court of Session Productions[6].

First the chapmen's societies of Scotland. I know of five such societies: The Fraternity of Chapmen in [sic] the Three Lothians, which is said to be the oldest; The Chapman Court of Fife meeting at Killconquer and The Fife Chapman Society meeting at Cupar, both dating from 1706 and mostly sharing the same rules; the Chapmen of Perthshire and The Fraternity of Chapmen in Stirlingshire, founded in 1726. The Lothians Society claimed to have been incorporated by a charter from King James V. In 1837 they write:

Owing to the late practise of opening so many retail shops in cities, towns and villages, it might almost be said, and even in hamlets, the number of respectable Travelling Chapmen is become small, and the old Members of the Fraternity of the Three Lothians fast dropping into the grave, which endangers the Society of soon sinking into oblivion in this part of the country, and their ancient and valuable Cross at Preston to stand, like the Pyramids of Egypt, weathering the storm, but unable to tell the wondering and anxiously inquiring traveller to whom it owes its origin.

Deeply impressed with such views as those, a few Gentlemen (Brethren and friends of the Incorporation), full of antiquarian spirit, requested the Lord of the Chapmen to call a Meeting of his Brethren, in order to admit new Members.

This reconstituted Society went down to Prestonpans once a year by train and held a fair round the Salt Preston Cross until about 1870. It also ran a widows' scheme, from the prospectus of which I have just quoted. All that I know of the Society's earlier history is that like the other chapmen's societies it elected a Lord and Brethren and made rules regulating the conduct of its members.[7]

Fortunately the minute-books of the Fife and the Stirlingshire societies have all survived from the beginning of each society. Those of the two Fife societies, whose rules or acts are virtually identical are rather disappointing, for though there are occasional acts referring to the setting up of stalls at fairs, the majority are concerned with regulating the behaviour and even the manners of the membership. The Stirlingshire Society was in some ways the most interesting. It had its own watchword solemnly hidden behind a flap of paper, and held dinners and horse-races at its annual meetings. Its acts included all those concerned with good manners which also appear in the Fife acts, but it concerned itself more with the regulating of fairs. On 20 September 1800 the Stirlingshire Society converted itself into a Friendly Society:

The Committee haveing taken into their consideration the present laws and Regulations of the Society, observe that they relate solely to Travelling Chapmen who have of late years greatly diminished in number, the business being almost now universally discontinued.[8]

The richest source for the details of the chapman's life is undoubtedly the memoirs. Scotland is fortunate in this respect in having unusually literate chapmen. The earliest of these was Dougal Graham. Dougal, possibly a hunchback — a number of chapmen had physical handicaps of one sort or another which disabled them for physical labour — wrote an eye-witness account of the Jacobite rising of 1745. His *History of the Rebellion* is a valuable account, though it gives little autobiographical information.[9] More important from our point of view is *The history of John Cheap the chapman*. This was attributed to Dougal Graham by George Caldwell, a chapbook printer of Paisley, in a conversation with William Motherwell, the Paisley poet, who published the information in his article on chapbook literature in the *Paisley Magazine*.[10] Dougal Graham was certainly a member of the Stirlingshire Society of Chapmen and possibly accompanied the Pretender's army in that capacity, though he later obtained the post of skellat bellman of Glasgow, a post well suited to a natural patterer. The chapbooks attributed to him, apart from the *History of the Rebellion*, are almost certainly not by him. They were first published in Edinburgh only a year or two before he died and at a time when tradition makes him skellat bellman of Glasgow.[11] Whoever their author was, they give a very lively picture of life in contemporary Scotland and particularly of chapmen:

John Cheap, the Chapman, was a very comical short thick fellow, with a broad face and a long nose; both lame and lazy, and something leacherous among the lasses: He chose rather to sit idle than work at any time, as he was a hater of hard labour.— No man needed to offer him cheese and bread after he curst he would not have it;

for he would blush at bread and milk, when hungry, as a beggar at a babee. He got the name of John Cheap the Chapman, because he sold twenty needles for a penny, and twa leather laces for a farthing. He swore no oaths but one, which was, Let me never sin. He used no imprecations, but Let me never cheat nor be cheated, but rather cheat. He gave bad counsel to none but children, and that was to burn the bane-cames, that their mothers might buy another wher he came that way again. He never fought with any but dogs, and the good wives daughters in their daffing, and that's not dangerous.

Alexander Wilson of Paisley, the poet and author of *Watty and Meg* and later better known as the father of American ornithology, tried his hand as a chapman selling drapery on commission, and included his journal for part of 1789 as an appendix to the second edition of his *Poems*. More important are his verses about chapmen, including two narrative poems spoken in the character of a chapman, *The Pack* and *The Loss of the Pack*. The latter was delivered at the Pantheon in Edinburgh, during a debate on the question 'Whether is disappointment in love, or the loss of fortune hardest to bear.' It should really be quoted in its entirety, but here is one brief extract:

> ... I wha stand here, in this bare scoury coat,
> Was ance a packman, wordy mony a groat:
> I've carried packs as big's your meikle table;
> I've scarted pats, and sleepit in a stable
> Sax pounds I wadna' for my pack ance ta'en,
> And I could bauldly brag 'twas a' mine ain.[12]

> [I who stand here in this bare dirty coat
> Was once a chapman, worth many a groat:
> I've carried packs as large as your big table
> I've scraped porridge pots, and slept in a stable:
> Six pounds I would not once have taken for my pack
> And I could boldly brag it was all my own.]

A lesser mind, but still important, was William Nicholson, the chapman poet of Galloway. Unlike Wilson, he remained a chapman all his active life, and finally like so many of his calling became an incurable alcoholic. He wrote nothing about his trade himself, but to the second edition of his *Poems* is prefixed a memoir which is particularly valuable. Nicholson's career was more typical than Wilson's and he expresses admirably the aspirations and failures of the trade.[13] The last memoir I want to mention is that of William Magee, a small Edinburgh bookseller. In 1830, he published a curious little pamphlet entitled *Recollections of a personal interview with the late Laird of Dundonnell, at his cottage in Lochbroom, during a tour through the North Highlands, in 1819–20. By an itinerant bookseller.* A disputed will in a case of some celebrity at the time depended on the state of mind of the late Laird of Dundonnell and particularly whether he could read and write. Its importance from our point of view is the part that chapbooks played in Magee's evidence. William Magee dealt principally in chapbooks and gives a very circumstantial account of his methods and stock, and incidentally of the hazards run by a chapman in the Highlands at the time.[14]

Chapmen were of as many kinds as the needs of the isolated communities they served. The commonest were doubtless the draper and hardwareman. The travelling souter [shoemaker], tailor, horn spoon maker, tinker and even bookbinders also travelled circuits, completing the work on hand before moving on, but as they sold nothing but only offered services they are not chapmen. The Scotch drapers, who sold clothes, taking payment in weekly instalments, were well organized, with their own apprenticeship system, societies with fixed circuits of regular customers and their own order books. They survived well into the twentieth century, working mainly in the north of England from the weaving towns of southern Scotland.[15] It is mainly the earlier chapmen that concern us: the travelling bookseller and the hardwareman and haberdasher who carried some books along with his small stuff. It was an attractive job for a young man who was not strong enough for manual labour or did not fancy it. Alexander Wilson, poet and author of *Birds of America*, had tried his hand as a weaver; William Nicholson had been a flax-dresser. If one worked hard at it one could hope 'Aeblins [maybe], through time, to warsle up a shop.'[16]

Many a topping draper and hardware merchant has begun his career by carrying the pack; and we have known provosts of "burrows towns" who have risen in this way from very small beginnings. The first step was to save a little substance; the second, to extend their credit and augment their wares; the third, to bundle the pack on the back of a horse, with the view of remaining longer out, and displaying a more imposing stock of goods; the fourth, if they throve, to harness the said horse to a wagon; and the fifth and last, to take a shop in a county town, and vegetate tranquilly behind the counter.

Thus the memoir of William Nicholson. He managed as far as the horse.

In the year 1812, he made a bold push to get on in the world, by purchasing a larger stock of goods than usual, and transferring his pack to a horse's back. But the speculation failed; and what is worse, the horse, on being turned out to graze in spring, unfortunately stumbled and broke its neck, in attempting to leap a neighbouring fence and thereby get to a richer pasture.[17]

What of a pack and its contents? In shape it could vary very much. William Nicholson describes the contents:

At length it was decreed that he should carry a pack, as the author of "Watty and Meg" had done before him, and drive a thriving trade in needles, pins, combs, thimbles, shears [i.e. scissors] and such like small gear. His capital amounted to the formidable sum of one pound one shilling sterling: and after paying six shillings for a wooden box, the reversion was expended in the purchase of such articles as are named above ... By degrees, he added neckerchiefs and gown-pieces to his stock.

William Magee sported a haversack and tells us what was in it:

My stock in trade at this period consisted of the following small publications:- *The Life and Prophecies of Mr Alexander Peden.... The Life and Prophecies of Mr Donald Cargill.... Ramsay's Gentle Shepherd.... The Life of Sir William Wallace.... The Life of Lord Nelson ... A Brief Memoir of Bonaparte.... The London Spy.... The Fortune-Teller* and a Dream Book. For the last mentioned six pamphlets I charged threepence each, and for the three former sixpence each. I had also six different collections of songs; but at present I only remember the name of three of them, viz.:- *The Mavis, The Blackbird* and the *Jovial Songster*. I had, moreover, a quantity of *Belfast Almanacks* for 1820. These I sold at threepence each, and the Song Books at fourpence each. With the exception of the Almanacks, all the above-mentioned little works were printed by T. Johnstone, Falkirk, or C. Randall, Stirling; and, with the same exception, were all purchased from one of the Magistrates of Forres. I had a considerable burden of them on leaving that town — as many as would bring, at the prices affixed, from fifteen to twenty pounds Sterling. Before I left Forres, I procured a sheet of post paper, ruled it carefully, and wrote out a catalogue of my books as legibly as possible. This I carried in my pocket, and occasionally in the crown of my hat, to save myself the trouble of opening my knapsack when any person inquired what I had for sale.[18]

Alexander Wilson's pack or 'wallet' consisted of a long pack of green canvas and he carried an elwand for measuring the cloth. Though Nicholson's pack was no doubt heavy, the draper's pack was both heavy and inconveniently bulky. A man is hidden in a draper's pack in James Hogg's gruesome tale of *The Long Pack*. In *The Loss of the Pack*, Wilson has his chapman narrator describe:

> My pond'rous pack upon the ground,
> I carelessly had flung;
> A wallet green, wi' straps fast bound,
> And neer't a hazel rung;

These packs were so large as to constitute a danger to their wearers in any perilous accident. Wilson once fell in a snow drift and had to loose the straps of his pack to extricate himself, spending a fraught quarter of an hour before he managed to find it again. One of Wilson's chapmen boasts, 'I've carried packs as big's your meikle table'. While, in 'A Midnight Adventure', Old Ralph

> ... sober he and grave, and large the load
> That lay unwieldy on his shoulders wide,
> And stoop'd him half to earth. A goat's rough skin
> Inwrapt the costly stores. Scissors and combs,
> And knives and laces long; sharp pointed awls,
> And pins arranged in many a glitt'ring row;
> Strong Shetland-hose, and woollen night-caps warm;
> Clasps, bonnets, razors, spectacles, and rings,

On arriving at a farmhouse, if he did not meet anyone of the house, the chapman would march straight into the kitchen. As Alexander Wilson puts it: 'on my arrival, without stopping to knock (a ceremony never practiced by pedlars, except when absolute necessity requires).' If a pedlar needed all his effrontery, he was at the best likely to be treated with scant courtesy. Alexander Wilson commented (in *The Loss of the Pack*):

> 'Ye're come frae Glasgow, lad, I true;
> (The pert gudewife presumes;)
> Ye'll be a malefactor too,
> Ye'll hae yer horse and grooms;
> What de'il brings siccan chaps like you,
> To lea' your wabs and looms?
> Wi' beggars, packmen and sic crew,
> Our door it never tooms,
>   The live-lang day.

> 'Nae doubt ye'll e'en right hungry be,
> I see your belly's clung;
> I hae some parritch here to gi'e
> As soon's a sang ye've sung.
> Come, lilt it up wi' blithesome glee;

Ye're supple, smart and young,
An gein ye please our John and me
Ye'se get the kirnan rung
    To lick, this day.[19]

[You come from Glasgow, I guess;
(The farmer's wife presumes;)
You'll be a manufacturer too,
You'll have your horse and grooms;
What the devil brings such chaps as you,
To leave your webs and looms?
With beggars, packmen, and such like,
Our door is never empty,
    The live-long day.

No doubt you'll also be very hungry,
I see you look starved;
I have some porridge here to give you
As soon as you have sung a song.
Come, sing up with cheerful glee;
You're supple, smart and young,
And if you please my John and me,
You'll get the porridge ladle
    To lick, today.]

As packmen went always where there were no regular inns or lodging houses they had to depend for board and lodging on the charity of their customers. To be successful they needed address, and an ability to accept almost any insult without retaliating. If they could play a musical instrument or sing it was all to the good, and youth was doubtless a great asset. It is interesting to note that Alexander Wilson had a pleasing singing voice, William Nicholson played the bagpipes, and William Magee had that rare accomplishment, the ability to play two jews-harps at the same time.

Even then the kindest reception might be for the chapman to be set down behind the backs of the family and be given the porridge ladle to lick, or perhaps receive a drop from each of the labourers' bowls after they had been served. After his supper he would seldom be allowed to sleep in the house. One cupboard bed would be for the farmer and his wife, the other for the maids, while the hired men would sleep in a bothy. If the farmer were generous, the chapman might be allowed to sleep in the barn.

If not, he might be offered the pig-sty, or turned out to find himself a ditch. John Cheap is eloquent on the chapman's life:

I made myself a chapman when very young, in great hopes of being rich when I became old; but fortune was fickle, and so was I, for I had not been a chapman above two days, until I began to consider the danger of deep ditches, midden dubs, biting dogs and bogles in barns, bangster wives and wiet sacks: And what comfort is it, says I, to ly in a cow's ouxter [literally: elbow], the length of a cold winter-night; to sit behind backs, till the kail be a' cuttied up, [the food was all divided out], and then to lick colley's [the farm dog's] leavings.... I went for East Lothian, and Tom for the West. My sorting of goods being very unsuitable for that country, I got but little or no money, which caused me to apply to the goodman for lodging and it being upon a Saturday's night was hard to be found till very late in the night, when I prevailed to get staid in a great farmer's house, about two miles from Haddington. They were all at supper when I went in, and I was ordered to sit down behind their backs. The goodwife then took a dish, went round the servants, and collected a soup out of every cog; which was sufficient to have served three men; The goodwife ordered me to be laid in the barn all night, but the bully-fac'd goodman swore he had too much stuff in it, to venture me there. The goodwife said, I should not ly within the house, for I would be o'er near the lass's bed, then the lads swore I should not go with them, for I was a forjesket like fellow, and wha kens, said they, whether he be honest or not? he may fill his wallet wi' our claiths, and gang his wa' or day light. At last I was conducted out to the swine's stye, to sleep with an old sow and seven pigs! and there I lay for two nights.

Two nights because it was a Saturday: travelling on a Sunday was a thing not to be thought of two hundred years ago. It was doubtful, even, if a hen could break the commandment by laying an egg on the Sabbath. Dean Ramsay tells the story of a highlander who gave this instance of the God-fearing character of his parish:

Last Sabbath, just as the kirk was skailin', there was a drover child frae Dumfries comin' along the road whustlin' an' lookin' as happy as if it was ta middle o' the week; weell, sir, oor laads is a God-fearin' set o' laads, an' they were just comin' oot o' the kirk — 'od they yokit upon him an' a'most killed him![20]

A similar fate might well have befallen John Cheap if he had travelled for a change of lodgings. The great temptations of a chapman's life were idleness and drink. Alexander Wilson's pack reminds him that he had:

> How aft lain dozin out yer wits,
> Disdaining to be hurried
> By ought, that day.[21]

The memoir of William Nicholson adds:

While journeying onward in a warm day, nothing can be conceived more innocent than for a packman to lay down his burden and rest ... and it is but fair to record of poor Nicholson, that rather than forego these enjoyments, he would have missed the sale of more than one gown-piece, and sometimes a good dinner to boot. ...It was on these occasions that he used to draw from his pocket the "Little Warbler," peruse some of his favourite songs, and after putting his pipes in order, strike up a lilt for his own amusement, and the edification of the birds and beasts around him.[22]

The temptation to drink was such that James McLevy was able to assert that all chapmen were dishonest or drunkards, or both.[23] William Nicholson became an alcoholic and suffered from delirium tremens. Dougal Graham's John Cheap was not above a heavy drinking bout:

We came to a place near Sutry-hill, where the ale was good, and where we met with very civil usage; our drouth being great, the more we drank, the better we lov'd it: And here we fell in company with a quack doctor, who bragged us with bottle-about, for two days and two nights; and when anyone fell drunk, we push'd and pricked him up with a big prin, to keep him from sleeping. He bought our hair, and we some of his pills and drugs, he having as much knowledge of the one, as we had of the other; only I was sure, I had as much of his article as would set a whole parish to the mug or midden' all at once:... But at last our money ran short, and the landlady had no chalk nor faith to credit us seeing by our coats, courage and conduct, that we would little mind performance against the day of payment, so then we began to turn sober and wise behind the hand,[24]

Many chapmen must, to use the phrase of a mid-nineteenth-century ballad, have 'perished the pack' or drunk all their takings and their stock.

At the other end of the scale, somehow one does not think of chapmen as owning horses, yet there are a number of references to horses in the literature. Patrick Walker, a seller of covenanting chapbooks, had a white pony on which he travelled round Scotland in the 1720s. The Stirlingshire chapmen, in their heyday, held an annual horse-race, and their Act 14th was 'Of chapmen travelling with horses'. As late as the middle of the nineteenth century, McLevy, the Edinburgh detective, tells a story called 'The Handcuffs' which features a chapman travelling on horseback.[25]

One problem for the travelling chapman was money. A chapman set out from his house on a circuit with a pack full of goods. Possibly, like Dauvit, he was always at home 'frae the last Monday o' the a'e month to the first Monday o' the other'. If he was good at his trade, two or three weeks later he had sold most of his goods and was carrying money. This was unprofitable as well as dangerous, as the money was standing idle. He would buy commodities which he could sell on, knitted stockings, or hare and rabbit skins, or a girl's hair to sell on to a barber for making wigs, or he might lend some of it to people whom he trusted. On the whole chapmen were able to go anywhere in safety under the old laws of hospitality, but exceptionally a chapman might be murdered. A Scots chapman, John Kilpatrick, was murdered in a 'petty public house', between Barny [Barnard] Castle and Richmond in Yorkshire in the early part of the eighteenth century.[26] He was well known on the road and had stayed there many times, and lent them nearly £20, which they still owed him at the time of his murder. His inventory contained 50 guineas besides silver, as well as goods.

On 19 March 1830, Hugh Macleod of Assynt, a young man of twenty-one who was badly in debt, murdered a pedlar, Murdoch Grant. The previous day he had met the pedlar and walked part of the way with him. Coming to a house, Grant said "I'll wager I'll sell something in this house." "Never mind that house" said Macleod, "it is only a widow that lives there and she can't buy anything from you as she is poor." But Grant knew the widow, Mrs Mackay, and though she protested that she had no money, insisted on showing her his pack, and in the end exchanged three and a half yards of cotton cloth for two pairs of the worsted stockings that she knitted for her livelihood. Macleod told Grant that if he would come to his house the following day he would make it worth his while by a large purchase. Grant offered to sell the contents of his pack for £2, to which Macleod agreed, and when Grant expressed surprise, Macleod said that he was getting married. The following day Macleod met Grant in a wild place, murdered him with a mason's hammer and sank the body in a deep part of a loch. He hid the pack under a cairn, taking out some handkerchiefs and some pairs of stockings which he wore, including the two knitted by Mrs Mackay, and spent the £10 which he found in Grant's pocket book, paying all his debts and buying clothes. When summer came again the body was discovered, having been preserved by the peaty water, and was recognized as Murdo Grant. Macleod was tried and executed at Inverness; among the witnesses who helped to convict him was that of the poor widow, Mrs Mackay, who was able to identify a pair of stockings in Macleod's possession as one of the pairs bought by Murdo Grant.[27]

The details above are taken from Macleod's confession, which gives a connected and circumstantial account of the whole affair. Grant lived at

Strathbeg in Lochbroom parish and he went to Assynt, at the beginning of spring, with the intention of returning to Strathbeg by St Patrick's market, which takes place in the middle of the spring. Assynt and Lochbroom, though respectively in the counties of Ross and Sutherland are adjacent to each other, so Murdo Grant's circuit was not very great. From Assynt Drumbeg is little over 40 miles, 50 perhaps if one goes by road, or 45 using ferries. His pack was worth about £40 when he left Strathbeg and he had in addition £15 or £16 inside a red pocket book, intending also to collect some debts that he was owed on the way.

The shortness of Murdoch's circuit is not unusual. There were a remarkable number of chapmen on the ground, and a great number stayed in a restricted area, where they would be known and could be sure of a welcome and a bed. The Stirlingshire Chapmen Society on its inception made a drive for members and enrolled all the chapmen who attended the fairs in the county of Stirling in that year; all without exception were domiciled in Stirling, and the associated county of Kinross. At the end of the eighteenth century, when the Lowlands were fairly well supplied with borough's touns and weekly markets and 'the Highlands were the place for meat', we find chapmen travelling considerable distances to circuits in remote areas, usually taking in a fair on the way. The chapman poet William Nicholson initially worked not only in the whole of Galloway, but in much of the counties of Ayr and Dumfries.[28] William Magee, who visited Stornoway in Lewis in December 1819, bought his stock of chapbooks at Forres, from one of the magistrates there, crossed the ferry at Fort-George over the Black Isle to Invergordon, and went west by Dingwall to Contin, where there is a fair held annually in January. Here he set up his stall opposite the inn; after the fair he went on to Ullapool, where he went from shop to shop selling his chapbooks. In the afternoon he crossed by the ferry to Polewe, returning from there, and the Stornoway packet not having arrived, he crossed the hills to Gairloch. Magee makes no mention of his return journey.[29] In total, the part of his journey that he describes took twelve days and he walked about fourteen miles a day.

John Magee describes a journey he took in 1808.[30] He lived at Paisley with his family and saw 'my family once a week, when convenient'. Paisley was a centre of the weaving trade at this time, but Magee was selling religious books. On Saturday 2 October he walked from Paisley to Greenock, a distance of eighteen miles, where he took ship to Ardentinny in the Cowal peninsula, in Argyle. He passed the Sabbath there, set out on the

Monday to Strachur, on Wednesday Lochfyne, the next day by boat to Inverary, on Friday travelled seven miles into the country: 'On Saturday I went to Portsonachan ferry, twelve miles from that place.' He then presumably passed over into Lorne, but the narrative ends at this point. After the first day, he never walks more than fourteen miles, and often much less, taking, as he had to, several ferries. A cautionary note about the distances covered is offered by John Howell in his tale 'The packman's journey to London', in which Bill Wilson says to his apprentice packman John Square: 'Our lodging for to-morrow night is Belford. I shall manage so that we shall reach it before dark. The direct distance is only fifteen miles; but we may travel thirty in quest of customers.'[31]

Fairs and markets had a very important place in the social structure of rural Scotland. Much of the population was virtually fixed and more or less evenly distributed throughout the countryside, engaged in subsistence agriculture, working full-time on the land and producing only marginal surpluses. Local shops did not exist except for the inhabitants of burgh-touns. Fairs provided markets for livestock and manufactured goods, such as surplus knitted stockings. They acted as a labour exchange and provided relaxation and a chance to buy manufactured goods, cloth, haberdashery, spectacles, bonnets, combs, pins — all the necessary small luxuries of life. They served also as a meeting place, a place to hear the latest ballad, to buy a pocket Bible or a small book of songs or prose.[32]

There were fairs in all parts of Scotland, and on almost every day of the year. On a good number of days there were several fairs in different places. One found out about them from almanacks, such as the Belfast almanack and Aberdeen almanack. Scottish almanacks were largely about fairs. They did tell the reader what day of the week the month started, and had tables of the phases of the moon and some perfunctory coverage of tides, but they principally started with announcements of new fairs, and then listed all the established ones chronologically under the months. There was an almanack in every house, next to the Bible.

Chapmen attended fairs assiduously. They represented the greatest accumulation of their customers to come together during the year. The chapmen's societies of Scotland were mainly concerned with the organization of fairs. Each society had its own Lord, its Depute and box holders, who were all elected annually. The regulations of the Perthshire Society enact that the first chapman on the site should reserve a stand for the Lord, and if he failed to do so that the Lord should have the pick of the stands

Fig. 2. A chapbook published by Charles Randall of Stirling, showing a family of ballad singers

that had been laid out. All the chapmen's societies also set out the rules of order and even of good behaviour. It was the duty of the Lord and his Depute to keep order among those keeping stalls (crames) at the fair. They held disciplinary courts, collecting dues, and taking ponds for offences against their rules. Their jurisdiction ran only among the sellers. The buyers were separately dealt with by the civil authorities.[33]

Not only chapmen sold chapbooks and broadsides. These were also sold by ballad singers, who sang the songs or ballads, and by patterers, who told a story. The best source for the lives of patterers in Scotland is in the literature that grew up round a gangrel (beggar) called William Cameron, but better known as 'Hawkie', after a cow in whose character he once wrote a chapbook. He wrote his autobiography, which was published in 1888 as *Hawkie: the autobiography of a gangrel* and was edited by a minor Scots novelist who called himself John Strathesk.[34] The catalogue of the National Library of Scotland, following that of the British Library, claims that it was in fact written by John Strathesk. This is not true. The autobiography is mentioned in the 1841 edition of *The Laird of Logan* by the publisher David Robertson, for whom Hawkie wrote it while in the Town's Hospital of Glasgow, and the original manuscript still exists among David Robertson's papers in Glasgow University Library, together with the tidied-up transcript that was prepared for John Strathesk's use.[35] Strathesk's alterations involve only the occasional substitution of a word to make the text easier for the general reader to understand, and the omission of a few passages whose violent anti-Irish sentiment the public would be unable to accept.

The patterer would buy a quire, or if short of money a dozen, of eight-page chapbooks at wholesale prices, twopence a dozen, and then sold them at a halfpenny each, so for someone who could tell a good tale it was a very profitable business. Here is Hawkie's account of how he started:

I went down to the street and saw an old man "calling" an eight-page book; I watched him, and he was selling tolerably well. I thought that, if he made a living by that, I would try and "breathe the same air". I went to him and asked "where he got the books?" It was to Jamie Blue I was speaking. His answer was "D—l send you news."

At this time I knew nothing about books, nor where I could get them. I went up the Saltmarket, into a bookseller's shop of the name of Hutcheson, and asked "if he had any eight-page books for crying on the street?" He told me that "he had eight-page ballads, but no books." 'I asked the price, and he told me "twopence a

Fig. 3. The binding of *Hawkie: the autobiography of a gangrel* (Glasgow, 1888). This is from the 15th thousand. The first edition, of the same year, is a paperback.

dozen." I bought a dozen, and had laid out my little all, with only one penny behind. What was to be done? They were ballads, and I could not sing.

In this dilemma I stood for some time; had it been a strange town, it would not have cost me a thought, but it was Saturday night, and Sabbath day approaching. There was no time for deliberation, and to work I must go.

I would not appear in the Saltmarket, and proceeded to the Cross, and up the Gallowgate. In several places I made a stand, but could not think of beginning till I reached Calton Cross. By this time it was six at night. I then started, but looked at no one, lest I should be damped by seeing any person whom I knew.

What the ballads were I never knew, but at that time I had a grand voice, and gathered a crowd. I told them a long tale, as I found them totally in hand. I held out the book, and in a few minutes I had sold the dozen. I returned and purchased three dozen, and went with them to the "Foot Barracks." I sold them in about half-an-hour, and returned again to the shop, where I purchased two quires; and was told that "if I wanted any more that night I would require to be there within half-an-hour, as they shut at eight o'clock."

I then "cast a gill in my neck," [drank a glass of whisky], went to the Cross, and started. I was no time in drawing three shillings; I returned to the booksellers' and got other two quires, took another gill, and started again. I sold the whole by a little past nine o'clock and returned to the "Flea Barracks" [the nickname of the common lodging house at which they were staying] where my wife was sitting in despair.

She had got 5s. from a friend, not expecting that I would have anything, but out of my twopence I brought home upwards of 6s. This was the first of my crying "specs;" I have continued at the trade ever since, and for long I spurned the name of a cadger. For many years this was a money-making business.[36]

Hawkie tells us something of his experiences as a chapbook author. The booksellers were always glad to have anything from his pen, but he never benefited much from it. On several occasions he made agreements that he should have the exclusive use of his own work for a period, but if the printer stood by the agreement other hawkers would buy a copy of the book and have it printed elsewhere, and the printers did not always keep to their bargain:

My next publication was in Edinburgh. A report spread in town and country that a man, dressed in a bullock's skin, with the horns fastened on his forehead, had robbed the house of a maiden lady, under the character of "Auld Clootie," [Old Nick] compelling her to give up her goods, or be carried off by him. A rumour was circulated of his apprehension and trial, and that he had been sentenced to stand in the pillory in the High Street of Edinburgh on a day specified.

The day came, and the streets were teeming with crowds at an early hour in the morning, to get a sight of his horned majesty in affliction. I drew out the account of the apprehension and trial of "Hairie's Counterfeit," and we hurried out to the streets, stating that the day of his punishment was that day fortnight.

Robert Menzies, in the Lawnmarket, who printed it, acknowledged that he sold six reams of the book that night, besides keeping his press going on it for three weeks.

I next published for a "Crispin" procession in Edinburgh the account of the "Ancient King Crispin" (patron saint of the shoemakers), in twelve pages of six-line poetry, but Menzies and I quarrelled about it. We brought it out, however, the day before the procession. I prohibited the printer from putting his name on the title page, for the criers not to find out where to get it.

I went out, and started opposite Bank Street. I was getting twopence a copy, as fast as I could take in the money, for about an hour; when on a sudden, the sale stopped, and I saw persons passing with copies in their hands. I turned round, and saw three criers selling them at the half of what I was crying. I put my books in my pocket, and went to remonstrate with the printer. He said, "He could not help it."

I was aware that other's money was as good to him as mine was, but it was never to their brains he applied for something that was needed. I took no more books from him, but went to Mr Glass, on the South Bridge. This circumstance brought Mr Menzies ten pounds that day, and the day of the procession; but Mr Menzies conceded too much afterwards to the criers, and he ultimately lost by them.

I did not enter Mr Menzies' door for six months after that, not that I had a spite against him, because he was of a discreet and gentlemanly turn.

Mr Menzies and I afterwards came to an understanding; and I next sold him a piece called, "The Adventures of a Temperance Gentleman from Edinburgh to Lasswade, on his horse 'Glanders' being a Coffee-drinking Excursion." This piece consisted of forty-eight pages, and it sold well, but the friends of the gentleman paid me to stop it.

Robert Menzies was at Brodie's Close, Lawnmarket, from 1810 to 1811, and at 304 Lawnmarket from 1812–36, possibly the same shop. This is diagonally across from Bank Street. He was actually in Bank Street at no. 20 from 1837 to 1844, but by then Hawkie was settled in Glasgow. It is possible that Hawkie, starting at Bank Street, gave away the source of his copies. Menzies, more than most, was dependent on the hawkers for his printing trade, most of his publications being handbills of a sensational nature. Once the other criers discovered that the book was printed by him they would have been in his shop clamouring for copies, and this may be why 'he could not help it'.

Hawkie also mentions a number of other chapbook printers. The day after his first experience of calling the ballad chapbooks of Robert

Hutchison, who sold them in the Saltmarket from 1816 to 1828, he was introduced by Jamie Blue to Thomas Duncan, whose shop was also in the Saltmarket, and who kept chapbooks much more to Hawkie's taste:

He kept a collection of the *best* old standard books of the "flying stationer" order in Scotland. I selected those which were most likely to take the market. An old copy of an eight-page book entitled "Willie Lawson's Courtship of Bess Gibb," was the first that I tried. It was a peck of ill-put-together nonsense, but I afterwards found that *nonsense* was the article that "took" best in the street. Of this piece I sold a number of reams, and cleaned out the shop; I have never seen it since, and it is a small loss to the public.

Thomas Duncan of an old-established Glasgow firm that had always printed chapbooks was at that address from 1817 to 1822, which corroborates Hawkie's dating. Indeed wherever Hawkie's narrative can be checked in detail, it proves to be accurate, though there is a minor inconsistency in his two accounts of his stay in Glasgow in 1818. Ebenezer Muir, another printer in the Saltmarket, whom Hawkie mentions as agreeing to print *The gauger's journey to the land of darkness* and then going away fishing for three weeks, is not known to have printed any chapbooks. Hawkie and Jamie Blue were employing him because they wanted to keep the text to themselves, and Duncan would have given it to the other criers. John Muir also in Glasgow, who is mentioned several times, printed mostly fly-sheets, and had his premises in Princes Street. Hawkie was for a time in Paisley. He probably first settled there in 1819, and there used to frequent George Caldwell senior, 'a bookseller, who had retired from business, and was living privately at the head of Dyers Wynd; but still kept a few small books to serve hawkers'. Caldwell's son opened one of the largest shops for chapbooks there in 1825, but by then Hawkie had probably moved on. While he was there George Caldwell had a book printed with Hawkie's help at Mr Neilson's. John Neilson printed many chapbooks between 1784 and 1831, many of them for other publishers.

In Dunfermline once Hawkie applied to

a bookseller's named Miller, for ballads or histories, but he had nothing but tracts. These were a *bad fit*, but the drink being in the "garret" I took four dozen of them, went into the street and began a long story. I soon gathered an audience, who relished the story, and many bought. One of the buyers spurned his bargain, and challenged me for an impostor, saying I had given him "John Covey" in place of what I was calling.

As a result Hawkie was put in the black hole for the weekend and ordered out of town on the Monday. John Miller, who set up in Dunfermline about 1815, was a member of the family of Miller of Haddington, and like them was devoted to 'cheap tracts calculated to promote the interests of religion, virtue and humanity'. Not a good fit.

Hawkie mentions various ruses used in 'calling'. On two occasions at least he sold old newspapers when he could not find books. He also gives long and gleeful detail of one occasion when a criminal called Robertson was to be hanged in Glasgow for housebreaking and theft:

The day before Robertson's execution Jamie and I were in Wilson Street, and in a bookseller's shop saw a [religious] tract entitled "A Reprieve from the Punishment of Death." As a reprieve was expected for Robertson, we considered that this tract was likely to sell. We asked the price and were told "three half-pence." We took four dozen each.

Naturally this caused an uproar, particularly since there was no reprieve for the unfortunate Robertson. Jamie Blue was arrested, and Hawkie was lucky to escape. Another ruse was 'Straw' selling, giving the book into the bargain:

"This is a most particular book, but I daurna' cry the book; 'deed, I daurna' either name the book, nor sell the book, but I will sell ony o' ye a *straw*, an' gie ye the book into the bargain." This "system" was new in Edinburgh, and I took money fast; the book I sold in this way was entitled, "Gilderoy, the Scotch Robber," of which I sold nearly twenty reams.

The disappearance of chapmen from the countryside was not a result of the legislation to license hawkers in 1850, but was due to various other factors. The movement of folk from the countryside into small towns, and from towns into industrial cities, concentrated demand and at the same time changed it. The population that had been gathered in small groups all over the countryside was now increasingly either dispersed to America, Australia or Canada, or within walking distance of a shop. Even where this was not so, the small chapman was being met on his own ground by the organized representatives of large firms. This process started early in the midland valley of Scotland, which by the end of the eighteenth century was beginning to resemble an English county, with prosperous farmers and market towns at no great distance from each other. In 1790 Alexander Wilson, who was offering good cloth at reasonable prices in the traditional way, had found trade very slow there. Still the highlands were a sure place, but even that changed with the clearances and the new preoccupation with sheep. That part of the highland population which was rehoused in the area was set up in small towns on the coast, with the intention that they should become fishermen. No doubt the chapmen were not even considered in this matter, but it had the effect of removing the highland market. Added to this there was the trade recession, which coincided with the rise of the textile factory in Paisley and district. The prosperous weavers of that area were not only rapidly impoverished, but the remnants were gathered into factories as machine-minders. The rising publishers in many cases took to the direct selling of books, in the same way that the Scottish drapers did to exploit the industrial markets of northern England, and the pickings for the old-style chapmen became very thin indeed.

According to the memoir of the Gallovidian poet William Nicholson, published in 1828:

The multiplication of shops in every quarter has so altered the channels of trade, that the more respectable class of packmen may say, with Othello, that their occupation is gone. At the remotest inns, we encounter what are called commercial travellers from London, Leeds, Huddersfield, Birmingham, Sheffield, Manchester, &c. &c., who, by means of samples, and the quickness with which they execute orders, put the humblest country merchant nearly on a level with his prouder brethren of Edinburgh and Glasgow.... In these circumstances, the jagger, chapman, or travelling merchant, has become, comparatively, an exploded character; and so far as my own observation extends, is chiefly useful in picking up hare-skins in gentlemen's kitchens, and selling them at a profit to the regular dealers.

This was not the end of popular literature. The new urban proletariat retained the same kind of taste for stories and for ballad literature, and this was catered for on the story side by such firms of wholesale stationers as Cameron & Ferguson of Glasgow, who produced the new Penny Dreadfuls, tales of romance and adventure, written in a version of the high-flown style popular among the novelists of the middle of the nineteenth century. These they sold locally, together with manuals for the accordion, and other popular musical instruments, and exported to the USA and Canada as dime novels. The verse side was supplied by the various Poet's Boxes, in Glasgow, Aberdeen, Dundee and Edinburgh. You sent for their catalogue, and then ordered by post the items you wanted, all money transactions being carried out in postage stamps.

When the chapmen disappeared is very difficult to say. They were in decline before the Act which licensed hawkers in 1850, but as we have seen, the decline had begun by about 1800. Different writers blame different causes for the decline. The truth seems to be that the trade died out slowly, and area by area. In 1789 Alexander Wilson found that he received little encouragement in the Lothians. In 1809 'the number of travelling chapmen [in Stirlingshire] is of late years much diminished'; by 1828 the Galloway chapmen had changed their trade and were going south into the north of England to be apprenticed as 'Scotch drapers'. But for many years before that the chapman could say with Wilson

> And as the Highlands was the place for meat,
> I ventured there in spite of wind and weet.

William Harvey could talk of the chapmen billies still being around at the beginning of this century and an Aberdeen firm continued printing chapbooks for sale at local fairs until the First World War. In the *Dundee Advertiser* of 30 September 1913 appeared an account of a meeting between an enthusiastic collector of chapbooks and an aged petty chapman. The article is signed 'F. S. A. Scot', and headed 'The flying stationer: last of the race'. The author was surprised to find that the chapman was well-educated and took an interest in the history of his calling:

I mounted my hobby-horse and touched upon the Flying Stationer with his humble literary wares.

"He's aff the road athegither," he explained. "You'll meet an anterin' yin [odd one] selling Orr's Scottish Almanac at the back-end o' the year, but as for the rest there's nane but the billies that cry the song sheets in the touns."

He turned to his battered box. The strap that held it was mended with cord that was frail in places. He untied it, removed the lid, and revealed his stock-in-trade — cotton and pearl buttons, tape, red and white and of different widths; thread of various colours done up in ha'penny hanks, cheap writing-paper and envelopes, and pen nibs, and a variety of other articles likely to be in demand at lonely farm towns and in remote upland bothies. These, resting on a tray, were lifted out, when there was disclosed an under-apartment or secret place. He looked at me with a sidelong glance, his eye closing in a wink that was pawkily "knowing." Instantly I was on my knees beside him.

"I carry them for the sake o' the chields that want them," he explained as he brought forth "The Comical Adventures of Lothian Tom," "but they are no' much in demand. Man!" and his eye glistened at the recollection. "I've seen the day when I could sell them by the dizzen."

Cheek by jowl with Lothian Tom were — "The Entertaining Exploits of George Buchanan," the greatest Scot of his age, who is known to the vulgar only as a buffoon; and the diverting "History of Buckhaven," which ridiculed the Fifeshire town to such an extent that the observant Hall had to flee from the wrath of the Kingdom when, on the occasion of his visit to the place, he inquired of the local bookseller whether a copy of the work was obtainable!

It was strange to find these and other chapbooks attributed to Dougal Graham on this lonely highland road. They are known to nobody but collectors, and are not to be had for love or money in our cities. Sir Walter Scott had a few, which he treasured. Motherwell, David Laing, Kirkpatrick Sharpe, and other literary students also found them of rare attractiveness. To-day one learns from the informing pages of "Who's Who" that the collectors include the unlikely Keir Hardie.

The chapbook is dead. The First World War seems to have marked its term, but wherever there are farms or crofts remote from shops, there still remains an empty niche for a chapman. An article by Ronald Faux in *The Times* of 28 October 1980 describes how small groups of Punjabis, arriving in Stornaway 30 years ago with suitcases bulging with goods, had been successful — by studying the timetables of the buses — in selling haberdashery from door to door and had won over the purses of the local housewives with their selection of Sunday hats. The children of the first among them are winning prizes for Gaelic recitation, and the small enclave of shops that they own is known affectionately as Mohammed Alley.

References

1. *The Oxford English Dictionary* (2nd edn, Oxford, 1989), iii, p. 28.
2. John Fraser, *The humorous chap-books of Scotland* (New York, 1873), quotes this from a 'novel by Miss Jean L. Wilson [*sic*: really Watson], *Round the Grange Farm: or the good old times* published in 1872'. It is included here as giving a valuable, if romantic, picture of a Scottish chapman. It is also reprinted, with some discrepancies, in William Harvey, *Scottish chapbook literature* (Paisley, 1903), pp. 127–30.
3. *The history of John Cheap the chapman, containing above a hundred merry exploits, done by him and his fellow traveller, Drouthy Tom, a sticket shaver. In three parts* ([Edinburgh]: Printed and sold in Niddery's-Wynd [by Alexander Robertson], 1772).
4. William Glover, *Journal through the counties of Berwick, Roxburgh, Selkirk, Dumfries, Ayr, Lanark, East, West, and Mid Lothians, in the year 1817* (Edinburgh, 1818).
5. William Magee, *Some account of the travels of John Magee, pedlar and flying stationer, in North and South Britain* (Paisley, 1826), and *An account of many wonderful instances of Divine Providence which have occurred to John Magee* (Glasgow, [no date]).
6. Court of Session Productions CS.96. It includes an Account Book 1761–9 (no. 1066); a Ledger 1766–73 (no. 1067); Journals 1768–9 (no. 1151), 1769–70 (no. 1068), 1770–1 (no. 1069); an index to the missing volume (no. 1070); and an Inventory of Goods (no. 1066). They dealt mainly in cloth and haberdashery.

7. Fraternity of Chapmen in the Three Lothians, *Prospectus of the Chapmen's rules, and Widows' Scheme* (1837). (National Library of Scotland (NLS) 5.560).

8. Minute Book of the Shires of Stirling and Clackmannan 1726–1816, NLS MS 197, fol. 101.

9. *The collected writings of Dougal Graham, edited with notes by George MacGregor*, 2 vols (Glasgow, 1883).

10. William Motherwell, 'Dugald Graham', *Paisley Magazine* (1828), pp. 662–3.

11. John Alexander Fairlie, *Dougal Graham and the chapbooks attributed to him* (Glasgow, 1914). The Glasgow burial register for 1779–82 has unfortunately been missing at least since 1828.

12. Alexander Wilson, *Poems, humorous, satirical and serious. The second edition with additions* (Edinburgh: printed for the author and sold by P. Hill, 1791). (NLS NG.1167.f.6); Alexander Wilson, *The loss of the pack: a true tale. By the author of Watty and Meg, Rab and Ringan, &c.* ... (Glasgow: printed for and sold by Brash & Reid, [c.1797]).

13. William Nicholson, *Tales in verse, and miscellaneous poems: descriptive of rural life and manners ... the second edition. To which is prefixed, A memoir of the author* (Edinburgh: published by Oliver & Boyd, 1828). (NLS K.191.d).

14. William Magee, *Recollections of a personal interview with the late Laird of Dundonnell, ... during a tour through the North Highlands in 1819–20. By an itinerant bookseller* (Edinburgh: published by William Magee, bookseller ... 1830). (NLS K.159.c).

15. There is an account of them and their organization from the *Glasgow Weekly Mail*, without date in Harvey's Collection of Cuttings vol. 1 (NLS RB.m.141). It is headed 'Scottish packmen. How they make a living. Their "hunting grounds" in England. What "John Bull" think of them.' There is a Hill and Adamson collotype of 'The Scotch Draper' in the Scottish National Portrait Gallery.

16. Alexander Wilson, *The loss of the pack*.

17. William Nicholson, *Tales in Verse*.

18. William Magee, *Recollections*.

19. Alexander Wilson, *Poems, humorous, satirical and serious* and *The loss of the pack*.

20. E. B. Ramsay, *Reminiscences of Scottish life & character*, 22nd edn (Edinburgh, 1874), p. 73.

21. Alexander Wilson, *Poems* (Paisley: printed for the author, 1790). (NLS F7.d.20).

22. William Nicholson, *Tales in Verse*.

23. James McLevy, *The Edinburgh detective* (Glasgow, n.d.), chap. 3.

24. *The history of John Cheap the chapman*.

25. James McLevy, 'The handcuffs', *The Edinburgh detective*, chap. 3.

26. *A cruel, barbarous, shocking, and inhuman murder, which was committed on the body of one John Killpatrick, a Scotchman, by 4 men and one woman at a publick-house betwixt Barny Castle and Richmond in Yorkshire. Which was committed in Jan. last* [no place or date]. (NLS L.C.2737(32)).

27. The NLS has a broadside, *Confession and execution of Hugh Macleod* (1830), and a sermon on the murder by the Reverend A. Clark, entitled *Macleod the murderer*. The most detailed account, however, is the *Life of Hugh Macleod, Assynt, embracing a report of his trial at the Circuit Court, Inverness, on 23rd Sept., 1831, for the murder of Murdoch*

Grant, pedlar, with evidence, including that of Kenneth Fraser 'The Dreamer', and an account of the execution (Inverness, 1882), which is based on and reprints all the documents of the case.

28. William Nicholson, *Tales in verse.*

29. William Magee, *Recollections of a personal interview.*

30. *An account of many wonderful instances of divine providence which have occurred to John Magee ... written by himself* (Printed by Thomas Duncan, 159 Saltmarket, Glasgow, [between 1817 and 1822]).

31. *Wilson's Tales of the Borders, and of Scotland, historical, traditionary, and imaginative,* vol. 9 (London, 1888), p. 188.

32. John Morris, 'The Scottish Fair as seen in Eighteenth- and Nineteenth-Century sources', *Scottish Studies. The Journal of the School of Scottish Studies, University of Edinburgh,* vol. 33 (2000), pp. 89–109.

33. The minute books of some of the Scottish chapmen's societies are in the National Library of Scotland. That of the Stirling Society, which covered Stirling and Kinross, is NLS MS 197 and those of the Fife Chapmen are MSS 198 and 199. The details of the Laws and Acts of the Chapmen of Perthshire are taken from Robert Fittis, *Illustrations of the history of Perthshire* (Perth, 1874).

34. William Cameron, *Hawkie: the autobiography of a gangrel edited by John Strathesk* (Glasgow: David Robertson & Co., 1888). (NLS L.C.3352.10; 15th thousand, Hall.242.g).

35. *The Laird of Logan: or anecdotes and tales illustrative of the wit and humour of Scotland* (Glasgow: David Robertson, 1841).

36. William Cameron, *Hawkie,* pp. 90–1.

The Book Trade in Public Spaces:
London street booksellers, 1690–1850

MICHAEL HARRIS

THIS ESSAY REPRESENTS an attempt to open up an area of the London book trade which is usually glossed over or misunderstood. It is not an easy task to bring into view the individuals working at street level in any trade and the dealers in books and related materials, who often sold a range of other things, are no exception. When I recently published a study of the barrow trade in books in London during the twentieth century, I rashly proposed that the materials for pushing the study back into the seventeenth century were simply not to be found.[1] This has turned out to be wrong, although it must be said that activities at street level only flicker fitfully through material accumulated for other purposes. Recently, some creative attention has been paid to the urban poor in eighteenth-century London. Tim Hitchcock has brought together a wide range of material and approaches which he presents as a new kind of analysis through which the most economically disadvantaged can be given substance and reality.[2] This essay is not concerned with the utterly desperate, nor with those who have been classified as 'outcasts', but it does make use of some of the documents in which they appear, alongside most other sectors of the population. In particular, I have used the records of trials at the Sessions House in the Old Bailey, which have recently been made available in electronic form. This project, run by Tim Hitchcock with the historian Robert Shoemaker, has opened up new possibilities for searching the text and has enabled me to revisit a source which I first examined in an earlier volume in this series.[3] The material has severe limitations, but even in the pre-electronic era it offered some remarkable opportunities for the study of the history of the London book trade.

At the other end of the period stands the monumental view of London street people constructed by Henry Mayhew in a paroxysm of activity from the late 1840s. His study of *London Labour and the London Poor*, which began in articles for the *Morning Chronicle*, developed as a separate serial and was first collected in book form in 1851, astounded contemporaries and has provided later readers with a vast mass of information about the life of the streets.[4] In his close, systematic and detailed investigation, the individuals whose living depended on the street sale of print were swept up along with others engaged in an almost manic variety of economic self-help. Mayhew's work has helped to define the modest target of this essay, which is not concerned with that sector of the self-identified 'paper workers' who moved constantly around the London streets and fell within his category of 'running patterers'. As Mayhew worked through his intricate subdivisions of the street-based traders, he identified clearly, for the first time, the group of individuals classified as the 'Street-sellers of Books on Stalls and Barrows' a group otherwise referred to in his text as 'Street Booksellers'. He took pains to distinguish this group, working from fixed sites within the urban core, not only from the mobile traders and hawkers but from the shop-based booksellers who used external, street displays of books as part of their business.[5]

Mayhew's distinction between shopkeepers with books displayed in the street and the specific category of street booksellers immediately introduces one of the reasons for the obscurity of the open-air trade across the long eighteenth century. In most usage, contemporary and historical, the word 'stall' may refer to any open-air display and this has tended to blur the distinction between the shop and street trade which was given some emphasis by Mayhew. The windows of many bookshops were covered by a wooden hatch which could be lowered to provide a platform for the display of books extending into the street. The use of such 'show boards', or of fixed tables standing in front of the window, which could provide precarious shelter for the very poor, were combined with a variety of shelves, racks or boxes. One such example of a shop, in which elaborate external decoration on the building itself was combined with an adjacent display of books and titlepages tucked into a covered gateway, was used to illustrate the valuable study by Giles Mandelbrote of the character of the London bookshop.[6] The open display area would have been referred to as a stall and various examples of this usage crop up in the trials. They include one involving Edmund Curll, whose peculiarities of speech and manner probably accounted for the amount of space given to a minor case of theft in the *Proceedings*.[7] Curll brought a case against his servant for theft and James Gibson for receiving, although it appeared during the case that Gibson was a carpenter and the book business was run entirely by his wife. Curll claimed that about 60 books had disappeared from the glass cases in his shop, which he was at a loss to explain "till going thro' Russel Court, I saw 17 volumes of 'em lying all a-Row upon Gibson's Stall'.

Bookbinders, usually working at a modest commercial level, often combined their trade with other activities, including the sale of new and secondhand books displayed in front of their premises. William Oxlade, a binder, sold books in this way and in 1776 prosecuted John Morton for the theft of a book on venereal disease from his stall outside his house in Holborn.[8] In evidence he deposed that, 'this book Syphillis was on a stall, which I kept a little girl of eight years old to look after; I was upstairs for about ten minutes, when I came down I missed it.' Street business has always been part of the shop trade and there has inevitably been some blurring of function. In eighteenth-century London this was compounded by the use of separate street-based stalls which came close in character to shops and were sometimes referred to as such.

The stalls at this upper level of the street trade were self-contained, free-standing units of variable size, large enough to contain a quantity of stock and one or more people engaged in the process of selling. They could be securely locked up and left overnight and were perhaps secured to a wall or some adjacent structure which could prevent removal or the sort of casual destruction that was applied to some watchmen's huts. The larger examples may have been similar to those which lined the walls of Westminster Hall, which were shut up and left when Parliament was not in session. In at least one case at the sessions in the Old Bailey the accused attempted to exploit the technicality that in the indictment the word 'shop' had been used, whereas in reality the units in Westminster Hall were stalls.[9] The Exchanges strung out along the Strand and the Royal Exchange in the City contained a large number of small spaces, but these units were an integral part of the structures in which they were located. There seem to be very few pictorial representations of street stalls and none showing the sale of books. One striking example forms the subject of a painting/engraving by Philipp Killian.[10] It shows a large open-fronted stall, about 10 feet high and 15 feet wide, from which tinware is being sold. The wooden counter runs the full length of the stall and two young women are shown dealing with customers. Behind them are racks of about five shelves from floor to ceiling groaning under the display of tin. The open front can be closed by lowering an upper and raising a lower flap to rest on slightly canted supports bolted into place at counter level, while the side-door into the selling space is secured by a solid wooden frame. The whole structure

may have been double-sided with a second stall unit facing the opposite
way. Assuming this to be a realistic representation, the scale of this stall
may suggest that it was intended to be a semi-permanent structure in a
market in which the stalls generally would be taken down and set up each
day. Next to it is a much smaller open-fronted unit with a pitched roof
from which a man is selling something which might be looking-glasses or
even, at a pinch, books. The lack of evidence about the appearance of the
smaller bookshops in sixteenth-century London has led Peter Blayney to
speculate on the character of the 'little and lowe' premises for use by John
Day in St Paul's Churchyard. However, this was not collapsible or trans-
portable and although Blayney is able to locate the site with great accuracy,
the external appearance of the structure is, as he points out, largely a
matter for guesswork.[11]

The absence of visual material in all periods underlines the value of
Killian's representation of the tinware stall, particularly as it seems that a
range of much more modest, box-shaped units from which books were sold
were scattered through the built-up area tucked into alcoves, placed against
blank walls or erected at locations where the streets widened out and
offered the street dealer greater public access. During the trials at the Old
Bailey sessions, references to stalls of this sort sometimes come into focus.
In 1740 William Jones, a bookseller who lived in Redcross Street near the
Barbican, was burgled.[12] He ran what he called 'a little Shop' in Holborn at
the corner of Staples Inn, which was broken into and 30 or 40 books
taken. Jones claimed that his total stock at this location amounted to
'about 2 or 3 hundred Books'. The watchman who made the arrest was
alerted by 'a clatter from a Shop' which, when he knocked, was opened by
the accused who claimed 'it was his Brother's Stall, and he came there to lie
that Night.' The indications are that the 'shop' was in fact a stall consisting
of a closed wooden structure containing a good stock of books of the sort
that probably characterized the upper levels of the street trade.

Some of the individuals who kept the street stalls were close to, or part
of, what might be described as the respectable book trade and some may
have been shop-based booksellers who extended their conventional retail
business in this way. At the same time, running a bookstall may have been
a means of moving up in the trade from street to shop. Among the high-
profile stall keepers of the first half of the eighteenth century were several
members of the King family. The details of their individual backgrounds
are not yet clear but they seem from the Stationers' records to have worked

for many years as booksellers and binders in Petty France in Westminster, as well as around Duck Lane and Little Britain. They were entered as masters and apprentices in the company records usually taking up their freedom by patrimony.[13] In 1725 Thomas King senior appeared in the Old Bailey sessions court as prosecutor of John Green for stealing his books. In evidence he deposed that he kept 'two Booksellers Stalls; one at the Corner of Token-House-Yard in Lothbury and the other in Petty-France'.[14] He kept the Lothbury stall himself while his son, Thomas King junior, kept the one in Westminster. Over the next decades both figured as prosecutors in shoplifting cases, as did John King who was probably another son of Thomas King senior and who in 1731 was in charge of the Lothbury stall.[15] Exactly how or why the move from street to shop was made is not clear. However, after Thomas senior died in 1743 Thomas junior and John King were running bookshops two doors from each other in Moorfields and were continuing to prosecute the perpetrators of the casual thefts of books from their shop windows.[16]

Whatever the precise circumstances leading to the Kings' change of commercial direction they must always have been the aristocrats of the street trade. Others passed them on their way down, moving remorselessly from shop to street. Such was the case of George Hammond who in 1779 came into court on charges of stealing a quantity of paper and books in sheets from the 'quire warehouse' of his employer, the Holborn bookseller William Fox.[17] The trajectory of his failure emerged in evidence. In May 1777 Hammond had taken a house in Peter Street, which ran between Saffron Hill and Cow Cross near Smithfield. It crossed the Fleet Ditch and was part of the neighbourhood swept away by nineteenth-century improvements. Here he set up as a bookseller with £15 or £16 worth of stationery wares and what was described as 'a great stock' of books. After about a year he fell into arrears with his landlord as well as with the local vestry through his failure to pay the rates. Before all his goods were seized and sold off by a broker, he removed the main part intending 'to re-assume my profession afterwards'. He stored his goods with Joseph Gaunt, a watchmaker who lived in Bridgewater Street near the Barbican and who testified to the quantity. Hammond, he said, 'brought so large a chest, I wonder he stood under it, for my apprentices and I had much a do to get it off his shoulders.' Hammond later brought a sack containing books, pamphlets and 'old magazines'. The drift of all this was to indicate title to the materials later found in his lodgings. Hammond claimed that in the confusion of events he had lost his catalogue which would have shown 'the number; denomination; the quality; the time when, where and at what price, I have bought my books.' Unfortunately, he remarked, he was 'deprived of that happiness'.

At all events, Hammond was obliged at this time to look for work, taking a job with Fox who employed him as a porter and to 'fold and sew, and fit books in boards for him'. Not long after, he left Fox and took lodgings in Oxford Road (now Street) and 'set up a bookstall'. It was here that his troubles began anew. John Cuttall, a bookseller in Middle Row in Holborn, bought a copy of Field's Bible from the stall and offered it for sale in his own shop. His neighbour William Fox saw it, identified it as his property, and launched proceedings against Hammond. The case when it came to court was lengthy and Hammond's penchant for flowery prose may have given it some public interest. He was found guilty and sentenced to three years' naval duty.

As well as the families and individuals moving up and down the commercial scale, whose experience of street bookselling marked off a phase in their careers, other bookstall keepers had a clearer link to the miscellaneous dealers whose living centred on the streets. One of these was Hugh Mattison of St Giles-in-the-Fields, who kept a bookstall in Lincoln's-Inn-Fields. He was not connected to any of the formal structures of the book trade and had what appeared to be an unscrupulous attitude to other people's property. In 1722 he was tried for receiving books in sheets stolen from the printer William Bowyer.[18] The evidence suggested that he was willing to buy anything that would sell in the way of books and that he had claimed that 'though he made but a mean Appearance yet he had great Acquaintance, and knew how to dispose of them.' His commercial activities were apparently comparable to those of the long-distance pedlars who spent part of the year in London and the remainder touring far-flung circuits buying and selling stock. He expressed a willingness to buy Bowyer's materials, it was said, 'because he was going to traffick beyond the Seas.' At all events, he was found guilty and sentenced to transportation.

Whether Mattison worked from a box stall does not emerge from the trial, although it seems possible, from the scale of his purchases, that he did. On the other hand, many of the stall keepers referred to in court probably kept the simplest form of display unit, which might consist of a table or similar platform of boards set up in any of the London thoroughfares. Many street sellers of goods and services worked from a botched-up handcart or wheelbarrow and any of the street booksellers may have done the same, participating in what has been described as the 'economy of makeshift'.[19] Even a convenient ledge or patch of open ground might have served the purpose. More searches of the records will have to be made if individuals at the lowest end of the eighteenth-century book business are to be brought into view. During a murder trial in 1756, a passing reference was made to a woman at the corner of Hatton Garden in Holborn who 'had a board with old books on it.'[20] It is unlikely that there is any further reference to this representative of the trade in the historical record. The non-specific use of the word 'stall' plays its part in blurring some of the issues, not least regarding their distribution through the streets. The court cases suggest a generalized dispersal of activity, mainly north of the river, with some concentrations in streets continuously full of people, in which other commodities such as fruit were also sold from stalls. It also seems that the street booksellers were drawn to locations where a number of modest, particularly secondhand, bookshops were already present. Holborn was one such thoroughfare while Charing Cross, where Francis Place watched the daily setting up of large food stalls from his window, was another.[21] However, through most of the eighteenth century the primary focus for open-air bookselling was to be found in the open space loosely designated as Moorfields.

On the northern edge of the City, Moorfields had been drained and turned into a public amenity early in the seventeenth century and, though undergoing something of a decline in its character, continued to provide Londoners with access to open space. By the time John Rocque's large-scale map of London was published in 1746, the area was still intact but had been given a sharper definition by the buildings around it. Adjacent to the City wall was the segment usually designated as Little or Lower Moorfields. Moorgate itself had been rebuilt in the 1670s with footpaths on each side of the main arch, while the accommodation it contained had been converted to use as a coffee-house by the early eighteenth century.[22] Then to the north came Middle Moorfields and finally, completing the corridor of open public space, came Upper Moorfields. This lay alongside what had become the New Artillery Ground which was walled off and used for the exercises of the City militia. Each part of Moorfields was enclosed by a low wall which formed a rough square and was crossed by diagonal walks lined with trees. The area closest to the City was the most formal in layout and was divided by balustrades into 'quarters'. The

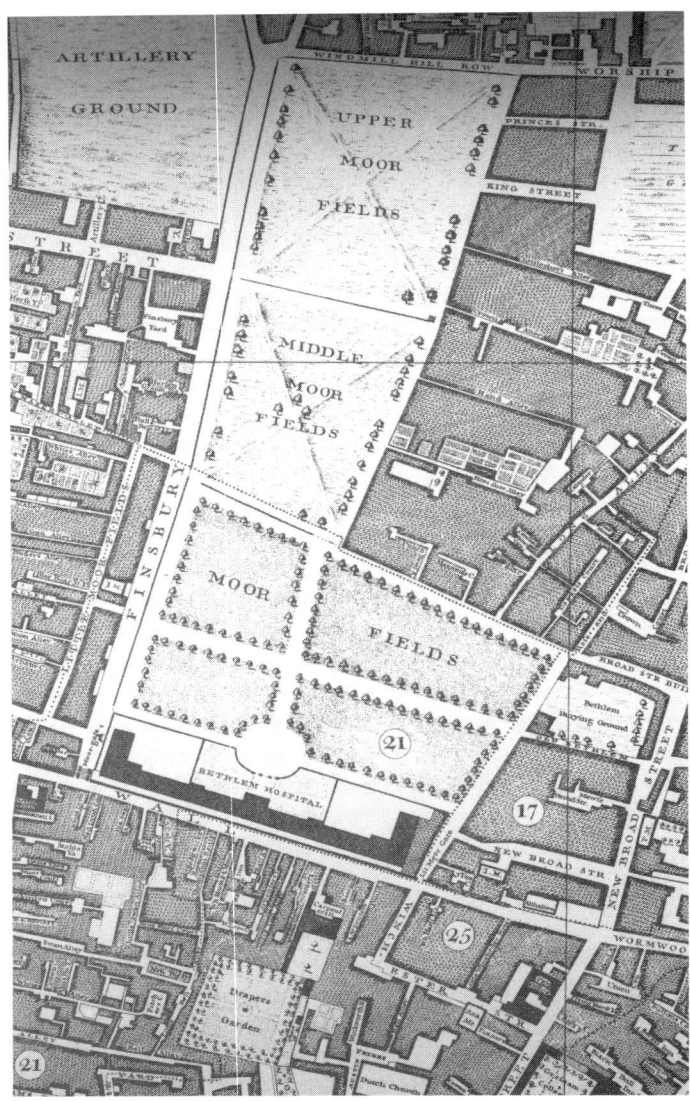

Fig. 1. Detail from John Rocque's 'Plan of the Cities of London and Westminster and Borough of Southwark' (1746)

dominant feature between Lower Moorfields and the City was the St Bethlehem Hospital for the insane known colloquially as Bedlam. It has been suggested that its blank walls through the eighteenth century were 'almost wholly covered by the dealers in old books.'[23] Though not part of the City, Moorfields was leased to the Corporation by the Prebendary of Finsbury and it was responsible for the maintenance and general oversight of what was technically referred to as the Liberty of Moorfields. The name was applied fairly indiscriminately to the street and houses that fell within the general neighbourhood and it is not always possible to know, in cases involving booksellers, what their relationship was to either street or open space.

By custom the fields had been left open for the benefit of Londoners and they became the focus for a wide range of sporting and related activities, of which gambling was the most prevalent. Some sport was formally organized and there was a wrestling ring and a wooden booth probably used for various kinds of combat.[24] The Middlesex Grand Jury took a particular interest in Moorfields during the 1730s and presented a number of groups and activities for punishment. These included vagrants, gaming booths, cricketers and 'unruly assembly of apprentices etc.'[25] Moorfields became associated with meetings of 'sodomites' and its use by criminals, particularly muggers and pick-pockets, made it a dangerous area after dark. As a stallholder in Moorfields remarked, 'there are a many carriby islands and places thereabouts, where people that do dark actions, love to go into.'[26] Below the fields were the vaults constructed originally to drain the area and bring in fresh water, but later used for storage and probably adding to the sinister aspect of parts of the open space.[27]

Even so, Moorfields also provided the locus for a very diverse range of commercial activities, although the details of its organization are only occasionally visible. Saloop, a drink sold to the poor by numbers of street traders, was available in Moorfields. Ann Hill, giving evidence in a trial in 1778, described how she went out each morning at 4 a.m. with her husband and daughter who helped carry the table from which the drink was sold for 1d. or 2d.[28] Rather less formally Isaac Levi, who was prosecuted for stealing 84 lb. of lead was seen in Moorfields with a sack which he rested on the rails before throwing it on the ground where he would have laid it out for sale.[29] Almost anything could be bought or sold in this location, beds, tables, chairs, looking-glasses, tools, lead, but perhaps the primary commodity sold in Moorfields was books.

This association was linked to the presence of a long-standing business in books, new, secondhand and antiquarian, in the nearby streets on the other side of Moorgate, centred on Little Britain and Duck Lane. It seems to be in this neighbourhood, not far from Smithfield, that Ned Ward found that '*Money for old Books* was writ upon some part or other of every Shop, as surely as *Money for live Hair* upon a *Barber's* Window.'[30] The layout and character of the small bookshops that riddled the neighbourhood have been effectively described by Giles Mandelbrote. My concern here is with the overspill activity in the fields themselves and in the pubs and shops around them. The integrated nature of the shop and bookstall trade from the customer's perspective at the end of the seventeenth century is evident from the diary of Robert Hooke, architect of the new Bethlehem Hospital which was opened in 1676. He recorded in laconic form how he 'rambled about bookes', buying numerous volumes in Moorfields and the adjacent streets as well as in Holborn, although it is not always possible to tell whether he was buying from shop or stall.[31]

Most of the 'houseless' booksellers were probably to be found in or adjacent to the area in front of Bedlam in Lower Moorfields. As Giles Mandelbrote has shown, books were laid out along the top of the balustrades as on a stall in the street. It was here that Hooke saw large numbers of Robert Boyle's Dutch and German books on chemistry, laid out for casual sale after the plans to sell his library at auction had been abandoned for some reason.[32] Some individuals identified at their trials as bookstall keepers in Moorfields may have sold books in this way, though other possibilities, including box stalls erected against any of the blank walls in the neighbourhood, remain viable in some cases. The Moorfields stallholders were not always at the end of their commercial tether. In 1732 Jacob Dowle stated that he 'formerly kept a Book-Stall in Moorfields, but was forced to leave off thro' Misfortunes.'[33] On the other hand, some of the book dealers probably reached Moorfields as a last resort, like Isaac Levi with his stolen lead, laying out books in a row to appeal as much to charitable impulse as reader interest. Somewhere along the spectrum of booksellers was the stallholder represented by Thomas Rowlandson towards the end of the eighteenth century in an ink and watercolour drawing of 'A scholar at a bookstall'.[34] It shows an elderly and shabbily dressed individual standing in the open air, engrossed in a folio volume. In front of him a bookseller is seated on a low pile of folios. A row of books appears behind the central figures, laid out on a shelf which may be a table but

Fig. 2. 'The Compleat Auctioner' by Sutton Nicholls (*fl.* 1680–1740). The print is undated, but was probably published *c.*1700.

which looks very like one of the 'rails' at Moorfields. The scene is both comic and depressing as the chances of any business being done seem slight.

Among the commercial activities carried out in the open spaces of Moorfields, and providing a direct link to street bookselling at the time of Henry Mayhew's survey, were those of the book auctioneer. The well-known engraving of about 1700 of the smartly dressed dealer, to whom the term of mountebank might almost be applied, showed him working from a table of books placed under a tree in Moorfields. It corresponds closely to the photographic image of a street book auctioneer published in Mayhew's survey.[35] This showed a top-hatted and smartly dressed individual, standing behind a gate-legged table covered in books. The stone surface suggests his table had been put up in the street and he is evidently engaged in the sort of quick-fire auctioneer's patter that Mayhew replicated in his text.[36] A difference between the two scenes is that Mayhew's book auctioneer is working at night.

There was, however, a larger underlying difference which the images, separated by 150 years, cannot indicate. By the middle of the nineteenth century Mayhew was only able to identify two street auctioneers in London whereas the trade had once been 'systematic and extensive'. This decline was linked directly to changes in the urban environment of which the obliteration of Moorfields was a particular and early symptom. Even at the end of the seventeenth century, the Corporation was working with potential developers in attempts to cash in on its leasehold interests. However, it was not until the 1760s that the interests, personal and corporate, of the Prebendary of Finsbury began to come into play and from the 1780s the process of building development began to accelerate.[37] The construction of Finsbury Square and Finsbury Circus rolled over Moorfields and by the 1820s only the controlled space of the Artillery Ground remained.

The topography and character of the metropolis was changing dramatically. The half million or so people of the 1690s had risen to about one million in 1801. By 1851, the year of the Great Exhibition and publication of Mayhew's survey in book form, it had reached about four million. The urban environment underwent continuous modification. Open spaces in the centre, including Moorfields, were squeezed while road building and associated improvements increased the pressure on the poor. New slums were formed in and around the urban core, as the old ones

Fig. 3. Engraved image of a street auctioneer working at night, based on a photograph and published by Henry Mayhew

were pushed aside by sanitary building programmes in which the railway played an important part. In tandem with this process, the self-help system of unauthorized street markets took shape, drawing in some of the peripatetic street traders. Mayhew listed 37 of these markets, 27 of them north of the river.[38] He referred to them as the poor man's markets. By the early years of the nineteenth century some new specialized but informal centres of street bookselling were taking shape, often in locations associated with the buying and selling of old clothes. Holywell Street off the Strand had begun to take shape as 'booksellers' row', providing a focus for the barrow and cheap bookshop trade. According to one of Mayhew's bookstall informants, customers often asked him for indecent books and he simply referred them to Holywell Street.[39] Among the street traders particularly badly hit by urbanization were the book auctioneers. They needed a crowd to get their modest income and by Mayhew's time they were restricted by the build-up in traffic to the suburbs and waste ground on the outer fringe of the built-up area. The two remaining practitioners were to be found most often at the yard full of caravans near the School for the Blind in Lambeth, or on the small space in front of the George Inn in the Commercial Road.[40]

Mayhew's survey recorded the shape of the street book trade at a time when it still recognizably reflected its seventeenth-century form. The metropolis was changing dramatically, but the 70 street booksellers whom he identified were still adapting as they squeezed themselves and their stock into the available spaces. As one street bookseller remarked to Mayhew, 'If there's what you might call a recess ... that's the place for us; and you'll often see us along with flower-stalls and pinners-up.'[41] There had been changes to the trade. Its geographical shape had been modified as the street booksellers colonized the busiest thoroughfares on the edge of London — the City Road, the New (Euston/Marylebone) Road, and the Old Kent Road. Equally, Mayhew's investigation is not concerned with interface between shop and street and he makes no reference to the free-standing box stalls or their later equivalents, although a variety of such structures may still have been scattered through the streets before they took on a new lease of life as the primary medium for selling books to railway passengers. Mayhew's focus is on the dealers who, like Hugh Mattison in the 1730s, came to the street as the primary focus of commercial struggle.

Mayhew provides the only systematic analysis of the organization and finance of the street trade in books in London. However, it is possible to extract some information about the eighteenth-century business from material scattered through the trials. One line of possible enquiry concerns the books sold and their value as a secondhand commodity. This is a notoriously elusive subject and the valuations linked to the many cases of book theft at the Old Bailey sessions give this material a particular interest. The valuation of stolen property was a key element in the prosecution and sentencing of the accused and in most cases a value was offered for stolen books, although titles were not always included. Such valuations could be challenged in court as too high. In the case involving Edmund Curll the values put on the books which were discovered on Gibson's stall were ridiculed by the bookseller Thomas Corbett. He pointed out that several of the books 'were odd Volumes, and therefore of very small Value.... But if the Sets had been compleat which Curll values at three Guineas a Set, I don't believe any Bookseller would have given half the Money for them.' Curll's retort was 'If you don't know how to make so much of them, I do.'[42] A point at issue here was that Gibson, by buying well below the market value, was implicitly acknowledging their status as stolen property.

The discrepancy between the estimated commercial value and the prices paid figured prominently in the case against the stallholder Hugh Mattison. Bowyer's stolen books in sheets consisted of four volumes of Anglo-Saxon laws, seven volumes of Bede's ecclesiastical history and a single volume of Bishop Bull's collected works in Latin. The total valuation amounted to £28 while Mattison had actually paid £3 5s.6d. An attempt was made to explain away the compromising cheapness of some of the books. According to Thomas Green, 'it was common for Books to be sold at a less price than they were subscribed for, in a little time after the Impression, and that he himself had been offered Leigh's History of Lancashire for 7s. in Quires, though it was subscribed to at 20s.'[43] The valuations of books at the sessions cover a wide spectrum and suggest the trickle-down process of price reduction that led towards street sale.

The cases underline the variety of materials that were to be found on the eighteenth-century London stalls: books in sheets, manuscript on paper or vellum, new books recently published as well as secondhand and antiquarian books of all sorts, perhaps with some emphasis on religious texts. The only criterion was cheapness and in the eighteenth century, as at the time of Mayhew's investigation, the predominant components of the stock of the street book dealers were 'old new books'. Sometimes in court cases, the valuations and titles are directly linked to the street booksellers and provide a random glimpse of the business, usually at the upper level. When Robert Wilson and George Murray were brought to court in 1740 charged with stealing books from William Jones's stall in Holborn a number of specimen titles and values were rehearsed in the charge. These were *The History of the Earls and Earldom of Flanders* (12*d.*), *A Voyage to Barbary for the Redemption of Captives performed in the Year 1720* (18*d.*), *The History of the Rights of Princes* (12*d.*), *The Divine Right of Episcopacy* (12*d.*) and volumes 1 and 2 of *The Guardian* (4*s.*).[44] Bookstalls were evidently filled with the cheaper elements of the routine stock of the secondhand bookshop trade.

This overlap appeared during the frequent prosecutions of shoplifters undertaken by the members of the King family. During the 1730s they took action over the thefts of books which, when specified, included Daniel Defoe's *History of the Pirates* (3*s.*6*d.*), stolen on two occasions, John Mapletoft's *Duties of the Christian Religion* (2*s.*6*d.*), Aphra Behn's *Novels* (not valued) and the three volumes of *The Letters of Cicero* (4*s.*6*d.*).[45] Such works were invariably stolen on impulse or because of opportunity rather than any deliberate assessment of value. Book thieves went for what appeared to be soft targets and this partly accounts for the constant leavening of bibles and prayer books which appear in the court records. In 1722 Mary Hyde stole two English prayer books (value 25*s.*) from the church of St Botolph, Aldgate.[46] They were advertised in the 'publick News' and found in Rag Fair, the repository of much stolen material including books, at the house of a dealer in 'Old Cloths Etc.'.

Mayhew's investigations included a review of the books he found on the booksellers' stalls, laid out spines upward as in a library or, in the case of sparser stock, laid flat with paper labels on the cover. He was interested in the changing patterns of demand and quizzed his informants closely on their experience of the market. In one instance, he was able to push back his enquiries to the middle of the eighteenth century through remembered conversations with an old street bookseller who had died at least 25 years earlier. From this very secondhand information, it appeared that the street bestsellers of the previous century had included *The Whole Duty of Man*, *A Tale of a Tub*, *Poems* by John Pomfret and Samuel Richardson's *Sir Charles Grandison*. However, these were all said to have been eclipsed by Richardson's immensely popular first novel *Pamela*. The same dealer emphasized the commercial potential of the writings of Tom Paine, which he kept out of sight in a drawer and which formed part of his highly profitable 'sly trade'. By the time of Mayhew's investigation some of the most commonly available books of the previous decades had fallen out of sight. Klopstock's *Messiah*, *The Young Man's Best Companion* and *The Death of Abel* were among those singled out as formerly high-profile works in the barrow trade. As one street trader remarked, 'I was dead sick of the "Death of Abel"... before I could get out of him.' There was some consensus that the best sellers on the mid-nineteenth-century London streets were old English classics and modern English poetry. The poetry in particular represented good business as it was available secondhand as well as in cheap modern editions.[47] Mayhew himself was unable to find much antiquarian or black-letter material, which his informants claimed was now being mopped up by the secondhand bookshop dealers. What he did find were the long-standing staples of the street booksellers, practical texts which included school-books and all kinds of dictionaries. The stock, he wrote, '[a]t some few of the street stalls, and at many of the shop-stalls, are boxes, containing works marked, "All 1*d*.," or, 2*d*., 3*d*., or 4*d*. Among these are old Court-Guides, Parliamentary Companions, Railway Plans and a variety of sermons and theological as well as educational and political pamphlets.'[48] Bibles and religious works, including the *Pilgrim's Progress*, were seldom found and were hard to sell. Old magazines, on the other hand, were very good sellers and when over 40 years old could fetch between 1*s*.6*d*. and 3*s*.6*d*. each, depending on size, binding and condition. As always the street booksellers' stock was full of odd volumes.[49]

A line of buying and selling which intersected with the street book-sellers' trade across the whole period was formed by the sale of waste-paper. By the mid-nineteenth century Mayhew found about 60 people employed in the street trade in waste-paper, most of their business concerned with recycling books, magazines and newspapers.[50] Demand among the retail trades of London was brisk: cheesemongers, fruiterers, pork butchers, fish-mongers, chandlers and many others created a permanent market for very large quantities of printed waste. Many of the stolen books in sheets went directly to these retailers, who often turned up in court as witnesses. At the same time, the street booksellers liked to buy print at waste-paper prices, generally, across the period, around 2*d*. per lb. The way in which this worked in practice was demonstrated in 1777 when a case was brought against the printer John Cook for stealing a huge quantity of printed paper belonging to the bookseller Thomas Becket.[51] Cook was followed to a cheese-monger's shop in Drury Lane, where he disposed of 102 lb. of waste for

17s. However, this included 600 numbers of the *Monthly Review*, for which Becket had to account to the proprietors at 9d. per copy, and therefore the total value of this material alone was over £20. Cook was found guilty and it appears that a great deal of printed material was moving around the secondhand trade in this way. Among those brought into court to testify on the purchase of printed waste was the ubiquitous William Rayner. In 1745 he stated that he had purchased thirteen bundles made up of sheets of Ozell's *Roman History* for £32 16s. What he wanted it for is unclear but it seems likely he was just after another slightly suspect bargain. He was back in court again as the end user of stolen waste in 1748.[52] The continuity of commercial interest at street level was reflected at each end of the period when stallholders were involved both in buying and in selling as waste official legal documents written on parchment.

In 1739 ' — Axtel', described as 'a Dealer in Books in Moorfields', went to the lodging of one of the 'hackney writers' in the Six Clerks Office at the Exchequer, where he was shown four bundles of unstamped documents.[53] They weighed 12 lb. 'for which he paid him a Shilling, and the Beer they drank [which] made the price come to 17d." Axtel sold the large pieces at a turner's shop to be used as drum heads, while the smaller pieces were to be sold to make glue. Just over a century later, a letter to *The Times* indignantly informed readers that exchequer records of the time of James I had been seen by the writer and 'purchased as waste paper price 4d. per pound from a book-stall keeper in Holywell Street, Strand.'[54]

The sources of supply of books and other materials sold by the street traders across the period were highly miscellaneous, but maintained a recognizable pattern. Auctions, which were held in London from the 1670s, were probably an informal and formal source of print throughout. Seepage from the auction accounted for the presence of Boyle's books in Moorfields in the 1690s and this sort of irregular, trickle-down effect, by which books were disposed of without the need to engage in the process of bidding, was probably as common in the seventeenth as in the twentieth century. Direct purchase of job lots at regular auctions was used to supply the street trade by Mayhew's time and the sale of at least part of Hammond's stock by a broker in the 1770s probably involved some sort of auction from which the trade could benefit. Casual purchase was and remained a primary source of books, not many of which came through the trade itself, although one of Mayhew's informants suggested there was some dumping of unsuccessful works on the street sellers by London publishers. During the eighteenth century a few men and women hawked what might be called bookshop books around the streets and probably, as proto-runners, played a small part in the supply of stallholders. This branch of street selling was said to have died out by the 1840s and Mayhew's interviews identified Jewish dealers in general secondhand goods as reliable sources, as well as tradesmen fallen on hard times. The beaten-down tradesman, it was said, would 'carry a basket-full of books to a stall-keeper, and say "Here, give me half-a-crown for these."'[55]

The business details of the trade of street bookseller are hard to find in all periods. The general reluctance to reveal financial information, combined with the fluctuations in trade and the variable levels of commercial activity, make the construction of any general picture extremely problematic. In terms of constraints on trade the street booksellers shared a number of problems arising directly from the location of their business. They were particularly vulnerable to casual thefts and information about their efforts to keep track of their stock sometimes formed part of their evidence in the Old Bailey sessions. There seems to have been a widespread use of coded marking of individual books. In 1740 Henry Warr, who kept a bookstall at the gate of the Royal Mews in Charing Cross, left a porter in charge while he spent half an hour in a nearby alehouse.[56] When he came back he found that his copy of Abel Boyer's *Royal Dictionary Abridg'd* was missing. He immediately 'went about among the Trade' to put a stop on its sale. The book duly turned up in Exeter Exchange, although identification was not straightforward. Warr claimed it was his, but although 'there were two Marks in it, when I lost it, which were made with Black-lead Pencil, on the 2 Covers, at the Beginning and End of the Book', these had been rubbed out by the time it was found. As the book was in a standard binding with no clear identifying features the case collapsed. William Jones marked all the books in his Holborn stall with 'an Alphabet Letter, — F, or M, or N. They are put in my Books both to distinguish the Prices and ascertain my Property; and they are such Marks as are peculiar to myself.'[57] Jones had put a Z and F in the two volumes of *The Guardian* and an M in Burnet's *Rights of Princes*. Such marks may have been general in the book trade but they had a special value in the street.

Theft was more containable than some of the other problems, particularly dealing with the general public. Most of the customers of the dealers interviewed by Mayhew were men: the experienced street bookseller who kept a stall in the City Road dealt mostly with bank and insurance clerks walking into the City. He described them as 'fairish customers' although he went on to remark that 'they often screw me.' Mechanics looking for self-help books were more amenable to the asking price, but the bookseller's main problem was with the people who stood around the stall for up to an hour at a time reading the stock and blocking up the space in front of the books. This group was usually composed of what his informant described as 'shabby genteels', perhaps of the type represented by Rowlandson's scholar. 'It's very trying when they take up room that way', the bookseller told Mayhew and described how a fellow stall keeper 'goes dancing mad, when he has customers of this sort, who aren't customers.'[58] Perhaps the principal difficulty faced by the outdoor trade was the weather. Rain, snow, and sharp and persistent falls in the temperature could deter all but the hardiest customers and the stock was particularly vulnerable to water damage. Street trading went on all the year round but the vagaries of the weather gave it an almost seasonal character. None of Hooke's purchases, which can be identified as out of doors, was made in the months from November to January. Equally, Mayhew's street auctioneers could only work in perfectly fine weather.

Until the searchlight of Mayhew's enquiry was focused on the street trade generally, and the street booksellers in particular, the financial shape of the business was largely conjectural. It is hard enough to find material relating to the shop trade in books and exhaustive searches over a long period have only brought a modest heap of pre-1800 information into view. Regular accounting was not part of the street business. However, the calculations by Mayhew represent the first and, to some extent, the only concrete figures for the street trade. The organization of his interviews imposed a structure on his apparently off-the-cuff record and consequently they usually contain some individual estimates of income and expenditure. Mayhew then uses this information, and any other material to hand, to extrapolate overall figures for each of his trading categories. There is something ramshackle about the outcome but it is consistent and there is no alternative source. Individual claims cannot be tested and there are some claims that may owe something to an understandable nostalgia.

As the general output of new printed works increased from the middle of the eighteenth century, the value of some of the standard secondhand titles seem to have been falling. At the same time, the income of the street booksellers may also have been in decline. The old trader working in London well before the turn of the century was said to have made two guineas a week from the sale of old books. The apparent ease with which he made his money regularly allowed him to celebrate the traditional rites of St Monday in a London tavern. The experienced street bookseller interviewed by Mayhew made a more cautious claim for the daily income from his stall: 'I dare say, one day with another, I earn 3s. the year through; wet days are greatly against us.'[59] Mayhew divided his seventy street booksellers into twenty who sold books from stalls, tables or some equivalent platform, and fifty who worked from barrows. The income of the latter he put at between 3s. and 5s.6d. a day. He calculated that although it was possible to earn 18s. a week as a street bookseller, it would need a 'tidy pitch' and a weekly turnover of at least £1 11s.6d.[60]

Mayhew's general tables, which offered a balance sheet for the business of each of the 23 categories of 'paper workers', included figures for the street booksellers.[61] They were intended to average out the capital and income for each classification and then to provide overall figures for the entire commercial sector. Even when moving towards his overall estimates, Mayhew's calculations can provide some revealing detail. His assessment of the value of each of the bookstalls themselves was 4s. and of the barrows themselves £1, with a further 3s. allowed for boards for the display of books. He put the average value of the stock of all 70 street booksellers at £2. On the other side of the equation, dealing with 'Income or Average Annual "Takings"', he based his calculations for the street booksellers on a weekly sale of 42 volumes priced at 9d. each. In the overall calculations the figures for the street booksellers are higher in both categories than any of the other paper workers, including the 120 street stationers and 250 sellers of songs and ballads. Mayhew estimated the booksellers' average capital at £201 10s. and their total annual income at £5,733.

Such an heroic attempt to get to grips with the economic experience of the poor, at a time of massive population growth and urban expansion, had to accommodate the increasingly authoritarian approach to social organiz-ation of government, both local and national. The pressures which were squeezing the street traders into the unauthorized markets were intensified by such new pieces of legislation as Angelo Taylor's Act of 1817, which was aimed at keeping the streets clear of obstructions, particularly stalls and barrows. The formation of a standing police force in 1828 aggravated the problems of the street traders generally and Mayhew's informants, including the booksellers, were forced to take account of changing circumstances. As one remarked, 'It's contrary to Act of Parliament to get an honest living in the streets now-a-days.'[62] One manifestation of the changing character of street bookselling was the increasing use of barrows instead of fixed sites. This had been forced on the trade by the 'commands of the police — that the men should "keep moving."'[63] The same informant stated that 'the well-known light form of street conveyance is now fast superseding not only the book-auctioneer, but the book-stall in the London streets.' The police played their part in the coalescence of bookselling within the street markets which was to reach its apotheosis in the Farringdon Road.

From the late seventeenth to the mid-nineteenth centuries, the street bookseller had a distinct but shadowy existence. In the street, though not always part of its hurry and bustle, the business was part of the London book trade which fell below the horizon and has remained largely outside the widening circles of historical bibliography. This tentative effort to give some substance to the street business in an early period has involved the use of sources not often applied to the history of the book trade. They have their problems, but they do at least suggest a starting point for an investigation of the rich and various trade in books in the London streets before 1850.

References

1. Michael Harris, 'The London Street Trade', in Giles Mandelbrote (ed.), *Out of Print & Into Profit* (London & New Castle, DE: British Library & Oak Knoll Press, 2006), pp. 75–89.
2. Tim Hitchcock, *Down and Out in Eighteenth-Century London* (London & New York: Hambledon and London, 2004).
3. 'The Proceedings of the Old Bailey, London 1674 to 1834': www.oldbaileyonline.org; Michael Harris, 'Trials and Criminal Biographies', in Robin Myers and Michael Harris (eds), *Sale and Distribution of Books from 1700* (Oxford: Oxford Polytechnic Press, 1984), pp. 1–36.
4. The edition of 1851 was collected from the parts and issued with a general title and portrait. Some purchasers bound in the extensive correspondence that appeared on the serial wrappers. Mayhew's contributions to the *Morning Chronicle* were republished in six volumes in 1984 by Caliban Books.
5. References here and below are to the extended edition of Henry Mayhew, *London Labour and the London Poor* (4 vols, 1861–2). The material on patterers and paper workers appeared mainly in the first volume and the section on 'Street Booksellers' in vol. I, pp. 292–8.
6. Giles Mandelbrote, 'Workplaces and Living Spaces', in Robin Myers, Michael Harris and Giles Mandelbrote (eds), *The London Book Trade* (London: British Library & Oak Knoll Press, 2003), pp. 21–43. See also his essay 'From the Warehouse to the

Counting-House', in Robin Myers and Michael Harris (eds), *A Genius for Letters* (Winchester & New Castle, DE: St Paul's Bibliographies & Oak Knoll Press, 1995), pp. 49–84.

7. *Proceedings* is one of the forms used to describe the printed record of the trials at the Sessions House in the street called the Old Bailey. More often, for purposes of reference, the phrase *Old Bailey Sessions Papers* (abbreviated to *OBSP*) is used and this will be adopted here, with the date of the hearing added. The long and entertaining report of the case involving Curll appeared in *OBSP*, 25 May 1732.

8. *OBSP*, 11 September 1776.

9. *OBSP*, 13 January 1721.

10. The print is reproduced in Claire Walsh, 'Shop Design and the Display of Goods in Eighteenth-Century London', *Journal of Design History*, 8 (1995), pp. 157–76. Among the enigmatic representations of trading places, is the Jewish dealer shown in the satirical print 'The Lady's Disaster'. He seems to be working in an open-fronted stall with a closed display case for his stock of toys. Reproduced in Judy Jowett, *The Warning Carriers* (*Silver Studies* 18, 2006) .

11. The detailed investigation appears in Peter W. M. Blayney, 'John Day and the Bookshop That Never Was', in Lena Cowen Orlin (ed.), *Material London, ca. 1600* (Philadelphia: University of Pennsylvania Press, 2000), pp. 322–43.

12. *OBSP*, 3 September 1740.

13. Entries for various members of the King family appear in D. F. McKenzie, *Stationers' Company Apprentices 1701–1800* (Oxford: Oxford Bibliographical Society, 1978). The complex network of relationships probably extends back to the previous century.

14. *OBSP*, 30 June 1725.

15. *OBSP*, 2 June 1731.

16. *OBSP*, 17 October 1744; 30 May 1745.

17. *OBSP*, 15 September 1779. Fox, who seems to have been a slightly erratic bookseller, was one of many working outside the structure of the Stationers' Company and therefore not recorded by McKenzie.

18. *OBSP*, 4 July 1722.

19. This is a term used effectively about the hand-to-mouth existence of London's poor in Hitchcock, *Down and Out*.

20. *OBSP*, 14 July 1756.

21. Place's childhood memory of Charing Cross, cited in Hitchcock, *Down and Out*, p. 13.

22. John Stow, *A Survey of the Cities of London and Westminster*, ed. John Strype (2 vols, 1720), I. 17.

23. Donald F. Bond (ed.), *The Tatler* (Oxford: Clarendon Press, 3 vols, 1987), II. p. 453. The quotation appears in a note and is attributed to 'Nichols' although no further information is given.

24. Reference to the ring and the booth appear in several of the trials, including *OBSP*, 6 September 1732. A threatening letter cited in another case on the same day referred to 'Yeatese's Booth'.

25. Presentations by the Middlesex Grand Jury to the Sessions of the Peace, London Metropolitan Archive, MJ/SP by date.

26. *OBSP*, 23 July 1783.

27. Stow, *Survey* (1720), I. 17.

28. *OBSP*, 16 September 1778.

29. *OBSP*, 7 July 1773.

30. Ned Ward, *The London Spy Compleat*, ed. Ralph Straus (Casanova Society, 1924), p. 115.

31. Robert Hooke's diaries record his purchases and rambles: Henry W. Robinson and Walter Adams (eds), *The Diary of Robert Hooke ... 1672–1680* (London: Taylor & Francis, 1935); R. J. Gunther, *Early Science in Oxford*, vol. 10, pt. 4 (Oxford, 1935) printed entries from 1688 into the 1690s.

32. Leona Rostenberg, *The Library of Robert Hooke: the Scientific Book Trade of Restoration England* (Santa Monica, California: Modoc Press, 1989), p. 11.

33. *OBSP*, 14 January 1732.

34. The picture was sold at Sotheby's on 30 June 2005 for £2,800 and was illustrated in the *Antiques Trade Gazette*, 16 July 2005.

35. Sutton Nicholls, 'The Compleat Auctioner' (*c*.1700), British Library, Bagford Collection, Harl.5947. Mayhew, *London Labour*, I. p. 296.

36. In the mid-nineteenth century the licence to sell by auction cost £5 a year on top of the hawker's licence of £4 for those who moved their stock from place to place. The street auctioneers attempted to evade the auction payment by moving the bids downwards from a high starting point, for example, from 2*s*.6*d*. to 10*d*. Mayhew, *London Labour*, I. p. 297.

37. A full and rather unexpected account of the building-over of Moorfields appeared in John Nichols, *Literary Anecdotes of the Eighteenth Century* (9 vols, 1812–14), IX. pp. 519–24. It forms part of a congratulatory account of the life of Dr Christopher Wilson, Prebend of Finsbury. From the material it appears that he was a fairly unscrupulous profiteer.

38. Mayhew's account of the London street markets and the character of the Saturday and Sunday trading appeared in *London Labour*, I. pp. 11–13.

39. Ibid., 295.

40. Ibid., 297.

41. Ibid., 292.

42. *OBSP*, 25 May 1732.

43. *OBSP*, 4 July 1722.

44. *OBSP*, 3 September 1740.

45. *OBSP*, 30 June 1725; 11 July 1750.

46. *OBSP*, 5 December 1722.

47. The old informant had worked as a hawker of books and could have been involved in the street trade by 1760. Mayhew, *London Labour*, I. p. 294. Those cited as achieving the readiest sale were Shakespeare, Pope, Thomson, Goldsmith (whose prose works were greatly in demand), Cowper, Burns, Byron and Scott.

48. Ibid., 295.

49. According to one informant, odd volumes of the *Spectator* sold better on cheap stalls than complete sets, whatever the price.

50. For a discussion of the books, manuscripts and other material forming part of the waste-paper trade see Mayhew, *London Labour*, II. pp. 113–15.

51. *OBSP*, 2 July 1777.
52. *OBSP*, 11 September 1745; 7 September 1748.
53. *OBSP*, 17 January 1739.
54. *The Times*, Tuesday 14 April 1840.
55. Mayhew, *London Labour*, I. p. 294.
56. *OBSP*, 22 May 1740.
57. *OBSP*, 3 September 1740.
58. Mayhew, *London Labour*, I. p. 295.
59. Ibid.
60. Ibid., I. pp. 296, 298.
61. Mayhew's general tables appear in *London Labour*, I. pp. 306–9.
62. Ibid., 297.
63. Ibid., 298.

Index

References to illustrations in *italic*